NASCAR This Ain't!

The automobile skidded around another curve in the race track. The rear wheels lost their grip on the surface, just as Janos had known carts to do on slippery cobblestones during a rain or in mud. But the carts had been moving slowly, not at—his eyes locked on the "speedometer" and froze at the sight—sixty miles an hour. The phrase didn't have a precise meaning to Janos, but he knew that was far faster than he'd ever seen an American drive such a contraption. And even at slow speeds, such a mishap could easily cause a sturdy down-time cart to break a wheel or axle.

The slide continued, the vehicle now clearly out of control. Janos clenched his teeth, his grip on the armrest as tight as he'd ever gripped a sword hilt or a lance on a battlefield. Under his breath, he began muttering the same prayer that he always muttered when a cavalry charge he was leading neared the enemy and his own death might be upon him, commending his soul to the Virgin's care. "*Ave Maria, gratia plena, Dominus tecum . . .*"

—From "T_____ ____ction"

BAEN BOOKS by ERIC FLINT

Ring of Fire Series: *1632 • 1633* with David Weber • *1634: The Baltic War* with David Weber • *1634: The Galileo Affair* with Andrew Dennis • *1634: The Bavarian Crisis* with Virginia DeMarce • *1635: The Ram Rebellion* with Virginia DeMarce et al • *1635: The Cannon Law* with Andrew Dennis • *1635: The Dreeson Incident* with Virginia DeMarce • *1635: The Eastern Front • 1636: The Papal Stakes* with Charles E. Gannon • *1636: The Saxon Uprising • 1636: The Kremlin Games* with Gorg Huff & Paula Goodlett • *1636: The Devil's Opera* with David Carrico • *1636: Commander Cantrell in the West Indies* with Charles E. Gannon • *1636: The Viennese Waltz* with Gorg Huff & Paula Goodlett • *1636: The Cardinal Virtues* with Walter Hunt • *1635: A Parcel of Rogues* with Andrew Dennis • *1636: The Ottoman Onslaught • 1636: Mission to the Mughals* with Griffin Barber • *1636: The Vatican Sanction* with Charles E. Gannon • *1637: The Volga Rules* with Gorg Huff & Paula Goodlett • *1637: The Polish Maelstrom*

Grantville Gazette I–V, ed. by Eric Flint, and *VI–VII*, ed. by Eric Flint & Paula Goodlett, and *VIII*, ed. by Eric Flint & Walt Boyes • *Ring of Fire I–IV* ed. by Eric Flint

The Assiti Shards Series: *Time Spike* with Marilyn Kosmatka • *The Alexander Inheritance* with Gorg Huff & Paula Goodlett

Worlds • Worlds II

With Dave Freer: *Rats, Bats & Vats • The Rats, the Bats & the Ugly • Pyramid Power • Pyramid Scheme • Slow Train to Arcturus*

With Mercedes Lackey & Dave Freer: *The Shadow of the Lion • This Rough Magic • Much Fall of Blood • Burdens of the Dead • Sorceress of Karres*

With David Drake: *The Tyrant*

The Belisarius Series with David Drake: *An Oblique Approach • In the Heart of Darkness • Belisarius I: Thunder at Dawn* (omnibus) • *Destiny's Shield • Fortune's Stroke • Belisarius II: Storm at Noontide* (omnibus) • *The Tide of Victory • The Dance of Time • Belisarius III: The Flames of Sunset* (omnibus)

Joe's World Series: *The Philosophical Strangler • Forward the Mage* (with Richard Roach)

Mother of Demons

With David Weber: *Crown of Slaves • Torch of Freedom • Cauldron of Ghosts*

The Jao Empire Series: *The Course of Empire* with K.D. Wentworth • *Crucible of Empire* with K.D. Wentworth • *The Span of Empire* with David Carrico

With Ryk E. Spoor: *Boundary • Threshold • Portal • Castaway Planet • Castaway Odyssey*

To purchase any of these titles in e-book form, please go to www.baen.com.

WORLDS
II
ERIC FLINT

Worlds II

A Baen Books Original

Baen Publishing Enterprises
P.O. Box 1403
Riverdale, NY 10471
www.baen.com

ISBN: 978-1-4814-8420-6

Cover art by Adam Burn

First printing, August 2018
First mass market printing, August 2019

Distributed by Simon & Schuster
1230 Avenue of the Americas
New York, NY 10020

Printed in the United States of America

10 9 8 7 6 5 4 3 2 1

Contents

To Judith

Preface

The opening sentence of the preface I wrote for my first collection of short fiction was this one:

"As an author, I'm almost a pure novelist."

Nothing has really changed in that self-assessment. The first anthology was titled *Worlds* —hence the title of this succeeding volume, *Worlds II*- —and it was published in February of 2009. Eight years have gone by since then, a period of time in which I have published:

> 27 novels
> 5 novellas or short novels
> 1 novelette
> 5 short stories

Twenty-seven novels and eleven of everything else put together. If I wanted to be really fussy about it, I could even claim I'd published twenty-four novels and only two novellas, because three of pieces in that category—the stories "Four Days on the Danube," "Sanctuary" and "Scarface"—were technically also novels. Officially, anything over 40,000 words is a "novel." In the real world, though, that's preposterous. To get a story published as a stand-alone novel in today's F&SF market, it needs to be at least 70,000 words unless it's YA (young adult)—and a lot of publishers insist on an 80,000 or even 90,000 word minimum.

A novelist I was, I novelist I am, and it seems pretty safe to assume that a novelist I will remain.

That said . . .

Three short novels, two novellas, one novelette and five short stories—is actually a pretty respectable output in and of itself, for an author. If you add them all up, the word count comes to around 225,000 words, which is about twice the length of an average novel.

Oh, happy day. That meant I had enough material to do another anthology of short fiction, even if I am a grubby novelist. Of course, I had to persuade my publisher that the project was worth doing, but she was amenable. The first anthology didn't sell as well as my novels—anthologies of short fiction rarely do in today's market—but its sales were at least respectable.

So, here we are. *Worlds II*. Never let it be said that authors can't be just as unimaginative as anyone else.

But if the title is a bit pedestrian, I don't believe the same is true of the stories themselves. I like each and every one of them. I liked them when I wrote them—in a few cases, as far back as thirty years ago, thereabouts—and I still did when I assembled them for this volume.

I hope you will as well.

Eric Flint
March 2018

THE
RING OF FIRE
SERIES

Author's note:

The 1632 series—often also called the Ring of Fire series—is my most popular work, and the thing I'm best known for. As of today, I've authored or coauthored sixteen novels in the series, along with a lot of shorter pieces. Four of them are included here. They are:

"The Austro-Hungarian Connection." The original purpose of this short novel when I wrote it was to develop the plot line in the series having to do with the evolution of the Austrian empire under the impact of the Ring of Fire. As invariably happens when you're working in a long series, a number of characters emerged who have continued to play a major role in the series since the story was published back in 2008. These include Noelle Stull, Denise Beasley, Eddie Junker, Janos Drugeth and, of course, the new young emperor of Austria, Ferdinand III. All of these characters have continued to appear and reappear in the series in a number of novels and stories including 1635: The Dreeson Incident, 1635: The Eastern Front, 1636: The Saxon Uprising, 1636: The Viennese Waltz and 1636: The Ottoman Onslaught.

"The Anatomy Lesson." This short story introduces Prince Rupert of the Rhine and his sister Elisabeth into the series. It's also the fourth and (so far) last of the Anne Jefferson stories, the first three of which were published in the original Worlds anthology. And, for those readers who are aficionados of the long-running in-joke among Baen authors, Joe Buckley gets killed off in the story. Again.

"*Steady Girl.*" This story continues directly from "*The Austro-Hungarian Connection*" and relates some of the later adventures of Denise Beasley and Eddie Junker. Using the term "*adventures*" in a broad and cheerful spirit.

"*The Masque.*" Here, we return to Prince Rupert and his sister, this time in an episode which is a lot more serious—not to mention grimmer—than the one recounted in "*The Anatomy Lesson.*"

The Austro-Hungarian Connection

CHAPTER 1. *The Track*

Vienna, Austria
October 1634

Fortunately, that part of Janos Drugeth's mind that always remained calm and controlled, even in the fury of a battlefield, was still there to restrain his panic. Indeed, it found the panic itself unseemly.

You are a Hungarian cavalry officer in the service of the Austrian emperor, that part of his mind informed Janos sternly. *A breed noted for its valor.*

It was all Janos could do not to snarl "so what?" aloud. He was not facing the familiar terrors of war.

You are not even unaccustomed to this, the stern inner voice continued. *You have ridden in automobiles before. In Grantville. Several times. Just a few months ago.*

Janos' grip on the handrest of his door to the vehicle grew tighter still. He was sitting on what Americans called the "passenger side" of the automobile. They also sometimes referred to it as "riding shotgun," he'd been told, a phrase that didn't seem to make any more sense than many of the up-timers' expressions.

True. He had. Four times, in fact, with three different operators.

But, first, those vehicles had been driven by Americans very familiar with their operation. All three of them filled with the sobriety of age, to boot. Not a young Austrian emperor whose personal acquaintance with automobiles was this one, and no other. The cursed thing had just arrived in Vienna the month before, not long before Janos himself returned from his inspection of the frontier forts facing the Turks.

Second, two of the vehicles had been large and stately things, moving not much faster than a horse and stopping frequently. What the up-timers called "buses." The third had been a "pickup" filled with people in the open area in the back, which moved not much faster than the buses. And the fourth had been large and roomy, almost the size of a proper coach if much lower-built, whose operator had been an elderly woman.

None of them had been a so-called "sports car" driven by a maniacal down-time monarch. Nor had any of them been driven on a ridiculous oval-shaped course freshly prepared for the purpose at the command of the crazed king in question. Ferdinand called it a "race track." The term was English, and unfamiliar to Janos. But his command of the language was almost fluent now, and he could easily determine its inner logic. Its frightening inner logic.

The automobile skidded around another curve in the race track. The rear wheels lost their grip on the surface, just as Janos had known carts to do on slippery cobblestones during a rain or in mud. But the carts had been moving slowly, not at—his eyes locked on the "speedometer" and froze at the sight—sixty miles an hour. The phrase didn't have a precise meaning to Janos, but he knew that was far faster than he'd ever seen an American drive such a contraption. And even at slow speeds, such a mishap could easily cause a sturdy down-time cart to break a wheel or axle.

The slide continued, the vehicle now clearly out of control. Janos clenched his teeth, his grip on the armrest as tight as he'd ever gripped a sword hilt or a lance on a battlefield. Under his breath, he began muttering the same prayer that he always muttered when a cavalry charge he was leading neared the enemy and his own death might be upon him, commending his soul to the Virgin's care. "*Ave Maria, gratia plena, Dominus tecum . . .*"

Fortunately, the muttered words were covered up by Ferdinand's squeal of glee. Fortunately also, while Ferdinand might be portly, he was young and had good reflexes. He turned the round steering mechanism abruptly—in the direction of the slide, oddly—and within seconds the vehicle had resumed its steady and straightforward course. They were still going at an insane speed, but at least the king now had the automobile back under control. And apparently they'd broken neither a wheel nor an axle.

Ferdinand squealed his glee again. "Ha!" He glanced at Janos, grinning. "I learned that trick from Sanderlin. It's not like a horse-drawn carriage, you know. The worst thing you can do in a skid is apply the brakes. That means restraining the mechanical horses under the hood." His right hand released the control mechanism and his forefinger pointed to the smooth dark-blue metal expanse in front of the window. "That's the hood, by the way. It's hard to believe, but there are more than two hundred mechanical horses in there."

To Drugeth's relief, the king had slowed the vehicle considerably. Ferdinand glanced at him again, still grinning. "Congratulations, Janos. You're the first person who's ridden with me on the track who hasn't said a word. Screamed a word, usually—and in the case of my wife and sister, cursed me directly."

Drugeth tried to return the grin. The result, he suspected, was simply a rictus. "Perhaps they were not cavalry officers." He managed to relinquish his grip on the armrest and slap his chest. "And Hungarian, too! We are a bold breed."

Ferdinand chuckled—and, praise the saints, continued to let the automobile's speed decline. "The first, no. You are the only cavalry officer to ride with me. The second explanation, I'm afraid, doesn't withstand scrutiny. Your uncle Pal Nadasdy has ridden with me, and I can assure you the hisses and screeches of terror he produced were no less profound than any German's."

They were nearing the stablelike building that the king had ordered constructed at the center point of one of the two long stretches on the oval track. What Ferdinand called by the English term "the straightaways," another expression that was unfamiliar to Janos but whose inner logic was clear enough. Three men were emerging from the very large and open double doors, holding some sort of tools and wearing peculiar one-piece garments.

The distinctive clothing went by the English name of "jumpsuits" and would have been enough in themselves to identify the men. But Janos had excellent eyesight, and recognized them even at a distance. The one in the center was Ronald Sanderlin, Jr., the up-timer who'd sold the automobile to the Austrian king and had agreed to move to Vienna to maintain it for him. He'd brought his wife and two children with him, although Janos didn't know their names. Drugeth estimated his age at being somewhere in the mid-thirties, although such estimates were always tricky with Americans. You simply couldn't use the easy gauge of the condition of their teeth.

The older man standing to Sanderlin's left was his uncle Robert, who went by the nickname of "Bob." He was unmarried, and seemed to be extremely taciturn. At least, on admittedly short acquaintance, Janos had never heard the man say a word in either German or English.

The third man was the most interesting of the three, from Drugeth's viewpoint. His name was Andrew Jackson "Sonny" Fortney, Jr. He was also married and had also brought his wife and two children. He was supposed to be a close friend of Ron Sanderlin's—plausible enough, at first glance, since they were approximately the same age—and Sanderlin had insisted that he come along to Vienna as part of the "deal," as he called it. There was even, from the Austrian standpoint, he'd argued, the additional benefit that Fortney had experience working with train steam engines, which was not true of either Sanderlin himself or his uncle.

Sanderlin had been quite stubborn on the matter. Istvan Janoszi, Drugeth's agent, had finally agreed to include the third man in the bargain. But he'd sent a private message to Janos warning him that Fortney might well be a spy for the United States of Europe. The man was known to have been visited on occasion by the USE's fiendishly capable spymaster, Francisco Nasi, for one thing. And, for another, despite Sanderlin's fervent insistence that Sonny Fortney was his "good buddy," Istvan had not been able to uncover any evidence that the two men had spent any time together prior to the summer of this year—which was to say, right about the time the Austrian proposal to the Sanderlins would have come to the attention of the USE's political authorities.

The issue was of sufficient concern that Janos had even raised it with the emperor himself, the day after he arrived back in Vienna. But Ferdinand had dismissed the problem.

"Let's be realistic, Janos. There was no possible way to keep secret the fact that three Americans with mechanical experience were moving to Vienna—not to mention the two complete automobiles they brought with them. Ha! You should have seen the huge wagons and their teams when they lumbered into the city. They could barely fit in the streets, even after I ordered all obstructions removed."

The emperor drummed his fingers on the armrest of his chair for a moment, and then shrugged. "The enemy was bound to fit a spy into the mix, unless they were deaf, dumb and blind—and if there's any evidence that either Michael Stearns or his Jewish spymaster are incompetent, it's been impossible to find. So be it. Vienna is full of spies—but now, in exchange for allowing another, we've gotten our first significant access to American technology. I can live with that, easily enough. At least, this time, we probably know who the spy is to begin with. That'll make it easier to keep an eye on him."

Janos had his doubts, but . . . Technically speaking, although the USE and the Austro-Hungarian Empire were political enemies, the two nations were not actually at war. Furthermore, from what he could tell, he thought the USE's Prime Minister Stearns was trying to keep an open conflict from breaking out, at least for the moment. That would be almost impossible, of course, if—as everyone suspected would happen next year—the USE's emperor Gustav Adolf launched a war of conquest on Saxony and Brandenburg. In that event, Austria would most likely join the conflict.

For the time being, however, Stearns seemed content to let the death of Ferdinand II and the accession of his son to the Austrian throne serve as a reason to keep the peace. The new monarch's surprising decision to publicly renounce any claim to being the new Holy Roman Emperor and replace that with his new title of "Emperor of Austria-Hungary" had no doubt gone a long way toward that end. Contained within the formalities of the titles was the underlying reality, that Austria realized the time it could directly control—or try to control—all of the Germanies was at an end. Ferdinand III's public renunciation of the title of Holy Roman Emperor meant, for all practical purposes, that the Holy Roman Empire itself was now a thing of the past. Henceforth, presumably, Austria's interests and ambitions would be directed toward the east and the south, not the north and the west.

The Turks hadn't been pleased by that announcement, to say the least. But the enmity of the Ottoman Empire was more or less a given, no matter what Austria did. The Turks had plenty of spies in Vienna too, which was the reason Ferdinand had sent Janos Drugeth on an inspection tour of the Balkan fortifications, the day after he made the announcement—even though that had required Janos to be absent from the scene during the later stages of the technology transfer from Grantville that he had largely developed. The emperor's decision to send off one of his closest confidants on such a tour of the fortifications was a none-too-subtle way of letting the Turks know that Ferdinand realized they would be furious at his decision. And they could swallow it or not, as they chose.

The automobile was finally gliding to a stop, just in front of the three American mechanics who stood waiting. From the placid looks on their faces, it seemed they hadn't been much impressed by the ability of Austria's new emperor to move faster on land than any monarch in this history of this universe.

That was as good a way as any to distinguish up-time mechanics from down-time statesmen and soldiers—or down-time fishwives and farmers, for that matter. Anyone *else* who'd seen Ferdinand III racing around a track like that would know that a very different man sat on the Austrian throne from the former emperor, these days.

Assuming they hadn't figured it out already, which

most of them would have, by now. In the first two months of his reign, Ferdinand III had forcefully carried through a major realignment of his empire in ways that his stolid father would never have imagined. The old man was probably "spinning in his grave," to use an American expression.

First, he'd pressured his father—on his deathbed, no less—to rescind the Edict of Restitution. At one stroke, at least in the legal realm, ending the major source of conflict with the Protestants of central Europe.

Second, within a week of his father's death, he'd renounced the title of Holy Roman Emperor—that was something of a hollow formality, since he hadn't had the title anyway—and replaced it with the new imperial title.

Third, and perhaps most important, he'd jettisoned his father's reluctance to even acknowledge the up-timers' technological superiority in favor of an aggressive policy of modernizing his realm. Ferdinand could move just as quickly on that front because, as the prince and heir, he'd set underway Drugeth's secret mission to Grantville. "Secret," not simply from the enemy, but from his own father. Had Ferdinand II learned of it, while he was still alive, he would have been even more furious than he was by his daughter Maria Anna's escapades.

Displaying better manners than Janos had seen displayed by most Americans in Grantville, two of the up-time mechanics opened the doors for the vehicle's occupants. Ron Sanderlin, on the emperor's side, and his uncle on Drugeth's.

"Nice recovery on that last turn, Your Majesty," said Ron, as he helped Ferdinand out of the seat.

"It worked splendidly! Just as you said!"

The older Sanderlin said nothing, as usual, and other than opening the door he made no effort to assist Janos out of the vehicle. Which was a bit unfortunate, since the contraption's bizarrely low construction made getting out of the seat a lot more difficult than clambering down from a carriage or dismounting from a horse. It didn't help any that Janos felt shaky and stiff at the same time.

Hungarian cavalry officer, he reminded himself. He decided that a straightforward lunge was probably the best way to do the business.

Somewhat to his surprise, that worked rather well. And now that he was on his feet, the properly stiff-legged stance of an officer in the presence of his monarch served nicely to keep his knees from wobbling.

Ferdinand III, Grand Duke of Austria, King of Hungary, and now Emperor of the Austro-Hungarian Empire, planted his hands on his hips and gave the newly constructed race track a gaze of approval.

"You were right, Ron," he announced. "We need to build up the banks of the track on the curves."

"Yup. Even at only sixty miles an hour, which is nothing for a 240Z, you almost spun out. Of course, it'll help a lot once we can replace that packed dirt with a solid surface. Tarmac, at least, although concrete would be better."

Ferdinand nodded. "We can manage that, I think, given a bit of time. We'll need to build spectator stands also."

He turned to Janos, smiling widely. "We'll call it the Vienna 500, I'm thinking. You watch! One of these days, it'll draw enough tourists to flood the city's coffers."

Janos Drugeth, Hungarian cavalry officer in the service of the Austrian emperor—a bold and daring breed, no one denied it—wondered what the "five hundred" part of that title meant.

But he kept silent. He was afraid to ask.

CHAPTER 2. *The Emperor*

A few hours later, in one of the emperor's private salons, Janos felt a similar terror. A greater one than he'd felt on the racetrack, in truth, albeit not one that was immediately perilous.

In the long run, though, what the new emperor was contemplating was likely to be far riskier than what he'd been doing a few hours earlier at the controls of an up-time vehicle.

"Driving," Janos recalled, was the term Ferdinand III and his American mechanics used to refer to that activity. They did not use the English term, just a derivative from the stout German equivalent verb *fahren*. In both languages, the verb had the additional connotation of half-forcing, half-cajoling someone or some animal to go somewhere they would not otherwise go.

In the afternoon, a young, portly, physically quite unprepossessing monarch had driven an automobile with flair. Tonight, he was proposing to drive an empire with the same flair. Indeed, in the full scope of his half-made plans, perhaps a fourth of an entire continent.

Slowly, Janos lowered the letter the emperor had asked him to read. The letter was a long one, and had been jointly signed by Ferdinand's oldest sister Maria Anna and her new husband. Don Fernando, that was—had been, rather, since he seemed to have dropped the honorific "Don" along with his former title of cardinal-infante. He was the younger brother of the king of Spain and a member of the Spanish branch of the far-flung and powerful Habsburg family.

Fernando I, King in the Netherlands, as he now styled himself, judging from the signature on the letter.

"Are you seriously considering this, Your Majesty?" Drugeth asked quietly. He resisted the temptation to glance at the two other men in the room. Whatever else, Janos knew, he had to be able to react to his monarch in this situation without being influenced by the attitude of others.

"Quite seriously, Janos. Be assured of that. Not that I feel bound by any of my sister and new brother-in-law's specific suggestions. They face a very different situation than I do, over there in the Low Countries. And while my sister is an exceptionally well-educated and intelligent woman, and was raised here, in the nature of things her knowledge of the Austrian empire was limited in many respects. Quite limited, in some. She has no close knowledge of military affairs, for instance." The new emperor chuckled, a bit heavily. "Of course, the same cannot be said of her new husband, who could legitimately lay claim to being the most accomplished military leader produced by the family in generations."

All that was true enough. Janos had encountered Maria Anna, and had been quite impressed by her forceful personality, as much the product of an acute mind as the self-confidence of a princess. What was even more true was that the situation in Austria and its possessions was quite different—radically different—from the one she now dealt with in her new domain.

There were but two or three languages in her new kingdom, for instance, and not too distantly related at that. Whereas in the Austrian empire, how many languages were spoken? And not by a handful of foreign émigrés or small groups in isolated pockets, either, but by entire regions and by powerful persons?

Janos didn't actually know, for sure. German and Italian, of course. Hungarian. A veritable host of Slavic dialects. Three very different groups of languages, with little similarities at all.

Maria Anna and her new husband only had to deal with a few religious strains, to name another difference. Catholicism and two brands of Calvinism. Some Jews. Almost no Lutherans. Whereas in the Austrian empire, although they'd been largely driven underground by the harsh policies of Ferdinand's rigidly Catholic father, there still lurked every variety of Protestantism, Christians who adhered to the Greek church, as many if not more Jews as there were in Holland—and, should the full scope of the successor's plans come to fruition, a great number of Muslims as well.

"*All* of the Balkans?" he asked, managing to keep any trace of quaver from his voice.

"Constantinople, too," said the emperor flatly. "The Turks have had it long enough."

Privately, Janos made a note to himself to try to limit the emperor's ambitions in that regard. He could see no real advantage to seizing the southern Balkans, beyond seizing territory for the sake of it. Especially given that the rest of the proposal was already so ambitious.

"Insanely" ambitious, one could almost say. Ferdinand proposed to overturn centuries of Austrian custom, social institutions and policies at the same time as he expanded Austrian power.

The older one of the other two men in the room cleared his throat. "I have read many of those same uptime history books, Your Majesty. I feel constrained to point out that, in essence, what you propose to do here in Austria is what another monarch in Russia would try to do at the end of this century."

"Yes. Peter the Great."

The man—Johann Jakob Khiesel, Count von Gottschee, who had served the Austrian dynasty as its principal spymaster for decades—cleared his throat again. "He failed, you know. In the long run, if not in his own time. His Romanov dynasty would be destroyed in two centuries—and, in great part, by the same forces he set loose."

The emperor nodded. "I'm aware of that. But simply because he failed does not mean that we shall. We have many advantages he did not possess. And please show me any alternative, Jakob? Given that those same histories make quite clear the fate of our own Habsburg dynasty. We were also destroyed, in that same conflagration they call the First World War."

Somewhere in Janos Drugeth's mind—perhaps his soul—he could feel the decision tipping. Pulled toward the emperor by Ferdinand's unthinking use of the pronoun "we," in a manner that made quite clear he was using it in the common form of a collective pronoun, rather than the royal We.

Although he'd only read some of the up-time accounts of the future history of Russia—which were fairly sparse, in any event—Janos was quite sure that Peter the Great had never done any such thing. The Russian Tsar had tried to transform his realm without ever once contemplating the need to transform himself and his dynasty.

That . . . might be enough.

Even if it weren't, Janos could not gainsay the emperor's other point. Drugeth had studied exhaustively every American account he could find—Austria had many spies in Grantville, and good ones, so he was sure they'd found most of them—and the accounts of the fall of the Austro-Hungarian Empire, and its likely causes, were clear enough. Insofar as anything was ever clear when it came to history.

If they continued as they had been, they were surely doomed. Not in their own lifetimes, probably, but so what? If a man had no greater ambition than to go through his life satisfying his personal wants and desires, ignoring what might happen to his descendants, Janos thought him to be a sorry sort of man. Not to mention a Catholic in name only.

The fourth man in the room put the thought to words. "I think we have no choice, Father. Like you, I can see all of the pitfalls and perils in the Netherlanders' proposal. But what choice do we have? And I will point out that if we have advantages that our counterparts in another universe did not have, we also have disadvantages." A thin smile came to the face of Georg Bartholomaeus Zwickl, the count's stepson and official heir. "They did not have to face Michael Stearns."

Stearns. Mentally, Janos rolled the harsh-sounding English name on his tongue. A former coal miner, now grown into a force that had struck Europe like Attila and the Huns a thousand years earlier. In his impact, at least, if not in his methods.

Janos had seen him, once, although only at a distance on the streets of Grantville. The man had been laughing at some remark made by his companion, the president of the USE's State of Thuringia-Franconia. That was Ed Piazza, whom Janos had met briefly and in person in the course of a casual social affair.

He'd liked Piazza's friendly and unassuming manner. Just as he'd liked the look on Stearns' face when he laughed, for that matter. Being fair, it was hard to imagine such a laugh ever issuing from the mouth of Attila.

Maybe...

He filed that possibility away. For the moment, and for the foreseeable future, Austria and the USE were enemies.

While silence filled the room for a time, Drugeth went back to scrutinizing the letter.

Very shrewd, many of those suggestions. Janos wondered who had actually originated them? For all their undoubted intelligence, he didn't think Maria Anna and Fernando would have thought of some of them. Being born and raised in royal families also created limits. They had—must have—at least one adviser who was capable of seeing beyond those limits.

"You have my full support, Your Majesty," he said. For the first time since he'd begun reading the letter, he looked directly at von Gottschee. The old man looked tired, more than anything else. As well he might, given that he'd served Austria's dynasty faithfully and well for so long—and now, almost at the age of seventy, he was being asked to undo much of what he had done.

Privately, Janos made another note. It was unrealistic to expect the count to do more than maintain Austria's spy network. Indeed, it might even be dangerous to try to force him to do more. Fortunately, Count von Gottschee had long been grooming his stepson to take his place. Janos got along quite well with Georg Bartholomaeus, who was in his late thirties.

Granted, their background and temperaments were quite different. For all his aptitude at the covert tasks Ferdinand had set him lately, Janos was still a Hungarian cavalry officer in the way he approached things. A soldier, not a spy, where Zwickl took to his stepfather's trade as if he'd been born to it. Still, he and Zwickl should manage to work together easily enough.

It might even be best to retire the count formally. Janos would raise that possibility with the emperor in private, at some later time. It would have to be done carefully, making sure that Johann Jakob was genuinely willing and did not resent being forced into retirement. Given the situation, there was probably no single individual who could do more damage to the dynasty, should his allegiances sour. Khiesel knew . . . almost everything.

Having made his decision, however, Janos was

immediately confronted by his major and immediate quarrel with the proposal.

"So," Ferdinand III stated, clapping his hands together. "We're agreed on the basic points, then? First—which I've already had done—repudiate the Edict of Restitution, so as to restore peace in our relations with our Protestant subjects. Second, retake Bohemia. Third—simultaneously, I should say—press forward with the technology transfer from the USE so we can begin the modernization of our economy and our army. Fourth, prepare for an inevitable war with the Turks. Finally, and most important of all, begin the process of drawing all of our peoples and classes into support for our cause. That will necessarily require the introduction of a great deal of popular participation in the empire's political affairs, although we will strive to keep it under control."

That was at least one too many tasks, Janos thought. And he knew, for a certainty, the one that he thought should be eliminated.

For a moment, he hesitated. Then, bracing himself, spoke it aloud. "Your Majesty, I strongly advise you to seek peace with Wallenstein and a stabilization of the northern frontier, rather than trying to retake Bohemia. I believe Wallenstein has no further designs on our remaining territory, and would agree to such an offer."

He was fudging a little, there. Janos was fairly certain that Wallenstein's ambitions lay to the east, not the south, true enough. But those same ambitions would almost require obtaining at least a part of Royal Hungary, or Wallenstein would have no way to reach the east. Not unless he was prepared to launch a war of conquest on the Polish heartland, at any rate, which Drugeth thought unlikely.

He was willing to make the fudge, nonetheless, if he could keep the emperor from such a rash and unwise policy. The truth was, so long as Wallenstein satisfied himself with seizing only the northern portions of Royal Hungary, Janos didn't care. Those lands were mostly inhabited by Slavs, not Hungarians. From a military standpoint, they were more of a nuisance than anything else.

True, there was an awkward personal matter involved. His own family's estates were mostly located in that very area. It would be a pity to lose the lovely Renaissance-style residence his father had built in Hommona. It was only twenty-five years old and had all the modern conveniences a man could wish for. But ceding a small portion of Austria's northernmost lands, even ones that included Hommona, was a small price to pay to get a stabilization of the northern borders.

The emperor would most likely find a way to compensate the Drugeth family for the loss, and what one architect had built another could build as well. But even if the emperor didn't, Janos would still argue in favor of ceding the northern portions of Royal Hungary. Being of the aristocracy, the way Janos viewed human relations bound a man to his duties far more than to his privileges. What overrode all other considerations, certainly mere personal ones, was that fighting the immensely powerful Ottoman Empire over control of the Balkans was going to be a mighty challenge in itself. The last thing Austria needed was to be embroiled simultaneously in a war with

Bohemia. Especially since Bohemia was allied to the USE, and they needed to make peace with the Swede also.

A heavy frown had formed on the emperor's brow. "Surely you're not serious, Janos? Wallenstein is a usurper and a traitor, whose claims to Bohemia are specious. Preposterous, rather!"

"Yes, they are, Your Majesty. But I feel compelled to point out that any war with the Turks will strain us to the utmost. I think it most unwise to get entangled with Bohemia also."

"Oh, that's nonsense, Janos. I don't propose to fight the Turks any time soon. We need Bohemia's resources. Surely, we can have it back in our hands within a year or two."

Surely we can't, Janos felt like snarling. He hadn't been present himself at the second battle of the White Mountain, since he'd been assigned to the Turkish border at the time. But he'd heard many accounts of it from his fellow officers who had been present. Granted, they were junior officers, who, as usual, were quick to criticize the failings of the top commanders in that battle. But the fact remained that while Austria might have won the battle with more capable commanders, it would still have been a savage affair. Nobody in their right mind dismissed Pappenheim lightly—not to mention that Wallenstein had proved himself to be one of Europe's most capable organizers of armies over a period of years. Any war with Bohemia, even a victorious war that resulted in a reconquest, would surely bleed Austria's armies badly. And that was the last thing they needed, if they intended to confront the Ottomans.

It was true that Bohemia had great resources, many of which were absent or scanty in the rest of the Austrian realm. But what good were resources that couldn't be obtained? By force, at any rate. If they established a stable peace with Wallenstein, Janos was fairly sure the Bohemians would be glad to provide those resources by way of trade—at a far smaller cost than the hideously expensive business of waging war.

Alas, one of the things those American future histories had contained was a clear record that Ferdinand III—still merely the king of Hungary, in that universe, since his father had lived a bit longer—had been, along with the cardinal-infante, the co-commander of the Habsburg army that had inflicted a massive defeat on the Swedes at Nordlingen in 1634.

That battle had not happened, in this universe, and never would. But the record had been enough to infuse Ferdinand with self-confidence in his abilities as a military leader which were simply premature in *this* universe. Janos didn't doubt that his new monarch indeed possessed a talent for military affairs. He was talented in many things. But "talent" and "experience" were not the same thing, in war perhaps more than in any sphere of human affairs.

"A year or two," the emperor repeated forcefully. "Watch and see if I'm not right."

Janos exchanged a glance with Zwickl. Some subtlety in Georg Bartholomaeus' expression made his attitude clear. *Let it go, Janos, at least for the moment. You're probably right, but you can't restrain him now.*

Drugeth decided Zwickl was right. As foolish and costly

as it might be, Austria's new ruler would simply have to learn some things for himself.

And probably more than once, too. The thought would have been a gloomy one, perhaps, had Janos not been a soldier. He'd seen very few officers—and certainly not himself—who'd learned their brutal trade without making mistakes. It was just the way things were.

"I simply felt it necessary to advance my opinion, Your Majesty," he said, trying to sound obedient but not submissive. "That said, in this as in all things, you have my allegiance and support."

Ferdinand beamed. "Well, good. In any event, Janos, it's not something you're likely to be worrying about. Not directly, at least." Here, the emperor exchanged a meaningful look with Count von Gottschee. "Since you've done so well in Grantville, I propose to hand the entire operation to you. Which Johann Jakob tells me is on the eve of coming to fruition."

Janos wondered what the emperor meant by "coming to fruition." The work that Janos had set underway in Grantville some months earlier was intended to produce a slow and steady stream of technology transfer—including some personnel—from the USE to Austria. It was not the sort of project that ever "came to fruition," as such.

Ferdinand rose from his chair and waved his hand airily. "I have an audience I need to attend. The count will explain it to you. But you'd best start packing, Janos. You'll need to head out for Grantville on the morrow."

After Johann Jakob Khiesel explained what had been happening in Grantville over the months since Janos had left for his inspection tour of the fortresses in the Balkans, Drugeth had to restrain himself from snarling again.

"In other words, in my absence, Henry Gage and Lion Gardiner—the benighted fools—allowed themselves to become cat's paws for a pack of American thieves."

Both Khiesel and his stepson looked startled. "But . . ." the count began.

"Don't you understand, Janos?" said Georg Bartholomaeus. "At one swoop, we will get a far greater transfer than anything we'd envisioned."

"And *then* what?" demanded Drugeth. He took a deep breath, reminding himself that neither the count nor his stepson had any personal acquaintance with Grantville or its up-time inhabitants. For them, as for most people in Europe, the Americans were a mysterious band of wizards. Drugeth had had the same impression himself, until the weeks he'd spent there had made the truth clear to him.

Grantville was a *town*, that's all. A town of people with knowledge and technical skills far advanced from any other in the world, true enough. But still simply a town— not of wizards, but of craftsmen. Simple folk, really, who understood in their bones something that most people who viewed them from a distance did not really understand at all. Their technical wizardry was the product of generations of skills compiled and passed on. Hard work lay at its root, not some sort of preposterous sorcery. There were no "secrets" in Grantville. No compendium of ultimate wisdom. No magic recipes, no magic spells, no magic wands—most of all, no sorcerer's grimoire that, once seized, opened all technical secrets to the possessor.

"What then?" he repeated. "By the very manner in which this escapade will take place—there is no way to avoid this—the Americans will surely put in place measures that make any further transfers ten times more difficult."

Finally, he did snarl. "Not to mention that we will have done the Americans the great favor of draining the worst sort of people from their midst, and planting them amongst us. For the love of God, these people are traitors and criminals. Who is to say they will not betray us in turn?"

For a moment, the memory of the three up-time mechanics whom he'd met at the race track earlier that day came to him. Janos was sure they knew far more than they were admitting, about matters that would be of direct benefit to Austria's power, not simply an emperor's whimsy. He knew, for instance, that while the three men insisted they were quite ignorant of all "aeronautical matters" that at least one of them, Ronald Sanderlin, had served for months as a mechanic at the USE's air force base in Wismar. He *had* to know how to construct at least the engine for a warplane, if not the plane itself.

But Sanderlin would keep that knowledge to himself, until and unless he became convinced that he could pass it on to Austrians without damaging his own nation. He was neither a traitor nor a thief.

Damnation! This was insane. They needed to make *peace* with the Swede and his Americans, not infuriate them. Just as they needed to forget the past and make peace with Wallenstein. The great foe of Austria was the Ottoman Empire—and would have been, even leaving aside the new emperor's determination to take the Balkans from them.

The two spymasters were still staring at him, obviously not understanding his concern. Spies and spymasters had their own limitations, he realized, produced by the very nature of their work. They dealt with criminals and traitors as a matter of course—which made sense, from the standpoint of spying, but made no sense at all from the standpoint of forging a new nation.

Janos made a note to remember that in the future. Always.

"Never mind," he said. "What's done is done. I'll be off to Grantville at first light."

CHAPTER 3. *The Elf*

Grantville, State of Thuringia-Franconia
November 1634

Noelle Murphy—Noelle Stull, now, having just changed her name legally—finished her report, and leaned back in her chair. Sitting at the desk in his office, Tony Adducci did the same. He looked to Carol Unruh, sitting in another chair facing the desk, at a diagonal from Noelle.

"Seems pretty complete to me, Carol. I'm not a lawyer, of course."

Noelle had to keep herself from smiling. "Not a lawyer" was putting it mildly. In point of fact, Tony Adducci's formal education extended to a high school diploma and two years at Fairmont State, from which he'd left to get a job in the mines without even picking up an AA degree. The main reason he'd been selected to be the secretary of the treasury for the New United States, not long after the Ring of Fire, was because he'd helped Frank Jackson keep the books for Mike Stearns' UMWA local. In those days—as was still the case, more often than not—Mike selected his administrators primarily because he thought they were solid men he could rely on, pedigrees and credentials be damned. And, in the case of posts like Tony's, knew that they were honest.

Noelle's suppressed smile would have been simply one of amusement, however, not derision. When all was said and done, Mike's crude method had worked pretty well. It had given the new government he'd been forced to set up in the midst of crisis and chaos a great deal of solidity and unity, however rough the edges might have been, and he'd simply shrugged off charges of "UMWA favoritism."

As the years had passed since the Ring of Fire, a number of those initial appointees had been gently eased out, when it turned out they simply weren't up to the job. But Tony had kept his post through all of the transformations—from the NUS as an independent principality, to its later status as a semi-independent principality within the Confederated Principalities of Europe, to its current (and hopefully final) manifestation as one of the provinces within the federal United States of Europe. Ed Piazza, who'd replaced Mike as the president of the SoTF after Mike became the prime minister of the USE and moved to Magdeburg, was no more inclined to replace Adducci than Stearns had been. He was capable, honest, and made up for his own lack of training by knowing how to use the skills of subordinates or associates who did have it.

Such as Carol Unruh, in fact, Ron Koch's wife although she'd kept her own name. Carol was the assistant director of the Department of Economic Resources, one of the branches of the Treasury Department. Her academic background might have been on the skimpy side for an equivalent position in the universe they'd come from. But by post-RoF Grantville standards, she was highly educated. She had a BA in mathematics and statistics and had taken graduate courses in the same subjects. She'd squeezed in the graduate courses on a part-time basis while she was bringing up her two children, but she'd always planned to go back full-time and finish her doctoral program once the kids were out of the house and she could really concentrate. Nobody much doubted she would have, either, except that the Ring of Fire had put paid to those plans as well as many others. Still, she was qualified enough to have been accepted as the University of Jena's instructor in statistics, whose male faculty was normally hostile to the idea of women teaching at the university level, outside of medicine and a few other special subjects.

"Oh, it's plenty good enough to put Horace Bolender behind bars," she said.

"*Keep* him behind bars," Tony growled. "Noelle and Eddie already got that much accomplished. The fucking bastard."

"He hasn't been convicted yet, Tony," Carol pointed out. "In fact, I think he's even going to manage to raise the bail money."

Again, Noelle had to fight to keep from smiling. Not at Tony's praise but at Carol's reaction. Unruh had the sort of prissy sense of duty that compelled her to add the caution—given that, in cold-blooded personal terms, she stood to benefit the most if Horace Bolender got convicted. Her title of "assistant" director was something of a formality these days. Bolender *had* been the director of the Department of Economic Resources, until Carol's suspicions and the investigative work by Noelle and Eddie Junker that those suspicions engendered had turned up plenty of evidence that the man had been using his post to feather his own nest.

Now, Carol was actually running the department, and everyone expected that it wouldn't be long before President Piazza made her the official director. Where a different sort of person in her position might have been pushing for a conviction, Unruh was being meticulously fair-minded and scrupulous.

That spoke well of her, of course, but Noelle still thought it was silly. She and Eddie had nailed the bastard, sure enough. It hadn't even been all that hard, once they started digging. Like untold thousands of officials before him, Bolender had been sloppy about his demands for kickbacks before he assigned contracts. That was due more to arrogance than actual stupidity, probably, but the end result was no different. It was easy for an up-time official to get careless on the subject of bribes, since most down-timers took bribing officials to be a routine cost of business.

He'd get a long, hard sentence, too. Bolender was not the first up-timer to have been caught breaking the law, but he was far and away the most prominent. Judge Tito was well known for his lack of leniency toward up-timers, because he was bound and determined to prove to the citizens of the SoTF—which had one million people in it all told—that the tiny percentage of them who were of American origin weren't going to be getting any special treatment or favors from the law.

Tony looked back at Noelle. "What else looks to be turning up? Besides Bolender and the Cunninghams and Norman Bell, I mean."

"Nothing definite, yet. But Eddie and I are still digging. We don't think we rooted it all out, by any means. We're almost certain that Stan Myers' tip regarding Mickey Simmons is a good one."

"How about Myers himself?" asked Carol. "It wouldn't be the first time a crook tried to deflect suspicion by fingering somebody else."

Noelle shook her head. "Eddie and I don't think Stan's dirty. For one thing, because we just don't. Beyond that, Stan's in charge of the fire department's training program. He simply doesn't have access to the kind of temptation to ask for kickbacks that somebody like Bolender did. He's got a hard enough time, as it is, getting volunteers for the fire department, given all the other economic opportunities around."

Tony chuckled. "True enough. I can remember my dad complaining when he had to pass the dispatcher a five-dollar bill to get work out of his union's hiring hall. Which was *not* the UMWA," he added self-righteously. "But those jobs paid well, so he thought it was worth the baksheesh. Most of the fire department posts are volunteer. Don't pay anything more than expenses."

Carol nodded. "I was just raising the possibility. I like Stan, myself, and I've never gotten any sense he was crooked. Mickey Simmons, though . . ." She made a face. "Well, I should keep personalities out of it, I suppose."

"He's a prick," stated Adducci. "He's always been a prick. Why the hell it took Lorraine so long to give him the heave-ho was always a mystery to me." He straightened up in his chair. "Just for the record. But I agree we should keep personalities out of it. There *is* such a thing as an honest assho—uh, butthead, here and there. But I won't be surprised at all if Mickey turns out not to be one of them."

He mused for a moment, apparently lost in remembrances of things past. "He really is a Grade A prick. But let's move on to the rest. How about the down-timers, Carol? Any decision yet from the attorney general?"

"I just talked to Christoph yesterday. He feels in an awkward position, given that he's a down-timer himself, so he stressed that he'd defer to your judgment on the matter. Still, he thinks it would be a mistake to press charges against any of the down-timers, if their only involvement was having their arm twisted into paying the kickbacks. I'm inclined to agree."

Adducci grunted. "Yeah, so am I. Not that seventeenth-century Germans haven't got at least as fine-tuned a sense of lawyering as any West Virginian ever did. They knew damn good and well they were breaking the law too. Still, you have to make allowances for the chaos caused by fifteen years of war half-wrecking the Germanies. People slide into bad habits in situations like that. For us to run around hammering everybody probably wouldn't be a good idea. Still, this is it, folks. You also gotta watch out for being paternalistic about these things. Down-timers ain't children. Once these cases break and we start putting people in prison, let's make sure the message gets out to every businessman in the province who's thinking of cutting a deal beneath the table. Do it again, and we'll bust you, sure and certain."

Noelle thought their attitude was probably the right one to take, though she was even more inclined than they were not to err on the side of paternalistic tolerance. *It's just their traditional ways,* baloney. Her partner Eddie Junker was a down-timer, and *he'd* never had any trouble recognizing that paying a kickback was just as illegal, if not perhaps as personally reprehensible, as demanding it in the first place.

That said, she was a little relieved. Her relations with Eddie had gotten awkward lately, and she was pretty sure she knew the reason. Now, with this decision having been made, she could see her way clear to straightening it out.

Adducci raised an admonishing finger. "But! That only applies to down-timers whose involvement was simply paying the kickback. Any of them who got more, what you might call enthusiastic and enterprising about the business, we'll go after them just like we are the up-timers."

For the third time in half an hour, Noelle had to fight to keep a smile from her face. *That* wouldn't be a problem for her, at least. Claus Junker might have been willing enough in the enthusiasm department, but when it came to "enterprise" it was just a fact that Eddie's father was a hopeless nincompoop. He bore about as much resemblance to a criminal mastermind as . . .

She tried to think of anyone she knew who could possibly be as inept as Claus Junker at the art of "making a deal." The only person she could come up with was her own mother.

She must have choked, or something.

"What's so funny, Noelle?" asked Carol.

"Ah . . . nothing. Just an idle thought."

Janos Drugeth's agents in Grantville, the Englishmen Henry Gage and Lion Gardiner, seemed bound and determined to waste more time continuing the recriminations.

"In particular," said Gage with exasperation, "I told you to stay away from the Barlow family!"

Gardiner scowled at him. "And I *did*—until I was approached by Neil O'Connor, who is part of the affair because *you* recruited his father Allen."

Gage looked defensive. "We need the O'Connors. Between the father's knowledge of steam engines and the son's experience working on aircraft, they'll be invaluable. And we need Peter Barclay and his wife, too. They both have experience in mechanical design."

"We *don't* need—"

Gage threw up his hands. "Of course we don't need their crazy daughter! But the Barclays insisted that their children had to be part of the bargain, or they wouldn't agree." Sullenly, he added: "It's *not* my fault. It's certainly not my fault that the oldest girl Suzi Barclay lives in a state of sin with Neil O'Connor, and she told *him*, and he told his father, and—"

He broke off there. Gardiner picked it right up, now with a sneer on his face.

"—and she also told her friend Caryn Barlow, who is almost as crazy as she is—not surprising, being the daughter of Jay Barlow—and she told her father and there we were. In the soup."

"Enough," said Janos stolidly. Rubbing the back of his neck, he looked around the small apartment his two subordinates had been renting on the outskirts of Grantville. At least they had enough sense to be packed and ready to go. "This is pointless—and we have little time remaining."

He gave Gardiner a cold eye. "Do restrain your indignation. It was you, after all, who recruited the Simmons fellow. Who has no skills I am aware of beyond embezzlement—and paltry skills at that, judging from the evidence."

It was Gardiner's turn to look defensive. "That wasn't *my* doing. The O'Connors insisted that their employee Timothy Kennedy should be included also. Seeing as he was very skilled in the steam work and was now disaffected from his wife—"

Seeing his chance, Gage interrupted with a sneer. "Who just happens to be the sister of Anita Masaniello, who just happens to be the wife of Steve Salatto, who just happens to be the American official in charge of administering Franconia."

Gardiner glared up. "As I recall, *you* thought recruiting Kennedy was a good idea at the time yourself. He seemed tight-lipped enough. How was I—or you—to know that he was good friends with Mickey Simmons and Simmons was up to his neck—"

"Enough!" growled Janos. He wiped his face tiredly. Part of his weariness was due to the rigors of the hard and fast journey he'd made from Vienna, much of which had been on horseback through forests and mountains to evade the USE's border patrols. Most of it, though, was simply weariness at the whole business.

He was still aggravated by Istvan's foolishness in having hired these two English adventurers as his direct agents in Grantville, as much as he was aggravated by the adventurers themselves. But, being fair to all parties, he also recognized that most of the problem was simply due to the nature of the work involved. This miserable business the Americans called "covert operations."

True, Gardiner and Gage were mercenary adventurers. On the other hand, they spoke fluent—now even idiomatic—English in a town of English speakers whose usage of the language was eccentric to begin with, by seventeenth-century standards. It was doubtful that any regular Austrian agents could have penetrated so deeply and quickly into the disaffected elements among the Americans. That was true even leaving aside the thugs who infested the so-called Club 250, who were automatically suspicious of any Central Europeans. None of the thugs themselves were of any particular interest to Austria, which could recruit plenty of thugs of its own. But the Club 250 served as something of a liaison venue for other disaffected up-timers that Austria was interested in. Gage and Gardiner could go there easily. Between their excellent knowledge of the American idiom and the fact they were English—for reasons still somewhat murky to Drugeth, the American bigots who patronized the Club 250 made an exemption for Englishmen—the two of them could habituate the place where, if Janos went himself, he'd likely face a fracas.

True, also, many—no, most; perhaps all—of the Americans they were seeking to recruit were not what any sane man would consider upright and moral persons. At best, their guiding motives were nakedly mercenary. For some of them, such as Simmons, you could add a desire to escape apprehension by the SoTF's authorities for criminal activity. For others, like the O'Connors and their employee Timothy Kennedy, their extravagant and careless spending habits had led them to drive a seemingly prosperous business into a state of near bankruptcy.

As for the "craziness" of the Suzi Barclay girl, a subject on which both Gage and Gardiner could expound at length, what was to be expected from the offspring of such parents?

He rubbed his face again. In the end, all the problems were simply inherent to the business itself. If a man insists on sticking his hand into a marsh looking for gold, he can hardly be surprised if he retrieves filth and leeches as well as the gold he was looking for.

And . . .

There was gold there, sure enough. Being fair to the two. Whatever the moral and mental characteristics of the up-timers whom Gage and Gardiner had recruited to move to Vienna and provide the Austrian empire with technological skills and advice, there was no question that they'd assembled an impressive group. Amongst them, there was extensive knowledge of American machining techniques, mechanical design, and steam engine design, not to mention the seemingly ubiquitous knowledge that American males had with regard to automobile engines. There was even a fair knowledge of aircraft principles, something which was in scant supply even among Americans.

Still, it was a mess. The original plan had been modified after the end of the war between the USE and the League of Ostend brought a period of peace. That, combined with the outcome of the Congress of Copenhagen and the decision of the SoTF to relocate its capital from Grantville to Bamberg, was producing a massive wave of emigration of Americans out of Grantville to other parts—and not all of them to somewhere else in the USE. It seemed as if every nation in Europe had launched a recruitment program here, even the French.

Most of those who chose to leave the USE, of course, went to either Prague or Copenhagen or the Netherlands. Bohemia and Denmark were allied to the USE; and, while the new kingdom in the Low Countries was not, it enjoyed quite friendly relations these days. Nowhere in Europe had the now-romantic figure of the Netherlands' new queen Maria Anna assumed such legendary proportions as it had in Grantville. "The Wheelbarrow Queen," they called her, often enough. Even the rambunctious and surly commoners of Magdeburg seemed inclined to favor the Netherlands, monarchy or not.

Janos had hopes that, eventually, that same romanticism might help relations between the USE and his own nation. Maria Anna was, after all, a daughter of the Habsburgs and one of the new emperor's two sisters. At one time—not more than a few months ago—an archduchess of Austria itself.

It was too early for that, of course. Everyone in the USE was expecting a new war to begin the coming spring, with Saxony and Brandenburg, and everyone was assuming—accurately, alas, unless Janos could persuade the emperor otherwise—that Austria would weigh in on the side of the USE's enemies. Still, Janos had hoped to keep tensions between Austria and the USE, especially its Americans, to a minimum. Sooner or later, he was sure Austria would have to seek peace with the USE, and he didn't want any more in the way of festering anger than was inevitable in the course of a war.

So, clearly and unequivocally, he'd told Istvan Janoszi to instruct his agents to keep any transfer of personnel and equipment from Grantville within the limits of the law, as the Americans saw it.

That hadn't seemed too difficult a project, at the time. The up-timers had sweeping notions on the subject of personal liberties, which included the right to emigrate and included the right to maintain personal property in the process. The key figures, the O'Connors and the Barclays, were in a position to do that. Simply move themselves and their businesses to Vienna. Impossible, of course, to move the actual physical plants, but they could certainly take with them all of their technical designs—"blueprints," those seemed to be called—and even much of the moveable equipment. Over time, if not immediately.

Unfortunately, what Janos hadn't foreseen was the

inevitability of what followed. Like anything dragged out of a swamp, be it gold-colored or not, the Barlows and the O'Connors were *sticky*. They had relatives and friends, the relatives and friends had their own such—and among them, what a surprise, were some individuals whom no one in their right mind would want to encourage to move into his own country.

And so, a legal enterprise had become an illegal one. Not only were some of these people going to be fleeing the authorities of the USE, they were going to be taking goods and possessions with them that they had no legal right to take.

For a moment, Drugeth considered simply forbidding any such goods. But he dismissed the idea almost as soon as it came to him. First, because that was bound to produce a quarrel with the would-be emigrants, and there was no time left for such a quarrel. Second, even more simply, because Drugeth really had no way to know which goods were legal and which weren't, in the first place. Once the expedition got to the Austrian border, he had a large cavalry unit waiting to escort them all the rest of the way to Vienna. But from here to the border, he'd have only Gage and Gardiner to assist him in keeping control over the up-timers.

What was he to do? Insist on a search of the wagons, not even knowing what he was looking for?

It was just a mess, that's all. A marshy muck. But Janos had crossed marshes and swamps often enough, since he took the Austrian colors. Though he was only twenty-five years old, he had plenty of experience as a soldier. He figured he could manage this, well enough.

"Tomorrow morning, then," he said. "We start to leave as early as possible."

CHAPTER 4. *The Biker*

Three days later, in the evening, over the sandwiches they were having by way of a working meal on the folding table in Noelle's apartment, she finally nailed her partner.

"All right, Eddie, spill it. I got the word from Carol Unruh over lunch today. For what it's worth, she and Tony Adducci and Christoph Wieland officially decided that no charges would be pressed against any down-timer unless they were actively involved as one of the arm-twisters. Just paying the bribes, we'll let it go. This time, anyway."

Eddie Junker laid his half-eaten sandwich down on the plate, then stared at it for a moment, before sighing.

"It has been difficult. I've felt bad about it. Not saying anything to you, I mean."

"Yeah, I can see that. How deep was your father involved?"

Eddie shrugged, uncomfortably. "Not as deep as I'm sure he would have liked to have been. Dear God in Heaven, when will my father learn that he has the business sense of . . . of . . ."

"My mother," Noelle said crisply. For a moment, they both shared a laugh. Noelle's mother Pat was to good sense what a junkyard was to orderly. The woman wasn't stupid. She just didn't seem to have a clue how to separate abstractions from their application to the real world.

In her favor, though, Noelle thought but didn't say out loud, at least Pat wasn't greedy. Something which couldn't be said for Claus Junker.

"The point is, Eddie, nobody's going to go after your dad. But I'd like to know if there are any leads there."

Eddie used the time it took to finish the sandwich to compose his thoughts. Then: "I think so, yes. Do you know a man—an up-timer—by the name of Jay Barlow? And another one by the name of Allen O'Connor?"

Noelle stared at him for a moment. "Jay Barlow, yeah," she said abruptly. "He used to be a car dealer before the Ring of Fire, mostly used cars—and he was pretty much a poster boy for what people think of used car dealers."

Eddie frowned. "Which is . . . what?"

"Never mind. Crooked sleazeball is close enough. The kind of guy whose stock in trade was passing off lemons."

"I thought you said he sold automobiles."

"Never mind, like I said. Some other time I'll enhance your vocabulary of up-time slang. But right now I want to concentrate on the other guy. Allen O'Connor, you said?"

"Yes. I think he's actually the more important of the two, although my father's direct dealings were with Barlow."

Noelle chuckled. "Well, yeah, I can believe that. In the TO of organized crime, like any other enterprise I can think of, you'll find the Jay Barlows of the world pretty regularly enrolled under the rank of 'foot soldier.'"

"What's a 'TO'?"

"Table of Organization. Like I said, later for the vocabulary lesson."

She scratched the tip of her chin, forgetting for a

moment her long-standing vow to eliminate that mannerism on account of it drew attention to her chin. She thought it was on the pointy side, which was especially unfortunate given the shape of her ears, which were also too damn close to being pointed. Add into the miserable bargain her too-slim figure, which she'd had since she was a kid, even before she started exercising regularly. She began that regimen after the scares she'd experienced in Franconia during the Ram Rebellion convinced her she'd better be in top physical condition.

All she needed, in her position, was for people to think she was some kind of elf.

Catching herself, she stopped. Then, tugged at her earlobe. Then, silently chided herself and brought the hand firmly down on the table. "O'Connor, on the other hand, has the potential to rise to higher levels. *Did* rise to higher levels, in fact, not long after the Ring of Fire, when he set up a steam engine business."

"So did Barlow," Eddie pointed out. "He's the partner and co-manager of the Grantville-Saalfeld Foundries and Metalworks—which is quite an important and profitable enterprise. More so than O'Connor's steam engine corporation, really."

Noelle sneered, forgetting momentarily her long-standing vow never to sneer on account of it made her look like an impudent elf. "Yeah, sure—but that's due to the *other* partner, Bart Kubiak, who's the brains of the outfit. I heard—never mind where—that the only reason Bart asked Jay to become his partner—and he doesn't have anything close to an equal share in the business, by the way, just a token amount—is because Billie Jean Mase sweet-talked him into it and Bart wanted her to relocate to Saalfeld to be his office manager."

She shook her head. "There's another mixed-blessing character for you. By all accounts, Billie Jean is a crackerjack office manager—"

"I thought those were a kind of cereal candy."

"What is it with your sudden obsession with learning every bit of American slang in one sitting? But whatever skills Billie Jean has in an office, she's a dumb blonde in the rest of her life."

Eddie was now eyeing Noelle's hair dubiously.

"Fine," she snapped. "It's sort-of blonde. It's just an expression. Some of the world's champion dumb blondes are brunettes and redheads. Trust me on this one, for just a moment. Who else but a dumb blonde would ever get hooked up with a guy like Jay Barlow? You can't even credit her with being a gold digger, since she brings in most of the gold."

She raised the fingers of her left hand and began counting them off with the thumb and forefinger of her right hand, forgetting also her solemn vow not to draw attention to her fingers because they were too slender and nimble and, well, sorta elflike.

"First, he's a loser. Second, he's a sleazebag. Third—"

"I thought the term was sleazeball," Eddie complained.

Noelle contemplated strangling him. Then, simultaneously concluded her hands were far too delicate for the task—Eddie was on the heavily-built side—and remembered her vow not to display them. Hurriedly, she put her hands back in her lap.

"Third," she said forcefully, "he's thirteen years older

than she is. Remembering my charitable Christian nature—"

Eddie was looking more dubious by the minute.

"—I will forego pointing out that his potbelly matches his age and then some. Fourth, he's lazy. Fifth—since after two months Bart Kubiak gave him the boot and told him to enjoy his piddly little share of the partnership back in Grantville where he'd be out of Bart's hair—he spends most of his waking hours lounging at the 250 Club, trying to pretend he's a tough biker even if the only part of 'biker' he has down pat is the boozing. Sixth—"

She broke off suddenly, and stared at the wall. Nothing there to look at, just getting an idea.

"What is it?" Eddie asked.

She started scratching her chin again, forgetting her solemn vow to work on her memory so it wouldn't resemble Swiss cheese. Just what she needed, having people think she was as flighty as an elf.

"I was just thinking, now that I think about it, that Jay Barlow is the mirror opposite of Buster Beasley. There's a guy who has 'tough biker' down pat every other way, except he finds most bikers pretty boring. So he doesn't hang out much at the 250 Club, true enough—but I'll bet he knows where all the bones are buried and whose skeleton is rattling which bike. He's honest, too. Well . . . allowing for a certain casual attitude toward mind-altering substances and stuff like that, but who cares? Those laws aren't in force anymore and even if they were you and I are working for the Treasury Department, not the old DEA."

"I am now completely lost," said Eddie.

Noelle flashed him a grin, forgetting her solemn vow to suppress her quick way of smiling since she thought that was probably the silly way that elves smiled if elves existed which they didn't but too many damn people had heard of them and thought they probably did and she was suspect number one.

"I'll introduce you." She glanced at the clock on the wall. "It's only eight. He's probably still at his storage rental place."

She got up, grabbed her purse and shrugged into her coat, then headed for the door. Eddie followed. "If we're lucky, maybe his daughter Denise is there too. There's a real pip."

Outside, Eddie asked: "What is a 'pip'?"

Noelle did her best to explain, as they walked. She'd never realized before, just how hard it could be to explain a colloquial term like "a real pip." But, when she was done, Eddie nodded sagely.

"Ah. Sort of an American elf."

"There's no such thing as an elf," Noelle snapped.

She thought his ensuing silence had a dubious flavor, too.

"Forget Simmons," said Buster Beasley. With the booted foot he had planted on an overturned crate, he kept rocking back and forth on his chair. Given that it wasn't a rocking chair, just a beat-up old wooden kitchen chair, and given Buster's heft, Noelle wondered how much longer it would last.

"Simmons is a clown," he continued. The light cast into the office of Buster's rental storage operation from a single naked light bulb in the ceiling threw his face into deep shadows, making him look more like a prophet than the middle-aged, long-haired, heavily-bearded and burly ex-biker that he was. If you ignored the muscular arms exposed by the cutaway denim jacket, anyway. Noelle was familiar with the lives of many of the saints and the Old Testament prophets, and she was quite sure not one of them had had a "Born to Raise Hell" tattoo on their shoulder, with or without a dagger through it.

"He can manage to slice bread on his own, I suppose, but anything more complicated would stump him for sure. The only reason he got that job heading up the training program for the Department of Transportation was because his ex-wife Lorraine talked her twin sister Lauren into getting it for him, even though she'd dumped the bum years ago."

Buster's fifteen-year-old daughter Denise was perched on an upended crate not far away, as was Eddie. Noelle had been given the one stool in the office to sit on. She'd have preferred a crate herself, actually, since the stool looked to be as rickety as the one and only chair in the office that was getting a workout from Buster.

"I don't get it, Dad," Denise said. The girl's expression was one of intense curiosity, which seemed to fit her face quite nicely. She shook her head a little, causing her long dark hair to ripple. "I mean, sure, I like Lorraine. Who doesn't? But where'd she get the pull to land an ex-husband—not even the guy she's married to now—a job that good?"

Denise didn't seem to think there was anything odd about her father calling another man a bum and clown.

This, despite the fact that Buster's office furniture consisted of upside-down crates and stools, a cheap metal cabinet that looked like an antique except no antique shop would have bothered trying to restore anything that badly stained and covered with rust spots, and a desk—Noelle was still trying not to grin at the thing—that was actually the bed of a junkyard pickup truck that Buster must have cut out with a torch and provided with legs made out of parts from the frames of old motorcycles. He ran a welding business on the side and was quite good at it. Good enough, in fact, that if he'd concentrated on that business he could have become very prosperous. But Buster valued his free time a lot more than he did money.

Noelle wasn't surprised by Denise's respect for her father, quite evident despite the relaxed and informal ease of their relationship. Buster Beasley, like Tom Stone, was one of those people who managed to live outside the normal boundaries of social custom without being considered a hopeless screwball. Screwball, maybe, hopeless—no. They were just too effective at managing their lives, each in their own way. In Buster's case, of course, the tattoos helped stifle vocal criticism, especially combined with the seventeen-inch biceps displayed by the cut-out jacket. Not to mention the scars.

Despite her appearance, which she'd inherited from her mother—slender and very attractive, where Buster was neither—Denise was a chip off the old block. She was just a few weeks shy of her sixteenth birthday. Most girls her age would have been either egotistical or confused by her good looks, and the effect it had on boys. Denise was neither. She took it for granted, didn't seem to care in the least—she certainly didn't pick her girlfriends based on *their* looks—and God help the overeager high school boy who didn't take "no" seriously. Denise was the only girl Noelle knew who'd been hauled in front of the high-school vice-principal for punching a kid out. Fortunately, there weren't too many boys stupid enough to harass Buster Beasley's daughter.

Buster gave his daughter a grin. "How many times have I told you not to underestimate networking skills?"

Denise snorted. "Coming from you!"

He shrugged. "I didn't say I was good at it, I just told you not to underestimate them. In this case, sure, Lorraine doesn't have any direct clout worth talking about. But—"

He held up his thumb. "Her twin sister Lauren owns and runs the town's best restaurant, along with her husband Calvin." He raised his forefinger alongside the thumb. "If there's a power-that-be in Grantville that doesn't hang out there, I don't know who it is." The middle finger came up to join them. "For sure and certain, Joe Stull—remember him? He's the secretary of transportation—eats lunch there practically every day."

Buster brought up the ring finger, somehow managing not to haul the little finger along with it. He was a very well-coordinated man, despite the graying beard and the muscle. "Moving right along, since Lauren and Calvin Tyler's daughter Rachel has all the sense when it comes to men that Lorraine doesn't, she married that Scot cavalryman Edward Graham, who—he ain't no dummy, either—immediately left the Swedish colors and wrangled himself a partnership in the restaurant with his new in-laws. And—"

Finally, the little finger came up. "That damn Scotsman could charm a rattlesnake, which Joe Stull ain't—and Graham makes it a point to be the waiter any time a bigshot shows up."

Denise was looking a little cross-eyed by now. For that matter, Noelle thought she might be herself.

The fingers started closing back down, one at a time, gracefully despite their heft. "So Lorraine talked to Lauren and she talked to Graham and Graham put in a word with Joe Stull, and I guess Joe must have been having one of his rare off days because he agreed to hire the clown. And that's how it happened."

Throughout, he hadn't varied in the slightest the metronome regularity of his chair-rocking. Now, he looked back to Noelle. "So, like I said, forget Simmons." He gestured with his thumb to the tattoo on his shoulder. "If Mickey had a tattoo, it'd read 'Born to Be a Small-Time Loser.' No, the people you want to start looking at are the Barclays."

Noelle frowned. "Pete Barclay? The guy who works for Dave Marcantonio?"

"Yup. Him and his wife Marina. She works there too, y'know." He finally ceased the chair-rocking and stood up, then picked up a big black flashlight perched on a shelf, one of those long, heavy Maglites favored by cops because they could double as a club in a pinch. Buster was holding it the way cops did, too, with the lamp cupped in his hand and the shaft perched on his shoulder, ready to swing forward if need be. So far as Noelle knew, Buster Beasley hadn't been in a brawl in years. But he'd been notorious for brawling in his younger years—if not for starting fights, certainly for ending them—and he clearly still had the ingrained habits.

The big ex-biker headed for the door, not bothering to put on a coat to fend off the autumn chill outside. "Come on. Let me show you something."

A minute later, they were staring into one of Buster's storage sheds. It was one of the big ones down by the end.

"There is nothing in it," said Eddie, puzzled.

"Not today, sure enough. But if you'd looked into it three mornings ago, you would have found it packed full. The Barclays showed up right when I opened, along with Allen and Neil O'Connor—I think most of the stuff belonged to them, actually, even though the Barclays are the ones who paid the rent—and cleaned it all out. They had three wagons for the purposes. Well-built wagons, driven by some down-timers I don't know. The guy who seemed to be in charge was a real dandy, dressed to the hilt. Fancy plumed hat, the whole works."

Noelle hissed. "The *O'Connors*? But . . ."

There seemed to be a thin smile on Buster's face. Between the beard and the darkness, though, it was hard to tell.

"But they have a successful business here? I wouldn't be too sure of that, the way they go through money like it was water. I can tell you this much, for sure. Since the Barclays rented this shed six months ago, they've been steadily filling it up with mechanical equipment—smallish stuff, of course, no big machines—tools, blueprints, diagrams, you name it. I'm pretty sure some of it was swiped from Marcantonio's machine shop, although I couldn't swear to it."

"Oh, wow," said Denise. "Dad, the fuckers are *defecting*."

"That's my guess. Got no idea where to, though."

Noelle's lips were tight. "You know, Buster, you *could* have maybe said something about this earlier."

He swiveled to face her. Whatever smile might have been on his face was gone now. "Said something to who? The so-called 'authorities'? Meaning no offense, Ms. Murphy—"

"It's Stull, now. I changed it."

"Good for you," said Denise. "I kinda like your mother, but her ex-husband—the guy who was supposed to be your dad and wasn't—is a complete shithead."

Clearly enough, whatever parental instruction Buster had felt it necessary to give his daughter had never included "proper language for a young lady." Noelle couldn't really fault Buster for that, though. He made a lot better father in everything essential than Francis Murphy had, she didn't doubt that in the least.

"Yeah, good for you," echoed Buster. "Your real dad Dennis is an okay guy, in my book. But like I was saying, Ms. Stull, I mind my own business. I'm as likely to go to the cops as I am to eat tofu for breakfast. I got along with Dan Frost well enough, once him and me straightened out a few issues. But I've generally got as much use for cops as I do for cockroaches. Especially since, in this case, I can't see where they were doing anything illegal anyway except for maybe some petty theft from Dave's machine shop."

He gave his daughter a stern look. "How is it 'defecting' when we're not at war with anybody any longer? People got a right to live wherever they want, you know—and take their property with them. You really oughta watch your language, young lady."

Noelle barked a laugh.

For his part, Eddie gave Buster a wary look.

"We're not actually policemen," he said. "No powers of arrest. We're just investigators."

Buster shrugged. "Like the guy said in that Muppet movie. Authorities is authorities."

"He didn't say that," Denise protested. "He said—"

"Do *you* want to help them?" demanded her father, gesturing with a thumb at Noelle and Eddie.

"Yeah, sure. I don't care what you say, Dad. Those fuckers are defecting. Buncha traitors."

"Then quit arguing with me about movie dialogue and get a move on." He turned back to Noelle and Eddie, smiling again. "If you want to catch them, you'd better plan on starting at dawn. They'll have three days' head start on you, wherever they're going."

"You have no idea?"

"Not a clue. Like I said—"

"You mind your own business. I heard you." Noelle tried not to sound too snappish and testy. Despite his appearance, Buster was generally an easy-going sort of fellow. Still. Aggravating a large ex-biker on his own property in the middle of the night when he was carrying an eighteen-inch flashlight in his hand did not strike Noelle as falling into the category of "good idea."

Eddie was scratching his head. "We'll need to alert the police, first. Then we'll have to figure out which way they went."

Denise grinned. "I'll find that out for you. Me and my bike. I'll get started as soon as it's light enough to see anything."

"Ain't she a pip?" said her father, admiringly.

CHAPTER 5. *The Nature of Plans*

Near Grantville, State of Thuringia-Franconia

"Fucking idiots, what they are," pronounced Denise. She finished the beer she'd ordered at Stephan Wurmbrand's roadside tavern just outside Grantville on the road to Rudolstadt and almost slammed the glass back on the bar. She glared around the room, as if defying any of its habitués to challenge either her use of language or her judgment of police chiefs and cavalry officers.

No challenge came forth, except from Lannie Yost, perched on a nearby stool. Owlishly, he peered at her empty glass. "Ain't you a little young to be drinking that stuff?"

Denise gaped at him. So did several of the other barflies in the place. In their case, because they were down-time Germans who thought the notion of anyone being under age to drink beer was silly—one of those up-time fetishes they'd thought must have died a natural death by now, three and a half years after the Ring of Fire. In Denise's case, because her father was Buster Beasley and *she* thought— so did Buster, actually—that she was practically abstemious when it came to substance abuse.

She was also gaping because she was outraged, of course.

"You! Lannie Yost, you're pie-eyed half the time! So-called test pilot. You got some nerve—"

"Hey, Denise, take it easy! I wasn't trying to pick no fight."

That wouldn't normally have done him any good at all, except he added hurriedly: "You got the right of it when it comes to Captain Knefler, that's for sure. Guy couldn't find his ass with both hands in broad daylight."

"That jackass. I *told* him I found their trail, leading south from Rudolstadt. But, noooo. Mr. Military Genius insisted they must have used those rafts the one guy—the one in charge, whoever he is—bought in Jena."

By now, the news had spread all over the area, including some of the details. "The rafts *were* gone," one of the down-timers pointed out. He was sitting with a friend at a table nearby.

Denise sniffed. "Big deal. All the guy in charge—and I think he's got more brains in his little toe than Knefler does—had to do was hire a few men to pole the rafts downriver. There's day laborers hanging around all over the place, in Jena. Probably told them they needed to pick up something in Halle and take it down to Magdeburg. Off goes whichever idiot came in pursuit—his name's Knefler, did I mention that? It's spelled 'k-n' like in numbskull— while the guy with the brains keeps heading up the Saale valley. Hasn't it struck any of you geniuses yet that Mr.-Whoever is good at this? Why would he have been wearing such a flamboyant outfit just to buy some cargo rafts—if he hadn't been trying to draw attention to himself?"

She was pretty proud of that deductive logic. Maybe she ought to become a detective when she grew up.

Finished growing up. Which she was practically there. She'd bet Minnie would partner with her.

On the other hand, she'd neglected to mention that Mr.-Whoever-He-Was had been wearing the same outfit when he arrived at her father's storage place to load the wagons. Obviously, just to make sure every idiot in Grantville connected Obvious Dot A to Blatant Dot B. The Grantville police chief and Captain Numbskull had squeezed that information out of her, despite her misgivings about what they'd do with it, but she saw no reason to weaken her case by divulging it to these layabouts.

Lannie took a swallow from his own beer. "You think?"

"Sure. What sort of lunatic would make his escape *further* into the USE?"

The same down-timer wasn't ready to let it go. "Not so foolish, that. Before he gets to Halle, he can offload the rafts and make his way into Saxony. Probably he's working for John George."

Denise opened her mouth, then decided it wasn't worth the effort to get into an argument with somebody who was obviously not playing with a full deck.

Right. Sure. That made sense. In six months, the elector of Saxony was staring in the face an all-out invasion by Gustav Adolf. Fat lot of good some tech transfer would do him at *this* stage of the game. Except give Gustav Adolf another Cassius Belly. Or whatever the name was of that ancient Roman guy who'd caused a war.

Denise might be willing to concede that John George was that stupid. But none of the up-timer traitors were that dumb, except maybe Jay Barlow and Mickey Simmons. Even Suzi Barclay wasn't that dumb, just nuts.

No, wherever the lousy defectors were going, it was someplace they figured could hold off the USE, at least for a while. That meant Austria, probably—that had been Noelle's guess—or maybe Bavaria.

Lannie finished his beer and stood up. The motion was just a little bit too exaggerated to be that of a completely sober man. Which, given Lannie, was no surprise. He wasn't actually drunk, just in his more-normal-than-not state of a pleasant buzz. Lannie's alcoholism wasn't so bad that he couldn't get by in life, with his rare skills. Jesse Wood hadn't been willing to accept him in the air force, but the Kellys used him for their test pilot.

"Okay, then," he said. "Give me a ride back to Grantville on your bike, kid. I'll nail the bastards for you."

Denise frowned. "What are you talking about?"

He slapped his chest. "When the cavalry falls down on the job, you gotta call in the air force. One of the planes at the facility—that's the *Dauntless*—is finished and ready to go."

Denise stopped laughing after a while, then shrugged. "Sure, why not? I'll take you there. I'm warning you, though. Those hands of yours better not move around any while you're holding onto me."

Lannie looked aggrieved. "Hey, there's no call for that. Besides, I ain't crazy enough to piss off your dad."

Denise squinted at him. "You start groping, and my dad will be the least of your worries."

The Saale Valley, south of Saalfeld

"It has to be them," Noelle pronounced.

Eddie sighed and wiped his face. His whole body ached, from spending three days in the saddle. Especially his thighs. "No, actually, it doesn't. They passed through Saalfeld yesterday evening, in bad lighting, and the guards we talked to didn't recognize anybody. Just three wagons, which they didn't give more than a cursory inspection if they gave them any at all, because they most likely got bribed. Those are not exactly elite troops in that garrison, now that nobody's worried any longer about another raid deep into the Thueringerwald. Even if they weren't bribed, they probably wouldn't have bothered to check the wagons anyway. You have any idea how many times heavily loaded wagons pass through Saalfeld?"

"It has to be them," Noelle repeated stubbornly. She swiveled in the saddle, the slight carefulness of the motion making it clear she wasn't feeling any too spry herself. "We should have gotten reinforcements by now. I guess Denise couldn't get anybody to take her seriously. Maybe I should have—"

"*You* weren't going to stay behind, since *you* can't resist the thrill of the chase. *I* couldn't stay behind, because somebody has to look after you. That left Denise—and we practically had to sit on her to get her to agree."

He wiped his face again. "And, yes, they probably didn't take her seriously. Given that she would have had to report to Captain Knefler, him now being the commander of the Grantville garrison, and Knefler is a jackass." He smiled. "Probably, after ten seconds or so, Denise started denouncing him. She's a real pip, that one."

Noelle eyed him suspiciously. "She's only sixteen years old. Not even that."

"All the more reason they wouldn't take her seriously."

"That's *not* what I was referring to. I was referring to the possibility of other men taking her too seriously."

"Don't be ridiculous."

The Saale Valley, near Hof

"Stop complaining," Janos said. He gave the wagon a cold, experienced eye. "The likelihood of having an axle break was very high, given the route we've taken and the speed we've made."

"And that's another thing," complained Billie Jean Mase. "You've been wearing everybody out."

Janos didn't bother replying to that accusation. In point of fact, while the pace he'd set had been hard by the standards of a commercial caravan, it was nothing compared to the pace Hungarian cavalrymen and their supply trains were accustomed to while on campaign. He was feeling perfectly well rested, himself. Granted, he'd been in a saddle, but Gage and Gardiner had been driving two of the three wagons and they were holding up well also.

Of the three drivers, the one in the worst shape was Mickey Simmons. He'd gotten the assignment because he'd boasted of the wagoneering skills he'd developed as a result of being the coordinator of training for the transportation department. Naturally, within less than four days he'd broken an axle.

"There's no time for this," Janos said curtly. He glanced up at the sun. "We'll camp here. We have perhaps three hours of daylight left to sort through the wagons, jettison whatever is least important, and repack the two surviving wagons."

Needless to say—he didn't think he'd ever met such self-indulgent people; they were even worse than Austrian noblemen—the Americans set up a round of protests and complaint. The gist of which was *we need all of it*.

He gave them no more than a minute before cutting the nonsense short.

"We have no means of repairing the axle. Nor can we seek the assistance of a wainwright in Hof, because there is a USE garrison there. By now, the alert will have reached them. Like most such garrisons, they will not exert themselves to search the surrounding countryside— but if we show up in the town itself, which is quite small, they will be almost certain to spot us."

He gave the assembled up-timers perhaps five seconds of a stony stare to see if any were stupid enough to argue those points.

None were, apparently. He revised his estimate of their common sense. Higher than carrots, after all.

"That leaves two options. The first is that we unload the contents of the broken wagon and pile them onto the two others."

"Yeah, that's what I was figuring," said Jay Barlow.

Sadly, the level of common sense did not attain that of rabbits.

Janos half-turned and pointed southeast toward a low range of mountains. "By tomorrow, we have to be well into the Fichtelgebirge. That terrain is considerably worse than we've been passing through, and the roads are worse yet. We are certain to break another axle, or a wheel, with overloaded wagons—and these are already dangerously burdened as it is. I leave aside the fact that we are now into late autumn. The weather has been good, so far, for which we can be thankful. But who knows when the weather might turn?"

The Americans squinted at the mountains. "We gotta go up *there*?" whined Peter Barclay's wife Marina. By now, Janos had come to recognize her as a champion whiner. She almost put his great aunt Orsolya in the shade. Not quite.

"Why?" demanded her husband.

Janos shook his head. "This close to Bayreuth, we can't stay in the lowlands or we run the risk of being spotted by a cavalry troop. Even in the Fichtelgebirge, there may be an occasional patrol. Once we enter it, we can take only a few days—no more—to reach Cheb by following the Eger."

The Barclays' daughter Suzi frowned. She was a bizarre-looking creature, who would have been an attractive young woman if it hadn't been for the short cropped hair dyed a truly hideous color, five earrings in her left ear and three on the right, two metal studs through her right eyebrow—and, capping it all, a tattoo of flames done in black ink reaching from the wrist of her right arm to the top of the right side of her neck. The woman was so attached to the grotesque decoration that she insisted on wearing a sleeveless vest instead of a coat, despite the November temperatures.

"That can't be right," she said. "I know somebody from Cheb, one of the girls—well, never mind that, but she's Bohemian."

"That is hardly surprising, since Cheb is in Bohemia.

It's an old fortress town that guards the western approaches. Good for us, in this instance, since the garrison is a mercenary company and its commander has been well bribed. We'll abandon these wagons in Cheb and replace them with several smaller ones, much better designed for travel in the mountains. We'll even have a cavalry escort while we pass down part of the Bohemian Forest until we reenter the USE near Kötzting. There, we will follow the Regen down to Regensburg, where we will exchange the wagons—that has also been arranged—for a barge that will take us down the Danube into Austria."

He'd already explained this to the leaders of the uptimers, the older Barclays and O'Connor and his son. But it seemed they either hadn't paid attention or hadn't considered all the implications.

"Hey, wait a minute," said Allan O'Connor. "We're coming *back* into the USE? What the hell for? I know my geography, dammit. Once we're across into Bohemia, let's just stay there until we get to Austria."

Janos stared at him. "Indeed. As a geographical proposition, that is certainly feasible. Follow the rivers down to Pizen. From there we could take a good road to Ceské Budejovice, the largest town in southern Bohemia. From there, of course, it is a short distance to Austria— and along a very good road, given the long and constant intercourse between Vienna and Prague."

O'Connor nodded. "Yeah, that's what I was thinking."

No rabbit had ever been this stupid, for a certainly. "You have missed the news, then. Of the war between Bohemia and Austria. Which has been going on for a year and a half, now."

The up-timers frowned at him. They looked like a pack of confused rabbits. All except Suzi Barclay, who just looked like a crazed rabbit.

Janos grit his teeth, reminding himself that he needed to remain on the best possible terms with these—these—people.

"Not a good idea," he said thinly. "The reason I could bribe the commander of the Cheb garrison is because no one expects hostilities to erupt between the USE and Bohemia, so that frontier post was given to a man who was competent enough but needed no further qualifications. Such as . . . what you might call a rigorous sense of duty. At Pizen and Ceské Budejovice, on the other hand, we would be dealing with Pappenheim's Black Cuirassiers."

The up-timers seemed to draw back a little.

"Ah. I see you have heard of them. Yes. We do not wish to have dealings with the Black Cuirassiers."

Enough! Still more time had been wasted. He pointed stiffly to the broken wagon. "So let us begin unloading it. Now. And discard from the other two wagons whatever is not essential."

CHAPTER 6. *The Mess*

High Street Mansion, Seat of Government for the State of Thuringia-Franconia
President's Office
Grantville, State of Thuringia-Franconia

After Grantville's police chief finished his report, Ed

Piazza, president of the State of Thuringia-Franconia, half-turned his swivel chair and looked out of the window in his office. That was the first time he'd so much as glanced outside since he showed up for work this morning. His schedule had been jam-packed even before this latest crisis hit.

The weather was still good, he saw. Clear, with not a cloud in the sky. Very crisp, of course, the way such days in November were, but not yet bitterly cold the way it would become in January and February.

Well, not "crisis," exactly, he mused. He and Mike Stearns had long known that there was no way to keep the USE's enemies from getting their hands on American technical knowledge—nor from suborning some of the Americans themselves. Among the thirty-five hundred people who'd come from up-time through the Ring of Fire, there was bound to be the usual percentage who were excessively greedy and not burdened with much in the way of a conscience. That was even leaving aside the ones—there were a lot of those, now—who'd accepted legitimate offers to relocate elsewhere. You couldn't keep people from emigrating, after all; not, at least, without building some sort of Godforsaken version of a Berlin Wall, which neither he nor Mike had wanted any part of.

Some people were surprised, even astonished, at the number of Americans who were leaving Grantville these days. They'd assumed that long familiarity, habits, family ties—not to mention modern indoor plumbing—would keep almost everyone from straying. But that was unrealistic. West Virginians, especially northern West Virginians, had been accustomed to moving around a lot, since the area was economically depressed except when the mines were working full bore. Most families had at least one person, in the past, who'd moved to one of the industrial cities to make a living. Often they came back, when things at home picked up, but sometimes they didn't.

And those had been relocations just to get decent-paying but usually hard jobs in a steel mill or auto assembly plant. Today, anyone with any skills was being offered salaries that were the down-time equivalent of the kind of money top-drawer technical and business consultants made back up-time. Often enough, with lots of perks and benefits attached. And since the prospective employers were rich—many of them noblemen, sometimes royalty—even the problem of leaving modern plumbing behind wasn't so bad. It wasn't as if the upper classes of the seventeenth century were medieval barons living in stone piles, after all. They had indoor plumbing, however rudimentary it might be by late twentieth-century American standards. And it would get better quickly, too, since the people offering the jobs had a keen desire themselves to get better facilities. Anyone in Grantville who had significant plumbing skills and experience practically had a *carte blanche* to go anywhere in Europe.

To add pressure to pull, most up-timers after the Ring of Fire had lost what they'd had in the way of a safety net back up-time. Which, for working class people like most of the town's inhabitants, had never been all that munificent in the first place.

Social Security was gone. Company pensions were

gone, except for a few companies headquartered in Grantville who'd been able to maintain them. Medicare was gone. That might not directly affect young people, right away, but most people in Grantville were part of families, often extended families. They had parents and grandparents and other elderly relatives who were in a tight situation, sometimes a desperate one—and now, Baron Whoozit or Merchant Moneybags or City Patrician Whazzisname was waving a small fortune under their noses, if they'd just relocate to wherever and apply their skills.

So, since the end of the Baltic war—the decision to move the SoTF's capital to Bamberg had been a prod, too—a great migration was underway. "Great," at least, in per capita terms if not absolute numbers. Some people were even starting to call it the "American Diaspora." What had been a trickle, in the first three years after the Ring of Fire, was now a small flood. By the time it was over, Ed wouldn't be surprised if half of Grantville's residents wound up living somewhere else, at least for a time.

Most of them were staying in the USE, true enough. But the number who were accepting positions in other countries was not inconsiderable, especially countries that had good relations with the USE like Bohemia, Venice, the Netherlands, and the Scandinavian nations now united within the Union of Kalmar. Some had gone to France and Austria. A few, even farther afield, to eastern Europe, Russia, Spain and Portugal, southern Italy—even the New World.

In fact, Ed was a little puzzled by the fact this batch of

emigrants had chosen to break the law by stealing things that didn't belong to them. Why? There was no legal barrier, as such, to moving to Austria, if that's where they went. The Sanderlins and Sonny Fortney had moved to Vienna not long ago, perfectly openly and aboveboard. They'd even hauled two complete automobiles with them.

Carol Unruh's suspicion, which she'd voiced two days earlier, was that at least some of them were going to wind up implicated in the legal fall-out from the Bolender arrest. She'd probably turn out to be right. But, whatever the reason, the immediate effect—and the thing that made it a problem for Ed—was that it transformed what would have otherwise have been a simple emigration into "defection" and even "treason."

What a stupid mess.

The worst thing about this episode with the Barclays and the O'Connors—assuming for the moment that they got away with it—wasn't actually the tech transfer itself. True, among the whole group of them, they had quite a bit of technical knowledge and skills, not to mention the stuff they'd taken or stolen. But it was hardly as if there was any one "secret" that was equivalent to a magic wand. One of the USE's enemies, probably Austria, would get a major boost to whatever modernization program they'd set underway. That was hardly enough, by itself, to transform them overnight into an industrial powerhouse—which was something of a double-edged sword in any event, for Europe's royal houses and aristocracy.

No, insofar as the affair constituted a crisis, it was a political one, not a military or technical one. Among the still-murky set of possible outcomes, one outcome was a certainty. Wilhelm Wettin and his Crown Loyalist party would pull out the stops to make as much political hay of it as they could. Wilhelm himself would keep within the limits of using the episode to argue that it showed Americans were nothing special, so what difference did it make if Mike Stearns' party had the support of most of them? A large number of the Crown Loyalists would go a lot farther than that, though, arguing that the whole affair cast suspicion on American loyalty in general.

And there were some elements within the CLs who'd take it to the hoop. It was well-known that reactionary elements were infiltrating that loosely-defined and none-too-disciplined party, now that nation-wide elections would be taking place within a few months. Some of them were outright extremists. They'd trot out their usual anti-Catholic diatribes, of course, given the high percentage of Catholics in the defecting group—even if most of them were lapsed Catholics. They'd probably also fire up the anti-Semitic propaganda, ignoring the fact that none of the defectors were Jewish or had any connection to Jews beyond purely casual ones. Logic was hardly the strong suit of that particular current within the politics of the Germanies.

Ed managed a chuckle, then, remembering one woodcut illustration of himself in a pamphlet put out by one of the reactionary outfits. The Knights of Barbarossa, if he remembered right. The thing had been quite charming, in its own way. The horns and the cloven hoofs and the forked tail were standard fare. Generic, really. But he'd thought the addition of a grotesquely "Jewish" hooked nose was a nice touch, given his rather puglike features. Not to mention showing him sacrificing a presumably gentile baby in some sort of religious rite, and never mind that he and his wife were lifelong Catholics and attended mass regularly.

He swiveled the chair back, to face Preston Richards and Carol Unruh, the two other people in the room. "What if Noelle's right, Press? And have we gotten any word from her since she left?"

"Nothing," said Carol Unruh, answering his second question. "Not a peep. We don't know where she is, really, except 'somewhere south of Rudolstadt.'"

The police chief grunted. "She hasn't passed through Saalfeld—or, if she did, she didn't stop for anything. We're in radio contact with the authorities there." His expression grew sour. "Not that it's likely to do any good. The garrisons in all the towns in the area are small and entirely mercenary, since—"

Ed waved that aside. "Yeah, Press, I know. Since the emperor is keeping most of the regular army units in the north because he wants them in position to attack Saxony and Brandenburg in a few months—and he's sending the ones he can spare down to reinforce the troops facing Bavaria and Bernhard. So we make do with what we can get. No point pissing and moaning about it all over again. I take it they haven't gotten off their butts and started scouring the countryside?"

"'Scouring,'" Carol jeered. "Their idea of 'scouring the countryside' is trotting a few miles out of town to the nearest watering hole, getting plastered, and reporting that they saw no signs of suspicious activity or suspicious persons passing through. Two or three days worth of getting soused later." Her expression grew more solemn. "I'm mostly worried about Noelle, Ed. She could get hurt, or even killed. I mean, you know what she's like."

Indeed, he did, having read the detailed report of her activities the previous summer and fall in Franconia, during the Ram Rebellion. Ed's wife Annabelle had once described Noelle Murphy—now Noelle Stull—as Grantville's distaff version of Clark Kent, absent the glasses. Primly-mannered maybe-I'll-become-a-nun young woman, zips into the phone booth, out comes Super-Ingénue. She'd even blown a torturer's head half off, when he attacked her partner Eddie Junker. Since Noelle couldn't shoot straight, she'd done so by the simple method of shoving the barrel of the gun under his chin and pulling the trigger.

Timid, she was not, appearances to the contrary.

"We'll just have to hope for the best," he said. "Captain Knefler took practically the whole garrison with him up to Halle. That just leaves the police force, which is under-strength to begin with, the way Grantville keeps growing."

Richards gave Carol an apologetic glance. "I did send a couple of officers over to Rudolstadt, and they were able to get the garrison commander there to detach three of his soldiers to accompany them. No more than three men, though, and no farther south than Hof, without the count's okay. I radioed Magdeburg to see if I could reach him, but it seems Ludwig Guenther and his wife are out of the city visiting relatives at the moment."

That was too bad. The count of Schwarzburg-Rudolstadt was a capable and conscientious man, and maintained good relations with Grantville. If he or his wife Emelie had been in residence at their castle in Rudolstadt, they'd have sent out the whole garrison to search for Noelle and Eddie—and the defectors, too, if Noelle was right and they were in the vicinity. It wasn't a big garrison, but it was a good one. Mercenaries, true, but a well-trained and disciplined company that had been in the service of the count for a long time, not a contractor's slapdash outfit.

The problem was that the State of Thuringia-Franconia—at least, the area around Grantville—simply didn't have much any longer in the way of military forces. In the months after the Croat raid on Grantville and its high school, more than two years earlier, the town had fairly bristled for a while with cavalry patrols, freshly built fortifications, sentinel outposts, the works. But two years was a long time in the war conditions of Europe. Soon enough, it became obvious that there was no immediate military threat to Grantville any longer. The key development had been Wallenstein switching sides in 1633. The same man who'd launched the Croat raid was now allied with the USE—and, given the number of Americans living in Prague today, some of them very closely connected to the new king, there was simply no way Wallenstein could organize and launch a secret attack even if he wanted to.

So that ended the threat from Bohemia, which was the most pressing one. Who else could launch a raid on Grantville? The Austrians would have to fight their way through Bohemia first—and Wallenstein had beaten their army at the second battle of the White Mountain. The

Bavarians were in no position to do anything more than try to hold their ground. That had been obvious even before Gustav Adolf's general Banér seized their fortress of Ingolstadt, which left the Bavarians without a bridgehead north of the Danube.

The Saxons were the only real possibility, and that was negligible. John George, the elector, had a full scale invasion coming and he knew it perfectly well. He was concentrating entirely on readying Saxony's defenses, not wasting energy on raids that would simply chew up his army. Holk's mercenary forces were really the only ones he had available for something like that, anyway. Holk would have to fight his way through sizeable forces—USE regulars, too—stationed in Halle, in order to reach Grantville or any of the towns in the Thuringian basin. Nobody thought he could manage that, and if he even tried he'd leave Saxony's frontier with Bohemia open to an attack by Wallenstein. There was no way the elector of Saxony would countenance such a thing. He'd hired Holk and his army in the first place, despite their unsavory reputation, in order to help protect his southern flank.

Who else? A few hysterics shrieked about the "French menace," pointing with alarm to Turenne's daring raid on the Wietze oil fields during the Baltic war, but that was downright laughable. Given the political tensions in France after the war, there was no way Richelieu was going to send his best general haring off on a long-distance raid. Even if he did, so what? Only somebody who was geographically-challenged and completely ignorant of logistics could possibly think that a raid from France to Grantville was anything like a raid into Brunswick. That

Turenne was an exceptionally gifted military commander had been proven in this universe, as well as being attested to by the historical records of another. That did not make him a magician, who could fight his way through the entire USE. It was three hundred miles from the French frontier to Grantville, even as the crow flies. At least half again that far, the way an army would have to travel.

No, aside from the mundane and everyday risks of living in a boom town, Grantville was about as safe as any place in Europe, these days. So, beginning in the fall of 1633, the military forces that had once protected it carefully had been almost completely drained away. They were needed elsewhere. The regular cavalry patrols were a thing of the past, the sentinel posts had been abandoned completely, and the outlying fortresses had no more than a handful of men detached from the small garrisons maintained in the towns of the basin—who were really there to keep order and double as a police force, more than to serve as an actual military defense.

"We haven't got a pot to piss in, is what it amounts to," he said.

"Not for something like this, Mr. President," agreed the police chief.

Carol looked fierce. "If those bastards so much as hurt Noelle and Eddie, I don't care what Mike says. I'm for firing up the war against Austria. Or whoever it is."

There'd be a lot of that sentiment, Ed knew, if Noelle and Eddie came to harm. Granted, assuming Austria was behind the affair, most people would hold a grudge about the mass defection in any event. But most of the grudge would be aimed at the defectors themselves, not the

Austrians. It wouldn't be the sort of thing that would set off any real war fever. Noelle and Eddie getting killed or badly injured would be a different kettle of fish altogether.

Ed contemplated the problem, for a few seconds. As a practical proposition, of course, launching any sort of immediate campaign against Austria was a non-starter. But "immediate" meant next year. The year after that . . .

He shook his head slightly. That was pointless speculation, right now. They still didn't even know what was really happening.

"I guess that's it then, for the moment." He straightened up in his chair. "Unless Denise Beasley— there's a real pip, for you—shows up with some more information."

Press Richards grinned. "Don't think that's too likely. I got no idea what she's up to now. The last I saw of her she was racing off on her bike, giving me and Knefler the finger. Most of her spleen wasn't really aimed at me, since Denise knows I haven't got the resources to do what she wanted. But she probably has me lumped in with 'the fathead' for the time being."

Carol's mouth made a little O. "Did she *really* call Captain Knefler a 'fathead'? I mean, to his face?"

"Oh, yeah." Solemnly, Press shook his head. "Wasn't all she called him, I'm deeply sorry to report. Girl's got a real potty mouth, when she cuts it loose. She also called him a fuckwad and an asshole and a motherfucking moron."

"She's not even sixteen!"

"She's Buster's kid," Ed grunted. "That's got to add a

decade or so, at least in the lack-of-respect-for-your-betters department. Thank God I'm no longer the high school principal. She's not my headache, these days."

Richards and Unruh both looked at him.

"Well, she isn't," Ed insisted. Hoping it was true.

CHAPTER 7. *The Wild Blue Yonder*

Kelly Aviation Facility
Near Grantville, State of Thuringia-Franconia

Denise stared at the object that was the center of the proposal Lannie had just advanced.

"No fucking way," she pronounced.

Yost shook his head lugubriously. "You really oughta watch your ˮ

"Don't fucking start on me, Lannie. Just don't." She pointed an accusing finger at the aircraft. "There is no fucking—or flibbertyjerking, if that makes you happier—way in hell I'm getting into that thing."

Lannie frowned. "What does 'flibbertyjerking' mean? And what's the matter, anyway? It flies. It flies just fine. I've taken it up plenty of times." After a two-second pause he added, "Well, maybe three times."

Denise scowled at him. "You said yourself. It's a *prototype*, remember?"

"Well, sure, but . . ."

He let that trail off into nothing. The truth was, except for being a boozer, Lannie wasn't a bad guy. And he did have the virtue of being a very loyal sort of person, even if Denise thought he had to be half-nuts to give his loyalty to Bob and Kay Kelly.

Kay was a harridan, and Bob was . . . Well. Impractical. Not hard to get along with, but the kind of guy who simply couldn't control his enthusiasms and seemed to have the attention span of a six-year-old.

She looked around the big hangar. There were no fewer than four planes in evidence, all of them in various stages of construction—or deconstruction, in the case of two—and every one of them bore the label "prototype." It seemed like every time Bob Kelly got close to finishing a plane he decided there was something not quite right about it and he needed to redesign it. Again. The slogan of his company might as well be *The Perfect Is the Enemy of the Good Enough—and We Can Prove it to You.*

The only reason he hadn't gone bankrupt three times over, since the Ring of Fire, was because of his wife. For reasons Denise couldn't begin to fathom, Kay Kelly seemed to have a veritable genius for drumming up investors and squeezing money out of the government.

"I'm *not* getting into it," she repeated.

Alas, some trace of uncertainty must have been in her voice. The third party present detected it and pounced immediately. That was Keenan Murphy, the mechanic who was the only other person in the facility that day. The Kellys had gone up to Magdeburg to lobby the government for more funds, and apparently the office manager had decided to take the day off.

"C'mon, Denise," said Keenan. "We gotta help Noelle. I mean, she's my *sister.*"

Denise almost snapped back, "half-sister," but she

restrained herself. First, because Keenan was giving her such a sad-eyed, woebegone look; second, because he was a sad-sack, woebegone kind of guy; but, mostly, because whether or not Keenan Murphy was a loser he was another one who had an exaggerated, irrational sense of loyalty.

As did Denise herself, and she knew it. In her own personal scale of things, the way she judged people, that counted for a lot.

She stared at the plane again, trying to imagine herself in it *up there*—what? maybe a mile high?—with a souse for a pilot and a low-achiever for a . . .

"Hey, wait a minute." She glared at the two of them. "I thought you said Keenan didn't know how to fly."

"He don't," said Lannie. "He's the bombardier. He'll ride in the back." He pointed toward the rear of the cockpit. Now that she looked more closely, Denise could see that there was a third seat there, behind the two side-by-side seats in front.

Her eyes widened. "You have *got* to be kidding. You want *me* to be the copilot? I don't know fuck-all about flying!"

Keenan Murphy shook his head. "Naw, not that. We need you to be the navigator. I can't see well enough, back there, and Lannie . . . well . . ."

Yost gave him a pained look. Keenan shrugged. "Sorry, Lannie, but it's just a fact. You get lost easy."

"Oh, swell," said Denise. She ran fingers through her dark hair, starting to wind it up into a bun. No, hell with that. She'd just put it in a pony tail, like she did riding the bike.

"Gimme a rubber band," she commanded. With a sneer: "I'm sure you got plenty around here, for engine parts."

"Hey, there's no call for—"

"Leave it, Lannie," said Keenan, chuckling. "I'll find you one, Denise. It might not be real clean, though."

She looked around the hangar again. Bob Kelly followed the Big Bang theory of design and manufacture. Out of chaos, creation—and, clearly enough, they were still a lot closer to chaos. The area was completely unlike her dad's weld shop, which was as neat and well kept as he wasn't.

"Never mind," she said, heading for the hangar door. "My bike's right outside. I got some in the saddlebags."

The Saale river, south of Halle

"I ought to have you arrested!" shouted Captain Knefler.

"For *what?*" demanded the burly boatman. Clearly, he was not a man easily intimidated by a mere show of official outrage. Not here, at least, while he was still within Thuringia-Franconia. In some provinces of the USE, not to mention the districts under direct imperial administration, he might have been more circumspect. But the laws concerning personal liberties were strict in the SoTF—and, perhaps more importantly, were strictly enforced by the authorities.

The *real* authorities, which did not include any cavalry captain who thought he could throw his weight around.

"You are part of a treasonous plot!" screeched Knefler.

Watching the scene, standing behind the captain where

Knefler couldn't see him, Sergeant Reimers flashed a grin at the two soldiers with him. None of them had any use for their commanding officer. This was entertaining.

"Oh, what a pile of horseshit," jeered the boatman. He waved a thick hand at the three rafts now drawn up to the river bank. "Your evidence, please?"

No evidence there, since the rafts were quite empty, except for some parcels of food and a few personal belongings. Unless something had been dumped overboard, the crude vessels obviously hadn't carried anything down from Jena except the boatmen themselves and their travel necessities.

Reimers' amusement faded a bit. To be sure, there was no chance the boatmen had jettisoned anything, since they couldn't have spotted the cavalry troop coming up from Grantville until it was almost upon them. Whereupon, Knefler had ordered them—with the threat of his soldiers' leveled carbines, no less—to bring the rafts immediately ashore.

Still, the captain was furious enough—he was certainly thick-witted enough—to order his men to start dredging the river for miles upstream. As useless as such a task might be, given their small numbers and lack of equipment.

The problem was that while Knefler was thick-witted, he was not a complete dimwit. He knew perfectly well that he now faced a major embarrassment. Probably not something that would get him cashiered, more was the pity. But certainly something that would not enhance his prospects for promotion.

The young American girl had told him the culprits had

fled to the south, in language that was still a delight to recall. But Knefler had dismissed her arguments and insisted on following his own reasoning.

Knefler was now wasting time glaring at the empty rafts. "I need no material evidence," he insisted. "There is the evidence of your actions. Why, if it were not part of a treasonous plot, did you leave Jena before dawn?"

He tried a sneer himself. "Of course, I am no boatman. But I doubt such is standard practice."

"Because our employer *paid* us to do so," said the boatmen. "A bonus, he said, to make sure we got to Halle in time to pick up—"

"Nonsense! Nonsense! You did it so there would be no witnesses! Nobody who could tell me that the rafts were empty!"

The boatman planted his hands on his hips and squinted up at the tall, almost-skeletal officer. "In other words, you were outsmarted. Not by me and my boys—we are innocent parties only accidentally involved—but by the man you're chasing. Not so?"

Knefler glared down at him. "You will have to answer for your actions. Prove your innocence."

The boatman's sneer was magnificent. "To the contrary, Your Mightyship. This is Thuringia-Franconia, or have you forgotten? *You* have to demonstrate my guilt, not the other way around."

Knefler was so angry he started waving his arms. "Even the silly fucking Americ—ah, the up-timers—accept such a thing as circumstantial evidence."

"Fine. There is the circumstantial evidence that we were hired to take rafts down the river to Halle to pick up a consignment of goods for early delivery to Magdeburg. Said deed being committed in Gerhard Pfrommer's tavern on the waterfront in Jena, by an man unknown to anyone there, who approached Gerhard asking for reliable boatmen and was pointed to us at a nearby table."

The sneer didn't waver once. "Said table, I might add, being right in the middle of the tavern—crowded, it was, that time of evening—so that any number of people heard the whole thing. He paid for the rafts, in addition to our labor. Bought them from Rudi Schaefer, also at the tavern, in a discussion also overheard by plenty of people. Good rates for the rafts and good pay for us, too, with a bonus for an early departure."

He took his right hand from his hip and gestured at the rafts. "So, we did. Why in the world would we refuse? I could show you the money. Still have almost all of it."

He made no movement to do so, of course. Even in Thuringia-Franconia, no sensible workman would gratuitously show money to an officer.

Stymied, Knefler went back to glaring at the rafts. "Describe the man who hired you," he commanded.

"Again?" The boatman's squint now verged on sheer melodrama. "Perhaps you should add more rosemary to your diet. It's good for the memory, they say."

"Describe the man again!" screeched Knefler.

Shrugging, the boatman did so. The description was identical to the one he'd given when he first came ashore. A handsome man, a bit taller than average, broad shouldered, appeared to be well built. Wasn't armed with a sword but carried himself like a nobleman. Long dark hair, dark brown eyes, a complexion that was not quite dark enough to be called swarthy but came close. Olive, you might call it. Maybe he was an Italian.

He wore fancy apparel, the most noticeable of which items were a red coat, expensive boots, and a feathered cap. The feathers were very large. You couldn't miss the fellow in a snowstorm. He spoke German—old-style, not Amideutsch—with something of an accent, at least to the boatman's ear. No, he had no idea what accent it was. There were dozens of German dialects, even among native speakers of the tongue. How was he to know? The man paid in good silver, which was a lingua franca accepted anywhere.

Finally, Knefler released the boatmen. He gave up trying to force them to return to Jena when their leader pointed out that he would then be taking responsibility for reimbursing Rudi Schaefer for the price the rafts would bring in Magdeburg. That being, of course, standard business practice for the disposal of rafts, and well established in law.

So, off the boatmen went, as cheery as could be. And why not? They'd been well paid to do nothing more strenuous than guide empty rafts following the current downriver. As work went, about as easy as it gets.

After they pushed off, Knefler snarled to Reimers: "First thing I'll do when we get back is teach that little whore a lesson. She'll learn the price for cursing an officer."

One of the soldiers cleared his throat. "Ah . . . Captain. I don't think—"

"Silence, Corporal Maurer!" bellowed the sergeant. "The captain gave you no leave to speak."

Maurer was suitably abashed, and shut up. Knefler sniffed at him and went for his horse.

About an hour later, on the ride back to Jena, Maurer drew his horse alongside Reimers. "Sergeant, you know who that girl *was*?" he asked quietly, after looking ahead to see that Captain Knefler was too far away to hear them.

Reimers smiled. "Denise Beasley. The daughter of Buster Beasley."

The poor fellow seemed confused. "But . . . if you knew that . . . remember the time . . ."

"This is why you are a mere corporal and I am a lofty sergeant," said Reimers. He nodded toward the captain in front of the little column. "Do *you* want the shithead for a garrison commander?"

The expression on Corporal Maurer's face was answer enough.

Reimers' ensuing chuckle had very little humor in it. "Sadly, the current fuck-up is probably not enough to get him discharged. But we can hope that his temper is still high when we get back to Grantville, so the idiot goes to chastise the daughter and discovers the father in the way. If we're lucky, we might even get to watch what happens."

It took Maurer a few seconds—he was pretty dull-witted himself, truth be told—but then he started smiling.

"Oh."

Kelly Aviation Facility
Near Grantville, State of Thuringia-Franconia

The take-off wasn't too bad, actually. Lannie would have

been in the air force except Jesse Wood didn't want any part of his drinking habits. But he did know how to fly, as such.

Denise suspected that "as such" probably didn't cover all that a pilot needed. But it was a done deal now, so there was no point fretting over it.

"That way," she said, pointing. "It's called 'south-east.'"

"You don't gotta be so sarcastic."

Fortunately, she'd thought to make sure they had a map before they took off. Lannie and Keenan, naturally, hadn't thought of that. Apparently, they thought Denise could navigate by feminine instinct or something—which was a laugh, since feminine instinct when it came to directions was just to ask somebody, and who was she going to ask up here? A fucking bird?

The map was on the grimy side, like most things in Kelly Aviation. At that, it was better than the seat she was sitting on.

Printed across the top of the map, the ink a little smeared, was a notice that read: *Property of Kelly Aviation. Unauthorized Use Will Be Prosecuted.*

"How'd you talk Bob into letting you use the plane whenever you wanted?"

"Well," said Lannie.

Behind her, Keenan cleared his throat. "It's an emergency, you know."

"Oh, perfect," said Denise. "The first recorded instance since the Ring of Fire of plane-stealing. I betcha that's a hanging offense."

Lannie looked smug. "Nope. I checked once. Seems

nobody's ever thought to get around to making it a crime yet."

"See, Denise?" added Keenan. "Nothing to worry about."

They even seemed to believe their own bullshit. Amazing. Did the jack-offs really think that somewhere in the books there wasn't a provision for prosecuting *Grand Theft, Whatever We Overlooked?*

But . . .

This was kinda fun, actually. Except for having to help Keenan attach the two bombs underneath. The bombs weren't all that big, just fifty-pounders, but they were still a little scary. What had been even scarier was watching Keenan do it. He belonged to the what-the-hell-it's-close-enough school of craftsmanship. Fine for chopping onions; probably a losing proposition over the long haul for munitions-handling.

Still and all, it was done. Denise couldn't remember a time she'd ever worried about water under a bridge. Now that she'd almost reached the ripe age of sixteen—her birthday was coming up on December 11—she was pleased to see no signs of advancing decrepitude.

CHAPTER 8. *The Cuirass*

Near the Fichtelgebirge, on the edge of the Saale valley

Janos Drugeth was trying to keep his temper under control. Despite his demands—he'd stopped just short of threatening his charges with violence—the up-timers had wasted so much time arguing over which items could be left behind that there had been no way to resume the journey until the next morning. And *then,* the idiots had wasted half the morning continuing the quarrel before they finally had the two intact wagons reloaded.

But, at least they were on the move again. Luckily, the USE garrison at Hof seemed to be sluggish even by the standards of small town garrisons. There'd been no sign at all that they were searching the countryside. They'd be a small unit, anyway, not more than half a dozen men with a sergeant in command. Perhaps just a corporal. As was the rule with sleepy garrisons in a region not threatened directly by war, they were mostly a police force and would spend half their time lounging in taverns by day and conducting desultory patrols of the town in the evening. The only time they'd venture into the countryside would be in response to a specific complaint or request.

It was even possible that they didn't have a radio. The up-time communication devices were spreading widely, at least in Thuringia-Franconia, but from what Janos understood of their operation—"reception" seemed to be the key issue—the sort of simple radios the Hof garrison would most likely possess might not be able to get messages sent across the Thueringerwald. Not reliably, at least.

So, hopefully, the delay would not cause any problems.

At the edge of the forest, on a small rise, he paused to let the wagons go by. Then, drawing out an eyeglass, he scanned the area behind them.

Nothing, so far as he could tell.

He was about to put the eyeglass away when his lingering animosity caused him to bring it back up and study the wagon they'd left behind, the way a man might foolishly scratch an itch, knowing he'd do better to leave it alone. It was still quite visible, being less than half a mile distant.

The only good thing was that at least they'd left the road by then and been making their way across a large meadow toward the forest when the wagon axle broke. Janos had ridden back to the road while the up-timers squabbled to see if the wagon was visible from there. The terrain was flat, but there was enough in the way of trees and shrubbery and tall grass to hide it from the sight of anyone just passing along the road—at least, to anyone on foot the way most travelers on that small country road would be. Someone on horseback would be able to spot it, if they were scanning the area.

Other than that . . .

What a mess. He'd tried to get the up-timers to repack the wagon with the goods they were leaving behind, so that if someone should happen to come across it they might assume the owners had just gone off to get assistance. If so, they'd either go about their business or— better still—they'd plunder the unguarded wagon. In the latter eventuality, of course, they'd hardly bring the attention of the authorities to their own thievery.

But, no. Careless in this as in seemingly all things, the up-timers had simply strewn the goods about. Anyone who came across it now would assume that foul play had transpired.

Nothing for it, though. Sighing, he started to put the eyeglass away, then, catching a glimpse of motion in the corner of his eye, looked back again.

Two horsemen were approaching the wagon. Not locals, either, since each of them was leading a pack horse.

He brought the glass back up. But even before he looked through it, he could see the flashing gleams coming from one of the riders. That had to be armor, reflecting the sun.

"What the hell are you doing?" asked Noelle.

Eddie shook his head and finished untying the cuirass from his pack horse. "You said it yourself, remember? 'That's got to be them!' Very excited, you were."

He started putting on the cuirass. "Do us both a favor and hand me the helmet."

When she just kept staring at him, Eddie looked up at her. "Think, Noelle. These are 'villains,' remember? Not likely to surrender simply because we yell 'stop, thief!'"

She stared back in the direction they'd spotted the wagon, then put her hand on the pistol holstered to her hip. "I thought . . ."

"Have to do everything myself," Eddie grumbled. Now that he'd gotten on the cuirass, he took the helmet from the pack. "I remind you of two things. First, you can't shoot straight. Second, while I can—"

He finished strapping the helmet on and started clambering back onto his horse. An awkward business, that was, wearing the damn cuirass. Eddie was trained in the use of arms and armor, but only to the extent that the son of a wealthy merchant would be. He was no experienced cavalryman.

"While I can," he continued, now drawing the rifle from its saddle holster, "you will perhaps recall that due to Carol Unruh's penny-pinching, the only up-time weapon I was allotted was this pitiful thing."

Noelle studied the rifle. "It's a perfectly good Winchester lever action rifle." A bit righteously: "Model 94. They say it's a classic."

"A 'classic,' indeed." Eddie chuckled. "The gun was manufactured almost half a century before the Ring of Fire. Still, I'll allow that it's a sturdy weapon. But it's only a .30-30, it has no more than six cartridges in the magazine, and while—unlike you—I can hit something at a respectable range, I'm hardly what you'd call a Wild Bill Hitchcock."

"Hickok," she corrected. "Hitchcock was the guy who made the movies." She looked back in the direction of the wagon. There still didn't seem to be anyone moving about, over there. "You really think . . ."

He shrugged, planting the butt of the rifle on his hip and taking up the reins. "I have no idea how they will react. What I do know is that if they see a man in armor demanding that they cease and desist all nefarious activity, they are perhaps a bit more likely to do so. I'd just as soon avoid another gunfight at the Okie Corral, if we can."

"'OK,'" she corrected. "'Okies' are sorta like hillbillies."

"And *will* you desist the language lesson?" he grumbled. "Now. Shall we about be it?"

Noelle hesitated, for a moment. She considered riding back to Hof and trying—

No, that was pointless. When they'd arrived in Hof early this morning, the garrison had still been asleep. Sleeping off a hangover, to be precise. All except the corporal in charge, who'd still been drinking. They'd be as useless as tits on a bull for hours, yet—and the traitors were almost into the Fichtelgebirge. Noelle was pretty sure there was no way she and Eddie would be able to get the garrison to go into the forest. That meant trying to get help from the soldiers at Saalfeld, and that was at least thirty miles away. By the time they got there, convinced the garrison commander to muster his unit, and got back, at least two days would have passed. More likely three, unless the garrison commander at Saalfeld was a lot more energetic and efficient than most such.

Two days, maybe three. Given that much lead time, it was unlikely they'd ever find the defectors. The Fichtelgebirge and the Bohemian Forest it was part of wasn't a tall range of mountains, but it was heavily wooded. Mostly evergreens, too, so they wouldn't get any advantage from the trees having shed their leaves. Assuming the man in charge, whoever he was, knew what he was doing—and there was no evidence so far that he didn't—he'd almost certainly be able to shake off their pursuit. There was enough commercial and personal traffic back and forth across the forest between Bohemia and Franconia that there would be a network of small roads—well, more like trails, really, but well-handled wagons could make their way through them. After the passage of two or three days, especially if the weather turned bad, it was unlikely they could figure out which specific route the defectors had taken.

"It's now or never, I guess." She started her horse into the meadow. "I'll do the talking. You just look fierce and militaristic and really mean and not too smart. The kind of guy who shoots first and lets God sort out the bodies, and doesn't much care if He gets it right or not."

• • •

"There!" hollered Denise, pointing across Lannie's chest out of the window on his side of the plane. "It's them!"

He looked over and spotted the wagon immediately. "Yup. Gotta be. Keenan, you get ready to unload when I tell you."

"Both bombs?"

"Better save one in case we miss the first time."

Denise wondered if they actually had the legal right to bomb somebody, without even giving them a warning. No way to shout "stop, thief!" of course, from an airplane doing better than a hundred miles an hour.

"Why don't we just call in their position on the radio?" she asked. "That way . . . you know. We could ask somebody up top how they want us to handle it."

"Well," said Lannie.

Behind her, Keenan cleared his throat. "The radio don't exactly work. Bob took some of the parts out of it so's we could—"

"Never mind," she said, exasperated more with herself than anyone else. She should have known better than to get into the plane without double-checking that all the details were up to snuff.

She'd once hitched a ride with Keenan Murphy into Fairmont, just a few weeks before the Ring of Fire. First, the tire had gone flat. Then, after borrowing a jack from a helpful driver passing by, which Keenan needed to borrow because he'd somehow or other lost his own jack, he discovered the spare was flat. Then, after the still-helpful passerby drove him to a nearby gas station where he could get the tire fixed, they'd continued the drive to Fairmont until he ran out of gas. Turned out the fuel gauge didn't work and Keenan had lost track of the last time he'd filled up the tank. She'd wound up walking the last three miles into town.

As for Lannie—

But there was no point in sour ruminations. Besides, what the hell. She had expansive opinions on the subject of "citizen's arrest." Why should the lousy cops get special privileges? If she'd heard her dad say it once, she'd heard him say it a million times.

"Now," commanded Janos. While Gage and Gardiner got off the wagons and untied their horses, he looked down from the saddle at the up-timers gawking up at him.

"Wait here," he said curtly.

"I got a gun!" protested Jay Barlow. As if that needed to be proven, he drew it from the holster at his hip. "Way better than that ancient piece of shit you're carrying, too."

Janos looked at the weapon Barlow was brandishing. It was what the up-timers referred to as a "six-shooter," a type of revolver, which the man had drawn from one of those holsters Janos had seen in the so-called "western movies." The ones slung low, for the "quick draw," tied down to the thigh.

Naturally, it was pearl-handled.

With his soldier's interest in weaponry, Janos had made inquiries during his weeks in Grantville. The man named Paul Santee had been particularly helpful on the subject of up-time firearms. On one occasion, when Janos had asked about "six-shooters," Santee had explained the careful distinctions to be made between serious revolvers and the sort of "Wild West bullshit pieces" that some of the town's more histrionic characters favored.

As for the wheellock Janos carried—he had two of them, actually, one in each saddle holster—the weapons were quite good and he was quite good with them.

"Wait here," he repeated firmly. The last thing he wanted was someone like Barlow involved. Janos still hoped the problem could be handled without violence. Barlow was the sort of man who would lose control in a confrontation—and then miss what he shot at.

Gage and Gardiner were ready. Both of them, from their long stay in Grantville, with up-time firearms. The weapons called "pump-action shotguns," which were much favored by soldiers. They'd be loaded with solid slugs, not pellets.

"Let's go," he said.

"Abandoned," Eddie pronounced. Given the broken axle and the goods strewn around the wagon, Noelle thought that as redundant a statement as she'd ever heard.

She didn't tease Eddie about it, though. She knew he'd really said it just to steel himself for the inevitable. They'd have to continue the pursuit into the forest.

Feeling more than a little nervous, she studied the terrain ahead of them. The Fichtelgebirge was not only a low range of mountains, it was an old one. Erosion had worn its peaks down to round forms, with not much rock showing. As a barrier to travel it wasn't remotely comparable to the Rocky Mountains, much less the Sierra Nevadas. It was more like the sort of terrain in most of Appalachia that Indians and early white settlers had never had too much trouble passing through.

But as ambush country, it did just fine, thank you.

Hearing a familiar and quite unexpected sound, she twisted in her saddle and looked up behind her.

Eddie had already spotted it. "Look!" he shouted, pointing toward the oncoming aircraft. "The Air Force has arrived!"

Her sense of relief was brief. She couldn't really see what good a warplane would be in the situation. There couldn't be more than one plane available. In fact, she'd thought the air force had all of their few craft stationed in Magdeburg or points north. Jesse Wood must have detached one to Grantville when he got news of the defection.

One plane would be almost useless trying to spot a small party in the forest, and even if it did spot the defectors it couldn't maintain the patrol for very long before it had to go back to refuel. By the time it returned, they'd have vanished again.

As the plane got closer, what little sense of relief remained went away altogether.

"That's not a warplane," she said. "It's got to be one of the Kellys'."

Eddie squinted at the oncoming aircraft. "You are sure? I didn't think any of theirs were operational yet."

Noelle shook her head. "Define 'operational.' Nobody ever said Bob Kelly didn't know how to build airplanes. The problem is he doesn't know when to quit. At any given time, he's got at least one plane able to fly—until he starts tinkering with it again."

The aircraft was heading straight for them, no longer more than a hundred yards off the ground. By now it was quite close enough to recognize the details of its construction. The USE's air force had a grand total of two—count 'em, two—models of aircraft. The Belles and the Gustavs. Even someone like Noelle, who'd never been able to distinguish one model of automobile from another unless she could see the logo or it was something obvious like a VW bug, could tell the difference between either one of them and the oncoming plane.

"No, it's one of the Kellys'. Couldn't tell you which model, except it'll have a name like Fearless or Invincible or something equally bombastic, but it's one of theirs."

Eddie was still squinting at it. "You're *positive*?"

"Yes, I'm posi—"

"The reason I ask," he interrupted, pointing his finger at the plane, "is because it's carrying bombs."

"Huh?" Noelle squinted herself. Her eyesight wasn't bad, but it wasn't as good as Eddie's. Still, now that she looked for it—the plane was close, and coming pretty fast—she could see two objects suspended underneath the fuselage.

Those *did* look like bombs, sure enough.

And now that she thought about it, the oncoming plane's trajectory . . .

"Let's get out of here!" she yelled. "They're going to bomb us!"

CHAPTER 9. *The Bomb*

"Bombs away!" shouted Lannie. Way too soon, in Denise's judgment.

Fortunately, Keenan objected. "Hey, make up your mind! You said only one—"

"Drop it!" Denise hollered, when she gauged the time was right. Lannie might have buck fever, but she didn't. Not with Buster for a dad, teaching her to hunt.

"It's off!" said Keenan.

By now, the plane had swept by, over the wagon and the two enemy cavalrymen guarding it.

Well, one cavalryman, anyway. The other one might have been a civilian. They'd been moving too fast for Denise to get a good look at them.

Lannie brought the plane around. As soon as they could see the effect of the bomb, he shouted gleefully. "Yeeee-*haaaaa*! Dead nuts, guys!"

Sure enough, the wagon had been hit by the bomb. If not directly, close enough. Denise wasn't sure, from the quick glimpse she'd gotten as they went over it, but she thought the wagon had already been busted. It had seemed to be tilted over to one side, as if a wheel or an axle had broken, and she thought some of its cargo was on the ground.

Now, though, it was in pieces. And something was burning.

One of the cavalrymen was down, too. His horse was thrashing on the ground, and the rider was lying nearby. Dead, wounded, unconscious, it was impossible to tell. The other cavalryman—well, maybe cavalryman—was dismounting to tend to his partner.

Denise frowned. There was something about the way that second cavalryman moved. . . .

"Fly back around," she commanded.

Keenan, even from his poor vantage point in the cramped bombadier's seat in the back, with its little windows, had been able to see the results too. "Jeez, Denise. I don't know as we gotta be bloodthirsty about this."

"Fly back around!" she snapped. "I just want to get a better look. And slow down, Lannic."

"Don't want to stall it out," he warned.

"Yeah, fine. So don't stall it out. Slow down and get lower."

"Backseat driver," he muttered. But he did as commanded.

"Wait," said Janos, holding out a hand. They were now sheltered beneath a large tree, not more than two hundred yards from what was left of the wagon. As soon as Janos had spotted the plane, he'd led them under the branches. Hopefully, they'd be out of sight.

"What a piece of luck," said Gage. "They bombed their own people."

Janos wasn't surprised, really. He knew from experience how easy it was for soldiers to kill and wound their own, in combat. In some battles, in bad weather or rough terrain, as many as a third of the casualties were caused by the soldiers' own comrades.

He'd never thought about it before, but he could see where that danger would be even worse with aircraft involved. At the speed and height it had maintained when it carried out the attack, the plane's operators couldn't have seen any details of their "enemy."

"What should we do?" asked Gardiner.

"Wait," Janos repeated. "The plane is coming back around. If we move out from under the tree, they might spot us."

That was the obvious reason not to move, and he left it at that. Still more, he wanted to see what would happen next.

Gardiner put up a mild objection. "That bomb was loud, when it went off. The garrison might come to investigate."

His tone was doubtful, though. Janos thought there was hardly any chance the explosion would alert the soldiers at Hof. Hof was miles away and while the sound might have carried the distance, it would have been indistinct. Thunder, perhaps. Of course, if the USE warplane kept dropping bombs, the situation would probably change. People would investigate an ongoing disturbance, where they would usually shrug off a single instance.

But Janos knew the plane couldn't be carrying very many bombs. By now, months after the Baltic war, Austria had very good intelligence on the capabilities of the up-time aircraft, and Janos had read all of the reports. Even the best of the enemy's warplanes, the one they called the "Gustav," was severely limited in its ordnance.

And this was no Gustav. Janos had seen one of them, on the ground at the Grantville airfield. Nor was it one of the other type of warplane, the one they called the "Belle." He'd seen those on several occasions, both on the ground and in the air.

Drugeth didn't know which type of airplane this was, but it couldn't have capabilities that were any better. In fact, if he was right in his guess about the object he could see under the craft's body, it had only had two bombs to begin with. He'd seen the bomb they'd dropped, although he hadn't spotted where it came from. But he was pretty sure it must have been the companion of the object he could see now.

As they came over the wagon again, moving as slowly as Lannie dared, they weren't going any faster than a car breaking the speed limit on an interstate highway. And Lannie had the plane not more than forty feet off the ground.

So, since he also obeyed Denise when she told him to fly on the side where she could see what was happening, she got a very good look at the second cavalryman when he looked up as they passed by. Glaring in fury and shaking his fist at them.

Except it wasn't a cavalryman and it wasn't a he.

"Jesus H. Christ!" Denise exploded. "We just bombed Noelle and Eddie!"

"Huh?" said Lannie, his mouth gaping.

"Well, shit!" screeched Keenan from the back. "Well, shit!"

"I'll kill 'em," Noelle hissed, as she went back to tending Eddie. Luckily—by now, she'd unfastened the cuirass—he didn't seem to have been wounded by the bomb itself or any of the splinters it had sent flying from the wagon when it exploded. At least, she couldn't see any blood anywhere, that she thought was any of Eddie's own. He did have some blood on one of his trouser legs, but she was pretty sure that came from his horse. One of the splinters or maybe a part of the bomb casing had torn a huge wound in the horse's belly. It had thrown Eddie when it fell to the ground. Kicked him in the head, too, in the course of thrashing about afterward, judging from the condition of his helmet.

At least, she didn't think that big a dent in a sturdy helmet could have been caused by his fall. The meadow had hardly any rocks in it.

Eddie's eyes were open, but he seemed dazed. Might have a concussion. And a broken left arm, from the looks of things.

Gingerly, she started unfastening his sleeve. Eddie moaned a little, but she got it peeled back enough to check its condition.

A broken forearm, sure enough. Noelle had broken her own forearm as a kid, falling out of a tree. She could remember insisting to her mother all the way to the hospital that the arm wasn't really broken. Just bent a little, that's all.

But it wasn't a compound fracture, and the break was obviously well below the elbow. Give it a few weeks, properly splinted, and it would heal as good as new.

The relief allowed her fury to resurge. She looked up, tracking the plane from its sound, so she could shake her fist at them again. The stupid bastards!

But when she spotted the plane, the gesture turned into a frantic wave.

"You stupid bastards! *Watch out!*"

The cramped interior of the cockpit seemed like bedlam to Denise.

"Jesus, Lannie, you bombed my sister! You bombed my sister!" Keenan kept screeching, in blithe disregard for the fact that he'd been the one who'd actually released the weapon.

Naturally, Lannie's response was to shift the blame himself. "She told me to do it! She told me to do it!" was his contribution.

"Shut up, both of you!" was Denise's own, trying to settle them down.

In retrospect, she'd admit to her best friend Minnie— nobody else—that she probably should have kept concentrating on the "navigating" side of the business.

Eventually, it did occur to her that she ought to see where they were going.

"*Lannie!*" she screeched.

"Fascinating," murmured Janos. He'd always wondered how fragile the devices were. Now, seeing one of the plane's wings partly shredded by its impact with a mere tree limb—a large tree, granted—his longstanding guess was confirmed.

As was his determination to remain a cavalryman. Say what you would about the stupid beasts, horses were rather sturdy. Nor did they move at ridiculous speeds, nor did they keep a rider more than a few feet from the ground.

"Jesus, Lannie, you wrecked the plane! You wrecked the plane!" was Keenan's current contribution, even more useless than the last.

"*Shut the fuck up!*" Denise hollered. "Just concentrate, Lannie. You can do it."

Fortunately, Lannie had left off his own shouting. Now that he was in a crisis, his pilot's instincts had taken over.

"We're going in, guys," he said. "Can't do anything else."

Even to Denise, it was obvious from the damage suffered by the wing on her side that he was right. "You can do it, Lannie," she said calmly. "And we got a big wide meadow here."

Lannie's grin was as thin as a grin could get, but she was relieved to see it. "Just better hope we don't hit a gopher hole. Got no way to retract the landing gear."

"There aren't any gophers in Europe," she said, in as reassuring a tone as she could manage.

"Yeah, that's right," chimed in Keenan from the back. "No ground hogs, neither." Thankfully, he'd left off the screeching.

Denise saw no reason to voice aloud her firm conviction that there were probably umpteen thousand things that could produce holes in a meadow. All but two of which *did* exist in Europe.

They'd be coming down in a few seconds. Lannie did have the plane more or less under control. Hopefully it'd be a crash landing they could walk away from, if nothing caught fire or—

"Drop the other bomb, Keenan!"

"Huh?"

"Drop the fucking bomb!"

"Oh. Yeah."

Watching, Janos didn't wonder for more than an instant why the up-timers had committed the seemingly pointless act of bombing an empty patch of meadow.

Judging from the way the first bomb had exploded, the device had been detonated by a contact fuse, probably armed by the act of releasing it. Not the sort of thing any sane man wants to be sitting atop when he tries to crash an aircraft as gently as possible.

The plane came down. And confirmed once again Janos' long-standing conviction that plans and schemes and plots are just naturally prone to crashing.

"Oh, hell," said Noelle. At first, she'd thought that the plane had come down safely. Almost as if it were landing on a proper airfield. Then—one of the wheels must have hit an unseen obstruction—she saw the still undamaged wing dip sharply and strike the ground. The plane skewed around, tipped up on its nose—*please God, don't let that propeller come apart in pieces and chew anybody up*—and seemed to balance precariously for a moment.

Then it looked as if the plane just more or less disintegrated into its component parts. The newly damaged wing broke off, the fuselage tipped and rolled, and the plane flopped down on its side. Most of the other wing broke off, as did part of the tail assembly when it hit.

Still . . .

There was no explosion. No flames. People had walked away from car crashes worse than that.

"Just wait for me, Eddie," she said. "And don't move. Your arm's busted."

She got on her horse and headed for the crash site.

● ● ●

Janos pointed to the enemy cavalryman still on the ground by the remains of the wagon.

"Gardiner, see to him. Keep him under guard, that's all. Do him no harm unless he attacks you. Gage, follow me."

He set off after the other cavalryman, toward the downed plane.

"What are we going to do?" asked Gage, loud enough to be heard over the sound of the cantering horses.

"Seize them and take them with us, any who survived. What else can we do? I don't think this is a reconnaissance patrol from a larger force following them. They wouldn't have sent just two men for that purpose. I'm not certain, but I think these are operating alone. If we let any of them go—and there's at least one of them in good condition—they'll take the alarm to Hof. Two bomb explosions, a crashed warcraft, even the sorriest garrison in Creation will react to that."

Gage was silent for a moment. Then, as Janos expected, he raised the other obvious alternative.

"We could kill them."

"Oh, splendid," said Janos. "Just what Austria needs. Half our army is facing Wallenstein on the north, most of the rest is facing the Turks to the south—and we ignite a new war by committing a pointless massacre."

"It was a thought," said Gage mildly. "Probably not a good one, I admit."

Drugeth's irritation with the Englishman was only momentary. He'd considered that solution himself. But he still had hopes they could complete this adventure without the sort of drastic measures that would trigger off an explosive reaction from the USE.

Firmly, he ignored his own hard-gained wisdom on the subjects of plans and their likely outcomes.

CHAPTER 10. *The Sword*

By the time Denise got done hauling Lannie out of the wreck, she was exhausted. Getting Keenan out hadn't been too bad, even though he'd been in the cramped rear of the cockpit. But Keenan had just been dazed and bruised, not pinned by some of the equipment that had been broken loose and all but completely unconscious.

Denise was strong for a girl her age and build, but the fact remained that the age was almost-sixteen and while the build was great for making girls jealous and boys drool— not that she appreciated either one—it wasn't that good for frantically trying to free a normal-sized man from wreckage and haul him out by bodily force. Not for the first time in her life, she wished she'd inherited more of her dad's bulk and muscle and less of her mother's appearance.

But, finally, it was done. Probably hadn't taken more than a few minutes, actually. With the last of her strength, she lowered Lannie onto the ground and half-spilled herself out of the fuselage. Fortunately, the meadow was pretty soft ground. On her hands and knees, she saw that Keenan was sitting up and holding his head. He was groaning a little, but so far as she could tell he didn't really seem to be hurt.

In the corner of her eye, she caught sight of a pair of legs. Looking over, she saw Noelle, with a very strained expression on her face.

"Hey, look," she said defensively, "I'm sorry. We didn't know it was you."

Belatedly, she realized that Noelle wasn't actually looking at her. She was looking over Denise's head at something off to the side.

Denise swiveled, flopping onto her side in the process, and propped herself up on one elbow.

"Oh, great."

The *something* Noelle had been staring out turned out to be two men, with two horses not far away behind them.

Both down-timers, obviously. Neither of them was smiling—hey, no kidding—so she couldn't see their teeth. That was usually the simplest indication, especially with a man somewhere in middle age like the one holding the very nasty looking and oh-so-very-up-time pump action shotgun, if not the younger one who was standing a little closer with a sword in his hand.

But it didn't matter. Leaving aside the clothes they were wearing and the hair styles, she would have known just looking at the way the young one held the sword. She didn't know any up-timer who held a sword like that. Maybe somebody like Harry Lefferts did, by now, with all of his escapades. But Denise hadn't seen much of Harry in a long time, and on the few occasions she had seen him Harry had been carousing in one of Grantville's taverns with the wine, women and song that seemed to accompany him like pilot fish did a shark. The wine and women, with complete ease, the singing a whole lot less so since Harry had a nice natural voice and could even carry a tune but somewhere along the way had picked up the silly conviction that he was one of those old-style Irish tenors who could make nasal sound good but he couldn't.

Her thoughts were veering all over the place, she realized, and she commanded them back to attention.

Concentrate on the fucking sword, idiot.

The damn thing didn't look any better when she did. This wasn't one of those fancy swords that a lot of down-time noblemen and wannabe noblemen carried about when they were trying to look impressive. Pretty, lots of decorations—even jewels, if they were rich enough—and looking as if they'd seen as much actual use as the kind of fancy china that people kept in a cabinet and didn't eat off of except once in a blue moon.

No, this sword looked like her mother's favorite kitchen knife, allowing for a drastic increase in size. Solid, plain, sharp as a razor and so often honed that the blade wasn't a completely straight line anymore. And the bastard was holding it just the way her mother did, too—or the way her dad held a welding torch or a tool he was using to work on one of his bikes.

Casually. The way no up-timer except maybe a few wild-ass screwballs like Harry could *possibly* hold a sword. The man wasn't flourishing it, wasn't brandishing it—didn't, really, even seem more than vaguely aware that he had it in his hand in the first place. A weapon so familiar and comfortable that it was just any other tool, used more by instinct than conscious thought.

Some tools chopped onions, some tools chopped metal, and this one wasn't any different except it chopped off heads and limbs and from the look of the miserable son-of-a-bitch any part of a human body he felt like chopping off.

She tore her eyes away from the sword and looked higher up, at the man's face. For a moment—one wild moment—she almost burst into laughter.

He looked for all the world like a rock star!

Dammit, it was true. Good-looking, in that sort of older-than-he-really-was way that indicated either dissipation or too much familiarity with the wicked ways of men—music recording executives in the case of rock stars; probably not in this guy's—and judging from the easy athleticism of his stance he didn't seem dissipated in the least, so scratch that theory.

Long, curly, dark hair. Flowing fucking locks, fer chrissake. A flaring mustache and a neatly trimmed full beard that'd look silly on almost anybody except genu-ine rock stars and guys who could hold a sword like that.

Just to complete the picture, soulful brown eyes. The kind of eyes with which rock stars sang to the world of their sorrow at the faithlessness of women and guys like this bastard looked down upon the corpses they left behind.

"Well, fuck," she said. "Just what it needed to make the day complete."

In German, she added: "And who are you?"

The swordsman had been staring back at Noelle the whole time Denise had been assessing him. Now he looked down at her.

"My name is Janos Drugeth. From the family with the estates in Humenné. Homonna, as we Hungarians would call it. I am a cavalry officer in the service of the Austrian emperor."

Hungarian. Denise didn't know much about

Hungarians, but she knew they liked to call themselves "Magyars" because they were descended from a tribe of nomadic conquerors. Like some biker gangs liked to call themselves "the Huns."

Perfect. Just perfect.

To her surprise, he added: "We may speak in English, if you prefer."

His English was good, too, if heavily accented.

Noelle stood very straight. "My name is Noelle Stull. I am an official for the USE government. Well, the State of Thuringia-Franconia. And I—me and my partner, Eddie Junker, over there"—she pointed toward the demolished wagon, some distance away—"are in pursuit of the criminals whom we believed to have been in possession of that vehicle. Please either assist us in that task or, at the very least, do not impede us in our duty."

Bold as brass. Mentally, Denise doffed her hat in salute. Not that she ever wore a hat.

The Drugeth fellow gave Noelle a sorrowful smile. "I will not dispute your characterization of the individuals in question. But I am afraid I cannot respond as you wish to either of your requests. Not only may I not assist you, I am afraid I shall have to detain you myself."

He slid the sword back into its scabbard. The motion was swift, easy, practiced. He hadn't even looked at the sword and scabbard as he did it, just letting his left thumb and forefinger guide the blade into the opening. The fact that he'd chosen to sheathe the weapon while explaining what he was going to do just emphasized his complete confidence that nobody would think to dispute the matter.

Which . . .

In point of fact, nobody would. Sure as hell not Denise. That sword could come out just as quickly and smoothly as it went in. And leaving that aside, the other guy still had the shotgun in his hands and didn't seem to be in the least inclined to emulate his leader's example and put it away. True, he didn't have the barrel pointed at anybody, but it was obvious he could in a split second. That was just good gun-handling, not carelessness.

He didn't look like a rock star, either. More like a record producer. Shoot you as quick as he'd shell out payola or cheat singers out of their royalties.

To Denise's alarm, she saw that Noelle's hand had moved to the vicinity of her holster.

That was crazy. First, that was no quick-draw holster. It was a safe-and-sound holster with a flap, and the flap was buckled. By the time Noelle got the pistol out, the older guy with the shotgun could kill them all. Assuming the Hungarian nomad-cum-rock-star hadn't sliced them up already.

And even if Noelle had been a quick-draw whizzeroo, so fucking what? The pistol was a dinky little .32 caliber and her marksmanship was something of a legend, in Grantville. The anti–Julie Sims. There were two schools of thought on the subject. The optimists insisted Noelle could hit the side of a barn. The other view was that she could only do it if she were inside the barn to begin with.

"Uh, Noelle . . ."

Fortunately, Noelle reconsidered. Her hand moved away. "This is an outrage!" she snapped. "You are on USE soil here, not Austrian. You have no right—"

"Please," said Drugeth, holding up his hand. "You are

wasting our time, and I believe you know it perfectly well. Although there have been no open hostilities in some time, Austria and the USE are enemies. I have been given the task of escorting the individuals in question to Vienna, and I intend to complete it successfully."

Noelle glared at him. "And you won't stop at outright abduction."

"Hardly 'abduction,' I think." He shrugged. Like the dark eyes, the gesture was sorrowful. Not really-sad sorrowful, just what you might call philosophically sorrowful. Exactly the same way, Denise imagined, the guy contemplated the bodies of his foes after he sliced them up.

"I will set you free, unharmed, as soon as we have reached a place where I can be confident you cannot bring troops in time to prevent our escape. If you will give me your parole, I shall not even disarm you. And please do not delay the matter any further. I point out"—here, he nodded toward Lannie and Keenan, and then toward the wagon—"that you have injured persons in your party, who should get medical attention. And I will also point out that none of the injuries were caused by me and my men."

Noelle shifted the glare to Denise.

"Hey, look, I *said* I was sorry. And he's right, Noelle."

For a moment, she even thought Noelle might start cussing. But she didn't, of course.

By the time they got back to the wagon, Keenan and Denise propping up Lannie along the way—he turned out to be okay except for a sprained ankle—Eddie Junker was up and moving.

Well. Sitting up and fiddling uselessly with his busted arm. There was another shotgun-toting sidekick of Drugeth's there, watching Eddie carefully but making no effort to assist him. Drugeth had probably told him to do that, and by now it was clear enough that anybody who worked for Drugeth followed orders.

"Cut it out, Eddie," said Noelle crossly, kneeling next to him. "It's broken. Denise, give me a hand."

"Why me?"

"Because you broke it, that's why."

"I don't know squat about setting a broken arm. Have Keenan do it."

Noelle looked at Keenan. Keenan looked alarmed. "I hate the sight of blood."

"There's no blood," Denise pointed out.

"I hate the sight of suffering. I'm not going to be any good at this."

"Enough," said the Drugeth fellow. He motioned Keenan toward Eddie. "All you have to do is help hold him down. You ladies as well. This will be painful, for a time."

Eddie looked alarmed. More by the sight of Drugeth approaching him with that sword on his hip than anything else, Denise thought.

"It doesn't need to be amputated!" he protested.

"Of course not," said Drugeth calmly. "Now do your best not to thrash around. Hold him, everyone."

Drugeth set the arm just as swiftly and smoothly as he'd sheathed the sword. It seemed like *zip-zip-zip* and it was done. By then, his shotgun-toting cohorts had found a couple of pieces of wood broken off from the wagon that would serve as a temporary splint, along with one of Suzi Barclay's flamboyant costumes that, sliced up, would serve to bind them.

One of the cohorts did the slicing, not Drugeth, using a simple knife he had in a scabbard. Clearly enough, the Hungarian's sword did not come out for any work less lofty than hacking flesh, still on the bone and twitching.

By now, Drugeth didn't remind Denise of a rock star at all. Just a good-looking nomad barbarian, who'd never once lost that serenely sorrowful expression even while Eddie had been screaming bloody murder. And who'd obviously set more than one broken limb in his day; which, given that he wasn't old enough to have seen all that many days, would indicate the days themselves had not been spent in the pursuit of serenity.

"It's done," he said, coming back up to his feet. "Good enough for the time being, at least. It's a clean break, so it should heal well."

Eddie was gasping, his heavy face pale and sweating. "You—you—" he said weakly, apparently searching for suitably vile cognomens to heap upon Drugeth. Then, he tightened his jaws, looked up and nodded. "Thank you."

That was classy, Denise thought. She hadn't known Eddie was that solid. Of course, she barely knew the guy.

Drugeth nodded in return. "Let us be off then. Gage, retrieve that rifle over there." He indicated a spot not far away. Denise hadn't seen it until Drugeth pointed at the thing, but she recognized an up-time lever action rifle. Must have been Eddie's.

"Then," the Hungarian continued, "you ride ahead and

make sure the party we are escorting is ready to go when we arrive. Gardiner, you ride alongside Ms. Stull. Ms. Stull, I would appreciate it if you'd lead my horse."

He even said it that way, too. "Miz," not "Miss." This guy knew Americans, somehow, even down to the subtle quirks of what you called career girls like Noelle.

"For the rest of us," Drugeth continued, "I recommend walking, since we have injured persons."

It was all done very courteously, but Denise didn't miss the fact that Drugeth's dispositions also meant he had all the USE loyalists under control. If Noelle tried to ride off, Cohort Gardiner could go in pursuit. He wasn't encumbered by having to lead another horse, and Denise didn't doubt for an instant he could ride better than Noelle as well as shoot better than she could.

And by remaining on foot, Drugeth was there—with the damn sword—in case any of the others decided to try something tricky that might throw off a horseman for a time. Like . . .

Who knows? Finding a hole dug by something bigger than a gopher—they had badgers in Europe—and trying to hide in it. Not likely, but Drugeth didn't seem like a guy who'd leave much to chance.

Eddie's horse was still thrashing a little. Cohort Gardiner went over and looked down at the poor animal, then looked at Drugeth.

The Hungarian officer nodded. *Clickety-BOOM,* and the horse was out of its misery.

As they headed toward the forest, moving slowly because of Eddie and Lannie, Denise decided things weren't so bad. Perhaps oddly, the fact that Drugeth's cohorts seemed just as familiar and relaxed in their use of up-time shotguns as Drugeth himself did with a sword, was somehow reassuring.

Whatever else they were, enemies of the USE or not, they obviously weren't wild-eyed desperadoes. Everything about them was experienced, controlled, disciplined—or self-disciplined, in the case of Drugeth.

True, that same control might lead to a quick, relaxed, practiced and easy execution squad too. But if they'd wanted to do that, they would have done it already. And would a man planning to kill her in a few minutes have bothered to give Noelle a courteous helping hand getting onto her horse? Denise didn't think so.

Besides, her assessment of Drugeth had shifted yet again. From rock star to nomad barbarian, it had tentatively come to rest on a label she was generally skeptical about but seemed accurate enough in this instance. Every now and then—not often—you did run across a down-time nobleman who actually lived up to the name instead of being a puffed-up thug with delusions of grandeur.

Drugeth had told them he would release them once his expedition got far enough away from any chance of pursuit. Okay, he hadn't officially "given his word." But Denise was pretty sure that the genuine articles when it came to noblemen didn't bother with silly flippery like solemn vows, except on formal occasions. He'd said what he would do, and so he would. To do otherwise would be a transgression of a code he took seriously.

Good enough, she decided, for a day that included bombing your own guys. Jesus, it'd take her *years* to live that down. Even Minnie would make fun of her, when she found out.

But when they reached the small clearing where the defectors had been waiting, things immediately got tense.

Unfortunately, even sober, Jay Barlow was nobody's idea of a nobleman—and he'd apparently spent the time since Drugeth left him with the others getting half-plastered. Him and Mickey Simmons. There was another prize for you.

"That's the fucking bitch!" he shouted, when he spotted Noelle. He thrust a half-empty bottle into Mickey's hand and took several steps forward. To make things perfect, he had his hand dramatically positioned to yank out the silly cowboy gun on his hip. He looked like something out of a Grade D western.

Drugeth moved up in front of him. "Enough, Barlow. Get back on the wagon. Now. We have to be moving."

"Fuck that!" Barlow pointed the forefinger of his right hand accusingly at Noelle. Unfortunately, he was left-handed and his left hand was now gripping the gun butt. "She's the one went after Horace! I say we shoot her now and good riddance."

Matching deed to word, he yanked the gun out of the holster.

Keenan squawked. Denise probably did too. She wasn't sure, because whatever she'd been about to say was stifled in her throat by Drugeth's sword.

Blurring like an arc. Barlow's gun and the hand holding it went sailing off somewhere. Barlow stared at the stump, gushing blood. His expression seemed one of amazement, not pain.

But it was Drugeth's expression that mostly registered on Denise. The Hungarian seemed to be in some sort of weird brown study. Just standing there, the sword in his hand, point down, dripping a little blood from the tip, while he contemplated Jay Barlow.

He shifted deftly to the side, the sword blurred again, and a fountain of blood gushed out of Barlow's neck. His whole throat looked to have been cut, from one ear to the other.

Paralyzed by shock, Denise realized that Drugeth had just been calculating whether to keep Barlow alive or not. The decision having come up negative, he'd shifted to the side so he wouldn't get blood all over himself.

And he didn't, not a drop. Barlow collapsed to his knees and then to the ground. He was effectively already dead.

Mickey Simmons was shouting, and clawing for something in the wagon. A gun, Denise assumed.

"Kill him," said Drugeth. Quietly, almost conversationally.

Gage and Gardiner's shotguns seemed to go off simultaneously. The heavy slugs hammered Simmons into the side of the wagon. He collapsed to the ground.

A lot of the American defectors were making noise now. Billie Jean Mase came running up to Drugeth, screaming at him. For a moment, Denise expected to see her throat sliced in half, too. But Drugeth simply planted a boot in her belly and that was that. She went down, gasping for air.

"*Silence*," said Drugeth. Not hollering, exactly, but the word carried like nobody's business. "You will all be silent."

That shut them up. Including Denise. Which was a good thing, or she might have giggled hysterically, because—well—there *was* something insanely amusing about the scene, if she ignored the gore. It was like watching a bunch of rabbits suddenly realize they'd pissed off a bobcat. Or a cougar.

Drugeth drew out a handkerchief and cleaned off the blade, then slid the sword back into the scabbard. Throughout, he did not take his eyes once off the defectors clustered around the two wagons in the clearing.

"I told Ms. Stull and her companions that they would be released unharmed once we were far enough from pursuit. So I spoke, and so it will be. And I am no longer inclined to tolerate any obstruction or dispute. I am in command, not you. You will obey me in all things, until we reach Vienna."

He waited a few seconds, to see if any protest would be made.

None was. What a shocker.

"And now, we must dig two graves. Mr. O'Connor, perhaps there is some tool in the wagon that might serve."

"We didn't bring any shovels," said Allen O'Connor uncertainly. His voice was a little shaky, maybe, but not much. He certainly didn't seem stricken by grief. Leaving aside the shock of the sudden blood-letting, Denise didn't think many of the defectors—leaving aside the cretin Billie Jean and Caryn Barlow—had any serious personal attachment to the two dead men. Simmons' wife was a down-timer, a widow he'd married the year before. But she wasn't in the group. Mickey must have decided to abandon her when he defected.

And the baby they'd had a few months ago. And his two step-children by his wife's first marriage.

The shithead.

Qualifying that, the now-dead shithead. And good riddance.

O'Connor's son Neil started digging amongst the goods piled in the wagon. "I'll find something."

Marina Barclay swallowed. "Are you sure, Mr. Drugeth? I mean, you were saying we needed to move as soon as . . ."

Her voice trailed off, as it must have dawned on her that she was perilously close to "obstruction and dispute." Nervously, she eyed the sword.

But either Drugeth was inclined to be lenient toward women—Billie Jean, still gasping for breath, supported that theory—or he was simply not given to bloodshed for the sake of it. That theory was supported by everything else Denise had seen.

Including his next words.

"They are not animals, to be left to scavengers. Time presses, yes, but God created time also. Everything we do is watched by Him."

Noelle got off her horse, holding a small spade that she'd retrieved from her saddlebag. "Let's get started," she said. "Officer Drugeth is right." She seemed quite calm, although with Noelle you never knew. She was the kind of person who clamped down her emotions under stress. She didn't so much as glance at Drugeth.

Less than half a minute later, having found a good spot,

she started digging. Drugeth came up and offered to replace her. But, still without looking at him, she shook her head.

"You can spell me when I get tired. This'll take a while."

Denise started digging alongside her—more like just breaking up the ground—with a heavy stick she found in the woods. Meanwhile, the two male O'Connors and Tim Kennedy dug the other grave, with some tools they'd found in the wagon and a spade that Gardiner had in his own saddlebags.

When Noelle did relinquish the shovel to Drugeth, maybe half an hour later, she finally looked at him.

"What *is* your rank?"

He was back to that sad-eyed sorrowful-look business. "It is quite complicated, and depends mostly on the situation. For now, 'captain' will do."

She nodded, still with no expression. "Why did you kill him, Captain Drugeth? You'd already disarmed him."

"Literally," muttered Denise; again, having to fight off a semi-hysterical giggle.

"I am not certain," was the soft reply. "I fear some of it was simply ingrained reflex, although I strove to contain it. First, because it would have been a struggle to keep him alive on the journey, with such a wound, and would inevitably have slowed us down. Second, because I decided if I didn't kill one of them now, I would have to kill one of them later. Perhaps more. They are undisciplined people, prone to emotional outbursts. That was bad enough before you appeared to make it worse. Clearly, they have an animus against you."

He took a long breath. "And, finally, because he was not essential to my mission. Not even important, really. Neither was Simmons."

The two of them stared at each other.

"Just like that?" she asked abruptly.

"At the time, yes. Just like that. In the time to come, of course, it will be different. I will spend many hours of my life thinking about the deed. And praying that I did not transgress His boundaries."

Noelle looked away, for a few seconds. "Yes," she said. "I understand."

She handed him the shovel and climbed out of the shallow pit. "I will give you my parole, Captain Drugeth."

"The others?"

"Eddie will too. So will Lannie and Keenan, probably, but I wouldn't believe Lannie or Keenan if they told me the sun rose in the east. It's not that they're dishonest. Just . . . forgetful."

He smiled. "Much like several of my cousins."

Now, he looked at Denise.

"You can take her word for anything," said Noelle. "If you don't mind it coming with vulgar qualifiers."

Denise scowled. "Well, thank you very much."

Drugeth just looked at her, saying nothing.

After a while, Denise shrugged. "Sure, why not? You've got my fucking word I'll be a good little girl."

He stroked his mustache. "Qualifiers, indeed," he said mildly. "Do I need to insist on qualifying the terms? No attempt to escape. No attempt to overwhelm us by force."

He even said that last with a straight face. "That sort of thing?"

Denise thought about it. "Nah," she said. "I hate all that legal dotting-the-I's and crossing-the-T's bullshit. But I'm okay with the spirit of stuff."

He studied her for a bit longer. Denise was primed to strip his hide if he started nattering about her potty mouth. Or asked her if her father knew the sort of language she used, when who the hell did he think she'd learned it from in the first place?

But all he said was, "I believe that will do quite nicely."

By nightfall, they were well into the Fichtelgebirge. They made camp just before nightfall.

Three camps, really, separated by a few yards from each other. One for the defectors, one for Drugeth and his two cohorts, one for Denise, Noelle, Eddie, Lannie and Keenan.

After they ate, Lannie and Eddie fell asleep. Between their injuries and the rigors of walking or riding a wagon along mountain trails for several hours, they were exhausted.

Denise and Noelle and Keenan stayed awake a while longer, mostly just staring into the little fire they'd made. All three of the camps had fires going. Drugeth had given permission to make them. He didn't seem too concerned they'd be spotted, given the thick woods around them.

And who'd spot them anyway? The ever-vigilant and non-existing USE park rangers? Overflying aircraft, when they'd already crashed the only one in Grantville that could get off the ground, and Jesse Wood only let even the air force guys fly at night in extreme emergencies?

But Denise's sarcastic thoughts were just her way of coming to a decision.

"I've decided," she finally pronounced. "Drugeth's okay."

"Scary son-of-a-bitch," Keenan grunted. "But. Yeah. He's okay, I guess. What do you think, Noelle?"

But Noelle said nothing. Denise wasn't even sure she'd heard them talking. She seemed completely preoccupied by the sight of the flames.

CHAPTER II. *The Prayer*

Two days later, after they'd made camp for the evening, Janos was approached by the Barclay couple and Allen O'Connor. They were the leaders of the up-time defectors, insofar as such a group could be said to have leaders.

The day before, Janos had heard Denise Beasley refer to them sarcastically as a "motley crew." The term being new to him, he'd asked for a translation. He'd found her explanation quite charming, especially the qualifiers that seemed to be inseparable from the girl's vocabulary. Even more amusing had been her pugnacious attitude. Clearly, she seemed to be expecting him at any moment to begin chastising her for her language.

Indeed, he was sometimes tempted to do so, when she lapsed into blasphemy. But he'd already learned from his weeks in Grantville that Americans had a casual attitude toward blasphemy, just as the rumors said they did. And despite his piety, Janos was skeptical—had been since he was a boy—that the way so many priests lumped all sins into unvarying categories was actually a reflection of God's will. Janos did not presume to understand the Lord's purpose in all things, and blasphemy was certainly listed as a transgression in the Ten Commandments. Still, he doubted that the Creator who had forged the sun and the moon made no distinction at all between blasphemy and murder.

As for the girl's profanity, he simply found it artful. Growing up as the scion of a Hungarian noble family in the countryside, he'd learned profanity from high-born father and low-born milkmaid alike. His were not a prissy folk. Janos himself avoided profanity, as a rule, but that was simply an expression of his austere personality. He didn't paint or write poetry, either. But he could still appreciate the skill and talent involved in all three of the arts.

Had Janos' father still been alive and been there, he might have had caustic remarks to say about the girl's language. But the old man would have criticized her for the sloppiness of the form, not the nature of the content. When it came to profanity, Janos' father had been a devotee of formal structure; Denise Beasley, of what the up-timers called free verse.

Jarring stuff, free verse, at first glance. But in the hands of a skilled poet, it could be effective. Janos had read some poems by an up-timer named e.e. cummings—he'd refused to capitalize even his name—and found them quite good. He'd even had a copy made of some of them to give to his uncle, Pal Nadasdy.

"We just wanted to tell you that Billie Jean's settling

down," said Barclay. "We were a little worried there, for a while."

Janos nodded. He'd been somewhat concerned himself. Caryn Barlow seemed almost indifferent to the death of her father, but that wasn't particularly surprising. Their relationship had obviously not been close. In fact, it had seemed to verge on outright hostility. She'd joined the group because of her friendship with Suzi Barclay, not because of her father's involvement.

The Mase woman, on the other hand, was an odd one. Clearly intelligent, in most things, even quite intelligent. But it had been hard to analyze her attachment to such a man as Jay Barlow as being anything other than sheer stupidity. It was not simply that the man had been unpleasant, since that was true of many husbands and paramours. He'd been feckless and improvident as well.

Marina Barclay shook her head. "There's a history of abuse, there. I think it's got her all twisted up."

Janos couldn't quite follow the idiom. "Excuse me?"

"Billie Jean's father . . . Well. It was pretty bad. God knows why that got transferred over to an asshole like Barlow, but I think that's what happened."

"Ah." That was somewhat clearer. It was certainly as clear as Janos wanted it to be. Up-timers set great store by what they called "psychology." They claimed it was almost a science. Janos was dubious, but supposed it couldn't be any worse than the astrology which so many down-timers used to guide their way through life.

"The point is," said O'Connor, "we don't think she'll be a problem anymore. Now that she's cried herself out, we think she's actually kind of relieved. That was a bad situation."

Marina's expression darkened. "He beat her, sometimes, when he got drunk."

Janos looked from her, to her husband, to O'Connor. "Does she have possession of a weapon? A gun, I mean." He was not concerned, of course, that she might have a knife.

"No," said Peter Barclay firmly. "We took that away from her right away. We didn't ... uh ..."

Janos was tempted to scowl, but didn't. *We didn't want her taking a shot at you because you'd slaughter all of us.*

As if he himself couldn't make distinctions! They were truly annoying, sometimes, in the way they insulted without even realizing they did so.

Barclay's wife immediately demonstrated the talent anew. "And, uh, thanks for not killing her at the time."

Janos kept his face expressionless, since he knew there was no intentional insult involved. True, there might come a time in his old age—assuming he lived that long, which was unlikely—when he would be forced to kill an unarmed woman who attacked him. But to do such a thing now, when he was twenty-five, an experienced cavalry officer, and one of the best swordsmen in the Austrian empire? She might as well have thanked him for not being a coward.

There was such a difference between them, and the ones he had captured. Eddie Junker he understood almost immediately. A few exchanges over the past two days had been enough for the purpose. A sturdy young fellow, from a good down-time family. Lutheran, true, not Catholic.

But Janos did not particularly hold that against him, since Junker retained the other virtues of the station he'd been born into. Loyal, quietly courageous, dependable, solicitous of his mistress' well-being.

In their own manner, the same was true of Lannie Yost and Keenan Murphy. A bit hapless in some ways, those two, as their actions with the plane demonstrated. But Janos had learned while still in his teens that some retainers could fumble at things, and one overlooked their failings for their virtues. The position of a nobleman was simply a transient charge given by God: gone in an instant, measured against eternity. In that, as in so many things, Father Drexel's *School of Patience* was a superb guide.

Young Denise had seemed a bit outside Janos' experience, at first. But eventually he'd realized that was because the fluid class relations of Americans always blurred one's view of them until you understood where to look. Ignore class, and she was not so strange at all. Neither was the Suzi Barclay creature, for that matter. Wild young noblewomen were not common in Hungary, and even less so in Austria. But they were hardly unheard of. What mattered was the way they shaped themselves as time went by. Some wound up quite well, as Janos thought Denise was likely to manage. Others were . . . hopeless. A nuisance to their families at all times, perhaps never more so than when they reached old age and the obnoxious wretches had to be cared for.

Mostly, he was intrigued by Noelle Stull. Such a perceptive one, she was. He was quite sure that it would never occur to the Barclays or O'Connor to ask him the question she had. Where they would thank him for not killing a woman, when the reason was obvious, she'd wondered why he had decided to kill a man. Even more, what he thought the cost would be.

She was attractive, too, in a way that some young Hungarian noblewomen were and a few Austrian ones. Pretty in a subdued sort of way; slender; far more athletic than most such. He wondered what she'd look like in formal court costume.

He was a little jarred when he realized the direction his thoughts were heading. Just so, a few times in the past, had he gauged a possible marital prospect. In one instance, an assessment that led to his marriage to his now-deceased wife Anna Jakusith de Orbova.

Anna had died a year and a half earlier. This was the first instance since that horrible time when he'd even thought of another woman in those terms.

The thought was preposterous on the face of it, of course.

He realized his silence was making the Barclays and O'Connor uncomfortable. They'd assume he was thinking about them; possibly, even contemplating harsh measures.

"I am pleased to hear she is settling her nerves. Please see to it, though, that she remains unarmed. Just in case."

They nodded.

"Are there any other problems I should know about?"

"Uh, no," said O'Connor. "Everybody else is fine."

Janos wasn't surprised. Barlow and Simmons had wound up attached to the group through happenstance. They were not and never had been part of the inner circles. Nor liked, for that matter.

Truth be told, the episode's outcome had been much as Janos hoped it would. The rest of the up-timers had been far easier to handle since the killings. That would improve their chances of reaching Austria safely.

Marina Barclay looked uncertain. "I guess I should tell you that Billie Jean's threatening to complain to the authorities—the Austrian authorities, I mean—once we get to Vienna. She says she'll press charges against you. Take it all the way up to the emperor, if need be."

"She will certainly have the right to do so, under Austrian law. Even the right to appeal to the emperor, although he rarely takes such appeals under consideration."

Now, all of them looked uncertain. After a few seconds, Marina's husband finally got around to asking.

"Do you, uh... know the emperor? Personally, I mean?"

"Oh, yes. We have been close friends since we were boys."

They stared at him, then started to turn away. Moved by a sudden impulse, Janos cleared his throat.

"Excuse me. If you would satisfy my curiosity? Noelle Stull. What is her family background?"

The three of them looked at each other. By whatever silent communication passed, Peter Barclay assumed the role of spokesman.

"Her family is, uh... Well. Strange. There are several families involved, actually. The Murphys and the Stulls and the Fitzpatricks."

The tale that followed was intricate; complex; even tortuous at points. More than it needed to be, really. It was clear that the up-timers assumed he would find almost all of it incomprehensible.

When they finished, he nodded. "I believe I understand the gist of it. Noelle's true father, Dennis Stull, was betrothed to her mother, Pat Fitzgerald—in their own eyes, at least. Then her family, largely for religious reasons, forced her into a marriage with Francis Murphy. By whom"—he glanced over at the five USE loyalists, readying their camp—"she gave birth to Keenan, over there. During the years that passed, meanwhile, her once-betrothed remained unmarried. Eventually, Pat—Murphy, now, not Fitzgerald, as is your American custom—abandoned her legal husband and went to live with Dennis Stull for many years. By whom she had her daughter Noelle, although the fiction was publicly maintained for over two decades that Noelle was Francis Murphy's daughter. Until it all—'blew up,' was the term you used?—because Francis Murphy was outraged that his long-estranged wife attended the funeral of her lover's mother when she had refused to attend the funeral of his father. So, in a drunken fury, he attempted to murder her at the funeral."

"Well, sort of," said Marina. "Stupid bastard shot into the funeral parlor from outside. The only solid hit he got was on the corpse in the casket. His own son Keenan was the one wrestled him down, and kept him from anything worse."

"The whole thing was a comic opera, really," added her husband, "although it wouldn't have been if Francis had been sober enough to shoot straight. As it is, the only thing they wound up charging him with was attempted murder and desecrating a corpse."

Janos stroked his mustache. "A reasonable legal decision. The latter is certainly a charming one."

The Barclays and O'Connor didn't seem to think it was the least bit charming. "That was Judge Maurice Tito. He wasn't anywhere nearly as prone to be lenient to poor Horace Bolender. Threw the whole damn book at him, the self-righteous bastard."

Janos decided not to pursue that. It was the common characteristic of thieves to believe that one of their own was roughly handled by the law, where favoritism was shown to others.

In truth, there was some substance to the charge. By their own account, the flamboyant conclusion to the long and complex family saga they'd narrated was the product of emotion and unreason, not cold-blooded and premeditated criminal intent. Austrian judges—certainly Hungarian ones—were prone to gauging the two differently also. As was Janos himself, for that matter.

"This must all seem weird to you," said Marina, smiling.

Janos shook his head. "It all sounds quite familiar, actually. I can think of several similar episodes involving Hungarian noble families. Rather mild escapades, actually, compared to other things that have been done by such. When we reach the Danube and can finally relax a bit, remind me to tell you the history of Countess Erzsebet Bathory. She is—was—my maternal grandmother. A Calvinist, true, not a Catholic. But I do not believe a fair man can ascribe cause to effect in this instance. My parents converted to Catholicism when I was two years old, and I was raised in the church. But one of her sons, my uncle Pal Nadasdy, has stubbornly remained a Calvinist to this day, unmoved by all of Ferdinand II's many proffered carrots and occasional brandished stick. Yet I have rarely met a more respectable man."

After they left, Janos stood there staring into the fire, mulling on the problem for a while. The up-timers, as usual, had not understood his question. They categorized families by their deeds, as if noble families did not typically have more outlandish members and histories than most peasant families; simply because they had more power, if for no other reason.

So. It was still probably a preposterous idea to entertain, for many political reasons. But if he persisted in contemplating the matter—which he very well might; he was an introspective man, and knew himself rather well by now—then, sooner or later, he would have to face the problem squarely.

It was a thorny one, given that he was Hungarian. In many of the Germanies, by now—elsewhere too in the western countries, he thought—the theory had taken hold that Americans as a class belonged to the noble ranks. At the very least, stood outside the class categories altogether. Hungarians and Austrians thought that nonsense, by and large, although Janos was fairly sure their resolve would start crumbling as time went by.

As such resolve always did, given realities and the passage of enough time. His own august family could trace its origins back to Naples. Three centuries earlier, they had come to Hungary in the entourage of Charles Robert of Anjou, when he assumed the throne of Hungary as King Charles I. Family tradition insisted they'd been a highly respected family in the Italian aristocracy. Perhaps it was even true. Given Italy, though, that was always suspect. That was a land steeped in commerce, quite unlike rural Hungary. Everything was for sale, including titles.

But even if it were true, what then? Trace it back still farther, if you could, and what would you find? No Christian family in Europe could claim, as did some Jewish ones, to be able to trace themselves back to the lords spoken of in the Bible. And who had made them lords, except the Lord Himself? Who had also made the Ring of Fire, through which came the man whom many Germans now called their prince. And whose soldiers had, just a few months earlier at Ahrensbök, shoved the title down the throats of haughty French noble generals.

But that took a lot of time, as a rule. Probably more than Janos would encompass in that span of his life that mattered. Soon enough, he would have to marry again. His little boy Györgÿ needed a mother, and given his position in the empire he really should produce more heirs in case misfortune took his son as it had taken his wife. For which latter purpose, unfortunately, if not the first, a morganatic marriage would probably not be suitable.

So. He flashed a quick grin at the fire he was staring into. A problem, then. Complex; complicated; even tortuous at points.

Janos enjoyed solving problems. He also took vows seriously, although he seldom made them formal ones. At the age of twelve, after he realized the full scope of his responsibilities, he had made a solemn vow that while he would be a faithful son of Hungary, he would not—would *not*—agree to marry a dullard. Be her rank never so high, or her station never more suitable.

He'd kept that pledge to himself when he married Anna Jakusith. The all-too-short time he'd shared his life with her had confirmed the wisdom of his youngster's vow. As a purely personal matter, and leaving aside the needs of state, he'd far rather remain a widower for the rest of his life than marry the sort of woman who, every morning and every nightfall, only made him think regretfully of the woman who was no longer there. He would remember Anna always, of course, so long as he lived, as he remembered her in his prayers every day. But he wanted a wife who could forge a place of her own in his life and affections.

"You're *kidding*," hissed Denise. Quickly, almost surreptitiously, she glanced at Drugeth. The way he was just standing there, not moving at all while he studied whatever the hell he found so fascinating in a campfire, matched Keenan's depiction perfectly. The expressionless, handsome, brooding face, half in shadows, the easy stance—*everything*. She could picture him just like that, standing in a castle in Transylvania. Which was part of Hungary, now that she thought about it. Well, parts of it were, anyway.

"Oh, wow." She took her eyes away from Janos, lest she draw his attention somehow. She didn't really believe in supernatural powers, but you could never be sure.

"Yup," said Keenan. "That's the whole story. I got it from Gardiner and Gage just an hour ago, while we were out foraging for wood. Janos Drugeth is a *vampire*."

Noelle sniffed. "Keenan, I am quite certain that neither Gage nor Gardiner said any such thing."

"Well, sure. Not in so many words. But what else could we be talking about? I mean, I've even *heard* of his grandma. The Blood Countess. She's almost as famous as Dracula himself. The one who sucked all those virgins dry of their blood so her complexion wouldn't get bad. *Dozens* of virgins."

Noelle sniffed again. "There are so many errors in what you just said that I don't know where to begin. For starters, she didn't 'suck the blood' out of anybody. She— uh . . ."

Denise had heard the story, too. "That's quibbling, Noelle. So she drained them dry with a knife and bathed in the blood. Big fucking difference. And it's a fact—well, that's what I heard, anyway—that when they caught her they didn't try to execute her 'cause they couldn't. So they walled her up in a room until she died of old age."

"Why didn't they drive a wooden stake through her heart?" Lannie asked plaintively. "That's supposed to work."

"There are no such things as vampires!" Noelle hissed. But Denise figured the reason she hissed it instead of shouting it was because Noelle was just as concerned as anyone else not to draw Drugeth's attention.

Denise glanced quickly at Janos again. He was still in that brown study he seemed to fall into about twenty times a day. Not surprising, really. Denise figured if she were a vampire she'd probably spend a lot of time contemplating the whichness of what herself.

How fucking exciting could it get? A *vampire*.

Well. Close enough, anyway.

Eventually, Noelle gave up. Even Eddie seemed dubious of her arguments.

Superstitious dolts!

She avoided looking at Drugeth for the rest of the evening, she was so exasperated.

But she found that she couldn't stop thinking about him, even after she rolled into her blankets, and that was even more exasperating.

The problem, she finally admitted to herself, was that while she absolutely did not—*Did. Not.*—believe in vampires, she also had to admit something else.

She doted on vampire stories. She owned every one of Anne Rice's books that had come out before the Ring of Fire, and had read none of them less than twice. Her copy of Bram Stoker's original novel was dog-eared.

She'd even once, in college, gotten into a ferocious all-night-long argument with three other female students over the subject of which actor's Dracula had been the best. Stupid mindless twits had been all ga-ga and gushing over effete fops like Bela Lugosi and Christopher Lee.

Even at that age, Noelle knew the truth. A *real* vampire—which didn't exist, of course—would be like the Dracula portrayed by Jack Palance. Medieval rulers, commanders of armies, swordsmen, guys with muscles as well as fangs. Not layabouts loafing in a castle somewhere.

Interesting guys. Exciting guys.

And just how deep, anyway, was she going to wallow in this idiotic fantasy?

She was a sane, sensible, rational modern woman. An official of the SoTF government. And *he* was an enemy soldier.

Period.

"Boy, do you look bedraggled," was Denise's greeting the next morning.

"I didn't sleep well," Noelle said grumpily.

Denise grinned at her. "You gotta admit, the guy's fascinating as all hell. If he weren't too old for me, I'd be checking him out myself."

That evening they reached a village in one of the many little valleys in the Fichtelgebirge. It was a Catholic village, with a small church.

The village was too small for a tavern, so they camped just outside it. After the camp was made, Janos went to the church.

Noelle followed him, after waiting a few minutes. *Not* because she was following him, but simply because she felt the need herself.

When she entered, he was in one of the pews, praying. She was quite certain he was praying for the souls of the two men he'd slain, a few days earlier. For his own, too, of course. But mostly theirs. There was still much about Janos Drugeth that was a mystery to her, but not everything. One of the prayers she'd be making here, as she had so many times since it happened, would be a prayer for the soul of the torturer she'd killed in Franconia last year. And for her own, for having done it.

So much for the idiots and their crap about vampires.

Even as quietly as Noelle was moving, he heard her come in. Being honest, the man really did seem to have preternatural senses. He turned his head and gazed at her for a while, his face as expressionless as it usually was.

Noelle did her best to ignore the scrutiny. She dipped her fingers in the basin, made the sign of the cross, and went to a pew some distance away from Drugeth. As far distant as she could get, in fact, allowing for the tiny size of the church.

She concentrated on her own prayers, and was pleased that she managed that pretty well. At least until the end, when she found herself fumbling because she was waiting for Drugeth to leave. There was no way she was going to leave with him.

Finally, he left. She waited perhaps five minutes before leaving herself.

Not that it did her any good. She discovered him waiting for her outside.

It would be silly to avoid him. So, she came up and nodded a greeting.

"I am told you are a devout Catholic," he said. "Have even contemplated taking holy vows."

"Ah . . ." She looked away, caught off balance by the unexpected question. "Yes, sort of. It's something I've thought about for years, off and on. Even though everybody who knows me says I'd make a lousy nun. Well, not that, exactly. They think I'd wind up very unhappy with the choice."

He said nothing. She was pretty sure that was because he didn't want to seem as if he were crowding her.

"What do you think?" she asked suddenly. And then

found herself caught even more off balance by her own question—*what are you doing, you ninny?*—than she had been by his.

"I think that decision, unlike many others, is one that only the person involved can make. We are all—those of us who are Catholic, for a certainty—obliged to follow the teachings of the Church involving matters of conscience. But not even the Church presumes to tell a man or a woman if they should take holy vows."

He smiled, in that gentle, half-melancholy and half-ironic way he had. "I grant you, for noble families and royal ones more so, that decision is often tightly circumscribed, even sometimes forced outright. Still, I will hold to the principle."

"You have no opinion?"

"I would not put in that way. Let us say I do not presume to advise. That is not quite the same thing as having no opinion."

He seemed on the verge of adding something. His lips even started to part open. But, then, he closed them firmly and just shook his head.

"I should speak no further on the matter. May I escort you back to the camp?"

Silly to refuse that offer, as well, so she nodded.

They said nothing on the way. By the time they reached the camp, though, Noelle was in a quiet fury.

Not at him, but herself. A decision she hadn't been able to make for years had somehow gotten made in that short walk of no more than two hundred yards. She knew it as surely as she knew anything.

• • •

Damn her impudent soul, Denise was waiting for her with that same aggravating grin.

"Yeah, right. Enemy of the state. Is he as cute in church as everywhere else?"

"Vampire, remember?" Noelle half-snarled at her. "As if a vampire would enter holy ground!"

Denise's grin didn't so much as flicker. "You're dodging the question. Nice try."

"What he is, is the most exasperating man I've ever met."

"Wow." Denise shook her head, the grin vanishing completely. "You've got it bad, girl."

CHAPTER 12. *The Date*

The Bohemian Border, near Cheb

A little after noon, three and a half days later, Drugeth called a halt and ordered a rest. The last stretch before they reached Cheb was going to be very difficult, and they couldn't afford to lose the last wagon due to someone's fatigue. The other one had broken a wheel two days earlier, and they'd lost two hours repacking the surviving wagon with the items that were too bulky or heavy to be loaded on pack horses. By then, fortunately, they had several of those. Foreseeing the likelihood that at least one of the wagons would not survive the trek across the Fichtelgebirge, Janos had purchased pack animals at any of the small villages they'd passed through which had one they were willing to sell.

They needed to stop, anyway, because it was time to release Noelle Stull and her companions. By now, Janos was sure that Noelle had figured out that his escape route was taking them into Bohemia. He wasn't concerned about that, in itself, because by the time she could return to a town that had a radio with which she could alert the USE authorities, his expedition would have long since left Cheb and would probably already be reentering the USE farther south. The main thing was that he didn't want her to realize that Austria had suborned the commander of the Cheb garrison.

Partly that was a matter of simple straight-dealing. Honesty among thieves, perhaps. But just as the up-timers had a witty saw that "an honest cop is one who stays bribed," it was equally true in the gray world Janos now spent more of his time in than he liked, that the man who bribes the cop is obliged not to carelessly betray him afterward.

Mostly, though, it was cold-blooded calculation. The future was impossible to predict, and Janos still hoped he could persuade the emperor to make peace with Wallenstein. But he'd probably not be successful in his effort, and the war with Bohemia would heat up again. In that event, as unlikely as it might be given the geography—but who could say where the winds of war might blow?—it could be highly advantageous to Austria to have the commander of the Cheb garrison on its payroll. Even if the man objected to flagrant treason, he could be blackmailed into ceding the fortress with the threat of exposure.

Janos was feeling a little guilty, actually, allowing

Noelle and her group to come this far. If one of them had a good enough knowledge of geography, they might be able to deduce that Cheb was his destination. He should have set them free the day before, in retrospect. Without horses—which he certainly wouldn't give them, even if he had any to spare—they probably still couldn't have gotten out of the Fichtelgebirge in time to cause any damage to his project.

But . . . he'd stalled, since there were so many "mights" and "probablies" involved on both sides of the equation. Looking back on it, he'd allowed himself to be influenced by a purely personal factor. He was reluctant to part company with Noelle Stull; it was as simple as that.

As the days had passed, his interest had deepened. He'd never thought about it before, but he'd come to realize that spending several days with a woman in a forced march, under considerable tension and strain— conflicting and complex ones, too—was as good a way as any to get a measure of her.

Which he had, at least to the extent possible in the few days they'd spent together.

Noelle was as perceptive as his dead wife had been, when it came to navigating difficult political waters. Demonstrated, in Anna's case, by her ability to work a compromise between the Catholic church and the many Orthodox inhabitants on their domains, which satisfied everyone well enough and kept the peace. In Noelle's case, by the way she maintained a workable relationship between her own captured party and the defectors. There was no love lost there, and she'd refused—quite firmly— to allow her people to be used in any of the labor directly connected to the defection. They'd taken no part, for instance, in the strenuous labor needed to repack the wagons again. But, that line drawn, she'd not been foolishly obstreperous about anything else.

So. Principles combined with flexibility where needed. A combination much rarer than one might think.

She also knew how to maintain authority over her own charges: smoothly, easily, and without either bullying them or ceding anything important. No easy task, that, given the nature of the people involved. Not a problem with Eddie Junker, of course. Although Janos was sure that Noelle would insist that Eddie was her "partner," as well as a close friend, the fact remained that the relationship was one of mistress and subordinate. Something which he was equally sure Junker himself understood—but was good-natured about because of the light hand of the mistress herself.

Lannie and Keenan, on the other hand, while they had the habits and temperament of subordinates by virtue of their origins and history, had not had a previous relationship with her, other than a family one in the case of the Murphy fellow. More than once—many more times than once—Janos had seen how awkwardly a new commander handled such a situation. In contrast to Anna, who had swept into her new position as the mistress of the estates at Homonna with complete ease. Within a short time, as the Americans would put it, she had the servants in the large household—even many of the peasants nearby—"eating out of her hand."

Noelle had even managed to keep Denise Beasley under control, for a wonder. And had done it, not by the harsh disciplinary methods a less perceptive person would have tried—and which would have succeeded poorly, if at all—but because she had the art of persuading a young, bright and rebellious girl that she was more in the way of a trusted older sister and a confidant than a substitute mother. It had been quite deftly done, and the fact that Noelle herself would no doubt be indignant if he suggested she was being manipulative, did not change the reality. The up-timers seemed to feel that "being manipulative" was a negative trait, even an evil one, but that was just one of their many superstitions. The ability to get other people to do what needed to be done was simply a valuable skill, that's all—especially for the wife of an important figure in a major realm.

Finally, there was her athleticism and quite evident good health. Anna had been less athletic than the average noblewoman, which, in and of itself, had not much bothered Janos. He was not one of those idle aristocrats who spent half their waking hours on the hunt, and wanted a wife who could ride with him. Where Janos was most likely to be riding at a full gallop was on a battlefield, where no wife could go or was wanted to go.

Unfortunately, Anna had been sickly, not simply sedentary. Had been since she was a girl. Janos had known that when he married her, but had chosen to overlook the problem in favor of her many other virtues. Having lost one wife after a short marriage, however, he had no desire to repeat the experience. That had been anguish such as he'd never felt in his life, and never wanted to again.

True, Noelle was not as physically attractive as Anna

had been. The woman was pretty, where Anna had been a real beauty. But that did not concern Janos. First, because it was a matter of flesh, and thus trivial. Second, because it was always transient, as was the nature of fleshly things. Finally, because given time it would be irrelevant in any event. The Americans could wallow in their romanticism, as they called it, but that was another of their odd superstitions. A good marriage produced affection and physical desire as naturally and inevitably as trees grew. Love was simply the fruit, which they confused with the seed.

There remained, of course, all the immense obstacles of a political nature. Which might indeed be too great to overcome. But he'd decided the matter was worth raising with the emperor. He'd need his permission to pursue the matter, anyway. Beyond that, Ferdinand was one of his closest friends and a man whose advice was often shrewd, sometimes uncannily so.

"I'm telling you, Noelle, you oughta ask him out on a date. Or finagle him into asking you out, if you're still hung up on proper gender roles on account of you're such an ancient."

"Why don't pharmacists develop the most useful drug of all?" Noelle grumbled. "The label would read: 'Eliminates shit-eating grins. Especially effective on teenagers.'"

Denise ignored that, of course. "Me, if I want to go out on a date with some guy—not often, but it does happen—I just tell him when I'm going to pick him up with my bike."

"He's an *enemy,* in case you've forgotten."

Denise waved her hand. "Wars come, wars go. True love remains."

"You are insufferable, sometimes. And shut up, will you? He's heading our way."

A few minutes later, after Janos explained that they'd be parting company, Denise's silly idea became a moot one as well.

Which made it all the more alarming, to Noelle, that she felt such a sharp anxiety at the news. Denise, at least, had the excuse of being sixteen years old. What was hers?

Firmly, she told herself she was simply worried about the practical aspects of the situation.

"I think it's outrageous, Captain Drugeth, that you are abandoning us without even a single horse."

He gave her that damned soulful smile that did annoying things to the primitive and ancient parts of her brainstem.

"First, Ms. Stull, it is rather absurd to use the term 'abandoning' when I am simply doing what you would have done yourself several days ago had you not given me your parole. Second, you don't need a horse to travel. Lannie Yost's ankle has healed and Eddie Junker's broken arm does not impede him from walking. Third, this is hardly a wilderness or a desert which must be crossed swiftly on pain of death. I am not, I remind you, depriving you of money with which you can buy food and shelter from any of the villages in the area. I am even allowing you to keep Eddie Junker's rifle and its ammunition, should you need to hunt for sustenance. Something for which, I can assure you, Austria's gunmakers would curse me if they found out."

Noelle sneered. Tried to, anyway. "You know perfectly well it's an antique."

He shrugged. "All the better, actually, from the standpoint of a down-time gunmaker using it for a model. As *you* know perfectly well, the USE's now-famous SRG is patterned after an even more antiquated design."

Which was true, of course. So Noelle fell back to glaring silently, feeling as if she were all of fourteen years old. Drugeth's conditions for releasing them were perfectly rational. Even somewhat generous, in fact. Her anger was just the way the underlying anxiety was working its way to the surface.

Why didn't the stupid pharmacists develop a drug that would anesthetize those useless brainstem parts?

Probably because we've been tested over and over again by evolution, and passed with flying colors, came the unwanted reply.

Out of the tension and confusion of the moment, like a thesis and antithesis struggling, came the synthesis.

"Very well!" she snapped. Her eyes became slitted. "But I warn you, Captain Drugeth. You haven't seen the last of me!"

"I look forward to that with great anticipation."

And off he went.

Denise shook her head. "Well, that's about the weirdest way I ever heard anybody make a date, but sure enough. It's a date."

"Shut. Up."

CHAPTER 13. *The Map*

High Street Mansion, Seat of Government for the State of Thuringia-Franconia
President's Office
Grantville, State of Thuringia-Franconia

"You should fire that whole garrison at Saalfeld," Noelle said testily. "For sure, get rid of that useless commander. I swear to you, Ed, if they'd been willing to get off their butts as soon as we arrived, I might have still caught the bastards."

"Not likely, Noelle. By then, they'd have been well into Bohemia—and there's the tiny little problem that while our relations with Wallenstein are good, they aren't so good that he'd take kindly to us sending a military unit into his territory without his permission. And getting that permission would have taken at least another week."

He shrugged. "Besides, it wouldn't do any good. The SoTF doesn't have the kind of money it would take to throw top wages at mercenary units to make sure we get good ones for mere garrison duty far from the war zones. If we fired Captain Stamm and his company, anyone we got to replace them wouldn't be any better in the raring-to-go department, and would probably be a lot worse in what matters, which is doing a decent job of keeping the peace locally without gouging the residents more than they think is reasonable."

He came out of his relaxed slouch and folded his hands

on the desk. "Relax, will you? I know you're like a bulldog when you set your teeth into something, but this is really not worth the amount of sweat you're putting into it. Look, you did your best, and the baddies got away. It happens. That said, it was not the crime of the century, the only people who got killed were baddies themselves — I almost wish I'd seen that; I really detested Jay Barlow—and the military impact of the tech transfer will be minor in the short run and probably not even that significant in the long run."

Noelle eyed him skeptically. "I notice you didn't say anything about the political impact."

Ed shrugged again. "So the Crown Loyalists are trying to make hay out of it. Big deal. That's the nature of politics, Noelle. You win some, you lose some, and when you do lose the other guy points with alarm and swears to the electorate that the sky is falling. I've talked to Mike about it, and I can assure you he's not losing any sleep over the affair. Neither am I. Neither should you."

Noelle sighed. "I *hate* giving up on something I started."

After a moment, she managed a smile. "At least Eddie's arm looks to be healing okay. The doctor told him it should be as good as new in a few more weeks. So I guess—I feel bad about it, even if it wasn't my fault—that the only real casualty on our side is that Lannie and Keenan are out of a job."

"No, they aren't. Didn't you hear? Kay Kelly had a conniption, of course, and demanded that her husband fire the two bums. I guess she was even making noises about filing criminal charges. But you know Bob. Hell of a nice guy, even if it does take him a month to screw in a lightbulb because he's got to redesign it to his satisfaction first. So he just plain refused, on the grounds that they meant well. And don't let anybody tell you that he doesn't wear the pants in that family, even if Kay could teach graduate courses in henpecking."

"That she could," said Noelle, grimacing. "I'll make it a point—even more than usual—to steer clear of her over the next few weeks."

"Unless you go to Magdeburg, you won't have to," Ed said. "She left yesterday, once she realized Bob wasn't going to budge."

"What? She's going to try to get the federal government to press charges?"

"Oh, hell no." Ed shook his head, smiling. "I don't like the woman, but nobody ever said she let any moss grow. She went up to Magdeburg to lobby the government to put in an order for the Dauntless line. Now that it's been field-tested and proved it could carry out a successful bomb run. Not the *plane's* fault the dummies piloting it bombed the wrong guys, after all."

"You're kidding!"

"Nope. One of her arguing points—you know how quick she is to level accusations of favoritism—is that that's more than Mike Stearns, playing his usual favorites game, ever asked Hal and Jesse to prove with *their* planes. Which he commissioned on nothing better than a prayer and a promise."

Noelle couldn't herself from laughing. "She's got brass, I'll say that for her."

The laughter finally broke her sour mood. She

gathered up her stuff and rose. "Well, okay. I guess you're right. And what I do know is that you're busy. So I'll get out of your hair. Besides, I'd better see if I can put in a word for Denise before her parents skin her alive."

But when she got to the Beasleys' place, one of those big double-sized trailers called "mobile homes" in blithe disregard for the cinder blocks it was actually sitting on instead of wheels, she discovered her mission was unnecessary. Denise's mother Christin had thrown a fit, sure enough. But Buster had taken it all in stride.

There were some advantages, it seemed, to having a father with an ex-biker's views on parenting.

"What the hell, Noelle, it's like I told my wife." He placed a large, affectionate hand on his daughter's shoulder. "It's not like she got pregnant or strung out on dope or started working for a pimp or even got in trouble with the cops. For that matter, her new tattoo she got yesterday's sorta reasonable."

Noelle eyed the tattoo on Denise's shoulder, easily visible because she was just wearing a tank top inside the warm trailer. That was the tattoo she'd gotten at the age of fourteen. A death's head with the logo *Watch it, buddy*. Completely tasteless, in Noelle's opinion, although she'd allow it might cause high school boys to think twice.

Buster had thought that tattoo was reasonable, too, Noelle remembered—and without the "sorta" qualifier. She didn't want to think—

"I love it!" exclaimed Denise. "Here, I'll show you."

With no further ado, she yanked up the tank top, exposing her slim midriff.

"Oh, dear God," was all Noelle could think to say.

It was a lot better from an artistic standpoint, certainly. The tattoo artist had quite a bit of skill.

Still.

The central image, right on the girl's belly, was that of a sexpot wearing a flying jacket—not that any flying jacket would expose that much bosom—pants that looked painted on, and spike-heeled boots. She was sitting with her legs crossed—lounging, rather—and holding a bomb in one hand, with a sputtering fuse.

Smiling seductively, of course.

That was bad enough. The logo was worse.

Above the image: *You can land here*

Below it: *If you don't crash*

Denise frowned. "You don't like it?"

"Well . . ."

Huffily, the girl dropped the hem of the tank top. "Just 'cause *you* can't keep from beating around the bush. How's Eddie doing?"

"Fine," said Noelle. Warily: "Why do you ask?"

"He's cute." She jerked a thumb at Buster. "My dad even says he's okay. I thought I might drop by on him later."

"You stay away from Eddie!"

"I bet *he'll* like the tattoo."

Noelle hurried away to warn Eddie of an impending visitation by a one-girl Mongol horde.

Alas, Eddie seemed unconcerned. "What's the problem? I like Denise. A lot, in fact."

"She's wild. And she's much too young for you."

"Don't be silly, Noelle. Denise is a bit wild, I suppose—although nothing like my cousin Kaethe—but she's not actually foolish. And I'm certainly not."

That last was true enough. Noelle started to feel relieved until she saw that Eddie's gaze seemed more than a little unfocused. As if he were contemplating in his mind's eye a certain tattoo that she had, perhaps unfortunately, described in great detail.

However the visit turned out—and Noelle wasn't *really* worried, since Eddie was to deliberation what a cow was to munching grass—he seemed his usual self when she visited him the next morning. He had a large map of the SoTF and the surrounding territories spread out across his table, and was studying it intently.

"What are you doing?" she asked.

"Just indulging in my curiosity. I'm as tenacious as you are, you know. I just don't have your compulsion to act on it at all costs." He lifted his eyes from the map. "Any more news from Bohemia?"

Noelle flopped onto the nearby armchair. "Nothing. Well, not 'nothing.' Wallenstein is certainly taking seriously the incursion of an Austrian expedition into his territory, even a small one. He and Pappenheim have the Black Cuirassiers scouring the whole area. But . . . nothing. Not a sign of them. We just got another lack-of-progress report on the radio an hour ago."

Eddie nodded. "I'm not surprised. I've been thinking about it, and considering the terrain. It finally dawned on me that Drugeth probably didn't stay in Bohemia for very long."

Noelle sat up straight. "What?"

"Come here. I can show you better on the map."
Noelle was there in a heartbeat. Eddie's finger started
tracing a route through the Fichtelgebirge. "He can cut
back across here, near this little town called Kötzting.
From there, he can just follow the Regen down to
Regensburg, and from there it's an easy barge-ride into
Austria."

"But . . . We have a *garrison* at Regensburg. A great
damn big one, too, and real soldiers."

"Indeed so. Because they have been assigned, no
matter the cost, to keep the enemy from crossing the
Danube by seizing the bridge there. Regensburg anchors
our left flank against Bavaria. Not likely, therefore—is
it?—that they'll be much concerned with anything else.
And there are no troops to the north until you reach
Amberg. A lot of military traffic between Amberg and
Regensburg, of course, but they'd be going along"—he
pointed to a river just west of the Regen—"the Naab. Not
the Regen."

Noelle stared at the map, while Eddie continued. "See
what I mean? He doesn't have to worry about anything
except the short time he'd be passing through Regensburg
itself."

"But . . . Damnation, the garrison at Regensburg was
warned to look for them."

"Noelle, be serious. Yes. The garrison at Regensburg—
along with a dozen others—received an alert over the
radio to keep an eye out for the possibility that a party of
up-time defectors might be passing through. Maybe. At a
time unknown. In wagons. Possibly with pack horses."

He tapped the spot indicating Regensburg. "First, they would have paid no attention to it. Even if they did, they'd be looking for 'up-timers' on wagons or horses. Given Janos Drugeth, what do you think the likelihood is that, by now, he hasn't obtained river transport and doesn't have the defectors outfitted as a party of down-time merchants?"

His eyes narrowed, as if he were gauging something. "If I'm right, he's already on the Regen. Should be passing through Regensburg today or tomorrow."

Given Janos Drugeth . . .

"That son-of-a-bitch!" Noelle yelped. Out the door she went.

After Eddie closed the door and sat back down at the table, he shook his head.

"Denise was right. She's got it bad."

CHAPTER 14. *The Bridge*

High Street Mansion, Seat of Government for the
State of Thuringia-Franconia
President's Office
Grantville, State of Thuringia-Franconia

"I'm afraid Mr. Piazza left for Bamberg this morning, Ms. Stull. He won't be in radio contact again until this evening, at the earliest. Carol Unruh went with him." The secretary folded her hands, in that inimitable and unmistakable way that they must spend a whole semester teaching people how to do in Executive Assistant College.

"I Am Afraid There Is Nothing I Can Do."

In caps. Noelle went out the door.

Municipal Complex
Police Department
Grantville, State of Thuringia-Franconia

"Gimme a break, Noelle," said Preston Richards. Grantville's police chief scowled at an assignment chart on the wall of his office. "You got any idea how stretched thin I am? No, I don't have any cops I can detach from duty on what sounds like a wild goose chase. And how would they get there in time anyway?"

Before she could keep arguing, he raised his hand. "I'll send another radio message to the garrison at Regensburg. But that's it. And I doubt very much that'll do any good. Word came yesterday that the Bavarians are moving more troops into the area."

No caps, but it didn't matter. Press Richards had a baccalaureate from Stubborn Like a Mule College. Graduated *magna cum laude.*

Noelle went out the door.

Regensburg
The Upper Palatinate, under USE imperial
administration

"Idiots," snarled Colonel Moritz Kreisler. "We've got at least three Bavarian regiments moving around just the other side of the Danube"—he pointed an accusing finger at the river, as if it were the guilty party—"and they want me to disrupt my disposition of forces in order to hunt down some fucking *thieves*?"

"I'm just passing on the message, sir," said the radio operator apologetically. "How should I respond?"

Kreisler took a deep breath, controlling his temper. He reminded himself that whatever the legal formalities might be, a message from any figure of authority in Grantville—even a miserable be-damned police chief—had to be handled diplomatically.

"Tell them we received the message." With an effort: "No, thank them for sending us the warning. Assure them we will do everything possible. Emphasize 'possible.'"

After the radio operator left, Kreisler went over to the window of his office and looked down on the Danube passing almost directly below.

They might be using a barge or other rivercraft.

"Oh, marvelous," he muttered, between teeth that were almost clenched. Just at a glance, he could see five such vessels on the river. Four of them were piled high with goods, and two of those were carrying a number of passengers as well. Did the cretins think that merchants and farmers and I-need-to-see-my-poor-uncle-before-he-dies suspended their activity because of a war?

Still, he should do something, just for the record. "Lieutenant Müller!" he bellowed.

His orderly appeared almost instantly.

"Send word to whatever squads are monitoring the river traffic—no, one squad should be enough; and make sure it's a squad right inside the city—I do *not* want the men watching the river up and down stream to be in the least bit distracted—to keep an eye out for a large party of American traitors—accompanied by a Hungarian officer; probably two or three other soldiers—who might attempt to pass through Regensburg on their way to Austria."

Lieutenant Müller was a little cross-eyed. "Yes, sir. Ah . . ."

"How should I know what 'American traitors' look like?" the colonel said testily. "Try to spot excellent teeth combined with a shifty expression. But if I were you, I'd concentrate on the Hungarian officer. You know what *those* look like, don't you?"

Müller practically sighed with relief. "Yes, sir. Of course."

"All right, boys, you heard him," said Corporal Brenner. "Keep an eye out for one of those Hungarian dandies. Can't be hard, since they're even more vain than Austrian noblemen."

As usual, Private Sandler looked confused. Sighing, the sergeant planted a large forefinger on the top of his helmet. "Just look for the plume, Jochen."

Kelly Aviation Facility
Near Grantville, State of Thuringia-Franconia

"Please, Bob. It's the only chance that's left."

Noelle felt like an idiot. Princess Leia, in a movie. *Please, Obi-Wan Kenobi. You're our only hope.*

Bob Kelly shook his head. "But . . . the authorities . . ."

"There *are* no authorities. Not in town that I can reach in time who have the clout to get anything done. But if I get there myself . . ."

Bob looked from her to one of the planes in the hangar. The one that looked as if they'd been working on it round the clock. Noelle had figured they might be, with Kay up in Magdeburg doing the full court lobbyist's press.

"Well . . . The *Dauntless II* is ready to fly, sure enough. But we haven't got it fitted with the bomb attachments yet. The best you could do would be to toss a grenade out the window."

Noelle set her teeth. "Bob, I am *not* planning to bomb anybody."

He peered at her nearsightedly, over the half-moon glasses he favored. He looked for all the world like a chubby middle-aged elf. Not one of the Tolkien-type heroic and dramatic elves, either. One of the Santa's-helpers elves. Exactly what Noelle was afraid she'd look like at that age if she let her figure go and didn't pay attention to her solemn vows to eliminate all elflike mannerisms.

"Then how do you plan to accomplish anything once you do get there?" he asked.

Good question. But Noelle was not to be thwarted.

"I'll simply summon the garrison to its duty. With an official from Grantville on the scene who's directly involved in the matter, I'm sure that'll be sufficient."

Which was a laugh, from Noelle's past experience with military commanders. They swore by Chain of Command the way other people swore by the Father, the Son and the Holy Ghost.

But she'd deal with that when she got there. First, she had to get there. By nightfall—and it was already two o'clock in the afternoon, in late November. They had just enough time.

Fortunately, Lannie piped up. "They do have a landing strip in Regensburg now, boss. Been operational for a month."

Kelly rubbed his jaw. "Kay'll have a fit, when she hears about it."

"Why?" Noelle tried to look as self-assured as she possibly could. She was pretty good at that, actually. "It'll just be another test of the capabilities of the Dauntless line."

She even said "Dauntless" without a waver.

"Well . . ."

But it was enough, she could tell. Bob Kelly had been smarting for years over the constant jokes about his unfinished planes.

"Yeah, sure. What the hell. The weather's clear and Regensburg's only a hundred and fifty miles away. Be there before sundown, easy. Lannie, take her there. Keenan, you go with them."

Unfortunately, Noelle didn't think to ask about the condition of the radio until they were half an hour into the flight.

"Well," said Lannie.

From the rear seat, Keenan's hand appeared over her shoulder, clutching a map. "I remembered to bring this, though."

Naturally, it was the wrong map.

"Never mind," she said, after checking to make sure— you just never knew with these guys—that the plane did have a functioning compass. "Just head south until we reach the Danube. Then follow it."

"Which way?"

Not. To. Be. Thwarted.

"I'll figure it out when the time comes."

She did, too. It wasn't even hard, since Noelle had a good knowledge of geography and she knew Regensburg was at the crest of a large northerly bend in the Danube. Between that and the compass, she could figure out where they were.

A bit too far to the east, as it happened. Here, the river was coursing southeast.

She pointed upstream. "Thataway."

Regensburg
The Upper Palatinate, under USE imperial
administration

Sure enough, the airfield was in good shape. Lannie brought the plane down as smoothly as you could ask for.

The soldiers guarding the field, of course, were practically jumping up and down with fury.

No one had informed them! They should have been notified of the flight plan by the radio!

But at least they weren't suspicious. Everyone knew that practically every country in Europe had started aircraft projects. But except for a handful of commercial craft operating out of the USE or the Netherlands, all the airplanes in existence were still in the USE's air force.

Besides, she'd brought a magic wand.

Documents. Official Documents. Testifying that she

was indeed an official for the State of Thuringia-Franconia and never mind exactly what her powers were and where her jurisdiction began and ended.

They even let her take one of the unit's horses to ride into town and summon the garrison to its duty.

"I am afraid that Colonel Kreisler has gone out of the city, checking some new reconnaissance reports. He is not expected to return until tomorrow at the earliest."

Lieutenant Müller clasped his hands behind his back. Allowing for variations, it was the well-known and detestable gesture. As were the capital letters.

"I Am Afraid There Is Nothing I Can Do."

Down at the river, on the great bridge that spanned the Danube, she considered whether she might prevail on one of the squads of soldiers below...

What a laugh.

Besides, now that she was here and could see it herself, she really couldn't blame the soldiers for their attitude. The Bavarians were in the area, after all, with sizeable forces. The USE's troops were concentrating on protecting the bridge and spotting any attempt to ferry large numbers of soldiers across the river.

True, there was *already* a small fleet of boats on the river—six of them that she could see, just on this side of the bridge looking upstream—but they weren't clustered the way landing craft would be. Just some of the many commercial craft that plied one of Europe's major waterways day in and day out, and had been doing so for centuries.

She glanced at a small barge just passing below the bridge. This one, for instance, looked to be carrying mostly—

"You son-of-a-bitch!" she screeched.

She raced over to the downstream side of the bridge, clawing at the flap of her holster. By the time she got the pistol out and steadied her nerves enough to check that the clip was in and the safety was off, the barge had reappeared.

Janos was standing at the very stern, looking up at her. Wide-eyed, as if in fear or astonishment.

Well, no. Not fear. Wide-eyed with astonishment.

Not for long, though. Suddenly he broke into a smile— a genuine grin; the first she'd ever seen on his face—and doffed his battered-looking cap. The sort any boatman might wear, although the flourishing bow that followed had obviously been learned in palaces.

She pointed the gun right at him, remembering to use the two-handed grip that was her only chance of hitting anything. He replaced the cap on his head, but otherwise just kept standing there, looking at her. His face had no expression, now.

He was maybe twenty yards away. Well, thirty or forty, allowing for the height of the bridge.

She'd probably miss. Worse, she might miss him and accidentally hit somebody else. There were kids playing on the river bank. Way off to the side, sure, but she'd heard all the Annie Oakley jokes people made about her. It wasn't likely, but she *might* hit one of the kids. Or hit a piece of metal on the barge that caused a ricochet that hit one of the kids.

She wondered if Janos had heard the jokes. He might very well have, in fact, as smoothly as he could finagle information from people.

That was probably why he wasn't making any attempt to take cover.

Well, no. She knew as surely as she knew anything that even if she'd been as good a shot as the real Annie Oakley, Janos Drugeth would have done exactly what he was doing.

She even knew why. A Hungarian nobleman's valor was only part of it. Two days after the encounter in the church, she'd told him about the torturer in Franconia. And the hours she spent in prayer because of it. They understood each other quite well, in some ways.

There was no way she was going to pull the trigger, and she knew it, and he knew it, and he knew she knew he knew it, and . . .

"You are the most exasperating man!"

She leaned way over the rail of the bridge, clasped the gun tightly in both hands, pointed the barrel straight below her, and emptied the entire clip. She even had enough presence of mind to make sure another barge wasn't passing through before she did it.

And she didn't miss the water, either. Not once. Hit the Danube every time, dead nuts.

She felt a lot better, then. She even used the gun to give Janos a little salute as the barge made its way down toward Austria. She didn't stop looking at him until it passed out of sight. And he didn't stop looking at her.

Then she giggled. "I guess Denise was right. Maybe I should get a tattoo."

• • •

When the others finally emerged from the shelter they'd taken behind the goods piled on the barge, Allen O'Connor came up to Janos, still standing in the stern.

"You got balls, I'll give you that. I told you the woman was crazy."

Janos said nothing. If a man couldn't recognize a sign from God, right in front of his face, what was the point of explaining it to him?

O'Connor shook his head. "No telling what she'll do. You ought to warn the emperor about her."

"Oh, yes. I most certainly shall."

CHAPTER 15. *The Motto*

High Street Mansion, Seat of Government for the
State of Thuringia-Franconia
President's Office
Grantville, State of Thuringia-Franconia
December 1634

"As long as the Regensburg authorities drop the serious charges," said Ed Piazza, "we won't contest the rest. We don't actually want to let people get the notion that officials of the SoTF can fire a gun anytime and anywhere they please."

Josua Mai, one of the down-timers who served the SoTF as legal advisers, seemed hesitant. "Ah ... Mr. President. I'm afraid that the charge of fishing without license and with equipment not approved by the fisherman's guild *is* a serious charge, in Regensburg. The fine is quite heavy."

"Is there any jail time, too?"

"Not if the fine is paid. Otherwise . . ." He grimaced.

Ed nodded. "So we'll pay the fine. It's not as if we're actually broke. Not even close, in fact."

The lawyer looked as if he might argue the matter. Despite his good humor, Ed was not in the mood for legal quibbling. "We'll pay it," he said firmly. "Noelle's gone way past her pay grade plenty of times, what she's been willing to tackle. The least we can do is return the favor. End of discussion."

He sat up straight, just to emphasize the point. "Any spin-off problems I need to deal with?"

Mai looked at his notes. "Well, Grantville will need a new garrison commander, but that's not something you need to deal with, Mr. President."

"I thought it was decided not to fire Knefler. Not that I'd mind it if he quit. Sure, he screwed up, but you can't fire officers just for making one mistake."

"Ah . . . the problem is of a different nature. It seems that shortly after he returned to Grantville he assaulted Denise Beasley with a quirt. Tried to, at least. According to the report I received from Chief Richards, the girl was actually doing a fair job of defending herself with—ah—" He rummaged in the notes and drew forth another sheet. "Seemingly, every loose object you might find in a roadside tavern, short of a full-size table."

Ed chuckled. "Boy, can I picture that. Girl's got a hell of an arm. Star pitcher for the girl's baseball team until she lost interest." Then, he scowled ferociously. "But what I want to know is why we *didn't* fire Knefler for that."

The lawyer was still examining the report. "He will be

discharged for it, Mr. President. After he gets out of the hospital. His injuries were quite severe. A number of bruises and a split lip inflicted by the girl—Chief Richards says she gave as good as she got—and then . . ." He cleared his throat. "Well. The father arrived. And was apparently in a very foul temper even before Knefler drew his sword. Tried to draw his sword, rather."

Both Ed and Carol winced. "Oh, Lord," she said.

After the lawyer left, Carol Unruh shook her head. "What was Noelle thinking? She's usually such a responsible person."

Ed leaned back, clasping his hands behind his head. After the news came of Noelle's arrest, he'd finally taken the time to visit Denise Beasley and get her version of the whole Noelle vs. Captain Drugeth Affair.

The full, complete, unabridged—nay, annotated and footnoted—Denise Beasley version.

"Domestic violence can be a terrible thing," he intoned solemnly.

Carol frowned at him. "What's that supposed to mean?"

"I don't know, actually. But it'll sure be interesting to find out."

The day after she got back to Grantville, Noelle did get a tattoo. She'd always secretly harbored a desire for one, she just hadn't seen any way she could pull it off. But she figured three days in the squalid jail Regensburg maintained for women—God only knew what the men's jail was like—gave her the needed credentials.

Denise guided her to the tattoo parlor. Offered tons of advice, too, but Noelle ignored almost all of it.

The design was entirely her own. A death's head—much more refined than Denise's, of course; ladylike, topped by a jaunty little feathered cap—with crossed pistols below and the logo above: *I Shot The Danube*.

The one and only piece of advice she took from Denise concerned the placement of the tattoo.

"Me, I put it on my shoulder, where all the pimply twits in high school could see it. You, on the other hand, got a lot more focused target. So put it way down on your hip, over toward the ass, where nobody will ever see it—"

The grin was as an impudent as ever. "Except."

Vienna, Austria

"Interesting idea," said Emperor Ferdinand III. He got up and went to the window in his palace, looking over the gardens. "Yes, I think so."

"Many suppositions, first," Janos cautioned.

"Oh, yes. And probably as many problems afterward, assuming it unfolds. But many opportunities also. And you sometimes forget—even you, Janos—who I am."

"Your Majesty?"

The emperor turned away from the window. "Majesty, now, yes. Go back five hundred years and I would have been a mere count in Switzerland or Swabia. Five hundred years before that, who knows? Certainly not a 'majesty.' The most ancient figure known in my line is a Carolingian. A nobleman, family tradition insists—but I can't help think that his cognomen of 'Guntram the Rich' casts some doubt on the matter."

He resumed his seat. "What I am ultimately, Janos, is a *Habsburg*. Something which I never forget. And what is our unofficial motto?"

Understanding, finally, Janos nodded. "*Bella gerunt alii, tu, felix Austria, nubes.* 'Let others wage war; you, happy Austria, marry.'"

"Precisely so. A guiding principle which has stood us in good stead for centuries. So why should we abandon it now?" Ferdinand made a small waving gesture. "At worst, you already have an heir. But I do not think it would come to that. The distinction between noble and morganatic marriages is already fraying. I have no objections to fraying it still more. In fact, I'm inclined in that direction."

So, that was that. Simply a problem, now.

"It wouldn't be anything quick, anyway," Janos mused.

The emperor chuckled again. "Not given the political situation."

Janos smiled. "I was actually thinking of the lady in question. The last time I saw her, she was shooting at me."

Ferdinand just gazed at him, looking very placid. He'd gotten the entire story by now.

"Well, not exactly that," Janos allowed. "Still, it was a dramatic gesture, you have to admit."

"When are you going to stop—what is that American expression . . . ah, yes, 'beating around the bush'—and ask my advice as well as my permission?" The emperor of Austria-Hungary spread his arms. "Here you are, alone, in the very seat of wisdom when it comes to such matters. If it weren't beneath my dignity, I could double the

Habsburg fortune—count the Spanish bullion fleets in it, too—by starting one of those American businesses... what are they called?"

"Marriage counseling."

"Yes, that one."

Janos hesitated. Despite the jocularity, the fact the emperor made the offer meant he took the matter very seriously indeed.

"I would deeply appreciate it, Your Majesty."

"For this—we're in private, after all—you'd best call me Ferdinand. Very well, my old friend. Start with a rose."

"Excuse me?"

"A rose, Janos. *Always* start with a rose. Then add something with just that perfect personal touch. And keep the accompanying note brief. Very brief. Lest, by your silly long-windedness, you make the recipient feel like someone hunted, instead of a weary traveler seeing an open door, spilling light to invite them in."

Grantville, State of Thuringia-Franconia
January 1635

Denise studied the three items spread out on Noelle's table, which had arrived that morning in a package.

There had been no return address, but that was hardly necessary.

"Gorgeous," she pronounced, after completing her examination of the first item. "Of course, you gotta subtract a few points since he probably got it from the imperial gardens. Still, that is one hell of a rose."

Next, she passed judgment on the note. All it said was: *Should we happen to meet again.*

"Way cool. Way, way, cool."

Finally, the third item, which she picked up and admired. "And this is just fucking perfect. Wonder where he got it?"

Noelle peered at the thing, not sure whether she should smile or frown or . . . what.

"By now, I'd imagine those could be found in lots of places in Europe. Certainly Vienna."

"Still. He even got the right caliber. And .32 caliber rounds are scarcer than you think. Most people want a heftier handgun."

Denise folded her hands on the table. "So. No point packing yet, of course, since we'll probably be at war again in a few months. Still, it's never too early to start putting together some nice luggage."

Noelle scowled at her. "I can't for the life of me remember why I asked you to come here and give me your opinion."

"'Cause it's the wisest opinion you can get. I got the advantage of the perspective of my years."

"All sixteen of them!"

"And barely sixteen at that," agreed Denise. "Exactly my point. When you figure what we got here are two people from about as two different places as you can imagine—we're talking centuries, girl, not just piddly geography—then what you got amounts to a couple of teenagers. D'you wonder why they call it 'sweet sixteen'?"

Noelle tried to remember how she'd looked at the world at the age of sixteen. "Well. No."

Denise smiled jeeringly, as only she could. "Never knew, I bet. Being a pious Catholic girl instead of a biker's kid. The reason's simple. It's because by the time you reach sixteen—at least, if you aren't dumb as a rock, which I'm not—you've figured out the basics and you're pretty much free and clear."

Her forefinger pointed to the rose. "That means he's got the hots, simple as that—but nicely expressed. Not a spot of drool on it."

The finger moved to the note: "That, the invitation. No, call it the ball's now in your court. Very classy guy. Understands that you play a game with somebody, not against them. Won't never be no backseat groping with this cool dude. Not ever."

She plucked the cartridge from the table and stood it upright, then planted her forefinger on the tip. "And just to make sure you understand, that's your insurance policy."

"Oh, nonsense!" exclaimed Noelle. "I didn't even try to hit him when I had the chance."

"Remedial Romance class, come to order. *He knows that*, you dummy. But he also knows you could have." She squinted at Noelle. "Well. Could have tried, anyway. The point is, he knew you had a choice."

With a little clipping motion, the forefinger knocked over the cartridge and sent it rolling over to the rose, where it nestled against the stem. "So the reason the cartridge came with it is so you'd know he knows you still have a choice. Like I said. Very classy guy. Best opening moves I ever seen in my life."

"All of sixteen years," Noelle tried again. Even to her, it sounded feeble.

Denise looked serious, for a change. "The last three of which—no, closer to four—have been a very concentrated educational experience. I've been good-looking since I was twelve, and every kid in school knew my dad was a biker. Sure, he scared 'em some, but they'd also heard all the rumors about biker chicks. You figure it out. I had to learn real quick and learn my lessons well."

Noelle looked from the rose to the note to the cartridge. Then back again.

The truth was, the girl's opinion *did* look shrewd.

"So what do you think I should do?" A bit crossly. "Now, I mean. Not in the maybe-never time after the maybe-war."

Denise got up and grabbed the tote bag she used instead of a purse. The one with the severed serpent and the *Don't Tread On Me* logo that Noelle would have assumed she'd picked up at a patriotic souvenir shop before the Ring of Fire except for what was on the other side. A dragon eating a knight, with the logo *I Love Hard Metal.*

"Come on. We're hitting the malls."

Noelle got her purse. "There aren't any malls in Grantville."

"That's the first thing. You gotta stretch your poetic license."

Noelle flatly refused to buy the specific item Denise recommended. No way in God's green earth was she going to send *that* book to Janos Drugeth. But she did allow that the general category was suitable. Even if the postage would be a little steep.

And she decided the girl's final advice was probably good, too.

"*Of course* you put on a return address." Denise slapped her forehead. "Jeez, Louise. You don't know anything. *He* didn't, because *he* was serving. Ball might have gone out of bounds, so he left you a graceful way to just pretend you didn't know where it came from."

She started more-or-less dragging Noelle toward the postal service. "But *you* decided to hit it back. So now we got a volley going. Can't do that without return addresses. Face it, girl. The game is afoot!"

Vienna, Austria
February 1635

"Oh, splendid," said Ferdinand, positively beaming. He turned another page of the beautifully bound volume. "I've always been very fond of Father Drexel's writings, myself. So is my sister, Maria Anna."

So was Janos himself, for that matter. But he was still puzzled by the gift.

Seeing the slight frown on his face, the emperor clucked his tongue. "Amazing, really. You're so shrewd on the fields of politics and battle."

He held up the book. "First, it reminds you of your piety. Whatever else, you are both devout Catholics. The most solid foundation there is, no?"

Well, that was certainly true.

The emperor turned the book, so Janos could see the title. "But there's the woman's subtle touch. I will even say, her wisdom. *The School of Patience.* Which you both will surely need."

Janos nodded. "Yes, now I see. The war, most likely. Then, even afterward, a difficult political situation."

Ferdinand set the book down on the table next to his chair and threw up his hands. "I have allowed a dolt into my chambers! No, Janos. You will need patience for a lifetime." He slapped the book. "And that offer, my friend, *that* is the gift."

"Oh." After a moment, finally understanding, he smiled. "It's going well, then?"

Ferdinand was actually rubbing his hands. "Yes, indeed. Happy Austria. Again."

The Anatomy Lesson

Amsterdam

"I've got a headache," Anne Jefferson announced.

Her fiancé, Adam Olearius, cleared his throat. "It might be better to say, you have at least two of them."

Anne removed the hands rubbing her temples long enough to glare at him. "Oh, very funny. Very, very funny." Then went back to the rubbing.

"I wasn't actually trying to be witty," he said. "It's just my diplomat's reflexes."

"You call piling another headache onto the one I've already got being *diplomatic*?" she grumbled.

"Not you, dearest. I was speaking of Europe." Olearius leaned back in the chair in Anne's salon, turned his head, and peered out the window.

"How shall I count the ways?" he mused. "It's a headache for the king in the Netherlands; for the prince of Orange; for Duke Ernst Wettin, the USE's regent in the Oberpfalz; and . . ." After a pause, he waggled his hand back and forth. "Probably even a headache for Gustav Adolf himself. Or his prime minister, at least."

"And me," Anne said forcefully. "Especially me."

Her tone was quite surly.

"And you, of course."

Brussels

"Yes, yes, gentlemen, I know it would be easiest if I simply forbade the girl and her brother to undertake their proposed change of residence to Amsterdam." Not quite glowering at them—almost, but not quite—Fernando I, King in the Netherlands, stared at the five advisers sitting around the large table in his council chamber. "Unfortunately, the situation is delicate."

"The emperor is not likely to go to war over the issue, Your Majesty," pointed out Pieter Paul Rubens.

"No, he isn't. If for no other reason than that it's convenient for Gustav Adolf to have the heirs to the Palatinate officially held captive by the Span—by the Netherlanders. It keeps them out of his hair."

The near slip did cause the king to glower at his advisers. He still hadn't gotten used to referring to himself as "Netherlander" rather than Spanish. Being, as he was, the younger brother of the king of Spain and having considered himself Spanish all his life until very recently.

That was hardly the fault of the advisers, of course. But Fernando figured that being glowered at from time to time was a reasonable part of their duties.

"*At the same time*," he continued, "the emperor of the USE—who is also, I will remind you, the king of Sweden and the high king of the Kalmar Union—is officially the protector of the dynastic interests of that family. Being, as they are, Protestant and not Catholic. And being, as they are, the family whose claim to the Bohemian throne was made null and void by the Holy Roman Emperor of the time, my now-deceased uncle Ferdinand II of Austria. And while it could be argued that their claim to the Bohemian throne was...what's that American expression?"

"Dicey," provided Alessandro Scaglia. "Your Majesty."

Fernando gave him a thin smile. "You needn't toss in the honorific every two minutes, Alessandro. Thin-skinned, I am not."

Scaglia nodded. "Sorry, Your—ah, my apologies. I'm afraid I'm still engrained with Savoyard court custom."

Fernando's smile expanded. The two Savoyard dukes whom Scaglia had served as an adviser, Charles Emmanuel and his son and successor Victor Amadeus, had both been notoriously fussy about protocol. Fernando's private opinion was that their prickly attitude stemmed less from personality than from the objective situation of the Savoy. An independent duchy located between France, Italy and Spain—and which controlled several strategic passes through the Alps—had damn well better be prickly about protocol. Fernando's own relaxed attitude was due in no small part to the security of his situation. Given the size of his army, his demonstrated military skill, and the difficulties which the terrain of the Low Countries posed to any invader, he didn't care that much how anyone addressed him, as long as they were polite.

All the more so given the influence of his new wife. Whatever Maria Anna's upbringing might have been, in the Viennese court, the former archduchess of Austria was almost shockingly informal. Perhaps that was a residue from her adventures during the Bavarian war, when she'd smuggled herself through war-torn regions with the help of commoners.

She exhibited the informality that very moment. Leaning forward over the table and giving Alessandro a rather arch look, she put into words what Fernando himself had left unspoken.

"Well, of course. If I'd had to do the dance the Savoyard dukes had to do to keep from getting swallowed up over the past few years, I'd be insisting you had to throw in every single title I might have a claim to in every other sentence. And pity the poor chambermaids! 'I shall empty the chamber pot now, Your Majesty and formerly Your Highness.'"

She gave her husband a sly smile. "Fine. It's an exaggeration. In the ever-so-modern Netherlands—in the palace, at least—we have actual plumbing."

Fernando chuckled. "And very good plumbing it is, too, since I took on the service of the Van Meter woman. Which, oddly, brings us back to the subject at hand. Because we can now toss that item onto the pile, out of which we seek to extract a coherent position. I'm thinking that it would ill behoove a monarch who chose to hire a woman to design and build the plumbing in his palace—"

"An *American* woman," Rubens interjected.

Fernando gave him an astringent glance. "—to object if another woman chooses to study medicine."

He now swiveled to face Rubens squarely. "And I'm

afraid your point about the Van Meter woman being an American speaks against your advice, Pieter, not for it. The Americans are the first to insist that they are not entitled to any special privileges." He raised his hand. "And spare me a recitation of the many ways in which, in the real world, they do get special treatment. That simply makes them all the more intransigent on the subject."

He leaned back in his chair. "The point being, that if I refuse to let the girl do as she wishes, I will incur the displeasure of the Americans as well as the emperor whom they advise. And, between us, I think I would rather risk Gustav Adolf's ire than theirs. I don't need a Swedish king's advice and assistance. I do need that of many of the Americans."

"That leaves the prince of Orange," said Scaglia.

The king made a face. "Yes, it does. And who knows what schemes Fredrik Hendrik has in mind, concerning this?"

It was a rhetorical question, not a real one. Fernando provided the answer himself. "But you can be assured it will be devious."

Breda

Had Fredrik Hendrik heard that last remark, the prince of Orange would have laughed sarcastically. He'd have appreciated the general sentiment, but would have filled the king's ear with a detailed explanation—nay, lament—concerning the impossibility of coming up with a devious scheme to take advantage of the blasted girl's stubbornness.

Not that he hadn't tried. Alas, the situation was too hemmed in by other factors to give him any maneuvering room.

You could start with the fact that he was glumly contemplating his options from the vantage point of his library in the House of Orange-Nassau's ancestral estate in Breda, overlooking the gardens. Which, appropriately enough, were rather bleak-looking at this time of year. Instead of being able to contemplate his options from the vantage point of the library in the small palace he maintained in Amsterdam, overlooking the harbor.

True, the harbor was an even bleaker sight, this time of year. But it was—even in mid-winter—a much busier and bustling sort of bleakiness. Vibrant with the energy of the Netherlands' largest and most dynamic city. A city which was now, for all practical purposes, *terra non grata* for the man who was supposed to be its prince, a figure second only to the king in his stature in the Low Countries.

"Well . . . not *that*, exactly," Fredrik Hendrik muttered to himself, staring at the flat landscape beyond the window. He was exaggerating out of irritation, and knew it. Whenever he visited Amsterdam, which he did quite regularly, the benighted Committee of Correspondence who actually ruled the city were always punctiliously polite. Gretchen Richter, for a marvel, was even cordial and friendly. But velvety as its cover might be, it was still her fist and not his that held the power in Amsterdam. And the woman was not hesitant to remove the glove when she felt it necessary.

As had been very forcefully demonstrated to the

burgomasters and patricians of the city less than two months earlier, when they tried to resume their previous positions of authority in Amsterdam after returning from their exile during the cardinal-infante's siege. Their self-selected exile, as Richter had bluntly pointed out. She and Amsterdam's commoners had remained in the city throughout the siege, after all. It was thanks to *them*—not the patricians and burgomasters residing comfortably elsewhere—that Don Fernando had never been able to take the city and had eventually agreed to the current settlement of the war.

"So you can go fuck yourselves," had been her final words, according to the many indignant accounts which Fredrik Hendrik had heard from the patricians afterward. "You can have your property, and that's it. Your posts and positions are either gone—and good riddance, since half of them were useless—or someone reliable and worthy now sits in your place."

He'd had little sympathy with the complaints. He'd *told* them they were fools to think they could march into Amsterdam this soon after the siege and get anything but a boot in the ass. And the fact that the boot was a woman's boot didn't matter in the least. She was a big woman and a strong one, and had the devil's fury to tap when she chose to do so.

"Well, not *that*, exactly," the prince muttered to himself. As tempting as it was, at times, he didn't really think Richter was Satan's minion. Just someone who had concluded that the near destruction of her family and her own rape and forced concubinage were outrages perpetrated not simply by the immediate parties involved, but by all of Europe's high and mighty. Who would now pay the price, whenever and wherever she could charge it. If nothing else, she owed that much to the young brother who'd been killed in the battle of Wismar.

And . . .

There really wasn't much anyone could do about it. The one time he'd raised the problem with the king, Fernando hadn't been much less blunt than Richter.

"It's your headache, I'm afraid, not mine. The displeasure and discomfiture of patricians and burgomasters is not much of a burden for me. Certainly not compared to the alternative. You know perfectly well that the Committee of Correspondence in Amsterdam can choose to secede from the Netherlands, if they feel pressed enough."

"They wouldn't dare!" one of Fredrik Henrik's courtiers had exclaimed. One of his soon-to-be-discharged courtiers. The idiot.

"Oh, wouldn't they?" the king had demanded frostily, giving the courtier in question a look that was downright icy. "As I recall, you were nowhere near the siege of Amsterdam at the time. While I, on the other hand, commanded the army besieging the city. For *months*, with everything I had—and I still couldn't take it. So don't tell me what Gretchen Richter and her people are and are not capable of daring. And, more to the more, doing."

He'd turned away then, and looked out over his own gardens in Brussels. "It wouldn't even be that hard for them. They have enough military strength in Amsterdam to close the city and keep it closed for months. More than they had, in fact, since I caught them off guard and today they are most certainly not. They've made an agreement with me—with us—and they're keeping to it. But Richter, whatever else she is, is very far from a trusting soul. Given her history, it's hard to blame her. So while she's kept the agreement—meticulously, in fact—she's also kept the city militia large and well-trained and has rebuilt and even strengthened the city's fortifications."

He shrugged. "Not forever, of course, if I brought the full weight of my army to bear. But they could certainly withstand a siege for as many months as they've already demonstrated they can—and long before then, they would have reached an accommodation with Gustav Adolf. There is no reason, after all, that Amsterdam couldn't become another province in his empire instead of a city in my kingdom. Not if the matter was pressed to the hilt."

The same courtier seemed to have no limit to his idiocy. "That's not possible! We've signed a treaty with him."

Again, came the icy royal gaze. "So we did. And so what? Treaties can be torn up. And while you may have forgotten that Gustav Adolf has an eye for acquiring new territory, I have not. And while you seem to have missed the sight of Admiral Simpson's ironclads patrolling the Zuider Zee—how did you manage that, by the way? the things are huge—have you even *been* to Amsterdam since the siege?—I have most certainly not. There is no way, unless you have overwhelming forces—which I do not—that a large port city can be taken by siege if the defenders control the adjoining waters. Only a lunatic would even try."

The courtier finally wilted away and the king turned back to the prince of Orange. "Anyway, you have my sympathies, Fredrik Hendrik. But my position as king— by the same terms you not only agreed to, but even insisted upon—give me only limited powers within the provinces, and even more limited authority with regard to the affairs of the towns and cities. And what internal powers I do have in the cities are what you might call negative. I can, by law, prevent a church from being suppressed. I cannot, by law, establish a church."

That was a major fudge, of course. Nothing, by law, prevented the king in the Netherlands from subsidizing and supporting a church—so long as he did it in his private capacity and using his own resources, rather than those of the state of the Netherlands. Given that the king was far and away the richest man in the Low Countries, the distinction was to a considerable degree a formal one.

"The burgomasters are therefore your cross to bear, not mine," the king continued. "And I'm not about to run the risk of another war over an issue like this one. Quite frankly, from everything I can see the Committee of Correspondence does a better job of running Amsterdam than the patricians did. The disease problem is certainly much better."

So, there it was. And while most of Fredrik Hendryk's advisers were well-nigh ecstatic at the recent news that Gretchen Richter would soon be leaving Amsterdam to return to her family in the Germanies, the prince himself did not share their sanguine expectations. Richter was, alas, a superb organizer, not simply a firebrand and agitatrix. By now, the Committee she'd forged was very

solid and durable. She'd be gone, but it would remain—
commanded by lieutenants whom she'd chosen and
trained personally. In a generation, things might change.
But they wouldn't change any time soon—and then, for
all he knew, the changes would be for the worse.

On that, for sure, the king had spoken truly. The
committee *did* run the city better than the patricians had.
Even most of the merchants and burghers were now
becoming reconciled to its rule, if they weren't highly
placed in the patricianate. Business was booming again,
and Richter had been very careful not to play favorites.

And if that left the prince of Orange with the
awkwardness of having a country whose provinces were
dominated by wealthy and conservative patrician families,
and whose principal city was the most radical in Europe
except for possibly Magdeburg and Grantville itself, then
so be it. He'd just have to scheme and maneuver around
the situation, as deviously as he could.

Which brought him back to the problem at hand. He
turned away from the window and picked up the letter
from the girl's mother.

Written in a very fine hand, on the best paper you
could ask for. The hand wouldn't be her own, of course,
although the signature was and she'd have dictated the
contents. But she'd have employed a secretary who,
among other things, had splendid handwriting. In exile or
not, officially in the captivity of the Netherlands or not,
she was still Elisabeth Stuart. Sister of the king of
England, the widow of the Elector of the Palatine and—
very briefly—the queen of Bohemia. Among her ancestors
she could name another king of England, a king and

queen of Scotland, several kings of Denmark and Norway, and the Lord only knew how many dukes and duchesses. Among the latter of whom could be counted the redoubtable Marie de Guise, another woman who'd plagued the counsels of Europe's rulers in her day.

He sighed and dropped the letter back onto the table. Given that she'd written it, there was no longer any point in trying to persuade the mother to dissuade the daughter. She wouldn't have written the letter at all if her daughter hadn't talked her into it. And, that done, the matter would no longer be of concern to Elisabeth. By all accounts, to use one of those picturesque American expressions, Elisabeth Stuart had the maternal instincts of a brick. Children were a burden and, what was worse, they piled still more burdens atop their mothers. This particular burden having been shifted to someone else, she was no more likely to reconsider the decision than a mule.

King Fernando could have forbidden the girl and her brother from making the trip to Amsterdam, of course. He and he alone could even have enforced it easily, since they resided in exile in Brussels, right under his nose and the nose of the many guards he'd placed over the family.

From the opposite end, Fredrik Hendrik could—in theory—bar them from entering any of those provinces assigned to the House of Orange to supervise. And—in theory—that would apply to Amsterdam as well, since—in theory—Amsterdam was simply one of many cities in the province of Holland.

Theory, theory, theory. In practice, the moment he did so the Committee of Correspondence would immediately issue an invitation to the pestiferous girl and her brother. Given Richter, they'd do more than just issue an invitation. They'd personally see to smuggling the two youngsters into the city and keeping them guarded against any attempt to get them out.

No, that alternative was just nonsense. Fredrik Hendrik disliked the prospect of having two such potentially important figures in European politics rattling around essentially unsupervised in a city like Amsterdam, especially given their ages. The girl was sixteen; the boy fifteen. Both ages at which even the dullest villager could get themselves into trouble.

But . . . all the alternatives were worse. Much worse.

He turned from the window and summoned his secretary, who'd been standing politely by the door some distance away.

"We'll need to write the girl a formal letter of invitation. Her brother also. I leave the wording to you. Just make sure to be polite, if not effusive. I'll sign it when you're done."

Magdeburg

Hands clasped over his stomach, Mike Stearns leaned back in his chair and gave Francisco Nasi that placid look that made anyone who knew him rather nervous, unless they knew him very well.

Since Francisco did know the prime minister of the United States of Europe very well, he remained unfazed.

"Explain to me again," Stearns said, drawling the words

a bit, "why time needs to be taken from my busy schedule to discuss what we think of the impending visit of two teenage noblefolk to Amsterdam. To put it as bluntly as I can, who gives a damn?"

"Well, first, some corrections needed to be made to your summation. Imprimus, they are not 'visiting' the city, they propose to relocate indefinitely from Brussels to Amsterdam. Secundus, to call them 'noblefolk' is to understate the reality. 'Royalfolk' would be a lot more accurate."

"The girl's not a princess and the boy's not a prince. In fact, I'm not even sure if they have any titles at all."

Francisco shrugged. "Like most Americans, unaccustomed as you are to the fine points of aristocratic etiquette, you're missing the key element. Titles don't really matter, in the end. What matters is blood line. Should they find it to their advantage—not likely at the moment, of course—there is not a royal house in Europe that would hesitate to marry off one of their princes or princesses to either one of those children. They have at least half a dozen kings and queens in their ancestry. It would take overheating my laptop to figure out how many dukes and duchesses."

Mike grimaced. "You're right. I keep forgetting that people in the here and now take that 'blood' nonsense dead seriously. Me, in my crude West Virginia coal miner's way, I figure the title makes the big shot, not the other way around."

Nasi grinned. Whatever his origins, Stearns was about as far removed these days from a rural bumpkin as the Ottoman emperor. He'd driven Europe's very sophisticated political elite half-mad, over the past few years. But he did enjoy putting on the act, from time to time.

He dropped the grin and leaned forward. "Mike, seriously, this is not trivial. Duke Ernst in the Oberpfalz has already written at least one vigorous letter of protest to the emperor concerning the matter."

"Why?" said Mike—who then proceeded to make nonsense of his own pretense at bumpkin ignorance. "The heir to the Oberpfalz is the oldest brother, Karl Ludwig. *He's* still in Brussels. *He's* not proposing to budge an inch from under the noses of his Spanish captors-although-we'll-pretend-they're-not. Neither does the mother, who's the official regent. If you look at it her way."

"Nevertheless. Ernst is worried about a precedent being set. He figures the last thing the Oberpfalz needs is to have any of the official heirs show up before he's had time to . . . ah . . ."

"Whip the province into good enough shape that the heir can't meddle with it. How's that? Of which dastardly scheme I approve, by the way. I'd far rather have one of those very capable Wettin brothers running the Oberpfalz than some royal flake. And from what you've told me in the past, Karl Ludwig is flaky even if he probably doesn't qualify as a flake-capital-F. I still don't see why it's any concern of ours what his younger brother and sister do."

Francisco squinted at him. Mike was normally more astute than this. "In other words, you do not think it's something to give any thought to. The fact that two youngsters in line of succession to the throne of England as well as the Palatine—you could even make a case for Bohemia—will be spending the next year or so in close proximity to an American nurse. And probably just as close proximity to the Amsterdam Committee of Correspondence, if I know Gretchen."

"She's leaving Amsterdam soon."

"Her spirit will remain—as you've said to me by now perhaps a hundred times."

Mike scowled. Francisco was heartened and pressed on.

"Not to mention close proximity to Thomas Wentworth, if the former—and very capable—duke of Strafford and chief minister of England can finally pull himself out of the dumps."

Mike glared at him, then unclasped his hands and sat up straight. "Well, thank y'all very much, Francisco," he drawled. "I was sorta hoping I might have a light day today."

Amsterdam

"At least agree to *see* the boy, Thomas," said William Laud. The archbishop of Canterbury—or former archbishop, if you listened to his enemies—shook his head at his friend Thomas Wentworth. "And you *must* cease and desist from this pointless melancholy."

Wentworth looked at him in silence, for a moment, through lowered lids. "He supported my execution, you know."

Laud threw up his hands with exasperation. "And people accuse *me* of being stubborn! That happened almost twenty years from now—"

"Sixteen years and six months." Wentworth smiled

sadly. "I don't keep count of the exact number of days. But I never forget the date. It comes to me when I wake up, each and every morning. May 12, 1641. The day I was beheaded."

Laud glared at him. "*And* in a completely different universe."

"Different, yes. Completely different? That's laughable, William, and you know it."

Before Laud could continue, Wentworth raised a hand. "Just to keep from having you natter at me endlessly, I'll invite the boy for supper. I'll even be polite to the murderous little bastard. But he may very well decline the invitation, you realize. And I'm hoping he does."

Brussels

"Good Lord!" exclaimed Rupert.

"You shouldn't blaspheme," reproved his older sister Elisabeth.

"But look at this!" The fifteen-year-old boy held up the letter he'd just opened. "Another invitation. And this one's from *Wentworth*, of all people."

"For someone who insists as mightily as you do that under no circumstances will you allow your former-or-somewhere-else historical fame as a soldier to determine your life in this existence—'nay, nay, I'll be an artist instead'—I can't help but notice that it's the invitations from political figures who excite your interest. *Not* the invitations from artists. Of which we've received any number, including from Rubens and Rembrandt."

The boy scowled. "Rembrandt's claim to fame comes

entirely from that other universe. In *this* one, he hasn't done anything worth talking about yet. Well, not much."

Elisabeth waited.

"Okay, Rubens is different. I admit."

"And stop using that hideous Americanism."

"Okey-doke." And then he burst into inane teenage laughter.

"I don't for the life of me remember why I asked you to come along."

"Because I'm your closest relative. Your best friend, too."

Elisabeth considered the matter. "True, on both counts. I still can't imagine what possessed me."

Rupert gave her a sly look. "You'll need me, Sister. You watch. When you puke your guts after seeing your first operation. I'll be there to console you and point out how ridiculous it was anyway, the idea of a girl like you becoming a doctor."

Amsterdam

"You get no special privileges," Anne Jefferson said firmly. "Not a one. You scrub like everybody else."

"Certainly, Madame Jefferson."

And that was *another* thing! The girl was invariably polite. Even gracious. For all that Anne wanted to work up a quiet and pleasant mad at being placed in this awkward situation, the damn girl wouldn't let her.

Even Elisabeth's appearance drove Anne nuts. Half-consciously, she'd been expecting someone . . .

Royal-looking. Anne wasn't sure what that meant,

exactly—a long nose being looked down was the central image, of course—but whatever it was, it certainly wasn't what had presented itself to her that morning.

Herself, not itself. Very definitely, herself.

For starters, the girl was *pretty*. Not stunning, not gorgeous, nothing mythical or legendary in the least. Just pretty enough to have gotten elected prom queen any time she ran for it, in any West Virginia high school Anne could think of. The kind of sweet-looking prettiness that attracted boys but didn't make other girls resentful.

But Elisabeth wouldn't have run for prom queen, because she was *shy*. She didn't look down at people, she looked up at them from a slightly lowered gaze.

What kind of damn princess is shy?

"Don't call me 'Madame.' I think that's only for married women and I'm not married yet."

"Certainly, Mad—. Oh, dear. What appellation would you prefer?"

Anne didn't have it in her. She just didn't.

"How about you call me 'Anne.' And I'll call you 'Elisabeth.'"

Slowly, a shy and gentle smile spread across the girl's face. "Oh, I think that would be splendid."

All the way there, the next day, Rupert was practically bouncing off the walls of the coach.

"Oh, how marvelous! I can't believe the luck! You're to be cutting up *Joe Buckley*!"

Elisabeth sniffed. "First of all, *I* shan't be cutting up anyone. Madame Jeff—ah, Anne—will be doing the anatomy lesson, not me. I'll just be one of the people observing. And, secondly, who in the world is Joe Buckley?"

Rupert clasped a hand to his forehead, in the overly histrionic way that a teenage lad will demonstrate shocked disbelief.

"I can't believe you've never heard of *Joe Buckley*. The rascal's exploits were *legendary*. In his prime, the most notorious cutpurse in London."

Elisabeth sniffed again. "I can't imagine why I'd be acquainted with the names and doings of a foreign city's criminal element. Or you would be, now that I think about it."

Rupert gave her his *girls-don't-understand* look. And a splendid one it was, too.

"Just accept it as good coin. The man's a *legend*."

"The man's dead, now. And how would a London cutpurse wind up the subject of an anatomy lesson in Amsterdam?"

Her brother looked a bit discomfited. "Well. He had to flee London a few years back, since he'd gotten too well known. Then had to flee Paris, after he gained too much notoriety there also. Apparently, he turned up in Amsterdam just a few weeks ago."

"Indeed. And they caught him and hung him, as he so richly deserved." Elisabeth frowned. "Or perhaps they behead them, here in Holland. Although I can't imagine that Anne would choose a corpse without a head for an anatomy lesson."

Rupert looked more discomfited still. "Well. Well. He wasn't either hanged or chopped, it seems. The story is that he got drunk a night or two back and fell into the harbor in a stupor. Drowned, before anyone could fish him out."

Elisabeth burst into laughter. "Some legend!"

Her brother got a sullen look on his face. "So what? He's still *Joe Buckley*. You watch, Sister. He'll be remembered long after you're forgotten by the world."

She turned her head and gave him a serene sort of look. "And you are forgotten also, no doubt. Given your firm resolve to devote your life to the higher pursuits instead of seeking fame and glory on the fields of war."

"Well."

Before he could come up with a lame remark, Elisabeth peered out the window. "Oh, look! We've arrived."

Rupert got another sly look on his face. He rummaged around in the sack he'd insisted on bringing with him, and came out holding a small bucket. "I brought this for you. To barf in, like you will."

There being no suitable rejoinder that wouldn't be undignified—worse still, might tempt her with blasphemy—Elisabeth just sniffed and prepared to disembark. As short as she was, that was always something of a chore, if modesty was to be preserved.

Brussels

Fernando chuckled, after reading the letter which had just arrived. "Well, that should relieve our good prince of Orange of a small burden, Pieter."

Rubens cocked an inquisitive head.

"That nurse of yours. Anne Jefferson. The one you used

as a model so many times. Apparently, a shrewd woman, and devious in her own way. It seems the prospect of having a royal student didn't appeal to her any more than it did to any of us. So—devious, as I said—she arranged the poor girl's very first introduction to the medical arts to be an anatomy lesson. Imagine it, if you will. Delicate little Elisabeth, having to watch at close hand while a human body is cut up into pieces."

Rubens' eyes widened. "That must be the same anatomy lesson that my young friend Rembrandt will be attending."

"Rembrandt? Why would he . . . ?"

"Oh, not as a doctor—although, like any good painter, he has a keen eye for anatomy." Rubens grinned. "No, this is his way of handling a problem I've had to handle myself."

It was the king's turn to cock an inquisitive head. Rubens elaborated. "He did that painting, in another universe. A very famous one, apparently. *The Anatomy Lesson*. As you know, I find that having to maintain my art under the suffocating weight of a body of work I'd done elsewhere and elsewhen is difficult."

The king nodded.

"Rembrandt faces the same problem, only for him it's even worse. He's a young man still, which I'm certainly not." The artist shrugged. "So, perhaps for that reason, his solution is different from mine. Where I avoid work I did, he seeks it out. He'll do, in this universe, the same painting that he did, in another—but without trying to copy it. And he'll let posterity decide which of the two is the better."

Fernando chuckled again. "Let's hope he leaves out of it the inevitable climax. When the girl starts vomiting."

Breda

Fredryk Hendrik's spies and informants in Amsterdam were even more numerous than the king's, and the city was closer. So he'd gotten the news the day before.

"Yes, it'll be happening . . ." He looked at the clock. "Right about now, I estimate," he said to one of his courtiers, sounding cheerful. "Remind me—at a suitable time, perhaps two weeks from now—to send that marvelous Anne Jefferson a short letter of thanks."

The courtier winced. "I hope someone thought to bring a bucket."

Amsterdam

"—lobes to the liver, as you can see. This liver is abnormal, however, because of the man's quite obvious alcoholism. If you look closer, you'll be able to detect—"

Elisabeth peered more closely, as instructed. It was absolutely fascinating!

Her brother, known as Rupert of the Rhine in another universe, the royalist hero of the first English civil war, had left the chamber some time back. Looking very pale, and taking the bucket with him.

Brussels

Three days later, looking philosophical, the king in the

Netherlands laid down the letter from Amsterdam which had just arrived, after reading it to Rubens.

"What's that American expression, Pieter?"

"It's Scots, actually. In their own way, the Americans are worse cutpurses than the man on the table. Penned by a poet named Robert Burns who won't be born—wherever that birth happens—until sometime in the next century. 'The best laid schemes o' mice and men, gang aft a-gley.'"

He said the rhyme in English, a language in which he was fluent and the king was now adept.

"Yes. That one."

Breda

Fredryk Hendryk, of course, had gotten the news much sooner. And was considerably less philosophical about it all.

"Well, there it is, I'm afraid. We'll need to develop a policy, after all. Whether we like it or not."

The courtier he favored least was the first to speak up—which explained a good deal of why he favored him the least. Would the man ever learn to think before he opined?

"The first thing, of course, is to see to it that the girl—and the boy, even more so—are closely supervised."

"In *Amsterdam*?" The prince of Orange glared at him. "Do I need to remind you again that, in Amsterdam, 'close supervision' is something that Gretchen Richter can do better than anyone. Much, much, much better."

There was silence, for a time. Then the courtier he

favored the most said the inevitable. "Best to ask Richter for a meeting, then. We can at least see to it that no harm comes to the two children."

"No physical harm, yes. Richter and her people can certainly see to that."

God only knew what they would do to their minds, of course. But he left that unspoken. Even his dullest courtier understood that much.

Magdeburg

"This is shaping up very nicely indeed," said Mike Stearns, almost chortling.

"Yes, not badly at all—for a matter I had to twist your arm originally to get you to pay attention to."

Alas, the needle was pointless, as such needles always were. Stearns simply grinned.

On some petty level, Francisco found that mildly frustrating. But only mildly so. Had he been in the service of the Ottoman emperor, as he'd once planned, he'd have been a lot more frustrated after needling his employer.

As frustrated as the term could possibly mean, in fact. Lying at the bottom of the Straits of Marmora, with a garrote around his neck.

So, all things considered, he did not regret the unexpected course his life had taken.

Amsterdam

By the end of the meal, as the servants were clearing away the plates and dining ware, Thomas Wentworth finally realized what an insufferable dolt he'd become. Odd, perhaps, that it took a conversation with a teenage boy to do what none of his closest friends or his wife or his children had been able to do.

But, so it was. And he thought he understood the reason. Those of his friends and associates who'd been famous enough to survive in Grantville's often spotty historical record, were all his age or even older. Here was a boy who'd been more famous than any of them—and he was fifteen, with his life fresh and still uncut.

Wentworth rose and went to the window, clasping his hands behind his back. The day had been clear and frosty, as was often true in Amsterdam this time of year. The moon was new, so the stars were quite clear, even through the window.

"We've not discussed political matters at all," he said brusquely. Without turning his head to look at the boy, he raised a hand. "Nor do I propose to do so, unless you'd care to. I didn't invite you here for that reason."

"Why did you, then?"

"To be honest? Because my friend William Laud insisted. But I'm glad he did, now."

He studied Orion for a moment. It had always been his favorite constellation. "It's difficult, isn't it? Having a life already recorded somewhere. Even more difficult, I imagine, for someone your age than mine."

There was a short pause. Then the boy said: "It's very difficult."

Wentworth nodded. "I imagine, at some point—no, six or seven points—you made yourself the same solemn vow I made to myself. 'No! I shall not read another blasted word of it.' And then, a short time later, found yourself digging through yet another record."

"Another scrap, it'd be better to say. The American records are ghastly poor."

Wentworth shrugged. "You can hardly fault them. It's not as if that town ever expected it would be plunged into this situation either. Their records of their own history are quite good, actually. But what they have concerning Europe—even England—is what you'd expect."

He went back to the table and resumed his seat. "It's like an addiction, isn't it? You swear you won't, and yet you do."

"I've made one vow that I intend to keep, though," said the boy, in that firm and certain way that only teenagers can manage. "I shall not—*shall not*—allow what I did in that other life to determine what I do in this one."

"An excellent vow. But be aware of the pitfall."

The boy frowned. "Which is . . . ?"

"Don't allow your determination *not* to follow that same course become what determines the life you have now. Who knows, lad? You may well find a day comes when your duties *here* require you to be a soldier. Should you shirk that duty, simply because you once followed it in another time and place, you are simply letting that other life guide you still."

"I . . . understand, yes." The boy cleared his throat. "I should say this aloud, I think. In that other universe, I was among those who called for your execution."

Wentworth shook his head. "That's putting it a bit too strongly, I think. I found no record that you *called* for it. It's true that when others did, you supported them."

The man and the boy studied each other, for a time. Then Wentworth rose from the table and went back to the window.

"You need to understand this. I have decided—just this evening, finally—that I have no choice—in this world—but to seek the overthrow of your uncle, the king of England. I will do my best, assuming I succeed, to avoid having your uncle suffer the same fate he did in that other world. But I can make no promises. Charles . . . is a very difficult man."

The boy's chuckle was far harsher than any chuckle coming from a fifteen year old throat should ever be. "Yes, I know. He parted company with me—or I, with him, the records aren't quite clear—when he refused to do the reasonable thing after our defeat at Naseby and make a settlement with Parliament."

Wentworth grinned, at that point. Like an addiction, for a certainty! He knew, as if he'd been there watching, that—time after time—the boy hadn't been able to keep his promise. Time after time, just as Wentworth had done himself, he'd been drawn back irresistibly to those scraps and pieces of a history that had not happened except in a world that God had sundered from this one. By now, he'd have his other life almost memorized. What was known of it, at least.

But there was still serious business at hand, so the grin was brief. He turned around to face the boy squarely. What had to be said next, could only be said looking him in the eye.

"I can make no promises, except one. Nor can you, except that same one. You may find a day comes, in this universe, when you are supporting my execution. Just as I may find a day comes when I walk to that scaffold. Or stand and watch, while another man of the time—perhaps Charles, perhaps even you—makes the same final walk. But let us never be able to say, either one of us, that we do it 'again.' Because, whatever we do, we will be doing it for the first time, and for those reasons that seem good to us in the universe that God chose to place us in. Not a universe that, for us, no longer exists. For you, at your age, one could almost say never existed."

He waited, to let the boy think. When enough time had passed, he said: "I can make that promise. Today, if not any day until now. Can you make it, Prince Rupert of the Rhine?"

The boy's smile was shy, almost gentle. He looked much like his sister, in that moment.

"I don't know if Prince Rupert of the Rhine could make it. But I'm just Rupert Stuart. And I can."

Thomas sighed. "I stand corrected. Very well, then, Rupert. Will you come to visit again, now that you'll be in Amsterdam for a time? We needn't discuss political matters, if you don't want to. I simply ask because I could use a good friend young enough to keep my own eyes on this world instead of another."

"Oh, I'd like that myself. As long as you don't ask me to attend another anatomy lesson."

Steady Girl

Noelle Stull's kitchen
Grantville, capital of the State of Thuringia-Franconia
June 12, 1635

"I'm telling you, Noelle, something's wrong with Eddie," Denise Beasley insisted. She stared into the coffee cup in front of her with all the intensity of a fortune teller reading tea leaves. "He's been acting weird for weeks, now. He hardly talks to me at all any more, he's so damn obsessed with making money."

In point of fact, there were tea leaves at the bottom of the cup and Denise had drained it dry enough that they could be read. Assuming she was a fortune teller, that is, which she wasn't. Indeed, she would have heaped derision on the suggestion with all the enthusiastic energy of which her sixteen-year-old self was capable.

That was a lot of enthusiasm and energy, which made her current mood all the odder. "Glum" and "Denise Beasley" were terms that normally couldn't be found in the same room. For that matter, the same football field.

Standing at the stove where she was bringing a kettle of water to a boil, Noelle Stull looked over her shoulder at Denise. A close observer might have spotted something unusual in that look. A hint of scrutiny. A trace of amusement. Perhaps also some concern and trepidation.

Denise, however, missed all that. She was too intent on staring at the tea leaves in her cup. "I don't like it," she concluded. "One damn bit."

Seeing that the water had come to a boil, Noelle used a folded up towel to lift the kettle off the stove and start another pot of tea brewing.

"I've had enough," Denise said. "I don't much like tea, anyway."

"I do," said her best friend, Minnie Hugelmair, who was sitting at the far end of the kitchen table. "Even if coffee weren't so expensive, tea is better."

"And since when is tea 'cheap'?" jeered Denise. "If you want 'cheap,' drink broth. The only reason Noelle can afford tea or coffee is because she's a government bureaucrat, living off the fat of the land—fat of the taxpayer, I should say—while she makes life miserable for the hardworking folk who produce all the real wealth by making them fill out useless forms for sixteen hours a day." She took a deep breath. "Thereby draining the nation's treasury, impoverishing its spirit and threatening its very soul, because nobody has time to do any real work."

Noelle started refilling her cup and Minnie's. "Been spending time with Tino Nobili lately, I see. How in the world did that happen?"

Denise made a face. "I had to go to the pharmacy to get some medicine for Mom and I got trapped."

"Exactly how does a sixty-five-year-old reactionary pharmacist with a potbelly and a bad knee trap a sixteen-year-old in very good health who is every truant officer's personal nightmare?"

"How do you think? He musta spent half a goddam hour mixing up Mom's stuff. The over-the-counter ibuprofen's long gone, you know. I would've left except her cramps are really bad this time. By the end, though, I was figuring I might die of starvation before Tino finished, on account of how I now understood that nobody actually makes anything any longer including farmers, who are idle in their fields. And it's all on account of *you*."

"Well, yes, that's true," said Noelle. "If anybody did any actual work instead of filling out my useless paperwork—which, oddly enough, consists of specialized forms filled out by less than one percent of the population, but never mind, a good Tino Nobili rant is a thing of wonder—then my stratospheric salary might get cut down to merely ionospheric proportions. And if that happened, I might have to settle for a town mansion instead of a country estate for my retirement home."

"You've got it all wrong," Minnie said firmly. "The ionosphere is higher than the stratosphere." She began gesticulating, as if she were stacking invisible books. "At the bottom, there is the troposphere. That's where we live. It goes up about ten miles and has more than three-fourths of all the air, measured by weight. Okay, *then* there is the stratosphere. It goes from about ten miles up to about thirty miles high. After that comes the mesosphere, the thermosphere and the exosphere. The ionosphere is part of the thermosphere. *Way* higher than the stratosphere."

Denise stared at her friend as if she'd suddenly discovered that an alien moved among them. Minnie shrugged. "I pay attention in class, even if you don't. Especially science class, because it's really interesting."

"And good for you," Noelle said. "Unlike Denise, you won't wind up with a brain like Tino Nobili's."

Minnie giggled. "All shriveled up. Hard as a walnut and just about as big."

Denise gave her a disgusted look. "Fat chance." She then transferred the look of disgust onto Noelle. "It's your fault. If you didn't overwork Eddie the way you do, he'd have some time to relax."

"As it happens," Noelle said mildly, "I'm barely working him at all, these days. He asked for as much time off as I could give him, and he got it. It's to the point now where I'm skirting the edge of fraud, the way I mark him down for working full days when he's not even close. Some days he barely shows up at the office at all."

Denise frowned. "Then what's he—"

"All kinds of odd jobs he picks up," said Noelle. "Mostly from his father's connections. Down-timers with money will pay a lot to get solid advice from another down-timer who understands up-time legal practices and the way to maneuver through the bureaucracy."

"See?" said Denise triumphantly. "You just admitted it yourself. It's a bureaucracy!"

"Well, of course it is. What else would government agencies be? A sports league?"

Minnie giggled again. Noelle took a sip of her tea. "Back up-time, I'd have to rein him in. Government officials are allowed to give advice to people who use their agency's services, of course, but they're not supposed to get paid for it. Down-time, though . . ."

Minnie grinned, being a down-timer herself. "Oh, come on. By today's standards, Eddie Junker is the soul of probity. He won't give anybody privy information and he won't take bribes to finagle contracts or juggle results."

"Yes, I know. That's why I look the other way."

"But *why?*" demanded Denise. "Since when did Eddie care that much about money?"

There was silence in the room. Noelle and Minnie glanced at each other.

Denise, naturally, spotted the glance. Despite the gibe, and leaving aside Denise's cavalier attitude toward formal education, there wasn't the slightest resemblance between her brain and a shriveled up walnut.

"Okay!" she said. "You guys know something! So *give.*"

Noelle sighed, then drained her cup and rose from the table to return it to the sink. "He wants to learn how to fly. And he figures flying lessons are going to cost him an arm and a leg."

"Bound to," said Minnie. "The air force won't teach him unless he signs up, which he's not about to do. Eddie hasn't got a military bone in his body, even if he does shoot a gun real well. That means he's got to pay the Kellys to teach him."

Denise frowned. "How much do they charge?"

"Who knows?" said Noelle, coming back to the table and sitting down. "There are no established rules or regulations, much less standard pricing, for flying lessons. They range all the way from a half-baked 'simulation' on somebody's computer to the sort of training pilots get in the air force. And you know what Eddie's like. He's not about to do something like this half-assed. He'll want to be trained by real pros like the Kellys."

"That means Kay Kelly will call the shots," Minnie added, "and you know what *she's* like. Eddie figures she'll want the equivalent in money of the pound of flesh nearest to his heart."

Denise's expression had been growing darker by the second. "You mean to tell me that Eddie Junker's been working like a dog in order to pay the Kellys for *flying lessons*?"

"That's the gist of it," said Noelle.

"We'll see about that!" Denise exploded. And off she went, up from the table and out the back door to Noelle's apartment like the proverbial flash. A few seconds later, they heard Denise firing up her motorcycle and racing off. Doing a wheelie, by the sound of it.

She'd been in too much of a hurry to even close the door. Noelle got up and shut it, then sat down again.

"You should have told her," Minnie said accusingly.

"Told her what?"

"You know. Why Eddie's doing it. As if he just decided to start flying for no reason!"

Noelle's lips tightened. "I don't approve in the first place, Minnie. You know that perfectly well."

"So what? I probably don't approve either. Not that I don't like Eddie a lot myself, but the whole thing's just silly. In a few weeks, we won't even be living here any more. We'll be in Magdeburg. A few months after that, we'll be in Prague."

Noelle's lips tightened still further. She knew the basic

parameters of the plans Minnie and Denise had made with Francisco Nasi. Now that Mike Stearns had lost the election and wasn't the prime minister any more, his intelligence chief had decided to go into private practice—in Prague, because Nasi also had some long-overdue personal matters to deal with, and Prague had the largest and most sophisticated Jewish community in Europe.

Personally, Noelle thought the man must be insane. Why in the world would he want to saddle himself with looking after two teenage girls? Especially *those* two. Either one of them was a handful and a half. Put them both together...

Noelle thought the wisecrack of one of the high school teachers about Denise and Minnie—*in tandem, they're the fifth horseman of the Apocalypse*—was overstating the case.

Probably.

"Who knows when we'll see Eddie again, after we move?" said Minnie. She shook her head. "That's going to be really hard on Denise. Since her father got killed, she leans a lot on Eddie even if she pretends she doesn't."

Noelle didn't say anything. Right there, she thought, was the heart of the problem. For all that there was no surface resemblance between stolid and level-headed Eddie Junker and Denise's ex-biker father, there were a lot more similarities than the average person might realize. However flamboyant Buster Beasley's reputation had been—and his death had been every bit as flamboyant—when it came to his daughter Denise, the man had been rock solid for the girl. As dependable as the tides.

There wasn't anything flamboyant about Eddie Junker. But he'd been Noelle's partner for some time now, and she knew him very well. They'd gone through the Ram Rebellion together, along with their adventure with the defectors and Janos Drugeth. If anyone had asked her to sum the man up, the first terms she would have used were "solid as a rock" and "dependable as the tides."

"Denise'll be okay, Noelle," Minnie said. "She's really smart, even if most people don't realize it because she gets bored in school and cusses like a soldier. Well, it doesn't help, probably, that she's beaten up a few boys, too. But only when they kept hitting on her after she told them to stop."

There was a lot of truth to that assessment, Noelle knew. But it still hadn't stopped Denise from . . .

Oh, let's see. Recently? Just in the last few months?

Picked a fight with an army officer. No verbal joust, either. A down home fist fight—well, Denise had gone to bar stools and salt shakers real quick—in a tavern.

Stolen an airplane.

Crashed said airplane. Well, fine, she hadn't been the pilot. Had participated in the crash of a stolen airplane.

What else of note? Noelle wasn't positive, but she was pretty sure from odd bits and pieces of data that had come her way—despite her innocuous-sounding formal title, she amounted to a secret agent for the government of the State of Thuringia-Franconia—that Denise had been centrally involved in the still mysterious episode involving Bryant Holloway's killing. The man had been "shot into doll rags," as one person who'd seen the body reported to Noelle afterward.

Could Denise Beasley shoot a man into doll rags? By all accounts, quite unlike Noelle herself, the girl was adept with firearms. So . . . yes. No doubt about it.

Would she do it, though? Knowing Denise as well as Noelle did . . .

Oh, yes, given the right situation. Noelle didn't have any doubt about that, either.

But all she said was, "I hope you're right."

The offices of Kelly Aviation
An airfield just outside of Grantville
June 12, 1635

"That's the most preposterous thing I've ever heard!" exclaimed Kay Kelly. "Ridiculous!"

She stopped striding back and forth and came to stand next to Denise, who was sitting in a chair in front of Bob Kelly's desk. Kay was a tall woman, and she loomed over the girl in a manner . . .

That might have intimidated another sixteen-year-old but affected Denise Beasley about as much as a light drizzle affects a duck.

"Oh, yeah?" sneered Denise. "You guys *bombed* him, remember? As in 'war crime.' The word 'atrocity' comes to mind, too. I know—I was there."

"You certainly were!" screeched Kay. She was starting to gesticulate a bit wildly. She had no way of knowing it, but the gestures would have seemed familiar to a number of high school teachers. Who had also, in the fullness of time, had cause to be exasperated by Denise Beasley.

"You certainly were!" she repeated. "That's because

you were *in* that airplane! Because you'd stolen it! In fact, you were the bombardier!"

"Oh, that's pure horseshit. Lannie Yost and Keenan Wynn stole the plane. I had no idea. I thought they'd borrowed it legitimately until we were already in the air and then it was too late. What was I supposed to do? Get out and walk? As for who was the bombardier, that was Keenan. I was just the navigator."

Had Denise been committed to an anal-retentive definition of truth-telling, she would have added that, well, yes, she'd actually been the one to give the command to drop the bomb. Seeing as how Lannie and Keenan were doofuses who couldn't hit the broadside of a barn with any sort of weapon. But Denise labored under no such silly notion. Truth was an expansive sort of thing, with lots of room around the edges.

Kay had resumed pacing back and forth, and was about to start screeching again. Fortunately, her husband Bob finally spoke up.

"Oh, calm down, Kay! Let's see if we can't work out something reasonable. Truth is, Eddie Junker *was* bombed by one of our planes, even if we hadn't given anybody permission to use it. We're all just lucky he didn't get hurt worse than a broken arm when his horse threw him."

Denise seized the moment. "Yeah, that was blind luck—as accurately as that plane of yours drops bombs, Mr. Kelly. It's no wonder the air force ordered a bunch of them."

She and Kelly exchanged big smiles. Bob was inordinately proud of his company's "Dauntless" line of aircraft—and, push come to shove, Denise had been one of the people who gave the plane its first real field test.

His wife Kay did not share in the momentary burst of good feeling. In fact, she hadn't even noticed it, as preoccupied as she'd been with her vigorous striding and gesticulating. "We're not—"

"Calm down, I said! We're not *what*? Liable?" Bob made a face. "If Eddie decides to sue us, it'll be a jury or a judge who makes that decision. You want to trust a judge or a jury? I sure don't. In fact, I'd just as soon keep the damn lawyers out of this altogether."

Kay pointed an accusing finger at Denise. "Let him sue! If he does, we'll sue *her*!"

"Oh, swell. We recoup our losses by stripping a sixteen-year-old clean of her possessions."

"Her mother—"

"Her mother? Would that be the Widder Beasley? Lemme see if I got this straight, Kay. You want us to fight it out in court with the widow and daughter of the hero Buster Beasley?" Bob shook his head. "Like I said. 'Oh, swell.' No, I don't think so."

His wife glared down at him, but the looming tactic was obviously just as useless with Bob as it had been with Denise. Kay Kelly was a rather formidable woman. But she and Bob had been married for a long time.

So Bob just ignored her and leaned forward in his chair, propping his arms on the desk and peering at Denise.

"You're sure about this? Eddie would be satisfied if we just provided him with flying lessons?"

"Yeah."

"How do you know?"

"I'm one of his best friends. Trust me. I know."

Kay hadn't quite given up. "Best friends! He's in his mid-twenties and you're way underage."

Denise looked bored. "He's twenty-three. That counts as 'early twenties,' not 'mid-twenties.' And there's no age of consent laws in the here and now and even if the seventeenth century had gotten around to that particularly stupid piece of so-called 'modern legislation,' it wouldn't matter anyway because we'd be under West Virginia law and the age of consent was sixteen. My sixteenth birthday was way, way back. Over seven months ago, now. And it's all beside the point, because Eddie and I aren't screwing each other. We're just real good friends."

Bob cleared his throat. "Kay, will you please let me handle this?"

His wife's lips tightened. But, after a moment, she went over to her own desk in the office and sat down. "Fine. Have at it."

Bob looked back at Denise. "I'm willing to bet you're doing this for Eddie, rather than him having sent you here." He held up his hand, forestalling any response on her part. "I'm not asking. Just don't think I'm a dummy, that's all."

"I never thought you were a dummy, Mr. Kelly," Denise said. That was quite true. Bob Kelly could sometimes be a walking definition of "absent minded" and he had plenty of other personal quirks and foibles. But nobody ever thought he wasn't smart. Dumb people don't design and build airplanes.

"What I'm getting at is this. If you and me reach a deal, I can assume that'll be okay with Eddie. Am I right?"

Denise nodded. "Yeah. Uh . . . Yeah. It will."

She had no doubt she was right. Given that Eddie didn't exactly know that she was doing this in the first place.

Well. Had no idea at all, if you wanted to get fussy about it.

"All right, then. I'll undertake to train Eddie Junker to be a pilot. And we'll understand that to mean that I'll train him until he's qualified for solo flight on a Dauntless." A bit stiffly: "I can't qualify him on one of Hal's aircraft, y'unnerstand?"

"Not a problem." So far as she knew, it wasn't. She had no idea why Eddie had gotten fixated on learning how to fly, but she was sure that as long as he could fly one type of plane he'd be satisfied.

And if he wasn't, well, dammit, *then* he could waste his own money on lessons.

She stuck out her hand. "It's a deal."

Kay spoke up again. "Junker pays for the fuel! Dammit, Bob, show a *little* backbone."

Denise did a quick calculation. Eddie could afford the cost of the fuel easily enough, she figured. And if she didn't leave him *something* to pay for, he was likely to go all stupid-male on her.

"Yeah, fine. Not a problem. Eddie pays for the fuel. Mr. Kelly, you drive a tough bargain. Surprised they don't call you Razorback Bob."

Rebecca Abrabanel's kitchen
Magdeburg, capital of the United States of Europe
July 2, 1635

"Does he not look splendid?" said Rebecca. The question

was purely rhetorical, judging from the way her eyes were admiring her husband. Who, for his part, was standing in the middle of the large kitchen and looking uncomfortable. "Michael, stop fidgeting."

"Damn thing *itches*," Mike Stearns complained.

"Of course it itches," was his wife's unsympathetic reply. "It is made of wool. You will be glad of it, once you are on campaign. It will keep you warm in the winter and it will handle water well."

Rhetorical or not, Francisco Nasi thought it would be wise to provide a suitable answer. Hell might or might not have no fury like a woman scorned, but woe unto whichever fool neglected to praise a wife's abilities as a seamstress—or, in this case, ability to select a good seamstress.

"Oh, yes," he assured the wife in question, in tones loud enough to be heard by all occupants in the room. "Splendid, indeed."

He didn't even have to lie. Mike Stearns *did* look good in his new uniform. True, the austere design of the uniform was a bit startling to someone raised according to seventeenth-century notions of proper male costume. All the more so for Nasi, who'd been reared in the Ottoman court. But Stearns was a well-built man, and taller than average. He was still muscular and not gone to fat despite being close to forty years of age and having spent most of the last three years seated behind a desk. The severity of the uniform simply emphasized that physique.

Rebecca looked pleased, but Mike was still in a grumbling mood. "I'm starting to feel like a traitor. First, we've got a flag that from a distance looks just like a damn Confederate flag—and now *this*."

After a moment, Nasi deduced that by "this" Mike was referring to the color of the uniform. It was solid gray, shading slightly toward green. If Francisco remembered correctly, the uniform worn by the soldiers of the Confederacy in the American civil war had been that color.

But perhaps not. Nasi could hardly be expected to remember every detail of books he had read about the history of another world's future.

"Oh, hogwash, Mike," said his friend and now fellow army officer Frank Jackson. "Those uniforms were butternut."

Mike's sneer was magnificent. "Izzat so? Ever hear of 'the blue and the gray'? The 'gray,' you'll note, not 'the blue and the butternut,' which sounds downright silly."

Jackson leaned back in his chair and shrugged. "Those were just officers' uniforms. The uniforms of the grunts were butternut."

The sneer remained in place. Indeed, it expanded, as Mike pointed at a cap perched on a peg near the kitchen entrance. "See the stars there on the front of the cap? Two of 'em, no less." The accusing finger now jabbed at the insignia on his left shoulder. "Same two we've got right here. They stand for 'major general,' old buddy. Since you're apparently going senile, a major general qualifies as an officer."

Frank grinned. "Aren't we testy? Will it make you feel any better if I tell you that I happen to know just how and why the army's quartermasters settled on gray uniforms?

Had absolutely nothing to do with our little American fracas, back when a couple of centuries from now. Seems they got their hands on some German history books and got swept up in a wave of future nostalgia." He pointed at Mike's tunic. "That color is officially '*feldgrau*,' fella. That means—"

"I know what it means," growled Mike. "My German is quite fluent by now, thank you. 'Field gray.' Swell. So now I find out that instead of being a damn Confederate, it seems I'm a damn storm trooper."

"Actually, feldgrau uniforms were common in the German Army way before the Nazis," Frank said. "But is there anything else you want to complain about? If so, better get it out quick, since Francisco needs a decision."

"No, I guess I'm done." Then, demonstrating that he had not lost all his senses, Mike bestowed a winning smile on his wife. "It's a nice uniform, Becky. Thank you."

He turned toward Nasi, and the smile faded a bit. "Francisco, I don't see any way you could buy one of Hal and Jesse's planes without the whole thing causing a stink."

"Hal's planes," Jesse Wood said mildly. "I got out of the business"—he looked at Nasi—"for pretty much the same reason Mike doesn't think you can buy one of the planes. Looks bad. Conflict of interest, that sort of thing."

"I am quite wealthy," said Nasi. "I assure you that I can pay the full price for one of the planes—and I am quite willing to have the figures made public. Indeed, for my purposes, the more public, the better."

Mike shook his head. "It doesn't matter, Francisco. We're just too closely associated, all of us. Me, you,

Frank"—he jabbed a thumb at Jesse—"even him, though I don't know if he voted for me in the election."

"In point of fact, I didn't," said the commander in chief of the USE's little air force. "I decided I'd follow General George Marshall's practice and not vote at all. I'm pretty sure Admiral Simpson did the same thing. But getting back to the issue at hand, Francisco, all of Hal's planes are spoken for by the air force, anyway, for at least another year's worth of production."

Francisco didn't argue the matter any further. He'd expected that answer. He'd only pushed the issue at all because he was reluctant to entrust his safety to any airplane that wasn't made by Jesse's one-time partner Hal Smith.

The alternatives were either Kelly Aircraft or Markgraf and Smith Aviation. Of those alternatives, Francisco had already decided he'd approach the Kellys, assuming Mike advised him that buying one of Hal Smith's planes was not a suitable choice. For his purposes, the new Dauntless aircraft was far more suitable than the slow and heavy cargo planes made by Markgraf and Smith.

That left the problem of finding a pilot. That wouldn't have been too hard if he'd been buying one of Smith's planes. Since the Gustavs were the standard models for the air force, quite a few people by now had learned to fly them. The same was not true for aircraft produced by the Kellys. Their test pilot was a man named Lannie Yost, about whom Francisco had heard many tales from his new assistant Denise Beasley. First and foremost among them, half-amused and half-awed accounts of Yost's alcohol consumption.

No, that wouldn't do.

"Piece of cake!" said Denise immediately. Her friend Minnie was vigorously nodding her head.

"You know someone?" asked Francisco.

"Eddie Junker," came the simultaneous reply from both girls.

"He's been learning how to fly from the Kellys," Denise explained. "By now, I betcha he's an expert on the Dauntless."

"He's been training for three whole weeks," concurred Minnie.

Francisco was dubious that "three whole weeks" constituted sufficient training for an aircraft pilot. He'd have to check with Jesse.

In the meantime . . .

He gave both girls a stern look. "And now, back to your lessons. I promised your mother"—that to Denise—"and Benny that I wouldn't let you slack off just because you were no longer formally enrolled in school."

Minnie was too polite to yawn, but she might as well have. Francisco had only added the name of her adoptive parent Benny Pierce in the interests of maintaining formal evenhandedness. Minnie was quite good about doing her homework. Not so Denise, to whom the comment had really been directed.

But the girl just grinned at him. Francisco, a renowned spymaster with a continental reputation, managed to keep a straight face.

Barely.

In point of fact, since moving with him to Magdeburg,

Denise had been quite attentive to her studies. It seemed that being an assistant to a renowned spymaster with a continental reputation made it fascinating to study exactly the same books she had previously scorned when they were assigned to a mere student. Such is the power of status change.

"It mostly depends on the student, Francisco," said Jesse. "If they've got a knack for it, and assuming they pay attention to their instructor, a person can learn to fly a plane a lot faster than you might think. The standard training for pilots in World War II was four and half weeks. Of course, that was continuous training, which I assume Eddie Junker hasn't been able to do since he has a job. The military wanted a pilot to have two hundred hours of experience flying a specific plane before they sent him into combat. Most civilian training courses are less demanding. They'll want a student to fly for ten to fifteen hours before they solo, and at least forty hours before they try to get a license."

That was much faster than Nasi had assumed. True, he still didn't know whether or not Eddie Junker had "the knack" for flying. But he did know that the Junker fellow was very reliable. For Francisco's purposes, a steady and reliable pilot was quite sufficient. He did not intend to fly a private plane into combat, after all.

So. Off to Grantville.

"Can we come?"

"No. You have your studies—which I promised your mother and Benny Pierce that you'd have completed before we move to Prague."

Minnie seemed unperturbed by the response. Denise scowled at him.

Noelle Stull's kitchen
Grantville, State of Thuringia-Franconia
July 9, 1635

"You bum," said Noelle Stull. For a moment, she looked as if she might snatch back the cup of tea she had placed before Francisco. "You dirty rotten bum," she qualified.

Nasi's tone was placid. "Oh, come now, Noelle. Surely you didn't expect Eddie Junker to work for you indefinitely."

"He doesn't work *for* me," Noelle snapped. "He's employed by the State of Thuringia-Franconia, same as I am. Technically, he's—excuse me, he *was*—my subordinate, but I always considered him my partner."

As heavily as possible for someone of her slender build, Noelle took a seat at the kitchen table across from Nasi. Her dark expression had not faded in the least. She still looked as if she were on the verge of snatching back the cup of tea she'd given Francisco. Even, possibly, throwing it in his face. For all the young woman's pleasant appearance—pretty, in an understated sort of way—she had a fearsome reputation.

True, her bad marksmanship was legendary. Still, she'd once managed to slay a torturer by shoving a gun under his jaw where she couldn't possibly miss—and there was always the chance that her aim with a teacup might be better than her aim with a pistol.

So, a bit hurriedly, Francisco added: "Surely you didn't

think I came here simply to inform you that I'd hired Eddie Junker. He could have done that much himself, thereby saving me"—here, he gave Noelle his most winning smile—"some possible, however unlikely, unpleasantness."

"'However unlikely,'" she jeered. "I oughta—"

She broke off the sentence and frowned at him. "Then why *did* you come here?"

"I would think it obvious. Surely you didn't think I was hiring Eddie simply to be my pilot? That occupation would leave him idle most of the time, after all. No, I did some research, and by all accounts he is very good at the work he's been doing—which, when you come right down to it, is not so different from the sort of work I'd have him doing."

"'Did some research,'" Noelle jeered. "'By all accounts,'" she jeered again. "Translated into realspeak, that means you asked Denise Beasley and she praised Eddie to the skies. Based on her sixteen—count 'em, sixteen—years of life's experience."

Francisco thought it best to make no direct response. True, he had asked Denise and, true again, she had praised Eddie Junker to the skies. But the praise had been salted by quite a few astute observations, as well. Sixteen or not—sixteen and a half, Denise herself would have insisted, being of an age where half-years loom large—the girl was generally shrewd when it came to people, and exceedingly shrewd when it came to people in whom she had a particular interest.

But there was no need to get into that. "However—again, by all accounts—it seems also true that Eddie's skills at his usual work are greatly amplified when he works with you. A true partnership, indeed. My research leads me to the conclusion that the two of you, working together, are quite formidable."

He cleared his throat. "Therefore, my visit."

Judging from Noelle's change of expression, Francisco judged it was now safe to drink his tea.

It was quite good, actually.

Office of the Director of the Department of Economic Resources
Grantville, State of Thuringia-Franconia
July 10, 1635

"You bum," said Tony Adducci. For a moment, he looked as if he might throw his chair at Francisco instead of leaning back in it. "You dirty rotten bum," he qualified.

Nasi's tone was placid. "Oh, come now, Tony. Surely you didn't expect Noelle to work for you indefinitely."

"There oughta be a law," complained the director of the Department of Economic Resources.

"Against what?" Francisco asked. "Wealthy private employers who pay generously?"

Adducci glared at him. "Conspicuous consumption."

"Ah. Sumptuary laws. Indeed, many realms in Europe have such in place." He could have added, *commonly aimed at Jews like me, in fact,* but that would have been quite unfair. There was legally no discrimination against Jews in the United States of Europe, and, at least in the State of Thuringia-Franconia if not all the USE's provinces, the law was enforced. Nor did Francisco have any reason to believe that Tony Adducci was himself a bigot.

Madder than the proverbial wet hen, yes, and the target of his ire was indeed a rich Jew. But that hardly constituted anti-Semitism, to any fair-minded person.

So all he said was: "Unfortunately for you, such laws are directed at the excessive acquisition of valuable clothing, jewelry, furniture, and such like material goods. Not," he cleared his throat, "valuable spies."

Office of the President, State of Thuringia-Franconia
Grantville
July 10, 1635

"That bum," said Tony Adducci. "That dirty rotten bum."

Ed Piazza, the president of the State of Thuringia-Franconia, leaned back in the chair in his office. He seemed quite relaxed and unflustered.

"Oh, calm down, Tony. People get hired away from government jobs into better-paying private employment all the time. Why did you think Noelle Stull and Eddie Junker would be exempt?"

"They're my best investigative team," Adducci whined.

"*Were* your best team," Piazza said. "Get over it, Tony. Your department will manage, well enough. And if you can tear yourself away for a moment from parochial concerns, you might want to contemplate the possibility that all this will work out pretty well for us in the future. Defining 'us' in admittedly factional terms."

Adducci stared at him. "Huh?"

"We're in a parliamentary system now, Tony. You *have* heard the phrase 'shadow cabinet,' haven't you?"

"Yeah, sure. The party in opposition keeps a cabinet going—in place, anyway—in case it has to step into power on short notice. What's that got to do with this headache?"

Piazza smiled. "Hasn't it dawned on you yet that what Francisco Nasi is setting up in Prague could be construed as Mike Stearns' shadow intelligence service? On the off chance, you know, that Willem Wettin's administration goes into the crapper on short notice."

"Oh."

A moment later, Adducci's sour expression cleared. Tony was another UMWA man, a former member of the mineworkers local union of which Mike had been the president before the Ring of Fire. Like most such, he was a fierce Stearns partisan.

"Well. I guess it's okay, then."

Boarding house kitchen
Magdeburg, capital of the United States of Europe
July 20, 1635

"How utterly cool is *this*?" Denise Beasley said happily. "Both Eddie and Noelle will be working for Francisco too! We'll see them all the time now."

Minnie Hugelmair nodded. "What's even better is that we'll probably wind up with Noelle as our boss. How cool is *that*?"

Denise's cheerful expression faded a bit. "Well... She'll be tough on us about homework."

"Tough on *you*," Minnie qualified. "I don't have a problem with homework."

"'Cause you're a suck-ass."

"Vulgar, vulgar, vulgar. You better watch out, or Noelle will wash your mouth with soap."

That was water off a duck's back. Denise Beasley's attitude toward threats of punishment could best be described as sanguine.

She jumped up from the table. "Let's go! Eddie and them should be landing soon."

Minnie looked at the clock perched on the wall of the kitchen. The landlady was inordinately proud of the thing. Personally, with tastes now heavily influenced by the Americans who had adopted her, Minnie thought it was also excessively ornate. "Baroque," the Americans often called such things, after an historical era that technically hadn't even started yet.

However, whatever she thought of the design, the clock worked perfectly well. Which meant they'd be spending at least an hour with nothing to do at the airport except look at the wind sock, as early as Denise would get them there.

But Minnie didn't argue the matter. She knew how much Denise had missed Eddie's company since they'd moved to Magdeburg this summer.

Magdeburg airfield

"That landing was pretty decent, Eddie," Denise pronounced, as soon as the pilot had clambered down to the ground. "All things considered."

Eddie Junker peeled off a flying cap, exposing a thatch of sandy-colored hair. His hazel eyes gazed down at her curiously. "All things . . . as in what?"

His tone was neither defensive nor hostile. One of the many things Denise liked about Eddie was that he was not easily flustered. His response to almost everything was careful, calm, deliberate, relaxed—in short, just about the exact opposite of her own reaction to things.

She beamed up at him. Eddie wasn't really that much taller than Denise—four inches, perhaps—but he was so wide-shouldered and stocky that he always seemed a little bigger than he really was.

"Oh, you know. Things that need to be considered. Like, Item One, you're still a tyro. Like, Item Two, you have a distaste for flamboyance—and what sort of top notch pilot isn't flamboyant?" She did an exaggerated search for some item of clothing on his person. "Like, Item Three, where's the requisite white scarf?"

Eddie shook his head. "It is quite false to say that I have a distaste for flamboyance. Far more appropriate words would be: horror, contempt and loathing. As for the scarf . . ."

He dug into the pockets of his jacket and drew forth a gray scarf. "Here it is. In case it gets too cold. Which it didn't, on this flight. It's mid-summer and I never exceeded eight thousand feet of altitude. I didn't even have to turn on the cabin's little heater."

Standing next to him, Francisco Nasi nodded. "Indeed, it was a most pleasant flight. And as for flamboyance—" He shuddered, a bit theatrically. "Imagine, if you will, my own horror, contempt and loathing for the trait. In my personal pilot, at least. I will admit that I found the quality sometimes quite charming in our former prime minister."

He shook his head. "Sometimes. But, speaking of which, I need to consult with Mike as soon as possible. Eddie, I don't think we'll be here longer than one day. Two, at the most."

Junker nodded. "I'll make sure the plane's ready to go on short notice. Where are we staying?"

"The boarding house!" piped up Minnie.

"We had the landlady hold rooms for you," Denise said proudly.

That was a slender claim to fame. Francisco had rented the rooms weeks earlier, and told the landlady he'd want them available at any time throughout the summer, whether he was present or not. But he saw no reason to correct the girl.

He looked around. "What? No fancy transportation?"

His two young female assistants showed a distressing lack of respect for their employer.

"Jeez, Mr. Nasi," said Denise, "this ain't Grantville with fancy bus lines and stuff. Besides, it's only a short ride."

She normally called him "Don Francisco." She spoke the term "Mr. Nasi" in the same manner one might speak of "the old geezer."

"They're good horses," added Minnie reassuringly. "Real mild-mannered. They probably won't throw you."

Francisco couldn't help but laugh. In point of fact, he was a better horseman than either of the two girls—if not, admittedly, in their league when it came to motorcycles.

"Lead me to these decrepit nags, then."

Boarding house kitchen
Magdeburg, capital of the United States of Europe

"So how soon are you coming back, Eddie?" Denise asked.

"More tea?" chimed in Minnie, holding up the pot.

Eddie extended his cup and Minnie refilled it. "Whenever Don Francisco wants me to bring him. Hard to say."

Denise frowned. "You're not his fucking slave, you know. Just ask him if you've got a week or two when he's not going to be needing you to fly him around. Then come up and visit us. Hell, he might even let you use the plane for that."

Junker shook his head. "Won't work, I'm afraid. I'm going to be tied up all summer."

"Huh? With what?"

"Painting lessons."

"What?" Denise was staring at him the way she might stare at a penguin which had suddenly appeared at the table.

"You heard me. Painting lessons." He starting making gestures with his hand. "Painting as in fine art. Not painting as in painting a house."

"What?" Denise's jaw was now sagging.

He peered at her closely. "That's odd. I don't remember you being particularly slow-witted."

Denise's jaw snapped shut. "Very funny, asswipe. There's nothing at all wrong with my wits. Unlike yours. Why the fuck do you need to take painting lessons, anyway?"

As always, Eddie was unfazed by Denise's coarse language. "In order to paint something, of course. Why else would I do it?"

Denise was practically speechless—for her, a highly unusual condition. "But—but—" The next words were almost wailed. "How many hours can you possibly spend in stupid painting classes?"

"Not very many," Eddie allowed. "No more than ten hours a week. But I need to work very hard and long hours to pay for the lessons."

Minnie had a puzzled face. "Since when does the school charge money for art classes?"

"I assume they don't. But I wanted private lessons from the best instructor I could find. And those do not come cheaply."

Denise's face looked like a pickle. As close a resemblance, at least, as was possible for such a very good-looking teenage girl. "Jesus H. Fucking Christ, Eddie! Do you have to do *everything* first class?"

Junker took another sip of tea. "I am usually rather frugal—as you know perfectly well, since your more common complaint is that I'm a tightwad and—what's that other colorful if grotesque American expression? 'Party-pooper,' I think."

"Damn right you're a party-pooper," said Denise. "You're ruining the whole summer!"

Junker and Nasi left early the next morning, flying back to Grantville. No sooner had the two girls seen them to the airfield and waved them goodbye, than Denise announced a new mission in life.

"How much does it cost to learn how to paint from a real pro, anyway?"

"How should I know?" said Minnie. "It probably depends what he wants to paint—and, in case you didn't notice, Eddie did his very best I'm-a-clam routine whenever you tried to pry it out of him."

"Well, fuck a duck. How can I find out?"

"I think Artemisia Gentileschi's in town," said Minnie. "Mrs. Simpson asked her to come up. Probably planning to parade her around the hoity-toities and maybe set up a showing. Or whatever they call it when they put up a lot of paintings on the walls and let people walk around and look at them. At least, people who are able to buy them."

Pointedly, she added: "Which excludes us."

Denise was chewing on her lower lip. "How well do you get along with the Simpson Grand Dame? I think she might still be pissed with me on account of that time I almost ran her down in Grantville because it's not my fault some people don't pay attention to traffic."

Denise Beasley's notion of "paying attention to traffic" was just as sanguine as her attitude toward threats. *She* was going about her necessary business whenever *she* was out on her motorcycle. It followed, as night from day, that it was therefore everyone else's business to stay out of her way.

"Not too well," replied Minnie. "I think I grossed her out that one time I took out my glass eye in front of her."

Denise frowned. "So how else can we get into Gentileschi's presence?"

"Knock on the door?"

* * *

Amazingly, that worked. Mrs. Simpson wasn't home to say yea or nay, and the servant ushered them right into the artist's presence. Who, for her part, was quite pleasant and suggested a cup of tea.

Mary Simpson's kitchen
Magdeburg, capital of the United States of Europe

"Oh, I hadn't realized Eddie was a friend of yours."

Denise and Minnie stared at Artemisia Gentileschi. "*You* know him, too?" asked Denise.

"Well, of course. He's one of my private students."

On the street outside Mary Simpson's residence
Magdeburg, capital of the United States of Europe

"Well, that didn't go so well, did it?" said Denise, almost snarling.

Minnie frowned. "We were reasonably polite. And I don't think Ms. Gentileschi was mad at us. Even though we tried to pry what she called privy information out of her for probably longer than we should have. Um. Probably a lot longer."

"That's not what I meant!" That sentence *was* snarled. "I can't believe that inconsiderate fucking bum is paying *Artemisia Gentileschi* for private painting lessons."

Teenage fury gave way, in an instant, to sixteen-and-half-year-old despair. "She's *world famous*, Minnie! They even got articles about her in encyclopedias that were written hundreds of years from now. It'll take him *years* to pay her off!"

Minnie nodded. "Probably. One or two years, for sure."

"You're no help at all!"

The door to the Simpson residence opened. Hearing the sound, the two girls turned and looked up the short flight of stairs leading to the front entrance.

Artemisia Gentileschi was standing there, smiling. "It occurred to me after you charged off, young ladies, that there might be a solution to your problem."

"Rob a bank?" said Denise, perhaps a tad sarcastically.

Gentileschi chuckled. "Oh, nothing that energetic. But I always have need of models. It's especially difficult to find suitable girls, because they're either street urchins— that won't do at all—or their families insist on chaperones, and that costs still more money."

She gazed down upon them. "In your case, however, I do not think chaperones will be necessary."

"Ha!" That came from Denise.

Minnie's response was more measured. "Assuming you could find any in the first place. Here in Magdeburg... maybe. Back in Grantville, the Babysitters Guild had Denise blacklisted by the time she was six."

"Splendid, then. I can simply deduct what I would pay you from the fee I charge young Junker. Will that suit you?"

Denise looked simultaneously ecstatic and suspicious. "Well, sure. But . . . what do we have to do? Exactly?"

"Just sit still."

Minnie shrugged. "Easy for me. I might have to hit Denise once in a while."

For her part, Denise was back to scowling. "I can't believe what I put myself through for that guy."

Prague airfield
Bohemia
August 26, 1635

"It's in much better shape than I expected," said Nasi, as Eddie Junker taxied the plane toward Prague airfield's one and only hangar. Francisco stuck his head out of the window and gazed down at the runway passing below. "It's been macadamized, I think."

"I'm sure you're right," said Eddie. He nodded toward a heavy piece of cast iron equipment parked near the hangar. "There's the roller they would have used."

Nasi looked over. "Water-bound macadam only. But knowing Wallenstein and his mania for all things modern, I won't be surprised if they make it a tarmac soon, one way or another. There must be a source of bitumen somewhere in Bohemia."

They had almost reached the hangar. There was a large welcoming party standing nearby. Morris and Judith Roth were there, along with a ferocious-looking officer whom Nasi presumed to be General Pappenheim.

Wallenstein himself had not come, of course. But Francisco didn't doubt that he'd be ushered into the king of Bohemia's presence soon enough.

Ushered again, to be precise—although, this time, the audience would be public rather than private, as had been his three previous meetings with Wallenstein. The airfield he'd just landed on had been the product of one of those meetings. Bohemia's new ruler, not surprisingly, had a keen interest in developing an aviation industry and his own air force as soon as possible. In the meantime, he and Nasi had reached a quiet mutual understanding that Nasi's ostensibly private airplane would retain all the equipment needed to make it a warplane on short notice, in the event Bohemia needed such to avert a threat.

That wouldn't be hard to do. After all, the Dauntless had been designed to be a warplane in the first place.

Most of the people gathered at the airfield to greet Nasi were Jews, naturally. From the looks of the throng, half the ghetto had turned out.

"Did you expect such an enormous crowd, Don Francisco?"

"Yes," he said smugly.

Eddie brought the plane to a stop. "How soon—"

"Two days. That should be enough time for you to get settled into your new quarters." Nasi smiled, a bit wickedly. "But if you wait any longer, the girl will probably strangle you. Had I realized your capacity for ruthlessness, young man, I would have hired you much sooner."

Eddie looked modest. "I've only done what was necessary, Don Francisco."

"Yes, I know. What was necessary—*all* that was necessary—and nothing more. That is the very definition of ruthlessness, you know."

It was time to climb out of the plane and greet the enthusiasts. Morris Roth was already waiting, grinning very widely.

As well he might. Were Morris a egotistical man, Francisco Nasi's arrival in Prague might have been cause for friction. Until this moment, Roth had been the preeminent Jew in the city, almost since the day he arrived. Henceforth, he would have to share much of that prestige.

But it was no matter. Francisco and Morris had had quite a few more than three private sessions, over the past few months. Theirs would be a relationship of partners, not rivals. Even friends, Francisco thought.

Eddie cleared his throat. "Uh, Don Francisco. Just to be sure—"

Nasi waved his hand. "I already said it was fine, Eddie. Indeed, I suspect it will simply add to the luster of the thing." As he started to open the door, he looked back and smiled again. "Given that the girl is a *shiksha*. Were she a Jewess . . . Oh, the scandal!"

An airfield just outside of Grantville
August 28, 1635

"Stop fidgeting, Eddie," said Artemisia Gentileschi. "I assure you I will have it done in time for your flight to Magdeburg tomorrow. Even with such a peculiar canvas."

Eddie flushed a little. "Sorry, I didn't mean . . . It's just . . ."

"Yes, I know. The girl can sometimes be the very definition of impatience. Once or twice I almost *did* order Minnie to hit her on the head to keep her still."

The artist contemplated the surface to be painted for a moment longer, and then began busying herself with her brushes and paints. "Be off, now. Shoo! Shoo!"

Eddie was back to fidgeting. "Maybe . . . I mean . . ."

"Shoo, I said! Come back just before sundown. I will show you where to place a few of the last strokes. That way, your claim to being the artist will not be entirely fabricated."

She gave him the sort of sly smile that a middle-aged woman of great experience bestows upon a young man with very little. "Not that she will ever ask."

Magdeburg airfield
August 29, 1635

"Prague is supposed to be a really pretty city," Minnie said. "I can't wait to get there."

Denise nodded, a bit absently. Most of her attention was on the airplane coming in for a landing. The same airplane that would—finally! this had to have been the longest summer on record—take them to their new home in Prague.

She glanced down at her suitcase. She and Minnie had done their best to follow the instructions Eddie had sent them concerning weight and dimensions. She thought they were well within the parameters, but . . .

With Eddie, you never knew. He could be such a damned perfectionist, sometimes.

The plane landed. Very smoothly, it looked like.

"I'll bet he's a really good pilot, even already," Minnie opined.

Denise wouldn't have taken that bet on any odds. She'd never known Eddie *not* to be good at something, if he really put his mind to it.

The plane taxied toward them, then, as it neared the hangar, swerved to the side.

Denise's jaw dropped.

"Oh, wow," said Minnie.

There was silence, for a few seconds, until the plane came to a stop not more than ten yards away. At that distance...

"It's *you*," said Minnie, in what Denise judged to be the most needless statement in human history.

It sure was. Denise Beasley, in the flesh—or as close to it, anyway, as a painting on a plane's nose could possibly be.

Yeah, sure, Denise had never worn an outfit like that and never would. Not that she minded the décolletage or the amount of leg showing. What the hell, she *did* have great legs. And if her bust wasn't exactly in Playboy Bunny territory, nobody had ever mistaken her for anything but a mammal since she was twelve years old.

The problem was simply that the fancy dress looked completely impractical. Denise Beasley didn't mind being scandalous but she drew the line at tripping over herself.

Still. Under the circumstances. She was not about to complain.

"Oh, wow," said Minnie. "Do you look great or what?"

Eddie was gazing down at her, now. Denise stared back up at him, not knowing what to say.

Minnie let out a whoop and clambered into the cockpit. A moment later, she reemerged, with a flyer's cap on her head and a big smile on her face and an upthrust thumb.

"There's a cap for you too!" she hollered.

Denise finally managed to speak. "Eddie, is—ah—*this* why you spent the whole summer... Not paying any attention to me. You know, if you wanted to impress me, you didn't have to do this."

"Sadly, that statement is quite false. Besides, I wasn't trying to 'impress' you, Denise. What good is that? I simply needed to make very clear that my intentions were . . . ah. What's the word?"

"Lustful," suggested Minnie. Again, she stuck up her thumb.

Eddie shook his head. "In part, yes. Absurd to deny it"—he leaned over and pointed down at the painting—"as I believe the illustration makes clear. But I assure you the principal thrust of my intentions are entirely what you would call 'honorable.'"

Denise stared at the painting. "Ah . . . Eddie. Is this . . . ah . . ."

"A German girl, I would simply have gotten a very nice pair of shoes to indicate my desires. Given that it was you . . ."

Again, he shook his head. "The quandary I faced. Even worse than the one Thorsten Engler faced, I think. At least Caroline Platzer considered herself an adult."

"So do I!" said Denise fiercely.

"Sadly, that statement is also false. Must be qualified, at least. Normally, it is true enough, you consider the age of sixteen—"

"Sixteen and a half!"

"I stand corrected for my grievous error. Sixteen and a half, to be well-nigh a synonym for 'maturity.' But there are other issues which cause you to flee into that tender age like a rabbit into a hole."

"Name one!"

"Me."

Denise opened her mouth, then . . .

Closed it.

What was she to say? Damn it, Eddie *was* twenty-three years old. Practically twice her age!

Well. Once and a half times, anyway. Still a cradle robber, no matter how you sliced it.

Not that she had any attachment to cradles, of course. But . . .

She realized, finally, just how high and rigid she'd made that wall. Eddie Junker, her best male buddy. Eddie Junker, whose company she enjoyed as much as Minnie's. Eddie Junker, whom she relied upon for . . . oh, so many things.

But not—but never—he was *way* older

"Okay!" she said, "I'll admit you probably did have to do something like this."

She searched her mind and soul. Sure enough. She *still* had no attachment to cradles.

"Eddie, I'm sorry. I'm just not ready to get betrothed yet." She swallowed, then added, in a small voice: "If I was, it'd be you, for sure. But I'm just . . . not ready. I'm only sixteen. Well, okay. And a half. But still."

As usual, Eddie's reaction was imperturbable. He simply nodded and said, "I figured as much. Not a problem. I am a patient man. I simply wanted to eliminate any misconceptions."

He hopped down from the plane. Very gracefully and lightly, for such a thick-looking man. Once on the ground, he grinned at her. "Such as any notions that I simply wish to be your good friend. And have no lustful designs on your body."

Denise grinned back. Lustful designs on her body, she

could handle. In fact, now that she really thought about it, she figured lust and Eddie Junker would go together about as well as bacon and eggs. As long as there were no cradles involved. Yet, anyway.

"Well, in that case. Let me explain an American custom."

After she was done with the explanation, Eddie looked back up at Minnie, who was still in the cockpit. "You will find some paints and brushes in the back. Hand them down to me, if you would."

The implements in hand, Eddie advanced upon the illustration.

"What are you doing?" asked Denise, a little alarmed. The more she looked at it, the more she really really liked that painting on the nose of the plane.

"It needs a caption."

"Oh. Yeah. Like *Memphis Belle,* you mean. Or the one on the plane that dropped the bomb on Hiroshima. *Nose Gay,* or something like that."

"I am not actually planning to destroy entire cities to demonstrate my affections, Denise. But I think this will do nicely." He went about his work.

When the caption was finished, Denise and Minnie studied it carefully.

My Steady Girl.

"Oh, wow," said Minnie. "That is just so cool."

Denise didn't say anything. Her mind was already at work, figuring the problem. Going steady, after all, had certain traditional obligations—if you insisted on using such a silly term for it.

"Can we postpone the trip to Prague? I need another day."

"I suppose," Eddie said. "Don Francisco will probably be curious, but he's a good boss. He'll accept any reasonable explanation."

He cocked his head, apparently expecting her to provide said reasonable explanation.

Which she certainly had—about as reasonable as reasonable ever gets—but she wasn't about to explain it to Eddie.

Artemisia Gentileschi, she figured. An up-timer would know more modern methods, sure. But, first, those methods were likely to be invalid before too long. And, second, they'd probably blabber. Denise and her reputation, yackety-yak-yak.

Denise thought Artemisia would keep her mouth shut. And she was sure that the artist knew what Denise needed to know. If ever a woman looked like she *really* had a reputation, it was Artemisia Gentileschi. But only had two kids to show for it. And she must be . . . what? At least forty years old, or some such astronomical age.

"Never you mind," she said. "If Don Francisco asks, I just needed to get some advice. And, uh, steady girl supplies."

She studied the illustration again. Amazing, really, how much leg he'd shown. Poor Eddie. He must have been thinking about it for months and months.

She smiled, sixteen-and-a-half going on forty. "A lot of steady girl supplies, I'm thinking."

The Masque

1

Anne Jefferson studied herself in the mirror, then turned sideways and spent a few more seconds with the examination.

"The colors are pretty drab," she announced "Comfortable, though, I'll give it that—way more so than modern-day Dutch women's apparel. At least it doesn't have a ruff. I hate those things."

She giggled. "I can't believe I just heard myself say 'modern-day' to refer to the year 1635."

Her husband Adam Olearius smiled at her reflection in the mirror. "I was born in this century so I can't say that I find the expression peculiar. Although people didn't use it much until you Americans came barging into the world. Changes came a lot more slowly before you arrived, so the distinction between past and present wasn't as great."

He studied her garments for a few seconds. "With the exception of fashion, of course. That's always changed rapidly."

Still looking at the outfit in the mirror, Anne shook her

head. "I'll tell you what's odd to me, though. In the world I came from, women's fashions changed all the time. But men's clothing changed slowly, and it was even more drab than this dress I'm wearing. Suits, suits, suits. The colors were black, gray, navy blue and one or another shade of white. If you were really daring, you wore a light brown suit. Whereas here! Men's clothing changes every bit as fast as women's and it's even more flamboyant."

Olearius curled his lip theatrically. "One of the great drawbacks of your democratic system! In our sane seventeenth century, male fashion is determined by princes—who are not about to bury their effulgent glory under dismal colors and sober designs. In your world, on the other hand, male fashion was dictated by businessmen. Merchants, that is to say, a class of people whose adventurousness is entirely restricted to pecuniary endeavors."

Anne chuckled but didn't argue the point. Leaving aside her husband's analysis of the causes involved, she didn't disagree with him on the substance of the matter. She thought male costuming in the here-and-now was a marked improvement over that of the world she'd come from. Thankfully, the codpieces prevalent in the last century had fallen out of fashion. That would have been . . . a bit much to take, for someone who still had a lot of West Virginia attitudes.

She turned away from the mirror altogether. "Talk about princes! I still can't believe Ben Jonson is taking a personal hand in this masque."

"Do not get your hopes too high. I've heard he's

declined a great deal from his glory days twenty years ago. That's the real reason he left England, I suspect, whatever he claims himself about the enmity of Inigo Jones and the earl of Cork."

Anne smiled. "It probably doesn't help that he's bound and determined to base the masque on that crate of stuff he got from Grantville. 'Memorabilia,' he calls it. 'Odds and ends,' is more like it."

"Or 'junk,'" added Olearius, perhaps uncharitably. He went to the door and opened it for her. "And now, my dear, we should go have an early dinner before making our appearance at the rehearsal. Even though"—his tone of voice was now definitely uncharitable—"I will be astonished if the esteemed poet has made much progress by the time we get there."

2

Ben Jonson studied the bizarre object in his right hand, his head propped up by the left. "Perhaps a token of esteem from the tritons . . ." he mused.

Standing behind him where the poet and dramatist couldn't see her, the young countess palatine Elisabeth rolled her eyes. It was obvious that Jonson was bound and determined to copy as much as he could of the masque he'd done thirty years earlier for King James, the famous *Masque of Blackness*. She thought the project was ill-conceived, herself. If for no other reason because the success of *The Masque of Blackness* had been due in no small part to the architectural genius of

Jonson's partner Inigo Jones. His stage settings had been magnificent.

Jonson's *then* partner, alas. The rupture between the two men had been deep; it was now deep and bitter, since Jones had won the favor of Richard Boyle, the earl of Cork. So now Jonson was in self-imposed exile in Amsterdam and the Dutch architects and artisans at his disposal were not really up to the challenge of designing the monumental stage settings he insisted upon.

It would help, of course, if he'd actually finish the blasted thing instead of dithering. There was another rehearsal scheduled for that evening, for which both she and her brother Rupert had donned their costumes. It would probably wind up being a disjointed semi-disaster like the two previous rehearsals.

Rupert was leaning over Jonson's shoulder. He had his chin cupped in his hand in what he presumably hoped would be seen as a gesture of thoughtfulness—but Elisabeth was quite sure her brother just wanted to stroke his beard. Still shy of his sixteenth birthday, Rupert was inordinately proud of his whiskers.

In truth, he had some right to be. He was already six feet tall and was showing that extraordinary musculature that would make him a military legend in another universe. *Prince Rupert of the Rhine*, they'd called him. Rupert had vowed he would not pursue the soldier's career he'd followed in that up-time world. But Elisabeth had noted that her brother maintained a rigorous regimen when it came to his exercises in the *salle d'armes* run by his Dutch swordmaster. Such vows were easy to make; not so easy to keep.

"I think you should rather make it a token of esteem from Oceanus," Rupert said. He pointed to the object in the poet's hand. "You could think of it as a symbol of the engirdling oceans in all their many hues."

Ben Jonson stroked his own beard. "Hm. Interesting idea, I agree."

In Elisabeth's opinion, the idea was idiotic—because *any* attempt to make the Rubik's Cube the center of a masque was idiotic. The ridiculous up-time contrivance was far too small to play that role. They'd do better to use the statue of the elf or even the club. What did Americans call the thing? A "baseball bat," if she remembered correctly.

The name was as idiotic as the Rubik's Cube. There'd been bats in two of the houses she'd lived in during her family's peripatetic existence following the expulsion of her father, the elector of the palatine Frederick V, from the throne he'd briefly held as King of Bohemia. The American club bore no resemblance to the creatures at all.

3

"George Monck's been executed," John Hampden announced, closing the door to the salon behind him. He came over to the big table in the center of the room around which a number of other men were seated and laid a radio message on the surface. "The news just came in. Thomas Fairfax, John Lambert and Thomas Horton were executed along with him. Horton was drawn and quartered first."

"*Bastards*," hissed Arthur Haselrig. "What about Denzil Holles? And Fairfax's son Ferdinando?"

Hampden pulled out a chair. "Still alive, I suppose. For how long remains to be seen." He sat down. "So far, the earl of Manchester is the only one who seems to have wormed his way into Cork's good graces."

"'Wormed' is the right word, too," said young Henry Ireton. "Unfair to worms, I suppose, but since 'swined' or 'toaded' aren't verbs it'll have to do."

There was real anger lurking under the humor. Still only twenty-four years old, Ireton was too young to have known any of the men executed by the earl of Cork. But like all of the men in the room, he'd studied the up-time accounts of the civil war that had begun in England— would have begun, rather, in another England in another universe—in the year 1642.

The history of that conflict weighed heavily on all of them, for all its insubstantial nature. Perhaps on none more than the man sitting at the head of the long table, Thomas Wentworth—who'd stopped calling himself the earl of Strafford because of it.

Wentworth studied young Ireton for a moment. In this world, the man was a lawyer—as he had been in that other. But so far he was only a lawyer, not the accomplished military officer he would become—would have become, had become, could have become—the grammar was maddening—in the up-timers' universe.

Wentworth suppressed a smile. And how must the youngster feel about having been Oliver Cromwell's son-in-law in that world? He'd never even met the Bridget Cromwell he would marry there. It would do him little good to do so in this one anyway, at least for the moment. The girl was still only . . .

Wentworth tried to remember the ages of Cromwell's children. Bridget was ten or eleven years old, he thought. Certainly no more than twelve.

If she was still alive at all. There'd been very little news of Cromwell since the escape from the Tower of London.

The men who'd recently been executed had played prominent roles in that civil war, as had the earl of Manchester. Would have played, it might be better to say. The reason Horton had been drawn and quartered was because, it that other universe, he'd been one of the commissioners of the High Court of Justice in 1649 and among those who'd signed the warrant for the execution of King Charles I of England.

In that universe, Horton had died of natural causes—disease, presumably; the American records were not specific—while serving in Ireland under Cromwell. In this universe, King Charles was still on the throne and his chief minister Richard Boyle, the earl of Cork, had seen fit to cut the matter short—along with the man himself.

In the universe the Americans came from, Horton's heirs had been deprived of their estate during the Restoration in the 1660s. Wentworth didn't doubt for a moment that they'd already been stripped of the estate in this one. Among his other charming characteristics, Richard Boyle was ravenously greedy. By all accounts, the king was mired in melancholia and paid no attention to the affairs of his realm. The earl of Cork had become for all practical purposes the military dictator of England and he saw to it that all property seized from "traitors" wound up either in his own hands or those of his close associates and followers.

"Why execute Monck at all?" asked Henry Vane plaintively. "Or Fairfax, for that matter? Both of them helped the Restoration in the end."

Wentworth exchanged glances with the man sitting at the other end of the table. That was Robert Devereux, the earl of Essex. He and Thomas Wentworth were more-or-less the two recognized leaders of the group. "More or less," because as yet the group itself was only more or less a group. It was still an association of like-minded individuals rather than the formally constituted revolutionary organization that both Wentworth and Devereux were striving to establish.

Robert understood the meaning of that glance. There was a great deal of personal friction between Thomas and Henry Vane, which stemmed from the fact that Vane had discovered in the course of perusing the American history texts that in that other universe he had disliked Wentworth for reasons having to do with the complex politics of the time. The cretin had chosen to adopt the same hostile stance in *this* universe—and never mind that none of the events which produced the hostility had happened in this world or ever would.

But it would be best to leave those embers unstirred. So Robert took it upon himself to answer Vane's question—and did so a lot more diplomatically than Thomas would have himself. It was a cretin's question, after all.

"Boyle's got his own ambitions, Henry, that's why. He doesn't want anyone at the court who could make a claim to the king's confidence, besides himself. Given the king's nature—even on his best days, which these aren't—that's not unlikely. Charles is petulant. Sooner or later, the earl of Cork is bound to annoy him. When that time comes, Boyle doesn't want anyone like Monck or Fairfax around whom the king might decide would make a suitable replacement for him."

Thomas Harrison grunted sarcastically. "Not all that likely, Robert! You're presuming that His Royal Idiocy has actually studied the up-time histories." He gave Wentworth a look that was not entirely friendly. "What actually happened is that he learned of the basic fact that concerned him—'they cut my head off!'—and then left it to Strafford here to learn the details and act accordingly."

Wentworth's jaws tightened, but he made no protest. It would be hard to do so, of course, since Harrison's account was fairly accurate. As for the harshness of the man's attitude . . .

Again, the weight of history. In this world, Harrison had had the good sense to flee England as soon as he heard of Pym's arrest. At the time, he hadn't read any of the up-time texts himself, but he'd sensed what was coming.

There was no guesswork involved any longer. In that other universe—and by now Harrison *had* read the texts—he'd been executed at the Restoration.

"There's no point in digging all that up," Devereux said mildly. "Thomas did as the king bade him do, which is the task of any minister. But he didn't go any farther than that, and he certainly didn't oversee the sort of wholesale slaughter that Boyle's been responsible for."

After a moment, Harrison nodded stiffly. "True enough. If I've caused any offense, Thomas, my apologies."

"None needed." Wentworth smiled ruefully. "It's not as if anything you said isn't true."

John Bradshaw had been silent, up till now. "I want to change the subject," he said. "What are we going to do about this *other* unpleasant news?"

Silence came over the room as the men sitting around the table exchanged glances with each other.

The "other unpleasant news" were the tidings that had arrived just this morning. Karl Ludwig, the oldest surviving son of the elector palatine, had assumed his father's title when Frederick V died less than three years earlier. Along with his mother Elizabeth, who was the daughter of King James and the current English king's older sister, he'd been residing in Brussels for years in what amounted to Spanish captivity. Very pleasant and genteel captivity, to be sure, but captivity nonetheless.

And now, it seemed, the eighteen-year-old Karl Ludwig had converted to Catholicism—taking with that conversion the best option the English exiles had to replace King Charles. No matter how unpopular Charles and his chief minister Richard Boyle might have become, there was no way the English populace would accept a Catholic monarch.

Harrison grunted again. Not sarcastically this time, though. The sound had an almost pleased quality to it.

"I never thought much of Karl Ludwig anyway," he said. "With him sworn over to the damn papists, that puts Rupert next in line—and I'll be the first to say I'd far rather have Rupert on the throne of England."

Wentworth sighed, and ran fingers through his hair. "So would I, Thomas, so would I. But Rupert will refuse if we raise the idea with him."

"Are you certain of that?"

"I'm afraid so. As most of you know, I've become rather close to the boy over the past months. I've never raised the possibility directly, of course—that would have been most inappropriate, with his older brother still in possible line of succession—but I know him well enough to know that he wouldn't accept. He's bound and determined to avoid the same career he had in the other world. He says he intends to become an inventor instead. Or possibly an artist. Or both."

"An inventor!" exclaimed Henry Vane. "That's absurd!"

Wentworth felt obliged to come to Rupert's defense. "Actually, later in his life—after the Restoration, I mean—Rupert became quite an accomplished inventor. And artist as well."

"It's still absurd," insisted Vane. "And he wasn't king in that world, anyway, so I fail to see the problem."

You wouldn't, thought Thomas. But he left it unsaid. Whatever else had or might change, the dictates of diplomacy had not, did not and would not.

Devereux pulled out a timepiece. "We need to go, gentlemen. It's almost five o'clock."

Wentworth rose from the table along with him. So did Hampden.

"Where are you off to now?" asked Bradshaw.

The earl of Essex made a face. "It's another of Jonson's masque rehearsals." His eyes widened. "But it occurs to me that since we'll be wearing masks anyway—

incredibly elaborate ones, to boot—that you could go in my place."

Bradshaw shook his head, smiling. "What? So I could stand around being bored while that decrepit old poet tries to remember what he's about? No, thank you." He waved an airy hand at Devereux, Hampden and Wentworth. "You three splendid—no, resplendent!— fellows are more than enough to attend to the needs of protocol."

"Have fun," said Harrison, chuckling.

Henry Vane looked envious. Certain proof, if any were needed, that the man was a cretin.

4

"Wentworth, Essex and Hampden," said Robert Clifford. He spoke softly, with his head canted slightly forward to bring his mouth closer to the three men listening to him. "Remember. Those are the key targets."

"And if we succeed with all three and have time to spare?" asked Matthew Bromley.

The corner of Clifford's lips twisted in the manner he had when thinking. After a moment he said: "It doesn't really matter that much. Laud, of course. But the reason I didn't place him with the first three is because he never attends these affairs."

While he'd been speaking, Bryan Neville had been keeping an eye on the windows of the large house in whose shrubbery they'd hidden, although nothing beyond shadows could be seen through the curtains. Now, he chuckled slightly. "God forbid the once-and-still-imagines-he-is archbishop of Canterbury should participate in such frivolous pastimes."

Bromley frowned. He was quite devout and disapproved of using the Lord's name in vain. But he made no open protest. The other three men present were not devout at all—their leader Clifford fell just short of being an outright freethinker—and they were quick to ridicule.

"How soon do we move?" asked the fourth man. That was George Wilchon, who'd once been a bookbinder's apprentice in Norwich before his uneven temperament had caused him to be dismissed. A week later he'd stabbed his former master to death in an alley by way of revenge and discovered his current trade.

Clifford glanced at the sky and then at the windows. At Amsterdam's latitude, twilight was a protracted affair. They'd crept into the bushes after sunset but had had to wait a considerable time before it was dark enough for their business. By now, though, night had fallen and since they were just three days past a new moon there wasn't much light in the streets.

All of their targets had arrived and judging from what Clifford could tell the rehearsal had finally gotten underway. He'd wanted to wait for that to begin just as much as he'd wanted to wait for full darkness. The demands of the rehearsal would keep everyone preoccupied while he and his men made their entry into the house.

"No reason to wait any longer," he said. He eased his way out of the shrubbery, heading for the narrow pathway that led around to the back. The house wasn't quite big enough to qualify for the term "mansion" but it came very close. Happily for their project, the kitchen was in an isolated extension of the house and there was a rear service entrance. They should be able to get inside without much in the way of noise or fuss, and they'd only counted two cooks.

The cooks were both men, and would of course be very familiar with knives. But Clifford foresaw no great difficulty. Skill at cutting meat was by no means the same thing as skill at cutting men.

5

"No, no, no!" exclaimed Ben Jonson. The old playwright limped toward the center of the room. "You!" he said, pointing at Rupert. Despite the mask he was wearing, the young prince's height made him quite recognizable. "You're supposed to be still, not capering about! Go sit down until you think you've mastered that meager skill."

Rupert restrained his temper easily enough. He wanted to sit down anyway. Jonson couldn't seem to make up his mind about what he wanted and Rupert's feet were getting sore.

He strode over to the wall where his sister was sitting and flung himself into the chair next to her.

"I was not 'capering about,'" he hissed. "Just . . ."

"Moving a lot," said Elisabeth. Rupert couldn't see her face because, like him, she was wearing a full mask. But he was darkly certain she was smiling.

His sister was smiling, in fact. It was not an expression

of derision, though, but one of sympathy. Elisabeth had had quite enough of Ben Jonson. The famous poet and playwright was irascible, bad-tempered—and worst of all, she didn't think he had all his wits about him any longer. He would yell at someone for not doing something Jonson had forgotten to tell them to do; and then yell at someone else for doing something he *had* told them to do but had since forgotten he'd done so.

She called it "senile" or "being in his dotage." Her instructor Anne Jefferson insisted that such terms were imprecise and unscientific and that Jonson suffered instead from one or another form of dementia brought on by his advanced years. Most likely something called "Alzheimer's disease."

Americans could be a bit tiresome. Had there ever existed a people more prone to making pointless distinctions?

Naturally, they had expressions for that too. *Splitting hairs. Crossing the t's and dotting the i's. Fussing over the fine points.*

"No, no, no!" Jonson yelled again, this time at a woman. Elisabeth wasn't sure because of the mask, but she thought that was Mrs. Hampden. She extended her unspoken sympathies still further with another smile.

6

As Clifford had foreseen, the cooks proved to be no problem. But there was a servant boy they hadn't expected, nine or ten years old and quick on his feet.

Luckily, his shrill peal of alarm was drowned out by a shouting voice coming from the salon and Bromley caught him before he could call out again or flee the kitchen.

His little corpse joined those of the two cooks in the root cellar.

"Quietly now," Clifford said. He entered the dim hallway leading into the rear quarters of the house.

7

As one of the servants guided Anne and Olearius through the house, Anne could hear Jonson's hollering while they were still twenty feet from the door leading to the main salon. That was a solid, heavy door, too.

She sighed with exasperation. "I am really getting sick of that man."

Her husband smiled and drew back one side of his coat. Anne could now see a pistol tucked into his belt. "Have no fear, dearest. Should the old reprobate misbehave again, I shall—what's that charming American phrase?—plug him full of holes. Well. One hole, anyway. It's just a single-shot flintlock."

Anne's eyes widened with alarm. Well. Some alarm. Her husband wasn't a hot-tempered man. "Oh, please! That old lecher? I assure you that I can handle him quite easily myself—as I did when he made his advances, remember? You really didn't need to bring that on his account."

They'd reached the door to the salon and the servant began to draw it open. Adam's smile widened. "I was only joking. I didn't bring the pistol because of Jonson. I just don't trust Amsterdam's streets at night."

They came into the salon. Jonson turned and glared at them. "You're late! And why aren't you wearing your masks?"

8

"*Now*," said Clifford. Neville, the biggest of them, kicked in the door to the salon leading from the back chambers. Clifford piled through, followed by Wilchon and Bromley.

The salon was packed with people. And most of them were wearing masks!

Clifford hadn't expected that. He and Wilchon had learned from casual questioning of one of the servants in a nearby tavern that their targets were among a crowd of people rehearsing a masque. But neither Clifford nor any of his companions had ever observed a masque in person, those being generally entertainments of the upper classes. Without thinking much about it, he'd simply assumed they weren't much different from the plays he'd seen performed.

One man sitting nearby was not wearing a mask and Clifford recognized him from woodcuts he'd been shown. That was the earl of Essex, Robert Devereux, one of their main targets. He aimed his pistol and fired. The bullet struck the earl in the chest. He threw back his arms, the chair tipped over, and he fell to the floor.

There'd be no time to reload and Clifford didn't want to use up his other pistol for such a target. Essex might already be dying anyway. Springing forward, he reached the earl, seized him by the hair and drew him up to a half-sitting position. Cutting his throat took but an instant.

Behind him, he heard his companions firing their pistols. He could only hope they hadn't wasted the shots by firing at random.

Masks!

Adam Olearius was a diplomat, not a soldier. He didn't lack courage but he did lack an experienced combatant's trained reflexes. So he was paralyzed for a couple of seconds before he thought to sweep his wife behind him with his left hand while he drew his pistol with the right.

That delay probably saved his life. The assassins *were* trained and experienced in these matters, so they ignored him. He seemed to pose no threat and they didn't recognize him as one of the men they sought.

Two of the assassins fired at the same man, a tall fellow wearing a rather flamboyant multicolored cloak. He slumped instantly to the floor. The third fired at a man standing perhaps eight feet away. From the long, dark and curly hair spilling out from behind his mask, Adam thought that was probably John Hampden.

The shot missed. Partly missed, rather. The man with the long curly hair cried out and clutched his left shoulder. Blood oozed from between his fingers.

His assailant threw down the pistol, drew another, and took aim again. It was all very quick—but by the time he could fire, a woman had arrived and was trying to pull the wounded man to the ground. The shot struck her instead, right in the middle of her back. She coughed. Blood burst from her mouth and splattered over the mask of the man she'd tried to protect.

That *was* Hampden. Adam recognized the costume of the woman who'd been shot while trying to save him as that of his wife.

Finally, he drew out his pistol. And, in his excitement and nervousness, dropped it onto the floor. But the man who'd shot Mrs. Hampden had ducked when he saw the pistol coming out, stumbled over someone who'd thrown themselves down in fear, and now stumbled onto his knees himself.

Both assassins who'd fired at the cloaked man had drawn new pistols and were advancing on Hampden. There was another assassin rising up behind them, too.

Rupert had no experience at all with this sort of bloody, brutal melee, and he was still only fifteen years old.

On the other hand, he'd been training with weapons for years and he was already immensely strong.

So he rose, turned, seized his chair and hurled it across the room. A great, solid oaken brute of a chair, as you'd expect to find in the salon of such a fine house.

The chair sailed across the room and struck the first of the two men about to shoot Hampden. He was knocked right off his feet and into the arms of his companion— who couldn't stop himself from pulling the trigger of his own pistol.

The bullet cut through the fleshy hip of his dazed partner, was deflected, and flew across the room to strike Rupert's sister Elisabeth in the head.

A glancing shot, luckily, and much of the bullet's force

had already been spent. Still, it was a bloody horrible sight. She clutched her head, blood spurted through her fingers, and she fell out of her chair.

Rupert roared with fury, seized Elisabeth's chair—which had not quite tipped over when the girl spilled out of it—and sent that one hurtling after the other.

This second chair struck the two assassins, who were still tangled together with one of them holding up his partner. Both of them were knocked flat.

There was a third chair nearby. Rupert seized it and smashed it against the wall. A heavy oaken wall, as you'd expect in such a house. The force of the impact was enough to shatter the chair. The prince came away from the wall with a chair leg in each hand.

Dear God, that bastard's strong! Clifford aimed at the tall figure striding toward him and squeezed the—

Damnation! Some old fool stumbled in the way and the bullet took the top of his head off.

No time to reload. Clifford hurled the pistol at his opponent and drew his dirk.

Thomas Wentworth hadn't come armed to the rehearsal. But the man who'd murdered poor Elizabeth Hampden had fallen to the floor and was now trying to rise not more than six feet away. Wentworth balled his fist, strode over, and struck the man behind the ear. Once, again, again, and yet again.

Wentworth was a large man, quite well-built, and he was in a fury. The blows knocked the killer senseless.

• • •

Rupert's training finally took over. He recognized the stance and knife-grip of the man facing him as that of an experienced bladesman. There was a straightforward way to handle such an opponent, when you had a sword—which the prince didn't, but a stout chair leg would substitute quite nicely.

Especially because he had two of them. He hurled the one in his right hand at the assassin's head.

The man ducked, and when he came up with the knife leading the way as it should, Rupert smashed his hand with the oak chair leg. The assassin cried out and clutched the shattered hand with his other. Rupert now smashed both hands.

The training left him. Rupert's opponent was helpless, the prince was very young, and the swine had foully murdered his sister. He drew back the club and brought it down with all the power of an arm that had just turned two oak chairs into splinters.

"Rupert, no!"

That was Wentworth. But he barely heard the voice. The club crushed the assassin's skull like an egg. About the only difference was that a ruptured brain came out instead of a ruptured yolk.

Adam Olearius finally brought up his pistol, ready to fire. But it was all over.

One man was obviously dead, another had been beaten unconscious by Wentworth, and the two whom Rupert had knocked off their feet with the chairs he'd thrown were now being . . .

Olearius winced. Beaten to a pulp, it seemed, by just

about every man in the room and a fair number of the women.

His wife Anne raced over, trying with the instincts of a nurse to halt the carnage.

Being honest, Adam couldn't wish her much luck in the project. It was all he could do not to race over himself and shoot one of the bastards.

Instead, he turned to help Elisabeth Stuart. Anne had glanced at her young protégé before running over to the mob in the center of the salon. With her experienced eye she'd immediately seen that while the girl's head wound was gory it wasn't really dangerous.

Once he reached her, Adam discovered that Elisabeth had come to that realization herself. "Just get me a cloth of some sort," she said, continuing to press her hand onto the wound. Her lips were tight but she seemed otherwise quite composed. "Preferably sterile, although I don't know where you'll find a sterile cloth in this chaos and confusion. Is my brother all right?"

"Well—"

There came a now-familiar roar from the center of the room. The tall figure of Rupert rose up from the mob assailing the two killers. He held one of the men above his head.

Another roar, and the man was sent flying across the room to smash into the wall and slide to the floor, bringing a large portrait of a prosperous burgher down with him.

The boy's strength was really quite astonishing.

"Well. Yes. I'd say he's in good health." After a moment he added: "I'm afraid Ben Jonson was killed, though."

The princess nodded, a bit gingerly. "I'm sorry to hear it."

"Perhaps it's just as well. His reputation won't be ruined now, the way it seemed it might be."

"Yes. And I didn't like him. But I'm still sorry."

For someone born of such royal lineage, Elisabeth Stuart was really quite a nice young woman. So Adam's wife had told him and he saw no reason to disagree.

There came another roar. Adam looked over. Rupert was rising up again, with the other assassin in his hands.

Another wall shook, and another portrait came down.

So was her brother, for that matter. Allowing for the occasional—quite justified, Adam thought—insensate fury.

Give him a few more years, and the prince would be a frightful enemy for those who drew down his ire.

9

"But Hampden himself is all right, yes? That's what matters."

Wentworth tightened his jaws, restraining his temper. Henry Vane could be trying.

To put it mildly. The term "ass" came to mind also. For that matter, so did "asshole."

The look that Thomas Harrison was giving Vane made it obvious that he was entertaining similar thoughts.

"I would strongly urge you not to say that in front of Hampden himself," Harrison said. "John's likely to take his rage out on you. He was close to his wife, you know."

Vane looked vaguely alarmed. But then, Vane often looked vaguely alarmed about many things.

Ireton leaned back in his chair. "It's too bad we couldn't get any useful information from the surviving assassins." He slapped the table with exasperation. "You'd think among the three of them that at least one would know *something*."

"Two of them, it'd be more accurate to say," grunted Bradshaw. "One of the swine the prince used to decorate the wall came out of the experience with his mentis pretty much compost."

Wentworth shrugged. "He probably didn't know any more than his fellows. It's clear enough that the one Rupert killed was the leader of the gang. These are just criminals, when all is said and done. Cut-purses and murderers-for-hire. Boyle hired them, obviously, but he would have worked through intermediaries. I doubt if even the ringleader knew who his ultimate employer was."

"Too bad." Ireton slapped the table again. "If we could just prove . . ."

Wentworth finally managed a smile. The first one, he thought, since those horrid events three days before. "I don't think it matters. The only person whose opinion is truly critical is the prince, and he's sure and certain—as only a teenage boy can be—that the earl of Cork was behind it all. Not to mention—"

Wentworth cleared his throat. This was perhaps a bit embarrassing. "Rupert, ah, also believes that he and his sister were among the assassins' targets. And he is purely furious about the assault on Elisabeth. Which he considers dastardly, unchivalrous, wicked, beyond all forgiveness—his terms, mind you—and for which he holds his uncle ultimately responsible."

Everyone at the table stared at him. Bradshaw cleared his throat. "I think it's almost certain that the assassins had no intention of harming the Stuart children. Probably didn't even know they'd be there."

"Supposition, supposition," stated Wentworth. "Who's to say?"

Ireton grinned at him. "And you're not about to suggest to the prince that his suspicions are unwarranted."

"No, I'm not. I believe Prince Rupert's thoughts are now running down an excellent channel and I see no reason to risk diverting that flow."

There was silence for perhaps a minute. Then Ireton grinned again. "It occurs to me that there never was a King Rupert of England in that up-time universe. Proving once again that predestination is as slippery as an eel."

Henry Vane frowned. He was clearly of the suspicion that theological error lurked somewhere in that statement by Ireton. Thankfully, he was not smart enough to figure out how or why.

10

"It's too bad about Wentworth and Hampden," commiserated Paul Pindar. "Would have been nice to get Laud too."

The earl of Cork shook his head. "The truth is, the scheme worked better than I thought it would. Essex alone is worth the cost."

The man who was England's ruler in fact if not in name rose and went to the window. From his vantage point in the royal palace at Whitehall he had a good view of Westminster as well as the City of London. He clasped his hands behind his back and spent a couple of minutes surveying his domain. The expression on his face was one of satisfaction.

"These sort of assassinations are always a toss of the dice," he said finally. "But even if they only partially succeed—or fail altogether, for that matter—there's no harm in trying."

THE
HONOR HARRINGTON
SERIES

Author's note:

"Fanatic" is a story which was designed and written with a specific purpose in mind. That was to bridge the development of the character of Victor Cachat from his initial appearance in David Weber's Honor Harrington series in my short novel "From the Highlands" to his later appearance in the trio of novels that David and I coauthored later in the series. Those are Crown of Slaves, Torch of Freedom and Cauldron of Ghosts, in all three of which Cachat is a major character.

David and I hadn't written any of those novels yet, but we knew we would be—and soon, in the case of Crown of Slaves. That novel was published in September of 2003, less than half a year after "Fanatic" came out in the anthology titled In the Service of the Sword.

In the first of the Cachat stories, "From the Highlands," he is a young man newly graduated from the Republic of Haven's State Security academy. In "From the Highlands," the reader follows his growing disaffection with Haven's ruling regime, which culminates in an impressive display of young Cachat's potential. Still, he's very young and very inexperienced, and it shows.

The Victor Cachat whom the reader encounters in the three Torch novels, on the other hand, is something very different. He's still young, but he is now an experienced, extraordinarily capable and when need be extraordinarily ruthless secret agent.

How did we get to this man, starting from the wet-behind-the-ears stripling we first encountered in "From the Highlands"? Well, read "Fanatic" and you'll find out. Hopefully, you'll enjoy the story as well, just on its own terms. For what it's worth, it's one of my personal favorites.

FANATIC

1

Citizen Rear Admiral Genevieve Chin stared at the holopic on her desk. Without even realizing it, she was perched on the edge of her chair.

Citizen Commodore Ogilve, slouched in a nearby chair in her office, put her thoughts into words:

"He looks like a real piece of work, doesn't he?"

Glumly, Chin nodded. The holopic on her desk was that of a State Security officer whose face practically shrieked: *fanatic.* The fact that it was the image of a young man did not detract from the impression in the least. Coarse black hair loomed over a wide, shallow brow; the brow, in turn, loomed over eyes as dark as the hair. The eyes themselves were obsidian flakes against an ascetic-pale, hard-jawed, tight-lipped, square-chinned and gaunt-cheeked face. Genevieve had no difficulty at all imagining that face in the gloom of an Inquisition dungeon, tightening the rack still further on a sinner. Or shoving the first torch into the mound of faggots piled under a heretic bound to a stake.

Chin couldn't detect any traces of the leering cruelty that had not been hard to find on the face of the officer's predecessor. But she took no great comfort from the fact. Even assuming she was right, that cold-blooded part of her which had enabled a disgraced admiral to survive for ten years through Haven's Pierre–Saint-Just–Ransom regime would have preferred an outright sadist to a sheer fanatic as the effective new head of State Security in La Martine Sector. One could at least hope that a sadist would be careless or lazy, too often distracted by his vices to pay full attention to his official assignment. Whereas this man ...

"Is he really as young as he looks, Yuri?" she asked quietly.

The third person in the room, who was leaning against the closed door to her office, nodded his head. He was a somewhat plump middle-aged man of average height, with a round and friendly looking face, wearing a StateSec uniform.

"Yup. Just turned twenty-four years old. Three years out of the academy. Unfortunately, he seems to have done splendidly on his first major field assignment and caught Saint-Just's eye. And now, of course ..."

Citizen Commodore Ogilve sighed. "Since all the casualties State Security suffered in Nouveau Paris when McQueen launched her coup attempt—what in *Hell* what was she thinking?—Saint-Just is throwing every young hotshot he's got left into the breaches." He wiped his face with a thin hand. "If we'd had any warning ..."

"And what good would that have done?" demanded Chin. "Sure, we could have seized this sector, and so what? As long as Nouveau Paris stayed under Saint-Just's control, he'd have the whip hand." Chin leaned back in her chair wearily. "God damn Esther McQueen and her ambitions, anyway."

She glanced at her desk display. It was dark, at the moment, but she had no difficulty imagining what it would have shown if she'd slipped it to tactical mode. Two State Security superdreadnoughts keeping orbit close to her own task force circling the planet of La Martine.

Admiral Chin's task force was much bigger in terms of ships, true—fourteen battleships on station, along with an equivalent number of cruisers and half a dozen destroyers. And so what? Chin was fairly confident that under ideal conditions she could have defeated those two monsters—though not without suffering enormous casualties. She had the advantage of handpicked officers and well-trained Navy crews, whereas the officers and crews of the StateSec superdreadnoughts had no real battle experience. They'd been selected for their political reliability, not their fighting skills.

But it was all a moot point. The StateSec warships had their impellers and sidewalls up and she didn't. They'd gotten word of Esther McQueen's failed coup attempt in Nouveau Paris before she had, and had immediately gone to battle stations . . . and stayed there. By the time she'd realized what was happening, it had been too late. Any battle now would be a sheer massacre of her own forces.

It had almost been a massacre anyway, she suspected. McQueen's coup attempt had immediately placed the entire Navy officer corps under suspicion; especially any officers who, like Chin herself, dated back to the old Legislaturalist regime.

But when her own People's Commissioner had been found murdered three days before the news arrived . . . As accidental as it may have been, the timing had been unfortunate—putting it mildly!

Ironically, Genevieve suspected, she owed her life to the Manticorans. If the Star Kingdom's Eighth Fleet hadn't begun their terrifying onslaught on the People's Republic of Haven, State Security probably *would* have decided just to destroy her chunk of the Navy. But . . . Oscar Saint-Just was between a rock and a hard place, and he'd probably decided he simply couldn't afford to lose any part of the Navy that he didn't absolutely have to lose.

That, at least, had been the gist of the message sent ahead to the two StateSec superdreadnoughts by Saint-Just's handpicked hatchet man.

She studied the holopic again. *No further action to be taken against Navy units or personnel until my arrival. Military situation critical.*

And so things had remained for a very tense three weeks, since the news of McQueen's coup attempt had arrived at the distant sector capital of La Martine. The entire Republican Navy in the sector had been under arrest in all but name. *All* of it, for the past week—the superdreadnought captains had demanded the recall of every ship on patrol. Genevieve Chin and her people had been under the equivalent of a prison lockdown, with two ferocious State Security SDs standing guard over them while everyone waited for the young new warden to show up.

"Do you know anything about him, Yuri?"

Yuri Radamacher, the People's Commissioner for Citizen Commodore Jean-Pierre Ogilve, pushed himself away from the door. "Personally, no. But I did find this record chip in Jamka's quarters. It's a personal communiqué from Saint-Just."

Ogilve stiffened in his chair. "You took that? For God's sake, Yuri—"

Radamacher waved him down. "Relax, will you? Now that Jamka's dead, I *am* the highest-ranked StateSec officer in this task force—in the whole sector, as a matter of fact, even if the captains in command of those two SDs aren't paying any attention to my exalted rank. The fact that I searched Jamka's quarters after his body was found won't strike anyone as suspicious. In fact, suspicion would have been aroused if I hadn't."

He pulled a chip from his pocket. "As for this . . ." Shrugging: "I'll have to destroy it, of course. No way to just put it back without leaving too many traces. But I doubt its absence will be noticed, even if Saint-Just thinks to enquire." Radamacher made a face. "Not only was Jamka a slob, but after anyone studies more than ten percent of the chips scattered all over his quarters they'll realize . . ."

He shrugged again. "We all knew he was a vicious pervert. Let Saint-Just's fair-haired boy"—motioning to the holopic with the chip—"wallow in that muck for a bit, and I don't think he'll be worrying about a missing private message from Saint-Just."

Yuri slid the chip into the holoviewer. After a moment, the image of the officer was replaced by another. The

same officer, as it happened. But this was not a formal
pose. What began playing was a recording of an interview
between the officer and Saint-Just himself, which had
apparently been made in Saint-Just's office recently.

"I'll give the kid this much," murmured Radamacher.
"He's StateSec through-and-through, but he doesn't seem
cut from the same cloth as Jamka. Watch."

Fascinated, Admiral Chin leaned forward. The sound
quality in the holoprojection was as good as the images
themselves—not surprising, given that Saint-Just would
have had the very best equipment in his own office.

The first thing that struck Admiral Chin was that the
head of Haven's State Security seemed a smaller man than
she remembered. Genevieve hadn't seen Saint-Just in
person for many years, and then only at a distance at a
large official gathering. On that occasion, Saint-Just had
been positioned behind a podium on an elevated dais, at
quite some distance from Genevieve. He'd looked like a
big man to her, then. Now, seeing him in a holoprojection
sitting behind the desk in his own office, he simply
seemed a small, unprepossessing bureaucrat. If Chin
hadn't known that Oscar Saint-Just was perhaps the most
cold-bloodedly murderous human being in existence, she
would have taken him for a middle-aged clerk.

That accounted for some of it. But Genevieve knew
that, for the most part, the reason Saint-Just seemed much
smaller to her was purely psychological. The last time
she'd seen Saint-Just she'd hated and feared him, and had
been wondering whether she'd still be alive by the end of
the week. She still hated Saint-Just—and still wondered

how much longer she'd be alive—but the passage of years and the slow rebuilding of her own self-confidence as she'd forged La Martine Sector into an asset for the Republic had drained away most of the sheer terror.

The door to Saint-Just's office opened and the same young StateSec officer whose face she'd been staring at earlier was ushered into the office by a secretary. The secretary then closed the door, not entering the room himself.

The young officer glanced at the two guards standing against the far wall behind Saint-Just. The Director of State Security was seated at a desk near the middle of the room, studying a dossier open before him.

Chin was impressed by the officer's glance at the guards. Calmly assessing, it seemed—just long enough to assure himself that the guards were not particularly concerned about him. Their stance was alert, of course. Saint-Just wouldn't have tolerated anything else from his personal bodyguards. But there was nothing visible in that alertness beyond training and habit; none of the subtle signs which would have indicated that a man about to be arrested or secretly murdered had just been ushered into Saint-Just's presence.

Chin knew she couldn't have maintained that much poise herself, in that situation, even with her advantage of many more years of life and experience. The StateSec officer was either blessed by a completely secure conscience, or he was a phenomenally good actor.

The officer marched briskly across the wide expanse of carpet and came to attention in front of the Director's desk. Genevieve noted that he was careful, however, not to get *too* close. The officer was not a particularly big man himself, and as long as he stayed out of arm's reach of Saint-Just, the bodyguards wouldn't get nervous. He would already have been thoroughly checked for weapons. It was quite obvious that neither of the two guards—much less both together—would have any difficulty subduing him if he suddenly went amok and tried to attack the Director. The guards were not precisely giants, but they were very big men. Admiral Chin had no doubt both of them were experts in close-quarter combat, armed or unarmed.

Which the officer standing at attention before the desk didn't seem to be, from what Genevieve could tell. He had a trim and well-built figure, yes; she could detect the signs of a man who exercised regularly. But Genevieve was an accomplished martial artist herself—had been, at least, in her younger days—and she couldn't detect any of the subtle indications of such training in the officer's stance.

Then, noticing something else, she cawed laughter. "They've removed his belt and shoes!"

Radamacher smiled sourly. "After Pierre was killed, I doubt if Saint-Just is going to overlook *any* possible danger." He paused the recording and studied it, then chuckled. "Is there anything sillier-looking than a man trying to stand at attention in his socks? It's a good thing for him the Committee of Public Safety did away with the old Legislaturalist custom of clicking your heels when coming to attention, or that youngster would look like a pure idiot."

But the humor was as sour as the smile. Idiotic or not,

Saint-Just's new version of the Committee of Public Safety had Haven and its Navy by the throat. And young men like the officer standing at attention before him were the fingers of that death grip.

Yuri started up the recording again. For half a minute or so, the three people in the room watched Saint-Just simply ignore the young man standing before him. The Director of State Security—now also Haven's head of state—was perusing the dossier spread out on the desk before him. The personal records of the officer himself, obviously.

Chin took the time to study that young officer. And, again, was impressed. Most young subordinates in that position would not have been able to disguise their anxiety. She knew perfectly well that Saint-Just was dragging out the process simply to reinforce that he was the boss and that his subordinate was completely at his mercy. A word from Saint-Just could destroy a career—or worse.

But from this youngster . . . nothing. Just an impassive face and stance, as if he possessed all the patience in the universe and not a trace of its fears.

Something indefinable in the expression on Saint-Just's face, when he finally raised his eyes from the dossier and studied the officer, let Genevieve know that Saint-Just's petty little attempt at intimidation had fallen flat—and Saint-Just knew it. For the first time, words entered the recording, and Chin leaned forward more closely.

"You're a self-possessed young man, Citizen Lieutenant Cachat," Saint-Just murmured. *"I approve of that—as long as you don't let it get out of hand."*

Cachat simply gave Saint-Just a brisk little nod of the head.

Saint-Just pushed the dossier aside a few inches. "I've now studied this report on the Manpower affair which you brought back from Terra. I've studied it three times over, in fact. And I will tell you that I've never seen such a cocked-up mess in my life."

Saint-Just's right hand reached out and fingered the pages of the report. "One of the pages in this dossier consists of your own record. Terra was your first major assignment, true. But you graduated almost at the top of your class in the academy—third, to be precise—so let's hope you can match the promise."

"Oh, hell," muttered Ogilve.

"'Oh, hell' is right." Radamacher grimaced. "The top five positions in any graduating class at the StateSec academy require a pure-perfect rating of political rectitude from every single one of your instructors. I graduated third from the bottom, myself."

He jabbed a finger at the recording, which he'd paused again. "And take a look at the kid's face. First time he's had any expression at all. This'll be news to him, you know. He'd had no idea where he stood at the academy, since it's the academy's policy not to let any of the cadets know how they're doing in the eyes of their superiors. I only found out my own standing years later, and then only because I was called on the carpet for 'slackness' and it was thrown in my face. A charge which, you can bet the bank, nobody's ever thrown at *this* young eager-beaver. Look at him! His eyes are practically gleaming."

Chin wasn't sure. There was something a bit odd to her in Cachat's expression. A gleam in his eyes, perhaps. But there was something... cold about it. As if Cachat was taking pleasure in knowledge for reasons other than the obvious.

She shook the thought away. It was ridiculous, really, to think you could make that much out of a hologram recording, even one of the finest quality.

"Start it up again," she commanded.

Saint-Just was still speaking. "So now you tell me the truth, young Victor Cachat."

Cachat glanced down at the dossier. "I haven't seen Citizen Major Gironde's report, Citizen Chairman. But, at a guess, I'd say he was concerned with minimizing the damage to Durkheim's reputation."

Saint-Just's snort was a mild thing, quite in keeping with his mild-mannered appearance.

"No kidding. If I took this report at face value, I'd have to think that Raphael Durkheim engineered a brilliant intelligence coup on Terra—in which, sadly, he lost his own life due to an excess of physical courage."

Again, that little snort. More like a sniff, really. "As it happens, however, I was personally quite familiar with Durkheim. And I can assure you that the man was neither brilliant nor possessed of an ounce of courage more than the minimum needed for his job." His voice grew a bit harsh. "So now you tell me what really happened."

"What really happened was that Durkheim tried to put together a scheme that was too clever by half, it all came apart at the seams, and the rest of us—Major Gironde and

me, mostly—had to keep it from blowing up in our faces."
He stood a bit more rigidly. *"In which, if you'll permit me
to say so, I think we did a pretty good job."*

"'Permit me to say so,'" mimicked Saint-Just. *But there
was no great sarcasm in his tone of voice.* "Youngster, I'll
permit any of my officers to speak the truth, provided they
do so in the service of the state." *He moved the dossier a
few inches farther away from him.* "Which I'd have to say,
in this case, you probably are. I assume you and Gironde
saw to it that Durkheim went under the knife himself?"

"Yes, Citizen Chairman, we did. Somebody in charge
had to take the fall—and be dead in the doing—or we
couldn't have buried the questions."

Saint-Just stared at him. "And who—I want a name—
did the actual cutting?"

Cachat didn't hesitate. "I did, Citizen Chairman. I shot
Durkheim myself, with one of the guns we recovered from
the Manpower assassination team. Then put the body in
with the rest of the casualties."

Again, Radamacher paused the recording. "Can you
believe the nerve of this kid? He just admitted—didn't
pause a second—to murdering his own superior officer.
Right in front of the Director! And—look at him! Standing
there as relaxed as can be, without a care in the world!"

Genevieve didn't quite agree with Yuri's assessment.
The image of Cachat didn't looked exactly "relaxed" to
her. Just . . . firm and certain in the knowledge of his own
Truth and Righteousness. She couldn't keep her
shoulders from shuddering a little. Just so might a zealous
inquisitor face the Inquisition himself, serene in the

certainty of his own assured salvation. The fanatic's mindset: *Kill them all and let God sort them out—I've got no worries where I stand with the Lord.*

Radamacher resumed the playback.

The room was silent for perhaps twenty seconds, with Saint-Just continuing to stare at the young officer standing at attention before him—and the guards with their hands on the butts of their sidearms.

Then, abruptly, Saint-Just issued a dry chuckle. "Remind me to congratulate the head of the academy for his perspicacity. Very good, Citizen Captain Cachat."

The relaxation in the room was almost palpable. The guards' hands slid away from the gunbutts, Saint-Just eased back in his chair—and even Cachat allowed his rigid stance to lessen a bit.

Saint-Just's fingers did a little drum-dance on the cover of the dossier. Then, firmly, he pushed the entire dossier to the side of the desk.

"We'll put the whole thing aside, then. It all turned out well, obviously. Amazingly well, in fact, for an operation you had to put together on the fly. As for Durkheim, I'm not going to lose any sleep over an officer who gets himself killed from an excess of ambition and stupidity. Certainly not when we're in a political crisis like this one. And now, Citizen Captain Cachat—yes, that's a promotion—I've got a new assignment for you."

To Chin's surprise, the recording ended abruptly. She cocked an eyebrow at Radamacher, who shrugged. "That's all there was. It you want my guess, I suspect the rest of it was none too complimentary to Jamka and Saint-Just saw no reason to let the bastard see the nuts and bolts of whatever he discussed with Cachat thereafter."

He popped the chip out of the holoviewer and put it back in his pocket. "Cachat's official new title may not have registered on you properly. *Special Investigator for the Director* is not a title used too often in State Security. And it's not one any StateSec officer wants to hear coming his way, let me tell you. This recording must have been made before Nouveau Paris got the news that Jamka had been murdered. I don't think Saint-Just was any too pleased with Jamka, and this was his way of letting Jamka know his ass was on the line."

"And about time!" snarled Ogilve. "I don't mind so much having a People's Commissioner looking over my shoulder—no offense, Yuri—" For a moment, he and Radamacher exchanged grins. "—but having a swine like Jamka around is something else entirely."

He gave Admiral Chin a look of sympathy. As the top-ranked naval officer in La Martine Sector, Genevieve had been saddled with Jamka as her People's Commissioner.

She shrugged. "To be honest, I didn't mind it all that much. The pig was usually more interested in his own—ah, hobbies—than he was in doing his job. And since he kept his vices away from me personally, I could pretty much just ignore him and go about my business."

She went back to studying the holoviewer gloomily. The original image of StateSec Citizen Captain Cachat was back. "This guy, on the other hand . . ." She sighed and slumped back in her chair. "Give me a lazy, distracted and incompetent commissioner any day of the week. Even a vicious brute." With an apologetic glance at Radamacher: "Or one like you, that the Navy can work with."

Her eyes moved back to Cachat's image. "But there's nothing worse I can think of than a young, competent, energetic, duty-driven . . . ah, what's the word?"

Radamacher provided it. "Fanatic."

2

Two days later, Victor Cachat arrived at La Martine. Eight hours after his arrival, Chin and Ogilve and Radamacher were ushered into his presence. The Special Investigator for the Director had set up his headquarters in one of the compartments normally set aside for a staff officer on a superdreadnought.

A part of Citizen Commodore Jean-Pierre Ogilve's mind noticed the austerity of the cabin. There was a regulation bed, a regulation desk and chair, and a regulation footlocker. Other than that, the compartment was bare except for a couch and two armchairs—both of which were utilitarian and had obviously been hauled out of storage from wherever the previous occupant had put them in favor of his or her own personalized furniture. *Official Staff Officer Compartment Accouterments, Grade Cheap, Type Mediocre, Quality Uncomfortable, As Per Regulations.*

The bulkheads showed faint traces where the previous occupant had apparently hung some personal pictures. Those were now gone also, replaced by nothing more than the official seal of State Security hanging over the bed and, positioned right behind the desk, two portraits. One was a holopic of Rob Pierre, draped in black with a bronze inscription below it reading *Never Forget*. The other was a holopic of Saint-Just. The two stern-faced images loomed over the shoulders of the young StateSec officer seated at the desk—not that he needed them in the least to project an image of severity and right-thinking.

Ogilve didn't spend much time contemplating the surroundings, however. Nor did he give more than a glance at the other occupants of the now-crowded compartment, who were seated on the couch and armchairs or standing against a far bulkhead. All of them were State Security officers assigned to the StateSec superdreadnoughts, most of whom he barely knew. People who—like the former boss of StateSec in the sector, Jamka—preferred the relative luxury and comfort of staff positions on the huge SDs to the more austere lifestyles of StateSec officers assigned to the smaller ships of the naval task force stationed in La Martine.

The young man sitting behind the desk was quite enough to keep his attention concentrated, thank you, especially after he spoke his first words.

There was this much to be said for Cachat—as least he didn't waste everybody's time playing petty little dominance games pretending to be busy with something else. There was no open dossier before him when they were ushered into the compartment. There were no antique paper dossiers in evidence anywhere, as a matter of fact. The desk was bare other than the computer perched on the corner, whose display was blank at the moment.

As Chin and Ogilve and Radamacher came forward,

Special Investigator Cachat's eyes swiveled to Radamacher.

"You're Citizen People's Commissioner Yuri Radamacher, yes? Attached to Citizen Commodore Ogilve."

The voice was hard and clipped. Otherwise it might have been a pleasant young man's tenor.

Yuri nodded. "Yes, Citizen Special Investigator."

"You're under arrest. Report yourself to one of the State Security guards outside and you will be ushered to new quarters aboard this superdreadnought. I will attend to you later."

Radamacher stiffened. So did Admiral Chin and Ogilve himself.

"May I know the reason?" asked Yuri, through tight lips.

"It should be obvious. Suspicion of murder. You were second-in-command to People's Commissioner Robert Jamka. As such, you stood to gain personally by his death, since under normal circumstances you would have— might have, I should say—been promoted to his place."

Ogilve was having a hard time thinking straight. The accusation was so preposterous—

Yuri said as much. "That's preposterous!"

The Special Investigator's shoulders twitched slightly. A shrug, perhaps. Ogilve got the feeling that everything this man did would be under tight control.

"No, it is not preposterous, People's Commissioner Radamacher. It is unlikely, yes. But I am not concerned at the moment with probabilities." Again, that minimal shrug. "Don't take it personally. I am having anyone arrested immediately who might have any personal motive for murdering Citizen Commissioner Jamka."

The hard dark eyes moved to Admiral Chin; then, to Ogilve himself. "That way I can quarantine the possibly personal aspect of the crime in order to concentrate my attention on what is important—the possible political implications of it."

Yuri started to say something else but Cachat cut him off without even looking at him. "There will be no discussion of my action, Citizen Commissioner. The only thing I want from you at the moment is your proposal for who should replace you. I will, for the moment, assume Citizen Commissioner Jamka's responsibilities for overseeing Citizen Admiral Chin, until a permanent replacement is sent from Nouveau Paris. But I will need someone to replace you as Commodore Ogilve's Citizen Commissioner."

Silence. The dark eyes flicked back to Yuri.

"*Now*, Citizen Commissioner Radamacher. Name your replacement."

Yuri hesitated. Then: "I'd recommend State Security Captain Sharon Justice, Special Investigator. She's—"

"A moment, please." The loose fists opened and Cachat worked quickly at the console. Within seconds, an information screen came up. Ogilve couldn't be certain, from the angle he was looking at it, but he thought it consisted of personnel records.

Cachat studied the screen for a moment. "She's attached to PNS *Veracity*, one of the battleships in Squadron Beta. A good service record here, according to this. Excellent, in fact."

"Yes, Special Investigator. Sharon—Citizen Captain Justice—is easily my most capable subordinate and she's—"

The hard, clipped voice cut him off again. "She's also under arrest. I will notify her as soon as this meeting is over and order her to report herself to this ship at once."

Yuri ogled him. Jean-Pierre was pretty sure his own eyes were just as round with disbelief.

Genevieve's eyes, on the other hand, were very narrow. Some of that was her pronounced epicanthic fold, but Ogilve knew her well enough to know that most of it was anger.

"For what possible reason?" she demanded.

Cachat's eyes moved to her. There was still no expression on his face beyond a sort of detached severity.

"It should be obvious, Citizen Admiral. People's Commissioner Radamacher may be involved in a plot against the state. The murder of his immediate superior Robert Jamka suggests that as a possibility. If so, under the circumstances, he would naturally name a trusted member of his cabal to replace him."

"That's insane!"

"Treason against the state is a form of insanity, yes. Such is my private opinion, at least, although it certainly wouldn't serve as a defense before a People's Court."

Genevieve, normally a model of self-composure, was almost hissing. "I meant the *accusation* was insane!"

"Is it?" Cachat shrugged. The gesture, this time, was not so minimal. And whether Cachat intended it or not, the easy heaving of the shoulders emphasized just how square and muscular those shoulders were. Much more so than Ogilve would have guessed from the holopic he'd seen a few days earlier. Ogilve was quite sure the man was a fanatic about physical exercise, too. Cachat's frame was naturally that of a rather slimly built man, and the muscle he had added was not massive so much as wiry. But the force of his personality was driving home to the commodore just how ruthlessly this young man would tackle any project—including his own physical transformation.

Cachat continued. "I can tell you that I spent most of my time on my voyage here studying the records on La Martine, Citizen Admiral Chin. And one thing that is blindingly obvious is that the proper distance between State Security and the Navy has badly eroded in this sector. As is further evident by your own anger at my actions. Why should a Navy admiral care what dispositions State Security makes of its personnel?"

Chin said nothing for a moment. Then her eyes became sheer slits and Ogilve held his breath. He almost shouted at her. *For God's sake, Genevieve—shut up! This maniac would arrest a cat for yawning!*

Too late. Genevieve Chin didn't often lose her temper. Nor was it volcanic when she did. But the low, snarling words which came out now contained all of the biting sarcasm of which she was capable.

"You arrogant jackass. Leave it to a desk man to think that in combat you can keep all the rules and regulations in tidy order. Let me explain to you, snotnose, that when you put people together in hard circumstances—for *years* we've been out here on our own, damn you, and done one hell of a good job—"

The State Security officers enjoying the privilege of being seated in the Special Investigator's presence began spluttering outrage. Two of the StateSec officers standing against the wall stepped forward, as if to seize Chin. The admiral herself, despite her age, slid easily into a martial artist's semi-crouch.

It's all going to blow! Ogilve thought frantically, trying to find some way to—

Wham!

He jumped. So did everyone in the room. The palm of Cachat's hand, slamming the desk, had sounded like a small explosion. Jean-Pierre Ogilve studied the Special Investigator's hand. It was not particularly large. But, like the shoulders, it was sinewy and square and looked . . . very, very hard.

For the first time, also, there was an actual expression on Cachat's face. A tight-eyed, tight-jawed, glare of cold fury. But, oddly enough, it was not aimed at Admiral Chin but at the two StateSec officers stepping forward.

"Were you given any instructions?" Cachat demanded harshly.

The two officers froze in mid-step.

"Were you?"

Hastily, they shook their heads. Then, just as hastily, they stepped back and resumed their position against the wall, now standing at rigid attention.

Cachat's hard eyes moved to the StateSec officers seated on the couch and two armchairs.

"And *you.* In case you have difficulty with simple geometry, it should be obvious that the proper relations between StateSec and Navy could not have collapsed in this sector without the participation of *both* parties involved."

One of the two StateSec officers granted an armchair in what Ogilve was coming to think of as *The Fanatic's Presence* began to protest. Jean-Pierre knew her name—Citizen Captain Jillian Gallanti, the senior of the two captains in command of the superdreadnoughts *Hector Van Dragen* and *Joseph Tilden*—but nothing else about her.

Cachat gave her as short a shrift as he was giving everyone else.

"Silence. Whether or not you can handle geometry, your grasp of simple arithmetic leaves much to be desired. Since when do two SDs need to keep their impellers up to handle a task force of battleships and cruisers? Leaving aside the useless wear and tear on the people's equipment"—the words somehow came out in capital letters, People's Equipment—"you've also kept the People's Navy paralyzed for weeks. *Weeks,* Citizen Captain Gallanti—thereby giving the Manticoran elitists free rein to wreak havoc on the commerce in this sector. All this, mind you, in the midst of the Republic's most desperate hour, when the blueblood Earl of White Haven and his Cossacks are ravening at our door."

Cachat's eyes narrowed a bit. "Whether your actions are the product of incompetence, cowardice—or something darker—remains to be determined."

Gallanti shrunk down in her chair like a mouse under a cat's regard. All the StateSec officers in the compartment now looked like furtive mice. Their eyes moving, if nothing else; desperately trying to avoid the cat's notice.

Cachat studied them for a moment, like a cat selecting

its lunch. "I can assure all of you that Citizen Chairman Saint-Just is no more pleased with the state of StateSec-Navy relations in this sector than I am. And I can also assure you that the man who created our organization understands better than anyone that it is ultimately *State Security* which is responsible for maintaining those proper relations."

After a moment, he looked back at Yuri Radamacher. "Name another replacement."

Yuri's lips twisted slightly. "Since Citizen Captain Justice didn't suit you, I'd recommend Citizen Captain James Keppler."

Cachat's fingers worked at the keyboard again. When the appropriate screen came up, he spent perhaps two minutes studying the information. Then:

"I will warn you only once, Citizen Commissioner Radamacher. Trifle with me again and I will have you shipped back immediately to Nouveau Paris and let you face the investigation in the Institute instead."

Mention of the Institute brought a chill to the compartment. Before the Harris assassination, the Institute had been the headquarters of the Mental Hygiene Police, and its reputation had become only more sinister since the change in management.

Cachat allowed the chill to settle in before continuing.

He pointed a finger at the screen. "Citizen Captain Keppler is an obvious incompetent. It's a mystery to me why he wasn't relieved of his duties months ago."

Like the admiral, Yuri seemed to have decided that he was damned anyway. "That's because he was one of Jamka's toadies," he snarled.

"I'll have Keppler assigned to escort my first set of dispatches to Nouveau Paris. Presumably the man can handle a briefcase shackled to his wrist. Which means I still want your recommendation for a replacement, Citizen Commissioner Radamacher. Your opinions on any other subject are not required at this time."

"What's the use? Whoever I recommend—"

"A *name*, Citizen Commissioner."

Yuri's shoulders slumped. "Fine. If you won't trust Captain Justice, the next best would be Citizen Commander Howard Wilkins."

A couple of minutes passed while the Special Investigator brought up another screen and studied it.

"Give me your assessment," he commanded.

By now, it was clear to Ogilve that Cachat had hammered Yuri into . . . not submission, exactly, so much as simple resignation. "Take my word for it or don't. Howard's a hard-working and conscientious officer. Quite a capable one, too, if you overlook his occasional fussiness and his tendency to get obsessed with charts and records."

The last was said with another little twist of the lips. Not sarcastic, this time—or, at least, with the sarcasm aimed elsewhere.

Cachat didn't miss it. "If that jibe is aimed at me, Citizen Commissioner, I am indifferent. Charts and records are not infallible, but they are nevertheless useful. Very well. I can see nothing in Citizen Captain Wilkins' record to disqualify him. Your recommendation is accepted. Now report yourself under arrest."

After Yuri was gone, Cachat turned to Genevieve. "I'll overlook your personal outburst, Citizen Admiral Chin.

Frankly, I am indifferent to the opinion anyone has of me other than the people of the Republic"—again, it came out in capital letters: The People Of The Republic—"and their authorized leaders."

Cachat gestured to the screen. "I spent a portion of my time on the voyage here studying your own records, and those of La Martine since you assumed command of naval forces here six years ago. It's an impressive record. You've succeeded in suppressing all piracy in the sector and even managed to keep Manticoran commerce raiding severely under check. In addition, the civilian authorities in the sector have nothing but praise for the way you've coordinated with them smoothly. Over the past six years, La Martine Sector has become one of the most important economic strongholds for the Republic—and the civilian authorities unanimously credit you for a large part of that accomplishment."

The Special Investigator glanced at Jean-Pierre. "Citizen Commodore Ogilve also seems to have excelled in his duties. I gather he's the one you normally assign to leading the actual patrols."

The sudden switch to praise startled Ogilve. It was all the more disconcerting because the words were spoken in exactly the same cold tone of voice. Not even that, Jean-Pierre realized. It wasn't cold so much as emotionless. Cachat just seemed to be one of those incredibly rare people who really *were* indifferent to anything beyond their duties.

From the expression on her face, he thought Genevieve was just as confused as he was.

"Well. I'm glad to hear it, of course, but . . ." Her face

settled stonily. "I assume this is a preface to questioning my loyalty."

"Do you react emotionally to *everything*, Citizen Admiral? I find that peculiar in an officer as senior as yourself." Cachat planted his hands on the desk, the fingers spread. Somehow, the young man managed to project the calm assurance of age over an admiral with three or four times his lifespan. "The fact that you were an admiral under the Legislaturalist regime naturally brought you under suspicion. How could it be otherwise? However, careful investigation concluded that you had been made one of the scapegoats for the Legislaturalist disaster at Hancock, whereupon your name was cleared and you were assigned to a responsible new post. Since then, no suspicion has been cast upon you."

Seemingly possessed of a lemming instinct, Genevieve wouldn't let it go. "So what? After McQueen's madness—not to mention Jamka found murdered—"

"*Enough.*" Cachat's fingers lifted from the desk, though the heels of his palms remained firmly planted. The gesture was the equivalent of a less emotionally controlled man throwing out his arms in frustration.

"Enough," he repeated. "You simply can't be that stupid, Citizen Admiral. McQueen's treachery makes it all the more imperative that the People's Republic finds naval officers it can trust. Do I need to remind you that Citizen Chairman Saint-Just saw fit to call Citizen Admiral Theismann to the capital in order to assume overall command of the Navy?"

The mention of Thomas Theismann settled Ogilve's nerves a bit. Jean-Pierre had never met the man, but

like all long-serving officers in the Navy he knew of
Theismann's reputation. Apolitical, supremely competent
as a military leader—and with none of Esther McQueen's
personal ambitiousness. Theismann's new position as
head of the Navy emphasized a simple fact of life: no
matter how suspicious and ruthless State Security might
be, they *had* to rely on the Navy in the end. No one else
had a chance of fending off the advancing forces of the
Star Kingdom. The armed forces directly under StateSec
control were enough to maintain the regime in power
against internal opposition. But White Haven and his
Eighth Fleet would go through them like a knife through
butter—and Oscar Saint-Just knew that just as well as
anyone.

Genevieve seemed to be settling down now. To
Ogilve's relief, she even issued an apology to Cachat.

"Sorry for getting personal, Citizen Special
Investigator." The apology was half-mumbled, but Cachat
seemed willing enough to accept it and let the whole
matter pass.

"Good," he stated. "As for the matter of Jamka's murder,
my personal belief is that the affair will prove in the end to
be nothing more than a sordid private matter. But my
responsibilities require me to prioritize any possible
political implications. It was for that reason that I had
Citizen Commissioner Radamacher and Citizen Captain
Justice placed under arrest. Just as it will be for that reason
that I am going to carry through a systematic reshuffling of
all StateSec assignments here in La Martine Sector."

The StateSec officers in the room stiffened a bit,
hearing that last sentence. Cachat seemed not to notice,

although Jean-Pierre spotted what might have been a slight tightening of the Special Investigator's lips.

"Indeed so," Cachat added forcefully. "Running parallel to an overly close relationship between StateSec and the Navy here, there's also been altogether too much of a separation of responsibilities within State Security itself. Very unhealthy. It reminds me of the caste preoccupations of the Legislaturalists. Some are always assigned comfortable positions here on the capital ships in orbit at La Martine"—his eyes glanced about the compartment, as if scrutinizing the little luxuries which he had ordered removed—"while others are always assigned to long and difficult patrols on smaller ships."

His eyes stopped ranging the bulkheads and settled on the StateSec officers. "That practice now comes to an end."

Jean-Pierre Ogilve had occasionally wondered what Moses had sounded like, returning from the mountain with his stone tablets. Now he knew. Ogilve had to stifle a smile. The expressions on the faces of the superdreadnoughts' officers were priceless. Just so, he was certain, had the idol-worshippers prancing around the Golden Calf welcomed the prophet down from the mountain.

"Comes—to—an—end." Cachat repeated the words, seeming to savor each and every one of them.

3

Ironically, the cabin which Yuri Radamacher was taken to by the guards after he left Cachat's presence was larger

and less austere than his own aboard the commodore's
flagship. That was always one of the advantages to serving
aboard an SD, where living space was far more ample.
This didn't quite qualify as a "stateroom"—at a guess,
some nameless StateSec lieutenant had been ousted to
make room for him—but it was still a more spacious cabin
than the one Yuri had occupied aboard Ogilve's PNS
Chartres.

Still and all, it was only a ship cabin. After the guards
left—locking the door behind them, needless to say—it
didn't take Yuri more than five minutes to examine it
completely. And most of that time was pure dithering; the
psychological self-protection of a man trying to keep the
little shrieks of terror in the back of his mind from
overwhelming him.

Soon enough, however, he could dither no more. So,
not having any idea what the future held in store for him,
Yuri sagged into the compartment's one small armchair
and tried to examine his prospects as objectively as
possible.

The prospects were . . . not good. They rarely were, for
a StateSec officer placed under arrest by StateSec itself.
Even the fig leaf of a trial before a People's Court would
be dispensed with. State Security kept its dirty linen
secret. Summary investigation. Summary trial. Often
enough, summary execution.

On the plus side, while he and Admiral Chin and
Commodore Ogilve had become a very close team over
the past few years—exactly the sort of thing State Security
did *not* like to see happening between naval officers and
the StateSec political commissioners assigned to oversee

them—they had always been careful to maintain the formalities in public.

Also on the plus side, while they had received vague feelers from Admiral Esther McQueen, they had been careful to keep their distance. In truth, they never *had* belonged to McQueen's conspiracy.

On the other hand . . .

On the minus side, there wasn't much doubt which way the admiral and Jean-Pierre and Yuri would have swung, in the event that McQueen had succeeded in her scheme. None of them particularly trusted McQueen. But when the alternative was Oscar Saint-Just, the old saw "better the devil you know than the devil you don't" just didn't hold any water. *Anybody* would be better than Saint-Just.

He tried to rally the plus side again. It was also true, after all, that they had never responded to McQueen's feelers with anything that could by any reasonable stretch of the term be characterized as "plotting."

Or so, at least, Yuri tried to tell himself. The problem was that he'd been an officer in StateSec for years. So he knew full well that Saint-Just's definition of "reasonable characterization" was . . . elastic at best. The fact was that there *had* been some informal communications between McQueen and Admiral Chin over the past year or so, which Ogilve and Radamacher had been privy to. And if the messages sent back and forth had been vague in the extreme, the simple fact of their existence alone would be enough to damn them if State Security found out.

If they found out. Yuri tried to find some comfort in the very good possibility that they wouldn't. The communications had always been verbal, of course, transmitted by one of McQueen's couriers. And always the same one—a woman named Jessica Hackett, who had been one of the officers on McQueen's staff. True, StateSec was superb at forcing information out of its prisoners. But there was at least a fifty/fifty chance that Hackett had been one of the many officers on McQueen's staff who had died when Saint-Just destroyed McQueen's command post with a hidden nuclear device. Not even a State Security interrogator could squeeze information out of radioactive debris.

Still, that was small comfort. Yuri knew perfectly well that StateSec would be on a rampage after McQueen's coup attempt. Heads were going to fall, right and left, and lots of them. The only reason Saint-Just had been relatively restrained thus far was simply because the critical state of the war with the Star Kingdom made it necessary for him to keep the disruption of the Navy to a minimum. But, as with everything else, Oscar Saint-Just's definition of "relatively restrained" was what you'd expect to find in a psychopath's dictionary.

Yuri sighed, wondering for the millionth time how the revolution had gone so completely sour. As a longtime oppositionist to the Legislaturalist regime—which had landed him for three years in an Internal Security prison, from which he'd only been freed by Rob Pierre's overthrow of the government—he'd greeted the new regime with enthusiasm.

Enough enthusiasm, even, to have volunteered for State Security. He chuckled drily, remembering the difficulty with which an inveterate dissident in his forties had struggled through the newly established StateSec academy, surrounded by other cadets most of whom were fiery young zealots like Victor Cachat.

Victor Cachat. What a piece of work. Radamacher tried to imagine how any man that young could be *that* self-assured, *that* confident in his own righteousness. So much so that in less than a day Cachat had succeeded in intimidating the naval officers of an entire task force and the officers of two StateSec superdreadnoughts.

Had Yuri himself ever been like that? He didn't think so, even in his rebellious youth. But he really couldn't remember anymore. The long years which had followed Pierre's coup d'état, as he slowly came to understand the horror and brutality lurking under the new regime's promise, had leached most of his idealism away. For a long time now, Yuri had simply been trying to survive— that, and, as much as possible, bury himself in the challenges posed by his assignment in La Martine Sector. Other, more ambitious StateSec officers might have been frustrated by being posted for so long in what was a political backwater, from the standpoint of career advancement. But Yuri had found La Martine a refuge, especially as he came to realize that the two naval officers he worked most closely with were kindred spirits. And, slowly, La Martine began to attract and keep other StateSec officers of his temperament.

They *had* done a good job in La Martine, damnation. And Yuri had found satisfaction in the doing. It had been one way—perhaps the only way—he could salvage what was left of his youthful spirit. Whether the Committee of Public Safety appreciated it or not, he and Chin and Ogilve had turned La Martine into a source of strength for the Republic. Despite its remote location, for the past several years La Martine had been one of the half-dozen most economically productive sectors for the People's Republic of Haven.

He wiped his face. *And so what?* Radamacher knew full well that Saint-Just and his ilk considered competence a feather, measured against the stone of political reliability.

Victor Cachat. It would be his decision, now. The powers of a StateSec Special Investigator, in a distant provincial sector like La Martine, were well-nigh limitless in practice. The only person who could have served as a check against Cachat would have been Robert Jamka, the senior People's Commissioner in the sector.

But Jamka was dead, and Radamacher was fairly certain that Saint-Just would be in no hurry to name a replacement for him. La Martine was not high on Saint-Just's priority list, being so far away from the war front. So long as Saint-Just was satisfied that Cachat was conducting the investigation with sufficient zeal and rigor, he'd let the young maniac have his way.

There was something ludicrous anyway about the idea of Robert Jamka serving as a "check" to anyone. Jamka had been a sadist and a sexual pervert. As well ask Beelzebub to rein in Belial.

And so the day wore on, as Yuri Radamacher sank deeper and deeper into despondency. By the time he finally dragged himself to his bed and fell asleep, the only thing he was wondering any longer was whether Cachat would offer him the honorable alternative of suicide to execution.

He wouldn't, of course. That had been the tradition of the Legislaturalist regime's Internal Security. Part of the "elitist privilege" which StateSec and its minions were determined to root out. None more so than men like Victor Cachat. Cachat's diction couldn't be faulted, but Yuri had had no difficulty detecting the traces of a Dolist accent in his speech. A man from Havenite society's lowest layers, now risen to power, filled with slum bitterness and rancor.

4

He was roused by Cachat himself, some hours later. The Special Investigator came into the cabin in the middle of the night, accompanied by a guard, and shook Radamacher out of his sleep.

"Get up," he commanded. "Take a quick shower, if need be. We have things to discuss."

The tone of voice was cold, the words curt; so much Yuri took for granted. But he was well nigh astonished by Cachat's offer to allow him time to shower. And he found himself wondering, as he did so, why Cachat was accompanied by a Marine guard instead of one from State Security.

For that matter, where had Cachat even *found* a Marine on a StateSec SD? Except for the rare instances when suppressing a widespread rebellion was required, State Security normally provided its own contingent of ground troops for duty aboard its ships. Saint-Just didn't trust the Marines any more than he did the Navy, and he wasn't about to allow large bodies of men armed and trained in the use of hand weapons aboard his precious StateSec superdreadnoughts.

He found out as soon as he stepped out of the shower stall, his hair still damp, and quickly got dressed.

Cachat was now sitting in Yuri's armchair. A pile of record chips was spread out on the small table next to him. Not official chips, but the kind used for personal records.

"Were you aware of Jamka's perversions?" demanded Cachat. His hand gestured toward the chips. "I spent two of the most unpleasant hours of my life examining these."

Yuri hesitated. Cachat's tone of voice was always cold, but now it was positively icy. As if the man was trying to restrain a boiling fury by layering it with an official glacier. Instinctively, Yuri understood he was standing on the edge of a crevasse. One false step . . .

"Of course," he said abruptly. "Everybody was."

"Why was it not reported to headquarters on Nouveau Paris?"

Can he be that much of a babe in the woods?

Something of his puzzlement must have shown. For only the second time since he'd met Cachat, the young man's face was filled with anger.

"Don't bother using the excuse of Tresca, damnation. I'm well aware that sadists and perverts have been tolerated—whether I approve of it or not, and I don't— on prison detail. But this is a task force of the People's Republic! Officially, on armed duty in time of war. The behavior of a deviant like Jamka posed an obvious security risk! Especially one who was also a sheer madman!"

Glaring, Cachat picked up one of the chips and brandished it like a prosecutor holding up the murder weapon before a jury. "This one records the torture and murder of a *naval* rating!"

Yuri felt the blood drain from his face. He'd heard rumors of what went on in Jamka's private quarters down on the planet, true. But, from the habit of years, he'd ignored the rumors and written off the more extravagant ones to the inflation inevitable to any hearsay. Truth be told, like Admiral Chin, a large part of Radamacher had been thankful for Jamka's secret perversions. It kept the bastard preoccupied and out of Yuri's hair. As long as Jamka kept his private habits away from the task force, Radamacher had minded his own business. It was dangerous—very dangerous—to pry into the private life of a StateSec officer as highly ranked as Robert Jamka. Who had been, after all, Radamacher's own superior.

"Good God."

"There is no God," snapped Cachat. "Don't let me hear you use such language again. And answer my question—why didn't you report it?"

Yuri groped for words. There was something about the youngster's sheer fanaticism that just disarmed his own cynicism. He realized, if he'd had any doubts before, that Cachat was a True Believer. One of those frightening people who, if they did not take personal advantage of their own power, did not hesitate for an instant to punish anyone who failed to live up to their own political standards.

"I didn't—" He took a breath of air. "I was not aware of any such murder. What went on dirtside—I mean, I kept an eye on him—so did Chin—when he was aboard the admiral's flagship—or anywhere in the fleet—which wasn't too often, he was lax about his duties, spent most of his time either on the SDs or on the planet—"

I'm babbling like an idiot.

"That's a lie," stated Cachat flatly. "The disappearance of Third Class Missile Tech Caroline Quedilla was reported to you five months ago. I found it in your records. You did a desultory investigation and reported her 'absent without leave, presumed to have deserted.'"

The name jogged Radamacher's memory. "Yes, I remember the case. But she disappeared while on shore leave—it happens, now and then—and . . ."

He forgot Cachat's warning. "Oh, God," he whispered "After I did the first set of checks, Jamka told me to drop the investigation. He said he had more important things for me to do than waste time on a routine naval desertion case."

Cachat's dark eyes stared at him. Then: "Indeed. Well, for punishment I'm going to require you to watch this entire chip. Make sure you're near the toilet. You'll puke at least once."

He rose abruptly to his feet. "But that's for later. Right now, we need to finish your investigation. The situation here is such an unholy mess that I can't afford to have an officer of your experience twiddling his thumbs. I'm desperately in need of personnel I can rely on." He jerked a thumb at the sergeant; scowling: "I even had to summon Marines from one of the task force vessels, since I can't be sure which StateSec personnel on this ship were involved with Jamka."

The scowl was now focused on Yuri himself. "That's

provided you can satisfy me of your political reliability, that is, and your own lack of involvement in Jamka's . . . I'm still calling it 'murder,' even if I personally think the man should have been shot in the head. As long as it was done officially."

Yuri hesitated. Then, guessing that Cachat would rush the matter, Yuri decided to take the chance to volunteer for chemical interrogation. And why not? Cachat could order it done anyway, whether Yuri agreed or not.

"You can give me any truth drug you want." He tried to sound as confident as possible. "Well, there's one I have an allergic reaction to—that's—"

Cachat interrupted him. "Not a chance. Among the people implicated in Jamka's behavior—there seems to have been a whole little cult of the swine—was one of the ship's doctors aboard this vessel. I have no idea how he might have adulterated the supply of drugs, precisely in order to protect himself if he came under suspicion. So we'll use the tried and true methods."

Cachat turned and opened the door. Without a glance backward, he led Yuri into the hallway. As Radamacher, following, came up to the big Marine sergeant, he suddenly realized that he recognized the man. He didn't know his first name, but he was Citizen Sergeant Pierce, one of the Marines attached to Sharon Justice's ship.

"Three squads of us from the *Veracity* just got called in by the Special Investigator," whispered Pierce. "Only been here four hours."

Radamacher left the room. Cachat was stalking down the corridor perhaps ten yards ahead of him. Just out of whispering range.

"What going on?" he asked softly.

"All hell's breaking loose, Sir. Been maybe the most interesting four hours of my life."

The citizen sergeant nodded toward Cachat. "That is one scary son-of-a-bitch, Sir. Would you believe—"

Seeing Cachat impatiently turning his head to see what was holding them up, the sergeant broke off.

Thereafter, they traveled in silence. Cachat set a fast pace, leading them through the convoluted corridors of the huge warship with only an occasional moment of hesitation. Yuri, remembering how he'd gotten lost himself the first time he came aboard the superdreadnought, wondered how Cachat was managing the feat.

But he didn't wonder much. It was a long voyage from Nouveau Paris, and he was quite sure the Special Investigator had spent the entire time preparing for his duties. Part of which, he was sure, involved studying the layout of the vessel he would be working in.

Duty. The Needs of the State.

He spent more time wondering about something else. He finally remembered that the woman who had been murdered by Jamka had *also* been attached to Sharon Justice's ship.

That was...odd. Not the fact itself. The fact that Cachat, after throwing Sharon Justice—and Yuri himself—under arrest, would then turn around and use Marine personnel from the same ship for—

For what, exactly? What the hell is he doing?

As soon as they entered the large chamber which was their destination, Yuri understood. Some of it, at least.

The chamber was normally used as a gym for StateSec troopers. In a way, it still was. Insofar as administering a beating could be called "exercise."

He stared, horrified, when he saw the person shackled to a heavy chair in the center of the compartment. It was Citizen Captain Sharon Justice, nude from the waist up except for a brassiere. He could barely recognize her. Sharon's upper body was covered with bruises, and her face was a pulp. Blood was splattered all over her head and chest.

"Sorry, Sir," whispered the Marine. Sharon's groans covered the soft sound of the words. "We'll go as easy as we can. But . . . it's either this or get what the good doctor got."

Yuri's brain didn't seem to be functioning very well. Despite State Security's reputation, there were plenty of StateSec officers like himself who were no more familiar with casual brutality than anyone else. Radamacher had never found it necessary to enforce discipline with anything more severe than a sharp tone, now and then.

There was a huge pool of blood around the chair Sharon was strapped into. Yuri groped for the answer . . .

How can she bleed so much?

Finally, the Marine's whispered words registered. Dimly, Radamacher realized that there were a number of other bleeding bodies in the compartment. He hadn't noticed them at first, because they'd been hauled into two of the compartment's corners and there were perhaps twenty other people crowded into the other two corners of the compartment.

"Crowded" was the word, too. They seemed to be

pressing themselves against the bulkheads, as if they were trying to get as far away as possible from the proceedings in the center. Or, more likely, as far away as possible from the Special Investigator. That they were all members of State Security, except for the Marine citizen major and three Marine citizen sergeants who had apparently administered the beatings, made the whole situation insanely half-comical to Radamacher. No wonder the Marine noncom had called it "maybe the most interesting four hours of my life." Talk about role reversal!

Then Yuri took a better look at the bodies in the other corner, and any sense of comedy vanished. The bloody and dazed people in the one corner had just been beaten. They were being attended to now by a couple of medics, but despite the bruises and the gauze he recognized all of them. Essentially, that little group constituted most of the top StateSec officers assigned to the naval task force. What Yuri Radamacher thought of as "his people."

The other group of bodies...

He didn't recognize any of them, except one woman he thought was one of the officers from the other superdreadnought. He was pretty sure they were all members of the SD personnel, who'd always kept their distance from "fleet" StateSec.

They were the source of most of the blood pooled around the chair, he realized. They'd all been shot in the head.

Jamka's accomplices, he was sure of it.

Dead, dead, dead. Six of them.

"Well?" demanded Cachat.

The citizen major overseeing the Marines was Khedi Lafitte, the commanding officer of the *Veracity*'s Marine detachment. He shook his head. "I think she's innocent, Sir." He gestured with his head toward the holopic recorder being held by a StateSec guard nearby. "You can study the record yourself, of course. But if she had anything to do with Jamka's killing—ah, murder—we sure couldn't get a trace of it."

Cachat studied the beaten officer in the chair, his jaws tight. "What about her political reliability?"

The citizen major looked a little uneasy. "Well...ah... we were concentrating on the Jamka business...."

Cachat shook his head impatiently. "Never mind. I'll study the record myself. So will whoever Citizen Chairman Saint-Just assigns to examine my report, once it reaches Nouveau Paris." He turned his head to the StateSec guard holding the recorder. "You *did* get a good record, yes?"

The guard nodded his head hastily. He seemed just as nervous around the Special Investigator as everyone else.

Apparently satisfied, Cachat turned back to study Justice again. After a few seconds, he twitched his shoulders. The gesture seemed more one of irritation than an actual shrug.

"Get her out of the chair, then. Put her with the others and see to it she gets medical attention. Thank you, Citizen Major Lafitte. I'll question Citizen Commissioner Radamacher myself. By now I'm almost certain we've cauterized the rot, but it's best to be certain."

Two of the Marine citizen sergeants, moving more gently than you'd expect from two men who had just administered her beating, unshackled Sharon from the chair and helped her toward the medics in the corner. Once the chair was empty, Cachat turned to Yuri.

"Please take a seat, Citizen Commissioner Radamacher. If you're innocent, you have nothing to fear beyond a painful episode which will end soon enough." There was a pulser holstered on his belt. Cachat lifted the weapon and held it casually. "If you're guilty, your pain will end even sooner."

Yuri took some pride in the fact that he made it to the chair and seated himself without trembling. As one of the sergeants fastened the shackles to his wrists and ankles, he stared up at Cachat.

Again, he ignored the Special Investigator's dictum. "Jesus Christ," he hissed softly. "You shot them *yourself?*"

Again, that irritated little twitch of the shoulders. "We are in time of war, at a moment of supreme crisis for the Republic. The security risk posed by Jamka and his cabal required summary judgement and execution. Their perversions and corruption threatened to undermine the authority of the state here. It *did* undermine that authority, as a matter of fact, when Jamka's behavior got himself killed."

Yuri had to fight not to let his relief show. Whether he realized it or not, Cachat had just stated that the significance of Jamka's murder was personal, not political—and had done so on the official record.

Cachat spoke his next words a bit more loudly, as if to make sure that all the StateSec officers in the room heard him.

"Citizen Chairman Saint-Just will naturally review the whole matter, and if he disapproves of my actions he'll see to my own punishment. Whatever that might be." His tone was one of sheer indifference. "In the meantime, however"—his eyes left Yuri and swept slowly across the crowd of officers watching in the corners, glittering like two agates—"I believe I have established that Legislaturalist-style cronyism and back-scratching between unfit and corrupt officers will no longer be tolerated in this sector. Indeed, it will be severely punished."

All three citizen sergeants were back. All of them donned gloves to protect their hands.

"Have at it, then," said Yuri firmly. For reasons he could not quite understand, he was suddenly filled with confidence. In fact, he felt better than he had in a long time.

The feeling didn't last, of course. But, as Cachat had stated, it was eventually over. Through one blurry eye— the other was closed completely—Yuri saw the pistol go back into the holster. And through ears that felt like cauliflowers, he dimly heard the Special Investigator pronounce him innocent of all suspicions. True, the words sounded as if they were spoken grudgingly. But, they were spoken. And properly recorded. Yuri heard Cachat enquire as to that also.

As Citizen Sergeant Pierce helped him over to the corner where the medics waited, Yuri managed to mumble a few words.

"Dink 'y noze id boken."

"Yessir, it is," muttered the citizen sergeant. "Sorry about that. We broke your nose right off. The Special Investigator's orders, Sir."

Cachat, you vicious bastard.

Later, after he was patched up, he felt better.

"You'll be okay, Sir," assured the medic who'd worked on him. "A broken nose looks gory as all hell at the time— blood all over the place—but it's really not all that serious. Few weeks, you'll be as good as new."

5

Radamacher spent the next several days in his cabin aboard the *Hector Van Dragen*, recovering from his injuries. Although he was no longer officially under arrest, and thus under no obligation to remain in the cabin, he decided that the old saw about discretion being the better part of valor applied in this case.

Besides, he got a full daily report from Sergeant Pierce anyway, concerning the events transpiring on the superdreadnought—indeed, throughout the entire task force. So he saw no reason to venture out into the corridors himself, since he had a perfectly valid medical excuse not to do so. Philosophically—especially with the aid of new bruises added to old saws—he thought that phenomena which went by such terms as "Reign of Terror" were best observed indirectly.

He got the term "Reign of Terror" from Pierce himself, the day after his interrogation.

"Just checking up, Sir," Pierce explained apologetically

after Yuri invited him into the room, "making sure you were okay." The sergeant examined his face, wincing a bit at the bruises and the bandages. "Hope you don't take none of this personally. Orders, Sir. We Marines never had no beef against you, ourselves."

The sergeant's wince changed into a scowl. "Sure as hell never had no beef against Captain Justice. He shouldna had us do that, dammit. It idn't proper."

The injuries to Yuri's face caused his ensuing snort of sarcastic half-laughter to *hurt*. Especially his broken nose. He added that little item to his long list of grievances against Special Investigator Victor Cachat.

"Ide 'ay nod!" he wheezed. "Ma'ines an'd zuppose do bead dey own ovizuhs." He steeled himself for more pain. "'Ow iz Zha—Gabban 'Usdis—doin'?"

"She's fine, Sir," the sergeant assured him, almost eagerly. "We went as easy as—I mean, well—the Special Investigator left before we started on Captain Justice, Sir. So he wasn't there to watch. So—"

Pierce was floundering, obviously feeling trapped between human sympathy and duty—not to mention the possible Wrath of Cachat. Yuri let him off the hook. Given the difficulty of speaking, he also decided to ignore the citizen sergeant's unthinking use of the forbidden term "sir." He understood full well the word was an indication of Pierce's trust in him.

"Nedduh mine, Ziddezen Zajend. Z'okay. Iz 'uh noze boke doo?"

"Oh, no, Sir!" Yuri had to force down another laugh. The sergeant seemed deeply aggrieved at the suggestion. "Pretty a woman as she is, we wouldn't do nothing like that. Didn't knock out none of her teeth, neither. Just, you know, bruised her up good for the recorder."

Feeling two missing teeth of his own with a probing tongue—they also *hurt*—Yuri was pleased at the news. He'd always found Sharon Justice a very attractive woman. So much so, in fact, that on more than one occasion he'd had to remind himself forcefully of the prohibition against romantic liaisons between officers in the same chain of command. That hadn't been easy. He was a bachelor beginning to tire of it, Sharon was a divorcée about his own age, and their duties brought them into constant contact. Just to make things worse, he was pretty sure his own attraction to her was reciprocated.

The citizen sergeant began moving about the cabin, fussily tidying up here and there. As if trying, somehow, to make amends for the events of the previous day. There was something utterly ludicrous about the whole situation, and another little laugh wracked pain through Yuri's face.

"Ncdduh minc, zajcnd," he repeated. Then, gesturing toward the door. "Wad's 'abbenin' oud deh?"

Pierce grinned. "It's a regular reign of terror, Sir. Look on the bright side. You're well and truly out of it, now. Whereas those sorry worthless bastards out there—"

He broke off, coughing a little. It was also against regulations for a Marine noncom to refer to the officers and crew of a State Security SD as "sorry worthless bastards."

Under the circumstances, Yuri decided to overlook the citizen sergeant's lapse. Indeed, with a lifted eyebrow, he invited Pierce to continue. Even went so far, in fact, as to invite the Marine to sit with a polite gesture of the hand.

For the next half an hour, Pierce regaled Radamacher with Tales of the Terror. He'd had a ringside seat at the proceedings, since he and the other Marines from the *Veracity* had continued to serve as Cachat's impromptu escort and ready-made police force.

"Got some StateSec people with us too, of course, making the actual arrests. But those are all okay folks. From the fleet. The Special Investigator brought 'em over from half the ships in the task force."

Yuri was puzzled. "'Ow did 'e know widge ones do ged?"

The sergeant's face flushed a little. "Well. Actually. He asked us, Sir—we Marines, I mean, especially Major Lafitte—which ones we'd recommend. If you can believe it. Then he went into Captain Justice's cabin—she's just down the corridor a ways—and cross-checked the names with her."

Yuri stared at him.

"It was weird as hell," Pierce chortled. "He went over the list with the captain just as calm as could be. Didn't even seem to notice the bandages."

No, the bastard wouldn't, Yuri thought sourly. Cachat would pass out beatings like he'd pass out any other assignment.

But there wasn't really much anger in the thought. Radamacher was just fascinated by the peculiarities of the whole thing. Cachat's actions were like a grotesque Moebius strip concocted in the mind of a torturer. First,

Cachat used the Marine contingent from Sharon's own ship to beat her into a pulp. Then, he turned around and consulted with those same Marines with regard to StateSec assignments—and cross-checked the recommendations with the same woman they'd just gotten through torturing!

Utterly insane. Not simply the actions of a fanatic, but of one who was unhinged to boot. It wasn't *precisely* against regulations for an officer of StateSec to rely on Marines for their recommendations for StateSec staff assignments. But that was only because it never would have occurred to anyone that such a regulation was needed in the first place. It just wasn't *done,* that's all. As well pass regulations forbidding stars to revolve around planets!

As the days passed and the citizen sergeant continued his Tales of the Terror, however, Yuri soon realized that Cachat was not a man to concern himself with "what isn't done." Results were all that mattered to him, and—fanatic or not; unhinged or not—results he was certainly getting.

Seven officers and twenty-three crewmen of the *Hector Van Dragen* arrested, for starters, within the first week. Two officers and seven crewmen from the other SD, the *Joseph Tilden.* One of those officers and four of the crewmen subsequently executed, after Cachat finished examining the evidence found in their quarters.

Most of the officers and ratings had been arrested for routine corruption. Theft and embezzlement, mostly. Those Cachat slammed with the maximum penalties allowable under the official rules for shipboard discipline short of court-martial. But the others had been implicated in Jamka's activities. Clearly so in the case of the officer. The evidence had been fuzzier for the crew members. From what Radamacher could determine, the hapless ratings had been mainly guilty of being too closely identified as "Jamka's people."

No matter. They were all shot. By a firing squad this time, selected from StateSec members brought over from the fleet, not by Cachat himself.

Radamacher wondered how much of Cachat's ruthlessness was dictated by typical StateSec empire-building. Guilty or not, the net effect of the purge was to completely shatter any residual Jamka network, and to intimidate anyone else from forming a different informal network. Or, at the very least, to keep it well under cover. By the end of his first week in La Martine Sector, Victor Cachat had established himself as The Boss, and nobody doubted it.

As cynical as he tried to be about the matter, however, Yuri didn't really think much if any of Cachat's behavior was motivated by personal ambitions. He noted, for instance, that although Cachat had ordered and personally overseen the beatings—okay, call them "interrogations"— of half a dozen of the top ranked StateSec officers attached directly to the task force, he had left it at that after pronouncing them all innocent. The Special Investigator had made no attempt to break up their own informal network, even though he was surely aware of its existence. As long as they were careful to mind their p's and q's—which all of them were doing scrupulously, now—he seemed willing to look the other way.

And thank God for that. Yuri still resented his bruises, and his broken nose and missing teeth. And he resented the bruises he saw on Sharon even more—which was every day, now, since they were both still on the SD and had cabins not too far apart. Still . . .

Any danger of being accused of being a McQueen conspirator was growing more distant as each day passed. Not just for Yuri himself, but for anyone in the task force. By hammering into a pulp the StateSec officers overseeing Admiral Chin's task force—and then declaring them all innocent of any crime—Cachat had effectively sealed the whole matter. Just as, by using task force Marines to do the blood work, he had effectively cleared them of any suspicion also; and, by implication, the naval officers in overall command of the task force. Neither Admiral Chin nor Commodore Ogilve had been subjected to anything worse than a rigorous but non-violent interrogation.

Granted, Saint-Just's regime didn't recognize the principle of double jeopardy, so any charges could theoretically be raised again at any time. But even Saint-Just's regime was subject to the inevitable dynamics of human affairs. Inertia worked in that field as surely as it did anywhere else. No one could question the rigor of Cachat's investigation—not with blood and bruises and dead bodies everywhere—and the matter was settled. Reopening it would be an uphill struggle, especially when the regime had a thousand critical problems to deal with in the wake of Rob Pierre's death.

Besides, whatever faint evidence there might once have been had surely vanished. By now, Yuri was quite certain that everyone in the task force who'd had any possible connection to McQueen had done the electronic equivalent of wiping off the fingerprints. Unwittingly—the young fanatic still had a lot to learn about intelligence work, Yuri reflected wryly—Cachat's week-long preoccupation with terrorizing the personnel of the two superdreadnoughts had bought time for the task force. Time to catch their breath, relax a bit, eliminate any traces of evidence, and get all their stories straight.

Radamacher was also aware that Cachat had made no move against either of the two captains commanding the SDs, even though Citizen Captain Gallanti in particular had made no secret of her hostility toward the young Special Investigator. Neither of the captains had been touched by Jamka's unsavory activities, and neither could be shown to be corrupt. So, punctiliously, Cachat had left them in their positions and did not even seem to be going out of his way to build any case against them—despite the fact that Radamacher was quite sure Cachat understood that the SD commanders would remain a possible threat to him.

When he mentioned that to Ned—he and Pierce had become quite friendly by the end of the week—the burly citizen sergeant grinned and shook his head.

"Don't underestimate him, Yuri. He might be leaving Gallanti and Vesey alone, but he's gutting their crews."

Radamacher cocked an eyebrow.

"Figuratively speaking, I mean," Pierce qualified. "You haven't heard yet, I take it, of what Cachat's calling the 'salubrious personnel retraining and transfer'?"

Yuri tried to wrap his brain around the clumsy phrase.

Somehow, the florid words didn't seem to fit what he'd seen of Cachat's personality.

The sergeant's grin widened. "We lowly Marines just call it SPRAT. So does the Special Investigator. In fact, he says he got the idea from the nursery rhyme."

That jogged Yuri's memory. From childhood, he dredged up the ancient doggerel:

> "Jack Sprat could eat no fat,
> His wife could eat no lean.
> And so betwixt the two of them,
> They licked the platter clean."

"Yup, that's it," chortled Pierce. "Except the Special Investigator says it's time to do a role switch. So he's transferring about five hundred people from the SDs over to the fleet, and about twice that number from the fleet over here. Even some Marines, believe it or not. A company's worth on each ship. I'm one of them, in fact."

"*Marines?* On a StateSec superdreadnought? That's.. . not done."

Pierce shrugged. "That's what Captain Gallanti said to him when he told her. She wasn't any too polite about it, neither. I know; I was there. The SI always keeps two or three of us Marines around him wherever he goes." Half-apologetically: "Along with the same number of StateSec guards, of course. But they're okay types."

Radamacher stared at him. *"Okay types."* He knew perfectly well that a Marine definition of that term would hardly match Saint-Just's.

His mind was almost reeling. Cachat was a lunatic! To

be sure, an SI's authority in a remote sector could be stretched a long ways. But it didn't really include decisions over personnel—well...unless severe problems of discipline and/or loyalty were concerned...and Cachat had just littered an SD's gym with dead bodies to prove that it was...

Still. It just *wasn't done*.

He must have muttered the words aloud. The citizen sergeant shrugged and said: "Yeah, that's what Gallanti said. But, as you mighta figured, the SI's a regular walking encyclopedia of StateSec rules, regulations and precedents. So he immediately rattled off half a dozen instances where Marines *had* been stationed on StateSec capital ships. Two of the instances at the order of none other than Eloise Pritchard, Saint-Just's—ah, the Citizen Chairman's—fair-haired girl."

Yuri's face tightened. He knew Pritchard himself, as it happened. Not well, no. But he'd been close to the Aprilists in his days as a youthful oppositionist, and she'd been one of the leaders he'd respected and admired. But since the revolution, she'd turned into what he detested most. Another fanatic like Cachat, who'd drown the world in blood for the sake of abstract principles. Her harshness as a People's Commissioner was a legend in State Security.

However, it was indeed true that Pritchard was, as the sergeant said, Saint-Just's "fair-haired girl." So if Cachat was right—and he'd hardly fabricate something like that—he might get away with it.

"You can bet the bank Gallanti's going to scream all the way to Nouveau Paris," he predicted.

Pierce didn't seem notably concerned. "Yup. She told

Cachat she'd insist on including her own dispatches with the next courier ship, and he told her that was her privilege. Didn't blink an eye when he said it. Just as lizard-cold as always."

The sergeant cocked his head a little, braced his hands on the edge of the seat, and leaned forward. "Look, Sir, I can understand where you'll be holding a grudge against the guy. What with a broken nose and all. But I gotta tell you that personally—and it's not just me, neither; all the Marines I know feel the same way about it—the SI's okay with me."

He grimaced ruefully. "Yeah, sure, I wouldn't invite him to a friendly poker game, and I think I'd have a heart attack if my sister told me she had a crush on the guy. But. Still."

For a moment, he groped for words. "What I mean is this, Sir. None of us Marines are gonna shed any tears over the shitheads he whacked. Neither are you, if you'll be honest about it. Scum, to call them by their right name. For the rest of it? He had a buncha decent people beaten up some, but—being honest about it— no worse than you mighta gotten in a barroom brawl. And then the slate was clean for them, and meanwhile he's been tearing right through all the crap that's piled up in these ships."

Yuri fingered his nose gingerly. "You must have been in some worse barroom brawls than I ever was, Ned."

"You don't hang out in Marine bars, Citizen Commissioner," Pierce chuckled. "A broken nose? Couple of missing teeth? Hell, I 'member a time a guy got his— Well, never mind."

"Please. I grow faint at the description of mayhem. And

remind me not to wander into any Marine bars in the future, would you? If you see me looking distracted, I mean."

The citizen sergeant snorted. "The only time I ever see you looking distracted is when Captain Justice is around."

Yuri flushed. "Is it that obvious?"

"Yeah, it's that obvious. For chrissake, Yuri, why don't you just ask the lady out on a date?" His eyes glanced around the room, then at the door, sizing up the surroundings. "I grant you, entertainment's a little hard to find on a StateSec superdreadnought. But I'm sure you could figure out something."

Yuri Radamacher had a little epiphany, then. The citizen sergeant veered away from the awkward personal moment into another tale of Cachat's Rampage. But Yuri barely heard a word of it.

His mind had wandered inward, remembering ideals he'd once believed in. How strange that a fanatic could, without intending to, create a situation where a Marine noncom would joke casually with a StateSec officer. A week ago, Radamacher had not even known the citizen sergeant's first name. Nor, a week ago, would that sergeant have dared tease a StateSec Commissioner about his love life.

The Law of Unintended Consequences, he mused. Maybe that's the rock on which all tyrannies founder in the end. And maybe freedom's real motto should be something whimsical, instead of flowery phrases about Liberty and Equality. There's a line from a Robert Burns poem that would do nicely.

● ● ●

"The best laid schemes o' mice an' men
Gang aft agleigh."

6

The next day, however, it was Radamacher's own half-assumed plans which suffered the mouse's fate.

The Special Investigator showed up at Yuri's door early in the morning. To his surprise, accompanied by Citizen Captain Justice.

As he invited them in, Yuri tried to keep his eyes off of the captain. Sharon's bruises were well on their way to healing now, and she looked . . .

Better than she ever had. Yuri realized that Citizen Sergeant Pierce's wisecrack the day before had broken through his last attempts at maintaining his personal reserve. To put it in the crude terms of a Marine, Yuri Radamacher had a serious case of the hots for Sharon Justice, and that was all there was to say about it.

The problem of what to *do* about it, of course, remained in all its stubborn intractability. So he told himself, firmly, as he forced his mind to concentrate on the unwelcome figure of the Special Investigator.

"Are your injuries sufficiently healed to resume your duties?" Cachat demanded. The tone of voice implied a sentence left unspoken. *Or do you still insist on malingering, mired in sloth and resentment?*

Yuri's jaws tightened. Law of Unintended Consequences or not, he just plain *detested* this young fanatic.

"Yes, Citizen Special Investigator. I am ready to resume my duties. I'll have my kit transferred—"

"Not your old duties. I have new ones for you."

The SI nodded at Sharon. "In light of her exoneration and your own recommendation, I've appointed Citizen Captain Justice—sorry, People's Commissioner Justice, now; the promotion is only brevet, but that's within my authority—to serve for the moment as Citizen Admiral Chin's commissioner. Citizen Commander Howard Wilkins will be replacing you as the commissioner for Citizen Commodore Ogilve."

Yuri frowned, puzzled. "But—"

"I shall require you to remain on board this superdreadnought. The *Hector Van Dragen* will be remaining in La Martine orbit while the *Joseph Tilden* accompanies the task force in its upcoming mission." Cachat scowled fiercely. "I cannot allow the needs of the ongoing investigation to impede the State's other business any longer. Three new incidents of Manticoran commerce raiding have been reported—even a case of simple piracy!—and this task force *must* be gotten back into action. There being no valid reason for both SDs to remain lounging about while Admiral Chin's task force resumes its work, I am assigning the *Tilden* to accompany them."

Radamacher scrambled to catch up. "But—Citizen Special Investigator—ah, no offense, but you're not a naval man—a superdreadnought really isn't suited for anti-raiding work. Not to mention—ah—"

Cachat smiled slightly. "Not to mention that the SD captains will raise a howl of protest? Indeed they will.

Indeed they have, I should say. I squelched them last night."

Yuri was fascinated, despite himself, at the smile which remained on Cachat's face. It was the first time he'd ever seen the Special Investigator smile about anything.

It was a thin smile, naturally. But try as he might, Yuri couldn't deny that it made the man's face look even younger than usual. You might even call it an attractive face, in that moment.

"As for the other," Cachat continued, "while I'm no expert on naval matters, Citizen Admiral Chin *is*. And she assures me that she can find a suitable role for the *Tilden*. Given her own experience and track record—and the fact that my investigation has turned up no reason to question either her competence or her loyalty—I have ordered Citizen Captain Vesey to place the *Tilden* under Citizen Admiral Chin's command."

Yuri tried to imagine how loudly Vesey must have shrieked at *that* news. True, Vesey wasn't as mulish and intemperate as Citizen Captain Gallanti, the CO of the *Hector Van Dragen*. But, like all commanding officers of StateSec capital ships, Vesey hadn't been selected for his friendly attitude toward the regular Navy.

Cachat's smile was gone, now, his usual cold expression firmly back in place.

"Citizen Captain Gallanti will naturally include her and Vesey's protests at my decision in their dispatches to Nouveau Paris. I authorized sending a courier ship today, in fact, to ensure that Vesey's remarks could be included before he left orbit. But until and unless my decision is overruled from StateSec headquarters, the decision stands. And I will see to it that it is enforced, of course, by any means necessary. Fortunately, Citizen Captain Vesey did not press the issue."

Hey, no kidding. Who's going to "press the issue" with a man who's already demonstrated he'll personally shoot six people in the head in the space of a few hours if he thinks it's in the line of duty? It's one thing for a mouse to bell a cat, if he thinks he can get away with it. But he's not going to debate the cat about it ahead of time, that's for sure.

Yuri stared at Cachat, wondering if the SI's own thoughts were running on parallel lines. They . . .

Might be. Cachat might not be an experienced naval officer. But Radamacher was quite certain that the young man had studied naval affairs just as thoroughly and relentlessly as he did everything else. If so, he'd understand perfectly well that a single superdreadnought attached to a flotilla the size of Admiral Chin's would be outmatched in the event of—ah, "internal hostilities." Especially since—*Jesus, is he possibly this Machiavellian?*—Cachat had also seen to it that the internal security squads for both superdreadnoughts were now composed of Marines and StateSec troops who got along well with Marines.

While . . .

Jesus Christ. He is that Machiavellian. Now that I think about it, by transferring all the worst elements from the SDs over to the task force, he's split them up and scattered them over three dozen different ships. With no way to communicate with each other, and . . . surrounded by Navy and Marine ratings who'd hammer them into a pulp

*cheerfully—or shoot them dead—if Chin or Cachat gave
the order.*

Which leaves . . .

He couldn't help it. A little groan forced its way
through Yuri's lips.

Cachat frowned. "What's this, Citizen Assistant Special
Investigator Radamacher? Surely you're not objecting to
a new assignment? You just got through assuring me your
health had recovered sufficiently."

"Yes. But—"

His mind raced wildly. Cachat was a lunatic. *Lunatic,
lunatic, lunatic!*

Yuri took a deep breath and tried to settle down. "Let
me see if I understand you properly, Citizen Special
Investigator. You're relieving me from my duties as a
commissioner in order to serve as your assistant. And
since I assume you will be accompanying the task force in
its mission—"

"That's essential." Cachat snapped the words. "I must
oversee the operation of this entire combined StateSec
and Naval force. In *action,* which is where it belongs. If
nothing else, I intend to make sure that this important
unit of the People's Republic is doing its duties properly
and according to regulations. Which I can't possibly
accomplish while everybody is lolling about in orbit
twiddling their thumbs. There is no Manticoran threat to
La Martine posed in the near future beyond commerce-
raiding, so leaving a single SD on station in the capital
should be more than sufficient to maintain order here."

He bestowed two piercing dark eyes upon Yuri. "The
more so if the investigation on the *Hector Van Dragen* is

concluded in my absence by a capable subordinate. You *do* have an excellent service record, Citizen StateSec Officer Radamacher. Now that any questions concerning your loyalty or possible involvement in the Jamka affair are resolved, I see no reason you can't accomplish the task quite successfully."

Cachat shrugged, as if moderately embarrassed to say the next words. "I dare say I've already rooted out the worst of the corruption and slackness aboard this ship. So all that really remains for you to do is oversee Citizen Captain Gallanti—"

She's going to love THAT! Yuri quailed a bit at the thought of Gallanti's temper.

"—and rigorously pursue whatever remaining traces of corruption and slackness you might uncover. To that end, I'll be leaving you the best of the new security units I've managed to put together. The best StateSec security teams—most of them from the task force, naturally, since the rot had festered too long here on the SDs—along with Citizen Major Lafitte and his Marines. I should think that would be sufficient."

That'll mean Ned Pierce will still be around. Thank God for that. I'll need his shoulder to cry on.

There didn't seem anything he could say. So, he simply nodded his head.

"Good." Cachat turned to leave, his hand on the door latch. Citizen Commissioner Justice began to follow, but not before giving Yuri a quick smile. Almost a shy smile, somehow, which was odd. Sharon Justice was normally a very self-assured woman.

The smile, even on lips still puffy from her beating,

made Yuri's heart lift. Even more, the warmth in her brown eyes.

A sudden realization jolted him.

"Ah—Citizen Special Investigator?"

Cachat turned back around. "Yes?"

Radamacher cleared his throat. "I simply wanted to make sure my understanding of regulations is clear. As an assistant now attached to your office, I believe I am no longer in the task force's chain of command. Is that correct?"

"Of course," replied Cachat curtly. "How could it be otherwise? You report to me, and I report to State Security HQ in Nouveau Paris. How could we possibly be responsible to the same chain of command we're investigating?" Impatiently: "An officer of your experience simply can't be that ignorant of basic—"

He broke off. Then glanced quickly at Sharon Justice. Then—

Yuri couldn't quite believe it, but . . . Cachat was actually *blushing*. For a moment, the young man looked like a schoolboy.

The moment didn't last long. Abruptly, as if summoned, the fanatic-face shield closed down. Cachat's next words were spoken in a very impatient tone of voice.

"If this involves a personal matter, Citizen Assistant Investigator Radamacher, it is no concern of mine so long as no regulations are broken."

He seemed to grope—the first time Yuri had ever seen the SI at a loss for words—then concluded in a half-mumble:

"I have pressing business. Citizen Commissioner

Justice, the task force will be leaving orbit very shortly. I'll
expect you to report for duty on time. Say, an hour from
now."

He opened the door—flung it open, more like—
slipped through, and was gone. Closing it firmly behind
him.

Yuri stared at Sharon. Her smile now seemed as shy as
a schoolgirl's herself. He suspected his own did likewise.

*What to say? How to say it? After three years of
scrupulously never crossing the line.*

And in an hour?! A lousy HOUR?! Cachat, you bastard!

Sharon broke the impasse. The shy smile dissolved into
a throaty chuckle, and all her normal self-assurance
seemed to return.

"What a mess, eh, Yuri? We're both way too old—too
dignified, too, especially you—to just hop into bed." She
eyed the cabin's narrow bed skeptically. "Leaving aside
the fact that neither of us have our youthful slender
figures left. We'd probably fall off halfway through—and
I don't know about you, but I'm still way too bruised to
want another set just yet."

"I think you look gorgeous," Yuri stated firmly. Well.
Croaked firmly.

Sharon grinned and took him by the hand. "An hour's
only an hour, so let's use it wisely. Let's talk, Yuri. Just
talk. I think we both need it desperately."

They didn't *just* talk. Before the hour was up, there'd
been a clinch or three tossed into the mix—and a very
passionate goodbye kiss when it finally came time for
Sharon to leave, bruised lips or not. But, mostly, they
talked. Yuri never remembered much of the conversation

afterward, although he always swore it was the most scintillating conversation he'd ever had in his life.

What was most important, though, was that after Sharon left and Yuri took stock of his situation, he realized that for the first time in years he felt just *great*. And, being by nature a cautious man but not a coward, was also sensible enough to ride that feeling out into the corridors and through the labyrinth of the SD's passages and into Citizen Captain Gallanti's office.

Even a newly enlarged and promoted mouse setting out to bell a cat has enough sense to do it with the wind in his sails.

7

Gallanti was not thrilled to see him.

"For God's sake!" she snarled, as soon as he was ushered into the stateroom she used for her command quarters when not on the bridge. "The maniac hasn't even left orbit yet and you're already here to give me grief?"

"There is no God," Radamacher informed her serenely. "Mention of the term is expressly forbidden in StateSec regulations."

That brought her up short. Her eyes rolled and Yuri could sense the woman's notorious temper rising. But he'd already gauged his tactics before entering the room, and knew what to do.

"Oh, relax, would you?" Radamacher gave her a wry smile—he had a superb wry smile; people had told him so over the years hundreds of times—and eased his way into an armchair. "For God's sake, Citizen Captain Gallanti, just once can you assume we're adults instead of kids in a schoolyard? I didn't come here to play dominance games with you."

That threw her off her stride, as he'd suspected it would. Gallanti stared at him, her mouth half-open. The stocky blonde's heavy brow was frowning more in puzzlement now than anger.

Yuri pressed the advantage. "Look, as you said: The maniac hasn't even left orbit yet. So let's take advantage of all the time we've got to get everything straightened up before he comes back. If we work together, we can see to it that by the time he returns—that'll be at least six weeks, more likely eight—not even that fanatic can find anything wrong any more. He'll blow on his way and we'll have seen the last of him."

Gallanti was as notorious for her suspiciousness as her temper. Her eyes narrowed. "Why are you being so friendly, all of sudden?"

He spread his hands. "When have I ever *not* been friendly? It's not my fault you don't know me. I couldn't very well invite *myself* over to your staff dinners, could I?" He left unspoken the rest of it. *Although you could have, Exalted SD Captain—if you hadn't been such a complete snot toward every officer in the task force since you arrived on station.*

Gallanti's heavy jaws tightened. That was embarrassment, at first. But, like anyone with her temperament, Gallanti was not fond of self-doubt, much less self-criticism. So, within seconds, the embarrassment began transforming into anger.

Yuri cut it off before it built up any steam. "Let it go, will you? If you think *you* can't stand the maniac, try getting a beating at his hands." He fingered his still somewhat swollen jaw, opening his mouth to let her see the missing front teeth. He'd already begun regeneration treatment, but the gap was still obvious. And Yuri had rebandaged his nose before leaving his cabin, taking care to make the dressings as bulky as possible.

That did the trick. Gallanti managed a half-smile of tepid sympathy; then, flopped into the chair behind her desk.

"Isn't he something else? Where in creation did the Citizen Chairman dredge *him* up from? The Ninth Circle of Hell?"

"I believe that's the circle reserved for traitors," Radamacher said mildly, "which I'm afraid is the one fault you *can't* find in the man. Not without being laughed out of court, anyway. It's been a while since I read Dante, but if I recall correctly, intemperate zealots were assigned to a different level."

Gallanti glared at him. "Who's Dante?" Without waiting for an answer, she transferred the glare to her desktop display.

"As soon as I'm certain that bastard's into hyper-space, I'm sending off a purely blistering set of dispatches by courier ship. I can promise you that! Vesey is doing the same." Half-spitting: "We'll see what's what after they find out on Haven what the maniac's been up to!"

Radamacher cleared his throat delicately. "I would remind you of two things, Citizen Captain Gallanti. The first is that it will be at least six weeks before we can expect any answer, travel times being what they are between La Martine and the capital. I'd guess more like two months. StateSec is going to study all the dispatches carefully before they send back any reply."

She was still glaring at him. But, after a couple of seconds, even Gallanti seemed to realize that glaring at a man for simply stating well-known astrophysical facts was foolish. Grudgingly, she nodded. Then, summoning up her still-moldering anger and resentment, she spat out: "And what's the second thing?"

Yuri shrugged. "I'm afraid I don't share your confidence that Nouveau Paris will be very sympathetic to our complaints."

That was a nice touch, he thought. In point of fact, Yuri Radamacher's name did not and would not appear on a single one of those "blistering dispatches." But, as he'd expected, a woman of Gallanti's mindset was always prepared to assume that everyone around her except lunatics would agree with her. So she took his casual mention of "our" complaints for good coin. That helped defuse her anger at his questioning of her judgement.

"Why not?" she demanded. "He had almost a dozen StateSec officers shot—"

"The figure is actually seven," Yuri countered mildly, "the rest were StateSec security ratings. Muscle, to put it crudely. And every single one of them was guilty—there's no doubt about this, Citizen Captain, don't think there is—of the most grotesque crimes and violations of StateSec regulations. You know as well as I do that Nouveau Paris will stamp 'fully approved' on each and every one of those summary executions."

Again, he cleared his throat delicately. "You'd do well not to forget that the Special Investigator is also—*has* also, I should say—sent dispatches of his own. I happen to know—never mind how—that those dispatches included a large sampling of the pornographic record chips found in the personal quarters of Jamka and his confederates. I don't know if you've seen any of those records, Citizen Captain, but I *have*—and I can assure you that the impact they will have on StateSec at the capital is *not*—not not not—going to be: 'why did Cachat blow their brains out?' The question is going to be of quite a different variety. 'Why was none of this reported prior to Cachat's arrival—*especially* by the commanding officers of the superdreadnoughts where the criminal activity was centered?'"

Finally, something seem to penetrate Gallanti's armor of self-righteousness. Her face paled a little. "I wasn't—damnation, it was none of my affair! I command an SD, I'm *not* assigned to the task force! Jamka was a people's commissioner—assigned to the task force—not someone under my command."

Try as she might, the words lacked force. Radamacher shrugged again.

"Citizen Captain Gallanti—do you mind if I call you Jillian, by the way, while we're speaking privately?"

Gallanti hesitated, then nodded her head brusquely. "Sure, go ahead. As long as it's private. Ah—Yuri, isn't it?"

Radamacher nodded. "Jillian, then. Look, let's face facts. We've all got our excuses, and you and I both know they aren't flimsy ones—not, at least, if you're willing to live in the real world instead of Cachat's fantasy one. But . . ."

He let the word fall into silence. Then:

"Face it, Jillian. Real world excuses always come up short against fantasy accusations whenever the fantasist can point to real crimes. So let's not kid ourselves. Cachat's rampage is going to go down very well in Nouveau Paris, don't think it won't." In a slightly cynical tone of voice: "Out of idle curiosity, I once did a textual analysis of several of our Citizen Chairman's occasional speeches to StateSec cadre assemblies. Back when he was still Director of State Security. Outside of common articles like 'a' and 'the,' do you know which word appears the most often?"

Gallanti swallowed.

"The word was *rigor*, Jillian. Or *rigorous*. So tell me again, just how sympathetic our boss is going to be when he hears us whining that the fanatic Victor Cachat was too *rigorous* in his punishment of deviants using StateSec rank to cover their misdeeds."

Now, Gallanti looked like she was choking on something. Yuri segued smoothly into the opening of what he thought of as "the deal." Prefacing it by sitting up straight and sliding forward in his chair. Nothing histrionic, just . . . the subtle body language of a man suggesting a harmless—nay, salutary and beneficial— conspiracy. Say better: *private understanding*.

"We'll have a lot more luck with what I'm sure you raised in the way of your other complaints. It *is* outrageous, the way Cachat's been swapping personnel around. You can be damn sure Nouveau Paris is going to look cross-eyed at the way he's been using the Marines."

"They certainly will! 'Cross-eyed' is putting it mildly! They'll have a fit!"

Yuri waggled a hand. "Um . . . yes and no. Cachat's a sharp bastard, Jillian, don't make the mistake of underestimating him. Fanatics aren't necessarily stupid. Don't forget that he was always careful to assign an equal number of hand-picked StateSec guards to serve alongside the Marines."

Yuri saw no reason to mention that the Marines themselves, in effect, had done the handpicking. He pressed on:

"Yes, Cachat bent regulations into a pretzel. But he didn't outright break them—no, he didn't, I checked—and he'll still have the excuse that he faced extraordinarily difficult circumstances because Jamka had corrupted the normal disciplinary staff. Unfortunately, five out of the seven executed officers— and all four of the ratings— belonged to the SDs' police details. He'll claim he had no choice—and the claim isn't really all that flimsy. Not from the distance of Nouveau Paris, anyway."

Gallanti fell into gloomy silence, slumping in her chair. Then, in a half-snarl: "The whole thing's *absurd*. The one thing the stinkbug was *supposed* to do is the one thing he didn't! We *still* have no idea who murdered Jamka. Somehow that 'little detail' has gotten lost in the shuffle."

Yuri chuckled drily. "Ironic, isn't it? And after Cachat's rampage, we'll never know. But so what? I assume you saw the medical examiner's report, yes?"

Gallanti nodded. Yuri grimaced. "Pretty grisly business, wasn't it? No quick killing, there. Whoever did Jamka was as sadistic about it as Jamka himself. From looking at the holopics of his corpse, I'd almost be tempted to say Jamka committed suicide. Except there's no possible way he could have shoved—"

Yuri shuddered a little. "Ah, never mind, it's sickening. But the point is—you know, I know, anyone with half a brain knows—that Jamka was certainly murdered by one of his own coterie. A falling out between thieves, as it were. So when you get right down to it, who really cares any more who killed Jamka? Cachat shot the whole lot of them, and there's an end to it. Good riddance. You really think *Oscar Saint-Just* is going to toss in his bed worrying about it?"

Glumly, the SD captain shook her head. Even more glumly, and in a very low voice, she said: "This is going to wreck my career. I *know* it is, damn it. And—" Her innate self-righteousness and resentfulness began to surface again. "It's not my *fault*. I had nothing to do with it! If that fucking Cachat hadn't—"

"*Jillian! Please.*" That cut her short. Yuri hurried onward. "Please. There's no point to this. My own career's on the rocks too, you know. Even when you're found 'innocent,' having an official 'rigorous interrogation' on your record is a big black mark. Worse than any on your record, when you get right down to it."

Gallanti almost—not quite—managed a smile of sympathy. Yuri decided the moment was right to strike "the deal."

This time, he slid all the way to the edge of his seat. "Look, the worst thing you can do is wallow in misery. There's still a chance to clean this up. Minimize the damage, at the very least. Cachat taking himself off on a romantic haring around after pirates and commerce raiders is the best thing we could have hoped for."

She cocked a questioning, vaguely hopeful eyebrow. Yuri gave her his very best sincere smile.

And an excellent one it was, too. Friendly, intimate without being vulgar, sympathetic; over the years, hundreds of people had told Yuri how much they appreciated his sincerity. Perhaps the strangest thing about it all—certainly in that moment— was that Yuri knew it for the simple truth. He *was* a sincere, sympathetic and friendly man. Using his own nature, since he was otherwise disarmed, as the only weapon at his disposal.

"I'm not a cop, Jillian. Cachat can plaster whatever labels he wants on me. I don't have the temperament for it. To cover my ass—everybody's ass —I'll find and bust up a few more pissant 'spots of corruption.' On a ship this big, there's got to be at least half a dozen illegal stills being operated by ratings."

"Ha. Try 'two dozen.' Not to mention the gambling operations."

"Exactly. So we'll fry a few ratings—slap 'em with the harshest penalties possible—while I go ahead with my real business."

"Which is?"

"I'm a *commissioner,* Jillian. And a damn good one. Whatever other beefs any of my superiors have ever had about me, nobody's ever given me anything but top marks for my actual *work*. Check my records, if you don't believe me."

That, too, was the simple truth. Radamacher didn't try to explain any of it to Gallanti, for the task would have been hopeless. By the nature of her assignment, even leaving aside her own temperament, Gallanti was a StateSec *enforcer*. That was how her mind naturally worked, and she'd inevitably project that onto anyone else in StateSec.

The reality was more complex. Yuri, unlike Gallanti, had spent his entire career in "fleet StateSec"—one of those handful of StateSec officers on each ship assigned to work and fight alongside the officers and ratings of the People's Navy they were officially overseeing. Many if not all of such StateSec officers, as the years passed, came to identify closely with their comrades in battle. For someone with Yuri's temperament, the process had been inevitable—and quick.

Gallanti was too dull-witted to grasp that. Oscar Saint-Just, of course, was not. He'd always understood that he held a dangerous double-edged sword in his hand. The problem was that he *needed* it. Because bitter experience had proven, time and again, that the StateSec commissioners who got the best results in the crucible of war were not the whiphandlers but precisely the ones like Yuri Radamacher. The ones who did not "oversee" their naval comrades so much as they served them as priests had once served the armies of Catholic Spain. Inquisitors in name, but more often confessors in practice. The people just far enough outside the naval chain of command that ratings—officers, too—would come to them for advice, help, counsel. Intercession with the authorities, often enough, if they'd fallen afoul of regs which were intolerant on paper but could somehow magically be softened at a commissioner's private word. Despite the grim "StateSec" term in his title, the simple fact was that Yuri had spent far more time over the past ten years helping heartsick young ratings deal with "Dear John" or "Dear Jane" letters than he had trying to ferret out disloyalty.

Yuri had pondered the matter, over the years. And, with his natural bent for irony, taken a certain solace in it. Whatever else the Committee of Public Safety's ruthlessness had crushed underfoot, it had not been able to transform basic human emotional reactions. Yuri doubted now if any tyranny ever could.

"So what do you want, Yuri?" Gallanti's words were gruff, but the tone was not that of a woman issuing a rebuff. It sounded more like an appeal, in fact.

"Give me free rein aboard the ship," he replied at once. "In name I'll be the 'assistant investigator' scurrying all over rooting out rot and corruption. In the real world, I'll serve you as your commissioner. I'm *good* at morale-building, Jillian, try me and see if I'm not. By the time Cachat gets back, I'll have a handful of 'suppressed crimes' to wave under his nose. But, way more important, we'll have a functioning capital ship again—and a crew, including all the transfers, who'll swear up and down that the good ship *Hector* is a jolly good ship and Cap'n Gallanti a jolly good soul."

"And what good will *that* do?"

"Jillian, give Victor Cachat his due. I'd do that much for the devil himself. Yes, he's a simon-pure fanatic. But a fanatic, in his own twisted way, is also an honest man. *The kid's for real*, Jillian. When he says 'the needs of the State,' he means it. It's not a cover for personal ambitions. If we can satisfy him that the rot's been rooted out—even that we've got things turned around nicely—he'll be satisfied and go on his way. The fact is that La Martine Sector *has* been a stronghold for the Republic's economy for the past few years. The fact is that you *weren't* personally implicated in Jamka's crimes—and Cachat said so himself, in his official report to Nouveau Paris."

"How'd you know that?" grunted Gallanti. Skepticism mixed with anxiety—and now, more than a little in the way of hope.

He gave her his best worldly-wise smile, which was just as good as any of his other smiles. "Don't ask, Jillian. I told you: I'm a *commissioner*. It's my job to know these things. More precisely, to make the connections so that I *can* know."

And, again, that was the pure and simple truth. Even under arrest and self-restricted to his cabin, a man like Yuri Radamacher could no more help "making connections" than he could stop breathing.

He knew what Cachat had said about Gallanti in his report because the SI had asked Citizen Major Lafitte for his input and the Citizen Major had mentioned it to Citizen Sergeant Pierce, and Ned Pierce had told Yuri. None too cheerfully, as it happened, because like all Marines serving on the *Hector,* Ned Pierce and Citizen Major Lafitte detested the SD's CO. But Yuri saw no reason to tell Gallanti *that*.

It was just a fact of life; and now, finally, Yuri Radamacher accepted it entirely. People liked him and trusted him. He couldn't remember a time in his life when they hadn't—or a time when he'd ever repaid that trust except in good coin.

It was odd, perhaps, that he came to accept it at the very moment when—for the first time in his life—he was consciously plotting to betray someone. The woman sitting across the desk from him, whose confidence and trust he was doing everything possible to gain.

But . . . so be it. There was, indeed, such a thing as a "higher loyalty," no matter how cynical Yuri had gotten over the years. Something of the fanatic Cachat had rubbed off on him after all, it seemed. And if a middle-aged man like Radamacher shared none of the young Special Investigator's faith in political abstractions, he had no difficulty understanding personal loyalties. When push came to shove, he owed nothing to Citizen Captain Jillian Gallanti. In fact, he despised her for a bully and a hot-tempered despot. But he did owe a loyalty to the thousands of men and women alongside whom he'd served in Citizen Admiral Chin's task force, for years now—from Genevieve herself all the way down to the newest recruit. So, he'd use his natural skills to create a false front—and then use that front to save them from Saint-Just's murderous suspicions.

And if Citizen Captain Gallanti had to fall by the wayside in the process, stabbed in the back by her newfound "friend" . . .

Well, so be it. If a fanatic like Cachat had the courage of his convictions, it would be nothing but cowardice for Yuri to claim to be his moral superior—yet refuse to act with the same decisiveness.

As he waited for Gallanti to fall into the trap, Yuri probed more deeply into his conscience.

*Well. Okay. Some of it's just 'cause I got the hots for
Sharon and I will damn well keep my woman alive. Me
too, if I can manage it.*

Gallanti fell. "S'a deal," she said, extending her hand.
Yuri rose, bestowed on her his very best trustworthy smile
and his very best sincere handshake—both of them top-
notch, of course. All the while, measuring her back for the
stiletto.

8

Yuri did, in fact, have an excellent record as a people's
commissioner. He had routinely been given top marks
throughout his career for his proficiency—at least, once
he got out of the abstract environment of the academy and
into the real world of StateSec fleet operations. The one
criticism which Radamacher's superiors had leveled
against him periodically, however, had been "slackness."

By some, that was defined in political terms. Yuri
Radamacher's actual loyalty wasn't called into question, of
course. Had there been any question about *that* he would
have been summarily dismissed (at best) from StateSec
altogether. Still, there had been some of his superiors, over
the years, who felt that he was insufficiently zealous.

Yuri could not argue the matter. He wasn't zealous at
all, truth be told.

But the charge of "slackness" had another connotation.
One which, several years earlier, had been put bluntly by
the woman who had been his superior in the first year of
his assignment in La Martine.

"Baloney, Yuri!" she'd snapped in the course of one of his personnel evaluation sessions. "It's all fine and dandy to be 'easy-going' and 'laid-back' and the most popular StateSec officer in this sector. Yeah, Citizen Mister Nice Guy. The truth is you're just plain *lazy*."

Yuri *had* argued the matter, on that occasion. And had even managed, by a virtuoso combination of razzle-dazzle reference to his record and half a dozen charmingly related anecdotes, to get his superior to semi-relent by the end of the evaluation. Still . . .

Deep down, he knew there was a fair amount of truth to the charge. Whether it was because of his own personality, or his disenchantment with the regime, he wasn't sure. Perhaps it was a combination of both. But, whatever the reason, it was just a fact that Yuri Radamacher never really did seem to operate, as the ancient and cryptic expression went, "firing on all cylinders." He did his job, and did it very well, yes—but he never really put in that extra effort to do it as well as he knew he could have done. It just somehow didn't seem worth the effort.

So he found himself amused occasionally, as the weeks went by, wondering what those long-gone superiors would think of his work habits *now*. Yuri Radamacher was still easy-going, and laid-back, and pleasant to deal with. But now he was working an average of eighteen hours a day.

He didn't wonder at the reason himself, though. With Yuri's love of classic literature, he could summon up the answer with any of a number of choice phrases. The one which best captured the situation, he thought, came from Dr. Johnson:

Depend upon it, Sir, when a man knows he is to be hanged in a fortnight, it concentrates his mind wonderfully.

Granted, Yuri Radamacher had more than a fortnight at his disposal. But how much more, remained to be seen. So, he threw himself into his project with an energy he hadn't displayed since he was a teenager newly enlisted in the opposition to the Legislaturalist regime.

A fortnight came and went, and another. And another. And still another.

And Yuri began to relax a little. He still had no idea what the future might bring. But whatever it was, he would at least face it from the best position he could have created. For most of those around him, not only himself.

More than that, it was given to no person to know. Not in this world at least; and, StateSec regulations aside, Yuri really didn't believe in an afterlife.

"Give me a break, Yuri," Citizen Lieutenant Commander Saunders complained. "Impeller Tech Bob Gottlieb is the best rating I've got. He can practically make those nodes sit up and beg."

Yuri looked at him mildly. "He's also the biggest bootlegger on the ship, and he's getting careless about it."

Saunders scowled. "Look, I'll talk to him. Get him to keep it under cover. Yuri, you know damn good and well there's *always* going to be an illegal still operating somewhere on a warship this size. Especially one that's been kept from having any shore leave for so long. At least we don't have to worry about Gottlieb selling dangerous hooch. He knows a lot about chemistry, too—don't ask me how or where he learned, I don't want to know. He's not a stupid kid who doesn't know the difference between ethanol and methanol."

"His stuff's pretty damn tasty, in fact," chimed in Ned Pierce, who was lounging in another armchair in Yuri's large office.

Yuri turned the mild-mannered gaze his way. The citizen sergeant was trying to project a degree of cherubic innocence which fit poorly with his dark-skinned, battered, altogether piratical-looking face. "That's what I hear, anyway," Pierce added.

Yuri snorted. "I need *something*, people," he pointed out. "Cachat'll be back any time now. I've got a fair number of screw-ups and goofballs on display in the brig, sure. But that's pretty much old stuff by now. About a third of them have almost served their time. And I'm telling you: nothing will soothe the savage inquisitor like being able to show him a freshly nabbed, still-trembling sinner."

"Aw, c'mon, Yuri, the SI's not that bad."

From the tight expression on his face, Citizen Lieutenant Commander Saunders did not agree with the citizen sergeant's assessment of Cachat's degree of severity. Not in the least.

Yuri wasn't surprised. Saunders had been present in the gym when Cachat personally shot six fellow officers of the *Hector Van Dragen* in the head. So had Ned, of course. But Pierce was a Marine, and a combat veteran. Personal, in-your-face mayhem was no stranger to him. Had Saunders been in the regular Navy, he might have encountered the kind of battering which capital ships often took in fleet encounters, where it was not uncommon for bodies to be shredded. But StateSec capital ships were there to enforce discipline over the Navy, not to fight the Navy's battles. That was undoubtedly the first time Saunders had seen blood and brains splattered all over the trousers of his uniform.

Citizen Major Lafitte cleared his throat. He and his counterpart, a StateSec citizen major by the name of Diana Citizen—her real name, that; not something she'd made up to curry favor with the regime—were sitting side by side on a couch angled next to Yuri's armchair. The two of them, along with Ned Pierce and *his* counterpart, StateSec Citizen Sergeant Jaime Rolla, constituted the informal little group which Yuri relied on to handle disciplinary matters on the superdreadnought. The SD's executive officer knew about it and had been looking the other way for weeks. The man was incompetent at everything except knowing which way the political winds were blowing. He'd quickly sized up the new situation and—wisely—decided that he'd be a nut crushed between Radamacher's skills and Captain Gallanti's temper if he tried to assert the traditional prerogatives and authority of a warship's XO.

Citizen Major Diana Citizen cleared her throat. "I've got a sacrificial lamb, if you need one." Her thin, rather pretty face grew a little pinched. "Except calling him a 'lamb' is an insult to baa-baas. He's a pig and a thug and I'd be delighted to see him slammed as hard as you can. Assuming you can figure out a charge that would stick. Unfortunately, he's slicker than your average shipboard bully. Keeps his ass covered. Name's Henri Alouette; he's a rating—"

"*That* fuckhead!" snarled Ned. "Me and him damn near came to it, once, in the mess room. Woulda, too, if the bastard hadn't backed off at the last minute. Too bad, I woulda—"

"Citizen Sergeant Pierce." Yuri's tone was as pleasant and relaxed as ever, but the unusual formality was enough in itself to draw the citizen sergeant up short. Normally, in this inner circle devoted to handling the nitty-gritty business of a warship's "dirty laundry," informality was the rule. Over the weeks, rank differences aside—even the traditional mutual hostility of StateSec and regular military aside—the five people involved had gotten onto very good personal terms. As usually happened with teams assembled by Yuri Radamacher and overseen by him.

"I will remind you that I've stressed—any number of times—the critical importance of keeping tensions between the regular military stationed on this ship and its StateSec complement to a bare minimum." He smiled easily. "Which I dare say having a Marine citizen sergeant pound a StateSec rating into a pulp—yes, Ned, I'm sure you woulda and coulda—might cut against."

"Don't count on it," piped up StateSec Citizen Sergeant Rolla. "Alouette's notorious all over the ship, Yuri. I'd give you three-to-one odds all the StateSec ratings in that mess room would have been cheering Ned on."

"You'd 'a won the bet," gruffed Ned. "Two of 'em offered to hold my coat. Another asked the fuckhead what blood type he was so he could make sure to tell the doctors in the ship's hospital."

Radamacher eyed Pierce for a moment. He'd been on

such friendly personal terms with the big citizen sergeant for so long that Yuri tended to forget what a truly ferocious specimen of humanity the man was. Jesting aside, he didn't have much doubt at all that anyone who'd apparently angered Pierce that much *would* be needing transfusions after the brawl was over.

"Still." Yuri swiveled his chair around and began working at the keyboard of his computer. "We've gotten morale to such a good point on the *Hector* that I'd just as soon avoid any possible interservice problems." He glanced over his shoulder, still smiling. "I'm sure I can find a better way to nail Alouette than have Ned here try to frame him up on a brawling charge. Not even Special Investigator Cachat would believe for a minute that somebody deliberately picked a fight with *him*."

He turned back, letting the easy laughter fill the room while he worked.

It didn't take long. Less than five minutes.

"I must be slipping," he muttered. "How'd I possibly miss *this*?"

"Working eighteen hours a day at everything else?" Major Lafitte chuckled. "What'd you find, Yuri?"

Radamacher jabbed a stiff finger at the screen. "How in the hell did Alouette pass his required annual spacesuit proficiency test when there's no record he's even been in a spacesuit once in the past three years? And how in the hell did he manage *that*—when he's rated as a gravitic sensor tech? Isn't external inspection and repair of the arrays sort of *part* of that specialization?"

He swiveled back around. "Well?"

The two Marines in the room had bland, blank *none-*

of-my-business expressions on their faces. The sort of expressions which polite people assume when another family's skeletons are spilling out of an opened closet.

Radamacher approved. This was StateSec's dirty laundry. As was obvious from the scowls on the faces of the two StateSec officers and—even fiercer—on the face of StateSec Citizen Sergeant Rolla.

"That rotten SOB," Rolla hissed. "Give you three-to-one—no, make it five-to-one—that Alouette's been intimidating his mates and the section chief. Probably threatened the rating recording the test results, too."

Citizen Major Citizen looked uncomfortable. "Yeah, that's probably it. I hate to say it, seeing as how I sure didn't shed any tears over those bums that the SI blew away, but their absence did hurt us a lot in security. It left holes all through my department, which I still haven't been able to get filled up all the way. Especially since I had to start from scratch coming over from the fleet."

"Nobody's blaming you, Diana," Yuri assured her smoothly. "Isolated little tumors like this are bound to turn up, now and then, when a ship's security department was in the hands of human cancer cells for years. Which is about the most polite way I can think of to describe Jamka's cronies."

He rubbed the back of his neck. "To be perfectly honest about it—cold-blooded, too—this is damn near perfect. Cachat'll rub his hands with glee over a bust like this one. Beats a penny-ante bootlegging case hands down. Inquisitors, you know, thrive on real *sin*."

"Aw, c'mon, Yuri—" Ned started again. "The SI's not—"

The sudden burst of laughter from everyone else in the room caused a look of grievance to come over the citizen sergeant's face. "Well, he's *not* that bad," he insisted.

Radamacher didn't argue the point. At the moment, he was in such a good mood that he was even willing to grant that Special Investigator Victor Cachat probably didn't really match up to Torquemada. His understudy, maybe.

He looked to Citizen Major Citizen. "You'll handle this, Diana? Mind you, I want a good, solid, rock-hard case against Alouette. Nothing flimsy."

She nodded. "Won't be hard. Assuming we're right, everybody in the section will fall all over themselves spilling the beans—as long as they're sure that Alouette will get put away for a long time. Somewhere he can't retaliate against them."

"Have no fear on that score. Just going by a minimum reading of regulations, if Alouette has been threatening his mates with violence in order to cover up his skill deficiencies—much less a senior rating like a section chief—he's looking at five years, at least. That's five years served in a StateSec maximum security prison, too, not a ship's brig."

Yuri's face was grim. "That's if he's lucky. But I think Alouette's luck just ran out on him. Because his case will be coming up after the Special Investigator's return, and Cachat has the authority to mete out any punishment he deems proper. *Any* punishment, people. After I got my new assignment, for the first time in my life I studied carefully all the rules and regulations governing the position of Special Investigator. It's . . . pretty scary. And Cachat's already made crystal clear how he looks on

StateSec personnel abusing their positions for the sake of personal gain or pleasure."

He studied the far wall of the stateroom. It was a wide bulkhead, as you'd expect in a top staff officer's suite in a superdreadnought. Almost as wide as the bulkhead which Cachat had used as the backstop for his firing squad.

Everyone else in the room seemed to share Yuri's grim mood, judging from the sudden silence.

Not for long, though, in the case of the two noncoms. "Hey, Jaime," whispered Ned. "Any chance I could volunteer—just the once—to serve on a StateSec firing squad?"

"S'against regs," Rolla whispered back. "But I'll put in a good word for you."

Yuri sighed. There were times—had been for many years, now—when he felt like a sheep running with the wolves. And wondering when someone was finally going to notice that his moon-howl was distinctly off-key.

The half-rueful, half-amused thought lasted for perhaps five seconds. Then the office hatch snapped open with no notice at all, a commo rating burst through the opening, and Yuri discovered that his long-extended fortnight had come to an end.

Dr. Johnson's proverbial hangman had finally arrived.

9

The rating's face was pale as a sheet. "The task force is back in the system. We just got a message from the Citizen Admiral. They expect to be back in orbit inside five hours."

Easy-going as Yuri was, the rating's lack of basic military courtesy was just too extreme to let pass unreprimanded. Yuri wondered what was wrong with the woman. The task force's return was hardly unexpected, after all.

"What is your name, Citizen Rating?" he demanded frostily.

The woman had apparently taken leave of her senses. She didn't even have the excuse of being a young recruit. From her age and the two hash marks on her sleeve, she'd been in StateSec service for at least six T-years. Even a wet-behind-the-ears newbie knew enough to recognize a superior officer's *you-are-about-to-be-fried-alive* tone of voice.

Utterly oblivious, it seemed. "You don't understand! The SI sent a message too. Ordering Citizen Captain Gallanti to disregard the message from the merchant ship—"

Yuri felt his stomach drop out from under him. He had a very bad feeling that the sensation was much like that of a man feeling the trapdoor open under the gallows.

"*What* message from a merchant ship?"

"—and stand down the impellers and sidewalls."

Citizen Lieutenant Commander Saunders bolted upright in his chair, his head cocked as if straining all his senses. He stretched out a hand and laid fingertips delicately against a bulkhead.

"She's right. The ship's getting under way. What the hell—?"

Impellers couldn't be detected in operation inside a ship. They were not reaction engines and produced no discernible noise or vibration. But the impeller rooms were close to Yuri's cabin and although Yuri himself still couldn't sense anything, Saunders was apparently picking up the subtle vibrations created by the various auxiliary engines. That was Saunder's specialty—although even he hadn't noticed until the rating brought it to his attention. Yuri didn't think to doubt him.

What was Gallanti doing? There was no logical reason for the *Hector Van Dragen* to be leaving orbit. And even if she were, why bring up the sidewalls unless . . .

Yuri forgot all his own by-the-regs proscriptions. "Jesus Christ," he whispered. Then, firmly, to the still-jittery rating:

"You're making no sense at all, woman! Settle down!"

That seemed to calm her, finally. She swallowed and then nodded abruptly. "Com Tech first-class Rita Enquien, Citizen Assistant Investigator. Sorry for the discourtesy. It's just—I'm not supposed to be here—the Citizen Captain finds out I left the bridge I'm dead meat—"

The sensation in Yuri's stomach was now definitely one of free fall. He wondered how long a man dropped before the rope ran out and the noose broke his neck.

"No problem, Citizen Tech Enquien," he said soothingly, in his best confessional tone of voice.

He realized, finally, what was happening. In general, if not the specifics. Something had completely panicked the rating and, in her confusion, she'd broken discipline and gone to the one person in the ship she'd come to trust in a pinch. Given that Yuri didn't know her, the woman's estimate was obviously based on what she'd heard from her shipmates.

Which meant . . .

The falling sensation vanished. Dr. Johnson's hangman be damned. Yuri had set out weeks ago to steal a capital warship right out from under its own captain, hadn't he? Just in case all hell broke loose.

All hell had broken loose, clearly enough. But the ship was there for the taking.

"Now, Enquien. Let's start from the beginning. What merchant ship are you talking about? And what message did it send?"

The woman's mouth made an "O" of surprise. "Oh. How stupid of me." Then, in a rush:

"A merchant ship arrived in the system just half an hour before we got the message from the Citizen Admiral. It's from Haven. There's been—a revolution, I guess. Coup d'état, whatever you call it. Citizen Admiral Theismann's taken over, they say. And—"

She swallowed. Yuri suddenly knew what was coming next. Exultation flooded over him. Yet at the same time, oddly, a wave of fear also.

At least the Devil you know is the one you know.

"Citizen Chairman Saint-Just is dead. Nobody knows exactly how, I guess. Well, by whom exactly, I mean. They know *how*, that's for sure. The merchant ship sent us the recording, it was played all over Nouveau Paris' HD networks. I saw it myself. It was Oscar Saint-Just all right. The face wasn't touched. Just a great big pulser dart hole in the middle of his forehead."

The rating shook herself, as if chilled. "He's dead, Sir!" she cried.

And, in her voice also, Yuri Radamacher could sense

the same conflicting emotions. His eyes scanned the room, seeing them on every face.

Exultation. The cold, gray, heartless man who had loomed over the Republic for years as the incarnation of murderous ruthlessness was finally gone. Dead, dead, dead.

Terror. And now what?

The paralysis lasted for perhaps five seconds. Then Yuri slapped his knees and rose abruptly.

"Oh, bullshit," he said, softly but firmly. "Now's the same as it always was. We do the best we can, that's all, with what we've got."

He looked at the rating. "I take it the Citizen Captain's gone berserk?"

Enquien jerked a nod. "Yes, Citi—uh, Sir. That's why I snuck out when she wasn't looking and came here." She hissed in a breath. "I'm scared, Sir. I think the Captain's really lost it."

Yuri sighed and shook his head. "I don't think she ever really had it, Enquien." Then, much like a priest might bestow absolution:

"Relax, you did the right thing. I'll take care of it."

The rating's taut face eased. Yuri turned to the other people in the room.

"Will you follow me?"

There was no hesitation. Five heads in unison— StateSec and Marine alike—jerked their own nods.

"Good. Citiz—the hell with it, the rating's got it right. Saint-Just is dead and his petty regulations went with him. Lieutenant Commander Saunders, I want you to return to your post and take control of the impeller rooms. Use whatever force you need to, in the event of resistance. Major Lafitte, you and Major Citizen go with him and see to it. Round up whatever Marines and reliable StateSec troopers you can. Whatever else, I want those impellers taken out of Gallanti's control. Understood?"

"Yes, Citizen Assistant Spec—uh, Sir." The stumbled phrase came in unison, and so did the rueful little laughs which followed.

The StateSec major grinned at her Marine counterpart. "This'll be worth it just so people won't keep making jokes about my last name." More seriously: "You're senior to me, Khedi. In years of service, anyway, and I don't know how else to figure this. Besides, you've got experience in boarding operations and I don't. So you take the lead and I'll follow."

Lafitte nodded. An instant later, the three officers were out into the corridor and hurrying in the direction of the impeller rooms.

Yuri looked to the two sergeants. A quick glance at their hips confirmed the fact that neither was armed. There had been no reason for them to be, of course. In fact, it would have been against regulations. Aboard a StateSec ship, unless expressly ordered otherwise, only StateSec officers were permitted to carry sidearms. And they were required to carry them. From old habit, in fact, Yuri had a pulser on his own hip, even though the regulations were not entirely clear as to whether the provision applied to an Assistant Special Investigator.

He was hoping that single pulser would be enough. But given Gallanti's temper . . .

He'd planned for that eventuality also. "Come here," he commanded, stepping over to a locker along one wall. Quickly, his fingers punched the combination and the locker opened. Inside—

Ned Pierce whistled admiringly. "Hey, that's quite an arsenal. Uh, Sir. You allowed to have this?"

Yuri shrugged. "Who knows? You wouldn't believe how vague the regulations get when it comes to specifying what Special Investigators—their assistants too, I presume—can and can't do."

He stepped aside from the locker. "This really isn't my line of work. So I'll let the two of you choose whatever weapons you think most suitable."

Pierce reached eagerly for a light tribarrel—about the heaviest man-portable weapon made (short of a plasma rifle, at any rate)—with a thousand-round ammunition tank. The tank was coded for a mixed flechette, armor-piercing, explosive belt, and the Marine's eyes glowed with anticipation. But—

"For Pete's sake, Ned!" Rolla protested. "You'll slaughter everybody on the bridge with that thing. You know how to fly a seven-million-ton SD? I sure as hell don't."

"Oh." Pierce's face looked simultaneously embarrassed and frustrated. "Yeah, you're right. Damn. I love those things."

"Just take a frickin' flechette gun, if you really *need* to splatter people wholesale," growled the StateSec sergeant, plucking a hand pulser out of the locker himself. "At least that way you won't blow any essential hardware apart, too! Or have you forgotten how to aim at anything smaller than a moon?"

"Teach your grandmother how to suck eggs," retorted Pierce. Quickly, easily, the Marine sergeant took out a flechette gun, examined and armed the weapon.

Then, he and Rolla studied each other for a moment. It was an awkward moment.

Yuri cleared his throat. "Ah, Sergeant Pierce, I believe you're senior to Sergeant Rolla. In terms of service, certainly—and, as Diana said, I don't see any other way to settle these things at the moment. Nevertheless—"

To his relief, Ned just shrugged. "Yeah, sure, Sir. Hey, look, I ain't stupid." He nodded at Rolla. "Jaime can have it. I really don't care."

"Good. What I *hope* we'll be dealing with is really more a police matter than a military one. Not to put too fine a point on it, but Sergeant Rolla has experience making arrests. Whereas, ah, you—"

Pierce's piratical grin was on full display. "I blow people apart. Don't worry about it, Sir. Mama Pierce's good little boy will follow orders."

Yuri's fears that they might face opposition on their way to the bridge proved to be unfounded. All they encountered, here and there, were a few small knots of StateSec ratings huddled and whispering. Clearly enough, some scraps of the news had begun percolating through the ship. Just as clearly, the scraps were just that—murky, muddled, impossible to make any clear sense from. The huge size of the superdreadnought added to the confusion. Wild rumors in a smaller ship might have stayed concentrated long enough for people to boil down the truth from them. In an SD juggernaut, rumors echoed down endless passages, becoming completely distorted and incoherent the farther they went.

He was a bit puzzled, at first. He would have expected Gallanti to have at least stationed StateSec guards at the critical access routes to the bridge. But . . . nothing, until they finally reached the hatch leading into the bridge itself.

By then, Yuri had figured out the reason, and so it was armed with that knowledge that he marched forthrightly toward the two StateSec security ratings standing guard by the hatch. The two guards were not from a special unit, summoned by Gallanti for the purpose. They were from the unit which was routinely stationed there—and these two happened to have the bad luck to be on shift when the crap hit the fan. They looked as nervous as mice when cats are on a rampage.

Gallanti was just a stupid, self-centered, hot-headed bully, that's all. The explanation was no more complicated than that. A woman who'd gotten her way for so long simply because of her rank and her overbearing personality that she wasn't giving a second's thought to the fact that she might be facing a *tactical* situation.

He was almost surprised he couldn't hear her screaming even through the closed hatch.

The Boss is blowing her stack, and when the Boss blows her stack everybody has to stand around and eat her shit. A law of nature, like gravity.

Idiot.

"Stand aside," he commanded, as soon as he came up to the guards. The words were spoken in a mild tone, but a very self-assured one.

The guards didn't think to question him. In fact, they were obviously relieved that he was there. Yuri jerked his thumb over his shoulder at Sergeant Rolla.

"You're now under the command of Citizen Sergeant Rolla. Is that understood?"

"Yes, Citizen Assistant Special Investigator." The replies came simultaneously. Then, seeing the figure of the commo rating following gingerly at the rear, their eyes widened.

Yuri opened the hatch and stepped through, followed by the two sergeants. Behind, he could hear one of the guards hissing to the commo rating.

"*Jesus*, Rita. You told us you were just gonna be gone for a minute. The Citizen Captain's ready to skin you alive. She finds out *we* let you pass—"

"Piss on Gallanti," Enquien hissed back. "I went and got the People's Commissioner. He's here now—and that bitch's ass is grass. *You watch.*"

The phrase she used made Yuri pause in midstep. Not "the Citizen Assistant Special Investigator." Just . . .

The Citizen Commissioner. No. Simply the People's Commissioner.

He found it all, then. All he needed for what had to be done. In that moment, for the first time in his life, he thought he understood that bizarre self-assuredness possessed by fanatics like Victor Cachat.

The People's Commissioner.

Indeed, it was so. For ten years he had carried that title, and made it his own. He had absolutely no idea what the future was going to bring, either for himself or anyone else, except for one thing alone. Whatever else happened, he was quite certain that the title "people's commissioner" was going to go down in history draped in the darkest of colors. As dark, he knew, as the term "inquisitors."

And rightly. Whatever the promise, the reality had turned it inside out. A post created to shield a republic from the possible depredations of its own military had been turned, not only against the military, but the republic itself. The old conundrum, reborn again. *Who will guard the guardians?*

Yet, he remembered reading of an inquisitor in the Basque country, in that ancient era when humanity had still lived on a single planet. Sent there by the Spanish Inquisition at the height of its power to investigate the truth behind a wave of accusations of witchcraft, the inquisitor had stopped the witch-burnings. Indeed, had insisted upon proper rules of evidence at all subsequent trials—and then released every supposed witch for lack of any such evidence.

Yuri had run across the anecdote in his voluminous reading. Years ago, that had been; but he'd taken a certain comfort from it ever since.

He even managed a chuckle, at that moment. Yuri Radamacher did not believe in an afterlife. Yet, if there was one, he was quite sure that at that very moment in Hell, some good-natured, round-faced, overweight, apprehensive little devil was being chewed out by Satan for "slackness."

It was time for the People's Commissioner to do his duty, then. The people of the republic needed protection against an officer run amok. Yuri advanced onto the bridge, with resolute steps.

The bridge was . . . quite a scene.

Citizen Captain Gallanti was standing in the center of it, glaring red-faced at a display split into two screens. One screen showed the bridge of Admiral Chin's flagship. Yuri could see Genevieve herself standing there, along with Commodore Ogilve and Commissioner Wilkins. At their center, seeming to be in the forefront, stood Victor Cachat.

Cachat, as always, was an imposing figure. Even through a holodisplay, the young man's intensity seemed to burn. But Yuri's eyes were immediately drawn to the other screen. Sharon Justice was in that screen, which was showing the bridge of the other StateSec SD, the *Joseph Tilden*. So he assumed, anyway, given that the SD's captain Vesey was standing next to her.

He was relieved to see that Sharon seemed in fine health. Even in good spirits, for that matter. Her facial expression was one of solemnity, but Yuri knew her quite well after all these years and could detect the underlying . . .

Excitement? Maybe. It was hard to tell. But whatever else, she certainly didn't seem gloomy.

Captain Vesey, on the other hand, did look on the gloomy side. The words "nervous, worried, and more than a little depressed" might capture the expression on his face a bit better.

One thing was clear, just from the body language of the two people alone. Whatever was happening on the *Tilden*, it was obvious that Sharon was calling the shots and not the superdreadnought's nominal commander.

That was good enough, for the moment. Yuri looked away from the screens and quickly examined the bridge of the *Hector* itself. All of the ratings and as many of the officers as could possibly manage it had their heads buried as far down as they could get them into their work stations. As long-beaten underlings will do, when their mistress is having another temper tantrum, trying their very best to be inconspicuous.

That was not possible, of course, for some of the officers. The nature of their duties required them to be directly attentive to the citizen captain.

The *Hector Van Drugen*'s executive officer was standing not far from Gallanti, bestowing upon her his well-practiced look of fawning vacancy. The man's name was as comical in its own way as that of the long-suffering Diana Citizen. *Kit Carson*, no less. Fortunately for him, Yuri Radamacher was one of the few people in the task force who had the historical knowledge to understand how ridiculous the name was, given the man's nature.

Yuri dismissed him from consideration. Carson was a nonentity. Of the other top ship's officers on the bridge, most of his attention went to the tac officer, Edouard Ballon. Partly that was because of the nature of a tac officer's duties, since Ballon controlled the ship's armament. Mostly it was because Yuri knew that if there was going to be trouble from anyone other than Gallanti herself, it would come from Ballon.

The tac officer was not precisely a StateSec "fanatic." Certainly not one cut from the same cloth as Cachat.

Ballon had no particularly strong ideological convictions. But he was the type of sour, nasty, mean-spirited person who tended to gravitate naturally to an organization like StateSec. Not a sadist, no. Just cut from the same cloth as the grim villagers who were always the first to raise the cry of "witchcraft!"—and always took satisfaction in the punishment of others. As if that validated their place in the world.

Neither Gallanti nor Ballon was watching him. Neither of them, in fact, had even noticed Yuri coming onto the bridge, they were so fixated on the screen. Yuri took the opportunity to nod toward Ballon while giving both the sergeants standing behind him a meaningful look. Sergeant Rallo nodded back, relaxed; Ned Pierce just smiled thinly and hefted the flechette gun in his hands a centimeter or two higher.

It's time, then. Do it.

Yuri turned back to face Gallanti. And suddenly—did life *always* have to be ridiculously awkward?—realized that the first obstacle he faced was simply the pedestrian problem of getting the damn woman to *hear* him. She was making enough of a racket herself to drown a bugler.

"—at's pure horseshit, Cachat! I don't give a flying fuck what fancy titles you carry around! I'm the captain of this ship and what I say goes! And if you think when there's treason all about I'm going to disarm a StateSec capital ship, you're out of your fucking mind! The impellers and the sidewalls stay up—and I'll tell you what else, wet-behind-the-ears errand boy. Your sugar daddy Saint-Just isn't around any longer to cover your ass. You're on your own now, punk. You try shooting me in the head with that piddly pulser of yours, I'll show you just what kind of hell on earth a superdreadnought can unleash! Go ahead, try me!"

Yuri saw Captain Vesey wince. To the man's credit, he tried to intervene. "Jillian, *please*. Until we find out what's really happening on Haven—"

"Fuck off, you gutless bastard! What? Does that bitch Justice intimidate you? She doesn't intimidate me! Nobody does—and that includes you. That scow of yours may technically be a sister ship of mine, but command is what matters, don't think it doesn't. If the gloves come off here—and we're getting real close—I'll tear that thing down around your ears before I turn Chickenshit Chin's task force into so much dog food. You'll see an SD turned into a funeral pyre faster than you can believe!"

Yuri had always heard about Gallanti's temper tantrums, but this was the first time he'd ever personally witnessed one. How in the world had this woman ever been given command of a capital ship? Even State Security should have had enough sense to realize she was unfit for such responsibility. If he wanted to be charitable about it, Yuri would have likened Gallanti to a spoiled five-year-old child throwing a fit.

Unfortunately, five-year-old children, no matter how spoiled, never had the terrifying power of a superdreadnought under their control. Gallanti did. Which made the situation deadly instead of simply pathetic. Under the circumstances, she was as dangerous as a maddened bear.

Gallanti finally took a breath, and Yuri began to speak. But before he managed to get a word out, Victor Cachat's audio-amplified voice filled the bridge.

As always, it was a cold voice. "What took you so long,

Assistant Special Investigator? I was beginning to wonder if you were slacking off again."

Yuri suddenly realized that he'd advanced far enough onto the bridge to enter the field of the comm pickup and become visible to those on the other two ships. Even though Gallanti herself hadn't noticed him until that very moment.

God, he was *tired* of that arrogant young voice.

"Have a certain regard for natural law if nothing else, would you, Cachat?" He took an admittedly petty pleasure in neglecting all honorifics. "I just got the news myself and got here as soon as I could."

The fact that Cachat didn't seem to take any umbrage at the lack of honorifics—didn't even seem to *notice*, damn the man—just irritated Yuri still further.

"And if you don't mind"—making clear by his tone that he didn't care if he did—"I prefer the title 'people's commissioner.' I don't really see where there's anything left to investigate, anyway."

Cachat stared at him. In the big display a capital ship could manage, the young fanatic seemed even larger than life.

Then, to Yuri's surprise, Cachat gave him a deep, slow nod. It had almost the sense of a ceremonial bow to it. And when his head lifted, for the first time since Yuri had met the man, Cachat's dark eyes seemed a warm brown instead of an iron black.

"Yes," said Cachat. "You have the right of it, Yuri Radamacher. Now do your duty, People's Commissioner."

Gallanti was gawping at Yuri. Then she burst into the start of another tirade.

"What the hell are you doing here? I didn't give you permission—"

Yuri had no desire at all to listen to more of that screech. When he needed it, he could manage quite a loud voice himself.

"You are under arrest, Captain Gallanti. I am relieving you of your duties. You are unfit to command."

That cut off her off in mid-screech. Again, she gawped.

Yuri, at the end, tried one last time. He put on his most sympathetic smile and added: "Jillian, please, there's no need for this. Just let it go and I'll give you my word I'll see to it—"

It was no use, and Yuri had a sick feeling that in his effort he'd simply condemned himself. Gallanti's hand was already grabbing the butt of her pulser—and, like a slack idiot, his own pulser still had the flap fastened.

"You fucking traitor!" Gallanti screamed. Her weapon was coming out of the holster and Yuri had no doubt at all she intended to fire. The woman had completely lost it. Out of the corner of one eye, as he scrabbled to get the flap of his holster open, Yuri saw the tac officer starting to rise from his chair. Ballon was reaching for his own sidearm.

Then—

Whackwhack. Whackwhack.

Small holes appeared in the foreheads of both Gallanti and Ballon, and the entire backs of their skulls exploded in a gory spray of splintered bone and finely divided brain tissue.

Rolla's doing, Yuri realized dimly. He'd double-tapped both of them. Yuri hadn't known the StateSec sergeant was that quick and expert a shot.

Brrraaaaaaaaaaaaaaaaaaa!

Before Gallanti's body could even begin to slump, Sergeant Pierce's short, lethally accurate three-round burst flung her five meters against a bulkhead, the deadly flechettes literally shredding the body along the way. No one else was standing there, thank God. Thank Pierce, actually; even in the shock of the moment Yuri understood that the experienced veteran had made sure he had a clean line of fire. Although at least three of the bridge's officers and ratings were frantically scraping bits and pieces of Gallanti off of them—now one of the ratings started vomiting—nobody else had actually gotten hurt.

"Ned," Yuri heard Rolla complaining, "can't you do *anything* neatly? What do you use when you go fishing? Missiles?"

"Hey, Jaime, I'm a Marine. This is what we do. You wanna transfer? I'll put in a good word for you—so will at least ten other guys I know. Probably even be able to keep the same rank."

Rolla started to make one of his usual retorts about the mental deficiencies of Marines, but broke off before he got through the first four words. Then, after a moment's silence, he said quietly: "Yeah, actually, I probably do. I've got a feeling State Security is about to get seriously downsized."

The StateSec sergeant had reholstered his pulser by now, there being clearly no other armed threat posed on the bridge. To Yuri's surprise, he pushed past him—not rudely, no; but firmly nonetheless—and came to stand at the center of the bridge staring at the figures in the display.

At Victor Cachat, to be precise.

"You tell me. Sir, or whatever else I'm supposed to call you. Who's running this show these days?"

Good question, thought Yuri.

"And what are we all supposed to do now?" Sergeant Rolla continued.

And that's an even better one.

10

Cachat didn't even hesitate, and Yuri damned him again. All the unfairness of the universe, in that moment, seemed concentrated in the fact that a twenty-four-year-old fanatic—*even now!*—never seemed to have any doubts about anything.

"I think the situation is clear enough, Sergeant—ah?"

"Rolla, Sir. Jaime Rolla."

"Sergeant Rolla. As for titles, I think we can all dispense with the curlicues." Cachat's razor-thin smile appeared. "I'll confess that I get tired myself of all those longwinded syllables. My standing rank in State Security is Captain, so I'll go with that. As for the rest—"

Cachat's eyes moved slowly across the people on the bridge of the *Hector*; then, briefly, at those he could see in his display on the sister SD; finally, at greater length, he looked at the naval officers standing next to him. Especially Admiral Chin.

Then he looked back at Rolla.

"Here's what I think. We have no real idea what's happened—or is happening—on Haven. The news brought by the merchant ship is simply too garbled. The only two things which seem clear at the moment are that Saint-Just is dead and Admiral Theismann holds effective power at the capital. But we still don't know what new government will emerge in its place—or upon what political principles that government will be based."

Genevieve's lips tightened. "I'll go with Theismann, myself."

Yuri could sense the StateSec officers on the bridge of the *Hector* stir a little. Not for the first time in his life, he found himself wishing that Admiral Chin would learn to be a *little* more diplomatic.

"Would you, Admiral?" Cachat demanded. "You know absolutely nothing about what sort of regime Admiral Theismann might—or might not—be putting into place. It might be an outright military dictatorship. Are you really so certain that's what you want?"

"It's better than Saint-Just!" she snarled.

Cachat shrugged. "Perhaps. And perhaps not. But Saint-Just is dead anyway, so he's irrelevant. Let's not all forget that our first responsibility—all of us—is to the republic and its people. *Not* to any organization within it."

"Fine for you to say! StateSec man!"

Yuri was practically grinding his teeth. *For Christ sake, Genevieve! We just barely averted disaster because one woman couldn't control her temper. Are you going to blow it now? In case you hadn't noticed—Admiral!—we've still got two fully armed StateSec SDs in this system. Yeah, sure, I might be able to control this one, seeing as how I've effectively created my own command staff. Except it's a jury-rigged hybrid staff, and if you start giving the*

*StateSec people the idea that the Navy and Marines are
going to start a counter-purge . . . Jesus, the whole thing
could dissolve into a civil war!*

He broke off the angry, desperate thought. Cachat was
addressing Chin again, still in that same calm, cold,
controlled tone of voice.

"Yes, I am State Security. But tell me, Admiral, what
is your grievance with *me*?" Cachat glanced at the screens.
"Or Commissioner Radamacher. Or Commissioner
Justice."

That—finally!—seem to rattle Chin. "Well . . . you had
my people beaten up!"

Cachat's eyebrows rose. "*Your* people? Admiral Chin,
I cannot recall a single instance where I had corporal
punishment of any kind inflicted on any member of either
the Navy or the Marines." He glanced at Ned Pierce, who
was also in line of sight of the display. "Well, I suppose
you could argue that I punished the Sergeant's knuckles
by having him pound a number of *my* people into a pulp.
Or have you forgotten—again—that Radamacher and
Justice are part of StateSec, not the military."

If Yuri had had any doubts whether he loved Sharon
Justice, she resolved them right then and there. She grinned
at Pierce and said: "Sergeant, if you'll forgive me your poor
knuckles, I'll forgive you my poor face. How's that?"

Pierce grinned back. "That's a deal, Captain. Uh,
Commissioner."

Sharon's head swiveled a little, to bring Chin's image
into view. Yuri was getting a little dizzy with this three-
way holographic discussion.

"Genevieve, cut it out," she said forcefully. "For six

years now, you've rebuilt your career—and probably saved your life—by trusting StateSec people you thought you could trust. Why are you screwing around with it now? For years now, we've all managed to spare La Martine from the worst of what happened, by working together. I say we stick with it."

Genevieve's temper was fading, now, and her usual intelligence returning. Yuri could recognize the signs, and drew a deep breath.

"Okay, fine," Genevieve. "But that only applies to—you know, *you.* The fleet StateSec people."

Cachat's face was impassive, as usual. Vesey, the CO of the *Tilden,* on the other hand, was looking distinctly uneasy.

"I believe Commissioner Justice has had no complaints against Captain Vesey," Cachat stated curtly. "At least, all the reports I received from her throughout our mission were completely positive. Am I not correct, Commissioner Justice?"

From her moment's hesitation, Yuri suspected that Sharon's reports to Cachat had been somewhat edited. He doubted very much if she'd found working with the stolid SD captain all *that* positive an experience. But she piped up cheerfully: "Oh, sure. I've got no problem with Captain Vesey. Neither do *you*, Genevieve. You told me yourself you were happy with the captain's work—especially the way he participated when we nailed that Mantie battlecruiser in Daggan."

Yuri's eyes flicked to the image of Chin, and he had to fight down a laugh. Chin's hesitation lasted longer than a "moment." Yuri was quite sure that whatever praise Chin had heaped on Vesey, it had been grudging at best. However, Chin also did not argue the point.

"Yes, yes. Okay. I've got no bone to pick with the *Tilden*." Genevieve was starting to think like an admiral again. "And since I see that Yuri's got the *Hector* under control—thanks for taking down the impellers and sidewalls, Yuri, that makes me a lot less nervous—"

Radamacher was startled. He hadn't ordered . . .

Then Kit Carson caught his eye and he *really* had to fight down a laugh. The *Hector*'s XO had his most ingratiating expression on. Ever attuned to the changing of the political winds, Carson had apparently ordered the SD to stand down while Yuri had been preoccupied with forestalling another disastrous explosion. It was one of the few times in his life where Radamacher was willing to sing hosannas to the virtues of lickspittles.

"—I guess we can all consider the military situation something of a stalemate," Genevieve continued. Frowning: "As long as everybody agrees to *remain* in stand down. And remain here, in La Martine orbit. Assuming the merchant ship's report that there's a truce on in the Mantie war is right also, we shouldn't need to run anti-raiding patrols for a while. And—ha!—after what we did in Laramie and New Calcutta, I doubt if any pirates are going to be stirring around here for a while either."

Yuri picked it up and took it from there. "I agree with Genevieve. Let's face it, everybody. The crews of *all* the Republic's warships here in La Martine are so thoroughly mixed up by now—"

Thanks to the fanatic. Ha! The Law of Unintended Consequences works its will again!

"—that as long as we all stay calm—as Genevieve says, stay together in one orbit and remain standing down— then nobody can purge anybody. And besides," he added, shrugging, "does anybody really have that much of a grudge left, anyway? Not for anybody here in La Martine, I don't think. So I see no reason why we can't just keep on maintaining this sector of the Republic in a state of peace and calm. Just *wait*, damnation, until we find out for sure what's happening in the capital."

The relaxation everywhere was almost palpable, on all three screens. Yuri took another deep breath. That was it, he thought. For now, at least.

Cachat's voice interrupted his pleasant thoughts.

"You're overlooking one final matter, Commissioner Radamacher."

"What's that?"

"Me, of course. More precisely, what I represent. I was sent here by personal appointment of Oscar Saint-Just, then head of state of the Republic. And leaving formalities aside, I think it's accurate to say that for some time now I have effectively ruled this sector by dictatorial methods."

Yuri stared at him, then snorted. "Yes, I'd say that's accurate. Especially the dictatorial part."

Cachat seemed oblivious to the sarcasm. His image in the display was still larger than life. The grim young fanatic face, especially, seemed to loom over everything else. On the bridge of the *Hector,* at least; but Yuri was quite sure the effect was the same on the *Tilden*—and probably even more so on the battleship where Cachat was standing in person. The man was just so forceful and intimidating that he had that effect.

"What's your point, Cachat?"

To his surprise, Sharon interjected herself sharply.

"Yuri, stop being an ass. Captain Cachat has been courteous to you, so there's no excuse for you to be rude to him."

Yuri stared at her. "He—the bastard beat you up!"

"Oh, for pity's sake!" she snapped. "You're behaving like a schoolboy. Instead of using your brains. And aren't you the man whose favorite little saying—one of them, anyway—is 'give credit where credit is due'?"

The image of her head swiveled, as she turned to the screen showing Cachat. "Are you really willing to do it, Captain? Nobody's asking it from you."

"Of course, I am. It's my simple duty, under the circumstances." Cachat made that little half-irritated twitch of the shoulders which seemed to be his version of a shrug. "I realize most of you—all of you, I imagine—consider me a fanatic. I neither accept the term, nor do I reject it. I am indifferent to your opinions, frankly. I swore an oath when I joined State Security to devote my life to the service of the Republic. I meant that oath when I gave it, and I have never once wavered in that conviction. Whatever I've done, to the best of my ability at the time and my gauge of the situation, was done in the interests of the people to whom I swore that oath. The *people* to whom I swore that oath, may I remind you. There is no mention of Oscar Saint-Just or any other individual in the StateSec oath of loyalty."

The square shoulders twitched again. "Oscar Saint-Just is dead, but the Republic remains. Certainly its people remain. So my oath still binds me, and under the current circumstances my duty seems clear to me."

He now looked straight at Yuri and a thin smile came to his face. "You're very good at this, Commissioner Radamacher. I knew you would be, which is why I left you behind here. But, if you'll forgive me saying so, you are not ruthless enough. It's an attractive personal quality, but it's a handicap for a commissioner. You're still flinching from the keystone you need to cap your little edifice."

Yuri was frowning. "What are you talking about?"

"I should think it was obvious. Commissioner Justice certainly understands. If you're going to bury an old regime, Commissioner, you have to bury a *body*. It's not enough to simply declare the body absent. Who knows when an absent body might return?"

"What—" Yuri shook his head. The fanatic was babbling gibberish.

Cachat's normal impatience returned. "Oh, for the sake of whatever is or isn't holy! If the mice won't bell the cat, I guess the cat will have to do it himself."

Cachat turned to face Sharon. "My preference would be to turn myself over to your custody, Commissioner Justice, but given that the situation in the *Tilden* is probably the most delicate at the moment, I think it would be best if I were kept incarcerated aboard the *Hector* under Commissioner Radamacher's custody. I think we should rule out Admiral Chin as the arresting officer. That might run the risk of stirring up Navy-StateSec animosity, which is the last thing La Martine sector needs at the moment."

Sharon chuckled. "Yuri might have you shot, you know."

"I doubt it. Commissioner Radamacher's not really the

type. Besides, my reference to a 'body' was just poetic license. It should do well enough, I think, to have the most visible representative of the Saint-Just regime here in La Martine under lock and key." Again, that little shrug. "And if Commissioner Radamacher feels compelled to have me rigorously interrogated at some point, I won't hold it against him."

For a moment, the dark eyes seem to glint. "I've been beaten before. Rather badly, once. As it happens, because a comrade and I were overseen by the enemy conspiring against them, and so in order to protect both our covers he feigned an angry argument and hammered me into a pulp. I spent a few days in the hospital, true enough—the man had fists like hams, even bigger than the Sergeant's over there—but it worked like a charm."

Yuri shook his head, trying to clear it.

"Let me get this straight . . ."

11

"Why," grumbled Yuri, staring at the ceiling of his stateroom, "do I feel like the poor sorry slob who got stuck with guarding Napoleon on St. Helena?"

Sharon lowered her book and lifted her head from the pillow next to him. "Who's Napoleon? And I never heard of a planet named St. Helena."

Yuri sighed. Whatever her other marvelous qualities—which he'd been enjoying immensely during the past month—Sharon did not share his passion for ancient history and literature.

Cachat did, oddly enough—some aspects of ancient culture, anyway—and that was something else Yuri had jotted down in his mental Black Book. The one with the title: *Reasons I Hate Victor Cachat.*

It was childish, he knew. But during the weeks since he'd arrested Cachat, Victor had found that his anger toward the man had simply deepened. The fact that the anger—Yuri was this honest with himself—stemmed more from Cachat's virtues than his vices only seemed to add fuel to the flames.

The fundamental problem was that Cachat *had* no vices—except being Victor Cachat. In captivity as in command, the young fanatic had faced everything resolutely, unflinchingly, with not a trace of any of the self-doubts or terrors which had plagued Yuri himself his entire life. Cachat never raised his voice in anger; never flinched in fear; never whined, nor groused, nor pleaded.

Yuri had fantasies, now and then, of Victor Cachat on his knees begging for mercy. But even for Yuri the fantasies were washed-out and colorless—and faded within seconds. It was simply impossible to imagine Cachat begging for anything. As well imagine a tyrannosaur blubbering on its knees.

It just wasn't *fair,* damn it all. And the fact that Cachat, during the weeks of his captivity, had turned out to be an aficionado of the obscure ancient art form known as *films* had somehow been a worse offense than any. Savage Mesozoic carnivores are not *supposed* to have any higher sentiments.

And they're certainly not supposed to argue art with

human beings! Which, needless to say, Cachat had done.
And, needless to say, had taken the opportunity to chide
Yuri for slackness.

That had happened in the first week.

"Nonsense," snapped Cachat. "Jean Renoir is the most
overrated director I can think of. *The Rules of the Game*—
supposedly a brilliant dissection of the mentality of the
elite? What a laugh. When Renoir tries to depict the
callousness of the upper crust, the best he can manage is
a silly rabbit hunt."

Yuri glared at him. So did Major Citizen, who was the
third of the little group on the *Hector* who had turned out
to be film buffs and had started holding informal chats on
the subject in Cachat's cell.

Well, it was technically a "cell," even if it was really a
lieutenant's former cabin on the SD. Just as it was
technically "locked" and there was technically always a
"guard" standing outside the hatch.

"Technically" was the word for it, too. Yuri had no
doubt at all that Cachat could have picked that simple
ship's lock within ten seconds. Just as he had no doubt at
all that nine out of ten of the guards stationed at the door
would be far more likely to ask the former Special
Investigator how he or she could be of service than to
demand he return to his cell.

Sourly, Yuri remembered the arrest itself.

"Arrest." *Ha!* It had been more like a ceremonial
procession. Cachat emerging from the lock with a task
force escort respectfully trotting behind him—and with

both Major Lafitte and Major Citizen's Marines and StateSec security units lined up to receive him.

Theoretically, they'd been there to take him into custody. But as soon as Cachat had stepped across the line on the deck which marked the official legal boundaries of the superdreadnought, the Marines had snapped to attention and presented arms. Major Citizen's StateSec troops lined up on the opposite side had followed suit within a second.

Yuri had been startled, since he'd certainly given no order for that courtesy. But he hadn't tried to countermand it, either. Not after scanning the hard faces of the Marines and StateSec troopers themselves.

He'd never understand how Cachat had managed it, but somehow . . .

So, he imagined, had the Old Guard always reacted in the presence of Napoleon. Reality, logic, justice—be damned to all of it. In victory or defeat, the Emperor was still the Emperor.

"If you want to see a genuinely superb depiction of the brutality of power," Cachat continued, "watch Mizoguchi's *Sansho the Bailiff.*"

Diana's glare faded. "Well . . . okay, Victor, I'll give you that. I'm a big fan of Mizoguchi myself, although I personally prefer *Ugetsu*. Still, I think you're being unfair to Renoir. What about—"

"A moment, please. Since we've ventured onto the subject—in a roundabout way—let me take the occasion to ask Commissioner Radamacher how much longer he's going to slack off before completing the purge."

"What are you talking about?" demanded Yuri. But his stomach was sinking as he said the words. In truth, he knew perfectly well what Cachat was talking about. He'd just been . . .

Procrastinating.

"You know!" snapped Cachat. "You're lazy, but you're not dumb. Not dumb at all. The fact that you've created a command staff throughout the fleet is fine and dandy. Fine also that, between the Marines and selected personnel from StateSec, you've put together a solid security team to enforce your authority. But this superdreadnought—and the *Tilden's* not much better; in some ways, worse—is still riddled with disaffected elements. Not to mention a small horde of pure hooligans. I'm warning you, Commissioner Radamacher, let this continue much longer and you'll start losing it."

Yuri swallowed. Cachat was speaking the truth, and he knew it. Both superdreadnoughts had enormous crews, whose personnel was entirely StateSec except for a relative handful of Marines. Some of those StateSec people—Major Citizen and Sergeant Rolla being outstanding examples—were people Yuri would stake his life on. *Was* staking his life on, as a matter of fact.

The rest . . . Most of them were simply people. People who'd enlisted originally to serve on a StateSec capital ship for much the same reasons that people from any society's lower classes volunteer for military service. A way out of the slums; decent and reliable pay; security; training; advancement. Nothing more sinister than that.

They'd all been willing enough to go along with the change of guard. Especially after it became clear that Yuri had engineered what amounted to a truce so that none of them need fear any immediate repercussions as long as they kept the peace.

But there were still plenty of SD ratings—and plenty of officers—who were not at all happy with the new setup. They'd *liked* being in State Security, and would be delighted to see its iron-fisted regime return—since they had every reason to expect they could resume their happy days as the fingers of that fist.

"Damn it," he complained—hating the fact that even to himself his voice sounded whiny—"I didn't sign on to carry out a Night of the Long Knives."

Cachat frowned. "Who said anything about knives? And they wouldn't need to be long anyway. You can cut a man's throat with a seven-centimeter blade perfectly well. In fact—have you forgotten everything?—that was the blade-length of choice in the academy's assassination courses."

"Never mind," sighed Yuri. "It's an historical reference. There was once a tyrant named Adolf Hitler and after he came to power he turned on the most hardcore of the fanatics who'd lifted him to power. The True Believers who were now a threat to him. Had them all purged in a single night."

Cachat grunted. "I still don't understand the point. I'm certainly not proposing that you purge *Diana*. Or Major Lafitte or Admiral Chin or Commodore Ogilve or any of the excellent noncoms—Marine and StateSec both—who are the people who lifted *you* into power. I'm simply pointing out what ought to be obvious: there are lots of sheer thugs on these capital ships and you ought to have the lot of them thrown into prison. A real prison, too—dirtside, where they can't get loose—not this silly arrangement you've got me in."

Diana Citizen's face looked troubled. "Uh, Yuri, I hate to say it but I agree with the Special—ah, Captain Cachat. I don't even care about political reliability, frankly. We're starting to have lots of problem with simple discipline. *Lots* of problems."

Yuri hesitated. Cachat's face seemed to soften, for a moment.

"You are a splendid shield, Yuri Radamacher," he said quietly. "But the republic needs a sword also, from time to time. So why don't you—this once—let a sword advise you?"

The young StateSec captain nodded his head toward the computer on his desk. The thing had no business still being there, of course. No one in their right mind would leave a computer in the hands of a prisoner like Cachat. Sure, sure, Yuri had slapped a codelock on it. Ha. He wondered if it had taken Cachat even two hours to break it.

But...

A computer was simply part of the dignity of a man like Cachat. To have removed it would have been like requiring Napoleon on St. Helena to sleep on the floor, or wear a sheet for clothing.

Cachat seemed to be reading his mind. "I haven't tried to use it, Yuri," he said softly. "But if you go into it yourself, you'll find my own records easily enough. The keyword is *Ginny* and the password is *Tongue*."

For some reason, Cachat seemed to be blushing a little. "Never mind. It was a personal reference I'd...ah, be able to remember. That will get you into the list of personnel I spent quite a bit of time assembling while I was operating on this warship. That list will only contain *Hector Van Dragen* personnel, of course. But you can find the same for the *Tilden*—more extensive, actually, since I had more time on that ship—stored away on the computer I used while on the *Tilden* during our mission."

The peculiar blush seemed to darken. "The keyword and password in that instance will be *sari* and, uh, *shakehertail*."

Diana burst out laughing. "Ginny—tongue—sari—*shakehertail*, no less. Victor, you dog! Who would have guessed you were a lady's man? I'd love to meet this girlfriend of yours, whoever she is."

The young man—for once, he didn't look like a fanatic—seemed on verge of choking. "She's not—ah, well. She's *not* my girlfriend. Actually, she's the wife—ah, never mind. Just a woman I knew once, whom I admired a lot." A bit defensively: "'Shake-her-tail' was a reference to her cover, and, uh, 'tongue' is because—well, never mind. There's no need to go into it."

For once, Yuri was inclined to let Cachat off the hook instead of needling him. Cachat the fanatic, he detested. Cachat the young man . . . was impossible to even dislike.

"Okay, Victor, we'll 'never mind,'" he said. "But what's on that list?"

The fanatic came back instantly. "Everyone I was planning to either arrest or, at the very least, break from StateSec service. Of course, I never thought I could do it all at once. Probably wouldn't even be able to do more than get started, since I had no idea how long Saint-Just would leave me on station here. But you can do the lot at a single stroke."

Radamacher eyed the computer. Then, sighing, he got up and went over to it.

"Well. I suppose I should at least look at it."

The first name and entry on the list was: *Alouette, Henri. GravSen Tech 1/c.*

"Damn," muttered Yuri. "I forgot all about him, things have been so hectic."

The rest of Cachat's entry read:

Vicious thug. Incompetent and derelict at anything else. Suspect him of conducting a reign of terror in his section, to the gross detriment of the section's performance. Arrest at the first opportunity. Most severe punishment possible, preferably execution, if sufficient evidence can be obtained. Certain it can once he is arrested and his section mates no longer fear retaliation.

"Damn," Yuri muttered again. "I've been slacking off."

The purge took place three nights later. On both capital ships simultaneously.

Major Citizen led the purge on the *Tilden*, since that ship was not as accustomed as the crew of the *Hector* to having Marines serving as a security unit. Captain Vesey, by then more relieved to see discipline restored than anything else, made no protest. Two of his bridge officers did, including the XO, but that was to be expected. They were led off the bridge in manacles, after all. Both of them had been high up on Cachat's list.

The purge on the *Hector* was, for the most part, carried

out by Major Lafitte's Marines. But it was officially led by
Jaime Rolla, whom Yuri had given a brevet promotion to
the rank of StateSec Lieutenant the day before.

Again, he'd been slacking off. Yuri had found Rolla's
name on another of Cachat's lists in the computer. This
one under the keyword and password of *hotelbed* and
ginrummy.

The list had been entitled: *Prospects for Advancement*,
and Rolla's name had been at the top of the list. Cachat's
entry read:

*Superb StateSec trooper. Intelligent, disciplined, self-
controlled. Commands confidence and inspires loyalty
from his subordinates. Absurd he still remains in the
ranks. Another legacy of Jamka's madness. Promote to
brevet Lieutenant immediately. Delay submission of name
to OTS. May need him here.*

Yuri had wondered at the last two sentences. He
thought of asking Cachat why he hadn't wanted to send
Rolla's name to Nouveau Paris as a candidate for
StateSec's Officer Training School.

Then, realizing how much *he* would miss Rolla's
steadying presence, he thought he understood. Although
. . . why would Cachat care, really? *He* hadn't faced the
problem of carrying through a revolution.

But he left the question unasked. He was irritated
enough with Cachat as it was, the way each reading of the
lists made him feel like a damn fool.

Just so, he was darkly certain, had Napoleon's jailor felt
whenever the emperor beat him at checkers on St.
Helena. Again.

• • •

Alouette was never arrested. Fleeing ahead of the arresting squad, finding himself cornered, the man tried to make his escape by climbing into his skinsuit, strapping on a sustained use thruster pack, and venturing onto the exterior of the *Hector*. Presumably—impossible to know—he'd hoped to make it across to the nearest commercial space station sharing orbit with the SD around La Martine.

It would have been an epic escape. Even a highly skilled and experienced EVA rating would have been hard-pressed to cross that distance in a skinsuit without a hardsuit's navigation systems to go with the SUT pack.

Alouette was neither superb nor experienced. He never even made it off the warship. Apparently in a panic, he jammed the jets into full throttle and rammed himself into a nearby gravitic array. There he remained for minutes, crushed against the array by the flaring SUT thrusters; which he was unable to turn off, either because he couldn't remember how or—if the fates had mercy on him— because the initial impact had rendered him unconscious.

It was a moot point. By the time his body could be recovered after the SUT ran out of fuel, the impact and the thrusters themselves had shredded the skinsuit with magnificent irony upon the very array the grav tech had *not* serviced in all his time aboard the *Hector*. Decompression had done the rest. The body that was hauled back into the *Hector* had been nothing but a broken, soggy mess.

It bought him no mercy. Again, Yuri decided to follow Cachat's advice.

"When you drive in a sword, Commissioner, drive it to

the hilt. Execute the corpse. Do it in front of a full assembly."

So it was. Ned Pierce got his wish, after all, emptying a full clip into the corpse of Alouette, propped up against a bulkhead.

The Marine sergeant did insist afterward—and loudly, too—that he got no satisfaction from the matter. But Yuri thought the cold grin on his face when he made the disclaimer belied the statement. And so, apparently, did the hundred or so of the *Hector*'s ratings who had been assembled in the chamber to witness the event.

True, the dozen of them who had been in Alouette's own section had raised a cheer. But even they looked a bit pale-faced at the time. And Yuri had no doubt at all that none of them would be in the least bit tempted thereafter to emulate Alouette. Or do anything which might draw the wrath of the new regime down on their heads.

He took no pleasure in the fact, although he did appreciate the irony. He'd read the ancient quip, that if Satan ever seized Heaven he'd have no choice but to take on God's characteristics. Now, he was realizing that the converse was true: *If God ever took over the management of Hell, He'd make a damn good Devil himself.*

And so the weeks passed, in the distant provincial sector of La Martine. No word from Haven. Nothing but wild rumors brought occasionally by merchant ships. The only certain things were that the capital system was still under the Navy's control and that a number of provincial sectors had burst into rebellion against the new regime, led by StateSec units.

But La Martine Sector remained tranquil. Within a month, the civilian authorities were even so confident that they began demanding that Radamacher—now called, by everyone, *the Commissioner for La Martine*—resume the anti-piracy patrols. There had been no incidents, true. But the commercial sector saw no reason to risk slackness.

When Yuri hesitated, the civilian delegation insisted on speaking to Cachat.

"Why?" Yuri demanded. "He's under arrest. He has no authority here. He doesn't even have a title any longer, except captain."

No use. The faces of the civilian delegation were set, stubborn. Yuri sighed and had Cachat brought to his office.

Cachat listened to the delegation. Then—needless to say—spoke without hesitation.

"Of course you should resume the patrols. Why not, Commissioner Radamacher? You've got everything well in hand."

Yuri almost ground his teeth, seeing the look of satisfaction on the faces of the civilians. Just so—just so!—would the fishermen on St. Helena have appealed from his guard to the Emperor, over a dispute regarding the proper repair of fishing nets.

But, he ordered the resumption of the patrols.

He had no choice, really. Yuri was coming to realize, slowly, that Cachat had been right about his own arrest also. In some indefinable manner, Yuri's own legitimacy somehow depended on the fact that he was seen as the custodian of the man who had been the final representative of Saint-Just's regime in La Martine.

Had the man he held captive ever protested, or complained, things might have been different. Yuri often found himself wishing that the news reporters who appeared frequently on the *Hector* to take yet another shot of Cachat In Captivity would produce a suitable image. That of a scowling, hunched, sullen tyrant finally brought to bay.

But . . . no. The images published in the newsviewers were always the same. A young man, stiff and dignified, looking more like a prince in exile than an incarcerated fanatic.

When he said as much to Sharon, she just laughed and told him to stop pouting.

Then, finally, official word came. A courier ship from Haven, bearing an official message from the new government.

As soon as the dispatch boat made its alpha translation, Yuri recognized the distinctive hyper footprint of a courier vessel. Nothing else that small was hyper-capable, after all, so it couldn't possibly be another merchantman . . . or a warship. Immediately, Yuri summoned all of the top commanders of the fleet to the bridge of the *Hector*. By the time the dispatch boat was within range to start transmitting messages, they were all present. Admiral Chin, Commodore Ogilve, Commissioner Wilkins, Captain Vesey, Majors Citizen and Lafitte. Captain Wright, recently promoted to replace Gallanti as the CO of the *Hector*. And Sharon, of course.

As Yuri began reading the first of the messages, he sighed with relief. The message began by stating that a new provisional government had been set in place by Admiral Theismann. A *civilian* government. There would be no military dictatorship, after all. Short of a return of the old regime, that had been Yuri's worst nightmare.

The message continued with a list of names—the officials of the new provisional government. The first of those names almost caused his heart to stop.

Eloise Pritchard, Provisional President.

The King is dead, long live the Queen. Saint-Just's fair-haired girl. Ring-around-the-rosy and we're right back where we started.

We're dead meat.

But his eyes were already continuing down the list, and he realized the truth even before he heard Sharon's shocked half-whisper.

"Jesus Christ Almighty. She must have been in the opposition all along. Look at the rest of those names."

Others were crowding around now, trying to read over Yuri's shoulders.

"Yeah, you're right," agreed Yuri. "I know a lot of them, myself, from the old days. At least half this list is made up of Aprilists. The best of them, too, at least those who've survived the last ten years. Hey—look! They've even got Kevin Usher. I didn't think he was still alive. The last I heard he'd been shipped off to the Marines in disgrace. I thought by now they'd have vanished him away somewhere."

"Who's Usher?" asked Ogilve.

"One hell of a good Marine, I know that much,"

growled Lafitte. "I've never met him myself, but I've known two officers who served with him for a while on Terra." Lafitte chuckled. "Mind you, they said he drank like a fish and was hardly the model of a proper colonel. Even got into barroom brawls himself, now and then. But his troops swore by the man, and the officers I knew—good people, both of them—told me they'd be delighted to have him in a combat situation. Which"—the growl deepened—"is what matters."

"I *do* know him," Yuri said quietly. "Pretty well, once. It was a long time ago, but . . ."

His eyes rested with satisfaction on Usher's name. With even greater satisfaction, on Usher's title. *Director, Federal Investigation Agency*.

"What's the 'Federal Investigation Agency,' do you think?" asked Genevieve Chin.

"I'm not sure," Yuri answered, "but my guess is that Theismann—or Pritchard—decided to bust up StateSec and separate its police functions from its intelligence work. Thank God. And put Kevin Usher in charge of the cops. Ha!"

He practically did a little jig of glee. "Mind you, that's like putting a chicken in charge of the foxes. Kevin Usher—a *cop*, of all things! But he's a very very very tough rooster." He grinned at Major Lafitte. "Pity the poor foxes. I can't imagine who'd be crazy enough to pick a barroom brawl with him."

While he had been basking in the pleasure of seeing Kevin's name, Sharon had continued to read down the list. Suddenly, she burst into riotous laughter. Almost hysterical laughter, in fact.

"What's so funny?" asked Yuri.

Sharon, none too steady on her feet herself, took Yuri by the shoulders and more-or-less forced him into a seat on the bridge. "You need to be sitting down for the rest of it," she cackled. "Especially when you get to the names of the provisional sector governors."

Her finger jabbed at a line. "Take a look. Here's La Martine."

Yuri read the name of the new provisional governor.

"Prince in exile, indeed!" Sharon howled.

Radamacher hissed a command.

"Get Cachat. Get him up here. *Now.*"

When Cachat entered the bridge, Yuri strode up to him and slammed the list onto a nearby console.

"Look at this!" he commanded accusingly. "Read it yourself!"

Puzzled, Cachat's eyes went down the list. Quickly, scanning, the first time through. Then, as he read it slowly again, Yuri knew the truth. Knew it for a certainty.

The hard young fanatic was gone, by the end. There stood before the commissioner only a man of twenty-four, who looked years younger than that. A bit confused; very uncertain.

His dark eyes—brown eyes—were even wet with tears.

"You swine," Yuri hissed. "You treacherous dog. You lied to me. You lied to all of us. Best damn liar I've ever met in my life. You played us all for fools!"

He pointed the finger of accusation at the list.

"Admit it!" he shouted. "It was all a goddam *act*!"

12

"Was it?" asked Cachat softly, as if wondering himself. Then, he shook his head. "No, Yuri, I don't think so. I told you once—it's not my fault if you never want to believe me—that I swore an oath to the *Republic*. I've kept that oath. Kept it here in La Martine."

His voice grew firmer, less uncertain. "I was specifically entrusted by the Republic to ferret out and punish traitors. Of which the two greatest, for years, were Rob Pierre and Oscar Saint-Just. Who stabbed our revolution in the back and seized it for their own ends."

No uncertainty, now: "Damn them both to hell."

"How long?" Yuri croaked.

Cachat understood what he meant. "I've been a member of the opposition since Terra. Since almost the beginning of my career. Kevin Usher was the commander of the Marine unit stationed at our embassy there and he— Well. Let's say he took me in hand, and showed me the way out. After I'd seen enough that I couldn't stomach any more."

Suddenly, Cachat's face lit up with a smile. A real, honest-to-God smile, too, not the razor Yuri had seen a few times before. "Though not before putting me in the hospital."

He gave Sharon a half-apologetic nod of the head. "If it'll make any amends, Commissioner Justice, I can assure you that Kevin Usher gave me a worse beating than you suffered at my order."

He looked back at Yuri, and shrugged. A real shrug. "Not, I admit, as bad as the one you got. But I'm sorry, Yuri, even before I got here I had you tagged as the key to the situation, and I needed to protect you as much as possible. So I used, on a broad scale, the same simple tactic Kevin once used on me. Had you—Sharon—many of you—beaten in order to establish your innocence."

"Why didn't you tell us?" asked Major Citizen, half-whispering. "I mean—after Saint-Just died and it was all over? All these weeks . . ."

"*Was it?* 'Over,' I mean." Cachat's eyes were very dark. "I had no way of knowing what sort of regime was going to emerge. For all I knew, I was still going to have to continue as an oppositionist. But since I'd done everything I could to prepare La Martine for any eventuality—including the possibility of a restoration of the old regime—I needed to maintain my cover. It was my simple duty."

Every officer on the bridge was now staring at him. Precious few of the ratings seated at their stations were making any attempt to hide the fact that they were listening also.

Cachat frowned. "Why are you all looking so confused? You know how thoroughly I do my research. By the time I got to La Martine—it's a long trip—I was pretty sure I understood what was happening here. And what I needed to do. It didn't take more than a short time here to confirm it."

Of all the faces on the bridge, Major Lafitte's was the only one whose eyes weren't wide. As a matter of fact, they were narrow with suppressed anger.

"Why the hell did you order *us* to do your blood work?" he demanded. Glancing at Sharon. "Especially on our own commissioner. Best damn ship's commissioner any of us had ever served with."

"Don't be stupid, Major Lafitte!" snapped Cachat. The fanatic was back, it seemed. "The first thing I needed to do—"

He broke off sharply. Turned, and bestowed a hard gaze on one of the commo ratings. "Are the recorders on?"

Hastily—she didn't even think to look at the ship's captain—the rating pushed a button on her console. "Not any more, Sir."

Cachat nodded and turned back. "If you don't mind, Captain Wright, I'd prefer there to be no official record of this." He continued on, not waiting for the SD's CO to finish nodding his approval. "As I was saying, Major, don't be stupid. Jamka's insane rule—the results of it, I should say—had given me the opportunity to destroy the worst elements of Saint-Just's treason here in La Martine. Of course—"

He shrugged again; but, this time, it was the shoulder-twitch of old. "I had no way of knowing—never imagined it, in fact—that Admiral Theismann would shortly be overthrowing the traitor. But, no matter. My duty was clear. Sooner or later, Saint-Just's regime was bound to collapse. At the very least, start coming apart at the seams. No purely police state in history has ever survived for very long. So Kevin Usher told me, once, and I believe him. Saint-Just, without Rob Pierre, was bound to fall—and fairly quickly."

Usher's right, thought Yuri. *Beria without Stalin didn't last for... weeks? I can't remember, exactly. Less than a year, that's for sure. Terror alone is never enough.*

"It was therefore my clear duty to do what I could to prepare La Martine for the coming upheavals," Cachat continued. "Sanitize the sector, if you will. Jamka's murder provided me with the perfect opening, of course. But—to come back to the point, Major—doing so required me to enlist the aid of his killers immediately. Those were the only people I could count on for sure. Partly, of course, because their actions indicated their good character. But just as much because they'd see my presence as the surest way to cover their own tracks. Indeed, the quickest way to complete the mission they'd set out for themselves. I'm sure you'd planned—over time, of course—to execute everyone involved in Ruting Quedilla's murder. Jamka was just the beginning."

The room was frozen. There was no anger left in Major Lafitte's face. Only shock. And Sharon's face was that of a ghost.

"Oh, Jesus," whispered Yuri. Half-pleading: "Sharon—"

"Desist, Radamacher!"

No one had ever heard Victor Cachat raise his voice. And this was a loud voice. Not cold in the least, but hot with anger.

"You slacker!" Cachat bellowed. Then, tightening his jaws and visibly clamping down on himself: "She only did what you *should* have done, Radamacher. You were second-in-command of State Security here in La Martine. It was *your* duty to have seen to the removal of a beast like Jamka, once his nature had become clear and the threat he posed to the people of the Republic was obvious. Not hers. *Yours.* Even if you had to go outside of channels to do it."

His nostrils fleered. "But, of course, you looked the other way. Slacked off. As always. *Commissioner.*"

The last word practically dripped sarcasm. But, as if that satisfied him, the angry contempt in his expression faded away within seconds.

"Oh, hell, Yuri," Cachat said wearily. "You are one of the nicest men I've ever met. But some day you'll have to learn that a shield without a sword is pitiful protection in a real fight."

Yuri was still staring at Sharon. She, staring back. Her face was still pale, but it was also composed.

"She was one of ours, Yuri," Sharon said quietly. "Caroline Quedilla was one of ours. When Jamka crossed that line—"

"A *shipmate*," Lafitte hissed. "And the best damn ship in the fleet, too." The major's shoulders seemed wider than ever, his big hands clasped behind his back. "Yeah, sure, Quedilla wasn't much of a rating and a screwball to boot. Always looking for thrills and a disciplinary pain-in-the-neck. Just the kind of nitwit that Jamka—he was a smooth, handsome bastard, if you'll remember; if you didn't know what lay beneath—could have suckered in while she was on shore leave. But she was still one of *ours.* God damn it! You don't *ever* let anyone cross that line." He took a slow, deep breath. "Not for something like this, anyway. If it'd been a matter of political loyalty or—or—"

The big hands seemed to tighten. "That's different. But this was just a monster at his games, thinking his position could protect him from anything. He learned otherwise."

The major swiveled his head to Cachat. "I had no idea you knew."

Cachat shrugged. "It wasn't hard to figure out, once I realized who the victim was. I'd already studied the personnel records, of course, on the voyage here. So I was aware of the *Veracity*'s record—and the fact that its Marine unit in particular had an exemplary combat record. Three unit citations, no less. I'm quite familiar with Marines, Major. I spent months in their company on Terra after the Manpower incident, before Saint-Just recalled me to Haven for reassignment."

Cachat glanced at Sharon. "Captain Justice's record as a commissioner just sealed the matter. I don't know exactly how it all went down—nor do I care to know—but I imagine she was the one who gave you the nod. She'd have kept it away from the *Veracity*'s captain, of course, to protect the ship as a whole in case it all came unglued. You would have organized the operation. Then—judging from the evidence I turned up over the next week or so, I'm quite certain Sergeant Pierce led the operation which executed Jamka."

He winced, slightly. "A bit flamboyant, that last part. But Pierce is a flamboyant sort of character. I certainly can't deny it was—ah—call it poetic justice. And the theatrical manner in which the killing was done—whether you or Pierce planned for it or not—did have the benefit of making it easy for everyone to assume that Jamka had fallen afoul of his cohorts." Cachat snorted. "It always amazes me how willing people are to jump to conclusions, as long as a handy conclusion is waved under their nose. The theory was ridiculous, of course. Jamka's cronies would have been the *last* people to kill him. His position and authority were what enabled them to operate with impunity. That's why I had them all shot at once, so they wouldn't have time to argue their case."

Yuri felt light-headed. "Evidence . . . ?"

Jesus, Sharon'll fry. Murder is murder, under any regime.

"Do you take me for an idiot?" demanded Cachat. "The evidence disappeared months ago. Vanished without a trace. I saw to that, I assure you. It was hardly difficult, since I was the Special Investigator assigned to handle the case."

Yuri was swept with relief. But only for a moment. His eyes began flitting around the large bridge. His stomach sinking as he realized how many sets of ears . . .

"And again!" Cachat snapped. "When are you going to learn?"

The fanatic—Yuri couldn't help but think of him that way; perhaps now more than ever—was giving him that cold, dark scrutiny. "Accept something as a fact, will you? I am far better at this than you will ever be, Yuri Radamacher. Better by nature, and then I was trained by the best there is. Oscar Saint-Just poured the iron, and— pity him!—Kevin Usher shaped the mold. So I know what I'm doing."

His eyes moved slowly over the bridge. As he came to each rating—none of them, any longer, even pretending to attend to their duty—most of them looked away. It was a hard gaze to face, after all. Oddly enough, though, Cachat's eyes seemed to lighten in color as they went. Black at the beginning; a rather warm brown at the end.

"There is no evidence," Cachat repeated, speaking to the entire bridge. "And there is no record of this discussion. I'm afraid all of you here are simply having a delusional experience. No doubt, wild and unsubstantiated rumors will begin appearing on this ship. No doubt, they will spread soon throughout the task force. Not much doubt, I'd say, they will eventually percolate throughout the Republic."

He turned back to the officers, smiling thinly. "And so? I see no harm to the Republic—none at all, as a matter of fact—if rumors exist that, even during the worst days of the Saint-Just tyranny, an especially vile leader of State Security was fragged by one of the ships' crews of the Republic."

For a moment, all was still. Then, as if they possessed a single pair of lungs, almost two dozen officers and ratings let out a collective breath.

Major Lafitte even managed a laugh of sorts. "Cachat, I don't think even Saint-Just—on his best day—or worst day, I'm not sure which—could have been that ruthless. *That's* why you used the *Veracity*'s Marines as your fist, from the very beginning."

"I told you. I was trained by the best." Cachat's own little laugh was a harsh thing. "No one suspects a torturer, Major, of any crime except torture. The work itself obliterates whatever might lurk beneath. As Kevin once told me, 'blood's always the best cover, and all the better if it's on your own fists.'"

He turned to face Yuri. "Now do you understand, Commissioner?"

Yuri said nothing. But his face must have conveyed his sentiments. *You're still a damn fanatic, Cachat.*

Cachat sighed, and looked away. For an instant, he seemed very young and vulnerable.

"I had nothing else, Yuri," he said softly. "No other weapon; no other shield. So I used my own character to serve me for both."

There seemed to be some moisture back in his eyes. "So, was it an act? I honestly don't know. I'm not sure I want to know."

"Doesn't matter to me," said Major Lafitte firmly. "As long as you're on my side."

Sharon seemed to choke. "I'll drink to that!" she exclaimed. Then, turning to Captain Wright: "What say, Sir? It's your ship. But I think a toast might be in order."

Wright wasn't exactly a "jolly good soul." Precious few commanding officers of a StateSec capital ship ever were. But compared to Gallanti, he was a veritable life-of-the-party.

"It's straining regulations, but—I'm inclined to agree that—"

He got no further before an alarm sounded. Commander Tarack, Ballon's replacement as *Hector*'s tac officer, started in his chair—his attention, like everyone else's, had been riveted on Cachat—and turned quickly to his console. Fresh datacodes blinked on his display, and he listened hard to his ear bug.

Then he paled.

Noticeably.

"Sir," he said, unable to completely disguise his nervousness, "I'm getting a very big hyper footprint. Uh, *very* big, Sir. And . . . uh, I think—not sure yet—that we've got some ships of the wall here. Uh. Lots of them. At least half a dozen, I think."

Whatever his other shortcomings, Wright was an experienced ship commander. "What distance?" he asked, his voice level and even. "And can you make out their identity?"

"Twelve light-minutes, Sir. Bearing oh-one-niner, right on the ecliptic. I won't be able to determine their identity, or even the actual class types, until the light-speed platforms report, Sir."

Twelve minutes later, Commander Tarack was able to determine the identity of the incoming task force. "They're Havenite, Sir."

The people on the bridge relaxed. Somewhat. It still remained unclear whether the task force was from the newly established regime or . . . who knew? There were apparently StateSec-led rebellions in several provincial sectors—one of which, at least, was not all that far from La Martine sector.

But, ten minutes after that, that uncertainty vanished also. The first message from the incoming flotilla had bridged the lightspeed distance.

"They're from Haven itself, Sir," reported the comm rating. "It's a task force sent out by President Pritchard, to—ah, it says *'help reestablish proper authority in Ja'al, Tetra and La Martine sectors, and suppress any disturbances, if needed.'* That's a quote, Sir. Admiral Austell's in command."

"*Midge* Austell?" asked Commodore Ogilve sharply.

The rating shook her head. "Doesn't say, Sir. Just: 'Rear Admiral Austell, task force commander.'"

"It's *got* to be Midge," said Admiral Chin. There was more than a trace of excitement in her voice. "I don't know any other Austell on the Captain's List. Didn't know she'd made admiral, though. Fast track, if she did."

"She could have, Genevieve," said Ogilve. His own voice sounded elated. "She never got smeared by Hancock the way we did, you know. She was too junior, at the time, just my tac officer in the *Napoleon*. So she didn't spend our time on the beach. God knows she's good enough. In my opinion, anyway."

"Here's another message, Sir," called out the rating. "Says that FIA Director Usher is accompanying the task force. *To reestablish proper police authorities in provincial sectors.*' That's a direct quote, Sir."

Cachat collapsed into an empty seat. "Thank God," he whispered. He put his face in his hands. "I am so very tired."

A last spark of anger almost led Yuri to demand: *From what? You haven't done anything for weeks except rest.*

But he didn't ask the question. Wouldn't have, even if he hadn't seen Sharon's eyes on him. Hard eyes; questioning eyes—still pleading eyes, too. Yuri and Sharon would have a lot to talk through, in the days to come.

But Yuri Radamacher did not ask, because the commissioner knew the answer. Victor Cachat had not slacked off. Cachat had done his duty, and done it to the full.

And now, even a fanatic was weary of such duty.

Cachat still seemed weary, five hours later, when the first pinnace from the arriving task force docked at the *Hector*. He was there with the rest of them in the boat bay gallery, but his normally square shoulders seemed slumped; his face drained and paler than ever.

The sight of the first person coming through the lock seemed to pick up his spirits, true. That sight certainly picked up Yuri's. He'd forgotten how large and excessively muscular Kevin Usher was, but the cheerful, rakish face was exactly as he remembered. Kevin Usher in a good mood could brighten up any gathering—and the man was obviously in a very good mood.

"Victor!" he bellowed, stepping forward and sweeping the smaller man into a bear hug. "Damn, it's good to see you again!"

He plunked the young man down and examined him. "You look like shit," he pronounced. "You're not exercising enough."

In point of fact, Yuri knew that Cachat exercised at least two hours a day. But Cachat didn't argue the point.

"I'm pretty worn out, Kevin," he said softly.

Usher's sharp eyes studied him for a few seconds. "Well, it's up to you. Your posting as provisional sector governor is rescinded, as of this moment. That was just an emergency stop-gap. You're not really the right type for it—as you and I both know good and well, heh—and we've got someone else in mind anyway. But I do need to appoint an FIA director for La Martine. I was going to offer the post to you, but . . . if you don't want it, you can return with me to Nouveau Paris. It's not like I don't have a thousand hot spots to squelch, and I do believe you've become one of my top firemen."

"I want to go home, Kevin." Cachat's voice seemed very thin. "Wherever home is. It's not here. Nobody here—"

He broke off, shook his head, and continued more firmly. "I'd rather return with you to Nouveau Paris and take on a different assignment. I'm tired of this one."

Usher studied him for a few seconds more, with that shrewd gaze. "Been rough, huh? I figured it might have been, from what I could tell at a distance. Okay, then. Name your replacement."

Cachat didn't hesitate. Just turned his head and pointed a finger at Yuri. "Him. He's—"

For the first time, Usher caught sight of Radamacher. "Yuri!" he bellowed. "Long time!"

The next thing Yuri knew he was being swept up into the same bear hug.

He'd also forgotten how *strong* Usher was. He couldn't breathe. But Yuri finally forgave Cachat for Sharon's beating. He didn't want to think what kind of punishment those huge hands had visited on the fanatic.

Usher plopped Yuri back on his feet. Then, one hand still on Yuri's shoulder, he shook his head firmly.

"Not a chance. We've got another assignment for this one, if he wants it. We're putting our own people in as governors for most of the sectors, but La Martine's been so rock steady that we decided we'd just leave Yuri here in place running the show."

Everyone in the La Martine delegation looked surprised. "How'd you know—?" Chin asked.

Usher laughed. "For Pete's sake, Admiral, rumor flies both ways. Must have been thirty merchant ships pass through Haven, all with the same story. *Commissioner Radamacher's holding the fort in La Martine, steady as she goes and business is even good.* That's why we've left you on your own so long. Sorry 'bout that, but we had way too many other problems on our hands to worry about a problem that didn't exist. Besides—"

The other big hand clapped down on Cachat's shoulder. "I knew my number one boy Victor was out here, lending a hand. That was worth an hour's extra sleep for me every night, right there."

To Victor: "Name somebody else."

Victor pointed at Sharon. "Her, then. Captain Sharon Justice."

Sharon was standing frozen. Radamacher likewise. In fact, everyone in the La Martine delegation had a strained look on their face.

Usher frowned. "What's the matter?"

Cachat glanced around, then flushed a bit. "Oh. Well. Bad memories, I imagine. I once asked people here to name their replacements and—well. It all turned out a bit, ah, unpleasant."

Usher grinned. "Ran you all through the wringer, did he? Ha!" The hand rose, fell, clapping Cachat's shoulder. "A real piece of work, isn't he? Like I said, my number one boy."

He focused the grin on Sharon. "Not to worry, I'm just passing out lollipops. La Martine Sector is the provincial apple of Haven's eye right now, don't think it isn't."

Now, to Yuri: "And you, what do you say? You'll have

to give up the 'commissioner' part of it, Yuri. The name, anyway. Can you live with 'governor'?"

Mutely, Yuri nodded. Usher immediately shifted the grin elsewhere. He seemed determined to complete his business immediately. Yuri had also forgotten how much energy Kevin Usher possessed.

"Okay, then. Admiral Chin, you're relieved of command and ordered to report back to the capital for a new assignment. It's ridiculous to keep an admiral of your talent and experience running a provincial task force. Tom—Admiral Theismann—no, he's the new Secretary of War—tells me he's got a Vice-Admiralty and a fleet waiting for you. Commodore Ogilve, you're promoted to Rear Admiral and will be taking over from Admiral Chin here. Don't get too comfy, though. I don't think you'll be here long. We can find somebody else to squelch pirates. We've got some rebellions to suppress—and who knows how long the truce with the Manties will last?"

Even somebody like Usher wasn't completely oblivious to such things as "formalities" and "proper chain of command." His grin seemed to widen, though, as if he took great pleasure in tweaking them.

"Of course, you'll be getting the official word from Admiral Austell, not me. That's Midge Austell—she's says she knows you, Commodore. She should be coming over on the next pinnace, which—ah. I see it's arrived."

Sure enough, the green light of a good seal flashed on the bay end of the boarding tube once more, and a woman swung herself from the tube's zero-gee into the bay. Piled through from the tube, rather, practically shoving Admiral Austell aside as she did so.

The woman was not wearing a uniform; was small; dark-skinned; gorgeous; and her face was tight with disapproval.

"Stupid red tape," Yuri heard her mutter. "Make me wait for the next pinnace!"

Then, loudly: "Where's Victor?"

She didn't wait for an answer, though, because her eyes spotted the man she was looking for.

"Victor!"

"Ginny!"

An instant later, they were embracing like long-lost siblings. Or . . . something. A close relationship, whatever it was.

"My wife," Usher announced proudly. "Virginia, but we all call her Ginny. She and Victor are good friends."

Yuri remembered various keywords and passwords. *Ginny. Tongue. Hotelbed. Shakehertail.* (True, *ginrummy* didn't seem to fit the pattern.)

Major Citizen happened to be standing right behind him. Diana leaned close and whispered into his ear: "You really don't want to know, Yuri. I mean, you really really really really don't want to know."

He nodded firmly.

Cachat and Usher's wife finally broke their embrace. Ginny held him out at arm's length and examined him.

"You look like shit," she pronounced. "What's the matter?"

Cachat seemed on the verge of tears. There was no trace left of the fanatic. Just a very young man, bruised by life.

"I'm tired, Ginny, that's all. It's been . . . real hard on

me here. I don't have any friends, and—God, I've missed you a lot—and . . . I just want to leave."

Yuri Radamacher had survived for ten years under the suspicious scrutiny of the Committee of Public Safety. It had been quite an odyssey, but it was over. He'd weathered all storms; escaped all reefs; even finally managed to make it safely to shore.

The experience, of course, had shaped his belief that there was precious little in the universe in the way of justice. But what happened next, confirmed his belief for all time.

Not even Oscar Saint-Just could have advanced such a completely, utterly, insanely *unfair* accusation.

"So that's it!" Ginny Usher's voice was shrill with fury, her hot eyes sweeping over the La Martine delegation.

"Victor Cachat is the sweetest kid in the world! And you—" She was practically spitting like a cat. "You dirty rotten bastards! You were *mean* to him."

FROM
POUL ANDERSON'S
MULTIVERSE

Author's note:

Given that I wrote an afterword to this story—see below—which says everything I would have said in this note, I see no reason to say any more since I'm not getting paid by the word here.

(Yes, authors think about such things. You betcha.)

(And there I went and wasted a few words I didn't get paid for . . . and now I just did it again.)

(Authors are grasping but unfortunately they tend to have a weak grip.)

Operation Xibalba

1

"Goddamn Matucheks," Frank Pianessa said wearily. He tossed the report I'd just handed to him onto the desk, without opening it, and reached for his coffee cup. The cup was resting on a pile of other reports in the same bile-green-colored folders the Department of Infernal Affairs had chosen to use for this particular purpose.

Appropriately chosen, if you ask me. The official name for the activity involved was "Unauthorized Incursions Into the Nether Reaches." Those of us assigned to deal with the ensuing messes called it either the "Darwin Award on Steroids" or "What Will These Idiots Think Of Next?"

Frank slurped at his coffee. "Summarize it for me, would you, Anibal? It's too early in the morning for me to fight my way through departmentese."

I couldn't help but smile. In the short period of its existence since it was created after the Matuchek Expedition, the prose of the DIA had become notorious even among federal agencies. Nobody else could produce something like—I'm not making this up, it's taken directly from an actual report—the following:

Subject incursee [that's DIA-speak for the moron involved, and never mind that an "incursee" would presumably refer to the person into whom the incursion was done, not the one who did it—but what do billions of people who speak proper English know?] *thereupon attempted to execute an extrapersonal ejection* [translation: the moron tried to fire or throw a missile of some sort] *intended to inflict uncertifiably mortal results* [tried to kill, a dubious prospect given the nature of the time, place and intended killee] *upon the demonic personage involved, tentatively classified as a minor fiend, thoracically enhanced variety, clawed ilk, ill-tempered branch.*

That last is pointless verbiage, since there's really no rhyme or reason to the construction—or possibly devolution—of the denizens of the hell universe. Clawed, spiny, bad-humored . . . Gee, a devil. Who would've guessed? I ran fingers through my hair. "This one's a doozy, boss."

Frank grimaced. "Don't tell me we've got another big game hunter on our hands."

One of our last cases—the one whose report I just quoted from, in fact—involved a man [tentatively classified as a minor cretin, cranially deprived variety, stupid ilk, suicidal branch] who tried to set himself up in business as a hunting guide. He'd undertake safaris in Hell, for any big game hunter tired of bagging the usual lion, bison, elk, or elephant.

He got three takers for his first and only safari. All of them were very well-armed indeed. Two of the hunters had double-barreled .600-caliber elephant guns, the third had a .50-caliber military-grade sniper rifle, and the guide himself was armed with a grenade launcher.

Fat lot of good it did them, in a universe whose geometry is not even remotely Euclidean. That's why the Matuchek party never tried to use missile weapons at all, not even with the spirits of Lobachevsky and Bolyai to guide them.

I shook my head. "No, I'm afraid it's a lot worse than that."

Frank set down his cup. "Oh, Gawd Almighty. Don't tell me we've got more missionaries on our hands."

You'd think any religious denomination that went in for proselytizing would understand that, pretty much by definition, the denizens of the hell universe are . . .

Well. Damned. That means "not subject to salvation."

But every few months we get another bunch of screwballs who hare off to save the unholy. By the time we get alerted and can track them down, it's usually too late. Since the would-be missionaries are deliberately trying to find demons, which are abundant in the nether regions (as you'd expect), they've already been slaughtered by the time we catch up to them. Or "martyred," to use their own terminology, which I personally consider preposterous. You might as well call a man who throws himself off a cliff to be a "martyr."

Again, I ran fingers through my hair. "Uh . . . no. It's a religious expedition of sorts, I suppose you could say. But they're not actually crazy. They've no intention of converting devils. They're seeking what they call 'morally neutral allies in the struggle against the Adversary.'"

"Huh?"

"'Morally neutral allies,'" I repeated patiently.

"What the hell does that mean?" he demanded.

"You remember how the Matuchek incident ended?"

"Yeah, sure. When all seemed lost, they summoned—called, rather—some enormous and presumably very powerful . . . Oh, dear Lord. You have *got* to be kidding me."

I shook my head. "Nope. It seems the head of this new expedition—his name's Rick Boatright, by the way—got into a conversation in a bar with a couple of the scholars who've been studying the data brought back by the Matucheks. They explained to him that they'd been able to tentatively identify the three beings summoned as godlings from an alternate universe. They don't know their names, but they think two of them have a European origin and the third one came from a pre-discovery New World society."

From the look of concentration on his face, Frank had been running that part of the Matuchek report through his mind. Now, he grunted. "I presume that's the weird-looking feathered snake."

"Yeah, that one. The same scholars think the being came from an analog of one of our own Native American cultures from the southwest or Mexico. And that's the being this new expedition went looking for. Apparently the logic involved—I'm using the term loosely—is that since Boatright and his party left for Hell from Yuma, that's the one they're most likely to run across."

Frank rolled his eyes. "Which part of 'non-Euclidean geometry' do people have trouble with? For Pete's sake, it doesn't matter where you leave from, when you set off for Hell."

I shrugged. "A disregard for basic geometry is pretty much a given with our clientele."

My boss scowled. "*Don't* call them 'our clientele,' Anibal. The term's silly. Clients are what doctors and dentists have."

"And psychiatrists," I pointed out. "Including ones who deal with schizophrenics. I'll say this much for Boatright—at least he had enough sense to take an IPS unit with him."

Frank's scowl darkened. "Talk about silly terms! 'Infernal Positioning System.' An oxymoron if there ever was one."

I shrugged again. "Hey, look, they *do* work. After a fashion. That's why we use them ourselves."

The operative phrase was *after a fashion,* though. IPS units were made by several different companies, each of whom claimed their unit had XYZ special feature or function that enabled—"enabled," *not* guaranteed; see fine print below—the user to navigate through the nether regions. We'd tried all of the models and had never found any of them to be all that useful. Granted, they were better than nothing, but that was about like saying that a walking stick was better than nothing when you set out to conquer Mount Everest.

The problem was that IPS units only worked in places where the geometry was relatively close to that of our own universe. Such places did exist in the hell universe—quite a few of them, in fact—but the problem is that those aren't the places in that universe where an expedition is most likely to wind up.

Why? Because such an expedition, or the rescue

expedition sent out after them, is looking for the denizens of the hell universe. Or, to put it another way, is looking for evil. And from what our scholars can determine, evil plays roughly the same role in the geometry of the hell universe that gravity plays in our own. Gravity isn't a "force" as such, it's the curvature of space-time produced by mass. It seems that wickedness is the analogous quasi-force in determining the geometry of hell.

You can see what that leads to. Mass is pleasantly stable, inert, mindless and without volition. Evil, on the other hand, is chaotic, willful, self-centered, and worst of all, often capricious. So, whenever you find a large enough concentration of devils, or even a single one if it's powerful enough, you'll find that the geometry of the hell universe starts flopping around unpredictably. At that point the IPS units give up the ghost, mechanically speaking.

In our experience, the most reliable method for navigating the hell universe is simply hard-won experience—emphasis on "hard-won." With enough experience, you learned to react based on moral instinct rather than eyesight. Oddly enough, with one exception, the people who turned out to be the best at it were people like me. Agnostics, with a low propensity for being judgmental. People with strong faith systems or rigid moral codes invariably got confused quickly once they entered the hell universe. A grand total of two—count 'em, two—missionaries have ever come back alive from the hell universe. One of them was missing both legs, both ears, all of his hair and—go figure—his appendix. The other was catatonic and has never recovered.

I'd always prided myself on being unprejudiced and

insistent on subjecting everything to rational analysis. I'd feel better about this except that the one exception sometimes made me wonder if there might be something wrong with me.

That's because the exceptions are outright psychopaths. To use the technical term, people who exhibit Anti-Social Personality Disorder. ASPD, for short.

No, I kid you not. For reasons that are presumably obvious, the DIA doesn't advertise the fact. We get enough accusations of being crazy as it is. I will add that psychopaths employed as guides by the DIA in the hell universe are strictly consultants, not employees of the department.

Still, it makes me wonder, sometimes. Especially when I discover, as I have on several occasions, that my own reactions to hell-universe geometic shifts—HUGS is the inevitable acronym; hey, look, we're a government agency—are more reliable than those of my psychopath guide.

Just to make something clear before we go any further, psychopaths are *not* necessarily serial murderers or even especially dangerous. It's the killers who get all the publicity, but the fact is that most psychopaths go through life without ever running afoul of the law. Quite a few are successful corporate CEOs, in fact.

Thinking about psychopaths naturally brought me to the inevitable end point of this meeting. Frank was bound to give me the assignment of tracking down Boatright and his people and hauling them (or what was left of them) out of the hell universe.

Not all psychopaths are the same. Most of them—well,

all of them, really—are thoroughly detestable people. But they are also usually charming, on the surface, and some are more charming than others. If you were lucky, the expedition might be short enough that the charm didn't wear off before the underlying personality emerged.

"Is Walt Boyes available?" I asked.

Frank shook his head. "No, he got arrested again."

"Too bad." I started working my way alphabetically through the list of psychopath guides. I didn't get any farther than David Carrico, though, before there came the sounds of a ruckus in the receptionist's office beyond the door.

"Yes, I know he's in a meeting," said a loud female voice I didn't know—and from its unpleasant edge, didn't want to. "That's why I need to get in there right now, before any further damage is done."

I heard the voice of Frank's receptionist, Mrs. Graves, although I couldn't make out more than one word in three. "...can't...have to...proper...*hey!*"

A moment later the door opened. Burst open, almost. A female—presumably the source of the unknown voice—strode into the office.

She was good-looking, in an intense sort of way. Somewhere in her early thirties, very dark hair, almost black, cut short; equally dark eyes; a slim but unmistakably female figure. All of it set off in a gray business suit cut along the same severe lines as her hair.

"Frank Pianessa?" she asked, looking at him. It was more in the way of a statement than a question, though. Before Frank's glare could turn into a verbal response, the intense black eyes were focused on me. "And you'd be Anibal Vargas. I'm assuming you're the one who'll be going on the expedition."

"*What* expedition?" growled Frank. "And just who are you to be asking in the first place?"

"I'm Sophia Loren, from the State Department. Please spare me the wisecracks. That's what my parents chose to name me and I'm too stubborn to get the name changed. As for the expedition, let's not play games. The one we're about to send off to snare Rick Boatright and his maniacs."

Frank's temper was rising, but my own was actually subsiding. Her comment about stubbornness concerning her name predisposed me in her favor. I'd grown up in a mostly Anglo neighborhood where my schoolmates—the ones who read, anyway, and those were the ones I hung out with—could never resist wordplay on the name "Hannibal." It didn't help that my high school girlfriend's last name was Alps.

"Assuming for the moment that such an expedition is in the works," Frank said, "what's it to you?"

"Are you serious? These people are planning to form an alliance with a non-human being from an alternate universe. A very powerful being. *Of course* the State Department is concerned."

Since this was not an unreasonable point, Frank reined in his temper and leaned back in his seat. "All right, I can see where State is legitimately involved. I assume you're concerned that such an alliance might upset the balance of power between Heaven and Hell."

"Nonsense," said Loren, waving her hand brusquely. "That's just Steven Matuchek's speculations based on—what, exactly?" With a slight curl of the lip: "His great knowledge of the Most High and the Most Low, deriving from his expertise in lycanthropy?"

Being a wereperson myself, that last remark brought my initial dislike for the woman back to the surface. Before I could say anything—if I decided to at all, which I probably wouldn't—Loren continued.

"The balance of power between the Highest and Lowest is far beyond our ability to affect significantly. If at all. But that says nothing about the ongoing struggle between the universes on a variety of lower levels. And on a number of those levels, the Boatright expedition could very well inflict a great deal of harm."

"On what?" demanded Frank.

She gave him the sort of look that is either bestowed on slimy disgusting creatures oozing from beneath a crevice, or people whose security clearances may not be up to snuff.

Frank recognized the look, naturally. "Give me a break," he said. "My clearance when it comes to infernal affairs is as high as it gets." He jerked a thumb at me. "So's his. That still leaves 'need to know,' but I presume if we didn't need to know you wouldn't have come here in the first place."

He had her over a barrel and she knew it. That was obvious from the look on her face. It was the sort of expression people had just before they underwent a root canal or divulged state secrets to someone in another agency.

"Yes, you're right. The reason Boatright poses a threat is because his expedition might cause problems for one of our existing alliances with forces in the netherworlds."

We both stared at her. After a couple of seconds, Frank said: "What alliances are you talking about? We don't have—"

Again, she made that abrupt gesture with her hand. "Of course you don't know about them. They're top secret and until now, there was no reason the DIA needed to know. Since you do know as of this minute, however, we can at least dispense with the nonsense of using lunatics as our guides in the hell universe. It's amazing you people get anything done."

I decided she really was an unpleasant woman, good looks or not and charming name or not. On the positive side, that would make my life easier, since I was obviously going to be dealing with her whether I wanted to or not.

When a heterosexually inclined single man like myself comes into contact with an attractive woman roughly his own age, an unstable situation automatically emerges. Unless he's taken holy vows, at any rate. First, curiosity demands to be satisfied. Is she herself heterosexually inclined? If so, is she single? If she is involved with someone, is the relationship officially monogamous? If so, is she open to cheating? If she is, do you want to get into that potential mare's nest?

It's exhausting just to think about it, especially because it may not stop there. If the answers are any one of yes, yes, no, yes and maybe, then the single heterosexually inclined single man has to go to work. Which can be *really* exhausting, usually unsettling, and often confusing.

But this situation was going to be no sweat. Since the answers across the board were: "Who cares? I don't like the damn woman anyway."

Frank's scowl was back in full force. "If you think I'm going to send one of my people into the hell universe with no better guide than an IPS gadget, you can damn well think again."

"No, of course not. The things are well-nigh useless." She turned, stuck fingers in her mouth, and blew a whistle.

A really impressive whistle it was, too, especially for a woman. The last woman—well, girl—I'd known with that good a whistle was Allison Alps. I felt my resolve to dislike Loren crumbling again.

There came another ruckus in the receptionist's office. Again, I could only catch one word in three. But I probably wasn't missing much in the way of intellectual content, because what I did hear was: "...*hey!...you don't...hey!...you can't!...what do you think...?...hey!*"

The door opened again and a creature waddled in. It stood about three feet high, was about three feet wide, and looked vaguely like a cross between a goose and a small troll. I recognized it as a svartálfar. They're sometimes known as "black elves," even though the color of their skin is slate gray. The darkness being referred to is a matter of the soul, not the body. They're generally nasty and invariably obnoxious. Most people don't associate with them willingly. I wondered why she did.

"You called, babe?" The creature twisted its long neck so that its grotesquely ugly face was cocked sideways as it looked up at Loren. Below the immense nose, thick lips twisted into a leer. "Finally getting horny?"

"In your dreams." Loren nodded toward me. "Meet Anibal Vargas. He's the agent from the DIA who'll be going with us. Mr. Vargas, this is my associate, Ingemar."

The creature now twisted the neck to bring its black and beady eyes to bear on me. It was the eyes more than anything—combined with that grotesque neck, of course—that brought the image of a goose to mind. There really wasn't anything very avian about the little monster.

"Hannibal, is it? I hope he's cannae-er than he looks."

I'd heard that one as far back as the ninth grade. But I hadn't expected to hear such an educated pun from something that looked like this creature.

"Be polite," said Loren.

"Why?" sneered Ingemar. "He'll just be another furball, like almost all these DIA field types. Dumber'n rocks."

It was true that most DIA field agents were therianthropes of one kind or another. People with degrees in sorcery or accounting tended to gravitate toward the FBI. But, true or not, I decided this snotty bastard needed to be put in his place right here at the outset.

Besides, the wisecrack about "furballs" was irritating.

I always wear were-adaptable clothing on the job, so I didn't need to strip. I just popped out my Polaroid flash, turned it on myself, and made the change.

The transformation is very quick although it seems much longer to the one undergoing the process. It wasn't more than a few seconds later that I came erect in my were form.

"*Arkh!*" squawked the little monster. He scrambled onto the filing cabinet against the door, that being the highest ground in the office.

Fat lot of good it would have done him. I swiveled my

head to gaze upon his partner. To her credit, Sophia Loren hadn't budged. She might have paled a little, although it was hard to tell with her olive complexion.

"I guess 'nice doggie' would be even more inappropriate than usual," she said. She turned to look at Ingemar. "Do you really think he can't get to you up there?"

The svartálfar gibbered something that sounded Germanic although I didn't recognize any of the words. Loren shook her head. "What difference does it make how high he can jump? He'd just bring the cabinet down." She studied my feet. "It'd be interesting to watch, actually."

This woman was quite confusing. I had a feeling my future might have some emotional exercise in it, after all.

2

"I didn't know it was even possible," said Loren the next day, as we waited for the State Department's witches to finish the ritual that would send us into the hell universe. We were using them instead of their DIA equivalents because the powers-that-be had pronounced this expedition to be under State's jurisdiction and control. Officially, I was just on loan as a field agent.

"I knew any sort of prehistoric therianthropy was rare," she continued, "and I just assumed they were all mammalian."

I shrugged. "Most are. Or I should say, almost all the few which exist are mammalian. But there are a handful like me."

"All velociraptors?"

"All dromaeosaurids, is the right way to put it. Velociraptors properly so-called were about the size of a turkey. The laws of physics, including conservation of mass and energy, aren't violated by therianthropy. A person who turned into a velociraptor would have to weigh no more than thirty to forty pounds."

"Okay. And that makes you . . . ?"

"I'm listed on the agency rolls as a *Deinonychus antirrhopus*. But the truth is, there's a lot of guesswork involved. Nobody really knows for sure."

I started to add something, but then saw that the sorcerers had reached the end of the ritual. I felt the universe beginning to swirl around us, in the by-now very familiar sensations of interplanar travel.

"And here we go," said Loren. She turned to her nasty little sidekick. "Are the goats ready?"

"Teach grandmothers to suck eggs," muttered Ingemar. He held up a sack and whacked the side of it. A couple of bleats emerged from within. "See?"

If you've read Steven Matuchek's account of the expedition he and his wife Virginia undertook into the hell universe to rescue their infant daughter, you'll remember his depictions of the terrain there. Those depictions are about as accurate as everything in his book. True as far as it goes, but it doesn't go as far as most people think it does. There's no such thing as "the" terrain of Hell, any more than there is such a thing as "the" terrain of Earth—or Mars, for that matter. In fact, the variation is a lot greater than anything you'll find in our own universe.

Because the witches had used personal possessions of Boatright in their cantrips, we came out in the same place in the hell universe that Boatright and his party had. Part of the cantrips also involved sending a homunculus through first to test the terrain's survivability in crude physical terms. The thing is mindless since its brain is no bigger than a pea, but its morphology and metabolism is otherwise completely human. They leave the homunculus in hell for twelve hours—hell time; it's only a second or two in our own—and then see what shape it's in when they bring it back. That's to make sure the party that goes through next won't immediately drown or suffocate in a vacuum or get poisoned by the atmosphere.

But beyond that, we had no idea what sort of environment we'd emerge in, and I was prepared for anything. So, it seemed, was my State Department companion. She'd exchanged her severe business suit for an explorer's jumpsuit that was cut every bit as severely but displayed her figure a lot better. I'd known already that the figure was slim, but now I could see that there was muscle there as well. Hers was the sort of slender build that came from a lot of exercise, not just genes and a good diet. Her gear wasn't too bulky and the only visible weapon was a machete slung across her back. Still, it must have come to somewhere around twenty pounds, and she was carrying all of it without apparent effort.

So far, so good. There didn't seem to be much chance that she'd just physically collapse under the strenuous conditions in the hell universe. I'd been worried about that. Foggy Bottom types like to sneer at we lowbrow DIA gorillas, but most of them think a strenuous workout consists of carrying a martini from one room to another in a diplomatic soiree.

I still had no idea what sort of experience she had in hell conditions. When I'd tried to enquire, she'd refused to answer. Politely, but I might as well have been interrogating a fire hydrant.

In the event, we arrived in a fetid jungle— just barely this side of a swamp. The soil underfoot was only "solid" in a technical sense. Walking on it would exhaust us within half an hour.

I turned to my companion and cocked an eye at her. Loren had insisted that she could and would provide transportation once we got to Hell.

She studied the terrain for a few more seconds, her lips pursed thoughtfully, and then said to Ingemar: "What do you think? I'm inclined toward the carpet myself, although the goats could probably manage the howdah."

The black elf peered suspiciously at the sky. What little he could see, which wasn't much given the solid low overcast. "I don't like the looks of it. Could be anything up there. I say we go with the howdah. It'll be slower but the goats can manage."

They sounded for all the world like a golfer and her caddy discussing which iron to use. After another few seconds and some continued lip-pursing, Loren nodded. "All right, let's do it."

With no further ado, Ingemar upended the sack in his hand. Two little goats fell out. I mean, *little*—neither one of them stood more than eight inches high. At a guess, they weighed about the same as small dogs. These were supposed to be our means of transportation?

"Stand back," Loren said, giving me a light warning push with her fingers. After I took a couple of steps back, she stuck her fingers in her mouth and whistled. A really piercing whistle, this one was.

The goats started growing. Really fast. Within fifteen seconds, they were both the size of elephants. Their morphologies changed as they grew also. By the end, they were still recognizably goats but their legs were disproportionately thick and their feet bore a closer resemblance to those of an elephant or a rhino than a goat's.

While that was happening, Ingemar had kept shaking the sack. The next thing that came out was a weird-looking contraption that looked like a scrunched-up haversack. By the time the goats finished their transformation, the haversack had turned into a howdah. Well...that's pushing it a little. Let's say it had the same resemblance to a proper howdah that a good tent has to a house. Still and all, it was clearly something a couple of people could ride in comfortably enough, even perched on top of a goat-cum-elephant.

It took another few minutes for the svartálfar to haul the howdah onto one of the goats and get it fastened in place. Then he reached back into the sack and hauled out something that looked like a fireplace poker. I recognized the device, although I couldn't remember what it was called. It was the tool used by mahouts to drive elephants.

Sure enough, a few seconds later he was perched in a mahout's position behind the goat's head, straddling its neck, and looking down at us with a sneer on his face. "What? You expect me to help you up, too?"

The jury-rigged howdah had a rope ladder hanging down from one side. Loren and I used it to climb aboard. No sooner had we gotten into the howdah than Ingemar set the goat in motion. Looking back, I could see the second one following. Apparently it would do so on its own, without a lead rope.

"We'll switch mounts after a few hours," Loren explained. "The beasts are tougher'n you'd believe, but they'll still get tired in this sort of terrain."

I looked ahead, and then to the sides. The terrain seemed identical anywhere you looked and I couldn't detect any sign of a trail. "Are you sure we're headed in the right direction?"

Loren sniffed. "As Ingemar said, don't teach grandmothers to suck eggs. First, the finding spell we used is the most reliable in existence. Second, Ingemar and the goats can find their way almost anywhere in Hell. Third, I know what I'm doing."

"An accomplished witch yourself, I take it."

"Me?" She gave me a look that somehow managed to be aloof and sly at the same time. "I haven't been a virgin since I was fifteen. If I'd even tried to apply to a good witch's program in college they'd have laughed at me. No, I'm a diplomat. What do you expect from the State Department? Think of me as a roving ambassador, if it makes you feel better."

It didn't. I didn't know exactly what the skill set of a diplomat consisted of, but I was pretty sure damn few of the skills would be any use here in the hell universe. Your average demon's idea of "negotiating" is arguing over whether you'll enter the monster's maw headfirst or feetfirst.

The remark about virginity kick-started my sternly suppressed single-male curiosity. As usual, this manifested itself in the form of a shifty-eyed glance and a suave "Aaaah..."

She chuckled. "I'm heterosexually inclined, single—divorced; not never married—currently unattached. Monogamous when I am, and no, I don't fool around. You?"

I cleared my throat. "Aaah...The same."

"Divorced for how long?"

"Two years. Not quite. Twenty-two months."

"It's been a little over three years for me. Okay, so divorce-shock shouldn't be too much of a problem. It's a deal, then. If you're still interested when this is over, ask me out on a date. The answer will be 'yes.' I've decided you're kind of cute, for a slavering carnosaur from the Cretaceous."

"Aaah..."

"Good thing one of us is a diplomat. Or are you under the delusion that a monosyllable is a good pickup line?" She flashed me a grin. "Get used to it, if you decide you're interested. Fair warning—I can be really annoying. Everyone says so. My ex-husband thinks the warning should be tattooed on my forehead. Every supervisor I've ever had would probably agree except for those who think it should be branded there. My friends, on the other hand, think a tattoo on the shoulder ought to be good enough if I agreed to always wear sleeveless dresses or tank tops."

A loud hoot from ahead drew our attention. Looking in that direction, we saw that a creature had emerged from the brush and was standing in our path. It looked more-or-less like a misshapen weightlifter with the head of an eagle and talons instead of fingers on its hands. At a guess, it weighed somewhere around four hundred pounds although that might be an over-estimate. Some demons with avian or partly avian morphologies have hollow bones.

"You gotta love this place," I said. "It's as predictable as the menu in a fast food joint."

"This monster being . . . ?"

I vaulted over the lip of the howdah and landed lightly on my feet. Well, allowing for a little squelch. Looking up, I saw that Loren was staring at me with surprise. Because of my size, people who don't know me don't realize how athletic I am. If I weren't just plain too massive, I'd have been an Olympic-level gymnast. As you'd expect, of course, given my genes.

"It's some variety of nisroch," I said. "This shouldn't take long."

It didn't.

A few minutes after we'd set back underway, Loren cleared her throat. "Well, I'd been thinking of recommending a nice sushi place for our date, but I guess that's not a good idea."

I grinned. "Rolled-up little fishie bits and tofu are really not my style. I'm pretty much a steakhouse kind of guy."

"Do you always eat the organs?"

"You have to stay away from the liver and spleen, with almost any kind of demon, and the hearts are just plain indigestible even for me. Other than that, though, yeah. The intestines are especially good because the hell universe has its own diseases and devil guts are the best source of antibiotics. Using the term loosely."

"But I'd think it must taste . . ."

"Horrible? Yeah, sure. But I'm eating them in raptor form. Think I care?"

That sly grin came back. I was starting to get fond of it, I decided, even though I could see where it might be annoying if you were in the wrong mood.

"I was wondering why the DIA had you listed as one of their top field agents," she said. "It's because you don't need much in the way of supplies. How many people can live off the land in Hell?"

"Not too many. In my defense, though, most of my rating is because of my brains. Believe it or not."

Her expression got more thoughtful. "Actually, I don't doubt that at all."

There came another loud sound from ahead of us. A screech, you might call it. A couple of seconds later, a huge falcon came flying into sight. It perched on a branch in a nearby tree, which sagged under the weight. Then it jerked its head around a few times and vomited a snake.

The snake landed on the soggy soil below and wriggled toward us. When it was no more than ten feet from the goat, it raised its head, jerked it around a few times, and puked up a toad. No sooner did the toad land on the ground than it made a prodigious hop onto one of the goat's horns and from there hopped onto the front side of the howdah.

That done, it jerked its head back and forth a few times—

"Oh, give me a break!" I said. Loren hurriedly leaned away from it.

—and vomited up a . . .

Louse? It sure looked like it.

The louse reared up and started speaking, in a much louder voice than you'd ever imagine such a tiny creature could produce. It sounded like gibberish to me, but Loren had a look of intent concentration on her face. I realized she was able to understand what it was saying.

Who the hell speaks louse? I didn't even know the pests had a language.

When the louse finally finished, Loren turned to me with a frown on her face. "What I was afraid of. That idiot Boatright managed to wander into a Mesoamerican region of the hell universe. A Mayan analog, at a first approximation. Of all the places to look for allies against the forces of evil!"

I understood her point. None of the early pagan religions were what you'd call filled with the milk of human kindness. But even in that crowd, the Mesoamerican deities and spirits were blood-curdling.

Literally, in many cases. The underlying belief system that had created them had for its main premise the idea that the universe was kept going by the gods, and the only thing that kept the gods themselves going was being fed with human blood. Human blood drawn from pain and suffering, to boot. No blood bank donors need apply. The blood had to come with shrieks of agony or it wasn't worth anything.

I dredged up what I knew about the mythos involved. If this region of the hell universe bore a close approximation to the Mayan region, I was pretty sure it would be ruled by the Lords of Xibalba. A cheery crowd, that lot. Among them would be a god of pain, a god of disease, a god of pus, a god of emaciation, a god of jaundice—you get the picture?

Loren's next words confirmed my guess:

"The louse is a messenger from the Lords of Xibalba. It says if we want to get Boatright and his people back we need to—"

"Undergo a series of tests. Yeah, I know. That's a pretty standard feature of this mythos."

It was clear from the expression on her face that she was familiar with it herself. "It is, indeed," she said. "Some of them will be straightforward tests of skill, but some will be ordeals and all of them are likely to be full of tricks."

"You do realize that there's already not much left of Boatright and his people? Not here."

She nodded. "Yes, I know."

"So why go on? I vote for an ignominious retreat."

"We can't. It's tempting, but . . ." She shook her head. "The problem is that too many of our netherworld alliances with pagan forces are based on rigid honor codes. Their codes, not ours, but if they start thinking we're prone to quitting when the going gets tough, the alliances will get frayed at the very least."

I put on my best sneer. "Who cares? There's a reason those silly buggers went out of business. Several reasons, actually. 'Rigid honor code' is probably right at the top."

She smiled thinly. "Oh, not right at the top. But I agree it's up there. It still doesn't matter, Anibal. We can't afford to lose those alliances, with all the chaos that's still reverberating from the collapse of the Johannine church after the Matuchek Incident."

Since she was officially in charge of the expedition, my vote didn't really matter. "Okay, you're the boss. Is this parasite our guide, or do we have to find our own way to the examination hall?"

"There'll be a guide of some sort, but not the louse. The creature was pretty vague—*whoa!*"

The howdah was lurching around wildly. The goat carrying it was bleating and the goat following was already half out of sight racing back in the direction from which we'd come. For his part, Ingemar was holding onto the goat's horns for dear life. He'd lost his prod in the process.

We were rising, too, very quickly. I looked down to see what was causing that, and then wished I hadn't.

The reason we were rising was because we were on the back of a gigantic crocodile. About the size of a battleship.

"And here we go," said Sophia.

3

The crocodile carried us for what I'd estimate was thirty miles—keeping in mind that the term "estimate" means exactly that, and under hell conditions to boot. Given the beast's size, though, that didn't take more than an hour or so. (See caveat concerning estimates above, with the added caution that watches are completely unreliable in the infernal regions.)

Eventually, we arrived in front of a great pit, at the bottom of which an enormous drunken revelry was taking place. There were about four hundred drunkards down there, not one of whom looked to be older than ten or eleven. They were all boys, too. Not a girl in sight.

"The Four Hundred Boys," said Sophia. "We're in a Mayan mythos, sure enough. Close analog, anyway. We won't go any further until one of us joins the celebration."

She turned to Ingemar. "Your job, this is."

He was already climbing over the side of the howdah, looking quite cheerful. "Good luck on the rest of your trip. Better you than me, heh! I'll be partying hard in support, be sure of it."

Once off the goat and on the crocodile, the svartálfar scampered down its spine until he reached the tip of the tail. From there, it wasn't too bad of a leap down to the ground. As soon as he was off, the crocodile started moving around the pit.

My knowledge of the Mayan mythos was on the sketchy side. "Who are the Four Hundred Boys?"

"The gods of drunkenness. Or the gods of alcoholic drinks, depending on the translation. The reason they're boys, according to State's scholars, is probably because they can't hold their liquor at all. The reason there are four hundred of them is probably to make sure not all of them are passed out at once. So far as we can tell, their diplomatic function is to waylay visitors, get them plastered, and then play nasty tricks on them. 'Nasty' as in frequently fatal or disfiguring."

"This is a diplomatic function?"

She grinned. "Leaving aside the murder and mayhem, it's really not too different from what happens at cocktail parties in embassies."

Not more than two miles past the pit, the crocodile came to a halt again. This time, in front of a large stone building. It swung its tail around until the tip of it was just before the building's only visible entrance.

The hint was obvious. So, Loren and I got out of the howdah and copied Ingemar's method of leaving the crocodile. As soon as we reached the ground, the gigantic reptile started moving away.

I was a little sorry to see it go. Despite its fearsome appearance, the monster had been perfectly well-behaved and I hadn't worried about being waylaid by anything while we were on top of it. Not even Hell's creatures are likely to pester something that size.

There being nothing else to do, we passed through the entrance. It wasn't a door, just a tall and narrow corridor through the stones that made up the structure. We emerged into a chamber about fifty feet across. Sitting on stools in a semi-circle at the opposite end were fourteen beings, staring at us.

I use the term "beings" because I can't think of anything more suitably vague that still conveys intelligence. The appearance of the fourteen figures varied wildly in every manner except one: they were all hideous.

You were expecting something else from the gods of

pus, pestilence, etc? Trust me, you don't even want to
think what the god of hemorrhoids looked like.

"At a guess," I said, "we're looking at the Lords of
Xibalba."

Sophia snorted. "You think?"

"What now?"

"I'm not sure. We need to greet all of them by name,
if I remember the protocol, or we'll be in immediate
trouble. But there's bound to be a trick involved."

"How good are you with languages?"

"That's one of my specialties. I'm not technically a
witch, but my abilities when it comes to speaking in
tongues are magical. For all practical purposes, I can
understand any language after I've heard a few words
spoken. Don't ask me how, because I don't know."

The germ of an idea came to me. A crudely direct idea,
I admit, but what else do you expect from a theropod?

"Okay, then. Let's see what happens." I pulled out my
flash and made the change.

Once in raptor form, I sprang over to the nearest Lord
of Xibalba and smelled it. For me, in that form, smelling
mostly meant licking it with my tongue.

At a guess, this one was the god of vomit. There was
no way I could have made myself smell the thing, much
less lick it with my tongue, if I'd still been in human form.
But theropods are to fastidiousness what monkeys are to
decorum. In a word, oblivious.

I then sprang over to the next one. At a guess, after a
couple of licks, this one was the god of edema.

The third one, even before my tongue could examine
it, I figured to be the god of acne. But before my tongue

reached it, the Lord of Xibalba waved me off frantically and started gibbering something at its fellow gods.

I swiveled my head to look at Sophia. She had that same expression of intent concentration that she'd had when she was listening to the louse. So, seeing no further role to play at the moment, I squatted down in front of the semi-circle.

When a human squats, he looks more harmless than usual. Not so, for a Deinonychus. He looks like he's about to spring into action.

All of the lords except the two at the far end were now gibbering wildly. Those two, on the other hand, were as inert as if they'd been made of the same stone the building was.

Which, as it turned out, they were.

"Okay," said Sophia. "I've learned all their names by now, since they used them in jabbering at one another." She pointed at the two silent ones. "Those are phonies. Mannequins. The other twelve . . ."

She moved to the center of the chamber, bowed, and addressed each one of the Lords in turn. I didn't understand any of it, but I found out later that the names were such charming monickers as One Death, Seven Death, Blood Gatherer—no St. Francis types in this crowd.

When she finished, the twelve real Lords of Xibalba starting gibbering again. After a few minutes of that, the racket died down and all of them looked at one of the Lords near the center of the semi-circle. This one was marginally less ugly than the others—you understand this doesn't mean much? like being the best-dressed hog in a pigsty—but made up for it by having a smoking obsidian mirror embedded in its forehead.

Smoking Mirror leaned forward on its stool and gibbered something at Sophia. She gibbered back, he gibbered, she gibbered, eventually they were done.

She came over to where I stood. By then, I'd changed back to human form.

"It's about what we figured," she said. "They'll hand Boatright and his people over to us if we pass some tests. To judge our worth—and don't ask me how they gauge worth in the first place, I haven't got a clue."

"How many tests?"

"They're being vague about that. Essentially, one test for every human they hand over. But for some reason they seem unable or unwilling to specify an exact number."

I frowned. "There's a gimmick in there, somewhere. Boatright had three people with him. Even monster gods dedicated to diseases should be able to count up to four."

She shrugged. "There's always a gimmick, dealing with the deities in this region of the hell universe. We'll just have to see how it works out."

Since I didn't have a better plan, I nodded. "Where's the first test?"

"From what I gather, as soon as we leave this edifice."

That test turned out to be a giant jaguar, the size of a big tiger. Piece of cake, even though I was outweighed by at least three hundred pounds.

It's not so much that dromaeosaurids are intrinsically more ferocious than modern predators—although they probably are. But the biggest factor is brains. A jaguar, even a giant one in Hell, is no smarter than any big cat. Even without a human intelligence riding piggyback, any dromaeosaurid can easily equal it. When you add the human intelligence, even as dimmed as it invariably is in were form, it's just no contest.

Except for bears, modern predators almost exclusively use their teeth as their killing tools. Their claws and talons are a means to hold prey, not weapons. So I knew the jaguar wouldn't be expecting me to shift to the side and disembowel it with one kick as it leapt at me. In Deinonychus form, the second toes on my rear feet have large sickle claws that will cut through almost anything short of thick metal or hardwood.

Normally, I would have just let the jaguar bleed out. Why take any risks at all? But since I figured time was pressing and had no idea what the rules of the test might be, I finished it off quickly with a bite to the neck. A Deinonychus has a bite force that's even greater than a hyena's, and almost equals that of a modern alligator of equal size. One bite was enough.

The next test required us to enter another stone edifice. Once inside, we found ourselves in a large chamber full of sharp obsidian blades. The blades were round and about the size of dinner plates.

"Oh, swell," said Sophia. "The House of Razors."

As soon as we entered, the blades lifted off the ground and started humming. Then, a few seconds later, they began a complex series of motions that I soon realized constituted an impenetrable barrier to anyone who wanted to get through them. It was like a moving version of the laser beam networks that are used in some security systems.

There was another door visible at the far end of the chamber. The nature of this test was depressingly clear.

While I'd been studying the pattern of the blades' movements, Sophia had gotten that now-familiar intent look on her face. I only half-noticed, though, until she nudged me with her elbow.

"I think I can talk our way through them," she said.

My contribution was: "Huh?"

But, sure enough, she started humming herself and before you knew it the blade pattern shifted to leave a narrow corridor in the middle. Sophia immediately hurried through, not quite running. After taking a deep breath, I followed.

Worked like a charm.

The next test went by the name of Cold House. The one after that, Bat House.

The first was full of hail the size of golf balls, freezing rain and winds just barely this side of hurricane force. That was purely a matter of endurance. The second one was full of—what else?—bats. Not fruit-eating bats, either. Vampire bats.

Wannabe vampires, I should say. Sophia started a godawful caterwauling that she told me later was the mating calls of lamias. That seemed to confuse the bats mightily. It would have scrambled my wits as well except that I shifted into were form. Theropods react to horrible noises about the same way they react to horrible smells:

the blithe indifference that generally goes along with being on top of the food chain.

When we emerged from the Bat House, we looked around.

Nothing, beyond a lot of trees crowded around the small clearing where the stone edifice was situated.

"Those rotten bastards," I grumbled. "We passed four tests. Boatright and his partners add up to four. So where are they?"

Sophia pointed to a tree off to our left. "Well, there's one of them. Part of one, I should say."

I followed her finger. There was a human head, perched in a fork of the tree about ten feet off the ground. A severed human head, to be precise.

"I think that's Boatright himself," I said. "Judging by the photos we had."

We went over to the tree. Even in human form, it wasn't hard for me to get up into the tree high enough to haul down the head.

"Yup, that's Boatright. I wonder where the rest of him is?"

Sophia spotted a trail leading out of the clearing. "Let's try that way."

That way led to the House of Fire, followed by the House of Snakes. Along the way, we picked up the head of one of Boatright's partners, the left foot of another and the upper body of a third. (They didn't belong to Boatright. Wrong size and in the case of the foot, wrong color.)

"This sucks," I said. "The Lords of Xibalba are going to work us to death."

Wearily, Sophia nodded. We were both a lot worse off than we'd been at the start. Leaving aside exhaustion, we'd picked up enough bruises and minor cuts to make us look like extras in a zombie movie. Judging from the number of body parts we'd collected so far, we weren't more than halfway there. I didn't think we could last long enough to finish. Not doing it this way.

I said as much. Sophia grimaced. "I don't disagree, but what's the alternative?"

"We need to take a fifteen-minute break anyway. Let me think about it while we're resting. There's got to be something."

It took me ten minutes to figure it out. Three minutes to explain the plan to Sophia. Five minutes to quell her doubts and objections.

Eighteen minutes all told, three minutes over my self-imposed time limit. Sue me. Watches don't work right in Hell anyway.

4

When we re-entered the first of the stone buildings—Greasy Grimy Godlet Guts House, I called it; 4-G for short—the Lords of Xibalba immediately started gibbering at us. They sounded angry to me; but then, they always sounded angry to me.

Sophia gibbered right back at them, and there was no doubt at all that her tone was hostile. Even the lords seemed to draw back a little from the fury in her voice.

"Guess I told them," she said with self-satisfaction, after her tirade wound down. She didn't bother to translate because I already knew the gist of what she'd been saying. It was my plan, after all.

You lousy bums are a bunch of cheats and chiselers and think you're pulling a fast one, but you just wait and see. You'll get your comeuppance. First, though, I have to sacrifice my loyal minion to regain my strength. Then I'll bring him back to life as good as new—and you just watch what happens next!

That was about the gist of it. Add maybe a thousand Xibalba equivalents of Anglo-Saxon four-letter words.

As soon as she was done, she pulled out her machete. I flopped to the ground and rolled over on my back. Playing the part of a loyal minion to perfection, if I say so myself.

Sophia looked down at me, her face tight with anxiety. She was definitely paler than usual, too. It was obvious despite her complexion.

I winked at her. "Relax. Pretend we're on our first date and I just made the crudest, grossest and most male chauvinist remark you ever heard. Hell, anyone ever heard."

That made her grin. That same sly grin I was getting really very fond of.

I held up the flash, and did the transformation. Once in were form, I did my best to stay on my back. I couldn't manage that very well, since the anatomy of a Deinonychus really isn't suited to a supine posture. But I got close enough for our purposes.

The machete came up. The machete came down. Right into my belly.

It hurt like you wouldn't believe. And I didn't stint on the howling and shrieking because that was pretty much *de rigeur* in this crowd.

Sophia must have been a butcher in a previous incarnation. Either that or—probably more likely—she just had a will of iron. It didn't take her more than a half a minute to hack her way into my abdomen, do the needed quick and crude surgery, and haul out a section of my intestines.

In dramatic terms, this would have worked better if she'd cut into my chest and taken out my heart. The problem is that therianthropes in beast form are more vulnerable than most people think. You don't *need* a silver bullet or blade to kill a were, it just makes things a lot easier and less chancy because you've got a metabolic poison working for you at the same time as whatever physical damage you've done. But enough physical damage in the right place will do the trick all by itself. Silver be damned. If you can stop a vital organ like a heart, a were will die.

But guts don't fall into that category. My intestinal tract was already healing. As long as I didn't transform back into human form until it was done, I'd survive. The process was very painful, but it really wasn't any more dangerous for me than a root canal.

I didn't think the Lords of Xibalba would know that, however. As deities went, these were some real lowbrows.

Sophia held the intestines high in her left hand, tilted her head, and squeezed some of the blood into her mouth. I don't think she hesitated more than a split-second, if she hesitated at all. Even in my pain and dizziness I was impressed.

That done, she cast the piece of gut aside as if it were so much trash and sprang to her feet. Before we'd entered the 4-G House, Sophia had taken a couple of the emergency stimulant pills she'd had in her supply kit. The chemicals would wear out in a few hours, at which point she'd be completely exhausted. But for those few hours, the pills gave her an enormous amount of energy.

It took about ten minutes for the effects to kick in. Right about now, in other words.

Oh, she was leaping and springing all over the place, gibbering with zeal and glee. To all outward appearances, a woman reborn. True, if you looked closely you'd still spot the bruises. But we'd figured the Lords of Xibalba wouldn't notice them at all. Why would something that looked like a chunk of shredded meat left out in the sun too long even think about a measly little bruise?

Me? I was already healed. The truth is, if I hadn't still been putting on the act of being at death's door, I'd have already been up and moving about in human form.

Eventually, Sophia left off her capering and came over to me. Then she started waving the still-bloody machete around and chanting what sounded like really serious incantations. I found out later they were actually curry recipes, spoken in the Caribbean Hindi dialect found in Suriname and Trinidad.

When she came to the climactic finale of her peroration, she spread her hands wide and shouted "*Arise, reborn!*" in standard English. Then, for good measure, she repeated it in Xibalba gibberish.

My cue. I rolled up onto my paws, Sophia used the flash, and a few seconds later I was back on my feet as a human being. To all outward appearances, completely unharmed.

Sophia started gibbering again. She'd now be telling them how we were going to charge back outside, knock down whatever other pitiful tests they had worked out for us, gather up the human parts we'd come for—boy oh boy are you guys screwed—and then come back and deal with them, dirty lousy conniving stinky cheaters that they were.

There was silence for a moment, when she finished. This was the critical moment. Would they fall for it . . . ? Or would they call our bluff?

If the latter, we'd have no choice but to return to our own universe with our mission unaccomplished. Or only partly accomplished, at best. We were simply too beat up to keep going for much longer. Being a therianthrope, I've got a lot more stamina than most people. But there are limits, even for weres. And Sophia would be completely out of gas, once the stimulants wore off.

I didn't think they'd be very smart, though, gods or not. You have to figure that a deity who embodies ulcers just isn't going to measure up intellectually against a god or goddess of wisdom. Or a reasonably bright twelve-year-old kid, for that matter.

And this was a mythos that took blood magic more seriously than any other the human race has ever produced. The thought of being completely revitalized by blood sacrifice would be incredibly attractive, even to godlings.

They started gibbering at Sophia again. She gibbered

back, making a big show of appearing reluctant and hesitant. Their gibbering got more and more animated until they sounded downright frantic.

Finally, bowing her head, Sophia yielded to their demands. She pointed to the lord on the far left of the group and motioned it into the center of the chamber. The creature—this one was the god of lice, I think—squirmed and oozed its way forward.

Once it arrived in position, Sophia wagged her finger at it and gibbered sternly. She'd be telling the critter—and all the others listening—that it couldn't expect as quick a recovery as her loyal minion had made. Being as I was accustomed to the process and they weren't.

Gibber, gibber, gibber. The machete came up, came down. Since she had no idea which portion of the creature's horrid body held critical parts and which didn't, she just sawed away merrily once she got inside. After a minute or so, she hauled out a quivering chunk of who-knows-what-and I-don't-want-to-know, and held it over the god's analog to a mouth. There was a bit of guesswork there too, but it didn't really matter because it was pretty obvious that the monster was already dead or as close to it as you could ask for.

Still, good theater is good theater. She took the time to squeeze out some blood—blood analog, rather; don't ask—into the gaping orifice before she cast it aside and summoned another of the lords to come forth.

Which, it did. Eagerly, in fact. She repeated the same process, again and again and again, allowing for the variations needed because no two Lords of Xibalba had the same form or anatomy.

It was a good thing she was on stimulants. That was more hacking and hewing of flesh—flesh analog, rather; really don't ask—than a meatpacker did in a full day's work.

Believe it or not, the Lords didn't get suspicious until there were only two left. But Sophia managed to sweet-talk—okay, sweet-gibber—one of them into undergoing the "revitalization" process. The one left finally realized that something was amiss and started putting up a fight. But this one was apparently the god of athlete's foot. A puny critter, when all was said and done. Measured, at least, by the standards of a two-hundred-and-forty-pound Deinonychus.

But I didn't eat the organs. Organ analogs, rather. Really really really don't ask. Even theropods have limits.

So ended the Lords of Xibalba. For a time, anyway. Given the underlying premises of this region of Hell, they'd almost certainly come back eventually. Reborn out of pain and suffering, so to speak. But that would take quite a while; far more time than we'd need to find and collect all the body parts we needed to bring back.

Then, we finally got a break. Within half an hour we came across the rest of Rick Boatright's body. It was wandering around the area with a gourd where the head used to be.

The gourd had facial features painted on. Someone, presumably a Lord of Xibalba or one of their agents, had even carved out a rough mouth.

The thing could talk, after a fashion. I couldn't

understand a word it was saying, but Sophia got that look of intense concentration again and we were off to the races.

Boatright—or should I say, Boatright-analog?—led us to the rest of his party. Their pieces, rather. Eventually, we collected them all and brought them back to the clearing in front of the 4-G House.

Unfortunately, for all her quasi-magical linguistic powers, Sophia wasn't an actual witch. If she had been, she could probably have figured out a way to return to our own universe from where we were. As it was, neither of us knew any better way than to return to our arrival locus. The State Department's witches would be keeping watch at that location and would be ready to draw us back into our own universe.

That left the problem of how to haul the stuff there. Whole or in pieces, four human bodies still weigh the better part of half a ton. If it were absolutely necessary, I was strong enough that I could probably carry it all back to our arrival spot. But I sure didn't want to.

Fortunately, there was an obvious alternative. We had the makings for a travois and the dumb beast to haul it.

Rick Boatright. His body hadn't been harmed and with a gourd for a head, he wasn't likely to argue his way out of the task.

He didn't even try. He just picked up the travois handles, lowered his gourd, and set off after us.

Along the way, we stopped at the pit to pick up Sophia's sidekick. By then, Ingemar had drunk all but a handful of the Four Hundred Boys under the table.

(Figuratively speaking. They'd actually been drinking from troughs made out of—never mind. Don't ask.)

I wasn't surprised. Despite the nickname, "black elves" are actually a variety of dwarves. No one in their right mind gets into drinking contests with dwarves.

5

It was slow going, of course. That would have been true over the best ground, much less this muck. But eventually we got there, the State Department's witches were indeed keeping a watch, and it wasn't long before we found ourselves back where we'd started.

"Oh, yuck!" screeched one of the witches, scurrying away from the travois.

Which...was a real mess. That part of the hell universe took death and dismemberment in stride, so to speak. That's the reason you could plant a gourd on the shoulders of a decapitated man, paint crude facial features on it, and expect it to walk around and even talk after a fashion.

But once we arrived back home, the conditions of our universe took over. The results were...

Unfortunate. Let's put it that way.

The first thing that happened was that the gourd rolled off Boatright's shoulders and Boatright's body collapsed to the floor. The gourd wound up underneath one of the chairs against the far wall and Boatright's body started spreading across the floor.

As did the body parts of all of his companions, oozing

out of the travois. The technical phrase is *advanced and enhanced decomposition produced by infernal conditions.* Colloquially known as Quick Rot.

Too bad for Boatright and his crew, of course, but from the cold-blooded standpoint of *Realpolitik* the outcome was just as good as if we'd brought them back alive. Not even the harshest Scandinavian or Slavic deity would fault us for the demise of the Boatright party. Such beings took violent death as a matter of course. What mattered was whether honor, just retribution and clan vengeance was satisfied. Bringing back all the corpses and putting paid to the Lords of Xibalba did that just fine.

Sophia told me a few weeks later that human embassies touring the so-called "morally neutral" portions of the nether regions universe were being feted everywhere they went. Especially in any mythos that placed a premium on sneakiness, treachery, and guile. Which was just about all of them.

Our first date went well, I thought. Extremely well, in fact. But I was clearly in for a protracted period of emotional exercise and probable exhaustion. The new lady in my life is never at a loss for words.

Fortunately, I have a theropod's stamina.

Afterword:

I've always enjoyed Poul Anderson's stories, which I started reading as a teenager. And in his case, I enjoyed just about everything he wrote.

That's unusual. With most authors I enjoy, I really only like a portion of their work. One story or novel but not another; one series or setting, but not another. With Anderson, I can't think of one that I didn't enjoy.

So, when Gardner Dozois asked me to contribute to this anthology, I had to think about it. Not *whether* I'd contribute something—that would be a pleasure—but in which of Poul Anderson's many universes.

It finally came down to a choice between the world Anderson created in *Operation Chaos* and the one he created in *The High Crusade*. (*Three Hearts and Three Lions* was a close third.)

In the end, I opted for *Operation Chaos*. I enjoy *The High Crusade* every bit as much, as a story, but I'd find it somewhat awkward to write my own story in that setting. More precisely, I'd find it difficult to write a story in that setting that stayed true to Anderson's own vision of it. And doing so, I think, is important for this kind of anthology.

I never met Poul Anderson, and never corresponded with him. But it's obvious just from reading his work that he had a different view of the political history of the human race than I do. He had a soft spot in his heart for feudalism. It might be better to say, was attuned to what he saw as its advantages. You could see that not only in *The High Crusade* but in such stories as "No Truce with Kings." That went along with an elegiac attitude toward the grandeur of dying regimes, which of course runs all through his massive Dominic Flandry series.

Me? I think the best thing about the medieval period is that it's gone. And as much as I enjoyed each and every one of the Flandry stories, the truth is, deep down inside

I was always rooting for the Merseians. The fading glories of the Terran Empire, so far as I was concerned, were just the trappings of another rotting, decadent empire. Pfui. History is littered with the cruddy things. Good riddance.

I'm sure Anderson and I would have spent a number of pleasant hours wrangling over the issues involved, if we'd ever met. Unfortunately, that can't happen now. And I wasn't comfortable at the idea of writing a story for an anthology commemorating an author that, no matter how subtly or indirectly, constituted a tacit critique of his work.

It's too bad, in a way. I would have had fun writing a story about the stalwart and quick-thinking alien peasantry rising up in rebellion against tyrannical and dirt-stupid human barons...

But, what the hell. I knew I'd have just as much fun writing about shapechangers and witches in the world of *Operation Chaos*—and *that* story was one I could write completely and fully in Poul Anderson's own spirit.

Such was my intent, at any rate. You've now just read the story, so you can decide for yourself if I succeeded or not.

—Eric Flint

FROM THE PEN
[OKAY, WORD PROCESSOR]
OF A GROUCHY
ATHEIST

Author's note:

I wrote these three stories many years ago, before my career as an author had really begun. In truth, I wasn't thinking about getting them published when I wrote them. The only one I even sent in to a magazine was "The Truth About the Gotterdammerung." I sent the story to The Magazine of Fantasy & Science Fiction and, a couple of months later, got back a very nice handwritten rejection letter from the magazine's editor, Kristine Kathryn Rusch. I wasn't a published author at the time, and getting that sort of personal rejection letter from a well-known editor was something of an accomplishment in itself. (Kris either had or would soon thereafter win a Hugo Award for Best Editor.)

The reason she gave for rejecting the story was that, although she personally enjoyed it and thought it was well written, she didn't think it was suitable for the magazine.

I could hardly object, since I agreed with her. I didn't think the story was suitable for the magazine either. I'd just sent it in on a whim.

The truth is, none of these three stories is really what you'd call "a proper story." I wrote each of them because one or another reactionary fundamentalist preacher said or did something that pissed me off. I don't remember which ones they were any more. Might have Jerry Falwell, or Pat Robertson, or Bob Jones, or any of those bums.

The stories did eventually get published, two of them in a couple of Esther Friesner's Chicks in Chainmail *series. I thought that was a happy home for them. As an editor, Esther handles propriety in publishing pretty much the same way Attila the Hun handled knocking politely on doors.*

So, here they are. A grouchy atheist's response to the twaddle that calls itself the literal truth of the Bible.

The Flood Was Fixed

"Still sore about Job, huh?" snickered Baalzebub.

The Prince of Darkness took a swipe at the archdevil with his tail, but his heart wasn't in it.

"It was a fluke," he grumbled. "A statistical freak. So what if God found one faithful man in a sea of sinners? I should have played the odds."

"How?"

"I should have bet Him on the whole lousy human race."

Baalzebub shook his head. "God never would have gone for it. Too much work, visiting personal suffering on all those people. He's lazy, when you get right down to it. Worked six lousy days, and thinks He ought to be able to lounge around the rest of eternity. Coupon-clipper. We proletarian types down here *never* get a day off."

Satan glowered about the stygian gloom of Hell. He'd gotten tired of Dante's Renaissance decor lately, so he'd gone back to Classic. Even the reek of brimstone and the screams of tortured sinners didn't cheer him up.

"I know, I know. That's why I agreed to bet on Job. I got taken to the cleaners."

Baalzebub hesitated. Not for the first time, the thought crossed his mind that being chief adviser to the Lord of Evil was not without its drawbacks.

"Maybe you should quit gambling with—"

He ducked Satan's pitchfork and dived behind a smoldering rock.

"He's God, dammit! You can't win. The house odds will get you every time."

But Satan wasn't willing to listen to reason. He never was, which (when you get right down to it) is why he's the Prince of Darkness instead of the Lord of Light.

"There's gotta be a way to beat Him," he snarled, after resuming his seat. "All I've got to do is figure out a way to get Him to bet on the whole miserable human race."

He cackled, rubbing his taloned paws. "Any bet on the whole bunch, I'm bound to win!"

Deciding it was safe, Baalzebub resumed his seat.

"Yeah, sure, no question about it. But it's like I said— He's a cloud potato. Hates to work up a sweat."

Satan slouched and stared at his cloven hooves gloomily. Suddenly, he sat up straight.

"I've got it! I've got it! I'll bet Him the human race will lose its faith in Creation!"

"Huh?"

"Don't you see? He's got such a swelled head over that genesis business that he won't be able to resist."

Baalzebub scratched his horns.

"I still don't get it. Of course He'll bet on it. Why

shouldn't He? He's bound to win. I mean, look at the thing!"

And so saying, Baalzebub exerted his archdevilish powers and brought before the superhuman vision of the Lord of Flies the entire vista of Creation, in all its glory and splendor.

"You see what I mean? Even creatures as stupid as humans aren't going to doubt for a minute that something this grand was created by a Creator. How else could it have come to be? Even a moron examining a watch is going to figure out that it took a watchmaker to—"

"*Will you shut up about the stupid watch?* I'm sick of hearing it!"

Satan hawked up a lunger and spit on a nearby sinner. A bit mollified, he watched the damned one's flesh boil away.

"I've already figured it out," he announced firmly. "All you have to do is provide humans with an alternate explanation, and they'll jump at it."

Baalzebub frowned with puzzlement. "What alternative explanation?"

Satan spread his arms in a grand gesture. "Evolution, that's what!"

"Huh? What's 'evolution'?"

So the Prince of Darkness explained to his chief archdevil the entire theory of evolution, which he had just thought up on the spot. (He's evil, but he's not stupid.) He explained mutations and natural selection and particulate inheritance and the double helix, and all the rest of it. By the time he was finished, Baalzebub was rolling on the ground, roaring with laughter.

"That's the most ridiculous idea I've ever heard!" he gasped. "Not even humans would fall for it."

Satan grinned. "They will if there's a shred of evidence."

"But there isn't any."

"There will be, once God makes it. It won't be hard for Him, either, so He won't be able to wriggle out of the bet. He's already made the universe, hasn't He? All He's got to do is fiddle with a few details. Throw in some old bones, things like that."

Baalzebub pondered his master's words. "You know, you just might be onto something here," he mused. Then he shook his head firmly.

"No, no. I go back to what I said earlier—there's no percentage in betting against the Almighty. He'll figure some way to welsh on the deal, no matter what happens."

But Satan was set on his course. Straight away he ascended to the heavens and bellowed for God to show His face. After the Lord of Creation manifested Himself, the Prince of Darkness explained the proposition.

God accepted the wager immediately. (He's not at all indecisive.)

ONCE A CHUMP, ALWAYS A CHUMP. WHEN ARE YOU EVER GOING TO LEARN, YOU PIPSQUEAK?

Instantly God set about creating the evidence of evolution. He caused great fossils to come into being deep in the bowels of the earth. He created DNA, RNA, the works. He created radioactivity, and then changed the laws of nature so that radioactive materials would decay at a precise rate. Because He's a sporting kind of Guy, He even made some peas smooth and some peas wrinkled, so that human dumbbells could figure out genetics.

When He was finished, he showed His work to Satan.

GOOD ENOUGH?

Satan examined the evidence and announced that he was satisfied.

"Once humans get a load of this stuff they'll dump the genesis story in a fast minute," he chortled. "Give humans a choice between musty old legends and the evidence in front of their own eyes, they'll trust their senses every time. Idiots."

NOT AFTER THEY SEE THE COUNTER-EVIDENCE.

"What counter-evidence?" demanded the Devil. "There wasn't anything in our bet about counter-evidence!"

SURE THERE IS. WE'RE BETTING HUMAN REASON VERSUS FAITH IN THE BIBLE, AM I RIGHT?

Satan scowled. He could smell a rat, but he wasn't sure just where it was.

"Well, yeah," he admitted.

ALL RIGHT, THEN! YOU EVER HEAR OF THE FLOOD?

Satan waved his hand dismissively. "That was just a heavy rainfall." He snickered. "It only happened because you forgot to turn off the water."

God glowered, but forebore comment. The truth is, He couldn't deny it. He'd gotten preoccupied with the creation of the Andromeda Nebula and had let the rain go on a wee bit longer than He'd intended.

But His reply was dignified, as you might expect.

NOT AFTER I REDO IT. THIS TIME I'M GOING TO DO IT UP GRAND.

And, it goes without saying, God was as good as His Word. He rolled history back a few generations to the time of Noah. (God is not limited by the Arrow of Time. As a mere human, you won't be able to understand how this works. That's why He's God and you're not.)

NOAH.

Noah scrambled to his feet. At his urgent gesture, his three sons stood to attention. Well, Shem and Japheth did, anyway. As usual, Ham slouched.

"Yes, Sir!"

DO YOU REMEMBER THAT HEAVY RAIN A FEW WEEKS BACK?

"Sure do, Chief. What a doozy! For a while there, I thought we were all going to drown. Heh, heh, heh."

IS THAT LEVITY, NOAH?

"No, Sir! No, Sir!"

I TRUST NOT. IN ANY EVENT, I'VE DECIDED TO REDO THE RAIN. WE NEED A MONSTROUS FLOOD, YOU SEE. DROWN EVERYTHING THAT MOVES ON LAND. EXCEPT YOU.

"Uh, yes Sir. Everything, Sir?"

ALL MEN AND BEASTS THAT WALK OR CRAWL UPON THE EARTH, OR CREEP WITHIN IT, OR FLY THROUGH THE AIR.

"Uh, yes Sir. If you don't mind my asking, though, why the hard line?"

THEY ARE SINNERS ALL.

Ham spoke up. "Uh, begging Your pardon, Sir, but I

actually think most of 'em are pretty devout. Look here, for instance!"

Ignoring Noah's glare, Ham pointed to a procession of beetles marching past, holding up icons and images of saints.

"And how about over there!" Ham pointed to a circle of baby hamsters, gathered about a gray-pelted oldster, learning to genuflect.

SINNERS, I SAID, SINNERS THEY ARE.

And, indeed, it was just as God said. That very moment the beetles plunged into a disgusting saturnalia. The baby hamsters (and the gray-pelted oldster!) began copulating shamelessly. In the air above, sparrows sodomized each other in mid-flight. Everywhere the eye could see, people were worshipping graven images. The soil erupted with earthworms, wriggling an obscene dance.

"I am shocked, Sir! Shocked!" cried Noah.

"Sinners all!" bellowed Shem and Japheth. Ham opened his mouth to say something, but fell silent at Shem's elbow to his ribs.

QUITE SO. YOU, HOWEVER, ARE A RIGHTEOUS MAN, AND SO SHALL I SPARE YOU. GATHER UP—

There followed a whole slew of instructions regarding the size of the ark to be built, the wood it was to be made of, how it was to be pitched, and so on and so forth. Accompanied by instructions to save two of every species, one male and one female.

Noah and his sons began scurrying around. Noah and Shem started chopping down trees. Japheth started boiling pitch in a cauldron. Ham—

—right off started causing trouble.

"Hey, Pop," he said, tugging at Noah's cloak. "I'm confused."

His father glared at him. "What could possibly be confusing, even to you? The Lord's instructions were very clear and precise."

"Yeah, I know. That's why I'm confused. He said the ark was supposed to be three hundred cubits long, fifty cubits wide, and thirty cubits high. Right?"

"Just so."

Ham held up his forearm and pointed to it. "That's how long a cubit is, right?"

"Just so."

Ham shrugged. "Ain't gonna work, Pop. There's millions of species on the earth. Sure, most of 'em are bugs. But even so—you got any idea how much room two elephants are gonna take up? And rhinos? And hippos? And crocodiles? And that's another thing. How are we gonna feed them? Take a lot of hay to feed a couple of elephants. And what about all the carnivores? They can't eat hay. We'll have to stock the boat with other animals for them to eat."

The little brat whistled. "It's a real paradox, Pop. The Lord said 'two of each kind of animals.' No more, no less. But if we only take two, most of 'em will be gobbled up for sure. By the tigers and lions and panthers and wolves and owls and falcons and snakes and—"

"Silence!"

"—which we ain't got room for anyway."

Noah cuffed his son. "The Lord will provide, dolt!"

"Gee, Pop," whined Ham, "I'm just trying to help."

"Then do so! Gather up all the animals!"

Ham was a lippy kid, but he knew when his father

wasn't fooling around. So, he obediently set forth to carry out his instructions.

There followed the most heroic saga in all of human history, unfortunately never recorded. The deeds of Hercules and Gilgamesh pale in comparison. For Ham was forced to wander all over the world collecting two of each animal that walked on the earth or wriggled in the soil. Most of which, alas, do not live in the Holy Land.

Ham headed south and traveled through the length and breadth of Africa. That took a bit of time, especially because he had to invent the microscope in order to examine all the continent's protozoa to determine how many separate species there were that needed to be saved. The most time-consuming part was examining their nonexistent sex organs to find out which of the asexual critters were male and which were female. In the end, giving up, he just faked it by grabbing two of each kind at random and hoped God wouldn't ask any hard questions.

At the Cape of Good Hope, assisted only by chimps, he built a boat of reeds in order to travel to Australia and the Americas. The voyage across the Atlantic was rough. Not because of high seas, but because the reed boat was much bigger than an aircraft carrier—how else could he have carried two of each animal in Africa?—and the animals weren't any help at all when it came to reefing sails and all that nautical business.

But he made it, eventually. He ordered the animals to stay put (which they did, naturally) while he traveled the length and breadth of North and South America collecting all the animals which lived on the millions of square miles of surface of those two great continents.

He met with setbacks, of course. Some of the animals refused to accept his invitation. The mammoths and mastodons told him he was an idiot. The giant ground sloths said they were too lazy to go along. The saber-tooth tigers got downright nasty.

"It's your funeral," Ham told them.

Eventually, he made it back to South America with all the new animals he'd collected. Then, of course, he had to build a much bigger boat. Fortunately, there's a lot of timber in the Amazon basin, so he was able to build a raft the size of Manhattan Island. He sailed around South America on the raft. Things got tough, beating around the Horn, but he had a lot of help from all the jillions of monkeys he'd picked up in the rain forest.

Across the Pacific now, making a quick stop at the Galapagos Islands to pick up some tortoises and finches he had on his list. Australia and New Zealand turned out to be pretty easy, once he got the kangaroos to settle down. The real snag came in Tasmania, where the local top predator proved to be recalcitrant. But, eventually, covered with bites and scratches, Ham dragged a couple of the monsters on board. (That's where the Tasmanian Devil got its name, by the way.)

Asia, next, after a more-or-less quick detour through Polynesia, Melanesia, the Philippines and the Indonesian islands. Up Malaya, through South-East Asia, China and all of Siberia, back down through Central Asia and into the Indian subcontinent. The tropical animals complained loudly, crossing the Himalayas. It wasn't the cold so much as it was the insults hurled their way by the local yeti. (That's how the Abominable Snowmen got their name, by the way.)

India was a piece of cake. Across Persia and the rest of the Middle East, and then—home at last.

"You forgot Europe, dummy," snapped Noah.

Sighing, Ham set off again. But after everything else, Europe was a milk run. Except for the Irish elk, who said their antlers would get all scuffed up, crowded in the ark like that.

By the time Ham was finished, the ark was ready. Ham took one look at it and shook his head.

"It's like I said, Pop. We're never going to fit 'em all inside."

But the faithless youth proved wrong. The Lord did, of course, provide. God changed the dimensions of the ark into cubits measured by *His* forearm, and there was room to spare.

YOU'D BETTER DISCIPLINE THAT LITTLE SNOT, said God to Noah. **OR ONE OF THESE DAYS, YOU'LL GET DRUNK AND HE'LL LOOK AT YOUR NAKED BODY.**

So, Noah set sail. But, because his lazy son Ham had loafed on the job, Noah was running a little behind schedule. He was in such a big hurry that he forgot one of the species.

Fortunately, the archangel Michael called him back.

"Noah! Noah! You forgot the *Anopheles* mosquitoes!"

So Noah turned back and picked up the mosquitoes.

"If Mark Twain finds out about this there'll be hell to pay," muttered Michael, as he handed over the deadly little insects.

The rest of the story, of course, is well known. The dove, and all that. About the only thing worth noting that happened while they were at sea was that, once again, Ham got himself in trouble. As usual, questioning the Lord.

"Hey, Pop," he said, leaning over the rail, "I'm puzzled about something."

"What is that, impious youth?"

Ham pointed to a school of sharks, rending flesh.

"How come they don't get drowned?"

The sharks themselves provided the answer. A moment later, the great killers were lined up at the rail, glaring.

"We are blessed in the eyes of the Lord," snarled a great white.

"Pious, the lot of us!" proclaimed a hammerhead. "Not like those sinful land animals."

And, indeed, it was so. That very moment, as the sharks resumed their feeding frenzy, the smell of incense wafted over the sea. A chorus of angels burst into songs of praise.

And Ham got another mark next to his name, in God's Little Black Book.

Which is, actually, not so little.

(About the size of M33.)

When it was all done, God was feeling mighty pleased with Himself. He even reorganized one of the very distant constellations to read:

NEVER GIVE A SUCKER AN EVEN BREAK.

Astronomers haven't seen it, because the light from the constellation hasn't reached the Earth yet. It's scheduled to arrive in the year 2222 AD at 12:01 AM on April Fool's Day. God enjoys His little Jokes.

● ● ●

But as the reports started coming in, in the late innings, He stopped being so pleased.

WHO?

"Cuvier, Sir," replied the archangel. "Georges Leopold Chretien—"

I KNOW WHO HE IS! I MADE HIM, DIDN'T I? OF ALL THE ROTTEN INGRATITUDE.

After a moment: **WHEN HE DIES, FRY HIM.**

But it wasn't just Cuvier. Soon, there was a whole flood of sinners. (If you'll pardon the pun.)

Darwin.

FRY HIM.

Wallace.

FRY HIM.

Huxley.

FRY HIM.

God was especially ticked off at Mendel.

HE'S A MONK! WHAT'S A MONK DOING PLAYING AROUND WITH SMUTTY-MINDED LITTLE PEAS?

Inevitably: **FRY HIM.**

In fact, the whole nineteenth century was pretty much of a big disappointment for the Lord. Queen Victoria was a bright spot, of course. And God was delighted with Richard Wagner. He loved the music (although He only listened to the orchestral excerpts, like everybody else except George Bernard Shaw), but he was absolutely ecstatic over the great composer's writings.

He even made *The Jew in Music* mandatory reading for all the residents of Heaven. That would have been a little tough on the Jews, but there aren't any in Heaven.

They have their own retirement plan, much to God's disgruntlement. After reading Wagner, He'd been really looking forward to damning Mendelssohn.

Satan, of course, was cackling with glee. Not only was he going to win his bet with God, but he was reaping a whole harvest of sinners. Much better class than he normally got, too.

Yes, sad to say, the theory of evolution was all the rage. All that faked evidence God had strewn around had completely turned the heads of mortal man, born in sin.

Of course, not everyone was swept up in the Devil's scheme. From the very beginning, there were those who stood by God's Word, starting with Bishop Wilberforce. By the time the late twentieth century rolled around, they had organized themselves into a movement called "creationism" or "intelligent design." It was an uphill battle all the way, but the creationists were a devout and plucky bunch.

Whenever creationists died, of course, they went straight to Heaven. Sat at the side of the Lord, they did, on account of they were God's favorites.

Still and all, it looked like the Devil had a sure winner.

But Satan was always a dummy.

Baalzebub tried to warn him: *you can't beat house odds*.

Because what happened, naturally, was that God changed the rules. Since the theory of evolution was sweeping the boards, God just went back in history and made evolution for real. Simple as that.

NOAH.

"Yes Sir!"

WE'RE DOING ANOTHER TAKE.

"Uh, excuse me, sir?"

YOU DEAF? WE'RE DOING THE FLOOD OVER.

Noah wasn't happy about having to go through all that hard work again. But he kept his mouth shut and did as he was told. He was a holy man, after all, and holy men know that arguing with God is a bad career move.

The scenario was a little different, of course. Since God had made evolution real, the earth was now covered with all sorts of dinosaurs and other uncouth beasts. Ham really had his job cut out for him, this time, what with all the tyrannosaurs and such that he had to round up. He probably couldn't have done it at all except that God had also made plate tectonics, so the continents were scrunched up together. No need to built giant reed boats and rafts, this time.

Then, all of Ham's hard work turned out to be wasted. Because, following the Lord's instructions, Noah set sail just before the dinosaurs could make it aboard.

It was kind of pitiful, really. All those big burly dinosaurs, blubbering like babies.

"Don't leave us! Don't leave us!"

Noah kept a straight face. But all the little nocturnal mammals leaned over the rail and blew raspberries.

"Nyah, nyah! Nyah, nyah! You're extinct, you're extinct!"

They shouldn't have done it, though. The jibes made the dinosaurs really mad, and things got a little hairy when Noah had to turn back.

Once again, he'd forgotten the *Anopheles* mosquitoes.

● ● ●

So that's how it all worked out. Satan lost the bet, big time. Of course, the Lord of Flies complained bitterly. Accused God of being a cheat and a swindler. But God is pretty much impervious to that kind of accusation, for two reasons:

First, Satan's not a friend of His, so He really doesn't care what the Devil thinks.

Second, He's God. So He really doesn't care what *anybody* thinks. Disapprove of Him? **FRY**.

Still, it wasn't all peaches and cream. There were a couple of flies in the ointment, from God's point of view.

First, He had to transfer all the creationists down to Hell, since the blasphemers had denied His handiwork. Broke His heart, that did, on account of He was really quite fond of them. But sacrilege is sacrilege, and that's that. Mortal sin. **FRY**.

The Devil was tickled pink. He's always happy to get a big new crop of sinners, of course. But he was especially happy to see all the creationists arrive, because he was suffering from a shortage of low-level goons and stooges and the creationists really worked out quite nicely, once they stopped whining and got with the program.

The other problem proved to be a lot trickier.

Because, naturally, Mark Twain *did* find out about the *Anopheles* mosquitoes. They might have slid it by him if they'd only screwed up once; but *twice*? Not a chance. And, naturally, he made a big stink about it.

After God read *Letters from the Earth*, He positively blew His stack. (That's what caused all the Seyfert galaxies.)

TWAIN'S TOAST.

You'd think the Devil would have been glad to see Mark Twain arrive. And he was, at first. But Twain turned out to be a real pain in the ass.

First of all, he had an attitude problem.

Even worse, he escaped.

It's true. The only escape from the Pit of Damnation in the historical record. Twain built a raft made out of petrified wood and set off down a great river of lava, accompanied by a runaway slave named Ham.

As soon as he learned of Twain's escape, Satan sent one of his chief devils in hot pursuit. A few days later the devil sent back a message. Helmuth announced that the fugitive Twain was in sight and that he had the situation totally under control.

Lucifer was delighted at the news. But not all of his top advisers shared his enthusiasm.

"He's made that claim before," sneered Gharlane. "And you know how that worked out."

Sure enough, Helmuth blew it again and Twain made good his escape. But that's another story.

The Truth About the Gotterdammerung

Since Loki's alibi was airtight, suspicion fell on God.

"That Bum's always had in it for us," grumbled Frey. Thor roared and bellowed, splintering tables with his hammer.

"Justice! Justice!" Valhalla rang with his thunderous basso profundo. As always, the gigantic hall was packed with heroes, who immediately took up the cry.

"JUSTICE! JUSTICE!"

Then:

"Death to the Christian God!"

At these words, the hall fell silent. Men and gods craned to see who had spoken. A huge and extraordinarily inebriated warrior clambered onto a feasting table. Several times, actually, before he finally managed the feat.

Swaying back and forth, spilling great quantities of mead from a tankard, this worthy spoke again.

"Hear me, gods and heroes! I am Hunkred Thorvaldsen, called the Cropped-Head, and I am accounted the fiercest berserk in my district! It was I who slew Gunnar Hairybreeks with one thrust of my spear through his liver after he took his sword and wounded my third cousin Ingmar, called the Reckless, after Ingmar cut off Gunnar's brother Harald's arm at the fjord with his ax after Harald killed my brother's wife's uncle's grandson's dog after the dog pissed on his leg after Harald stole a bone from the dog at the midwinter festival after the dog had seized it fairly from the feasting table after Harald's nephew Bjorn, called the Ungenerous, refused the dog his fair portion."

Great applause resounded throughout Valhalla. Many toasts were drunk to the downfall of miserliness. After falling off the table three more times, Hunkred Thorvaldsen resumed his wobbly stance and continued his speech.

"Therefore do I, Hunkred Thorvaldsen, called the Cropped-Head, call upon the gods and heroes of Valhalla to avenge the murder of our beloved deity"—here the berserk, sobbing tears, pointed to the pallid corpse of the god Loki which was lying face down upon the floor of Valhalla, a knife sticking out of its back—"and seek satisfaction upon the mangy body of God, called the Almighty."

As one man, the heroes of Valhalla leapt to their feet, tankards held high.

"DEATH TO GOD!"

The excitement of the moment was irresistible. Heroes seized their weapons and charged out of the hall, led by the gods Heimdall and Thor. The former blew his great horn, the latter swung his hammer gaily. Taking his place at the head of the entire parade was Odin, riding his eight-legged horse Sleipner. His two great wolves, Freke and Gere, paced by his side.

As the gods and heroes poured out of the great feasting hall, the goddesses and Valkyries hastily donned their breastplates and rushed out to bid them farewell.

Wincing, most of them.

"Breastplates and fond farewells are a lousy match," grumbled Odin's wife Frigga, after the gods and heroes were gone.

"You're telling me?" groused Thor's wife Sif, trying—gingerly—to pry her breastplate loose. "Breastplates are a lousy match with anything civilized. At least your husband isn't a damned weight-lifter."

As he led the procession across the heavens, Odin's expression was grim and stern, as befitted the Allfather of gods and men. It grew grimmer and sterner at the words of the ravens perched on his shoulder. Hugin and Munin, they were called.

"This is a bad idea," observed Hugin.

"A *really* bad idea," added Munin.

"Shuddup," growled Odin. "What do you know, anyway? You're just a couple of stupid birds."

"They don't call God the Almighty for nothing," pointed out Hugin.

"Omniscient, omnipotent, omnipresent," added Munin.

"Not like you, Odin, who's just a—"

Odin's divine temper boiled over. His spear missed the ravens, although a few tail feathers went flying. The birds cawed derisively and flew back toward Valhalla.

"Don't say we didn't warn you!"

"And they call us bird-brains!"

But Odin had no more time for impudent avians. Even now was the mighty host drawing up before the Pearly Gates of Heaven, so rapid is travel through the outer planes of creation.

High atop the Pearly Gates stood the resplendent figures of two angels. The one on the left held a great trumpet. Gabriel, his name. No doubt in the hopes of abashing the lout, Heimdall blew a mighty blast with his horn. But even before the sound of Heimdall's horn faded, Gabriel was improvising upon the tune, developing themes and variations which were not only dazzling in their divinity and awesome in their cunning, but which also—especially the little riff which he added as a coda— exuded musical derision.

"O Heavens!" cried the other angel, Azrael. "We are besieged by a mighty host of flea-bitten barbarians!"

"O, what shall we do?" sobbed Gabriel.

The two angels convulsed with laughter. The assembled heroes of Valhalla bayed with fury. But at a gesture from Odin, they fell silent.

"Stand aside, lackeys!" cried the Allfather. "Open the Pearly Gates! We've business with your Boss!"

Azrael sneered. "God's busy."

"Deciding the fate of the universe," added Gabriel.

"Not that it's really necessary," mused Azrael, "seeing as how He figured it out right from the start when He made the whole thing. But He likes to check His work."

"A real precisionist." Gabriel.

"Not like some deities I could name." Azrael.

"And isn't that a good thing!" cried Gabriel. "Can you imagine the lopsided universe created by a god with only one eye?"

The insult was too much to bear. With a great curse, Odin hurled his spear at Gabriel. Alas, he missed. By quite a large margin, actually.

"Just like you said, Gabriel," giggled Azrael. "No stereoscopic vision."

Odin's curse was now joined by a multitude of others. A hailstorm of spears and axes was hurled at the Pearly Gates. With no noticeable effect, alas, although Thor's hammer did produce an impressive booming sound.

The ensuing comments by Azrael and Gabriel did little to improve the temper of the assembled gods and heroes of Valhalla. They were especially affronted by the angels' offer to find Thor a job ringing the bell in a cathedral, provided he agree to abstain from sin and grow a hunchback.

But their fury was suddenly stilled by the manifestation of an infinite Presence.

"Now you've done it," complained Azrael.

"God's here," added Gabriel. Quite unnecessarily, for the Presence of the Almighty is a unique and unmistakable phenomenon.

WHAT'S UP?

(Quotation marks cannot properly be used to indicate God's Voice. He is, after all, Unlimitable.)

The charges against Him were babbled forth in an unruly and not entirely sober manner.

YOU THINK _I_ STABBED THIS—WHAT'S HIS NAME?—LOKI CHARACTER IN THE BACK?

There was an overwhelming sense of infinite amusement.

WHAT A BUNCH OF CLOWNS.

The assembled gods and heroes of Valhalla suddenly found themselves attired in the ridiculous costumes of circus clowns. Odin's mount was now an eight-legged elephant wearing a fez. His wolves were poodles, yipping with rage at the absurd cut of their pelts. Thor's hammer was a rubber mallet, with which, seized by an overpowering compulsion, he began hitting himself on the head. Heimdall's great horn was a carnival noisemaker.

Other indignities followed, but there is no need to dwell upon them. Suffice it to say that the assault of the gods and heroes of Valhalla upon Heaven turned out very badly in the end, even as foretold by the ravens.

On their way back, slouched and miserable, Frey complained to Odin: "When you made yourself the father of the gods, why didn't *you* assume omnipotence?"

"Do I look like an egomaniac?" snarled Odin.

"He's not the only Almighty, you know," came a voice. Turning, Odin and Frey beheld a slender but well-muscled stripling striding alongside.

"Who're you?" demanded Frey.

The stripling swelled his chest. "I am Lothar Halversen, called the Skinny, and I am recognized as the fiercest berserk in my district. It was I who slew Knut Ohtheresen, called the Heavy-Sleeper, after—"

"Forget all that!" roared Odin. "What did you mean—when you said God wasn't the only Almighty?"

The youth grinned gaily. "Oh, there's at least one other.

Goes by the name of Allah. I heard about Him when I was raiding in Spain. The Moors are some fighters, you know? Of course, that didn't stop me from slaying twenty-eight of them at—"

"Shut up! I never heard of him. Allah, you say? And He's another omnipotent god?"

"According to the Moors, even more than God. And they say this Allah hates God with a passion."

Odin's grim face grew stern with thought.

"It's worth a try," he muttered.

And so it was that the host of heroes and gods of Valhalla came to Paradise, and sought an audience with Allah. This they were immediately granted, without obstruction by insolent servants, for Allah runs a strictly One-God show.

Alas, it went badly. No sooner had Allah heard Odin's proposal that He lead a charge on the Pearly Gates than the universe was filled with an overwhelming sense of fury. Allah's voice filled the infinite void.

GOD'S A HERETIC AND AN INFIDEL, BUT AT LEAST HE'S NOT A PAGAN.

And so saying, Allah visited a rain of toads and brimstone upon the heroes and gods of Valhalla, followed by locusts and seven lean years.

On their way back from Paradise, the gods and heroes of Valhalla regained some of their strength by eating the stripling Lothar Halversen, called—unfortunately—the Skinny. Such is the lot of those who give bad advice to ill-tempered gods and heroes.

"Still and all," mused Frey, picking his teeth with one

of Lothar's fingerbones, "the kid's general idea wasn't bad. Just picked the wrong Almighty, that's all. But there must be one omniscient, omnipotent and omnipresent Deity around who'd be willing to take a crack at the Pearly Gates."

And so it came to pass that the gods and heroes of Valhalla sought out the various Almighties for aid and assistance in their quest to seek justice for the foul murder of Loki. Finding these Almighties proved simple. True, the Void is infinite and eternal. But, on the other hand, it is in the nature of Almighties to be omnipresent.

Finding them, therefore, proved easy. Obtaining their help, on the other hand, proved otherwise.

The interview with Yahweh went sour right from the start. The gods and heroes of Valhalla offered Yahweh a feast of pork baked in goat's milk, with steamed shellfish on the side, and it was all downhill from there.

"What does that Guy manage to eat, anyway?" grumbled Thor, as they crawled their boil-infested way across the limitless desert into which Yahweh's wrath had cast them.

But it is well said of the northern gods that they are a stubborn lot, and so they persisted in their search. All to no avail.

The Hindu Trinity couldn't seem to agree on anything, and Shiva wouldn't go it alone even though he was all for the idea. The Buddha just babbled nonsense, and Confucius wouldn't stop droning on and on about filial piety.

The time came when the gods and heroes gave up the

hopeless quest and made their way back to Valhalla. Imagine their outrage when they finally came home— much the worse for wear—and saw that their great feasting hall had been turned into a Victorian mansion.

Odin stormed through the door, calling for his wife Frigga in a tone which boded ill for domestic tranquility. But he didn't get far before he was confronted by a huge wolf, fangs bared.

"You're ruining the carpet!" snarled the wolf, who was— as all the gods and heroes immediately recognized—none other than the great monster Garm.

"You're supposed to be guarding the Hel-Gate!" roared Thor.

A look of satisfaction came upon Garm's horrid visage. "Got a better gig," he said smugly. Then, eyeing Odin's wolves, who were yipping at him fiercely, Garm announced that he was in the mood for raw poodle. Freke and Gere immediately shrank back, wagging their pom-poms furiously.

"Out of my way!" bellowed Odin, who made to push past the great wolf. But Garm seized his leg in his maw and brought the Allfather down.

"I said," growled the wolf around Odin's leg, "you're ruining the carpet."

"What carpet?" demanded Odin, vainly trying to pry the great jaws loose. "There's no carpet in Valhalla!"

"There is now!" came a shrill voice. Looking up, Odin beheld his wife Frigga. Her appearance made him goggle. She was wearing an elaborate gown, with high heeled shoes and—and—her hair—

"What'd you do to your *hair*? What happened to the

braids? Why are you wearing shoes?" With a particular air of complaint: "*And where are your breastplates?*"

Frigga ignored the questions, gazing down at her husband with a look of immense disfavor.

"I suppose we'll have to go through this unpleasantness," she snapped. Then, making an imperious gesture:

"Oh, let him go, Garm!"

The wolf obeyed. But no sooner had Odin scrambled to his feet, swearing sulphurously and promising great mayhem upon the person of his spouse, than Frigga drew forth a tiny bell and tinkled it vigorously. A moment later, a giant stepped into the foyer. (And that was another thing the gods and heroes were outraged about—who ever heard of a foyer in Valhalla?)

"Thrym!" cried Frey.

"King of the Frost Giants!" exclaimed Heimdall.

"Why are you wearing that ridiculous outfit?" demanded Thor.

Thrym gazed down at his formal suit. "I'm the butler," he replied complacently. "And if you don't mind, I prefer to be called James."

Frigga clapped her hands briskly. "James, see these— *gentlemen*—into the parlor, if you will. But I insist that they remove those muddy boots before they ruin the entire carpet."

The scene which ensued was most undignified, for the gods and heroes of Valhalla objected strenuously to the removal of their boots. After Thor began hammering Thrym (James, rather) with his rubber mallet, the butler felt it necessary to call for assistance. Moments later the foyer was flooded with fire and frost giants who proceeded to forcibly remove the boots of the gods and heroes of Valhalla. Not too gently, either, for the giants were much aggrieved at the damage inflicted upon their nice new footmen's uniforms.

And so it was that the gods and heroes of Valhalla were ushered into the parlor which was located where the feasting hall used to be. "What's a 'parlor,' anyway?" groused Tyr.

"And will you look at that?" demanded Heimdall. "It's a—what *is* it, anyway?"

"It's called a piano, sir," sniffed James.

Even at that moment the fire giant sitting at the piano brought a dazzling mazurka to a close. The audience, which consisted of goddesses, dwarves and giants dressed in evening wear, burst into applause. An enormous serpent which encircled the entire room hissed its mighty approval.

"Watch it, Odin!" murmured Heimdall. "That's the Midgard Serpent."

But Odin's concern over the presence of the great reptile was immediately overridden by Thor's bellow.

"Surtur, get your filthy paws off my wife!"

The thunder god's fury was understandable, for the pianist—who was actually Surtur, the King of the Fire Giants, although the gods and heroes hadn't immediately recognized him because he was wearing a tuxedo and the flames which formed his hair were shaped into long flowing locks—was stroking the back of the goddess who was leaning over him. She, for her part, was cooing admiration of his musical artistry.

"And why aren't you wearing your breastplates?" roared Thor at his wife.

Sif looked up and glared at him.

"I'm not your wife, you loudmouth! I got a divorce three weeks ago!"

Thor's eyes bugged out. He gabbled incoherently. Sif giggled.

"Look at him!" she exclaimed, She gazed around the room. "Can any *civilized person* blame me?" The murmurs of the assembled giants, dwarves and goddesses indicated their profound agreement with her sentiments. Sif ran her fingers through Surtur's flaming hair, which is the kind of thing goddesses can get away with, but is not recommended for mortals.

"Surtur is so much more genteel," she said. Then, laughing gaily: "And much more passionate! You won't ever find *him* complaining that I'm not wearing those stinking breastplates."

"It's my artist's soul," murmured Surtur.

Thor lost his temper completely at that point and set upon the King of the Fire Giants. But the affair went badly, for Surtur insisted upon a proper duel and before you knew it the two opponents were facing each other across the room, Thor hurling his rubber mallet and Surtur firing one unerring shot after another right between Thor's eyes with his dueling pistol.

No harm came to the thunder god, of course. It's one of the advantages of being immortal. But it certainly made him look foolish.

Then all the gods and heroes felt even more foolish when it occurred to one of them (Rolf Gunuldsen, called the Bigfoot, who was accounted the fiercest berserk of his district because he slew—well, never mind) that since the bullets weren't actually hurting Thor, even though he looked like a jackass, that it was a mystery how a knife in the back had done in Loki who was, after all, also immortal.

No sooner did Rolf utter these words than the gods and heroes of Valhalla heard a snicker behind them. Turning, they beheld Loki himself, entering the parlor with a beautiful giantess on his arm.

"I was wondering when you saps would finally figure it out," sneered the god of discord and strife. He advanced to the center of the room, scratching his back.

"Still itches," he grumbled.

"Try wearing breastplates!" laughed Frigga. "You want to talk about *itching*?"

Loki smiled sympathetically, then said with a laugh:

"And will you look at these idiots? They find me with a knife in my back, which isn't the kind of thing which would do any real harm at all to an immortal deity, and the cretins not only jump to the conclusion that I've been murdered but that the culprit was none other than God Almighty Himself."

Loki bestowed a great sneer upon the assembled gods and heroes of Valhalla. "Let me explain something to you, dimwits. When God Almighty decides to do somebody in, He does not—repeat, *not*—stab them in the back with a knife."

I CERTAINLY DON'T, came a voice which filled the universe.

The gods and heroes of Valhalla jumped with surprise.

"Where'd He come from?" demanded Frey.

I'M OMNIPRESENT. ALSO OMNIPOTENT, WHICH IS WHY I DON'T STAB PEOPLE IN THE BACK WITH A KNIFE. MUCH PREFER HEAVENLY CATASTROPHES—COMETS, ASTEROIDS, THE OCCASIONAL SUPERNOVA. BIT INDISCRIMINATE, I ADMIT, BUT I HAVE A REPUTATION TO MAINTAIN.

"Then who stabbed Loki in the back?"

"I did," said Thrym (James, rather). "It was Loki's idea, of course, but we all thought it would be appropriate for me to do the actual deed. After all," he concluded proudly, "I'm the butler."

"But why?" cried Odin.

"To get you out of here!" snapped Loki. "So we'd have some time to set everything right."

"Not to mention some peace and quiet!" exclaimed Frigga. "It's been so heavenly since you left—no more sleepless nights caused by your carousing and brawling."

A furious chorus from the assembled giants, dwarves and goddesses indicated their complete agreement with these sentiments. The goddesses and Valkyries seemed especially aggrieved on the subject of breastplates.

Needless to say, the assembled gods and heroes of Valhalla were not slow to indicate (even more loudly) their own sentiments, which were quite the opposite. Indeed, the whole thing turned into quite a scandal, but when all was said and done the gods and heroes found themselves pitched out of Valhalla with firm instructions not to come back.

The goddesses were adamant on this last point, each of them whipping out a bill of divorce on the spot. They weren't printed on mere paper, either. Each bill of divorce was engraved on a brass placard made from melted-down breastplates.

"You can't divorce me, Frigga!" cried Odin. "No power in the Universe can divorce the Allfather of the Gods from his wife!"

OH, YES I CAN, came the voice of the Almighty.

"That's not what the Pope says," complained one of the heroes. "I know, because when I was raiding in France I tried to force this priest to marry over this hot wench to me but he said he couldn't because she was already married and the Church had forbidden divorce."

A slight tinge of pink embarrassment colored the entire universe, for just a split second.

WELL, THE POPE TENDS TO BE A LITTLE RIGID. AND IT'S A FACT THAT I DON'T GENERALLY APPROVE OF DIVORCE. BUT I MAKE EXCEPTIONS IN EXTREME CIRCUMSTANCES, OF WHICH YOU CERTAINLY FIT THE BILL. I WOULDN'T FORCE A PIG TO STAY MARRIED TO OAFS LIKE YOU. MAKING YOUR WOMEN WEAR BREASTPLATES WAS THE FINAL STRAW! HOW WOULD *YOU* LIKE TO HAUL AROUND TEN POUNDS OF BRASS ON YOUR TITS? A FLAGRANT CASE OF DOMESTIC VIOLENCE, WHAT IT IS. THESE ARE MODERN TIMES, YOU KNOW.

And that was that. The gods and heroes of Valhalla eventually got it into their thick skulls that things had changed, and they slouched off into the wilderness.

But they made a comeback, of sorts. Once they calmed down enough to think about it, they realized that the worst thing was the damage to their reputations. It wasn't as if any of them were actually going to miss their wives, after all. Making love and breastplates were a lousy match.

"The old story of Ragnarok was so much more dignified," wailed one of the heroes. "Now we're gonna look like chumps!"

It was Bragi, the god of poetry and song, who came up with the idea that saved the day.

"There's no point in fighting progress," he explained.

So Bragi went down to Middle-earth and brought back an opera composer named Richard Wagner. After Wagner heard what the gods had to say, he assured them that he could take care of the whole problem.

"For money, of course."

After the gods agreed to his terms, the detailed negotiations began. Wagner was particularly adamant about protecting his artistic reputation.

"It's great for people to think I have divine inspiration, but it can't look crass. So we'll have to figure out a way to launder the money."

And that's why Odin the Allfather caused King Ludwig of Bavaria to go mad and shower Wagner with patronage and largesse.

Wagner also insisted that the opera had to be in German, which would involve some changes in names.

"Wotan," mused Odin. "Wotan," he said again. "It kind of rolls off the tongue, doesn't it? Okay, I can live with that."

For their part, the gods were deeply concerned that the opera put forth the proper moral lessons.

"The giants and the dwarves have got to be the bad guys," insisted Tyr.

"Piece of cake," said Wagner.

"The women have to come to a bad end," demanded Thor.

"How's being burned alive grab you?" snickered Wagner.

"I get to sing a lot," specified Odin sternly. "After all, I'm the Father of the Gods."

"No sweat," assured Wagner. "I'll call it 'Wotan's Narration.' It'll go on and on and on and on and on and on and on and on and on. Then we'll repeat it. Over and over and over and over and over again."

Finally, after the gods were satisfied that Wagner was their kind of composer, Odin turned to the assembled heroes.

"How about you mortals?" he asked. "Got any requests?"

The heroes of Valhalla talked it over and, after they came to agreement, they appointed one of their number to act as their artistic spokesman. This fellow was muscled like Hercules and had no discernable forehead.

"I am Siegfried Siegmundsen, called the Brainless," he said, "and I am accounted the fiercest berserk in my district. It was I who slew Fafnir the Hutmaker after that lousy snake in the grass demanded payment for—"

"Shut up!" roared Odin. "Get to—"

"No, no, let him talk!" cried Wagner. "I'm getting an idea."

So Siegfried Siegmundsen was allowed to finish his very, very, very long but monosyllabic recitation of his accomplishments. Wagner took copious notes. At the end, Siegfried explained the central concern of the heroes regarding the opera.

"We just want to be sure the hero won't be some kind of pansy," he growled. "No eggheads, fretting over all kind of silly stuff. A stout, simple hero type. That's what we want."

"Absolutely!" exclaimed Wagner. "In fact, I'm going to model the hero after you personally. Uh, how well did your mother know her brother?"

The hero's face turned beet red.

"I knew it!" shrieked Wagner, clapping his hands with glee. "Oh, it's going to be the greatest opera ever written! Very profound. Very uplifting. Worthy of my genius!"

And that's how the gods and heroes of Valhalla managed to salvage their reputation. They all agreed that Wagner did a magnificent job. In fact, attending the season at Bayreuth has become their favorite pastime. You can always spot them in the audience, if you're in the know. Look for a crowd of beefy middle-aged men obviously uncomfortable in their suits, tugging at their ties. Their breath will smell like a brewery, and they'll be complaining loudly about the avant-garde set design.

That's them. The Aesir.

The Thief & the Roller Derby Queen

An essay on the importance of formal education

The problem, in a nutshell, was that he had a lousy formal education. It didn't help, of course, that he suffered from delusions of grandeur. But if he'd stayed in school, he would have taken enough tests to realize that he was a dunce.

Being a dunce is okay, but you have to know your limitations. If you choose thieving as a profession, shoot for hubcaps instead of the Crown Jewels. For sure, don't try to steal from Satan. But that's exactly what he did.

Why did he do it? Well, partly because he was an egomaniacal dunce. But, mostly, he did it because of his girlfriend.

So it's time to introduce her: Loretta Minisci. Twenty-two years old; five feet, ten inches tall; raven-black hair; brown eyes; beautiful; shapely; and possessed of an all-consuming passion to become the greatest witch who ever lived. *Her* problem, in a nutshell, is that while she was incredibly bright she didn't have any higher education either. And despite what you may have heard, it really takes a lot of book learning to be a great witch—much less the greatest witch who ever lived.

So, she was frustrated. Her spells never seemed to work quite the way they should (when they worked at all). And she couldn't use a lot of spells, because the really good spells are written in arcane languages, bizarre runes, and the like. You really need a Ph.D. to work through that kind of stuff, and she was a high-school dropout.

The worst of it, from Loretta's point of view, was that she wasn't able to summon demons. She tried, once, but the affair went badly. She followed all the instructions in the grimoire, including the part about being naked while you do the incantation. That last was a piece of cake, for her, because she made her living as an exotic dancer in between roller derby matches. But because her education wasn't up to snuff, she didn't quite understand what a pentacle is. Stumbling through the words in the grimoire, Loretta made the word out to be *tentacle.*

So there she was, when the demon materialized, surrounded by a pile of fried calimari.

"That stuff's like rubber," complained the demon. Then, ogling Loretta: "But what a babe!"

Things didn't go as badly as they might, because Loretta was used to fending off the advances of lustful males. And even though she wasn't wearing her roller derby pads, she still had a mean knee and a really vicious elbow smash. But it was sticky for a while, and she was always afraid to summon demons thereafter.

But what kind of great witch can't summon demons?

She brooded about the problem for several weeks. Then she decided that what she needed was a piece of brimstone. It's not clear where she got that idea. It's not in the literature, that's for sure. But Loretta had a tendency to invent her own recipes, which was one of the reasons her boyfriend insisted on eating out. (The other reason is that he felt a great thief should eat in fine restaurants, even if he couldn't read the menu.)

Now, mind you, fooling with recipes is no big deal when it comes to cooking. But it's really not a good idea when you're dealing with the underworld.

Loretta was just as stubborn as she was smart and good-looking. Once she got something in her head, that was that. Right off she started pestering her boyfriend to go to Hell with her and steal a piece of brimstone. She didn't actually know what brimstone was, but she remembered from her Sunday school days (which were a long way back) that there was lots of it in Hell.

The thief refused, at first, so Loretta withheld her affections (as they say). Eventually, he gave in. Loretta thought it was because he was terminally horny, but the truth is that the more he thought about the job, the more it appealed to his vanity. He liked to call himself the Cat, but his friends called him the Pussy (which, among his crowd, didn't have the same connotation at all).

"I'll show 'em," he muttered to himself. And he went to Loretta and agreed to do the job. "*Provided* you can get us into Hell."

"That's easy!" she exclaimed.

And it was. Any half-educated witch can get into Hell. The trick, of course, is getting back out.

Even then, she botched it. Loretta still hadn't figured out what a pentacle was, so when they arrived in Hell they were surrounded by fried calimari. Naturally, the smell drew every imp within range, because imps love seafood and there's a real shortage of it in the Pit of Damnation.

That's probably what saved them, for the moment, because the imps were so busy gobbling down the calimari that they didn't think to grab the trespassers until Loretta and the thief were on the lam.

Still, things looked bad.

Loretta and the thief were trying to make their escape across a field of ice. The thief was grousing and complaining the whole time because he'd dressed for what he thought Hell would be like, and sneakers and a bathing suit just didn't cut it. Loretta didn't hear him, however, because after the first five seconds she had skidded completely out of sight. *She'd* come to Hell in her roller derby outfit. (Damn what the book said; she wasn't about to deal with demons stark naked again.) And while the knee and elbow pads kept her from getting too badly scraped up, her roller skates were completely useless. Although, as it happens, they're probably all that saved her.

But we'll get to that in a moment. First, let's reexamine the moral of the tale.

The problem? *Lack of formal education*. Both Loretta and her boyfriend had gotten their ideas about Hell from watching TV evangelists late at night when there wasn't anything else on the tube. And the truth of it is that televangelists have the silliest ideas about Hell, as well as everything else. That doesn't hurt *them*, of course, since they always go to Heaven because God likes them even if they are a lot of con artists. (He's willing to forgive a pious scam. And it's not even a scam, anyway, because God favors faith a long way over brains so even the jerks who send in their money get to Heaven.)

But it was tough on Loretta and the thief. If they'd read Dante's *Inferno*, of course, they'd have known that Hell was a frigid wasteland.

Again: *lack of formal education*. Because if you trace it all back, you find that the preachers from whom they'd gotten their ideas were a poorly educated bunch themselves. Their ideas of Hell they'd gotten from the only book they'd ever read, which is the Bible. And while the Holy Book was accurate enough at the time it was written, you've got to stay abreast of the literature in your field. Satan does. Once the Devil read Dante's description of Hell in the *Inferno* he redecorated the whole place. Calls it Renaissance Chic.

Loretta got out okay due to blind luck. As it happens, the ice fields of Hell are almost frictionless. That's because the coefficient of   Never mind. No point going into the physics here. (The kind of people who'd buy a book like this—I haven't even seen the cover yet, but I'll guarantee it's covered with half-nekkid women wearing S&M gear—wouldn't follow it anyway.) (Oh, sure. Tell me it'll be on the coffee table when the guests arrive. Along with your leather-bound copy of Kant's *Critique of Pure Reason*.)

Like I said, frictionless. Two great roller-derby-queen-type strides into it and she was off her skates—*wham!*—right on her ass, sailing across Hell. Loretta steered herself as best she could, using her knee and elbow pads, but within five minutes she reached the Wall. (Yes, Hell has a boundary. It's flexible, of course.

Depends, any given day or night, on the precise equation between damned souls and saved souls but, again, we'll skip the math. See reasoning above.)

She hit the Wall feetfirst. Anybody else would have broken their ankles. But Loretta was a roller derby queen, and she knew just how to handle collisions. Next thing you know, she was skating up the Wall making her getaway. (Gravity works differently in Hell. Just trust me.) The Wall is infinite, of course, but she was saved by divine intervention. Once she got high enough to be noticed, an angel came and took her back home. Sports fan, he claimed, even though Loretta thought he was a regular in the club where she did her dancing, hiding his face at one of the back tables along with all the televangelists. Maybe not.

For the thief, on the other hand, things didn't go as well. At first, he was full of confidence. He always liked to brag to his friends that he'd never been caught. His friends always said that was because he never managed to actually steal much of anything. And it was true that he was better at the getaway part of the job than he was at the actual getting. (Which, when you think about it, kind of defeats the whole purpose of being a thief in the first place, but he was never smart enough to figure that out.)

The thief took one look at Loretta flying off and decided to try a different route. So he plunged into a snowdrift. Bright guy, like I said.

Soon enough, the thief was floundering around in the snow, freezing his ass off. He didn't get far, of course. After they finished gorging themselves on the calimari, the imps set off in hot pursuit. They had no trouble tracking him. They didn't even bother following his footsteps, they just followed the smell of suntan lotion. Imps know exactly what sun block smells like, because all surfers go to Hell.

(Yes, *all* of them. It's not that God has anything in particular against the sport. It's just that He hates the music of the Beach Boys, and He tends to overreact.)

(Hey, it's true, He does. Read the Bible. A little hanky-panky in Sodom and Gomorrah? BRONZE AGE HIROSHIMA. Eat the wrong fruit? LIVE BY THE SWEAT OF YOUR BROW, CHILDREN BORN IN SORROW, PMS—the whole nine yards. Violate the building code? ALL LANGUAGES CAST INTO CONFUSION; MILLENNIA OF TRIBAL WARFARE. Eat shellfish? LOCUSTS. Jaywalk? SEVEN LEAN YEARS. Don't recycle? PLAGUE. Do this, ETERNAL DAMNATION; do that, ETERNAL DAMNATION. Strict is one thing. That Guy's into leather.)

Back to the story.

After they caught him, the imps straightaway hauled him up before the Prince of Darkness. The whole thing moved way faster than the thief expected, being, as he was, accustomed to the pace of the criminal justice system. Naturally, the dummy tried to cop a plea. (This is what's called "unclear on the concept.") The devils immediately convulsed with laughter.

"Wrong court, chump!" they howled.

The Prince of Darkness wasn't at all what the thief expected. No horns, no cloven hooves, no barbed tail. Just an ordinary-looking fellow, middle-aged, dressed in a navy blue Brooks Brothers suit. With a red power tie, naturally.

He was sitting in an executive swivel chair on a raised mound in the very center of Hell, eating lunch off a TV tray. Around him, as far as the eye could see, stretched a horde of sinners squatting naked on the ice.

No, Satan didn't look like much, but the thief wasn't fooled for a minute. He wasn't bright, but he'd kicked around a lot. The Devil's lunch was the first tip-off. What you call a *real* power lunch: Satan was tearing the leg from a roasted baby and devouring it like a wolf.

"Unbaptised toddler." He burped. "My favorite."

That was bad enough. Then the thief spotted the tasseled Gucci loafers and the Rolex and knew he was really in deep trouble.

"I want a lawyer!" he cried. "Is there a lawyer anywhere around?"

Satan's minions started howling again. Two thirds of the horde of sinners scrambled to their feet. In less than a minute, a gigantic brawl erupted on the field of ice, millions of naked attorneys battling each other over the fee.

Eventually a wizened old character fought his way through the mob.

"Corporate lawyers," he sneered. "Punks."

"I'll take your case," he announced, extending his hand. "I'm Clarence Darrow."

Ignorant as he was, the thief had heard of Clarence Darrow. (Defense lawyers were of interest to him, given his profession.)

"But—you're famous! What are you doing here? You're supposed to be a good guy."

Darrow shrugged. "God's got a different opinion. At first I thought it was because of the Scopes trial. But then

I found out it was really the Leopold and Loeb case that ticked Him off. The Lord views the insanity plea as a Personal affront, seeing as how He made man in His own image."

Clarence Darrow really was a great defense lawyer. Right off he entered a plea of not guilty on grounds of mental incapacity, arguing that only a moron would think of going to Hell to steal brimstone. Satan immediately agreed with him, but pointed out that Hell was the assigned eternity for imbeciles.

"It's not fair," admitted the Lord of Flies, "but I don't set the rules. God does. And you know how He feels about retards."

So then Darrow changed the plea to not guilty on the grounds that there was no crime involved anyway, seeing as how there wasn't any brimstone in Hell to steal in the first place. "It's like charging a man in a desert with trying to steal water," he argued.

This led to a long wrangle. The Devil responded that intent is as important as action in assessing a crime. That developed into a discussion of the metaphysical priority of mind vs. matter, which Darrow would have lost in a minute if he were in Heaven where (it goes without saying) Mind comes a long way before Matter. But he was a canny old lawyer, and he knew that Satan placed great store in things of the flesh.

Eventually, the Devil admitted the plea. The thief started to breathe easy, but not for long, because Satan right away charged him with trespassing.

"That's just a misdemeanor!" squealed the thief, before Darrow could shut him up.

"You dummy," growled the lawyer.

Sure enough, the Prince of Darkness and all his satanic subordinates were glaring at the thief like—well, like devils. "*A misdemeanor!*" bellowed Satan. He shredded what was left of the two-month-old sinner and hurled the hideous gobbets at the thief.

"Let me give you a taste of the punishment reserved for trespassers," he snarled.

The next instant the thief found himself transported into a realm of Hell that is so horrible and gruesome that even Dante couldn't bring himself to describe it. At the time, the thief thought it was for an eternity, but when he was hauled back Satan glanced at his Rolex and said: "How'd you like *that* thirty seconds?"

The thief was shaking all over. Tight-lipped, Darrow leaned over and whispered in his ear: "They're real big on the territorial imperative down here, stupe. From now on, keep your mouth shut and let me do the talking."

That said, Darrow went right back on the offensive, entering a plea of not guilty on the grounds that there were no signs posted informing the unwary traveler that Hell was private property.

The Devil spluttered. "What are you talking about, you lousy shyster? I don't need signs—everybody knows I own this place!"

Bingo. Jackpot. *Clarence Darrow for the defense!*

Because, naturally, as soon as God heard the Devil say that (He hears everything, of course) He blew His stack and intervened. Which was exactly what Darrow had counted on—winning on appeal to a Higher Court.

A great Presence manifested Itself.

NO YOU DON'T, BUM. I OWN THIS PLACE. I MADE IT, DIDN'T I? YOU JUST COLLECT THE RENT. (You can't put quotation marks around God's dialogue. He's unlimitable. First offense gets a rain of toads.)

Satan tried to squawk about jurisdiction, but that's really a flimsy argument when you're dealing with the Lord Almighty, Creator of the Universe. The Devil's usually a lot smarter than that, but he was caught off guard. In the end he irritated God so much that the Lord Above changed the terms of the lease.

FROM NOW ON, BUM, YOU DON'T GET THE UNBAPTISED BABES. (And that's how Limbo got created, in case you ever wondered.)

Satan gibbered with rage, which is an absolutely terrifying thing to see unless you happen to be God. After the display had gone on for a while, God got impatient.

ARE YOU FINISHED? IF NOT, I'LL CREATE A BIB TO CATCH THE DROOL.

Satan clamped his jaws shut.

THAT'S BETTER. NOW. WHAT'S THIS ALL ABOUT, ANYWAY?

God already knew what it was all about, of course. He's omniscient. But He gets some kind of weird kick out of acting dumb. (Always been like that. Remember the time, early on, when He was wandering through the Garden of Eden? Silly. A full-grown Supreme Being, acting like a Kid playing tag: "Yoo-hoo! Adam, where are you?")

Before the Devil could open his mouth, Darrow started talking. It was a great closing argument, too.

Then God announced His decision. He found in favor

of the defendant on the grounds that while he was guiltier than sin the whole thing tickled the Lord's fancy. But the thief didn't get off scot-free, because God sentenced him to ten years in Purgatory before he would be released back to earth.

"What for?" whined the thief.

BECAUSE YOU'RE AN IDIOT.

Then God smote the Devil with a bolt of lightning. Contempt of court.

Finally, He glowered at Darrow. (Actually, God's immaterial. It was more that the whole Universe took on a sense of all-pervading **GLOWER**, aimed at Darrow.)

YOU RAT. YOU LOUSE.

The old man was a plucky character, you've got to hand it to him. "What did I do—besides win another defense case?"

THAT'S THE WHOLE POINT, DARROW. AS YOU WELL KNOW. MAN IS GUILTY OF ORIGINAL SIN, SO HOW CAN HE BE INNOCENT? YOUR WHOLE LIFE WAS AN AFFRONT TO ME, AND YOU'RE *STILL* DOING IT!

Darrow sneered. "So damn me to Hell, then."

God was silent. After all, what could He say? It's the ultimate problem in penal science, when you think about it. How do you punish a lifer who's already dead?

In the end, of course, Darrow caught it from the Devil after God left. Satan was purely furious about the whole affair.

"You're promoted," snarled the Prince of Darkness, and he gave Darrow the premier spot in Hell, on the ninth level. Satan even added a fourth mouth to his clone (which, contrary to Dante, isn't actually the Devil himself) so that Clarence Darrow could join Cassius, Brutus and Judas Iscariot as a chewee.

But Darrow wasn't fazed. Right away he introduced himself to his neighbors.

"Boy, am I glad to see you," said Judas.

"It was temporary insanity!" cried Cassius. "Caused by eating junk food. Shakespeare's my witness. He said himself I had 'a lean and hungry look.'"

"I had a warped childhood," whined Brutus. "Too much privilege."

As for the thief, he had ten years to think over the course of his life. Ten *long* years, because Purgatory is a doctor's waiting room. And he never got any time off for good behavior because he screwed up. (Tried to steal a six-year-old copy of *Sports Illustrated*. Wasn't even the swimsuit issue.)

But eventually, he served the time, and was materialized back in Loretta's cellar.

And found that the cellar was now the TV room of a very large and muscular truck driver who immediately beat him to a pulp. Partly for trespassing, but mostly because he materialized in front of the TV set in the last ten seconds of the Super Bowl with the go-ahead field goal on its way. The truck driver had four friends with him, too. Raiders fans.

A few days later, when the thief got out of the hospital, he went looking for Loretta. It took him weeks, but eventually he tracked her down to a very fancy house in a very nice part of town.

His tongue was practically hanging out as he rang the doorbell. Ten years' abstinence, you understand.

Loretta was there, all right. She even opened the door wearing her roller derby queen gear, all the way down to the knee and elbow pads. That had him salivating immediately. He'd always loved that outfit! I've got to tell the truth, now that we're getting to the end of the story. That thief was a warped, depraved, degenerate, kinky sicko. The only books he ever bought had covers just like this one.

Alas. She wasn't Loretta Minisci, stripper, would-be witch, anymore. She was still a roller derby queen—*the* roller derby queen, in fact—but she was also Mrs. Loretta White, Ph.D. (Harvard—*summa cum laude*, *Phi Beta Kappa*, the whole shot). It turns out that a week after she got back from Hell she met a chemist at the supermarket and while they were chatting in the cashier's line he explained to her that brimstone was just another word for sulfur, which, (hey, what do you know?) he happened to have a lot of in his laboratory and before they even got there she'd fallen in love with the mousy little guy and one thing led to another and ten years later she'd not only earned her Ph.D. in chemistry but had been able to apply her talent for witchcraft to revolutionize the entire science, and, no, she'd love to talk (*How have you been, anyway? Still stealing?*) but she had to catch a plane for the Olympics where she was going to win the gold medal—she'd gotten the sport internationally recognized just last year, *isn't that great?*—before she had to catch another plane to Stockholm to accept the Nobel Prize. *Bye*.

The thief went berserk at that point and tried to force

his affections upon her (as they say). But that's really not the best seduction technique to use on a roller derby queen. A few knees and elbows later, Loretta was off to catch her plane and the thief went back into the hospital for a few more days.

Things went downhill from there.

He started thieving again, but the truth is that it's a young man's game and he was over the hill. Ten years out of practice, too. So he got caught. Hubcaps, believe it or not. He tried to steal them off a slow-moving car in the inaugural parade—yeah; Limo One. Sent up for three years. (Would have been way more—assassination attempts get twenty, easy—except the psychiatrist informed the court that the thief didn't know the names of any presidents since Abraham Lincoln led the war of independence against George Washington III.)

After he got out, he lasted on the streets for six weeks before he was sent back to prison. Stealing hubcaps, again. In the pits, at the Daytona 500. Five years. No time off for good behavior because they caught him trying to steal—never mind. You wouldn't believe it.

The next time he got caught he was a three-time loser and so they sent him up for life in the toughest prison in the state. He survived six, count 'em, six hours. After finding himself with two cellmates wearing "Aryan Nation" tattoos and reading weird books about women in armor, he got into a religious discussion in which he explained that he had met Satan personally and could assure them that the Devil was a white man.

● ● ●

So there he was, back again, a thief in Hell.

"I want Darrow!" he cried.

But the Devil just laughed at him. "Not this time, chump. You've already been convicted. No trial. No rights. No appeals. And I've been waiting for this day to come."

Satan rubbed his hands together with glee. It sounded like a rattlesnake. "Boy," snickered the Lord of Flies, "have I got plans for you."

And he did, too. Grotesque plans. Horrible plans. Indescribable plans. The worst thing you could imagine.

He made the thief listen to one performance of Wagner's *Parsifal* (which, of course, lasts for eternity).

It all goes to show the importance in the modern world of getting a formal education.

Although, now that I think about it, maybe it wouldn't have made much difference in the thief's case. Ignorance can be fixed. Stupid is forever.

THE
RATS, BATS & VATS
SERIES

Author's note:

Both of these stories, albeit in very different ways, are part of the Rats, Bats and Vats series which I coauthored some years ago with Dave Freer. The heart of the series is a trilogy which begins with the novella "Genie Out of a Vat" (initially published in Cosmic Tales: Adventures in Far Futures, *edited by T.K.F. Weisskopf) and continues with the novels* Rats, Bats & Vats *and* The Rats, the Bats & the Ugly.

The second of the stories included here, "Crawlspace," takes place about a century after the events related in the trilogy. The first story, "A Soldier's Complaint," isn't technically part of the series at all. What it is, instead, is the inspiration.

I wrote this story a long time ago, mostly for my own amusement. I did send it in to a magazine, Analog Science Fiction and Fact, *but (not to my surprise) they rejected it. Being honest, if I'd been the editor I probably would have rejected it myself. It's very short—about 1,500 words— very lightweight, as they say, and depends too much on the final punch line.*

After getting the rejection from Analog, *I set the story aside and pretty much forgot about it until, years later, I encountered Dave Freer in the discussion area of Baen Books' web site, "Baen's Bar." Dave and I were both newly published authors with Baen, got along well, and Jim Baen suggested we coauthor a novel together. In the course of discussing the possibility, I sent Dave my story*

"A Soldier's Complaint" because I thought the basic idea might make a good premise for a light-hearted science fiction adventure novel. He read the story, thought the same thing, and we developed the RBV series out of it.

A Soldier's Complaint

I don't care what the genetic engineers say, I think it's a bad idea.

I didn't mind the rats, once I got used to them. (Yes, yes, I know—they're not rats, they're engineered from primitive insectivore stock. Only genetic engineers would know the difference. They look like rats, don't they? So as far as we grunts are concerned, they're rats.)

The truth is, most human soldiers get along fine with the rats. First of all, rats have a dark and pessimistic view of life, which any foot soldier can appreciate. From the first day, they fit right into the gripe sessions, predicting doom and disaster like seasoned veterans.

Maybe a little too much on the grim side, your rats. Even by grunt standards. Personally, I think it comes from ancient racial memories of being the favorite prey of practically every small carnivore in creation. But when I raised the idea with Corporal Laughs-At-Digitigrades (and don't ask me why rats insist on these silly names— we just call him Lad for short) he immediately sneered. Well, actually, he wriggled his whiskers in that particular

537

mode which conveys "sneer" better than any human sneer ever could.

"What a lot of crap," he chittered. He took a hefty swig from his stein. (And that's another thing I like about rats—they've got a proper appreciation for brew. Not like this new bunch! But I'll come to that in a moment.)

He made a big production of wiping the beer off his whiskers. Then he leaned back in his chair and emitted that disgusting bray which rats have instead of a laugh. It's their worst characteristic, in my book. The sound is bad enough, but the sight of those huge yellow incisors!

"Humans are so stupid."

"We invented you, didn't we?" I grumbled.

"Your only intelligent move, in a racial lifetime of blunders. It's like they say—put a monkey in front of a typewriter long enough, and eventually he'll write all of Shakespeare's plays."

I didn't get offended. Before they integrated our battalion, they gave us lectures on how to get along with rats. Stripped of the psychobabble, the gist of it was: don't get offended. Even if they are a lot of offensive rodents.

"The fact is, Sergeant Johnson," he continued, "rats never gave a thought to predators. We had the world on the run! Any biologist will tell you that. The most successful order of mammals ever known—the rodents. And the rats were the most successful of the rodents."

Another sneering twitch of the whiskers.

"Humans are so stupid! Always worrying about lions and sharks and crocodiles. Ha! Between the diseases we spread around and the famine we caused by gobbling up your food, we rats bumped off a thousand times more of you monkeys-with-delusions-of-grandeur than all the predators in the world put together. Kings of creation, the rats. Think we lost any sleep worrying over cats and owls? Ha! Sure, they'd catch one of us now and again. So what? The way we breed?"

He finished off his beer. "I mean, look at them!" He gestured with his snout toward the corner where a handful of mutated felines were sitting at a table. One of the cats caught Corporal Lad's eye, and he chittered at him. The cat looked away, hunching his shoulders.

"Make love, not war—that's the ratly road to triumph." He emitted a great belch and chittered for more beer. The falconoid running the bar stumped over with another pitcher. The big bird avoided the Corporal's eyes. I hate to admit it, but the truth is that once the rats arrived they terrorized the cats and the birds to the point where all the predators are good for is being mess orderlies.

"The rats don't fight fair." That's the complaint you always hear from predators. "They gang up on you."

And what can you say? It's true. That's why rats make such good soldiers and predators don't. You put a cat or a raptor on a battlefield and the silly bastards right off start trying to engage the insects in honorable single combat. An insect's idea of single combat is let's you and my swarm fight. God only knows what their notion of honor is. Doubt if they have one, actually. The universe's great pragmatists, the bugs.

It's odd, really, how the whole thing turned out. When the bugs invaded the earth (they started in Poland, naturally—do those people ever get a break?), and after the Umpires of the Galaxy intervened and explained that weapons were forbidden in ecological warfare for bizarre theological reasons that nobody's ever been able to figure out (but there's no point arguing about it, as the Umpires made clear when they nuked Paris and Butte, Montana— and why Butte, anyway? Paris I can understand), the genetic engineers right away charged out and mutated cats and dogs and bears and owls and falcons.

Disaster followed upon disaster. The bugs made mincemeat out of the mutated predators in no time. Oh, sure, the predators look great. But the simple truth is that they make worthless soldiers. No discipline. No sense of teamwork. And talk about lazy! A cat'll kill one bug and sleep the rest of the day. And the raptors are so disgruntled over the fact that they can't fly because they're too big that they don't do much except sulk and write letters to the editor.

Yeah, things were looking bad for the home team until Professor Whitfield finally convinced SACRECOEUR (Supreme Allied Command, Reunified, Ecowar Europe— the French insisted on the acronym; like I said, I can understand nuking Paris) that they were approaching the whole problem upside down.

In his words, which have become as famous as $e=mc^2$: "To kill bugs, breed bugkillers."

Naturally, the idiot geneticists started off by engineering giant intelligent frogs. "Intelligent frog" is an oxymoron. Not only do the amphibious dopes stay in one place waiting for a bug to come within reach of their tongues (which they never do, because there's nothing wrong with *their* brains, which you'd expect from a collection of species that mastered *interstellar* travel), but the frogs can only fight when it's warm. And since the bugs aren't really bugs, but a group of species which descended on some far distant planet from a rootstock of warm-blooded arthropods, they just waited until the sun went down and—voila! Frog legs for dinner. That's how we lost the Ukraine.

So then the geneticists charged out and—well, that's when the jokes got started.

You know the ones:

"How many genetic engineers does it take to screw in a lightbulb? Eleven—one to do the work, and the other ten to figure out why it doesn't have a double helix."

"What's the definition of a virgin genetic engineer? A nerd with too many pocket protectors."

My personal favorite: "Why did the genetic engineer cross the road? To get to the other slide."

Fortunately for the vertebrate world, Professor Whitfield came to the rescue again. His immortal words:

"To fight low, think low."

Bingo. We got the rats, the rats started breeding, and we stopped the invasion in its tracks. Natural soldiers, rats. Born bug-killers. And, like I said, not bad guys once you get to know them.

But enough's enough. I hate to say it, as much as I admire Professor Whitfield (and who doesn't?), but I think his latest idea is just plain goofy.

Yeah, yeah, I've heard all the arguments.

"The greatest insectivores in the entire history of the vertebrate phylum." "The greatest night fighters ever produced by evolution." Blah, blah, blah.

That may all be true. Probably is—I'll admit these new

guys are a terror on the battlefield. The bugs won't even move at night, anymore.

But I don't care. Study your history and you'll find that it's always the morale factor that ultimately prevails in warfare. Don't take my word for it—read Clausewitz. Or Napoleon.

And these new guys are just wrecking the Army's morale. This is not shape prejudice! Sure, the new bunch are uglier than sin, but that's not the problem. The rats are ugly too—but do I care? Not in the slightest. Some of my best friends are rats.

The problem isn't the way the new guys look. It's their lousy sense of humor.

That's all, you say? All right, smart-ass civilian. Let's see you get any sleep at night, lying in your bunk, with the new guys hanging from the rafters, chuckling and chortling, telling the same stupid joke over and over again:

"I vant to trink your bludd."

Crawlspace

by Dave Freer and Eric Flint

Act I, Scene 1:
Enter rats, scampering through the darkness.

In the narrow tunnels deep inside a nineteen by five mile asteroid, long pipes snaked endlessly into the blackness. At the tunnel junction a naked globe hung, plainly jury-rigged into the cable tacked to the low roof. A woman's body lay there, sprawled, a little blood leaking from the retroussé nose. In the shadows, the light reflected off two sets of ferally red eyes, looking at the corpse.

"Well? What do we do with it?" asked Snout, not moving forward with her little barrow.

"It's solid waste," said Mercutio. "'Tis what we do. Remove it."

She always asked those sort of questions of him. Well: Just because one could think didn't always mean one wanted to.

Snout sniffed critically. "Well, not that solid. Parts of her look positively malnourished. Especially around the waist."

Mercutio shrugged. The Siamese-cat sized, long-nosed,

rattish creature, stepped forward and prodded the dead woman's waistline. "Humans like to be like that. Anyway, 'tis corsetry, Snout."

"Of course 'tis," nodded the other cyber-uplifted elephant shrew. "Not natural to be that thin around the middle." She stalked forward while her companion methodically rifled the pockets in the blouse top and then investigated the dead woman's purse. He was about to tuck what he found there into a pouch of his own when his companion hissed at him. He split the bundle of notes, roughly. She tucked her share of it into her own waist pouch.

"Wonder why she was killed, and yet they left the loot?" he asked, professionally.

"Probably done in because she's not a very pretty sight. Short little nose." Snout patted her own magnificent protuberance. "And no tail, poor thing. I don't care what humans say, this," she prodded the corpse's well-rounded derriere, "Is not a tail."

A thought plainly crossed Snout's mind. Mercutio pretended not to see her hasty glance at him. It would avoid a fight. She felt inside the corpse's low neckline, brought out something that made a plastic crinkling sound to his carefully listening ear, and hastily tucked it into her bag. She kept talking, obviously in the hope that he wouldn't notice. "What was she doing here?"

"Dying, I would guess," said Mercutio, searching the lip of the corpse's stockings to no avail.

"Do we tell someone?" Snout removed a silver filigree butterfly shaped hair-grip and tucked it next to her ear. "One of the humans. She is a human, so they might want to know."

Mercutio snorted. "Oh yes. And you know what they'd say: 'Why did you rats do it?' And then they'd put us into durance vile."

"But we are in durance, at least while the siege holds. It is fairly vile. And you usually did do it, Mercutio," she said, with that impeccable if twisted logic that comes from adding cybernetic memory and processing to an organic brain that hadn't gone a long way beyond thinking of its next meal or mating.

Mercutio was uplifted far enough to know that it was irritating, even if he did it himself. "That's not . . ."

Snout froze. "Hist," she said in a sibilant whisper. "Something this way comes."

Both rats ghosted away into the darkness as someone came climbing down the metal staples.

Act I, Scene II:
A sparsely furnished rock-hewn chamber, somewhere on the same large asteroid in the Olmert system.

Captain Rebecca Wuollet, HAR Marine Corps, was making a very credible effort to not tear off the head of Colonel De Darcy. First, because he was a superior officer and secondly because . . .

Well, technically he was right. You could see his point. If you walked around with blinkers on.

She made another attempt to use persuasion instead of violence, tempting though it was. That temptation was made easier to resist by the fact that the colonel was a combat vet himself. "Look Sir. I'm a combat demolitions specialist. I've been in the Corps for the whole of my adult life. I don't do . . . civilians. Sir."

De Darcy gave her the benefit of his famous crooked smile, complete with his famous crooked teeth. "I'm not a civilian liaison officer either, Captain. And this isn't about liaison. This is about the fact that we have fifteen thousand humans, mostly civs, God knows how many rats, about three hundred bats, and some fifteen other liberated races on this rock, which is under military control for the duration of the siege. We need some sort of security, and you're hard-assed enough to do it. Besides if I don't give you something to do, you'll lose that shiny new pip on your shoulder faster than you put it there."

He raised his eyebrows and shifted the famous crooked smile to its normal nastiness. "Look on the bright side. I could have put you in charge of the militia. I could still change my mind and shift Major Gahamey off the job and give him security."

"Um. Maybe security isn't so bad, sir." On this vast asteroid they only had a thousand seven hundred and thirty Marines, who had been caught up in the mess when the attack on Epsilon Theta had gone ass-haywire. Stuck here with twenty times their number of civ refugees, and a bloody big rock to defend, they needed a militia. But the population of rock-rats, fortune-hunters, whores and sharp-dealing traders they had to draw from, was going to drive Scotty Gahamey over the deep end. Well, maybe not. He was a real bastard and half over the deep end anyway. But it would certainly drive her there PDQ.

"I thought you might see it my way, Captain. Congratulations. You are now the chief of police for the duration, or until I decide otherwise. Not that I intended you to have any choice in the matter."

The colonel emitted an evil chuckle. "You do realize that you're only going to get the sick, lame and lazy from me to help you to do the job? You'll need to draw in civs to run patrols, and keep fights and petty crime to a minimum, especially between soldiers and civs. We're thin enough stretched just running a defense perimeter. But with all the trouble that's cropped up, the civilians' council sent a delegation to ask me to appoint someone to deal with the situation."

Rebecca felt the short hairs on her neck rise. "What situation, sir?"

"Someone is killing the joy-girls from the Last Chance. The locals suspect that it's one of us," he said dryly.

"And is it, sir?" she asked, equally dryly

The colonel tugged his moustache. "That's for you to find out. It could be true. If it is, you're going to have to stop it quietly and hard. Or the Korozhet won't have to take this lump of rock by force. Oh, and there are some hard drugs circulating. Civs do what they please out here. It's a long way from the law Earthside or on HAR. But I can't afford addicts in the Corps. You're as much law as this rock has. Stop the hard stuff."

She gritted her teeth. "Anything else I ought to know, sir?"

He thrust his hands into his pockets. "A lot. But you're going to have to find it out for yourself, Captain." His expression softened slightly. "You're a pain in the ass at times, Captain. But I chose you for this because you get results. I need them. I know that I can rely on you."

"Sir." It might be a lousy job, but De Darcy was always sparing with praise. She stood a little straighter.

He turned back to his desk and scooped up a datacube that he held out to her. "That's what I've got from them. There is also a list of personnel available to you in a file marked 'security personnel.' They're not all useless."

She took the cube, warily, as if it could just turn and bite her. He gestured at the door. "Get to it, Captain."

Rebecca saluted and turned.

As she did, De Darcy said, "One last thing, Captain. Try to use some of that tact you're famous for not having."

Act I, Scene III:
In a large Korozhet command ship among the myriad asteroids that make up the Olmert system.

"Considering these reports it would seem that it is indeed essential that we recapture it. Although why the scientists could not have told us before the system was abandoned, I do not know. It would appear that laxity has taken place. That or resistance." The deep purple reclined further into his saline bath.

"It may be that they were deceived by the scale of the object and its exterior, High Spine," said the maroon.

"I trust they have been eaten," said the purple.

"Difficult. They are the experts and training new ones takes time."

The deep purple acknowledged the sad truth of this with a clack of his anterior spines. "Well, they must be suitably punished."

"I believe this has occurred, High Spine."

The Korozhet bent its eye-spines to peer at the report-screens. The data was not encouraging.

"The best option still appears to be a siege and our traditional means. And of course probing attacks, to take advantage of what we can. We have plenty of expendables."

"Less than we used to have," said another of the purple, humping up off her last meal.

"We may have to resort to more care in slave-handling, but things have not reached that point yet," said the purple in charge of alien resources. "They still breed and we have taken steps to prevent their subversion ever happening again."

"Maybe we need to see if we can insert some into the artifact," said the maroon, risking an opinion in this high council of his elders.

It was a sign of just how worried the Korozhet were that he was not disciplined for this breach of hierarchy. "It would be difficult," said one of the purple. "There may however be implanted escapees that could be turned to our purposes."

"Investigate the possibilities."

"It will be done, High Spine."

Act I, Scene IV:
  In the tunnels and cavernous tavern and house of ill repute.

"Sergeant Holmes."

The mountain of flesh saluted. So, despite appearances,

it was human and alive. "Captain," he said in a carefully neutral voice.

This just had to be De Darcy's sense of humor, thought Rebecca sourly. He probably didn't find anyone called "Watson" among the enlisted men. Well, the one thing going for this man was his size. He could intimidate just by being there.

"Did you volunteer for this billet, Sergeant?" she asked suspiciously.

"With my name, the study of the criminal mind has always been my interest, Captain," said Sergeant Holmes calmly.

"Oh, and how do you do that?" She rocked on the balls of her feet, her hands clasped behind her.

Holmes lifted a meaty hand. "I knock it out of their ears and then look at it, Ma'am. It seems more effective than all this magnifying glass stuff I've read about."

"I'm beginning to revise my initial opinions about you, Sergeant. I think you could be an asset to the criminal investigation section. Which is, as of now . . . you. Assisted by me if it goes as far as murder. I have your first case awaiting you, just as soon as I finish with the patrol briefing."

"Maybe I should have chosen to go to brig after all, Captain," said Holmes amiably, confirming her suspicions about the able-bodied men she'd been given. Well, set a thief to catch a thief, and a drunk, disorderly and assaulting-the-guard Marine to catch others of the same kind. If you could stop them joining them, that is.

Twenty minutes later, after the patrols made up of one

civ volunteer and a Marine apiece having been dispatched, they set out. Her first ever criminal investigation, she thought, led straight to the Last Chance Saloon Bar. Anyway, it would be a good opportunity to see how many of her patrols ended up in the place. She had half an hour before her meeting with the civic authorities, whoever they might be, among this rabble of refugees.

The Last Chance was an eloquent testimony to the ingenuity of rockrats. They'd created a visual masterpiece to get blind drunk in. The murals painted and projected around the room made it an almost believable walled garden, visible through French doors. There was even an ivy hung garden door, and distant green vistas over the top of the painted mossy stone wall. By the time you'd had three of the overpriced drinks it probably would fool you. There was of course a full length polished stone bar on the other wall, and a number of stone tables and benches that probably defied the strongest drunk's effort to use them for combat weapons.

The furniture was large. The proprietor was not. He was a tiny, soft-looking man.

"Honest Laguna at your service," he said obsequiously, bobbing and rubbing his plump hands.

"I'm the new head of internal security for the rock," explained the captain, absorbing the unlikely name.

Laguna his shook his head. "Big job. Make that huge and impossible job, Captain."

"Why?" she asked.

"Well, the thing about this rock that most people just don't get is just how big it is. When the first prospectors came into the system just after the Crotchets' pull-back, they thought this place must be what the Crotchets and their bugs had been mining. Took a while, and a lot of boys getting lost in these here tunnels, to figure out that the diggings might even be older than the Crotchets. Who knows? Anyway, it's a regular warren. I been here from the very beginning, taking advantage of that. Not mining, of course. It's dug out of easy ores, even if there are still some heavy metals in the rock. There's plenty more heavy-metal rocks out in the asteroid belt, some even bigger than this one. But this is the only mined-out one we've found. Still, it is a good place for the rock-rats to come and breathe something other than their own gas, and find out that easy ores ain't always cheap."

He gurgled like a drain at his own joke. "Before the Korozhet counter-attack there were maybe five hundred permanent residents on the rock. Some weird ones. Aliens. We kept getting them wandering in from deeper down for weeks after we set up here. The Crochets left in a hurry, you bet."

This was news to Rebecca. Not that it had anything to do with murdered hookers. But she'd always thought that the Korozhet slaves had been all liberated at once . . . not showing up like a trickle of lost souls, hungry, thirsty and confused. She'd bet they'd not received the milk of human kindness from of this little son-of-a-bitch with his false smile and laugh.

"What the hell did they live on?" asked Holmes, showing that thought processes did happen inside that huge form.

"Hell, boy, I don't speak Crotchet and they didn't speak human. They could mop floors and wash dishes okay,

which is all I cared about. Now, you two wanted to talk to
me about those two dead girls. I reckon that it's one of
your boys has got himself a twisted hate of the women.
Like her."

He pointed out of the windows—what the hell you
needed windows for in a damn cave puzzled her—at the
fluttering protestor outside. You could tell that the bat was
a protestor by the sign she was carrying with her feet.

Pro life-choice!
End female subjugation now!

It seemed to be a one-bat protest. "You could start
improving security by getting rid of her." He scowled.
"She's always coming around and pestering the girls."

It was unusual to see a civ bat. No bandoliers, no
insignia . . . just a poster. The bats had taken the war
against the Korozhet as a holy crusade, and joined almost
to the last bat. The uplifted rats were a different matter.
They were deadly fighters, if they wanted to be. But they
were not soldiers by nature, and most of the time it took
the prospect of lots of loot to inspire them at all. But the
bats . . .

If Rebecca had learned anything in the military it was
not to get involved in dealing with a single-minded bat.
She'd seen better officers than her try it. She ignored the
bat, and turned to Laguna. "I have been told that two
women aged between twenty and thirty Terran years, who
had been working here, were found dead in the tunnels."

"And another one is missing," said Laguna,
lugubriously, wiping an eye. "Cindy-Jane."

Sergeant Holmes cracked his knuckles. Looked at the captain. Looked at Laguna. "I think I'd better examine his mind," he said. "Even if he is a bit on the small side."

"Sergeant," said Rebecca. The huge bar was relatively empty at this time of day. But "relative" only to what it could hold. There must be fifty miners in here, even now. The Marines were tough, but these rockrats, even the human ones, were almost certainly bar fight veterans. "As head of the serious crimes unit . . . Stick with asking questions for now, before you use your magnifying glass technique. Besides, think of what happened to the victims. It would take a fairly strong man."

The girls had been raped, robbed, and then been beaten to death, and dropped up a shaft. Things were backwards here. You got dropped up a shaft not down one, because of the centrifugal spin. It was a pity the murders weren't backwards, but this little shrimp would probably not be able to beat up a granny in a wheelchair, let alone a healthy young woman. He also would certainly never need to resort to rape. And robbery was something he was doing in the open here, on a grand scale, judging by his prices. It probably wouldn't be worth his while to go in for petty larceny, let alone kill one of his sources of income.

Holmes blinked. And then nodded, and set to his new technique of questioning verbally. "Who saw them last?" he asked Laguna.

"Oh, they were good girls. Only ever slept with two clients."

"Who?" asked Holmes, skeptically.

"The Marines and the rock-rats." Laguna cackled and

slapped his own thighs. "Boy, this isn't the hick town you come from. This is the wild frontier, or it was until the Korozhet put the place under siege. These girls came here for one reason, and it wasn't to powder their noses. You ain't gonna trace their last movements, nohow. I can tell you it was probably up and down, though."

Act II, Scene I:
Amid drunks, hookers, cutpurses and thieves and other municipal officials. In the presence of death and disorder.

The civic authorities, Rebecca discovered, included the bat she'd seen protesting outside the Last Chance. The council weren't going to cut it in any big mayoral parades in more civilized parts. The mayor, dressed in patched holey coveralls and a vast beard, which covered more of him than the coveralls, looked like a rock-rat. It was what he had been until about two weeks ago, and would almost certainly be again as soon as the siege lifted. Still, after the initial chaos this unlikely group had put together some kind of election and got a roughly working civil system up and running. Good enough to at least see to a sewage system and get water and food rationing implemented. There were plenty of gold chained mayors who would have done worse.

"I don't see why you don't have your own policing," she said directly.

The mayor scratched his bald head. A rat poked its long nose out from under his beard and whiffled its nostrils at her. "Well, it's difficult, you know," said the mayor. "Ain't easy to get anyone to take orders from another rock-rat. And the problems that we don't sort out for ourselves tend to come from when the Marines and locals clash. So we figured it might be best if we got you to take the blame, and do the work."

It was pleasant to meet with honesty at least, but . . .

"There is a rat peeping out of your beard," she said.

"Oh. That's just Firkin." The mayor reached under the giant beard and producing a sharp-nosed rat in an outfit that included fountaining flounces of lace. Or rather, flounces that included a little outfit. "My partner in prospecting. She's not on the council but she's kind of hard to keep out of the meetings. Firkin, meet Captain Wuollet."

The rat bowed. "Nice uniform. You could use more lace, though." She sat down on the table, produced a bottle of amber fluid from a sleeve and drank with lip-smacking appreciation.

Several councilors eyed the bottle with naked lust, even if they showed no suicidal desire to attempt to snatch it, or even the folly of trying to cadge a drink. Rats had a certain reputation. The tall, cadaverous one shook his head and said admiringly: "And she never seems to get any drunker than she is now."

"Methinks I have a harder head than you," said Firkin. "Which is not hard to imagine, Slim."

The rest of council plainly could imagine it too, by the grins.

"Anyways we'd take it kindly if you'd find the Marine behind these killings and string him up, before we do. There was talk last night of lynching the whole boiling lot of you," said the tall skinny Slim, obviously keen to move the subject away from his tolerance of liquor. He was sitting next to a little man in a skull cap with long locks of hair next to each ear.

With a shock, Rebecca realized that she recognized the man. Well, she'd seen his picture, anyway. Without the side locks or the skull-cap, but definitely the same face. She never forgot a face. This one she had reason to remember—along with the entire board of Intersolar Mining and Minerals, arrayed behind him and his father.

"But we did stop it," he said with a quiet smile. "Even though Slim here said it was undemocratic to put it to the vote."

"But you only survived by a narrow margin," said the bat. "And next time I might not vote with the entrenched exploiters." She glared at the young man under the skull-cap. "And I am in charge of the portfolio for security and social upliftment."

"Services. Social *services*, Zed," corrected the mayor.

She stared down her nose at him, which is easy to do if you're hanging upside down from the roof. "How many times do I have to say Ms.? Ms. Davitta Ze . . ."

"I reckon putting 'em down would be lot better than upliftment," interrupted Slim, combatively. "Especially you lot." This was addressed at the blue-furred Jampad swinging placidly from a roof-chain at the foot of the rock-table.

There was a grumble of agreement from one or two of the other council members, and a hiss of outrage from the bat.

The mayor slapped his hand down on the table. "Now you all hush up. Ain't no one here who fought better than Meredeth and his friends in the fall-back on the Rock. Like with the Marines, we might have come off second if they hadn't taken a hand."

"They were fighting for their own survival," said the jowl-faced bull-dog of a woman at the end of the table.

"And so were we," said the little man in the skull-cap. "Except for those who were running and hiding."

"I was fetching more ammunition!" said Slim.

"In the Last Chance. Looking for Laggy's bolt-hole, which you didn't find," said the bull-dog woman, with a derisive smile.

The mayor slapped both of his palms down on the stone table. "Now, you two. I'll throw you both out, like last time. Captain, I reckon you'd better leave us to our work. Maybe you want to take Ms. Zed with you and talk to her. She knew one of the victims."

"I had had a note from one of the victims. I did not know her," said the bat.

"Anyway, methinks the place will be more tranquil without her," said the flouncy rat snippily.

The bat grimaced at her, and shook a clenched foot. "Sellout," she said, fluttering from her perch. "Let's go, you imperialist lackeys," she said to the two Marines. "It'll be to drinking and fighting they'll fall without me, so I need to get back to it." Her tone suggested she might just enjoy at least one of the activities, and felt that she was missing out.

In a chamber far enough away that they could only hear the occasional bull-like bellows of the mayor, they paused. The bat found a piece of roof to cling to and turned her gargoyle-like black face to them. "I really cannot stay away long. Firkin and Abe will do their best but they need my voice too. You have to find this killer, and find him fast," she said seriously. "It's little enough success I have had with Laggy's exploited women. They'll not even dare speak to me, normally. But right now they're frightened to death. I was to be meeting Ms. Candy, the night that she was killed. And I had a message that the next woman killed needed to see me, urgently. They're frightened indeed if they are prepared to risk Laggy's wrath."

"Laguna?" asked Rebecca sitting on one of the empty boxes that littered this part of the "Civic center." "This is the 'Laggy' that you're talking about? The little man at the Last Chance?"

"Indade," said the bat, in the traditional fake Irish accent. She scowled. "He'd be my prime suspect."

"Look, the guy is a cess-pit, but he's too small to threaten anyone. I know that to you bats we humans all look large . . ."

"Ach bah," the bat spat. "It's not his strength they fear. He holds them in chemical bondage, Captain. He'll withhold their drug supply if they dare to cross him."

"Oho. So he's the supplier, is he?" asked Rebecca, like a terrier scenting rats. She'd get him for something, at least. And solve another of her problems in the process.

The bat wrinkled her face, folding it even more than it was folded already. "Say rather that he supplies the women he holds in bondage. There are several purveyors of these things," she admitted with reluctant honesty.

"It's something else I'm supposed to investigate and put a stop to," said Rebecca.

The bat shook her head. "You need to find the murderer first. The miners are indade close to a lynching. A Marine badge was found at the last killing."

"That we can follow up. Why wasn't I told?"

The bat shrugged her wings. "It is all a little muddled, yet. Slim told us of it."

"Both of these women wanted to see you," said Holmes, taking the initiative and calmly treading it underfoot. "Why?"

The bat shrugged her wings. "I do not know . . ."

Rebecca's communicator bleeped insistently. "Captain Wuollet," she said, pressing the send button.

"Alpha 3 patrol here, Captain. We've found a dead body. A woman. It looks like she's been raped and murdered."

"Hell's teeth. Where are you?"

"Punching the co-ords through to you, Captain," said the Marine, his voice full of relief at the idea that would soon be someone else's problem.

"We'll be right there. Don't move her or touch anything."

"And so will I," said the bat. "Someone needs to report on the brutality of th' polis," she said self-righteously. "Polis I name you, and not a Garda of our own."

They tramped through the rock-hewn corridors, away from the more settled level, where many rockrats had taken up residence in some of the larger galleries. "The very least that they should give me for this job is a groundcar," grumbled Rebecca. "Who ever heard of a police-chief walking to the scene of the crime?" There were vehicle tracks in the dust.

"Indade, there are a bare handful of such vehicles," said the bat. "And those belong to the entrenched exploiters that had already settled on this den of vice. They have to repair them themselves, as no facilities are to be found here for doing that.

"Nasty smelly things," she said with a lofty sniff. "The rock-rats scattered across the system had no need for wheels, or space for anything but ore-cargo. Besides, the price of importing such a thing was too expensive for any but the obscenely wealthy."

"So we walk, except for those who can fly," said Holmes, hunching to avoid hitting his head on the tunnel roof. "Why did they have to make these tunnels so low?"

The bat found this amusing. "There are many which are much lower. The ones the first two bodies were found in were narrower. And they were not built for human convenience."

"Why the hell does anyone go into them then?" asked Rebecca, ducking.

"They often widen out into what were plainly ore-chambers," explained the bat. "They make good rooms. You know, the prospectors had just found a similar rock, but without airlocks, in the second belt when the Korozhet attacked. It's the way the Korozhet mined. They were not worried by their slaves' comfort."

They'd at least worried about their slaves' air and had an amazing system of airlocks, reflected Rebecca. The asteroid siege would have been a short conquest, without those miles of corridors filled with air that contained too much oxygen and enough helium to alter the pitches of their voices. Inside the rock that air got scrubbed . . . in some place in the maze of internal passages as yet unmapped. The colonel had been doing some interesting swearing about that. They didn't even know if they had all the airlocks located. There were enough of them. And the Marines' supply of heavy weapons to defend those they'd found was very limited. How they'd hold off a major landing, heaven alone knew. But with strange gel-curtain airlocks every hundred yards or so, landing and capture would be two very different things. The miners didn't have much in the way of missiles, but they did have a personal arsenal each, and a number of heavy-duty tripod-mounted mining lasers. The attacks—so far—had been on the main landing bay, now crowded with little miner-ships, and Marine landing craft. Quite a few of the miner-ships had had some external weapons. This had plainly been a rough neighborhood.

"We need to go down here," said the bat, pointing to a shaft. There were metal staples in the wall. Not very big staples and too close together for human climbers to have set them there.

"How do you know?" asked Sergeant Holmes, blinking, looking at the position co-ords on his palm-comm.

"I can hear the voices of several people, arguing. The word murder has been used." The bat flew up into the hole. That was down—if you took the core of the asteroid as "down." Centrifugal force provided an alternative to gravity here.

Bats did have hyper-keen hearing. Or she might just have known, concluded Captain Wuollet. Something about the black-faced bat activist smelled. Not necessarily of murder, but the bat knew more than she was telling. Rebecca reached up and began to climb. Better get there fast.

That was a good decision, it turned out, even if Holmes was not designed to run down a corridor this high or wide, complete with pipes to trip over. The scene was angry and heading to the point of shooting.

"The captain," said a voice, uncertain and plainly tense, "is coming to look at the crime scene . . ."

"Screw your captain," interrupted someone. "You just step aside and let us take the poor dead girl back to the Last Chance, and you don't get hurt, see."

Rebecca poked the burly speaker hard in the kidneys. Hard enough for him to turn and crack his head . . . and see the tunnel entirely full of Holmes behind her. "Your chances of screwing me are slightly lower than your chances of surviving beyond the next ten seconds. And those chances are not good, if you're still here by the time I count to ten. One."

"Now see here, Captain," said an angry voice, from elbow height.

"And that means you too, Mr. Laguna," she said icily. "We'll return the body to the Last Chance when we've finished inspecting the crime scene. Two."

"But . . ."

"Three." One of the advantages of Holmes being outsize, besides sheer intimidation, was that it was impossible to see if there was a whole squad . . . or no-one, behind him in the narrow tunnel.

Grumbling, Laguna and his mini-mob retreated down the far passage. "You haven't heard the last of this!" shouted someone.

"Alas, 'tis probably true," said the bat. "They'll be back at the Last Chance drinking more courage. You'll have trouble presently."

The Marine who had called her grinned. "Good thing you got here fast, Captain. And good thing Larry was here with me." He put a hand on the shoulder of the stocky miner who had gone on patrol with him. It was not the same Marine who had left their base cave an hour before, looking like he'd been inflicted with a boil or a toothache for company. "That lot said I'd done it, and they were all for lynching me. Larry talked them out of it." He looked at the tunnel. "If I was going to do that I'd choose somewhere where I could at least stand up."

Rebecca was on her knees examining the corpse. It was at times like this it paid to be a combat vet. It still wasn't a pretty sight. Someone had hit the victim very hard with a piece of rock. Hard enough to smash her skull. There wasn't much blood. Odd for head wound, that. She pulled the victim's skirt down. The dead woman had little enough dignity left to her, and Rebecca could do nothing much about the ripped filmy blouse. There wasn't a lot of spare material. "What were you two doing in here anyway?"

"It's a shortcut across to where they're setting up the ag caves," explained the miner. "The roof is a bit low, but if you follow the pipes it'll save you ten minutes walk."

It made a sort of sense, except that it did mean that this was not the quiet private spot the attacker must have assumed. That in itself suggested that the attacker was a

Marine. "I suppose there is nothing much else for us to see. Let's get her out of here."

"Captain," said Holmes from his knees back in the tunnel. He was far too tall to stand there. "I need to show you this first." He pointed to a hose-clamp on one of the pipes. A gossamer shred of material clung to it. A piece of blouse. "She got dragged in here."

Rebecca looked intently at it. "So," she said after some thought. "He must knocked her down, dragged her in here, and then killed her with that rock. See if you can see any other signs of dragging."

"I'll have to go out backwards, Captain. There is not enough space for me to turn around."

"Look as you crawl, Sergeant."

The passage, however, was relatively dust-free. The rock-floor was not particularly even, but there were no other pieces of material snagged there—which, considering the filmy flimsy nature of the clothing was surprising. Even more surprising was the arrival of yet another visitor. In flounces. "I had to stop and eat, and follow you by scent," said Firkin crossly. "You humans run too slowly and for far too long."

Rats had speed, but not stamina.

The rat pushed past the sergeant. "This is your new method of advancing? Methinks you are showing your best features to the enemy."

The rat looked at the corpse. "Cindy-Jane. A lot of miners will be mightily upset, and the Last Chance will lose a fair bit of turnover. She was almost rattish in her appetites. Made up for the price with volume."

Rats were not known for their sensitivity, thought

Rebecca. It at least made them accidentally honest. "Well, let's get her out of here. She was dragged in. I suppose we can drag her out."

She took an arm, deciding by the look on the miner and young Marine's faces, that it was a good time to lead by example. She was grateful that all her years in the service had at least taught her how to control squeamishness. As she pulled the body it rolled slightly, to reveal a brown billfold. She twitched it out from under the corpse with the other hand and opened it.

It revealed two things. The first was a Marine ID card. The second was even more puzzling.

Money.

Tucked inside the inner flap were three hundred C notes. Not a fortune, but surely enough to pay for a cheap tart.

"I want Private Samson, 4655573490."

"Plooks?" said the Marine who'd called her to the scene. "He's out on patrol, Captain."

"He's one of mine?" she asked, already knowing the answer. Wouldn't this do the credibility of her fledgling force the world of good, she thought sourly.

The Marine looked uncomfortable. "It was you or staying in the brig, Captain."

"He should have stayed in the brig," she said coldly. She called her ops room, and told them to call Samson in, and place him under arrest.

As she put the comm device back in its pouch, she stood up and banged her head. She ground her teeth in irritation, feeling the bump. "Now can we get the body out of here," she said, reaching down to take an arm again.

"Captain, I think you'd better come and have a look here," called Sergeant Holmes. "I had a look in the next passage, while I was waiting for you to come out."

"Inborn investigative urge overwhelming you, Sergeant?" she said, covering the fact that she'd banged her head yet again with sarcasm.

"Needed a leak, Captain," said Holmes with innate honesty. "There is more of that blouse material back there. That's where it happened, I reckon. The body has been moved."

"Hell's teeth!" said Rebecca when she look into the dark passage that Holmes pointed out to her. "Why did he move her? They'd not have found her in there until she started to smell "

"Indade," said Ms. Zed, wrapping her wings around her and shivering. "Unless, as I'd be thinking, someone wanted her found."

Captain Wuollet looked at the single electric bulb tacked into the cable at the intersection. She thought of those blissful days when she'd been a mere boot and only had to deal with grueling Marine drill, instead of coping with this mess. She was going to need a lot of things that she didn't have, to handle this, like an elementary knowledge of forensic practice for a start. All she knew about was shaped charges and detonators, not catching murderers. "Better search the other corridors too," she said resignedly. "Next thing we know we'll find more bodies."

They didn't. But they did find a small wheelbarrow and a shovel. A very small wheelbarrow. "Maybe a garden gnome did it," said Holmes thoughtfully.

NCOs were of course allowed a sense of humor. Just not in public or with their superior officers. She decided to ignore the comment. "And moved her on the barrow, which is easier than dragging," she said dryly. The barrow looked far too small to move a body. "Better have a look for wheel tracks," she sighed.

Holmes shone a focused beam of light down the center of the dusty tunnel. Shook his head "It's been wiped. There is one footprint, fairly small. And mine, of course. He must have carried her."

"A man with small feet and a strong back," said Rebecca rubbing her jaw. "So . . . what is the barrow doing here. Who does it belong to?"

"'Tis a rat-miner's barrow," said Firkin. "I have such a one myself. We purchased it from Abe." She eyed it speculatively. "As it is lying about, methinks the owner has no further need of it," she said cheerfully. "I'll have it."

"Looter. Despoiler. Capitalist," said the bat. "To take thus from those less fortunate than you."

The rat jerked a thumb at the corpse that the miner and Marine had just carried out. "She doesn't exactly need it any more. Besides, methinks Cindy-Jane would have been willing to try anything, but a position involving a small wheelbarrow taxes even my imagination."

It taxed hers too, admitted the captain to herself. "It's evidence. I'll hold onto it," was all that she said, however.

"Tch," said the rat, producing her amber-fluid filled bottle and having a good chug. "Well, do tell me if you ever work out just what a hooker needed a rat miner's barrow for. I've heard of fetishes, but . . ."

"Shut up, will you? Let's get a blanket and carry the corpse out of here. Sergeant. Bring me that incriminating barrow. Let's go and talk to Private Sampson," she said grimly.

Private Sampson might actually not have had enough money in that wallet. He was an acne-cure advertiser's dream, poor kid. And he was just a kid, thought Rebecca. A kid with a black eye, and a cut on his cheek. Maybe the girl had got a last few blows in. "This yours, Private?" She held out the wallet. He blinked. You could almost see the thoughts crossing his mind, using heavy levers to shift the expressions on the spotty face. He beamed. And reached for it. "Yeah! Thanks, Captain. I thought I was in trouble or something."

She pulled the wallet back. "Not so fast, Marine."

His expression turn woeful. "I guess my money's gone then."

"How much was there?" she asked speculatively.

"About twenty in front flap. But," he said, doing his best attempt at a cunning expression. "I got some more in the secret place at the back. Three hundred."

"You lost the twenty," she said. "But the rest is still there. So, tell me when you last had your wallet."

He was smiling again. "That's the rest of my pay. I reckoned I'd lost it all."

Either this kid was the best actor in the world, or he was a damn stupid young fool who nearly got strung up. "When did you last have it, Marine?" she asked again.

He looked wary. Something in her tone must have finally gotten through to him. "Me and a couple of the boys slipped off to the Last Chance last night. I don't remember too well, but I didn't have it this morning."

"When you woke up in the brig," she said, trying to keep her face expressionless.

He nodded. "They said if I volunteered for security duty I was off the hook, Captain."

It looked like she had her murderer after all . . . or maybe more than one of them. "Just who was with you, Sampson?"

He looked wary. "The colonel said we was all off the hook, Captain." His voice said: You do not split on your mates. Not if you want to live.

She restrained herself from solving his pimple problem forever by starting to squeeze at the neck. "I'm not playing games now, Private Sampson. I need to know. And I need to know now. I can look in the unit records if I have to. You're wasting my time."

Her answer came from another source, though. "Private Ogumba, Private Wilkins and Private Mikes," said Sergeant Holmes. "It was Mikes who found the body, Captain. He's still here. Shall I haul him in?"

"Body? I didn't kill no-one, Captain . . . did I? I was in a fight . . . I think," said the boy. He was now pale, beginning, finally, to realize that he might be in deep trouble.

Holmes brought Private Mikes through to her office-cave. The entire thing was obviously preying on Mikes' mind so much that he barely managed to salute before he blurted out:

"I been thinking, Captain," he said. "It can't be Sampson. Me and Gumbo only got separated from him once, just after the fight when we got thrown out. And we found him maybe fifteen minutes later. He was blind-drunk, Major. Plooks can't hold much. Gumbo and me, we took him back to camp. He couldn't hardly stand when we got thrown out. And then he got into a fight with one of the Guard Commanders . . ."

"Me," said Holmes, with a nod. "They were all in the brig at 22:00 hours." His expression said that he considered this a ridiculous time to be drunk and arrested by.

"That still gave him fifteen minutes." Or them, she thought to herself.

"Indade," said the bat, quietly from the corner. "Except that she was still alive at 22:30. I saw her then. I was doing my picket."

"Are you sure?" asked Rebecca.

"Sure as death," said the bat. "I don't get times wrong."

Bats didn't. Their soft-cyber chips had inbuilt clocks. She knew that well from dealing with bats on the demolitions course. Bats made up most of the sappers. They regarded humans as ludicrously vague about time and memory, as that part of them was cybernetic. She sighed. "We'll have to try to confirm it, Private Sampson. But it looks like you may just have got your wallet back, and escaped a hanging. That's a lifetime's ration of luck. Stay out of the Last Chance from now on, see."

The youth nodded earnestly. "Yes, Captain. The drinks is cheaper in the Miner's Rest anyway."

Why did she feel she was better off talking to the rat, even it laughed at her? "Get out of my office, Private. Stay here at ops. And stay out of all of the bars," she added, knowing that order was pointless.

"Can I have my wallet, Captain?"

In the grim certainty that only the absence of money would keep him out of the bar, she shook her head. "No. It's still evidence in a robbery, rape and murder trial. You may get it back, if we ever find the culprit. You nearly got hanged for losing it last time, you brainless idiot."

When he'd gone, saluting sheepishly, and accompanied by his fellow genius of the night before, Rebecca sat down on the makeshift desk and swore. She was not surprised to see the flouncy rat appear from under the desk and clap appreciatively.

She tossed the "evidence" wallet down. "Well. That's the wallet. Stolen during or after the fight. The owner was locked up when the crime happened. Which leaves the damned wheelbarrow. And no matter what that rat says," she said, pointing at Firkin, "I refuse to even consider it as a sex toy."

"What about the little shovel, then?" asked Firkin with her favorite evil laugh.

Rebecca decided it was best to just ignore her, if she could.

"It might have been there by accident, Captain," said Holmes, keeping his face carefully expressionless.

"'Tis likely," said the rat. "Well, as you've no further use for that wallet . . ."

Wuollet slapped the reaching paw away. "Do you loot everything? Don't answer that. I already know the answer."

The rat shrugged. "'Tis rattish nature, methinks. If it is not tied down one steals it."

"And it had better be tied down very thoroughly." Rebecca sighed. "How about if you do some asking about who has lost a barrow?"

Firkin yawned. "A waste of time, methinks. But I will ask about who is trying to steal one."

The rat sauntered out. That was no guarantee that it had actually gone anywhere, of course. She could hope, though.

"Someone deliberately planted that wallet, Captain," said the sergeant.

"That much is elementary, Holmes. Someone wanted the Marines to take the rap. Colonel De Darcy didn't realize what a live, pin-less grenade he'd handed me," said Rebecca, wishing she had enough hair to pull out. "The big question is whether they were just letting us take the rap or whether they wanted to try and get rid of us. Whether we are dealing with murder, or treason."

Act II, Scene II:
An arras, or possibly a rattish bar.

"Thou hast the most unsavory similes," said Snout loftily, returning—as rats would under pressure—to the Shakespearean downloads that had once made up their linguistic source. "To think that I would indulge in such things, sweet wag."

"Ask, morelike, when you have ever done anything else," said Firkin, yawning. "I know you were there, you and your paramour Mercutio. I smelled it at the time, but said nothing."

"A good idea, my flouncy bit," said Mercutio, from the shadows. "Keep it thus. We did a little looting, nothing else."

"Methinks that was enough. You will need to tell her that," said Firkin, knowing that this would be dangerous ground.

"And be put into durance vile. I think not," said Mercutio. "Humans have odd ideas about property."

Firkin had to admit that that much was true, even if it was unlikely anything else Mercutio volunteered would be. "Mayhap a deal can be arranged," she said, heavily. Not likely. Humans should understand rats better, as they were so ratlike themselves.

Act II, Scene III:
Enter various gentlemen of Verona, Chicago, Dublin, Bangbanduc . . . heck. Miners and prospectors. Don't ever ask where they come from.

"You could take the barrow to Abe," suggested the bat. "Maybe he can tell you more about it."

"This Abe is the one who sold it?" asked Holmes, examining the little barrow he held in one hand.

The bat scowled. "He is the entrenched capitalist exploiter of the downtrodden masses, or the miners at least, yes. He sits on the council. With his skull-cap and ear-locks." Her innate sense of justice had a brief wrestling match with her conscience. "There are worse," she conceded.

Coming from her that was probably high praise. "Let's go, Ms. Zed," Rebecca said, pulling aside the curtain that served the ops-cave as a door.

"That's not actually my full name . . ."

She broke off. A large mob was marching down on them, led by Laggy and several of his search party from their earlier encounter. "We hear you got the man who done it, Captain. Hand him over to us. We'll deal with him," said Laguna.

Rebecca wished really hard for some nice shaped demolition charges—set in the tunnel just ahead of this lot. She stepped into the middle of the passage and spoke loudly and clearly. "That rot-gut of yours is making you hear things, Laguna. What I did catch was a set-up. Unfortunately, they set up a man who definitely couldn't have done it, because at the time he was behind bars back at the camp. Now, *you* tell me who told you that we had the man. That must be the one who actually did this. And I'll take him into custody. There'll be no lynching."

The mob stopped dead.

A beard came racing around the corner, followed somewhat later by the rest of the mayor. "Huh . . . huh— what's going on here?" he panted. "Break it up now!"

"It was him," said Laggy. "Or rather it was that rat of his. She told me."

The worst of it was that it could possibly be perfectly true. Firkin had known about it. And she did seem to be a rat that was familiar with Laggy's girls if nothing else. Anything that lacked virtue would attract a rat. And, looking at the mayor and then his feet . . . if anyone was short enough to stand upright in the tunnels, and was strong enough to carry a harem, let alone one woman, it would be him. It could be, after all. He might want complete control over the rock and have seen this as a way to get rid of the Marines.

"Lynch him!" yelled one of the front-men of the mob. "The bastard has been killing our women!"

Rebecca stepped in front of the mayor. "The first person to try any lynching on my watch is going to be dead." Her voice could have cut across three parade grounds.

"There's more of us than you," said one of the mob, fingering the butt of his flechette-pistol.

"Yep," said Holmes stepping out of the office cave, cradling a Mark 24 automatic flechette rifle. "But who will be first to die?"

The Mark 24 made an impression on the mob. It was normally tripod mounted.

"You said you'd arrest whoever told us," said Laggy sulkily.

"I will take him in," said Rebecca, wondering if the colonel had known just what a treasure he'd given her in Sergeant Holmes. "And that rat too, and hold them until I get some answers. But the rat was here when I found out that it was a set-up. So tell us what you heard?"

"That you had found a Marine's wallet under her." That was said by a gangling man with a planar face and an outsize nose.

Rebecca raised her eyebrows. "Oh? Full of money, no doubt."

That got a laugh from the crowd. "Not likely!" said planar face.

"Well, you've told me all I needed to know," she said, reflecting that they'd told her something anyway—that the information had come from someone who either hadn't wanted to mention the money or hadn't known about it. "Now get along with you. The mayor will stay right here with me."

Act II, Scene IV:

In some shady hostelry, where you might find the likes of Doll Tearsheet.

"It took me long enough to find you," said the bat crossly. "I should have known that you'd be off carousing, when Albert needs you!"

Firkin sniffed and raised her goblet. "Zed, methinks that there is very little that Albert cannot do for himself. I am his partner, not his nursemaid."

"Ah. Even though they were after lynching him for those murders?"

"What!" Firkin leapt off her stool, spilling drink onto the bat, who spluttered, and swore and fluttered up to the ceiling, to shake off her wings with an expression of distaste. "Where have they taken him, Zed? Come here, you blasted winged teetotaler!"

"He's with the polis," Davitta answered, flying higher. "The captain kept him from the mob."

It went against her socialist and revolutionary instincts but the authorities had been very welcome then. She'd been unsure what to do. Albert, for all that he was a reactionary sellout, was none too bad a mayor.

"Methinks it is the first time that I have heard of them being useful," said Firkin, shaking out her ruffles. "I'd better go and find Mercutio."

"That blackguard!" Davitta exclaimed. "What need do you have of him?"

Firkin yawned artfully. "Firstly, because he's a blackguard, a weasand-slitter and a rogue. I've a feeling that I might have need of him to deal with this poxy mess that Albert has wandered into. Secondly, he has another property, more unusual in rats. He can think. And thirdly, he was there. I smelled his presence at the scene. He and that doxy of his, Snout. Officially, they traffic in ordure, and that makes them quite noxious."

Davitta nearly fell out of the air "Why didn't you say so to the captain?" she squawked.

"Why?" Firkin raised her nose. "We rats stand for ourselves, and the devil take the hindmost. I will not betray a rat to the constabulary. A policeman's lot should not be a happy one, anyway."

"And such is honor among rats," said the bat, sardonically. "Well, let us find him without delay then, because the mob will be drinking themselves into courage for a second try."

Act II, Scene V:
Enter a merchant with all the perfumes of Arabia.

"I've come to see the prisoner," said the small man with the side locks and skull-cap. "You can call me his lawyer if you have to. I did train as one once, although I don't usually admit to it."

Rebecca studied him. Regrettably, he had large feet for a relatively small man. "He's not strictly a prisoner," she said. "I decided that he would be safer here than out there. At the moment I am using him as a tea-boy."

Abe shook his head in mock horror. "A clear infringement of his rights. Tell him I take two sugars." He lifted a heavy flechette rifle from his shoulder and leaned it against the wall. "They'll be back, you know. That's actually why I came with this. I can't shoot very well, but at least I'm an extra man."

With questionable motives, she thought. Everyone had questionable motives in this darned case! But all she said was: "Then leave the shooting to us. The passages are narrow and—"

He interrupted. "And you're dealing with miners, Captain. According to your colonel, you know how to use explosives. So do they. They probably have even more experience than you do."

That was true enough, she supposed. "So we need to take action first."

"Perhaps by finding the murderer."

"Or by laying mines in the passage," said Rebecca sourly. Did everyone have to assume that she knew the first thing about detection? "Where is that rat when I need her? I need know what, if anything, she said to Laggy. If it wasn't for a lack of motive and his size I'd suspect him first. You couldn't tell me anything about a little wheelbarrow could you?"

"A miner's barrow? Rat-size? If it is one of mine—it will have a serial number. I guarantee them."

"Let's hope it is one of yours, then," she said. The way this case was going it wouldn't be.

He smiled with quiet confidence. "Bound to be. I've

cornered the market. My competitors don't understand that quality and a reasonable price almost always trumps them."

"Besides, the rats all think that sooner or later they've got to put one over him," said Albert, handing him a mug of tea. "The barrow is in the corner. It's one of yours. Smells a bit."

"Rats need something to hope for," said Abe, going to look at the barrow. He took a mini-stylus-pad out of his pocket and tapped a number into it. "Here you are. Snout. She's one of the supposed sewage maintenance team your Firkin recruited, Albert. They work in the narrow tunnels better than people."

To Rebecca, he explained: "And sewage doesn't offend them. People were just using empty passages at first, and something had to be done about it. Too much disease risk, apart from the smell, otherwise. Anything else you want to know?"

Rebecca looked carefully at that bland face. "Just one thing. What is the deputy chairman of Intersolar Mining and Minerals doing here?"

He hesitated. "You must be mistaken."

She shook her head. "Not likely. I never forget a face. And yours takes some explaining. There might even be a motive for murder there."

He looked at the puzzled face above the mayor's beard, then sighed. "Well, if I can't trust Albert, I can trust no-one. I was getting back to my roots, that's all. It's about an old leather suitcase, I suppose."

He seemed to think he'd said enough. Rebecca looked at him, unblinking. "Explain."

He laughed softly. "The inquisition had nothing on you. I am beginning to think you were well chosen for this job. Very well. I found an old leather suitcase, in what had been my grandfather's office, when we moving to the new corporate headquarters . . . well, rather the movers found it. It was a cheap thing, and one of them asked me what should be done with it. It was full of old papers and pictures, he said."

He took mouthful of his tea. "I opened it. Looked inside—and found the life story of a man in there. My great-grandfather. Founder of the company, a few name changes back. It was his suitcase. I found out that we had not always been ultra-wealthy corporate moguls."

"Most of us were something else before we got to be rockrats," said the mayor. "We don't ask what a man's family history was."

Abe acknowledged this with a wry smile. "My great-grandfather had been a pack-peddler. He sold his wares across the Northern Cape, selling to diggers across the semi-desert that was the Kimberly diamond-fields. I started reading the letters in that case. Letters from his family in Poland, letters from the board of the synagogue he helped to found in Kimberly, letters from his wife, letters from miners, letters from farmers and suppliers. I got the picture of a man. He was devout, happy, and strangely, a much-loved man."

Abe took a deep pull at his tea-mug. "I can't say there are many people who loved Intersolar Minings and Mineral's deputy chairman."

"No," said Rebecca, hoping that she was hiding her feelings on that subject.

Maybe she didn't succeed. Or maybe he just read people well. He waved a placatory hand. "It's a good thing I am not that any more."

She had a job to do. Not payback time. Yet. "And the side locks and skullcap?" she asked.

He shrugged. "An affectation. A reminder that when great-grandfather went out there, blacks and Jews were everyone's kicking boys. I didn't mean to become a Korozhet target though. Is that enough?"

"Not really." But she was impressed in spite of herself. It was too weird to make up. "It's a pretty story, but unlikely."

He allowed that faint smile back onto his face. "You really are suspicious enough to make a good detective. There was more to it all, of course, but I don't think that I need to waste your time with it." There was a finality in his tone which suggested that torture wouldn't work either. "Perhaps we need to go and look for the rattess Snout. Now."

Act III, Scene I:
Enter the great detective.

"She's dead." said Mercutio, quietly. "Snout is dead." Davitta had had other brushes with Mercutio. He was normally urbane and slightly sinister, as befitted a prince of the underworld of ratly crimes. Now his voice shook.

A furry face precluded any sign of paleness, but the voice suggested that the rat was going to pitch face forward any moment. "Sit down," said the bat, practically.

"And drink some of this and take heart," said Firkin, producing a bottle from her sleeve flounces.

A slap would hardly have shocked Mercutio more. "You . . . giving out drink?" He hastily snatched the bottle and swigged. And spluttered. "It's cold tea!" he said both incredulously and indignantly. "Not even some vile sack. Art trying to kill me?"

"And do the world a favor." Firkin snatched the bottle back. "Why did you kill Snout?"

"T'was not I. I would have done the thing quietly and eaten the evidence. Methinks . . . she may have been murdered. Come."

He led them to a chamber—which one might have passed ten times without finding it, as the door was so neatly hidden in a fold in the rock. There, within, was an Aladdin's trove of loot. And a small female rat, sprawled. Dead.

"Out, brief candle," said Firkin, quietly. "What killed her?"

"I don't know. But I will find out," said Mercutio with grim certainty.

"The polis . . ." said Davitta, fluttering her wings.

"Methinks I'll solve my own problems."

Firkin shook her head. "Nay, methinks that it is we, and they, who need you to solve theirs, Mercutio. They have Albert, accused of these murders. We need whoever did that. I was on my way to beg your help."

Mercutio looked her in the eye. Nodded slowly. "Twas done by the same hand, methinks. Let us go to the Last Chance."

"I am not very welcome there," admitted Davitta, thinking, not for the first time, that even the heroes of the

Easter Rising had it easier than a bat trying to follow her conscience. Doing so seemed to have unforeseen consequences, like discovering that your official worst enemies were your friends, and actually drank cold tea.

Mercutio snorted. "Methinks Laggy does not welcome any non-human. But there is another entrance, and I have connections."

"Comrades in thievery, no doubt," said Davitta.

"Naturally." The rat led them off down a passage far too narrow for humans, and too narrow for comfortable flying either. It brought them out a few yards from the Last Chance, in time to see a drunk being ejected through the bat-wing doors. Davitta wondered, as she had many times before, if it was possible to sue the door-makers for slander.

The drunk must have truly believed he was seeing things, when the bat and two rats pushed stubby digits into four little holes on a low bit of wall, and then disappeared into the hole that appeared . . . and then the wall sealed up again.

"What's this?" squawked Davitta. "Are we trapped?"

"Be still," said Mercutio. "Methinks it is just a part of the air recycling system. We have found a few such ducts, but there are doubtless many."

"But why have they hid it thus?" The bat fluttered down the dim passage filled with machines, some of which plainly were still working.

"Without intent, mayhap. It is just neatly cut, we think with a laser. The chamber Laggy has turned into the Last Chance was perhaps a machine room or a dormitory. Be careful of that machine over there. 'Tis hot."

"But . . . but where does the power come from?" asked

Davitta. This was a whole world that she'd not known existed. It was a little alarming to think that they relied on this abandoned Korozhet machinery.

The rat shrugged. "Why should we care? I was interested for a while when I heard you say, some time back, that all power corrupts, but I stole several batteries and, as yet, I have seen nothing but decay, and not one single offer of a bribe."

Mercutio sounded suitably disappointed in this further betrayal by the English language. "Ah. Here we are. The kitchens. The drains. Laggy used what was here. He plainly explored it well."

"Ach, that old voyeur. He explores everything well. He has minicams concealed in the girls' rooms, I have heard tell," said Firkin.

"Hush," said Mercutio. "We need to go up the stairs. Cookie is a friend of mine."

Cookie was short and rotund. And brown. With pink sugar frosting. Well, it probably wasn't sugar frosting, though with alien life forms you couldn't be too sure. The alien must have had eyes somewhere, even if Davitta couldn't see them, because it spoke to them. Or maybe it used some other way of detecting them.

It spoke in Korozhet, which was still the default language of the soft-cyber units which the Korozhet had used for uplift and enslavement. The enslavement module had been cracked in the rebellion on Harmony and Reason, but the language remained. Hearing it set Davitta's sharp white teeth on edge.

"Tell it to speak a decent uncivilized language," she snapped.

Mercutio shook his head. "Cookie can't. That's why he has to put up with working for Laggy. He was one of the left-behinds when the Korozhet cut and ran. He cleans here."

"He is in bondage, you mean?" demanded the bat.

"Nay. Though a couple of the girls will do that, if the price is right."

"I meant a slave," she explained coldly.

Mercutio considered this. "I don't think he is, in the strictest sense of the word. He just doesn't speak anything but Korozhet and Laggy feeds him. At first there wasn't anyone else, and I don't know if he has figured out that he has any other options now."

Davitta hissed angrily, despite knowing that it made her sound like an exploding kettle. "And I don't suppose you saw fit to tell him."

Mercutio blinked. "No. Never thought of it. We've got a bit of barter and exchange going with him. There is good loot around this place."

"Rats!" she snarled. Mercutio was probably merely being truthful. Rats were the epitome of natural selfishness—not that they couldn't rise above it, it just never occurred to them that there was any need to. "I will liberate him!"

"Good luck finding the words," said Firkin. "Anyway, aren't you supposed to be solving a murder and saving Albert's groats, seeing as us rats are too idle."

The language was literally the problem. The word "liberty" was not in the Korozhet download. It might not even exist in the Korozhet language. It was very hard to think about something you had no word for. She sighed. Was nothing simple?

"Very well. But as soon as we have this sorted out, I'll talk to the Jampad about this. They'll free him even they have to blow the place up to do it." The humans and even the rats would support that—or at least not prevent them from doing it. Slavery was something abhorrent, especially for the miners that had come from the Korozhet-invaded world of Harmony and Reason. Admittedly, the rats only worried about it happening to themselves, but they had been brought to think that if it were done to others, they just might be next.

"You will do what you will do," said Mercutio, shrugging.

Act III, Scene II:
Into a den of lyings.

"Only a rat will ever get information out of another rat," said Abe with a shrug. "If they have decided not to tell us where the rattess Snout can be found, we're not going to find her."

Rebecca shook her head. "That's not why I said I'd be damned. It was that . . . bar."

Abe snorted in amusement. "The pictures on the walls don't leave much to the imagination, do they?"

"Not if you're a lonely rat miner, no," said Albert with perfect seriousness. "So what do we do now?"

"Sun Tzu," said Rebecca.

"What?" said the mayor, puzzled. Military strategy was not one of his interests, obviously.

"We take the battle to them," said Rebecca. "The

center of all of this is the Last Chance. It's not the only brothel around, is it?"

They both looked a little taken aback at the question. The mayor found his wits first. "No. There are nine such establishments and a fair number of freelancers," he said.

Abe coughed and continued: "It's a refugee colony now, but it was a miners R&R place. That's what they wanted and they had the money to pay for it. Demand creates supply."

"Yet all the murdered women came from just one of those places," said Rebecca. "I smell a rat, and it isn't just Firkin, or the missing Snout. Let's go to the Last Chance and ask some awkward questions."

"Man, but that's a lynch mob brewing in there!" said the mayor uneasily.

"Exactly. Is there one place a guilty man wouldn't go, as bold as brass?" asked Abe, grinning. "Besides, as the mayor, tasting the local brews is your civic duty."

"That's part of the problem," said the mayor, tugging his beard nervously. "No one knows exactly where Laggy stashes his still. God alone knows what goes into the stuff. Evil bastard. He's changed since the Epsilon III rush. I met him back then. He used to be a nice bloke. They called him 'honest' back then because he was too dumb to cheat even the local tax men. He's learned a lot since then, that's for sure."

"Unusual for a man to learn to have brains," said Abe, as they walked towards the flashing light outside the bar.

"He used to drink a lot," explained the mayor. "Always had his own still. I reckon he drank some bad stuff. He's given up. Or at least he barely drinks now."

"Could happen, I suppose," said Abe.

"Unlikely," said Holmes, with a look that said he'd known a few serious drunks.

They walked through the bat-wing doors and into a sudden silence—from what had been a tumultuous racket moments before.

Laggy appeared from the midst of what had been the hubbub. "What do you want here, Captain?" he demanded, with a nasty edge to his voice.

"Just pursuing my enquiries, Mr. Laguna," she said, evenly. "I have several lines of enquiry that lead me ... here."

"The girls weren't killed anywhere near here!" protested Slim. The crowd stirred like an angry beehive.

"No," said the captain, calmly, "but they all came *from* here. Unusual, I gather for them to even be out of your establishment—and it's only women from this place who've been attacked, even though there are others working the corridors and tunnels. I've seen them."

There was silence again. Some thoughtful looks.

"They were all lured out of here," Laggy insisted. "By that bat."

It was such a pity that he lacked the physique to have done the deed.

Laggy stuck his hand in his pocket. "I was just going to show the boys. I found this note from that bat in Cindy's things."

He pulled a piece of paper from his pocket and handed it to her. "That bat lured them out to their death," he said, as Rebecca untwisted the screw of paper.

"It sounds to me as if you have a grudge against the

council," said Abe evenly. "First the mayor and now Zed."

"It's obvious. They're in it together. They want to destroy my enterprise."

"Indade, not!" snapped the bat, fluttering out of an air-vent. "You're a blackhearted vile exploiter."

Laggy gaped at her. "I won't have any non-humans in my bar!" he snapped.

"No, you'll keep them as slaves and cleaners instead," hissed the bat.

Laggy went white. "I . . . I . . ." He fumbled for his flechette pistol.

"That's enough," said Rebecca. "I'll remove the bat once we have discussed a few matters. Firstly, would you like to clarify a few matters as concerns this wallet?"

"I heard that rat of his," said Laggy, pointing at the mayor, "tell that it was found under the body."

Act III, Scene III:
Enter the element of surprise, possibly not Watson, but Mercutio.

"I'faith you have mighty keen ears, to hear something I have not said," said Firkin loftily, from the air-vent. "I bite my thumb at you, Sirrah. But Cookie tells me that he found the wallet here. It was, as is the custom with such items, placed in the container on the bar."

There was a silence. Several people looked at the big glass jar on the end of the bar.

"Who are you going to believe? Me or some rat?" demanded Laguna.

"Knowing you, the rat, I reckon," said one wag, grinning.

"They're rogues and liars!" shouted the offended proprietor of the Last Chance saloon.

"Yes, I am," said Mercutio, appearing next to Firkin. "But who better to set to catch one?"

He leaped onto the table—a prodigious jump, but one he was easily capable of. "Attend!" he said to the crowd. "Methinks, you have reached several wrong conclusions. Firstly, you assumed that because the victim was robbed, robbery was part of the motive for the killing."

"But they *were* robbed. All of them," said Slim. "Are you trying to tell us they were robbed before they were attacked? I might believe that happened once . . ."

"The bodies were robbed after death. After they had been murdered. Not by the murderer."

"Who would do that kind of thing? Anyway, we found them," said Slim, waving at several friends of his in the crowd.

The rat reached into his pouch and flung a rather distinctive silver filigree hairgrip on the table. Several people plainly recognized it by the gasps. "Ah, but methinks you did not find them first. Ask then of the captain. What artifact did she find at the last murder?"

"A rat barrow," supplied the captain.

The rat nodded. "Rats move through the passages. They will loot. You all know that."

The crowd laughed.

"Indade. As it happens a rattess named Snout did find the last body. She did rob it. And she too has been killed," said the bat. "We seek her murderer."

"Who cares if another bloody rat is dead? They're scavengers and thieves. And what does it matter if they robbed the victims?" Laggy calmly reached for a bottle and began filling glasses, as if nothing could ever upset his equilibrium.

"Methinks it matters because if you are wrong about the sequence of events of one part of the crime, you could be wrong about another," said Mercutio.

"No way that they were raped by rats," said Slim dismissively, over the rim of his full glass. "Even if you all think you're hung like Errol Flynn."

Mercutio shook his head, looking thirstily at the glass. "'Tis true that most rats are destined to be hung. But it was not a rat that killed them."

"It was a bloody great rock that someone smashed their skulls with," supplied another drinker. "Too big for a rat."

"Indeed. And that too was not what killed them," said Mercutio, grimly.

Laggy laughed. "You might live on as a bit of head-plastic after your brain gets smashed in. But the rest of us would be dead," he said with a sneer.

"Oh, the rock would have killed them," said Mercutio, digging in his pouch again, and producing a small cellophane packet of white powder. "But this already had."

"What?" demanded Captain Wuollet.

Mercutio held the packet up. "This is what killed them. They were killed by the drug, the same one that killed Snout, when she tried to use what she'd stolen from the last victim. The rest was mere fakery to make it look like a crime of rapine. You did it." He pointed at Laggy.

The proprietor of the Last Chance laughed again. "Don't be ridiculous. Why would I kill them? Anyway, how can you prove it?"

"There was very little blood where we found the body," said the captain, quietly. "And head wounds bleed. You all know that. What you may not know is that dead bodies don't."

Mercutio nodded. "Anyway. We—Snout and I— saw and robbed the body. There was no mark on her. She had not been violated. We heard someone approach and ran off lest we be caught. Methinks, if you offer sufficient reward and impunity among the rats, the looters of the other bodies will come forward. But you may be certain that the last victim was killed *before* her skull was broken. You had it all backwards."

"Why didn't you tell someone?" demanded Captain Wuollet.

"And be blamed? 'Tis not our business."

"It's drivel," said Laguna. "I mean yes, maybe the dust did come from the women, and might have overdosed your rat. But look, what reason do I have for killing them? They're my business. They were raped and someone killed them to hide his ID. It had to be someone strong, that they knew or could recognize."

He pointed at Holmes. "Someone like him. There is no other motive."

Mercutio shook his head. "It is indeed a question of motive. But you have the motive. One of the women stumbled on your unpleasant secret, and thought she'd blackmail you. She threatened to tell Miz Zed. Even sent her a note. You killed her, and her friends, because, reviewing your disc of voyeurism, you saw that she'd talked." Mercutio reached into his pouch yet again, this time holding up a recording-minidisc. "I have it here."

"Give me that," yelled Laggy, his face ashen. "Thief!"

"At least he is just a thief, not a murderer and slave-holder," said the bat, grimly. "As you are. You also forgot that there was a witness. Or perhaps you thought you were safe as he was an alien who cannot speak English. You forgot that we too can speak Korozhet, although we choose not to."

Captain Wuollet held up her hand. "Stop right there. Mr. Laguna told me that he didn't speak Korozhet."

"That is correct," said Mercutio tugging his long whiskers. "Mr. Laguna does not. Unfortunately, Mr. Laguna is dead so what he speaks is of no matter."

"What?" said Abe, just seconds ahead of several others.

Mercutio held up his stubby paws. "'Tis, methinks, both simple and obvious." He pointed at the short, plump proprietor. "This is not Mr. Laguna."

Everybody still looked puzzled. "What?" said Slim finally. "This is my buddy, Honest . . ."

"No," said Mercutio, with the air of someone explaining to a simpleton—or a group of simpletons. "The man you call Honest Laguna is a former Korozhet slave who was found by the real Honest Laguna. Laguna was drunk, and trusting. This man—free now because the Korozhet had run off without their slaves—was found by the real Laguna. The slave he helped killed him, stole his clothes and possessions, including his still, and set up shop here. The act was witnessed by a fellow slave . . . one who is still here."

"What?"

"It would appear to me that their brains are stuck on that word," said Firkin. "Laggy here was a slave. He's got a few more slaves himself."

"But slaves are totally forbidden in human space," said the mayor.

"Methinks that you have a veritable nugget of fact there." Mercutio fluffed his whiskers. "One that is motive for murder. He has not told them they've been liberated. He uses them in his drug manufacturing process, and to run his stills." He gave his audience a ratty grin. "Just because you have been a slave yourself does not mean that you are a good man. According to Cookie, he was a Korozhet trusty. When the Korozhet fled . . . well, the two of them were found by Laguna, who was drunk. Laggy here was much the same size and build, and for reasons as yet unknown killed him."

"You've just got his crazy rat's word for all this," said Laggy, backing against the bar. "How could I kill the girls? I've got alibis for my time. He lies."

Mercutio regarded him askance. "We eat, perforce, rations. They are scarce, while the hydroponics are getting going. Methinks you will find scant witnesses to your presence during the dinner sittings." He pointed with a stubby pawhand to the door in the painted mural. "Let us look behind the door then and ask the others if I lie."

That gesture proved to be a mistake. All the eyes in the place followed, and people stopped looking, for an instant, at Laggy. Captain Wuollet was one of the first to realize it. And thus caught the full blinding force of the magnesium flare. And something hit her flak-jacket really hard.

● ● ●

There was, by the noise—she couldn't see anything—a lot of chaos. Which included things like "after the bastard," and "he went that-a-ways." It sounded like Laggy's well-oiled lynch mob was being put to excellent use, thought Rebecca, as she struggled to clear her vision.

By the time she could see again, Holmes had removed his large body from shielding his commanding officer. The bar was empty, with the exception of two rats, one with a large glass of cognac, and the other with her flouncy arms in the till, never mind her fingers. The bat was fluttering around the door in the wall-mural. And what was obviously a weird retinal after-burn shaped just like a cupcake was standing talking gibberish to the bat.

"What happened to the mayor and Abe?"

"The mayor was leading the pack. He might even stop it being an onsite lynching. And Abe was looking for some tools." Sergeant Holmes closed the cash-register and narrowly missed making Firkin a little short-handed.

She sniffed irritably at him, and showed teeth. "Spoilsport."

Abe returned with a small tool kit, and walked over to the mural door. Rebecca saw that the bat was pointing at some small holes she'd never noticed before. "At least you could help instead of indulging in petty larceny!"

Mercutio preened his whiskers. "I never indulge in petty larceny," he said loftily. "This is hundred year old cognac. And you know as well as I that Cookie told us that Laggy has somehow locked that one. Methinks it will take explosives."

Rebecca looked at the rat. "You have some explaining to do."

He cocked his head. "Is Mercutio headed for durance vile?"

"I'll settle for explanations," said Rebecca. "And a glass of that loot. This time. If you stop Firkin trying to open the till again."

Firkin sat down on the bar and pulled a bottle out of her sleeve and drank some of the amber fluid in it. She looked at Mercutio very intently as she did it.

"Art sure you would not have a stoup of this stuff?" he asked.

"Methinks I will stick to my own brew," said the rattess. There seemed to be a hint of menace in that statement, although Rebecca could not put her finger on just why.

"I think," said Mercutio, "That the largest part of my explanation is that things are not always quite what they seem by first appearance. And if you can see motive... the picture gets clearer."

"I'm still faint but pursuing as to what the picture actually is, and just how he was able to do it." Rebecca took the cognac from the faintly sinister rat. "I assume you found the motive on the disc."

Mercutio shook his head. "I did but deduce it. I know not what is on that disc. Probably the rutting of some miners and one of wenches. There must a hundred of them in his room. I guessed what his reaction would be. I was right."

"Methinks they have great resale value," said Firkin, snatching it up and dancing away.

"I'll resell you," said Rebecca. "Give it back."

"No wonder no one likes the constabulary," said Firkin,

tossing it down. "So explain, Mercutio. How then did little Laggy kill the girls, if we grant him the motive?"

Mercutio savored the cognac. "It was a matter of arranging a rendezvous and waiting for the drug to kill them. The note, methinks you will find came from him, not the claw of Zed. I hath seen her script, which the girls had not. I caught a bare glimpse of the note when Laggy gave it to you, but it was neat and handwritten. Wingclaws or feet do a poor job of writing. Zed uses an electronic scripter, even for her picket signs. Did the note offer a great deal of money perchance?"

"Yes," admitted Rebecca. He was too astute for his own good, this rat.

"So that is how he killed them," said Holmes. "But how did he move them then. Mister rat?"

Mercutio shrugged. "He has a vehicle, and he repairs it. I think you'll find he has a slider. Look carefully in the tunnel on the sides and you may see the tracks . . ."

"But we did. For the barrow," said Holmes, shaking his head.

"With a narrow torch beam," said Firkin. "I was there, I saw you do it. The tracks will be on the edges of the tunnel if they are there at all . . . not where a barrow would leave them, which was what you looked for."

Holmes shook his head again. "God, what a sick bastard. You think he . . ."

It wasn't something Rebecca wanted to think about, either. "Without a forensic expert we won't know. I suspect he found the first body had been robbed, when he went to hide it, and saw a bright way of getting someone else to take the blame."

"We'll ask him, very politely, of course," said Holmes. "When I examine his mind. If they haven't killed him."

Firkin snorted. "They'll not catch him."

"Then I will," said Rebecca, grimly.

"Or the rats will find him. For a fee, of course," said Mercutio.

"Got it!" said Abe. The painted door in the mural swung open to reveal a room full of lab paraphernalia, and a still. And three terrified looking aliens. Of course, expressions could be hard to read accurately on alien faces. But the cowering wasn't. Cowering crossed the species and interplanetary divide.

Maybe the easy answer was just to pay the rats to bring the bastard in dead, thought Rebecca grimly. She turned to Mercutio. "I'm thinking of giving you a job in the police force."

Mercutio seemed distinctly unwell, and looked around hastily for an exit. "Me? Art diseased in thy mind? My reputation, Iago . . ."

...AND MORE

Author's note:

I got to know Mike Resnick while I was editing Jim Baen's Universe *magazine*, whose first issue came out in June of 2006. Very soon after we launched the magazine, Mike submitted a story titled "All the Things You Are." In his accompanying email, he said he thought the story had a real shot at getting nominated for a Hugo Award.

I knew who Mike was, of course, but we'd never met or had any interaction prior to that moment. I sent him a reply saying that if he thought he had a shot at a Hugo with the story he ought to send it to one of the prestigious magazines like Asimov's or Analog or *the* Mag of F&SF. I told Mike there was no way a newly-launched electronic magazine coming out of Baen Books was likely to have the chops to get one of its stories considered for a Hugo.

(Yes, there's a pecking order when it comes to which venues are more likely to get awards. Yes, there's a lot of politicking around literary awards. If you are shocked by discovering either of these things you have either been living in a fool's paradise all your life or—sorry you had to hear it from me—you're really not too bright.)

Mike's reply, stripped to its essentials, was: "Screw that. You guys pay better'n anyone else."

Thus was born a friendship which has lasted all the years since—better than a decade now, and still counting—and wound up with the two of us collaborating on a lot of things. Mike eventually became my coeditor on Jim Baen's Universe, *we also coedited an anthology of short stories titled* The Dragon Done It, *we're both judges in the Writers of the Future Contest, and we recently had a novel published by Baen Books titled* The Gods of Sagittarius.

But the first thing we ever did together was write this story. Not long after I bought Mike's story "All the Things You Are," he sent me an email saying that Pyr Books was willing to commission us to write a story for their upcoming anthology, Sideways in Crime. Would I be interested?

Sure, I said. And then . . . forgot all about it.

Some time later, Mike sent me another email reminding me that we had to turn the story in to the publisher. . . . Well, in about three days. And I was leaving on a trip abroad in . . . two days.

So I told him I'd write the first half of the story that night and send it to him by the morning. It was up to him to finish it because I was going to be in the southern hemisphere. But I told him not to worry because I'd put everything in the story including the kitchen sink so he'd have plenty to work with.

Which, I did. And, finish it he did. On time.

The result is before you. I hope you enjoy reading it as much as I enjoyed writing the first half and reading the second half after I got back from New Zealand and Australia.

Conspiracies:
A Very Condensed 937-Page Novel

by Mike Resnick and Eric Flint

PROLOGUE

If you go to the northern end of Praslin Island in the
Seychelles, a thousand miles off the coast of East Africa,
there's every likelihood that you'll chance upon a pudgy,
gray-haired man holding a cigar in one hand and a cold
drink in the other. You can nod a greeting to him, but if
you try to start up a conversation, you may find yourself
spending the next few years in a jail on Mahe, the main
island in the chain.

So we figure it's our job to tell you who he is and what
he's doing there.

1

"It was a dark and stormy night."

The alien lapsed into silence, thereafter. It seemed

sullen and brooding, simply staring at a blank wall of the chamber with its peculiarly small eyes.

After a while, Fuyd turned to the interrogator. "What is the meaning of 'stormy'? I thought it referred to a tempest."

"It does, more or less."

Fuyd looked back at the lumpy, ugly creature. "That makes no sense at all. How can the simple effect of a planet's rotation be tempestuous?"

The interrogator rippled its neck in the manner by which his species indicated uncertainty. Fuyd found the gesture vaguely unsettling. But then, she found much about the gnuzzit unsettling. It didn't help that their names were unpronounceable by her species. By any other species, actually.

"This human seems prone to obfuscation, Mistress Fuyd. Very little that it tells us seems to convey any sensible meaning."

"Try again," Fuyd commanded. "More severely."

The gnuzzit interrogator joggled a lever. The torture device's arm stretched out and began twisting the slender body parts growing out of the human's head. Some sort of feeding cilia, obviously. The pattern was not an uncommon one. They would be acutely sensitive to pain.

The brutish creature's eyes seemed to narrow. Other than that . . .

Nothing.

Quite an astonishing pain threshold. Fuyd was tempted to order an anatomical analysis of the monster, on the remote chance its body type was unique among its species. But that would be in clear contravention to the Drasspunt Accord, and the matter simply wasn't important enough to risk an altercation with the liucuz, and certainly not with the always-belligerent jatts.

Frustrated, she leaned forward and hissed at the creature. "Why did you murder the first Kennedy one? Did the jatts pay you to do so?"

They were the most likely culprits. The liucuz and the kly—not to mention the miserable flappa—were equally aggressive players of the Great Game, but were not prone to such crude and direct methods.

The human creature answered. But, again, the reply made no sense.

"Snoopy's on the doghouse and his bowl is empty."

Other than the term "Snoopy"—perhaps it was a name—all of the words were recognizable, even the peculiar "dog house" with its odd connotations. But the statement as a whole conveyed no sensible meaning.

"Perhaps," suggested the gnuzzit, "it is implicating the first Kennedy's spouse. 'On the doghouse' might be a reference to marital tensions. Perhaps she was his direct employer, recruited by the jatts because of her animosity and acting on their behalf."

Fuyd considered the scenario. Unlikely, but . . .

There was no reason not to investigate. The Drasspunt Accord carried no prohibition against testing for trace elements. Not even the excessively legalistic tlatla advanced such a claim. Naturally, there was no prohibition against violating the quaint customs and taboos of playee species. Their anatomies could not be probed, but their reliquaries could.

"Disinter the first Kennedy spouse and examine the corpse for trace elements of our opponents."

2

The newly-elected President of the United States had expected any number of surprises once he assumed office. He'd even made a joke to his wife that maybe he'd finally know the truth about Roswell and Area 51.

It had been a *joke*.

He stared at the national security adviser—not *the* National Security Adviser, who was just as new as he was to her post and whose eyes were as round with surprise as his own—but at the wrinkled little man who seemed to be at least eighty years old and was apparently the official keeper of the nation's deepest secrets. His name was H. Saddler. Just "H." It seemed that not even the President of the U.S. was cleared to know his first name. Nor his actual title.

"Do you mean to tell me," the President said, managing not to splutter outright, "that *we* abducted Jimmy Hoffa?"

The little old man seemed to wince. At least, two or three more wrinkles appeared on his face.

"Please, Mr. President. *We* did not abduct Hoffa. The aliens did. We simply fingered him to them. On account of the Kennedy assassination and what he might know about it which we'd just as soon he didn't talk about."

"Which might be *what*?" demanded Janet Dailey, the new NSA. "You told us not more than an hour ago that the nation's security specialists were certain there was no conspiracy to assassinate John Kennedy."

"There wasn't," came the firm reply. "Lee Harvey

Oswald acted on his own, sure enough. But there were a lot of conspiracies *around* the whole JFK business, if you know what I mean. Most of which involved us versus the Cubans—very delicate stuff, you understand—and it's almost certain Hoffa had his thumb in at least one of them." The old man's expression grew pious. "Being as how he had it in for Mr. Kennedy on account of him being a crook and the Kennedys being the bane of his life. That's why Robert Kennedy got assassinated, we're pretty sure."

The President thought his head might start spinning. "*Hoffa* ordered RFK murdered? Sirhan Sirhan was supposed to have been acting alone also."

"Well, sure, he was. Guy was a complete fruitcake. And I didn't say Jimmy Hoffa did it. Would have been a neat trick, since he was still in prison at the time. What I meant was that we're almost certain Sirhan Sirhan was abducted and brainwashed by the aliens—a different set, we think—so that by killing Robert Kennedy they could cast suspicion on Jimmy Hoffa."

Now, the President's head *did* feel like it was spinning.

"That makes no sense at all, Mr. Saddler," protested the National Security Adviser.

"I know that, Ms. Dailey." The old man's tone was lugubrious. "They're *aliens*, like I said. We're not sure if they're actually stupid or just barking mad. I'm inclined to the latter suspicion myself, seeing as how the whole thing apparently started with the Lincoln assassination, 'way back a hundred and fifty years ago."

"*Lincoln* was assassinated by aliens?"

"No, ma'am." Saddler gave her a reproachful look. "Abraham Lincoln was assassinated by John Wilkes

Booth. Everyone knows that. But after what happened at Roswell—that's tomorrow's briefing—"

"I can't wait," muttered the President.

"—we got suspicious about some of the inconsistencies and ordered the disinterment of Edwin Booth's body from where it was buried in Massachusetts, as well as all of his relatives that we could find." Somehow, the pattern of wrinkles exuded triumph. "Sure enough. John Wilkes Booth's older brother was not human. Close, mind you, but no cigar. The body had too many bones in the feet. Which means he wasn't actually his brother at all."

The President and the NSA stared at Saddler. The old man shrugged. "We don't think the older Booth brother himself—or *it*self, maybe—had anything to do with the Lincoln assassination. Which, like I said, we don't actually have any suspicions was anything other than it looked to be. But we're now dead certain that Edwin Booth— maybe his alien confederates—must have brooded about the matter afterward. And that's why they assassinated Garfield and McKinley."

"You're referring to *Presidents* Garfield and McKinley," said Janet Dailey. Her voice sounded a little feeble.

"Well, sure. Garfield the cat's still alive and he isn't real anyway. We're not positive about the Garfield business, I need to add by way of caution, on account of the only parts of his assassin Guiteau's body we could get hold of were his skeleton, brain and spleen. They kept them in a jar, so to speak, at the museum at Walter Reed hospital. The spleen's suspiciously large, but that's not much to go on. There's no question about the McKinley assassination, though. First, because Leon Frank Czolgosz—he was the assassin—was just about the silliest caricature of an anarchist you can imagine. He actually voted Republican! The stated motive didn't make any sense at all."

Apparently, unlike the President himself, Ms. Dailey was beginning to make sense out of this lunacy. "Another case of alien abduction and brain-washing, you're saying?"

Mr. Saddler smiled at her approvingly. "Yes, ma'am. It's obvious. Sulfuric acid and lye were thrown into his coffin, you know, and all of his possessions were burned. Letters, clothes, the lot. There's only one logical reason to do that: Cover up the evidence."

Forcibly, the President reminded himself that he had been elected not only by a landslide in the electoral college but by almost 56% of the popular vote. Leadership was called for here.

"You're contradicting yourself, Mr. Saddler," he said sternly, trying to sound as if he were following the logic instead of thinking he'd fallen into a rabbit hole. "If Cholo—whatever his name was—had to have his body destroyed, then presumably he was an alien himself. Not an—ah—*abductee*."

Saddler went back to his lugubrious head-shaking. "No, sir. They would have destroyed the body and the possessions to eliminate any traces of their own DNA— or whatever they have instead of DNA. Like with the feet, it's close but no cigar. In fact, we're almost sure there are at least three species of aliens involved, from the stuff we found at the Roswell crash. From the sets of almost-like-DNA traces, you understand. As I'll explain tomorrow. Well, tomorrow and the day afterward. It's pretty complicated stuff."

The President and the NSA stared at him again. Eventually, the President said: "This is sheer lunacy."

Mr. Saddler nodded his head. "That's what the Rand people think. The gist of every one of their analyses is that all these aliens are just plain bonkers. I have to admit there are times I almost think they're right, especially when I go back over the Alydar case. Can't call it a murder, of course."

Seeing the blank look on the President's face, he added: "Alydar was a race horse, Mr. President. Pretty famous one, if you're a racing fan. He got euthanized after breaking his leg twice in a stall when he was the leading sire in the country. Foul play was suspected on account of the insurance involved—there was a tidy $45 million pay-out, and eventually there was even a conviction. But we dug up the carcass and, once again, there are just too many damn bones. But why would aliens kill a horse, unless they were simply insane?"

"This is *all* 'simply insane,'" snarled the President. "Mr. Saddler, I have to tell you—"

There was an interruption, as one of the President's staff entered the Oval Office.

"Excuse me, Mr. President," Raul Sanchez said apologetically. "This isn't normally something I imagine you'd—well—"

The young man seemed nonplussed. That wasn't perhaps surprising since he was just as new to his post as almost everyone in the White House, starting with the President himself. Sanchez didn't really have any more of an idea what was "normally something" than anyone else.

"Well," he concluded diffidently, "I thought you'd want to see it anyway."

He laid the newspaper he was holding down on the desk, the front page facing up.

It was the morning edition of *The Washington Post*. The President stared down at the blaring headline.

JACKIE O'S GRAVE DESECRATED
President Kennedy's grave left untouched by vandals

Mr. Saddler rose from his chair just enough to read the title. Then, looking very self-satisfied, he slouched back into it. "Like I said, Mr. President."

3

"In other words, you got no rights at all."

The gnuzzit interrogator wriggled its neck. "What are 'rights,' Master Hoffa?"

The squat little human shook its head. "Just call me Jimmy, willya? I'm a labor man. Can't organize your way out of a paper bag, you insist on formalities."

The Hoffa human reached up and scratched its head. It could do that because after Mistress Fuyd had left the chamber, the gnuzzit had released the shackles on the human's upper limbs.

Dubiously, the interrogator eyed the head-scratching. The cilia were being given a treatment almost as rough as they'd gotten from the torture device.

"That is not painful?"

"Meaning no offense, Jock, but you guys aren't exactly the sharpest pencils in the box. That includes Missus

Toadstool."

The phrase about pencils made little sense. Neither did the cognomen "Jock," which was not even an approximation of the interrogator's name. But the gnuzzit had come to understand by now that the Hoffa human was two things.

First, it was peculiar. Second, it was extremely intelligent. Much more so than the interrogator, and certainly more so than Mistress Fuyd.

So, the Hoffa human was worth listening to. The gnuzzit was still puzzled by "rights," but it had no trouble at all understanding the concept of "grievances," which Hoffa had introduced the first time Mistress Fuyd left the interrogation chamber.

"So, if I've got this right, if you guys tried to fight for a decent contract, the other side would just refuse to negotiate."

"What is 'negotiate'?" asked the gnuzzit. "Whatever it is, the bluipta don't do it. Neither do the jatts or the liucuz or the kly or the flappa. Not even the fussy tlatla. If any of the servant species fail to perform as expected, any of the master species will have the offender exterminated."

"Right." Hoffa lowered its hand. The creature's thick chest rose and fell in a peculiar manner the gnuzzit had noticed before. It was more pronounced than the human's regular breathing. Perhaps that indicated frustration or aggravation. It was hard to know, of course, with such a bizarre lifeform. The gnuzzit still found it upsetting to watch the creature move about on only two legs.

"Right," the human repeated. "So we gotta start with the ABCs. Damn, I wish you'd snatched Farrell Dobbs too. I never held with his commie ideas, but he'd sure be handy in this situation. Guy knew his stuff."

"What is 'commie'?" asked the gnuzzit.

For the first time since he'd met the human, Hoffa's face expressed something other than stolidity. It would have been extremely alarming, actually, except the teeth displayed were so blunt.

"You are," said the human, its voice seeming to gurgle a bit. "Regular Bolshies, all of you downtrodden gnuzzit, starting from this moment forward."

"What is 'regular Bolsh—'?"

"We'll get to that," interrupted Hoffa. "First, I gotta explain some of the basic ingredients. We'll start with 'general strike.' Then we'll move on to 'insurrection.'"

4

As he always did when he came into Roswell, Ken Phipps grinned at the sign just outside the town limits. The Chamber of Commerce put up the billboards, in a feeble attempt to maintain a semblance of respectability.

WELCOME TO ROSWELL!
Dairy Capital of the Southwest

Ken drove past the billboard, looking for the first signs of the town's true principal industry. They started appearing almost immediately. Every other storefront, one way or another, was hawking something related to aliens. The pious and stodgy Chamber of Commerce notwithstanding, Roswell's real business was milking tourists, not cows. If he didn't know better, Ken would have suspected the whole thing was a hoax invented by some of the town's more ingenious inhabitants.

As he usually did unless he was in a real hurry, Ken stopped for lunch at the big restaurant located at the town's main intersection. The Cover-Up Café, that was, whose menu was a faithful reflection of the name. Beneath the clever plays on aliens and cover-ups, of course, the food just amounted to the standard burger-and-fries fare one found in any small American town. Still, it tickled Ken's fancy.

After paying the bill and leaving a generous tip, he wandered down Main Street, window-shopping as if he were any tourist. Eventually, satisfied that no one was following him, he slipped into one of the more nondescript gift shops on the street.

"Hi, Jock," he said to the proprietor, who was sitting on a stool behind the cash register. "How's tricks?"

The proprietor frowned—tried to, anyway; he still didn't really have the expression right. "I do not understand the relevance of 'tricks' to the question. And my name is not Jock, as you know."

There was no heat to the complaint. This was an old routine, by now. Ken simply shrugged.

"Nobody can pronounce your name. And that means *nobody*, according to you."

"We are a much oppressed people," said the proprietor sullenly. For a moment, he lost control and his neck did a little wriggle that would have instantly alerted anyone not in the know that this was no human being in front of them.

"Yeah, that's what they all say," replied Ken. "Life's hard and all that. Mr. Henderson still wants to know why you're short-changing him." He mustered his best gangster glower—which was in fact very good. Given that he was a no-fooling gangster, that was hardly surprising.

The gnuzzit managed an actual sneer. Ken was impressed.

"Fucking coyotes." The alien had mastered essential gerunds and participles early on in their acquaintance. "We have decided to discontinue paying Mr. Henderson his smuggling fees. They are unconscionably high. Besides, we have decided to adopt a different course of action."

Ken's sneer was way better, of course. "'Unconscionably,' no less. Listen, snake neck. It costs money to smuggle aliens into the United States, especially no-fooling alien aliens. Mr. Henderson even provides them with jobs."

"Washing dishes. Making beds. Mowing grass."

Ken shrugged. "You got no other skills. Other than running spaceships and things like that that don't exist here. Whaddaya expect?"

The store proprietor—which he was, too; even legitimately—pushed a button on the cash register. A little chime sounded.

Stalling for time, obviously. Ken did his best gangster threatening hunch, which was every bit as good as his glower. "And enough already. I'm warning you, Jock, Mr. Henderson's not a man to waste time arguing. He'll just—"

He felt himself seized, as if by a giant pair of hands, then lifted into midair.

"Hey! What are you up to?" He twisted his neck, but couldn't see anyone behind him.

"You are being abducted," said the gnuzzit. "The man wants to talk to you."

5

"You can't be Jimmy Hoffa," Ken protested. "You disappeared more'n thirty years ago—and you wasn't no spring chicken then. You'd have to be . . . jeez. . . ."

"What's the date?" asked the square-headed man sitting across from Ken at what seemed like a table except Ken couldn't see any legs holding it up.

The man *did* look like Jimmy Hoffa, from a few photos Ken remembered.

"What's the date?" the man repeated.

"Uh . . . Well, I don't know how much time passed since they . . . uh . . ."

"The *date*, asshole!"

Now he really did look like Hoffa. *The* Hoffa.

"It was August 2 on Thursday."

"What year?"

"Huh?"

"Jesus, they snatched me a dimwit," muttered Hoffa to himself. "I told 'em I needed muscle, but I didn't mean between the ears."

Ken wasn't even offended, for some reason. "2007."

Hoffa nodded. "I was born in 1913. February 14, Valentine's Day. Means I'd be ninety-four and a half years old." He grinned, very coldly. "Funny how time flies. Last time I looked in a mirror—which they ain't got on this ship—I didn't look a day over sixty."

Ken stared at him. The truth was, Hoffa *didn't* look much over sixty.

The burly labor leader—ex–labor leader?—shrugged. "What I can tell, the way these alien ships move around, there's some kind of time tricks involved. I think Einstein explained it once."

Actually, Ken had some serious problems with the Special Theory of Relativity, but nobody wanted a hit man who could quote Shakespeare and argue quantum mechanics, so he put on his most thuggish expression and tried to remember not to use any three-syllable words.

"So, okay. What do you want, Mr. Hoffa?"

Finally, there came a smile. "Call me Jimmy, why dontcha? Never been much of one for formalities."

6

"And you're Kenny, right?" continued Hoffa, making an easy transition from the previous chapter.

"Kenneth, actually."

"Kenny, right," repeated Hoffa. "And you were brought here by a guzzler."

"A gnuzzit," Ken corrected him.

"Yeah, a guzzler," agreed Hoffa. "Stupid race, even for godless aliens."

"You believe in God, Mr. . . . . Jimmy?"

"Fucking-A right I do!" said Hoffa firmly. "But you could fill a book with what God doesn't know about organizing." Suddenly he smiled. "In fact, I think someone has. Called *The Capital*."

"You mean *Das Kapital*?"

"Yeah, that's what I said. Anyway, we got us some work to do, you and me, kid."

It had been a long time since anyone had called Ken a kid, but he decided not to mention it. Even up here, you didn't mess around with Jimmy Hoffa.

"So what, exactly, am I here for?"

Hoffa stared at him. Ken felt like the burly man was staring *through* him.

"Why dontcha ask what you really want to know?"

"I beg your pardon?" said Ken.

"Don't," admonished Hoffa. "It's a sign of weakness. Now ask."

"Okay," said Ken. "What does the job pay?"

Hoffa grinned. "That's more like it."

Ken waited a moment, then said, "Well?"

"Quiet, Kenny. I'm doing the math." Hoffa closed his eyes, frowned, moved his lips almost imperceptibly, and then looked at Ken. "Here's the deal. First, you get to live."

"Was that ever in doubt?" asked Ken, suddenly nervous.

"Don't interrupt. Second, you get five percent of my rake-off." A brief pause. "Ah, hell—make that seven percent. You're probably the only human-type person I'm going to be dealing with. And third, when we're done, I'll give you a planet of your own. You can be King of the kbajics, or Muscha-Muscha of the silky spaxxora." Hoffa leaned forward. "What do you say, Kenny?"

"My own planet?"

"Your own planet," replied Hoffa. "Of course, you'll have to pay your annual dues to the Brotherhood."

"What Brotherhood?" asked Ken.

"The one you're here to help me organize," answered Hoffa. "The United Brotherhood of Godless Alien Scum."

"It needs a more dignified name," suggested Ken. "Sir," he added quickly.

Hoffa frowned. "You really think so?"

"Absolutely."

"Maybe you got a point, Kenny." A thoughtful pause. "How about the Federated League of Godless Alien Heathen?"

7

In Chapter 7 Ken stumbles into an orgy involving a jatt, three flappas, a kly, a fussy tlatla, an underage gnuzzit, two liucuz of the Southern variety, and Paris Hilton. It breaks the tension and serves as comic relief, as everyone knows you need at least five flappas—one of each gender—for any kind of sexual encounter at all, but since it would take fourteen pages to set up the scene, even in this condensed form, we elected to leave it to the reader's—and Ken's—imagination.

8

"He's up to something, that much seems clear," said the gnuzzit.

"How can he be?" replied Mistress Fuyd. "I mean, after all, he's our prisoner, isn't he? At this point in the interrogation, he should be a pushover."

"The Kennedy creature thought he was a pushover too," remarked the gnuzzit.

"Which Kennedy creature was that?"

"The one with too much hair who couldn't keep his hands off females."

"Oh," she said, ashamed of her ignorance. "*That* one. Of course."

"I wonder why the Hoffa requested this other human, this Ken thing?" continued the gnuzzit. "He seems obsequious, yet we know from our background check that there is no crime of which he is not guilty, possibly excepting bestiality."

"Possibly?"

"You didn't see his last bedmate," answered the gnuzzit.

"What do we propose to do about him—or is it *them*?"

"We'll keep a watchful four or five eyes on Hoffa, and if he tries anything deleterious to the ship or those aboard it, we'll torture him."

"That could be fun," she said. Then she frowned—as much as an animated Fig Newton *can* frown—and said: "We'll have to apply new methods. Cutting the cilia from his head and chin elicited no reaction whatsoever."

"I know," answered the gnuzzit. "But I've been observing him carefully. Have you seen those hardened protrusions at the end of his mandibles—you know, the ten manipulative tentacles? I may just take something sharp and cut off a sixteenth of an inch or so. *That* will have him screaming in agony."

"Can I watch?" asked Mistress Fuyd eagerly.

9

"Now, you got that straight, Kenny?" said Hoffa.

"I contact all the gnuzzits and wichtigos . . ."

"All the gonzos and witches, right."

"And I tell them that if they're tired of working long hours for short pay and taking orders from the bluiptas and the rest of them, they should meet in your room after dark."

"You left out the part about owning a full and equal share of the ship, a percentage of all the trade with Earth, and regaining their self-respect and being able to walk with their heads held high."

"Jimmy, have you gotten a good look at the wichtigos? Both of their heads are on top of their feet. You get one of them to walk with his head held high and it means he's been decapitated."

"So think of something else to say. Don't hassle me with details, Kenny. I've got my eye on the big picture."

"Well, there's one more detail I have to bring up," said Ken.

"Yeah? What?"

"You want everyone to meet in your room after dark."

"That's what I said."

"Yeah, well, where we are, it's been after dark for ten billion years, give or take a month."

Hoffa looked out a viewport. "Okay," he said. "When you're right, you're right." His expression became threatening. "Don't be right around me too often, unless you're agreeing with me. Got it, kid?"

"Got it." Ken paused. "So when should I tell them to show up?"

Hoffa pondered the question for a moment. "Tell them to show up when they're sick of things as they are, and want their rights, their self-respect, and especially a sizeable piece of the action. Then stand aside so you don't get trampled."

"They're aliens, Jimmy," said Ken. "Do they *care* about that stuff?"

"Kid, there are three truisms in the universe. Two of them have to do with women. This is the third. Trust old Jimmy on this."

Ken had planned to tell every member of the crew below the rank of *quaslodit*. But after he told the first dozen aliens he met, he had to flatten himself against a bulkhead to avoid the mad dash to Jimmy Hoffa's room.

10

"Do you really think it'll work?" asked Mistress Fuyd.

"It worked every time I tried it back home," said Hoffa. "Maybe the bliptas and the floppies and them others call the shots, but *you* carry the mail."

"All of our mail is electronic," the gnuzzit pointed out.

"Don't interrupt," said Hoffa. "Like I said, you carry the cargo—even if the cargo is nothing but a bunch of bloodthirsty gnuzzit and wichtigo scum, meaning no offense. If you go on strike, commerce and conquest both come to a stop. The wheels don't roll."

"We don't have wheels," pointed out another gnuzzit.

"Shut up," said Hoffa. "The wheels don't roll, the wings don't flap, the nuclears don't pile. Choose whatever fits."

"What do we do when the bluipta or the fussy tlatla come after us with a punishment party?" asked Mistress Fuyd.

"How are they gonna get here? You control the ships. You control the gas pumps."

"We don't use gas."

"Okay, you control the plutonium pumps. Don't hassle me with details." He looked around the room. "Think about it. How are they going to *make* you go to work?"

"They'll threaten to torture and kill us," answered the gnuzzit.

"See?" said Hoffa with a triumphant smile. "A dead man can't fly a ship! You've won already."

"So they'll stick to torture," said the gnuzzit.

"How are you gonna read a chart if they gouge out your eyes? If they cut off all your hands, do they think you're going to push all these little buttons with your nose?"

"Actually, we could," said another gnuzzit.

"That's defeatist talk!" snapped Hoffa. "I'm telling you, we can bring the galaxy to a standstill. Maybe even the whole solar system."

"Somehow I think there must be more to it than just killing our engines and demanding better treatment."

"Right," agreed Hoffa. "The very first thing we need is a pension fund. Since none of you have had any experience in that area, I'll take the job myself, onerous as it is." He paused once more. "All right," he continued. "Now it's time to elect a leader, someone who will call the shots. I modestly put myself forth as a candidate. Are there any others?"

One of the wichtigos seemed about to step forward. Ken immediately walked over to it and let it see that his hand was gripping the hilt of a knife he had in his pocket.

"None?" said Hoffa. "Then I guess I'm elected."

"And you're *sure* that a general strike always succeeds?" asked Mistress Fuyd.

"Always."

"And unions are always successful?"

"Every single time," answered Hoffa.

"I have checked your record," said Mistress Fuyd, "and your own race incarcerated you."

"Pure jealousy," answered Hoffa. "And if you checked *all* the records, you'll see that the Teamsters continued to run even while I was in stir. *That's* why I offered to be your leader. I'll take the heat, and you'll keep on truckin'. Or jettin'. Or whatever."

A wichtigo stepped forward. "Why are you here at all?" it asked. "Why aren't you back on Earth, organizing strikes and pension funds and whatever else it is that you do?"

"You want the truth?" asked Hoffa.

"Please."

"I'm a modest man, and I was so popular people wouldn't leave me alone. Gorgeous oversexed women kept breaking into my house to thank me for helping them obtain full dental care. Politicians from both parties kept asking me to run for President. *Fortune* and *Business Week* were always after me for interviews, and *The Christian Science Monitor* wanted me to write a daily column on the strong moral code that led me to become such a successful man of the people." He paused and shrugged. "What could I do? They had become too dependent upon me. So I faked my own death, took just enough money from the pension fund to meet my modest needs, and I was leading a humble incognito life under an assumed name in the Presidential suite of the Hong Kong Hilton when one of your gonzos—"

"Gnuzzits."

"Gezundheit," said Hoffa. "Anyone, a gonzo snatched me and brought me up here."

"And all that is absolutely true?" said the wichtigo dubiously.

"As God is my witness," said Hoffa, holding his right hand up.

"I guess we'll take your word for it," said the wichtigo. "For now."

"You don't take anything at face value," said Hoffa. "I like that in a man— or a whatever-you-are. You got a name, son?"

"Mercortule."

"I'll remember it," promised Hoffa. "Anyway, I think this has been a successful first meeting. My vice chairman Kenny here will let you know when we're having the next one. But I got a good feeling about this. I wouldn't want to be a floppy stockbroker a month from now."

"Flappa," Mistress Fuyd corrected him.

"Flappa to you, too," said Hoffa, shaking what passed for her hand. "Thank you all for coming." After they had filed out, Ken approached Hoffa.

"So you faked your death!" he said. "Everyone always wondered."

"The feds wanted me dead, the Mafia wanted me dead, even the Teamsters wanted me dead. I figured the only way I was gonna survive my murder was if I committed it myself." He looked around to make sure the room was empty. "Now to business. You know that little bastard, Mercantile?"

"You mean Mercortule?"

Hoffa nodded. "When everyone's asleep, find an airlock and put him in orbit." He grimaced. "If there's one thing I hate, it's a lippy alien."

11

It took seven months for the Brotherhood of Enlightened Aliens to bring the galactic economy to a screeching halt.

It took two weeks of negotiations before the races that ruled the Sevagram, or at least the Spiral Arm of the Milky Way, agreed to supply medical and dental care to the gnuzzits, the wichtigos, and the other oppressed races of the sector, as well as vacation time, sick leave, personal days, profit sharing, and 401Ks. They dug their heels in—not that any of them actually *had* any heels—at committing never to deal with a non-union shop, especially since there was only one union, but after another general strike they capitulated.

Things went swimmingly—which is probably a poor way of stating it, since there were a lot of things in the galaxy, and many of them spent their entire lives immersed in water or more noxious liquids, coming to the surface only to chat with fishermen, sing folk songs, and sign up for the union. Let us say, then, that things went smoothly—yes, that's the word: smoothly—for the better part of a year. Everyone, even the toothless raxiia, received dental care; everyone, even the muskagogees, who laid four thousand eggs a month, got paternity leave. Everyone worked, everyone got a handsome pay raise, everyone looked forward to a retirement in which every need was taken care of thanks to astute management of the union's assets.

And then one day the pension fund was gone, and so was Jimmy Hoffa.

12

The President followed H. Saddler into the small fourth-floor room in the Executive Office Building. It was 4:05 AM, and there was no one there except a lone guard who was totally loyal, to Saddler if not the President. Even the Secret Service had been ordered to remain in the underground passageway leading to the White House.

"Are you sure this is necessary?" asked the President.

"Mr. President, it is more than necessary. It is essential. Even if you weren't at a twenty-three percent approval rating in the polls, this is an opportunity you can't pass up."

"It's not my fault!" muttered the President. "Paraguay and Uruguay sound so much alike! Someone should have corrected me when I gave the order to attack."

"That's in the past," said Saddler. "As is Uruguay, alas. But what you're doing now will make you the most important President since—"

"Truman?" interrupted the President hopefully.

"Think bigger."

"The Roosevelts?"

"Bigger still."

"Honest Abe himself?"

Saddler nodded.

"And you're saying this one meeting will accomplish that?"

"This one meeting will be the first step in accomplishing that."

"And how did you hear about this, Mr. Saddler?" asked the President. He wanted to be informal, to call the man by his first name, but he didn't know his first name, and it seemed awkward to just called him "H".

"I have my sources." Saddler looked at his wristwatch. "He's due here any minute."

"It occurs to me that the guards will never let him in."

"Then it's fortunate that I sent them all home, isn't it?"

"But . . . but what if some thief sneaks into the building while they're gone?"

Saddler smiled. "This is the Executive Office Building, Mr. President. You don't really think there's anything worth stealing here, do you?"

The President considered it. "No, I suppose not."

"When you get right down to it, the most valuable thing here is a list of the better escort services in Washington DC—and even if someone steals a copy, there are 400 more in the building."

There was a knock at the door.

"Come in," said Saddler.

Jimmy Hoffa entered the room, peering into the

darkened corners to make sure no one besides Saddler and the President was there.

"Mr. President, say hello to Mr. Hoffa."

"*The* Mr. Hoffa?" asked the President.

"Call me Jimmy," said Hoffa, pulling up a chair.

"Mr. Hoffa has a proposition that I think will meet with your approval, sir," said Saddler. "Jimmy?"

"Right," said Hoffa. "I've spent the last few years . . . well, *elsewhere*. And in the process I learned a lot of things that affect the security of the United States, which I love as if it was my own country."

"It *is* your own country," said the President.

"Don't interrupt," said Hoffa. "Anyway, I had to leave my last position in a hurry, and I have reason to believe some of my former associates are gunning for me—especially one called Kenny."

"Should I know why?" asked the President.

"It's not important," said Saddler. "Go on, Jimmy."

"Anyway, I didn't come back empty-handed," said Hoffa. "I'm prepared to make a deal."

"What have you got that we could possibly want?" asked the President.

"A list of every illegal alien in the country—names, addresses, ID's, everything."

"And in exchange?"

"You get me the best plastic surgeon on the East Coast, give me a new face and a new identity, and put me in the witness protection program."

"All that, just for identifying a few illegal aliens?" said the President dubiously.

"There are more than a few, Jock," said Hoffa.

"Even so, they're just illegals. We've got fifteen million of them."

"These guys are a little more."

The President looked confused. "More illegal?"

"More alien."

"Where is this list?" asked the President.

"In a safe place," said Hoffa. "Now, do we have a deal?"

The President looked at Saddler, who nodded almost imperceptibly.

"We have a deal," said the President.

And that is the story, true in every detail, of how Jimmy Hoffa faked his own death a second time and saved America from an alien invasion, the magnitude of which had not been seen since the prior year along the Mexican border.

EPILOGUE

Praslin Island really isn't known for much except the Coco de Mer, and since this is a G-rated story, or at least PG, we're not at liberty to tell you why all the Victorian explorers were fascinated by it. (But it's a really neat story. Remember to ask us about it over a drink. Your treat.)

Still, it's a relatively untouched tropical paradise, and one of the things that remains most untouched is the burly, gray-haired gentleman with the brand-new face who spends most of his time lounging on the northern beach under a huge umbrella, his every need catered to by three unbelievably gorgeous bikini-clad women whose signet rings identify them as members of the most secret branch of the CIA.

Occasionally some tourist finds himself within a couple of hundred yards of the burly gentleman, and is promptly carted away for questioning, then released on neighboring La Digue island with just enough time left on his visa to get home.

Only one visitor is ever allowed to come closer. He usually carries a briefcase, and his suit and tie show him to be a stranger to the tropics. His passport displays only an initial for his first name, but no one ever challenges it.

He was there again just the other day. The burly man welcomed him, had one of the girls to fetch a pair of beers, and lit up a cigar.

"What is it this time?"

"Your information about the Kennedy brothers, John Lennon, James Dean, Amelia Earhart and Alydar checked out, but I still have a couple of questions about the Garfield assassination. Can you point me in the right direction?"

"Sure can," said the man.

"What is it going to cost this time?"

"I don't know," said the burly man, leaning forward and smiling. "Let's negotiate."

Author's note:

The following story also came about because of my connection to Mike Resnick. A few years ago, Mike became the editor of PhoenixPick, an imprint of ArcManor, a publishing house run by Shahid Mahmud. The basic premise of PhoenixPick is to publish a line consisting of paired stories—novellas, instead of the usual novels—in which a well-established author works with a new author in a common setting.

Mike asked me if I'd be willing to anchor one of the volumes. I agreed, in part because I had recently started collaborating on a novel with a new author named Chuck Gannon. (Charles E. Gannon, to be formal; Dr. Charles E. Gannon, if you want to go all tails and white tie about it.) And—oh, happy day—Chuck had just told me he was working on what sounded like a really nifty steampunk setting.

I'd never written a steampunk story and had a hankering to do so. Here was my chance, by God. So, Chuck and I signed the contract, produced our stories, and they were then combined in a volume titled The Aethers of Mars which was published in May of 2014.

Which—ahem—is still in print as well as being available electronically. You really owe it to yourself to read Chuck's half of the work if you enjoy the story you're about to read.

In the Matter of Savinkov

CHAPTER 1

"Look, Charlotte! Look!" said Adrian Luff. "It's the aethership!"

Charlotte went to his side and peered up at the area of the sky he was pointing to through the window. She had to stoop a little to see under the swell of the gasbag. Her eleven-year-old brother was short for his age, and she was tall for a fourteen-year-old girl.

She had to restrain herself from exhibiting the same public enthusiasm as her brother. Charlotte was quite excited herself, of course, this being her first extraplanetary voyage. But she was a young lady now, no longer a child. Adrian could behave indecorously, but she needed to maintain a proper demeanor.

After a moment she spotted what he was indicating. "I don't think . . ."

By then their father Edward was at their side. Being a large man, he had to stoop quite a bit more than Charlotte in order to bring the object into his view.

"That's not the aethership, Adrian," he said. "That's the transfer station."

Adrian frowned. "Are you sure?"

Impatiently, Charlotte was about to answer of course he's sure! But her father placed a hand on her shoulder and said genially, "Well, I could be wrong, of course. Let's ask someone who'd be certain." He looked about, spotted one of the stewards on the observation deck, and waved him over.

That was typical of him. He was very careful not to be overbearing toward his children, especially since their mother had died. But while Charlotte generally appreciated his attitude, there were times . . .

Especially involving her brother!

Of course that wasn't the aethership. After her father had told his children that his researches would be taking them all to Mars, she'd read up on the famous vessel that would transport them to the red planet. The craft they were approaching was much too small, for one thing. Now that the airship they were riding in had come closer, and she'd had more time to examine the object, she had a better sense of scale. That thing was not much bigger than their grandparents' house in East Finchley. Taller, to be sure, but no bigger in terms of volume.

Granted, that house was large; much larger than the average home in England. Their mother Emily's parents had been quite wealthy.

Charlotte made a face. She didn't like her grandparents. They were polite to her and Adrian, when they visited, but were never very welcoming and certainly not warmhearted.

From things her parents had let slip in her presence, from time to time, Charlotte knew that the Danbrooks—

the entire family, not just her grandparents—had disapproved of Emily's marriage to Edward Luff. True, he came from a respectable middle-class family, but he was a scholar—which is to say, from their viewpoint, barely this side of penury.

Had he been an economist, or a respectable historian of Britain—at least France or Germany—they could have let the matter slide, perhaps. But . . . but . . .

An historian of South Asia? A man who mucked about in the legends and myths—you could hardly call them histories—of Hindoos and Mohammedans?

Had Charlotte's mother still been alive, the family's scandal would have become even worse. After Cecil Rhodes publicly revealed his expeditions to Mars and the existence of intelligent creatures on the planet, in April of 1900, Edward Luff had shifted his field of study and become one of the world's very first "areologists," as such people styled themselves. That is to say, from the standpoint of the wealthy and oh-so-respectable Danbrooks, an outright charlatan—and never mind that his change of scholarly focus enabled him to obtain much larger grants to pursue his new field of studies, such as the one from the Meredith Foundation that had made this voyage possible. The Danbrooks viewed such financial acquisition as no better than swindling or embezzlement.

The steward arrived. "What may I do for you, Mr. Luff?"

Stooping again, Charlotte's father pointed . . .

"Oh, it's now out of sight." The airship had come close enough for the huge gasbag to have completely obscured the view. Her father straightened back up. "I was wondering—my son and I were wondering—if the ship we were nearing—are nearing, I should say—is our aethership or the transfer station?"

"That would be the transfer station, sir. You'll have a four- or five-hour wait there before the *Agincourt* arrives."

"Why so long?" asked Adrian. He wasn't being cross, simply curious.

For her part, Charlotte was wondering why the BEPC, the British Extra-Planetary Company, named their aetherships in such impolitic ways. Among the other dozen or so were included the *Poitiers* and the *Crécy*. Did Cecil Rhodes have some special animus against the French? To be fair, on the other side of the ledger was the *Hastings*. Then again, from what she knew of the famous man's racial views, Rhodes probably didn't consider the Normans to be French.

She'd asked her father once. He'd shrugged and said: "I don't know. But it's not as if anyone really cares what the French think. Politically speaking, at least, their nation is the joke of Europe."

Which was also impolitic, of course—but at least it was said in the privacy of a home, not blazoned across the flanks of the world's most famous and glamorous vessels.

Did one refer to the sides of vessels as "flanks"? She'd have to find out.

". . . the delay," the steward was saying. Charlotte had missed the first part of his response in her musings. "You were supposed to be the last airship, but there will be another coming, it seems. It's expensive for an aethership to come this close to the surface, so the *Agincourt*'s captain decided to wait until the final passengers were aboard the transfer station."

Less than half an hour later, the airship docked at an entryway located on the very top of the hovering transfer station. It struck Charlotte as an odd arrangement—she'd been thinking more in terms of a traditional gangway by which one might board a steamship—but with the hindsight of this new experience she understood the logic. The huge gasbag that provided their airship with its buoyancy would have made it impossible to come alongside the transfer station. This way, aligning the bottom of the airship with the top of the spindle-shaped transfer station, they could lower themselves onto the station through a hatchway in the deck of the airship. Much the way Charlotte imagined one might board a submarine.

Once aboard the transfer station, they were greeted by a steward who murmured polite and vacuous phrases, ending with: "Do make yourselves comfortable." He gestured in the direction of chairs bolted to the floor some distance away, and then moved off to attend to other duties.

There were quite a few of the chairs; fifty or sixty, arranged in three arcing rows that spread across half the space of the transfer station's central chamber. The chamber itself was perhaps twenty yards in diameter. The chairs were upholstered and looked very sturdy and well-made, with headrests, but were simple in design. Most of them were taken up already by other passengers waiting for the aethership to arrive.

Charlotte's attention was drawn to one end of the seating arrangement, occupied by a large group of rather exotic-looking people. They seemed to be an extended family, judging by their obvious familiarity with each other.

As they drew near the chairs, Charlotte tried to determine the language the group was speaking. It was certainly not Slavic, although the people looked vaguely Bulgarian to her. But then, for whatever peculiar reason, all dark-skinned Caucasians looked vaguely Bulgarian to her. She had no idea why, since she'd never actually met a Bulgarian. The closest she'd come were a couple of her father's academic associates. One of them was a visiting professor from Poland; the other, a Russian of uncertain profession who worked at nothing Charlotte could discern. She suspected he was a refugee from the Tsar's notorious secret police, being given shelter at the university. But when she'd inquired of her father, he'd been unusually close-mouthed and claimed he knew nothing himself.

That was nonsense, of course. Charlotte's father knew something about everything.

Leaving aside the group's national origins, Charlotte also wondered as to the reason for their presence here. They ranged in age from a trio of elderly women to several small children. There was even a babe in their midst. And they looked . . . well, not poverty-stricken. But certainly not well-to-do, either. For one thing, they were carrying an alarming amount of baggage, presumably because they hadn't wanted to pay the—quite modest—surcharge of having their belongings handled by the BEPC's staff. That was what Charlotte's father had done, even though he'd had to pay for it out of pocket. The voyage itself was being financed by the Meredith Foundation, but they didn't cover what they presumably considered frills.

Edward Luff had inherited very little from his wife. Her family had seen to it that when she married him against their wishes she was provided with nothing more than a modest annuity—which they discontinued immediately after her death. Yet, even on the none-too-fulsome salary of a university professor, he hadn't hesitated to pay the luggage surcharge.

That meant—had to mean—Charlotte prided herself on her skills at deduction—that this family (or group of whatever kind; she cautioned herself not to jump to conclusions) was of limited means. So how were they managing a voyage to Mars aboard the prestigious flagship of the BEPC's fleet of aetherships? And why?

Had they been about to cross the seas in a steamship—say, to America—Charlotte would have thought the hypothetical family of Bulgarians would be traveling in steerage. But she was fairly certain there was no such thing as "steerage" on board an aethership.

Variations in the quality of the cabins, certainly. Even great variations—the sumptuousness of the Founder's Cabin was well-known. That cabin was always reserved for Rhodes himself on the now-rare occasions he returned to Earth from his retreat on Mars. But even the smallest and most austere cabins on the *Agincourt*, such as the ones they'd be taking, were quite expensive.

Travel between the planets was still very new, and there just weren't that many aetherships in existence yet.

Great Britain had less than twenty, all told, most of them owned by the BEPC and the rest by the Royal Navy. The Germans, less than ten. The Russians, no more than a handful, and the same for the French. She thought the Americans had three or four and the Italians perhaps as many. And that was about it, so far as she knew.

There were certainly not enough aetherships to allow for the luxury—using the term in a perhaps ironic manner—of having poor people crossing to the other planets in steerage.

Would that be called "steerage" on an aethership? She'd have to find out.

Then, alas, her father demolished her pleasant exercise in deduction. Spotting someone in the little mob, he smiled and strode forward, his hand outstretched.

"Vijay!" he exclaimed. "I thought you'd be aboard the *Agincourt* already."

A short, slender man about her father's age rose from one of the chairs and the two men shook hands. He looked rather harassed. "I had expected to be, Edward. Yesterday, in fact. But . . ."

He made a vague gesture toward the rest of the group. "I'm afraid that herding a Brahmin family is akin to herding cats. Argumentative cats, at that."

Charlotte's father studied the group, now smiling widely. "You brought them all?" He nodded toward one of the women in the group. Her black hair was streaked with gray at the temples. Charlotte made a tentative hypothesis that she was the Vijay fellow's wife. She seemed older than he was, but certainly not old enough to be the man's mother. His sister, perhaps . . . except they didn't resemble each other in the least, other than both being Indian. And the fact that she was older than her husband wouldn't be surprising. She knew from comments made by her father that Indian customs on these matters were often quite different from those of Europeans.

"Sumati," her father said. "You're looking well."

The Sumati woman looked even more harassed than her husband. (Tentatively classified husband, Charlotte reminded herself; one mustn't jump to conclusions.) "I most certainly do not, Edward. But I thank you for the pleasantry."

Charlotte's father turned his attention back to Vijay. "How..."

"The Nizam insisted. He's a young fellow, you know, very full of modern ideas—and insistent that Hindus take their rightful place in the human race's solar expansion. I think he has daydreams that by shipping to Mars an entire clan—well, smart part of one, at any rate—he will somehow have advanced that project."

He shrugged. "He may even prove right, in the end. All I know, at the moment, is that trying to conduct a scholarly quest"—here he winced slightly, as a babe squalled—"in the midst of chaos is not what Sumati and I had in mind. It would be nice if the Nizam's purse were as expansive as his notions, so we could have afforded a few nannies and more than one tutor. As it stands... grandmothers and great-aunts make excellent caretakers of children, but they invariably have demands of their own."

Edward Luff chuckled. "You have my heartfelt sympathies. And now, some introductions are in order."

He turned back to face his son and daughter. "Charlotte, Adrian, allow me to introduce you to Vijay Shankar and his wife Sumati. They are two of the world's preeminent scholars of Mars. Vijay is an historian like myself; Sumati, a linguist. Vijay and Sumati, this is my daughter Charlotte and my son Adrian."

He smiled slyly. "All that I brought with me of my own small clan, happily. And"—he nodded toward a heavy-set woman approaching them—"I even managed to persuade the Foundation to let me bring our nanny. Her name is Mrs. Smith. Helen Smith."

"Oh, lucky fellow," muttered Shankar.

Mrs. Smith arrived. She also looked harassed. But then, she usually did.

"When will we be boarding?" she asked. She hadn't heard the earlier exchange with the steward because she'd been busy fussing with another steward who'd been overseeing the entryway. About . . . something. Charlotte made it a point not to investigate the source and nature of Mrs. Smith's fusses. First, there were too many. Second, they were invariably boring.

"Soon," her father replied.

Four or five hours was not Charlotte's conception of the term soon. But Mrs. Smith seemed satisfied. She moved over to one of the chairs and lowered herself into the seat.

Time moved differently for Mrs. Smith than it did for Charlotte. As long as the woman had no tasks or chores to perform, she seemed quite content to sit and do nothing at all, for hours on end. It would drive Charlotte mad.

She was not an unpleasant woman, Mrs. Smith. Quite

conscientious in her duties; and if she was not what one would call enjoyable company, she was not nasty or rude either. Just . . . boring.

CHAPTER 2

The expression on the face of the airship's officer was decidedly unfriendly, as Alexander Evalenko and his companion Ilya Drezhner came aboard. But he said nothing, and Alexander thought silence on his own part was the best course. It was hardly surprising that employees of Great Britain's premier transportation company would be irritated at having the departure of their flagship delayed in order to await the arrival of two unexpected passengers.

Alexander wasn't happy about the situation himself. If word got out, as it almost certainly would, the conclusion anyone would come to was that political pressure had been brought to bear. There was no doubt at all that their quarry would draw that conclusion. And, having drawn it, be made more alert to the possibility that he was being pursued.

Alexander moved toward the other side of the airship, seeking to get away from the unfriendly scrutiny.

"He seems a bit testy," Drezhner said softly.

Alexander's mouth quirked. "Puzzled, too, I suspect. He's probably trying to figure out how the Russian government could bring enough pressure to bear to make such a schedule change. Given that we are not—ah—held in any great regard in Britain these days."

Relations between the United Kingdom and Russia were always shaky, despite the two nations being officially allied. Right now they were on particularly edgy terms, given the tensions over the Peshawar Incident. Even the Irish nationalists, normally so pragmatic in accepting aid from any party in their quarrel with the English, were hostile to Russia. As such malcontents almost invariably were, the Irish were rabid republicans—and the Tsar of All the Russias was universally considered the world's premier autocrat.

As it happened, although political interference had been necessary to get the last airship shuttling passengers and supplies to the *Agincourt* to delay its departure, it had not been pressure from the British government. So far as Alexander knew, the British authorities were quite unaware that the BEPC's premier interplanetary aethership's schedule had been altered.

"Luckily for us," Alexander said, in the same soft tones, "Cecil Rhodes thinks well of the Okhrana. Rachkovsky himself sent the radio message to Rhodes—a polite request, no more—and, *voila, c'est fait.*"

His French was fluent and unaccented, as you might expect of one of Russia's top secret agents in Paris.

He and Drezhner came to a stop against the windows on the far side of the airship cabin. The craft had lifted as soon as they came aboard and they were now at least a thousand meters high. Through the panes they could see the soft countryside of southeastern England below them.

"I hadn't known that," said Drezhner. "About Rhodes. I thought he despised Slavs. What did he call us? One of those most detestable . . ." He waved his hand in a gesture that indicated a minor loss of memory.

Alexander smiled wryly. The pronounced racial views of Cecil Rhodes were a byword in Europe. To be born English is to win first prize in the lottery of life was his best-known axiom on the subject, but he had many others.

"The phrase he used was 'the most despicable specimens of human beings.' He wasn't singling out Slavs, however. And the man's theories have their quirks as well as their . . . ah, fervor. He's quite partial to Germans; considers them almost as good as Englishmen. And while he generally sneers at Slavs, he makes an exception for the Russian aristocracy."

"Ah." Drezhner smiled. "That old business about Kievan Rus being ruled by Nordic conquerors and adventurers."

"Exactly so. And since the Okhrana officially recruits only from the Russian army, and the army does not allow Jews in the officer corps unless they convert to Christianity, Rhodes has concluded that the Tsar's secret police are stout fellows. It doesn't hurt at all, of course, that we generally cooperate with his own intelligence service."

Alexander spent a moment contemplating the view before continuing. "The odd thing—the man has his foibles, there's no doubt about it—is that Rhodes is not particularly hostile to Jews. Or, at least, no more so than any English gentleman. It's that he presumes—so I was told by Rachkovsky, who knows him rather well—that the Russian army's anti-Semitism indicates a generally stringent attitude toward the acceptance of lesser breeds. By his logic, if you won't find Jews among the Russian secret police, you won't find lowly purebred Slavs and Mongols, either."

"Ah." After a moment, Drezhner said: "But we have a number of Jews in our ranks. Including—"

"No names, please."

There was silence for a bit, as the airship continued to rise, heading toward the transfer station. When they were perhaps three miles high, Drezhner commented: "Can't say I much care for the yids myself."

Alexander shrugged. "Such is the world we live in."

The steward who welcomed them aboard the transfer station was more polite, or at least more diplomatic. As they came into the main waiting room, they were greeted with the sight of three rows of chairs, all of them now occupied.

"Marvelous," muttered Drezhner. "A tribe of gypsies. How on Earth did they get aboard?"

In point of fact, the people in question were obviously South Asians, not gypsies. Hindus, at a guess, although they might be Muslims. But by now, more than a week since they'd made their acquaintance, Alexander understood that his new junior partner was something of an ignoramus as well as a bigot.

The second fault was minor. The first was not. Especially since, in Alexander's estimation, Drezhner's ignorance was willful. Lack of knowledge could be repaired. Willful ignorance was not far removed from outright stupidity.

But such was the nature of the world he lived in.

Vera knew who they were—had to be—the moment the two men came aboard. She hadn't been expecting them, precisely, but from the beginning there had been a chance the Okhrana would learn of the project. Not learn very much, probably, but enough to send a team in pursuit of Gavril Savinkov.

She wasn't especially worried that the Okhrana agents would be able to spot Savinkov. But she'd have to take steps to evade detection herself. Fortunately, the arrival of the new party presented her with a better opportunity than trying to fit herself into the large group from Hyderabad. That had been her best option prior to their arrival, but it hadn't been a very good one. Her features could pass as those of someone from South Asia, but her skin tone was far too light.

Being careful not to move too quickly and draw attention to herself, she slid into a seat behind a tall young girl sitting next to a man she assumed to be her father. The girl was pretty, in a modest sort of way. Northern European, clearly: pale skin; dark blonde hair; blue eyes. Not one to draw the attention of most boys immediately, but a girl who'd have no trouble fascinating any boy who did become attracted to her.

Vera leaned over the shoulder of the girl and asked: "How much longer will the wait be, do you know?"

The girl turned to look at her, a bit surprised. She hadn't heard Vera take her seat. "I'm not really sure, Madame. But I don't have the impression it will be much longer."

"Let's hope not." Vera smiled ruefully. "These chairs are sturdy but not very comfortable for long stretches." The rueful smile expanded into something more cheerful. "Fortunately, I am—ah, how to put it in English?—'well-padded,' perhaps? In my native German, I would say zaftig."

Vera extended her hand. "I am Vera Duchesne."

The girl extended her own and they shook hands. "Pleased to make your acquaintance. I am Charlotte Luff. I thought Vera was a Russian name, not German."

Vera took a brief moment to wish a silent curse upon all precocious girls. Only a brief moment, though. Having been one herself, the curse was half-hearted anyway.

The best way to deal with such girls was to intrigue them. Trying to fend off their curiosity was pointless.

"You're quite right—although the name is widespread across the Slavic lands, not just Russia. My given name, however, was Verena." Here a bright, gleaming smile, hinting that the girl was being drawn into conspiracy. "Which, despite its Latin origin—from vereri, it's thought—is now properly Teutonic. But my late husband was half-Russian on his mother's side and since he thought the name was a bit grandiose—"

The girl clapped her hands gleefully. "Oh, yes! If it's from the Latin, it would mean 'to fear' or 'to respect.' Certainly nothing a husband would favor."

Vera took a brief moment to wish a silent blessing upon all precocious girls. "Exactly what he said himself. So he insisted on substituting Vera. Being honest, I prefer the name myself. 'Verena' is so . . . so . . ."

"Stand-offish," the girl supplied.

"Precisely." Now joined in mutual conspiracy, the plump middle-aged woman and the slender teenage girl exchanged gazes of mutual admiration.

Mission accomplished. Immediate mission, at least.

The girl shifted on her own seat. "They're really not very comfortable, are they? I think they're designed this

way in case of emergencies. Look—they even have some
sort of safety harnesses."

The spirited discussion Charlotte was having with
Madame Duchesne drew her father's attention. He'd left
off his discussion with Mr. and Mrs. Shankar and taken a
seat between Charlotte and Adrian. He looked over
Charlotte's shoulder and smiled.

"Indeed, they are," he said. "Aetherships have difficulty
with strong magnetic fields at times. The engines which
keep this transfer station in the air are essentially the same
as those in aetherships. If the Earth's magnetic field gets
unruly, which can happen from time to time, the transfer
station could undergo rather severe turbulence. Hence
the design of these chairs. They keep the passengers from
being flung about and injured."

Adrian's attention had also been drawn and, as usual,
he became obstreperous. "But that doesn't make sense,
Father. Shouldn't they have them all around, then, instead
of only on one side?"

"I imagine the weight in those compartments across
from us fairly well counter-balances our own, Adrian,"
their father replied. "In any event, as heavy as this transfer
station is, I doubt if the weight of the passengers is all that
great a concern."

"How fascinating," said Madame Duchesne. She
returned Edward Luff's smile with a very friendly one of
her own. For a moment, Charlotte wondered if the
woman might be trying to flirt with her father.

No, that would be ridiculous, she decided. Madame
Duchesne was apparently a widow and she was attractive

enough, in a fleshy sort of way. She had intelligent eyes, so dark a brown they were almost black. Quite striking, really.

But—

She was much too old; at least five years older than her father.

It was too bad, really. After Charlotte's father celebrated his fortieth birthday, just a few months earlier, she had set herself the goal (among many) of seeing to it that he remarry. Madame Duchesne was an interesting woman—quite perceptive, obviously—and would have otherwise made a suitable match. Preliminarily speaking, that is. Inquiries would have had to be made, naturally. A woman from the Continent—formerly married to a Frenchman—one never knew what one might encounter under such circumstances.

It would have made for an interesting investigation, actually. But there was no point to it, given the age difference between her father and Madame Duchesne. Five years. Practically an eternity, even for someone at the mature age of fourteen. Had the genders been reversed . . . possibly . . .

But, no. Out of the question. They were not Hindus, after all.

CHAPTER 3

The wait aboard the transfer station seemed to take forever to Charlotte. Very soon, Madame Duchesne was drawn into a conversation with her father and the Shankar couple concerning the intricacies of Martian history. It turned out the widow was a scholar of sorts herself. She was an amateur, not a professional like Edward Luff and Vijay Shankar. But amateurs played a prominent role in areological studies, at least if they were wealthy enough to devote themselves to the pursuit. Apparently Monsieur Duchesne had left his wife a sizeable inheritance.

There really wasn't anything to do aboard the vessel, whose furnishings were as austere as those of a small-town train station. There wasn't even that much to see out of the viewports. The craft was kept hovering far above the ground—eight and a half miles, Charlotte was told by one of the stewards—and within a short time after their arrival the cloud cover had filled in completely below them.

But, finally, a dong-dong-dong announced the arrival of the *Agincourt*. Like most of the passengers, Charlotte moved back to the observation windows to observe the aethership. But she made it a point not to rush eagerly and gawk avidly as did her brother.

It was hard not to gawk, though, when she caught sight of the craft. The aethership was huge, much bigger than the transfer station or even the airship. And whereas most of the airship's volume—you could hardly call it "bulk"— was composed of the gasbag, the *Agincourt*'s hull was made of steel.

Charlotte had studied the ship before they left Earth. Being the BEPC's flagship, there was a great deal of literature on the *Agincourt*. So she knew the vessel was really no larger than an ocean liner—and smaller than the very largest of those. She weighed a little under 15,000 tonnes, about the size of the German ocean liner SS

Kaiser Wilhelm der Grosse but only three-fourths the size of its sister ship the SS *Kaiser Wilhelm II*. And the *Agincourt* would be almost dwarfed once the Cunard Lines launched their Olympic-class super-liners, a trio of ships which would include the *Titanic* and the *Britannic*. Those would each weigh around 46,000 tonnes.

That was measuring solely in terms of weight. The *Agincourt*'s design was radically different from that of a sea-going ship. It was much longer than any ocean liner, measuring just over three thousand feet from the tip of one aether-drive chamber to the other. One couldn't refer to them as "fore" and "aft" chambers because they were quite interchangeable. An aethership, unlike an ocean liner, could readily move in either direction.

Most of that length, however, consisted of the slender pylons that connected the aether-drive chambers to the main body of the *Agincourt*. The powerful electromagnetic forces involved in propelling a spacecraft through the aether needed to be kept at a considerable distance from the living quarters.

The main body of the *Agincourt* also bore no resemblance to any ocean-going craft. It was shaped like a stubby cylinder, two hundred feet from top to bottom (front to back? hard to say, since the ship was completely ambidextrous, propulsively-speaking) and approximately three hundred feet in diameter. One might, somewhat fancily, depict the *Agincourt* as being a can of tinned meat with two long rods sticking out from the center of the top and bottom of the can—understanding that "top" and "bottom" were arbitrary terms in this application—which ended in two knobs.

But such a depiction would be a gross simplification. For one thing, the outer rim of the cylinder—the "tin can" of her fancy—contained the hydroponic gardens that provided the ship with breathable air and some of its food. Its huge water tanks also provided the living quarters located in the interior with shielding against radiation. Most of the dangerous radiation encountered in space travel was shielded against by the aether-drives themselves, but having a water bulwark could be critical in case of unexpected solar flares or bursts of cosmic radiation.

At the moment, the great windows that would be exposed in the voyage to provide the gardens with sunlight were covered by steel shutters. The insides of those shutters also served as mirrors that would concentrate the light as needed, when the ship moved far enough away from the sun, or would serve as photoelectric power sources whenever the sunlight alone was sufficient for the vegetation. Charlotte had seen photographs of what an aethership looked like once the shutters were fully exposed. The "tin can" of her analogy would then look far more like some sort of bizarre coral formation than any sort of neatly defined cylinder.

For another thing, the term "knobs" was also a gross oversimplification, referring to the shape of the aether-drive chambers. True, the chambers were roughly spherical in design. But they had a multitude of protuberances and whatnots which served the engines in whatever peculiar manner was needed to make them work.

• • •

The *Agincourt* docked with the transfer station by extending a long tube from a hatch in its flank to the same entryway at the very top of the station that they'd used to gain access to it. Two long tubes, rather—there was a much smaller one extended to a narrower entry not far away. Charlotte's guess that this smaller tube would be used to transfer supplies and luggage was confirmed by her brother. As was to be expected of boys his age, Adrian was a font of excessively detailed information about all things mechanical and electrical.

The bigger tube, of course, was the one used to transfer passengers and crew. It was rather exciting, actually. The tube was flexible—like a stiff garden hose, not a flimsy stocking—which made the process something of an adventure. It was as much like climbing a rope ladder as a set of stairs.

Charlotte's father handled it with aplomb. He assisted Madame Duchesne as well, although from what Charlotte could see the widow didn't seem to need any help at all. That was male gallantry at work, even if it was quite wasted under these circumstances in romantic terms.

But perhaps she was being unfair to her father and his gender. Edward Luff extended the same assistance to several of the elderly Shankar ladies, after all.

Those ladies were not shy about expressing their displeasure with the whole business. Silly of them. What did they expect? A barge to take them across?

Adrian didn't help things at all when he piped up to explain to the Shankar women that their fretting and fussing over the unsteady footing was completely misdirected.

"The worst that a fall or slip caused by a sudden sharp flex in the tube would do you would be a broken leg." The wretched boy rapped the wall of the tube with a knuckle. "This is what should be making you nervous. If such a flex were to rupture the wall . . ."

He waved his hands and widened his eyes in the silly melodramatic manner that was so typical of eleven-year-old males. "Whoosh! We're at almost twice the elevation as the very tip of Mt. Everest. The air outside is much too thin to breathe. Not to mention the temperature! Be a race to see whether we froze to death or died gasping for breath."

"Enough, Adrian," chided their father. He bestowed a reassuring smile upon the now-more-worried-than-ever Brahmins. "Don't listen to him. It's quite safe. There's never been a mishap in such a transfer—"

"But that's not true, Father," protested her brother. "Just last year—"

Charlotte's father got a pained expression on his face. "Involving any BEPC vessel," he continued firmly. Again, the reassuring smile made its appearance. "The unfortunate incident my son is referring to involved naval maneuvers. Entirely different matter."

The Shankar ladies didn't seem mollified. But at least their heightened apprehension caused them to fall silent as they concentrated on the task at hand.

And, eventually—it probably didn't take more than a couple of minutes, really—they came aboard the aethership.

"Welcome to the *Agincourt*," said a hearty voice. Looking up, Charlotte saw a ship's officer extending a hand. With a little lift, he helped her make the final step up into the vessel.

At last—everything she'd been expecting. The entry chamber she now stood in was everything the transfer station had failed to be.

No provincial train station environs here! The carpet underfoot was thick and luxurious. Gleaming brass everywhere you looked. Except the lamp fixtures, which looked to be gilded.

"Oh, how splendid!" exclaimed Adrian, following on her heels. He pointed to the side. "Look at that magnificent barometer, Charlotte!"

Leave it to her brother to marvel over the one and only instrument in the room. And the only item that seemed to be completely utilitarian.

This would be their environment for the next several weeks.

Weeks. Their cabins would be on the small side, of course. But they were probably even more luxurious— and the food aboard the *Agincourt* was reputed to be superb.

Weeks, without any of Mrs. Smith's sturdy but unimaginative cooking to endure.

On the other hand . . .

Weeks, putting up with her brother in close quarters.

Weeks, with nothing for Mrs. Smith to do—which meant weeks watching her stare at nothing like a cow in the fields.

Madame Duchesne came aboard. Charlotte must have been frowning, because the widow placed a friendly hand on her shoulder and murmured. "Just think, Miss Luff.

We'll have so much time for conversation, with no chores to distract us."

Charlotte wondered what sort of "chores" a wealthy woman such as Madame Duchesne had to deal with. But the thought wasn't sarcastic. In truth, she was looking forward to those conversations herself. Duchesne was interesting—for a girl like Charlotte, without question the cardinal virtue in a traveling companion.

CHAPTER 4

Alexander Evalenko examined his cabin with distaste. The furnishings were luxurious, true enough, and the bed—it might be better to say, deluxe cot—looked comfortable. But the room seemed more like a glorified closet than anything Alexander associated with the term "cabin."

His claustrophobia was heightened by disorientation. The peculiar design of the cabin made the cramped quarters seem ever worse. He understood the reason for that design: the furnishings needed to be swiveled around and work at a ninety-degree angle once the aethership was in outer space and was set spinning to mimic gravity. But that knowledge did little to alleviate his discomfort.

Perhaps that was just the residue of his provincialism at work. He'd been raised in the countryside on a large estate in Perm Guberniya. His family, although part of the hereditary nobility, had not been wealthy and had lived in rather primitive wooden dwellings. But even for the peasants in the region, a "cabin" had been spacious compared to this room. And there had certainly been nothing exotic about its construction.

On the positive side, he wouldn't have to share the room with Ilya Drezhner. The cabin was barely big enough for one person, much less two. Alexander found Drezhner's company increasingly tiresome. The man was intelligent, technically speaking, but full of so many biases and fixed notions as to make him effectively a halfwit.

Ah, well. The life of a secret agent tasked to seek out and destroy anarchists, revolutionists and agitators was not an easy one. Alexander had known that from the moment he decided to resign from the army and join the Okhrana. He reminded himself that Drezhner was a veritable sage compared to the imbeciles he'd had to contend with in the cavalry.

Once he'd packed away the few belongings he'd brought with him, he drew out the message that Drezhner had brought to him in Paris. The only reason he was looking at it again was from long habit. He'd found that if he studied a message several times, over a period of two or three days, he could destroy it without fear of forgetting anything.

The note was from one of Okhrana chief Semiakin's assistants. The exact identity of the assistant was unfortunately not specified. Drezhner had not thought to inquire, and his description of the man could have fit any of three clerks stationed at the Okhrana's headquarters in St. Petersburg. One of those assistants was brilliant, one was competent, and the third only had his post because of family connections. Alexander would have liked to know which of the three had composed this message.

Gavril Savinkov reported en route to Mars. Probable conveyance BEPC vessel. Probable destination Tryddoc Aru or Crenex. Probable targets include:

Cecil Rhodes
Prince Mikhail Ivanovich Vorontsov
Prince Pyotr Pavlovich Saltykov
Count Vasily Fedorovich Kamensky
Count Pavel Andreyevich Shuvalov

Arrest Savinkov if possible for questioning. Essential his mission be thwarted by whatever means necessary.

The last part was straightforward enough. Obviously, it would be ideal to apprehend the man and subject him to questioning in hopes of learning the identity of his accomplices and associates. But, above all else, his plot had to be stopped. If that meant killing him on the spot, so be it. Savinkov was a leader of the Socialist-Revolutionary Party's Combat Organization and its most notorious assassin.

The first part of the message was also reasonably straightforward. The Okhrana's sources, whoever they might be, had not been able to specify the exact vessel Gavril Savinkov would be taking. That was unfortunate, of course, but in this instance not especially troublesome. There simply weren't that many aetherships available for someone to travel to Mars. Narrowing the possibilities to those craft owned by the British Extra-Planetary Company was also helpful. It hadn't taken Alexander

more than an hour to ascertain that there were only two
possible vessels unless the assassin was willing to wait
another three months, which he thought highly unlikely.

And, of the two possibilities, the second aethership—
that would be the *Blenheim*—was a much smaller vessel
than the *Agincourt*; and, better still, would not set off to
Mars for another two weeks. That would give the Paris
bureau of the Okhrana, the largest in Europe outside of
Russia itself, plenty of time to assemble a sizeable
counter-assassination team.

The problem lay with the *Agincourt*. It was scheduled
to depart . . .

Alexander had literally yelped when he discovered the
Agincourt's departure date. It was leaving on the
morrow! There had been just enough time for he and
Drezhner to race across the Channel and board the
airship bringing the last passengers aboard—and even
then, they'd only managed it because Rachkovsky had
put through an emergency message to Rhodes to get the
needed delay.

It was the middle part of the message, however, that
was now causing Alexander's worries. Five possible
targets, in two different cities—and he had only one agent
beside himself. Once they reached Mars, they'd have no
choice but to split up, each to a different city.

Hopefully, of course, they would have apprehended
Savinkov—or killed him, which Alexander thought to be
more likely—before they arrived at their destination. But
he was not sanguine about the prospect of doing so. Any
assassin as successful as Savinkov would be expert at
disguising himself. Insofar as the phrase "disguise himself"

had any meaning at all in this instance. The Okhrana had never gotten a clear description of the man.

There were hundreds of passengers aboard the *Agincourt*. It was even conceivable that Savinkov had somehow managed to infiltrate the vessel's crew. That was extremely unlikely, in Alexander's estimation, but the possibility couldn't be ruled out altogether. For someone with the assassin's skills, hiding himself in plain sight aboard the *Agincourt* would not be difficult.

Had this been a Russian imperial vessel, Alexander could simply have applied force majeure. When need be, Tsarist officials would not hesitate to sequester an entire crew and complement of passengers and subject them all to rigorous interrogation until the assassin was uncovered. But that wouldn't be possible here. Rhodes' willingness to cooperate with Russian police agencies only went so far. The man was fiercely proud of his fleet of aetherships, especially its flagship. There would be no chance he'd agree to tarnishing his reputation, as he'd see it, by allowing Okhrana agents to effectively take control of the *Agincourt*.

Barring good fortune, therefore, Alexander had to assume that Savinkov would successfully complete the voyage to Mars. They'd have to catch him after he began his operation. The point where an assassin's target was in greatest danger was also the point where the assassin himself was most exposed and vulnerable.

He'd take Tryddoc Aru, of course. That was the most important Martian city other than the multi-city area in the Vallis Agathodaemonis known as the Octad Gentillus and the city of Crenex, which dominated the rich lands around the Ogygis Regio depression.

More to the point, it was the city which Cecil Rhodes had seized outright in his initial expedition to Mars in 1898. He'd even killed the local despot himself, although Alexander had been told that was more a matter of surprised self-defense when the despot attempted treachery rather than any derring-do. The despot must have been mad to make the attempt. His forces had been overwhelmed by Rhodes' mercenaries, hardened by years of fighting Boers and Zulus in southern Africa and armed with lever-action repeating rifles and revolvers that completely out-classed Martian weaponry.

Martian societies were highly ritualized and the customs in most Martian lands gave great weight to their version of a code duello. That gave Rhodes' coup d'état something in the way of cultural legitimacy, given his personal killing of the potentate. He'd made Tryddoc Aru his capital and the city had become a major commercial as well as political center under his rule. Rhodes maintained his own residence there, as did the Russian imperial envoy to the planet, Prince Vorontsov. Count Kamensky, the prince's military adviser, resided there as well.

That would be Gavril Savinkov's most likely destination. It certainly provided him with the richest targets.

Prince Saltykov and his own military adviser, Count Shuvalov, resided in Crenex. They were much less important figures and he thought it unlikely Savinkov would be aiming for them. The Esers, as members of the S-R Party were commonly called, were perennially short of funds. They wouldn't have spent the money to send an assassin to Mars to attack a secondary target.

He spent a minute or so considering the possibility that

Rhodes himself was the target. The Esers might be engaged in a complex tit-for-tat, allied at least temporarily with a non-Russian revolutionary organization. They'd kill Rhodes in exchange for their allies targeting a very prominent Russian official. The logic being that Rhodes' security service and the various Russian police agencies would be looking for danger from the usual parties, not foreigners who had no personal involvement or motives.

It was certainly true that Rhodes had no shortage of enemies. What was left of the Boers hated him with a corrosive passion, for a start. While their own paramilitary forces had largely been crushed or dispersed, some Boer individuals had escaped with their fortunes, mostly to the United States. Any one of them, or a small cabal, could have financed a sole assassin's voyage to Mars.

There were other possibilities, too. Rumors continued to swirl that Rhodes had been involved in the assassination of Queen Victoria, despite the official finding that Fenians had been responsible. What was no rumor at all but well established was that it was Rhodes' aetherships which had bombed from orbit and destroyed or badly damaged several naval units from the North Fleet. The units had mutinied after the newly-formed Loyalty Party used its majority in Parliament to pass sweeping new laws and ordinances which shredded ancient British liberties and legal customs. Most of the United Kingdom's military had accepted, however grudgingly, the new black uniforms decreed by the Loyalists—but it was open knowledge that many British officers and enlisted men still considered themselves "redcoats." A cabal emerging from those disaffected ranks might have decided to employ Russian terrorists instead of risking direct action on their own.

All possibilities, certainly. But Alexander thought they were unlikely. Occam's Razor applied just as much to assassination as it did to other areas of human activity. The more complicated you made a scheme, the more likely it was to fail.

Furthermore, Rhodes' Martian stronghold was heavily guarded by his own security forces, whereas all the Russian officials on Mars had by way of protection was a small number of guards. Not more than half a dozen in any one place—and Cossacks to a man, to make things worse. Alexander didn't doubt the Cossacks were splendid on a field of battle, but for this sort of work they were well-nigh useless.

No, he was sure the target was Vorontsov. The prince was a detested enemy of Russian revolutionaries. As one of the chief lieutenants for Police Director Vyacheslav von Plehve, during the early 1880s Vorontsov had been responsible for the destruction of a number of terrorist groups affiliated with Narodnaya Volya—the so-called "People's Will" organization. Two decades had gone by since then and Prince Vorontsov had left the Interior Ministry fifteen years earlier for the Tsar's diplomatic corps. But the Socialist-Revolutionary Party had been founded largely by former members of Narodnaya Volya after they were released from imprisonment. They had long memories and were as unforgiving as a Siberian winter—which many of them had experienced firsthand, thanks to Vorontsov.

That explained why the Esers would send Savinkov. If

anyone working alone could succeed in assassinating a Russian official on Mars, it would be Savinkov.

There was a knock on his door. Opening it, he saw Drezhner standing in the corridor outside. The young agent had a crooked smile on his face. "Weird cabins, ha? When will they shift all the furniture around?"

"It'll be a while yet." Seeing no reason to remain cooped up in the tiny cabin, Alexander came into the corridor and closed the door behind him. Then, after making sure it was locked, he headed toward the center of the ship. "We may as well go to the main observation deck and see if we can find out anything."

The corridor was just as peculiar as the rooms. Ladders—rungs built into the walls, rather—ran horizontally along the ceiling of the corridor. Once the *Agincourt* began to rotate, the corridor would become a vertical shaft and they'd move to and from their cabins using those ladders. There were a few spiral staircases as well that would come into play, but none of them were nearby.

"What an adventure!" said Drezhner cheerfully.

CHAPTER 5

Charlotte's reaction to her cabin was very different from Alexander's. She found it all quite exciting, and was especially charmed by the complex design that allowed the cabin to function with two different axes of gravity. Or centrifugal force, she reminded herself. One had to be careful to understand the distinction, even if in practice it would mean very little while they were in flight.

"Oh, look here, Mrs. Smith." She pulled a drawer out all the way in order to better examine the mechanism. "It's on some sort of gimbal system. After we pack away our belongings they'll remain undisturbed even when the ship begins to rotate and our present floor becomes a wall."

The governess with whom she was sharing the room stared at her. It was obvious she hadn't understood anything Charlotte had just said.

Well, it had been foolish to make the statement. Charlotte reminded herself to accept Mrs. Smith's limitations. It was hard, at times. The limitations were so . . . so . . .

Limited.

"Yes, dear," said Mrs. Smith. She continued to stow away their belongings, quite oblivious to the sophisticated engineering that had turned a simple closet and cabinet drawers into mechanical masterpieces.

Charlotte didn't offer Mrs. Smith any assistance. That wasn't laziness on her part, simply long experience at work. The governess had fixed views concerning what her duties consisted of, and those views did not allow for the possibility that a teenage girl might be perfectly capable of packing away her own clothes.

"I think I'll go down to the observation deck."

"Yes, dear."

The first thing Charlotte did when she came onto the observation deck was subject it to the scrutiny she'd given the closet and drawers. She was delighted to discover that the same marvelous engineering had been applied here also—except on a much grander scale.

The deck was huge, with a ceiling about sixty feet high. That was more than a quarter of the overall length of the *Agincourt*'s central hub, measuring from bow to stern.

Or should that be top to bottom? She wasn't sure if sea-going terminology applied to spacecraft. She'd have to inquire. It was important to get these things right.

The reason for the towering ceiling was obvious at a glance. Once the vessel entered deep space and began to rotate, centrifugal force would turn that sixty-foot wall into the floor of the observation deck. The ceiling would then become the forward wall. She knew that once in flight, the observation deck would also serve the *Agincourt* as its main dining room. None of the chairs and tables were present at the moment, though. They'd have to be attached directly to the wall to keep from falling off in the ship's present configuration.

There were windows all along the deck, forming the final six feet or so of each wall/floor. Heavy steel borders joined them together where they met at a ninety degree angle. One would be able to look through them either way the ship was . . .

What term should she use? Heading? Flying? Proceeding? Configurating? It was a bit confusing.

Most of the people on the observation deck were standing, although there were a few comfortable-looking chairs scattered about. The reason for that was also obvious—the observation deck circumnavigated the entire hub and people were walking slowly along the rail that kept them from stepping onto the windows.

The Earth was not visible from Charlotte's current position. The ship was already rotating, but very slowly;

not enough to provide any significant centrifugal force, just enough to eventually bring any part of the deck into sight of the planet below them. Most people, however—as Charlotte planned to do herself—were not waiting for that to happen but were walking toward it.

There had been perhaps thirty people visible from where she had first come onto the deck. Once she got a third of the way around and came into sight of the Earth, the population got much thicker. There were at least a hundred people crowding at the rail, looking at the spectacular view below them.

Far below them, Charlotte saw, once she squeezed her way into a space at the rail. The *Agincourt* must have begun its departure almost as soon as the last passengers came aboard. The transfer station, hovering some 45,000 feet above the planet's surface, was no longer in sight. They were very high by now. The curvature of the Earth was quite visible and the sky had not a trace of blue left in it. Stars were appearing against the darkness of space.

She'd known in the abstract that aether drives produced very little in the way of acceleration—not more than one or two percent of standard Earth gravity. They did not operate by applying brute force to the laws of motion, the way a cannon or rocket did, but by seizing hold of the very fabric of space and drawing the craft forward. Hence the supremely smooth manner of its motion. Undetectable, really, unless you had instruments or could visibly see the progress.

Her brother tugged at her elbow. "Let me see, Charlotte. Please let me see."

Reluctantly, she allowed Adrian to take her place at the rail.

"Oh!" he exclaimed. "We're already in outer space!"

A man next to him looked down and smiled. "We're still in the atmosphere, in fact. What they call the mesosphere—that's the part above the stratosphere but below the thermosphere."

He was a rather nice looking man, younger than Charlotte's father but no longer in his twenties. His English was fluent and idiomatic, but had some sort of accent Charlotte couldn't place. A bit Frenchy, but there was something else. Not German, she didn't think.

"Really?" Adrian looked profoundly disappointed. "When do we reach outer space, then?"

"That depends on your definitions," the man continued. "The term 'deep space' is ambiguous. It's generally agreed that low Earth orbit begins about one hundred and sixty kilometers—that would be one hundred of your English miles—above the surface. Anything lower than that, and your orbit degrades very quickly. But even low Earth orbit is still in the highest reaches of the atmosphere, so you get some drag. You need to get two thousand kilometers away from the planet before your orbit is really stable."

"So that's where outer space begins? Two thousand kilometers?"

The man shrugged. "So some would say. But the diplomats wrangling over the matter seem to be settling on a definition that would begin much lower, at one hundred and sixty kilometers—that is to say, low Earth orbit. On the other hand"—he smiled again, more widely—"space voyagers themselves seem to believe that 'outer space' is a purely practical term, which they define as that point at which they begin rotating their craft and centrifugal force replaces gravity from the standpoint of the vessel's crew. And passengers, in our case."

"When is that?"

"It varies from ship to ship. At five hundred kilometers altitude your weight will only have decreased by a little over ten percent. There'd be no point in beginning the centrifugal rotation, since the most that will achieve is between ten and thirty percent of standard Earth gravity, depending on the radius and speed of the rotation. You need to wait until the gravitational force of the Earth has declined below that."

Adrian was frowning, as he tried to follow the logic. Charlotte was a bit at a loss herself and had to concentrate on maintaining a smooth brow. Frowning was uncouth, in her opinion, especially for girls.

"Well, then . . ." Adrian shook his head. "When will this ship start rotating?"

"I don't know, since I've never traveled on it before. But it'll be quite a while, I suspect. The *Agincourt* is a luxury liner, not a naval vessel. Spinning too rapidly makes a lot of people uncomfortable"—his easy smile reappeared—"which is not something the BEPC wants to inflict on wealthy customers. So they'll use a very modest rotation. I don't believe the resultant centrifugal force will exceed fifteen percent of gee. That's just enough to counteract the medical problems caused by microgravity, at least for a voyage lasting weeks instead of months or years."

Charlotte was able to make sense of that, thankfully. More for the sake of seeming intelligent than because she really cared about the answer, she asked: "Couldn't they increase the centrifugal force if the ship had a bigger radius?"

Now, the man chuckled. The sound was good-natured rather than derisive, however.

"In theory, yes. But this is already—by a large margin—the biggest spacecraft in existence. Its hub has a diameter of one hundred meters or so. That's more than twice the diameter of any other space vessel." He waggled his hand. "Well, at least vessels using the torus-on-a-spindle design. There are some ships using other designs, that can attain much greater gee force. But those aren't very practical for large passenger vessels."

He seemed a pleasant man. Charlotte decided introductions were in order.

"I am Charlotte Luff. This is my brother Adrian."

"I am Alexander Evalenko. From Russia, although I've lived in Paris most of my adult life."

That explained the accent. Slavic with a heavy French overlay. Charlotte was pleased with her perspicacity.

"We're accompanying our father," Adrian said. "He's Professor Edward Luff. He's a scholar of Martian history."

"I am on a business trip, myself." Alexander made that same hand-waggling motion. "Too complicated to explain easily."

Alexander thought that sounded better than I am here to apprehend or execute a notorious terrorist. Probably the latter. They seemed like nice children.

A large man came up and placed a hand on Adrian Luff's shoulder. "There you are! I've been looking all over for you."

If that was a reproof, the tone was mild. As it should be, given the boy's response:

"I did wait for you, Father. But you and Mr. Shankar got—"

"Yes, yes, I know." The person now revealed to be Professor Edward Luff grimaced ruefully. "We got rather preoccupied. But all's well that ends well. What a magnificent view!"

"Isn't it?" Charlotte gestured toward Alexander. "This is Mr. Evalenko, Father. He was kind enough to explain some of the—ah—astronautical matters to us. He's a businessman. From Russia originally, but he's lived mostly in Paris."

The professor extended his hand and Alexander shook it.

So. The first suspect could now be eliminated. Under other circumstances, Alexander would have given Luff a careful and thorough scrutiny. Youngish—somewhere around forty—and of a seemingly athletic build despite his reputed scholarly status. Perfect British accent but Savinkov was reputed to be a superb linguist.

But Alexander couldn't imagine even the most ruthless assassin bringing his own children on a mission. And these had to be his children. The boy couldn't be more than ten or eleven years old; not the age for the sort of hardened accomplice such a mission would require. As for the girl . . .

Alexander recognized the type. Teenage; precocious;

not as mature as she fancied herself but not so far off, either; given to questioning established wisdom but only within acceptable limits; rather charming, in a gawky sort of way. The sort of girl the English seemed to produce as if they had a factory for the purpose.

If he'd still been a teenage boy, Alexander would have found her very attractive. But those days were far behind him now. What remained as evident as the full moon in a cloudless sky was that Charlotte Luff was no sort of revolutionist, much less an Eser fanatic with a revolver or bomb always ready to hand.

He looked around, examining the crowd without seeming to do so.

He spotted Drezhner some distance off. He was sightseeing! All his attention fixed on the slowly receding blue orb below them.

To a degree, Drezhner's distraction was understandable. This was, after all, the young Okhrana agent's first voyage into space where it was Alexander's third—albeit the first to another planet instead of Russia's orbital station. He could well remember how exciting, even exhilarating, he'd found the first such experience. Still, even then, he'd never let himself lose sight of his mission—which had been a far less critical one than the task they'd been charged with here.

The damn fool. This was probably the best opportunity they'd have to detect Savinkov, or at least narrow the number of possible suspects. Most of the passengers, having found their cabins and stowed their belongings, would be coming to the observation deck. Until they neared Mars, this was the most splendid sightseeing opportunity they'd have on the voyage. "Outer space" sounded very dramatic, but there was only so much time one could spend staring at stars wheeling slowly across the view as the ship rotated.

He gave the professor and his children a polite smile. "I must be off. Business to attend to, I'm afraid."

The Luffs paid him no mind at all, outside of an answering smile from the daughter. They were quite engrossed themselves in the magnificent vista.

He'd have to give Drezhner a subtle elbow as he passed him by, since they couldn't risk being seen engaged in conversation this early in the voyage. Part of the reason they had separate cabins was to establish that they didn't know each other. The main reason, of course, was that Okhrana field offices—even the Paris office—were also chronically short of funds. The only exceptions were the occasions when members of the imperial family traveled abroad. At such times the Okhrana was showered with money to make sure no harm came to whatever grand duke insisted on enjoying the glaciers on the Ile St. Louis or the view of the Eiffel Tower from the Trocadero.

Alexander was skeptical that the deception would work very well. The problem, as always when Russian agents operated in western Europe, was that the accents were almost impossible to disguise—especially an accent as pronounced as Drezhner's. It usually worked better to employ local agents; mercenaries, hired for pay. But such people would have been unusable for this sort of mission.

He gave Drezhner the requisite elbow, then passed on

his way without looking back to see if the idiot got the hint. In any event, he was preoccupied with trying to spot someone who might be Savinkov in the crowd pressing against the rail on the observation deck.

Savinkov had considered staying in the cabin but decided that might look suspicious. Almost no passengers except those ill or indisposed or blasé from many space voyages—there couldn't be more than a handful of those in the entire world—could resist the urge to see the Earth receding from view as the spacecraft departed for Mars. All an Okhrana agent would have to do would be to get access to the cabin logs to see which passengers had stayed in their cabin. At one stroke, they could narrow down the list of suspects far more quickly than they could looking for their target in the mob.

So, a sightseeing jaunt it would have to be. Besides, Savinkov could use the opportunity to start gauging the members of the crew. Before this voyage was over, there was a good chance the SRP agent would need to suborn one of them, in whatever manner proved possible.

Blessedly, Cecil Rhodes shared the most common characteristic of great capitalists. He was a cheap, chiseling bastard when it came to paying his own employees, however much largesse he might spread elsewhere.

The tools of the trade the public at large associated with revolutionists were incendiary pamphlets, incendiary devices, bombs and pistols. In Savinkov's experience, however—very extensive experience—they were often cast in the shade by the humble bribe.

CHAPTER 6

As the hours passed while the *Agincourt* moved slowly away from the Earth, Vera kept a wary eye out for the two men she was almost certain were with the Okhrana. They would be looking for Savinkov, not her, but it was still essential that she do nothing to draw their attention. If at any point the Okhrana agents took an interest in her of a political nature, they might be able to ferret out the identity and whereabouts of Savinkov.

The younger agent seemed like something of a dolt, from what she could see of him. To begin with, he apparently found it next to impossible to spy on people surreptitiously. Where a glance should have done, he stared. And if the object of his scrutiny was an attractive female, the stare bordered on an outright ogle.

That was all to Vera's advantage, though. She was in her mid-forties, much older than the young Okhrana agent, and her figure had long ago lost what it had ever possessed in the way of supple nubility. But it was still, as it had been since she was fourteen years of age, a demonstrably—one might even say, flamboyantly— female figure. Her clothing, moreover, though certainly respectable, had been designed to subtly emphasize her impressive bust. She was sure that the not-really-glances the agent sent her way whenever he passed near her had failed to register anything about her beyond her membership in the biological class of mammals.

The other Okhrana agent, unfortunately, was a

different matter. He was older, for one thing. Still quite a few years short of Vera's own age but no longer a callow youth, if he'd ever been one at all. He had an intelligent air about him, and the glances he sent at the people he was inspecting—quick glances; no dull-witted staring here—seemed to absorb a great deal in a small amount of time.

From his appearance and habits, she was fairly sure she even knew his identity. He was probably Alexander Evalenko, one of Rachkovsky's top agents.

Thankfully, she'd been able to attach herself to the Luff party before Evalenko caught sight of her. No matter how shrewd a man might be—even a woman—it was exceedingly difficult not to let first impressions sway one's assessments unduly. The first sight he would have had of Vera would have been her conversing with a vivacious teenage girl; and the second, the obvious interest taken in her by the girl's father. The fact that the father was several years younger than she was wouldn't matter. A man entering middle age; with children; a woman somewhat further into that period of life but still very "well-preserved," as the expression went.

The exact nature of the relationship would be unclear to Evalenko. But the one thing that would have registered on him was *not the one I'm looking for*. Not Savinkov, certainly; not anyone of interest.

She'd need to maintain the connection with the Luffs, at least in public. But Vera didn't expect that to be a problem.

She'd first considered encouraging the father's interest. Vera was not exactly what the French meant by the term femme fatale, but she was not far removed. A member of the genus, as it were, if not the species. Given Professor Luff's obviously healthy and active constitution, she'd probably have a good chance of seducing him.

That was still an option. But there could be complications, and to follow that course at the outset would almost certainly alienate Luff's daughter, whom Vera judged to be a simpler and easier target. All she had to do, really, was be herself—at least, part of herself. Besides, the girl seemed likeable and might very well prove to be more enjoyable company than her father. Such men could sometimes be . . .

Tiresome. She should know, being the widow of a university professor. The fact that her husband Vladimir had died in a Tsarist prison because of his revolutionary sympathies did not alter the fact that he'd often been buried in the minutiae of his scholarly pursuits. During the worst of such periods she might as well have been married to a cabbage.

Yes, the girl, definitely. That meant dealing with the brother as well, of course. But Vera was of an age where the behavior of boys was no longer very annoying. It was certainly no worse than the behavior of academics.

By the time the *Agincourt* reached the turnover point, Alexander had come to the same assessment of his associate's abilities as Vera Duchesne. To put it simply, Ilya Drezhner was a dolt.

Other terms came to mind as well, in several languages. Lummox, dummox and dimwit, from English. Dummkopf, from German. Durak from his native

Russian. And of course imbecile was always ready to hand from English, French—oh, any number of languages.

Was it impossible for the man to examine someone without calling attention to himself? Couldn't he understand that at this stage of their endeavor all they could hope to do was a rough winnowing of the terrorist chaff from the innocent—or at least irrelevant—wheat? All they could do at the moment was narrow down the potential suspects to a manageable number.

There was no chance that Savinkov would expose himself in any obvious manner. So what was the point of drawing attention to oneself by an excessively drawn-out scrutiny of the persons on the observation deck?

He'd even managed to irritate one fellow enough to cause a small verbal ruckus. Thankfully, that had resulted from Drezhner's ogling of the man's wife, not the man himself. Since the woman in question was obviously not Savinkov, Alexander could hope that if Savinkov had been present and witnessed the affair he would simply conclude that Drezhner was a boor rather than a Tsarist agent

Not that the two were mutually exclusive. The Okhrana had its full share of boors.

Still, most of those boors were at least competent at their work. If only the Paris office hadn't been so short-handed when the news arrived! Alexander could have picked one of his known associates to accompany him rather than this numbskull just arrived from St. Petersburg.

Ah, well. Such was the life of an Okhrana agent. It was still better than dealing with cavalrymen and the slightly dumber beasts they rode.

● ● ●

"Attention! Attention! Ladies and gentlemen, may I please have your attention."

The hubbub of conversation on the observation deck died away. Everyone present in this section of the deck turned to look at a ship's officer who'd just stepped onto a small platform he'd positioned by the railing. Not much more than a stool, really.

In the distance, both to her left and right, Charlotte could hear the voices of other officers calling out the same summons.

Attention! Attention! Ladies and gentlemen, may I please have your attention.

Attention! Attention! Ladies and gentlemen, may I please have your attention.

The observation deck went all the way around the ship, and there was no way to see all of it from any one vantage point. Apparently the passengers were being assembled in several groups simultaneously.

The officer addressing Charlotte's part of the deck continued:

"We have reached the turnover point and we will shortly be reorienting the ship. As you have no doubt noticed, your weight has been steadily dropping as we've moved farther from the Earth."

He gave them all the too-sweet smile of a man pleased that his charges had not behaved badly over the past period. "Let me take the occasion to thank all of you once again for not indulging yourselves in potentially dangerous gymnastics."

That had been a bit hard to resist, in truth. The constant reiteration by the ship's officers and crew of the perils of cavorting in low gravity had been counter-productive, in Charlotte's opinion. They served more to remind the less responsible passengers of the possibilities at hand than to deter them from partaking in them.

At one point, their father had had to physically restrain Adrian from leaping about. When a boy his age discovered himself weighing not more than a fifth of what he'd weighed back on Earth, he was inevitably tempted to emulate a gazelle.

No one had been forced to physically restrain Charlotte, needless to say. But she'd not deny having been tempted herself.

"We are now ten thousand miles removed from the Earth's surface," the officer went on, "and effective gravity has dropped to approximately ten percent of that experienced on the planet's surface. Hence, it is now time to begin rotating the ship and substitute centrifugal force for gravity. As I'm sure most of you know, prolonged exposure to null or even very low gravity is deleterious to health."

"How fast will we be rotating?" asked a portly middle-aged man a few yards away from Charlotte. He shook his head irritably, realizing that he'd posed the question badly. "What I mean is, what will be the effective gravity produced by the centrifugal force of the rotation?"

"About fifteen percent of standard gee," replied the officer.

"Will that be sufficient?" nervously asked a woman standing next to the man who'd spoken. She was probably his wife, judging from her matronly appearance. "In terms of our health, I mean."

"For this length of voyage, most certainly. If we were an exploratory ship headed for the outer planets with the prospect of a voyage duration of months rather than weeks ..." The officer's expression indicated some mild uncertainty—you could hardly call it apprehension. "I suppose we might want a somewhat faster rotation."

Adrian leaned over and whispered to her: "Ha! I'd like to see that, on this ship. Start spinning the *Agincourt* like a top! Half the people here would start puking their guts, you watch!"

He obviously found great satisfaction, even glee, at the thought.

Boys.

Charlotte knew what he was referring to, since she'd taken the time to familiarize herself with the basic issues involved in space travel. She'd done so partly out of curiosity but mostly to forestall her brother from bombarding her with loftily knowledgeable and exasperating little lectures.

The range within which a spacecraft could establish what amounted to artificial gravity using centrifugal force was determined by several factors.

First, obviously, diameter of the craft. Diameter of the rotation, rather, using the term "diameter" loosely. The *Agincourt*'s torus design was the most common but not the only one possible. You could accomplish the same thing by spinning two nacelles around each other connected only by a pylon or even a cable.

The limits here were set partly by engineering but mostly by economics. Building an aethership the size of the *Agincourt* was fiendishly expensive. The cost of building one that significantly exceeded its torus diameter was simply not practical. Not today, at least.

Second, the existing diameter determined the possible centrifugal force by adding the simple element of rotation. It would be very easy to rotate the ship fast enough to achieve a full standard gravity at the rim of the torus. Theoretically, you could do that with a ship whose diameter was much smaller than the *Agincourt*'s.

Unfortunately, a large percentage of people simply couldn't handle rapid rotation. They got queasy, even sick. A naval vessel or exploratory vessel could select its crew from those people who were resistant to such effects. But not a passenger vessel; certainly not a luxury liner.

In practice, it was not possible to rotate a ship the size of the *Agincourt* at a speed much greater than one revolution per minute. That was enough to produce an effective gee force of about fifteen percent of standard Earth gravity. As the ship's officer said, just enough to counteract the medical risks of microgravity.

There was a slight bustle at the edges of the crowd as a few newcomers made their appearance. Mrs. Smith was among them, looking quite aggrieved.

"They made me leave the cabin," she complained. "Quite rude about it, they were."

Charlotte discounted that last. Their governess was firmly of the opinion that anyone who contradicted her desires, unless that person was her employer, was by definition being rude. Never mind how politely they spoke or comported themselves.

"We've moved all passengers out of the cabins and assembled everyone here on the observation deck," explained the officer. "This is the best place for everyone to be as we make the transition from one configuration to another."

"Oh, this'll be splendid fun!" said Adrian.

It was rather entertaining, actually—although certainly not to the extent Adrian imagined it to be.

All the passengers were first assembled against the railing. Then, the crew brought out bizarre-looking staircases—portable steps, rather—that could be swiveled to span the gap between the railing they were against and the railing above them that stood out from (what was now) the wall of the deck at a ninety degree angle.

Then, very slowly at first but soon picking up speed, the ship began to rotate. As the stars began wheeling past, Charlotte could feel the centrifugal force starting to force her against the railing. (In that direction, rather; there were two rows of people between her and the railing itself.)

Once the force became palpable but before it became a problem, crewmen extended the staircases and began assisting passengers in making the combined climb and transfer over to the wall that was becoming a floor for the newly-configured observation deck.

Had the existing gravity remained at one gee and the centrifugal force been of equivalent effect, the result would have been calamitous. Particularly athletic or agile people—Charlotte herself, for instance—could have made the transition without mishap. But most people would have suffered injuries of one sort or another, up to and including broken bones.

At an effective gravity of 0.1 gee in both directions,

however, even the plumpest and most sedentary person could manage the business quite easily. At least, with the assistance of crew members.

Not without complaint, however. Many complaints; great complaints; constant complaints. The clientele of a luxury aethership like the *Agincourt* was mostly made up of very wealthy and (self-)important people. That is to say, the class of people for whom complaint, reproof and criticism of their lessers comes trippingly off the tongue.

Charlotte refrained from blowing any raspberries or making other rude and ribald remarks at the expense of the complainers.

Her brother did not. And for once—she had to be honest about this—Charlotte was pleased by Adrian's rambunctious behavior.

So, she was quite sure, were the ship's crewmen.

Finally, it was done. The transition complete; fancy chairs and tables brought forth to provide solace to the passengers as they rested from their labors; the finest delicacies and drinks made available to assuage all grievances and griefs.

"Oh, what a splendid adventure!" said Adrian.

CHAPTER 7

It didn't take Charlotte very long to figure out three Profound Truths about space voyages that would last for weeks and keep what was actually quite a small number of people, somewhere around five hundred passengers and one hundred and fifty crewmen—once you factored in "weeks" and "rather limited space"—in close proximity forever and ever and ever.

The first of the Profound Truths was that confining hundreds of people for long stretches of times in an enclosed space which could not in the nature of things be aired out—the vacuum of space not being suitable for the purpose—produced aromas that could most delicately be described as "fatiguing." Privately, she did not disagree with her brother's preferred term of "stinky" but she found his constant use of it also fatiguing.

The perfumes and colognes that many people started slathering on to compensate for the problem only made it worse.

The second of the Profound Truths was that listening to scholars like her father and the Shankar couple discuss the arcane complexities of their field was to tedium what little brothers were to aggravation.

The third of the Profound Truths was that sophisticated, intelligent, friendly, middle-aged women of somewhat exotic origin were to salvation from boredom what water was to thirst in the desert.

The only fly in this ointment was that Adrian figured out the Truths as quickly as she did. Still, even little brothers were not as irritating as usual when you had someone like Madame Duchesne around. The German widow handled Adrian's eleven-year-old lack of couth gracefully and easily, without ever needing to neglect her primary mission on this voyage, which was to keep Charlotte herself from going mad.

* * *

"Oh, no," Madame Duchesne said, smiling. "German bureaucrats aren't everything legend makes them out to be. I assure you, they don't refuse to eat breakfast until their wives have presented them with the menu in triplicate."

She paused, to admire a particularly striking vine that wove all through the grid making up the side of the corridor. Charlotte was not familiar with the vine, despite its flamboyantly-colored flowers. That was not surprising, since they were in a portion of the hydroponics promenade that was tropical in its temperature and humidity. None of the flora was remotely English.

Still examining the vine, Madame Duchesne pursed her lips. "Well... Prussians, maybe. But certainly not Bavarians or Swabians. Do be careful, Adrian. That glass panel—"

Turning her head, Charlotte saw that her brother was reaching out to touch one of the huge glass panels that allowed sunlight reflected from mirrors to bathe the hydroponic garden.

"Oh, it can't be that fragile," scoffed Adrian, "or it'd be too risky—ow!"

He snatched back his hand and stuffed his forefinger into his mouth.

"—is likely to be quite hot," Madame Duchesne finished, in a mild tone of voice. "They have some sort of shielding embedded in the glass to deflect radiation. Quite effective, but it tends to absorb a lot of energy. You do need to be cautious in space, you know."

Adrian winced, and kept sucking on his finger.

Served him right!

• • •

"It has to be one of those four men," insisted Ilya Drezhner. "Who else could it be?"

Alexander stifled his temper. By now, halfway through the voyage, practically anything Drezhner said was aggravating, due to the man's insufferable self-assurance. For Drezhner, all things came in clear hues and tones. He recognized the existence of gray, yes—but for him, gray had no shades, no indistinctions. It was a color every bit as clear and sharp-edged as black or white.

Alexander didn't even disagree with him, in this instance. He was almost sure himself that Gavril Savinkov had to be one of the same four men Drezhner's suspicion had fallen upon. But . . .

There was always a "but," in their peculiar occupation. The only colors one encountered in counter-revolutionary work were hues of gray.

The simple truth was that there were no clear descriptions of Savinkov, despite the assassin's notoriety. The man was reputed to have organized the assassination of Dmitry Sipyagin, the Minister of the Interior, as well as that of two provincial governors and a deputy commander of the Imperial Corps of Gendarmes. Yet, somehow, less was known of him than any other top leader of the Socialist-Revolutionary Party or any member of the SRP's Combat Organization.

According to the reports available, Savinkov was male, probably of average height and build, probably in his late thirties or early forties. If various rumors were to be believed, he was probably Jewish too, but that was of little help. A very high percentage of Russia's revolutionaries were Jewish in their origin, though almost none of them observed the faith any longer.

It was the commonly held opinion of the cavalry officers whose company Alexander had once shared that Jews could be easily detected by their mere appearance. One only had to look for a large, hooked nose, dark and close-set eyes, and a shifty expression. The same cavalry officers, of course, also subscribed to every idiotic superstition known to man or beast. Most of them could have been outplayed at checkers by their mounts if the horses had only had opposable thumbs to move the game pieces.

Alexander knew a great many Jews, partly because he encountered them as enemies and partly because the Okhrana employed many Jews. (Of necessity, and regulations be damned.) Of that number, only one of them shared any resemblance at all to the stereotype— and that was simply because the man's nose did have a distinct curve, although it was not especially large.

The problem with Savinkov's description was not even so much that it was hopelessly vague. Could it even be trusted at all? Years of experience had taught Alexander that revolutionists could at times be fiendishly clever. (Also, at times, incredibly foolish—but only an incompetent agent or one who was a fool himself relied on his enemy to make mistakes.)

It was possible, therefore, that Savinkov was tall, or fat, or bald. It was possible that he was considerably older than the reports. It was also possible that he was a young man, although that was unlikely given his long string of accomplishments.

For that matter, it was even conceivable that all the reports were entirely inaccurate and "Gavril" Savinkov was actually a woman. Russia's revolutionary organizations had many women in their ranks, some of whom had become assassins themselves. As far back as 1879, in one of Russia's very first terrorist incidents, Vera Zasulich had seriously wounded Colonel Theodore Trepov, the governor of St. Petersburg.

Zasulich had been captured but later escaped. In fact, she was still at large.

Alexander was quite sure Zasulich herself was not aboard the *Agincourt*. Her description was not only well-known, he'd seen photographs of the woman.

But it simply couldn't be ruled out entirely that the Okhrana's intelligence was wildly off the mark. Perhaps Savinkov was actually a woman. Perhaps he was indeed a man, but a woman impersonating him was undertaking this mission. For that matter, perhaps the whole mission was a figment of the Okhrana's imagination and he and Drezhner were wasting their time altogether.

Perhaps—perhaps—perhaps—

Such was the inescapable epistemology of the counter-revolutionist's trade.

To which truth his companion Ilya Drezhner seemed completely oblivious. Why had this man ever joined the Okhrana in the first place? He seemed ideally suited for leading cavalry charges.

Alexander reminded himself that another of the great truths of the counter-revolutionist's trade was that you worked with the material available, as inferior as that material might be. He'd once even had to work with a

Lapp reindeer herder, who had been completely illiterate and possessed of an odor that was quite indescribable.

But—he suppressed a sigh, here—the Lapp had actually been a rather intelligent man, given his limitations. He'd certainly not suffered from Drezhner's rigidity of thought. It seemed that herding reindeer was a profession that taught a man to avoid dogmatic assumptions, whereas riding horses did the exact opposite.

Back to the matter at hand, he told himself firmly. His reservations and caveats were simply the product of the scrupulous intellect of a good agent. On balance, he did not really think the accepted assumptions about Savinkov were incorrect.

Which meant . . . he was indeed one of the four men Drezhner had pointed out.

"Look here, Edward," said Vijay Shankar. "It's a passage from the Black Yajur Veda." He swiveled the volume on the table between them so that the writing faced Luff, then tapped his finger on a particular line of text.

Edward Luff's knowledge of Sanskrit was passable, but only that. It took him a moment or two to understand the meaning of the lines indicated.

From Earth I have mounted to the atmosphere;
From the atmosphere I have mounted to the sky.

"And here," Shankar said, laying a second, more slender volume atop the first. "This is in the White Yajur Veda." Again, he tapped his finger on a line.

The line was very short:

Earth! Ether! Sky!

Luff made a face. "That all depends on the translator, Vijay. The term 'ether,' I mean."

"True. But what's indisputably clear is that a tripartite—not a dual—distinction is being made. Earth and sky, which is common to any ancient tradition. But then there's something in between. Something else."

"And it's not just a reference to air, either," said Vijay's wife Sumati. She leaned over the table and flipped a few pages in the book, then mimicked her husband's finger-tapping. "Look at these lines."

From earth to air's mid-region have I mounted,
And from mid-air ascended to heaven.
From the high pitch of heaven's cope
I came into the world of light.

Edward had to admit, the passage did seem like a description of interplanetary travel. The first journey, via an airship, to a transfer station; then the journey into space aboard an aethership.

Except . . .

"Doesn't this all seem very . . . call it vague, if you will. Why use such poetic ways to depict what is ultimately a mundane matter? Would you use iambic pentameter and a slathering of classical allusions to depict a train journey?"

Shankar shrugged. "We know very little of Indian history during the Vedic period—any part of it, much less the earliest stages. The Rig Veda is the oldest of the sacred texts and it dates back at least three and a half thousand years."

Sumati chimed in again. "And remember that if our theory is correct, what we're calling the Martian period would have antedated Vedic civilization, possibly by thousands of years."

"Almost certainly by thousands of years," said Vijay. "Which means that the references in the Vedas came much later than the activities they depict. The analogy might be with Homer's epics, which were almost certainly composed long after the events they speak about."

"Except, if you're right," mused Edward, "the gap between the actual events and the Vedic record was measured in millennia rather than centuries. That would certainly explain the imprecision of the texts. In essence, you have people in a technologically primitive period trying to depict what their ancestors remembered of an ancient society whose science and industry was highly developed."

He chuckled. "And, of course, your theory has a built-in explanation for the lack of an archaeological record."

The Brahmin scholar shrugged again. "Yes, granted. But the mere fact that it's convenient to our theory doesn't make it incorrect."

"No, no," Luff agreed. "It is indeed true, as counter-intuitive as it might seem to most people, that the archaeological remains of primitive civilizations will long outlive the remains of highly advanced technical societies. The pyramids of Egypt have survived for three thousand years and will undoubtedly survive at least that many years into the future. Whereas if modern civilization collapses, none of its works will survive much more than a few centuries except some gold, silver and jewelry—items which will reveal very little of the technical development of the society which produced them."

He leaned back in his chair. "Is there more?"

Sumati brushed back her long hair. "For one thing, there are frequent references throughout the Vedas to two worlds."

"Sometimes multiple worlds," said Vijay. He smiled. "And before you raise the objection that most religions make a distinction between this world and a more spiritual one, these references seem—to use your term—rather mundane. It can't be proved, but the . . . call it 'feel' or 'flavor' of the texts seem to be matter-of-factly referring to two actual worlds. That is to say, physical worlds."

Luff nodded. "And what else?"

This time, it was Sumati who took the larger of the two books and flipped through the pages until she found the one she was looking for. She laid the book down in front of Edward, after turning it so the text faced him again.

Her finger tapped three times in quick succession, indicating three separate lines. Luff leaned over and studied them.

> *That most auspicious One whose hue is coppery*
> *and red and brown*
> *May he who glides away, whose neck is azure,*
> *and whose hue is red*
> *Homage to him the Azure-nested, the thousand-*
> *eyed, the bountiful*

When she saw that he was finished, Sumati leaned over and flipped a few more pages, then tapped twice. "These two lines also."

> *Pursuer, Lord of Soma juice, thou cleaver,*
> *colored blue and red*
> *   . . . their necks are blue, their throats are white*

He leaned back again. "Vague, so blasted vague. But . . ."

He cocked a semi-skeptical, semi-fascinated eye at the Hindu couple sitting across from him. He was by now quite oblivious to the murmuring voices that surrounded them. The table they occupied was just one of many in the crowded observation deck. "Do you really think these are references to the so-called Old Ones?"

Shankar raised his hands and spread them in a gesture that somehow mirrored Luff's expression: half-doubt; half fierce interest.

"At the moment, I can't say. Ask me in a few weeks— best say, few months—when I've had a chance to examine the Martian texts in the vaults at Ghlaktora. But one of the things that all references to the Old Ones that I've seen share in common is their coloration. It's always red— or reddish, at least—but especially blue."

"The necks in particular?"

It was Vijay's turn to chuckle. "Alas! One of the things the texts definitely do not share in common is a morphological depiction of the Old Ones, other than a general sense they were monstrous. It's not clear that they even had 'necks' at all, at least as we use the term."

"The clearest description seems to picture them

standing on four legs," said Sumati, "with a torso of some kind and a head at the top. But the shape does not seem to have been a terrestrial one. From what I can tell, the torso went straight up from the legs, the way a camera sits on a tripod—not the way you'd picture something like a centaur or a sphinx."

She spread her hands also. "Whether there was any sort of neck is entirely unclear."

"If they existed at all," said Luff.

"If they existed at all," agreed Shankar.

CHAPTER 8

The voyage to Mars had now lasted six weeks, and the *Agincourt* was much closer to its destination than to its planet of departure. Savinkov felt confident, therefore, that the two Okhrana men still had no idea concerning the real identity of the notorious assassin.

The problem that remained would surface at the moment of their arrival. The passengers would then scatter to their various destinations, and unless steps were taken there was the risk that Savinkov would be exposed because the agent had no clear destination. More precisely, had no clear reason to choose that destination in the first place.

Had Savinkov known the Okhrana would manage to place two agents aboard the aethership before it left Earth, the assassin might have chosen a different cover identity. That of a reporter, perhaps. But it was too late now.

It was not a large risk, granted. Savinkov was not headed for Tryddoc Aru, which was the obvious place an Eser terrorist would go. Still, the older of the two Okhrana agents was shrewd. That was Evalenko, one of Rachkovsky's chief lieutenants. Just the sort of man whose suspicions would be aroused by anyone behaving in a manner whose logic wasn't readily apparent. It was best to be careful.

So.

Savinkov had planned for this and placed the necessary bribes—the first, three weeks ago; the second, yesterday; and the third and last would come after the deed paid for had been done. That would happen shortly before their arrival at Mars.

As deeds went, it wasn't a particularly dark one. Nonetheless, Savinkov felt a certain amount of regret at the necessity. The victim of the upcoming deed was quite blameless in the affair, with no connection at all to the bitter struggle between Russia's revolutionary forces and the Tsar's instruments of oppression and reaction.

But, it had to be done. The goal of the mission was too important. Savinkov couldn't afford to take any chances that might in any way be forestalled or mitigated. The scheme was clever; clever enough, the agent was sure, to continue deflecting Evalenko's attention elsewhere.

As it happened, Alexander Evalenko's attention had now settled almost exclusively upon two men. There was only a fortnight left in the voyage, and the Okhrana agent no longer had the luxury of taking his time and carefully weighing all possibilities.

The first possibility was the man known as Klaus Kuhn, who claimed to be a Swiss pharmaceutical representative. To begin with, Kuhn was the right age and had the right appearance—at least, insofar as that term could be applied to someone whose description was as vague as Savinkov's.

The same could be said of several other men on the ship, of course. But Kuhn's behavior had been suspicious throughout the voyage. He was rarely seen, spending most of his time in his stateroom—which was all the more odd given that his stateroom, 17 F, was one of the smaller ones. When he did appear, it was only at odd hours. He'd make brief visits to the cafés on the observation deck and hydroponics promenade and order very little besides coffee. Alexander had spied on him and seen the man, on one occasion, steal some of the bread and fruit that were placed on the tables to attract customers. The word "steal" seemed appropriate, even though the food was given out at no charge, because Kuhn surreptitiously slid the items into the pockets of his coat and took them away. Presumably, he'd eat the stuff later in the privacy of his cabin.

Clearly enough, this was not the behavior of a pharmaceutical representative. Certainly not a Swiss one.

His speech seemed wrong, too. His German was fluent and idiomatic, as was Alexander's own. But something about Kuhn's accent didn't seem right for someone from Switzerland. Alexander wasn't sure exactly what it was, since his own accent was far worse.

But—but—but—

The fact that Kuhn's behavior could be explained as the behavior of a Eser assassin didn't mean that it couldn't be explained as something else as well—which they were missing because they didn't know the man's history.

By way of analogy, a man is seen to gesticulate and speak to no one in sight as he walks down a street. Clearly this is the behavior of a lunatic. But when accosted by the police and questioned, the man—now quite embarrassed—explains that he has to give a speech to a luncheon club and was practicing on his way, not realizing how publicly he was behaving.

The problem with Kuhn as their suspect was that he was too suspicious. Would an Eser terrorist—any of them, much less Savinkov—behave in such a manner?

Steal food? That made no sense at all. The SRP's Combat Organization was not that short of funds. If they could afford to send their top assassin to Mars by way of the human race's most prestigious aethership, they could certainly afford to give the man enough money to pay for meals along the way.

No, Kuhn wasn't their man. That he was guilty of something or other, Alexander didn't doubt at all. But whatever Kuhn was up to, he wasn't working on behalf of the SRP. Or any organization, for that matter, revolutionary or otherwise. His semi-desperate behavior was the earmark of a man running on the edge, entirely on his own.

So, finally, Alexander settled on his other principal suspect, a man going by the name of Antoine Jelinek. He was supposed to be a Frenchman of Czech extraction; a dealer in exotic art, heading to Mars in search of extra-terrestrial—i.e., super-exotic—objects of art.

The story was not that implausible, actually. The reason Jelinek had drawn Alexander's attention was that the story's very plausibility provided the Frenchman with an excellent rationale for traveling anywhere on Mars he chose to go without creating any suspicion. He could be in Ogygis Regio one day, over in the Great Spillway a short time later, then in Protei Locus—hopping all over the red planet like a flea, losing anyone who might be curious about him . . .

And then, suddenly, he appears in Tryddoc Aru. Bringing with him strange objects of Martian art that could easily be used to smuggle weapons and explosives into the most carefully guarded city on the red planet.

"I'll follow Jelinek, once we arrive on Mars," he told Drezhner. "You go after the Underwood fellow. He's the only one we know for sure is headed for Crenex."

"I still think Kuhn—"

"Forget Kuhn. I've told you already—he's behaving too suspiciously to be Savinkov."

From the expression on his face, Drezhner was going to continue protesting. But Alexander had lost patience with the man. It was time to simply use his authority.

"Enough," he said coldly.

Drezhner was nothing if not stubborn. His contrary nature having been thwarted on the matter of Kuhn, he chose to plant himself on different ground. Much the way a mule, barred from the house, might try to force its way into the barn.

"But you said yourself the most likely place Savinkov was headed was Tryddoc Aru."

"Yes, I know—and so it is, still. But we are now nearing the end of our voyage, after having spent weeks investigating what we could. This means that we now have facts at our disposal as well as pure logic. And the facts are these."

He began counting off his fingers. "Fact One. The only people aboard the *Agincourt* who have indicated their destination is Tryddoc Aru are people we do not suspect of being Savinkov. Or have you changed your mind and decided that Reginald Barnes and Bertram Stans—one or the other or perhaps both, if their inseparability is a sign of mystic coexistence—are really our Russian master terrorist?"

Ilya glared at him. Barnes and Stans were two English bankers traveling together. The chance that either one of them might be Savinkov was nil. Their bona fides were too well-established, too solid—not least of all, too easy to check. Prominent bankers in the City of London were anything but obscure people.

"Now let's move on to Fact Two. Of the remaining suspects—leaving aside Jelinek, Underwood and Kuhn, for the moment—none of them are men of a suitable age or constitution to be active assassins. Unless you suspect that Edward Luff's two children are actually Eser midgets—well, one midget, anyway; the girl's close to full grown—who came along to provide Savinkov with a cunning disguise."

"If Luff is actually Savinkov, those probably wouldn't be his own children at all," Ilya said sourly. "Have you ever thought of that possibility?"

"I did, as a matter of fact. By that scenario, the

Duchesne woman would be an auxiliary Eser agent, who came along to spirit the children away when the proper time arrives so that Luff—Savinkov, that is—would have a completely free hand. But it didn't take me long to conclude that such a scheme was too elaborate, too ornate—not to mention too expensive. And how do you explain Luff's connection with that mob of Hindus? Is he planning to strike down Russian officials on Mars by the sheer tedium of their scholarly debates?

"Besides, Ilya"—Alexander waved his hand impatiently—"we know Luff's travel arrangements. You were the one yourself who bribed the purser's assistant to find out."

"That just tells us where their luggage is supposed to go."

"So? Terrorists need to change their clothes on occasion just like anyone else. Especially since on Mars they'll find precious little in the way of garment shops or laundries."

That was purely a guess on Alexander's part. He had no idea how native Martians handled such matters. But it didn't matter. The notion that Edward Luff might be Savinkov was so outlandish that Alexander saw no reason to waste his time and mental energy trying to come up with detailed and careful rebuttals. Drezhner himself wasn't that stupid. He was just being pigheaded.

He was still glaring at him, too. What an insufferable man!

This was a waste of time. "Just do as you're told," he commanded Drezhner. "After we land, you follow Underwood. There's a radio station at our embassy in Crenex which you can use to report to me."

"Report to you where? You said yourself that Jelinek will be moving about."

Alexander managed to restrain himself from responding angrily. It was a legitimate question, after all, even if he was sure Drezhner had only raised it to be obstreperous.

Unfortunately, radio communication on Mars was difficult, and could only be done at all by using large transmitters—which meant there weren't many of them. The problem, he'd been told by the technical expert at the Paris office, was the planet's ionosphere. Unlike Earth's, it was ill-suited to transmit long-range radio signals. Even the powerful radios at the Russian embassies and consulates on Mars had poor and erratic reception if the signal came from any great distance.

"We have a consulate at one of the cities of the Octad Gentillus in the Vallis Agathodaemonis. Mooktar, it's called. It's less than thirty kilometers from the city of Coprates, where we'll be landing. You can send a message there as well as to the embassy at Tryddoc Aru."

Tryddoc Aru was located in the Sinus Aurorae region. With the embassy at Crenex and the consulate in Coprates, the three radio stations made a roughly equilateral triangle with each other. In the event Drezhner had to communicate with him, Alexander should be able to get the message soon enough no matter where he went.

Soon enough, at least, given that he didn't think his subordinate was going to encounter anything that required an urgent response. The likelihood that Underwood was Savinkov was quite low, in Alexander's estimate. He was almost certain that Jelinek was the assassin—if Savinkov was on Mars at all, which he might well not be. The longer the voyage had lasted, the less confident Alexander had become that the Okhrana's intelligence was accurate.

He was not dismayed by the prospect that their mission might turn out to be completely pointless, however. Blind alleys and fruitless expeditions—what the English called a wild goose chase—were simply part and parcel of the life of an Okhrana agent. One might as well be dismayed by the sunset or the tides.

CHAPTER 9

"So where will you go first, Vera?" asked Edward Luff. The voyage was almost over and he'd long been on first name terms with the Duchesne widow. "Vallis Agathodaemonis or the mountain?"

"I'd do Nix Olympica, for sure!" exclaimed his son. "It's not only the solar system's greatest mountain—it's a volcano." A moment later he added, "Not active at the moment, though."

He sounded quite disgruntled, as if having a gigantic volcano erupt in their midst would be some sort of splendid adventure. Charlotte rolled her eyes.

Madame Duchesne just smiled at the boy, however. She had the patience of a saint.

"For you, perhaps, Adrian. But I'm a creaky old woman."

"Oh, I'd hardly say that!" protested Edward. No token protest, either. It was by now obvious to Charlotte that her father had become attracted to the woman in the course of their voyage. To the point where Charlotte herself was beginning to reconsider her previous assumption that the age difference involved was an insurmountable obstacle.

Smiling more widely now, Duchesne fluttered the fingers of her left hand. "Well, perhaps 'creaky' is overstating the matter. But I'm still of an age where sightseeing among the exotic cities of the Octad Gentillus is more enticing than climbing up the side of a mountain that is approximately the size of Iceland and three times higher than Mount Everest."

Adrian rubbed his hands gleefully. "Not to mention that at its peak, Nix Olympica sticks up out of Mars's atmosphere! That's how tall it is!"

Charlotte was startled—enough, in fact, to express herself out loud, something she tried never to do in response to one of her brother's inane factoids.

"You're joking!" she exclaimed.

"I am not!"

"Not joking perhaps," said their father, in a tone of mild reproof. "But you are exaggerating. I believe at the very top of Nix Olympica that the atmosphere still exists, although it's only ten or fifteen percent of the planet's normal atmospheric pressure."

Madame Duchesne made a face. "Either way, much too thin for me. I'm a creature of bistros, not barometers. I can only hope that bistros—or some reasonable equivalent—exist on Mars. But if they do, I think my best chance of finding them would be somewhere in the Octad Gentillus."

They were all sitting at a table which they shared with Vijay and Sumati Shankar, as well as Mrs. Smith. The rest of the Hindu group was seated at three adjacent tables. Outside the windows that surrounded the observation deck, the stars wheeled by. The magnificent view of Mars which they'd enjoyed for the past few days was no longer in evidence, however. The *Agincourt*'s crew had carried through the reconfiguration of the ship the day before. The planet they were nearing was now located beneath the floor of the observation deck; not visible unless one was standing at the railing.

A choking sound came from the other end of the table from where Charlotte was seated. Leaning over and looking to her left, she saw that Mrs. Smith had her hand on her throat. Her eyes seemed to be bulging a little. She seemed quite pale, too; more so than usual.

Again, the woman made that peculiar choking sound. As if something were lodged in her throat, although her mouth was open and she was breathing normally. Well, perhaps not normally—but she was breathing. She couldn't be choking on something.

"Are you quite well, Mrs. Smith?" asked Charlotte's father. He was frowning slightly, as a man does when he's concerned but not yet really alarmed.

Mrs. Smith looked at him. A bit desperately, Charlotte thought. And, again, she made that choking sound.

"Something is wrong," said Madame Duchesne. Her tone was firm; even decisive. She rose from her chair and went around the table to take Mrs. Smith by the shoulders.

"Come, dear. We must get you to the infirmary."

Madame Duchesne shifted her grip under the woman's arms and lifted her up out of the chair. She did so with complete ease, from what Charlotte could tell. The German widow's ample figure obviously included quite a bit of muscle.

By now, Charlotte's father had risen and come over as well. "She's absolutely right, Mrs. Smith. We must get you to the infirmary at once."

The governess gave Charlotte's father an apologetic grimace. She then tried to take a few steps away from the table, with Edward Luff's hand under one arm and Madame Duchesne's under the other.

And promptly collapsed.

Fortunately, Charlotte's father caught her before she fell to the floor. As he held her up, Madame Duchesne inspected her face.

"She's breathing but she's unconscious, Edward. We need to hurry." Charlotte's father picked up the governess and cradled her limp body in his arms. He was a large man, and rather strong despite his sedentary occupation.

Vera was already moving toward the infirmary. But within seconds, three stewards arrived. One of them offered to carry Mrs. Smith, but Charlotte's father shook his head.

"I'm fine. Just clear the way to the infirmary."

Edward Luff returned to the table half an hour later and resumed his seat.

"What's wrong with Mrs. Smith?" Charlotte asked.

"They don't know. Something, clearly. She's still unconscious. Fortunately, all her vital signs seem . . . well, adequate, at least. She's apparently not in any immediate danger. But . . ."

He seemed a bit lost. "But . . ."

"But she won't be able to resume her duties tomorrow. When we land on Mars." That came from Mr. Shankar.

"Ah . . . no. I don't imagine there's any chance of it. In fact . . ."

"She may not recover for some time," Mr. Shankar said. "Days, possibly weeks."

Charlotte's father sighed. "Yes. Exactly. There is a hospital—for humans, I mean—at Coprates. Where we're landing. It's in the city itself, of course, not out at the aerodrome."

"I think it's 'astrodome,' Father." That was her brother Adrian's utterly useless contribution to the crisis.

"Yes, yes," her father replied distractedly.

"Where's Madame Duchesne?" Charlotte asked.

"She's staying with Mrs. Smith for the moment. I told her I'd be back as soon as possible."

He still looked distracted. Charlotte saw Mr. and Mrs. Shankar exchange what seemed to be a meaningful glance. Then Mrs. Shankar leaned over and said softly, "Charlotte, why don't you and your brother go see to Mrs. Smith yourselves, for a short while."

Charlotte might have protested, but she was fairly sure she understood the purpose behind Mrs. Shankar's suggestion. She'd given the matter some thought herself, over the past few weeks, and while she hadn't come to any definite conclusion she was inclined toward the positive.

"Come along, Adrian," she said, rising to her feet.

Naturally, her brother—oblivious as boys were—put

up a protest. But their father seconded Mrs. Shankar's suggestion. Rather firmly.

After the children left, Sumati got straight to the point. "I hope Mrs. Smith will recover soon, and suffer no permanent ill effects. But I have to tell you honestly, Edward, that I think of this as something of a blessing. Given"—here she looked very stern—"that you've been incapable thus far of making what seems to both Vijay and myself a clear and simple decision regarding a clear and simple matter."

Edward smiled crookedly. "Leave it to a woman to call such a thing 'clear and simple.' I think it's anything but that."

He looked to Vijay, seeking support from another male. But the Brahmin scholar shook his head. "I am an Indian, Edward. On this subject I share my wife's hard-headed and practical attitude, not the phantasmagories of you Englishmen."

"I don't think 'phantasmagories' is a real word, Vijay," Luff said.

"Perhaps not in London. But I assure you that in my native Punjab it comes quite trippingly off the tongue of those Indians who speak English at all, after they meet their first Englishman in the flesh."

"Ours was an arranged marriage, as you know," said Shankar's wife. "I think it's turned out very well. Vijay and I met for the first time at our wedding. He was a seventeen-year-old virgin and I was the nearest thing possible, being the widow of a first husband who was sixty-three when I married him and not in good health. So what are you complaining about? You've had weeks to contemplate the subject of Vera Duchesne. Weeks. In close and constant proximity, to boot."

"Is it her age that concerns you?" asked Vijay. He smiled at his wife. "Sumati is almost ten years older than I am. Trust me. It's never been a problem. To the contrary—there are many advantages to having an older wife."

Luff shook his head. "No, it's not that. To tell you the truth, I never think about Vera's age any longer. She's . . . ah . . ."

"Quite attractive." That came from Sumati. Stated firmly, flatly—something not to be disputed.

"Well. Yes."

He sighed and ran fingers through his hair.

Hair which was beginning to grow a bit thin. Edward was still in good health, but he was no longer a young man.

"Your children are already fond of her, you know," said Vijay.

"Yes, I know. Don't think I haven't thought about that. Especially in terms of Charlotte. It's hard for a girl her age, not to have a mother to turn to for advice when . . . well. When she needs to."

A throaty little laugh came from Sumati. "And when it involves matters she's not about to raise with her father."

"Well. That. Yes."

Again, he ran fingers through his hair.

Sumati leaned over and placed a hand on his arm. "Edward, you don't have to propose to the woman within the next hour. You need simply ask her if she'd be willing to forego her tourist plans in order to accompany us to our destination. Because with Mrs. Smith being ill, and you committed to your work—you have no leeway in the matter, given that the Meredith Foundation is paying for it all—you desperately need help with the children."

"And what if she declines?"

Sumati sat back and shrugged. "Then that is the answer to your unspoken question along with the spoken one."

She left unsaid the obvious corollary. If Vera Duchesne said yes, she'd also be replying to an unspoken question as well as the one spoken aloud.

Edward wasn't sure which made him the most nervous. But he wasn't actually obtuse, despite being a male, a scholar, and an Englishman. The very fact that he was nervous about both outcomes made it clear he needed to ask the question.

"Yes, Edward. Of course I'll come with you to Ghlaktora." Vera Duchesne waved her hand airily. "My own plans were simply those of a bored, well-to-do widow. I can always be a tourist again. If need be."

The English governess had had a worse reaction to the poison than was normal. The waiter who'd placed it in her food came to Savinkov's cabin in a panic late that night.

"You said she wouldn't die!" he hissed. He was quite agitated, but trying to keep his voice down. His gaze shifted nervously back and forth, scanning the corridor for passersby.

"And she won't," the assassin replied confidently, trying to soothe the fellow. "She's just having a bad reaction. A few people do. It will pass, in a few days, and she'll be fine again."

"They'll investigate. Suspicion will fall upon me."

The waiter's anxiety was excessive. If all the people at his table had been affected, he might indeed come under suspicion. One person falling ill could be caused by anything. But there was no point wasting time in an argument.

"Wait here." Savinkov went back into the cabin and emerged perhaps ten seconds later, with a small vial in hand. "Take this. Place a bit of it in the food of . . . let's say four people, at breakfast. Make sure most of them are seated at tables served by other waiters."

The waiter took the vial and stared at it, wide-eyed. His expression was apprehensive—but also, at the edges, hope was emerging.

"The symptoms will be the same, but milder. The ship's doctor will conclude that some sort of illness was spread around. Food poisoning of some kind, most likely." Savinkov's soft laugh had an acid tinge to it. "At that point, of course, the BEPC will squelch any further investigation. The last thing they want to get bruited about is that their precious *Agincourt* had problems of that nature."

The waiter still looked uncertain. "But . . . the port authorities . . ."

"In Coprates? Because of the spaceport, the city is practically an outright fiefdom of Cecil Rhodes. In case you've forgotten, he's the man who owns the BEPC in the first place. The largest shareholder, at least. The authorities in Coprates will do exactly what Rhodes instructs them to do."

After the waiter left and Savinkov retired back into the

cabin, the assassin spent the first half hour in bed considering the best way to handle the situation.

What most people would assume to be the natural inclination of an assassin was more likely to cause problems than solve them. In any event, Savinkov had strong ethical principles and was unwilling to kill anyone except in self-defense or if they were legitimate political targets. Killing the waiter would be murder, pure and simple.

And there was no need for it. Another bribe, passed to the waiter just before leaving the ship, should do the trick. When in doubt, in Savinkov's experience—very extensive experience—the humble bribe was usually the most reliable option. The terrorist's equivalent of Occam's Razor, you might say.

CHAPTER 10

Alexander wanted to make sure he was one of the very first passengers to disembark from the *Agincourt*. That required a bribe to the head steward, which he explained to the man as being due to vaguely defined commercial competition, but the steward didn't really care anyway.

As the favor asked was a small one, it didn't need to be a large bribe—thankfully, since Alexander's funds were starting to run low. He was hoping he'd be able to replenish his purse once he made contact with the Russian embassy at Tryddoc Aru. Prince Vorontsov was a wealthy man, and given the nature of Alexander's mission here on Mars—which began with *protect Prince*

Vorontsov—he was fairly confident the prince would be reasonable.

Only fairly confident, though. Vorontsov was known to be a prickly man, difficult in his dealings with subordinates. "Difficult" was the term Rachkovsky had used. Translated from the diplomatese that the head of the Okhrana's office in Paris tended to use when referring to high-ranked Russian nobility, the term meant "the man's an ass."

The Martian magnetic field was so weak and localized that the enormous aethership was able to land directly on the planet without any need for cumbersome transfers. That was another thing Alexander was thankful for, since trying to maintain surveillance on their suspects in the course of two vehicular transfers—aethership to transfer station, transfer station to airship—would have been difficult. As it was, Alexander would be able to disembark before any of their suspects and place himself in position to observe them as they came off the *Agincourt*.

Meanwhile, his junior partner Drezhner would leave the ship after their suspects had done so, to keep them under observation. There was no real need for that. But Alexander had managed to keep his connection to Drezhner veiled throughout the long voyage and saw no reason to undo that work by having them be associated during the disembarkation. One never knew what might develop. There was no point in losing an asset for no purpose.

Besides, it meant he didn't have to be in Drezhner's company any longer. Once they'd quit the *Agincourt*, they'd each be going their separate ways. Yet another thing to be thankful for.

• • •

When the gangway ramp came down, the Martian daylight flooded the large disembarkation compartment— using the term "flooded" loosely. The light was rather feeble compared to Earth's. It reminded Alexander of the illumination produced by a late autumn sunrise near the Arctic circle. While still a cavalryman, he'd once been stationed in Archangel, on the White Sea. (For no good reason he'd ever been able to determine; but such was the nature of cavalry service.)

Alexander didn't pay much attention to the light, however. Following closely on its heels came the aromas of Mars. Those were . . .

Not feeble. At. All.

Behind him, he heard several people gasp and one person even gag a bit. But Alexander was made of sterner stuff. True, sewage was clearly present among those odors. Raw, open sewage and quite a bit of it, judging from the stench. But you couldn't be a soldier for long— certainly not a Russian cavalryman—without becoming intimately familiar with vile smells. And while the other odors he detected were not always pleasant, Alexander found them intriguing. They were unfamiliar, exotic, hinting at adventures to come. He was reminded of the time, as a very young officer, that he first arrived in the Tsar's holdings in central Asia.

One of the *Agincourt*'s officers began to speak.

"Ladies and gentlemen," he said, "you are now free to leave the ship. Please make your way steadily to the bottom of the ramp, where you will find your personal luggage. Any freighted goods can be claimed with the aid of the assistant purser, whom you will find at the cargo ramp amidships. Please observe caution . . ."

Alexander ignored the rest, it being nothing more than the usual speech given by officials of a commercial establishment on such occasions. The gist of it, translated into the common tongue, was: you've been duly warned so don't even THINK of filing a lawsuit if you stumble and break some bones.

Alexander was the third passenger to set foot on Mars. Where the first two immediately began gawking at their surroundings, however, he picked his suitcase from the pile at the bottom of the ramp and made his way to an overhanging shelter positioned some thirty meters from the bottom of the ramp. The shelter looked for all the world like the sort of shelter provided for people waiting at a train station, but there were neither trains nor rails anywhere in sight. The Okhrana agent had no idea what its purpose was, but he didn't care. Right now, he just needed a place from which he could observe the disembarking passengers without being easily seen himself. Once he took position deep within the shelter, he would be well-nigh invisible to anyone who casually looked his way.

He was too preoccupied with the task at hand to give much attention to anything not immediately relevant to his purpose. That was bizarre, looked at a certain way. The first time he'd visited Paris, years before, Alexander had spent a full day just wandering around and sightseeing. Yet now, visiting for the first time not a foreign capital in a country which was not really all that different from his own but another planet, he barely noticed the landscape and the inhabitants. But on that visit to Paris he had simply been reporting for reassignment to another bureau, not on a critical mission with narrow time constraints.

Some idle part of his brain which had somehow escaped the lash of the taskmaster did observe a few things:

The native Martians looked astonishingly humanlike. He thought the term was humanoid. They were skinny to the point of being skeletal and had some facial features—especially the ears—that went outside any human parameters. Still, if you dressed them in winter clothes and put a hat on their heads, passersby would pay no attention to them. Not in cosmopolitan Paris, at least. People would simply assume the Martians were Asians of some sort, perhaps Malays: short of stature, their skin color ranging from ochre to a dull yellow, eyes which at a casual glance seemed to have the distinctive Oriental appearance.

He could see almost nothing of the terrain itself, because of the nature of Martian construction. The natives favored tall, very slender buildings made mostly of some sort of reddish stone—and then built them right next to each other. The roofs were flat, which was not surprising given that they never had to worry about the accumulation of snow. The surface of the ground looked to be covered everywhere in that same reddish stone. You couldn't really use the term "cobblestoned," though, because the stones were flush with each other and very tightly fitted. It was almost like walking on tile.

Even here, at what passed for a landing site, the Martians crowded the area with their edifices. No human nation—no civilized one, at any rate—would allow dwellings and commercial buildings to be erected so close to a field where enormous craft landed and took off. But the natives were either oblivious to the danger or simply chose to ignore the risk.

That indifference might result from necessity. The population density was astonishing. It brought to mind tales Alexander had heard about Calcutta and Cairo. Everywhere you looked, natives seemed to be scurrying about. "Scurrying" was the best term to describe their locomotion, too. Alexander didn't spot a single Martian who looked to be on a casual outing or a simple stroll. All of them seemed intent on whatever their business was, and all of them were moving quickly.

While the landscape surrounding Coprates couldn't really be seen, the sky was almost overwhelming. The color was a light rose, quite striking in itself. But the centerpiece was the low clouds. Those were colored a bright scarlet due to airborne algae which lived within them. High above were other clouds, wispy and colored white much like the clouds of Earth.

Alexander had read of the scarlet clouds of Mars, but had assumed that was poetic license. He'd been expecting something that, while certainly reddish in color, would be far duller than the tales.

But, no. Those clouds were scarlet, and they floated in a rose-colored sky that was almost as bright as the blue sky of Earth.

Among the first passengers to come down the ramp after him was Klaus Kuhn, the supposedly Swiss pharmaceutical representative whom Drezhner had suggested might be

Savinkov. Alexander thought the notion was ludicrous, but he did keep an eye on Kuhn while he continued his surveillance of the other disembarking passengers.

As a result, he didn't miss the altercation that erupted when Kuhn tried to retrieve his luggage from the midships bay. He was almost immediately accosted by a man in the distinctive black uniform which had been recently adopted by the English military. A sergeant, if Alexander was reading the insignia properly. He was apparently overseeing a squad of men belonging to Rhodes' private little army, which was theoretically a security force for the British Extra-Planetary Company. On Mars, apparently, the distinction between Rhodes' men and the official military blurred at the edges.

Alexander was too far away to hear the words being spoken, but he didn't think the exchange was a friendly one. That much became obvious a moment later, when two of the BEPC soldiers seized Kuhn by the arms and the British blackcoat drew his revolver. Some more words were spoken. Then the two English bankers, Stans and Barnes, came up to the group and joined in. Alexander still couldn't hear whatever was being said, but the Kuhn fellow was looking more unhappy by the moment.

With good reason, as it turned out. The sergeant suddenly drove the barrel of his revolver into Kuhn's belly, almost doubling him up. Not more than a second or two later, the soldiers in his squad began beating the man with their rifle-butts. Very soon, he was on the ground and unconscious, whereupon two of the BEPC troops seized him by the ankles and began dragging him out of sight.

The dramatic conclusion of the affair drew the attention of many of the passengers who had by now disembarked. That was a fortunate break for Alexander, because it meant that dozens of people were milling around, gawking at the scene by the midships bay—and paying no attention at all to him. He was able to carefully examine everyone to see what they were about.

But ... there were no surprises, no mysteries. Jelinek and Underwood both made their way to the area that had been cordoned off for people who wanted to take one of the Martian airships to their destination. Alexander would be joining them himself before long, but there was no need to hurry the matter. None of the airships would attempt to land in the area until the huge bulk of the *Agincourt* was gone.

The large group of Hindus drew his attention for a short while. Edward Luff and his children were with them, as was the Duchesne woman.

Nothing suspicious there. Alexander knew the widow had been planning to sightsee the cities in the Octad Gentillus, but once the Luffs' governess came down with whatever malady had struck several of the *Agincourt*'s passengers, Duchesne had agreed to help the English scholar. Ilya had found all that out by questioning one of the cabin boys. He'd expressed some suspicion of the whole thing, on the grounds that he could see no reason a wealthy woman like Duchesne would agree to such a thing.

But that was just Drezhner being obtuse again. The widow's motives were obvious. She'd developed a personal interest in Edward Luff; it was as simple as that—and hardly an unusual story.

By the time Drezhner made his appearance coming down the ramp, almost the very last passenger to do so, all the persons involved in l'Affaire Kuhn had vanished, and the crowd of onlookers had broken up. Alexander was grateful for that. The last thing he needed was to get into an argument with Drezhner about Kuhn. It was a given that Ilya would think the fracas suggested Kuhn was Savinkov, when it was blindingly clear it demonstrated the exact opposite. No Eser agent as canny as Savinkov would have gotten himself into such a mess in the first place. Whatever had aroused the suspicions and antagonism of the English sergeant, it certainly had nothing to do with Russian affairs. At a guess, he'd been caught smuggling something that either the English authorities or Rhodes' people didn't want on Mars.

Once Drezhner left the *Agincourt*, Alexander hurried after Jelinek. He could rely on Drezhner to catch up with Underwood and follow him to Crenex. Ilya was an unimaginative blockhead—it might be better to say, an excessively imaginative blockhead—but he wasn't incompetent when it came to the basic skills of counter-espionage. Besides, as tailing assignments went, this one was easy. Approximately one fourth of the passengers disembarking from the *Agincourt* were headed for Crenex. There was only one airship scheduled for that trip today, and it wouldn't be leaving for almost two hours. Drezhner would have plenty of time to mingle with the crowd and keep Underwood under surveillance without needing to behave in a suspicious manner.

Alexander's assignment, on the other hand, was much trickier. He'd been able to find out that Jelinek's first stop was Kralladin, a small city located just a bit more than two hundred kilometers from the easternmost of the Octad Gentillus cities. The problem was that there was no regular airship travel to Kralladin. The dirigibles that were used by Martians for travel between major cities, such as the one Drezhner and Underwood would be taking to Crenex, were designed roughly like human airships. But they were generally used for major and regular travel routes. For something like the short trip from Coprates to Kralladin, Martians used their version of aerial tramp steamers. These were oddly designed airships that looked like nothing so much as airborne canoes or longships. The vessels were carried aloft by collections of long, slender hydrogen-filled tubes.

Such a design would never have worked in Earth's heavy, turbulent atmosphere. But they did well enough on Mars, with its thin atmosphere and much more predictable weather and wind patterns.

The problem posed immediately, however, was that such vessels were small. They normally didn't carry more than a dozen passengers, if that many. It would be impossible for Alexander to travel on the same ship that Jelinek took without being immediately noticed. And while he might be able to explain his presence there— once—he could hardly do so if he kept reappearing on vessels that Jelinek took as he followed his purchasing route up the complex of canals called the Aromatus, which brought water from the Great Spillway down to the rich benchlands of Sinus Aurorae and Vallis Agathodaemonis. The Aromatus stretched roughly west by northwest, and between the Octad Gentillus and Tryddoc Aru there were many cities, but none large enough to require a regular route by one of the large dirigibles.

If Alexander had enough money, he'd hire one of the longship-style airships for his own private use. But even on Mars, where European currencies stretched very far, such a vessel would be much too expensive.

There was no help for it. He'd have to take whichever small longship was the next to make the run to Kralladin, and hope that he arrived before Jelinek had left. If his quarry had already departed, he'd have to do whatever investigation was necessary to discover where he'd gone.

Were this pursuit taking place in almost any country in Europe—and a fair number in Asia and the Levant—Alexander would have been quite confident he could manage well enough. Here on Mars . . .

Who could say? He had no idea how difficult it would be to ask questions of the planet's peculiar natives, even assuming he could find ones who spoke one of the human languages he knew.

Such was the life of an Okhrana agent. It was never easy, even on his home planet.

On the positive side, he reminded himself, there were no horses on Mars. Hence, no cavalrymen.

CHAPTER 11

Charlotte found the journey to Ghlaktora absolutely fascinating, especially the last stretch when they had to use the Martian riverboats. From Coprates to the main city in Protei Locus, Uddakit, they'd been able to travel on one of the Martian dirigibles. That was quite engrossing in its own right, although the native airships of that design weren't too different from human ones.

If the design of the dirigible wasn't too different from anything you'd find on Earth, the same could not be said for the terrain. The landscape of Mars was far more stark than anything Charlotte had ever seen on her own planet. At least in western Europe, she had to caution herself. She'd never been anywhere else on Earth.

Everything seemed to divide into two sorts of regions, very different from each other: the lowlands and the tablelands. She knew that there were also some huge mountains on Mars and some vast basins in the northern hemisphere, but those were not within sight. Their airship was traveling down one of the benchlands—she wasn't sure of its name—following the canals that seemed to run all along its length. Whether from the action of the canals or the nature of the terrain itself, the result was a huge valley: about twenty miles across and stretching up and down as far as the eye could see.

Although the dirigible was following the valley, they were high enough in the air that Charlotte could see over the rims that marked both sides of the benchlands. There lay the famous Martian tablelands, the terrain that covered most of the planet's surface.

Their appearance was rugged, but quite uniform: rocky, barren, dry, mostly a sort of red-orange in color. There seemed to be very little life out there, of either a plant or animal nature.

The outstanding exception to that general lifelessness was the area immediately adjacent to the rims of the benchlands. There, for perhaps a mile back on both sides, the vegetation was quite lush. Even at this distance Charlotte could see large animals moving about, although she could make out little of them beyond their size.

When she remarked upon the matter to her father, he said: "That's called the floramargin. It's quite dangerous, apparently, if you travel through it on foot. And look there!"

Charlotte following his pointing finger and saw in the distance ahead of them a peculiar structure. As they neared, she could see that it was a combination of an enclosed staircase rising up from the benchlands below and what looked to be a small citadel on the very edge of the rim.

"That's one of their hunting lodges," her father explained. "Only the top nobility can afford to build and maintain them. They retire to them during the worst time of summer—it's much cooler up there, as you might expect—and amuse themselves in the chase. Apparently, being a noted hunter of the sort of large and dangerous game found in the floramargin brings considerable status."

Once they got to Uddakit, everything changed.

(Apparently, the proper Martian pronunciation would have been something like Oo'h!dha?kgit. The "!" indicated a Martian guttural inhalation that Mrs. Shankar said was roughly equivalent to the clicks used by Hottentots and some of the Bantu tribes of southern Africa. The "?" indicated a glottal stop not too dissimilar to those used in Arabic and a number of other tongues. It was all quite interesting but Charlotte was perfectly happy to use the practical "Uddakit.")

Uddakit served the Protei Locus region as something in the way of a capital city, although Mr. Shankar said the term "capital city" didn't really capture the heart of the matter. To humans, that term signified a town or city that served as the seat of government for a distinct geographic realm, be that realm a fully sovereign state or a region within it such as a province, district or prefecture. But Martian political relationships were more fluid. Nations in the sense that humans used the term didn't really exist on Mars. Instead, the planet's population was organized politically in a multitude of what humans would consider city-states, all which had the most complex—it might be better to say convoluted, sometimes even tortuous— relations with each other.

So, according to Mr. Shankar, Uddakit could more accurately be depicted thusly:

The dominant metropolis of the Protei Locus region, understanding that "dominance" in this context is a complex phenomenon which can be better measured as the sum of mutual debts and obligations in which Uddakit is what you might call the principal creditor, rather than a simple matter of command and obeisance.

To get from Uddakit to any of the subordinate cities of Protei Locus one could no longer travel by dirigible unless one was prepared to risk life and limb in the bizarre Martian airships which looked more like inflated canoes than anything else Charlotte could think of. Naturally, her brother Adrian was keen to do so, but fortunately their father put his foot down.

"I don't think so, Son," he said genially. "Mind you, I wouldn't mind trying it myself"—he was ever the diplomat dealing with Adrian—"but don't forget we have all of the Shankars to deal with. They'd hardly agree to risk it, especially the elderly ladies."

So, they travelled by barge—understanding by the term "barge" the Martian rivercraft that were much narrower in their beam than any human vessel of that name. They reminded Charlotte of the wherries you saw on English rivers and canals, except the bows were squared off like punts. They were propelled by two Martians standing in the stern of the boat using oars, much like pictures she'd seen of Venetian gondolas, except the gondolas only had one oarsman.

That was not surprising, though, given how small Martians were compared to humans. They weren't all that much shorter than humans, but they were built along more slender lines, to the point of seeming gaunt. She didn't think any of them weighed more than seven stone.

She found them to be a bit horrid, actually. The problem was that they looked so human, allowing for a few notable differences. The most outstanding of those were their ears, which were foxlike: very tall—the tips often rose above the crest of the skull—and very thin, although they were as hairless as a human's. The eyes were set wide apart and were also quite thin. They brought to mind the eyes of Japanese or Chinese, except there was no epicanthic fold.

It was the Martians' close resemblance to humans that bothered Charlotte. She thought she'd have been less unsettled if they'd been distinctly alien in their appearance.

She made a comment to that effect to her father and

he said: "Well, they are related to us, you know. Much more closely than any of the great apes, in fact."

They were standing in a group on a pier along one of the many small rivers that passed through Uddakit. Mr. Shankar was standing next to them, and he overheard her father's remark.

"Be careful, Edward!" he said, smiling slyly. "If the august professors at Oxford learn of your heresy, you'll never hear the end of it. Wouldn't surprise me if you were denounced by name at the next meeting of the Royal Society."

"What's the Royal Society?" demanded Adrian. Snoopy as ever, her brother had overheard the exchange.

"It's short for 'The Royal Society of London for Improving Natural Knowledge,'" said Mr. Shankar, smiling more widely still. "Founded in 1660. It's considered the most prestigious learned society in the entire world—"

"Not by me," grunted her father.

"—by all save hopeless cranks who advocate such preposterous theories as continental drift and the common ancestry of humans and Martians."

"Blithering idiots," said her father. "It's blindingly obvious we're of the same evolutionary lineage as Martians. The number of morphological features we have in common number literally in the hundreds. How else—"

"Convergent evolution, convergent evolution," said Mr. Shankar, intoning the phrase as he might a religious incantation.

"Blithering idiots, I say it again." Her father was frowning rather fiercely. "The odds that convergent evolution would produce such a huge number of common traits is literally astronomical. There's as much chance that two people born next door to each other of completely different parents were as close as identical twins."

Mr. Shankar shrugged. "I don't disagree with you, Edward. But it will take a great deal of work to overturn the existing biases—all the more so, given that the political authorities and economic powers have a vested interest in maintaining the notion that humans and Martians are species as separate and distinct as oysters and buffalos."

"Why is that?" asked Adrian.

Her father and Mr. Shankar looked at each other. Then her father shook his head. "I'll explain some other time, Son. It's a somewhat delicate matter, and"—he pointed his finger—"I do believe our boats have arrived."

To Vera Duchesne's relief—mild relief, since she'd been expecting it; but relief nonetheless—the two Okhrana agents were left behind as she and her large party departed from Uddakit on the three boats that Luff and Shankar had hired to take them to Ghlaktora. Apparently they'd persuaded themselves that other people were more likely candidates for being Savinkov, or harboring Savinkov. That was true enough, to be sure, but there was always a certain element of chance in these things.

And they might still change their minds, however unlikely that might seem at the moment. She'd need to remain vigilant once they arrived at their destination. But, for the moment—really, for the first time since she'd boarded the *Agincourt*—she could relax.

"Look, Madame Duchesne!" exclaimed Adrian. The

boy was pointing toward something in the distance. "I think it's a real Martian!"

His sister frowned, glancing at the two Martians in the stern of the boat, rowing them forward. "Be polite," she hissed at her brother.

Adrian responded with a magnificent sneer—or what he imagined to be one, rather. It was really not possible for someone his age to produce the sort of lip-curling expression that caused foes to reel in dismay and subordinates to cringe and abase themselves.

"Those aren't real Martians," he stated firmly. "Didn't you listen to Papa? They're just funny-looking almost-people."

Again he pointed into the distance. Far away, across the bleak landscape they were now passing through, Vera could barely discern some sort of creature moving slowly along the skyline.

It looked . . . odd. Very odd. The creature—was it intelligent? should she rather think of it as a "being" than a creature?—seemed to be stumping along on four equidistantly positioned lower limbs. The movement reminded her more of the way a sensate derrick might locomote than anything she'd ever seen an animal on Earth do.

"Be quiet, Adrian," Charlotte hissed again. "You're being rude."

Vera had grown quite fond of the Luff children. Charlotte more than Adrian, but that was probably just a passing thing. She remembered her own two brothers at the age of eleven. Vexatious creatures, they'd been—and in their case, "creatures" was indeed the right term to use.

But she forced those memories away. Along with them came too many other, more painful ones. Valentin had died in the Tsar's prisons when he was only eighteen. Of disease, the police said, but the bruises and abrasions on his corpse suggested otherwise. Her older brother Dmitri had survived the three years he spent in Siberia, but he'd never been the same afterward.

He'd been badly beaten also, on several occasions. The Russian police and prison officers were brutes, always quick to use the knout. He'd survived reasonably intact—measured in physical terms, at least. But mentally . . .

He seemed to have aged a decade for every year he'd lived in exile. It was seeing him return home when she was nineteen that had crystallized her own attitude toward the Romanov dynasty and the brutal regime it oversaw. She'd hated them since she was a girl. Now, she resolved to work toward their overthrow. She'd joined the SR Party less than a month later.

"What are you thinking, Vera?" asked Edward Luff, his voice tinged with concern. "You seem very sad all of a sudden."

She shook her head, more to remind herself of the need to remain vigilant than anything else. The company of friends carried its own perils.

"It's nothing, Edward. I was just remembering my brothers. One of them died very young and the other . . . well, he's been sickly since he suffered some mishaps."

On impulse, she took Luff's hand in her own and gave it a little squeeze. He returned the grip and leaned a little closer.

She still hadn't made a decision regarding that issue.

The problem wasn't an emotional one. Not any longer. Luff was a fine man whom it would be easy to come to love as time passed, and she was already attached to his children.

The problem was Savinkov, as always for her these past few years. What was she to do with the man? Her obligation toward him and everything he represented outweighed everything else.

Still, she did not relinquish her grip on the hand of the man standing beside her. Not even she, after all that had transpired, was immune to sentiment and feeling.

They arrived in Ghlaktora on the morning of the third day after they disembarked from the *Agincourt*. It had been a slow voyage—the Martian canal boats were no faster than their earthly counterparts. But Charlotte had found it to be a pleasant one nonetheless.

The ever-growing closeness between her father and Madame Duchesne was now so obvious that even her obtuse little brother had noticed. And, for once, had not been a nuisance.

"I like her a lot," he'd declared. So he'd not be an antagonist, after all, as she schemed and maneuvered to bring about the logical and beneficial end result.

No one would ever really be able to replace her own mother. But Vera Duchesne would serve splendidly as a stepmother—she'd be a vast improvement on Mrs. Smith!—and what was more important was that her father's loneliness needed to be brought to an end. He was not by nature well-suited to being a widower.

Charlotte came to that final conclusion before they

reached Ghlaktora. Quite a bit before, in fact. She spent the last day and a half of their journey basking in the glow of her own maturity. Already rather wise, she was—though still two months shy of fifteen.

Earth months, that was. Did they have months on Mars? She'd have to find out.

CHAPTER 12

The five days Alexander spent chasing after Jelinek managed to be simultaneously nerve-wracking and tedious. Nerve-wracking, because following the art dealer as he worked his way through several small Martian cities was hard to do without being spotted. Tedious, because all of that tense work produced absolutely nothing in the way of results.

By the third day, Alexander had stopped placing quotation marks in his own mind around the phrase "art dealer." He no longer had any real doubt that Jelinek's profession was exactly what he claimed it to be. The man not only stopped at the places an art dealer would frequent, but he also made the sort of purchases you'd expect him to make.

By the fourth day, Alexander's suspicions that Jelinek might be Savinkov had faded almost entirely away. The only logic behind those suspicions had been the possibility that Jelinek/Savinkov might use whatever art objects he acquired to smuggle weapons into Tryddoc Aru.

A nice theory, in the abstract—and brought down, as theories so often were, by a crude fact. In this case, by the fact that Jelinek turned out to be a very specialized sort of art dealer. He didn't seem to be the slightest bit interested in Martian sculpture or the peculiar carvings they made from the knobby outer bark—if such it was; Alexander was not a botanist—of the gnarled and stunted trees—if such they were; the same caveat applied—that grew on the planet's arid tablelands.

Either of those could have served as hiding places for weapons and explosives, especially the carvings. But the only objets d'art that Jelinek seemed interested in were the small tapestries that Martians used for curtains in their homes. The tapestries might have served to disguise weapons or munitions, if they were accumulated in sufficient number. But as soon as Jelinek bought one, he immediately had it mounted in a thin frame made of some Martian substance that seemed like a cross between heavy cardboard and thick leather. Protection for the long voyage home, presumably.

Nothing much deadlier than a large knife could have been hidden in those flat parcels, and no one armed only with a blade was going to pose any threat to Russian officials on Mars. Not important ones as closely guarded as Prince Vorontsov, at any rate, and an assassin like Savinkov wouldn't have come all the way to Mars simply to murder a minor consulate officer. Cossacks had limits, but dealing with men wielding blades was not one of them.

So, by the fifth day, Alexander was more than ready to relinquish the chase—if the term could be used at all. Happily, Jelinek ended his travels by returning to Mooktar and Alexander was able to reach the Russian consulate before noon. From there, he'd be able to check on Drezhner's progress and, more importantly, reopen communication with Rachkovsky. The Paris bureau of the Okhrana had a very powerful radio at its disposal; powerful enough to reach Mars with Morse code.

As it happened, when he arrived at the consulate there was already a message waiting for him from Rachkovsky, along with another from Drezhner.

He read the one from Rachkovsky first.

SAVINKOV DISCOVERED TO HAVE DIED
TWO YEARS AGO. IDENTITY AND MISSION
OF SRP AGENT ON MARS UNKNOWN, IF HE
EXISTS AT ALL. MAY BE A RUSE. TAKE
WHATEVER MEASURES SEEM NECESSARY.

Alexander stared at the slip of paper. Savinkov... dead? So for the past two years...

Who had been taking his place? Who had been responsible for the reports—not many, but some—that had trickled in to the Okhrana placing Savinkov in various places?

He shook his head. This would take some contemplation. In the meantime, he might as well see what Drezhner had been up to. Nothing very useful, most likely.

Drezhner's message was also in Morse. It didn't take Alexander more than a few seconds to read it.

"That cretin!" he exclaimed.

YOU WILL HAVE SEEN MESSAGE FROM

RACHKOVSKY. NOW OBVIOUS EDWARD LUFF
IS SAVINKOV. I AM IN PURSUIT.

Alexander felt like tearing out his air. It should have been obvious to Drezhner that the most likely situation was that they had been chasing a phantom all along. Didn't the message itself caution *if he exists at all*? But even if one assumed that there was an unknown SRP agent on Mars—Savinkov or someone else, it mattered not—the notion that the English scholar was the agent was . . .

He groped for a suitable term. "Moronic" came to mind immediately. The more long-winded "fevered fantasies of an imbecile" came right on its heels, followed by "monumentally stupid."

Drezhner was likely to cause an international incident. Alexander turned to the embassy clerk who had handed him the message. The consul himself, Evgeny Kireyev, was standing right next to the clerk, but Alexander had already taken his measure. Kireyev was the sort of minor nobleman who filled such unimportant posts for the Russian empire. By mid-day, they were usually drunk.

By now, it was afternoon and Kireyev was sodden. The clerk was likely to be more useful.

"What's the fastest way to get to Ghlaktora?" he asked.

"Where's Ghlaktora?" The clerk was not inebriated. But obviously not an intellectual titan, either.

"It's one of the smaller cities in Protei Locus," Alexander explained impatiently. "It's famous as a repository of ancient Martian texts."

"What's Protei Locus?"

Fortunately, the consul had something in the way of a functioning brain, awash as it might be in vodka.

"Part of the Aromatus," he said, then belched. Then: "Were me, I'd hire a—belch—gondola thing." He waved his hand vaguely. "You know. One of those funny-looking airships with the gasbags on the bottom instead of the top where—belch—they should be."

"What do they cost?"

Bleary-eyed, the consul looked at the clerk. That worthy now demonstrated that his brain, minuscule thought it might be, did hold at least a few facts.

"About eight ootyuk a day. Twelve, if you hire a crew as well, which I'd recommend."

"And an ootyuk is . . . what, in Russian currency?"

When told the sum, Alexander decided he could manage the business—with the assistance of Kireyev. Consulates always had a certain amount of discretionary funds at their disposal.

Kireyev put up a protest, but between his drunkenness and Alexander's insistence, he capitulated soon enough.

Not soon enough, though, for Alexander to hire a "gondola thing"—which was called a fluybakh in the local tongue, as it turned out—and set off for Ghlaktora the same day. By the time he finished haggling with the fluybakh's owner and captain the sun was setting. And as it turned out, Martians were unwilling to fly by night. Not, at least, in a fluybakh.

Alexander wasn't clear on the reason for that attitude. It might just be superstition. But he didn't press the matter. He could use a night's rest—not to mention the services of the consulate's laundry.

Tomorrow would be soon enough, he figured. Not even Ilya Drezhner could get into that much trouble in just a few days.

Edward Luff stared down the long corridor that had been carved out of stone below the edifice in Ghlaktora that served Martians as the analog of a human library. Analog, not equivalent. Repositories of ancient texts seemed to have a religious function on Mars, not simply a secular one. But Edward couldn't place the function exactly, since Martian religions seemed to operate on different principles than those of any human religion Edward was familiar with.

"How far does it go?" he asked, his tone hushed.

The Martian who was serving as their combined guide, text analyst and spiritual adviser—or perhaps that should be, metaphysical councilor; it was hard to tell—made the wrist-rolling motion that seemed to serve Martians as a shrug. "No one knows," he said.

Joedheg's English was surprisingly good, if not quite fluent, but Edward had to strain a bit to understand the fellow. Martians, at least in this region, spoke English with a pronounced accent. It reminded Edward somewhat of the way a German spoke English, but with a sibilant undertone quite foreign to any German-speaker he'd ever known.

"These halls are ancient," the Martian continued. "We believe some of them date back as far as the Second Epoch."

That would place them in a time of pre-history rather than history, properly speaking. The Second Epoch was the period in Martian history when the planet was conquered by the Old Ones, according to their legends. The identity of the Old Ones was not clear, although the texts seem to agree that they came from somewhere else in the solar system.

Somewhere other than Mars—and other than the Earth, as well. The same legends generally agreed that Martians had founded colonies on Earth during the Second Epoch, and it was from those colonies that the liberation of Mars from the Old Ones was finally achieved.

So who were the Old Ones? The most common theory posited a race emerging on Europa, or possibly Titan. But no one really knew, because Martians had lost whatever capacity for interplanetary travel they might once have possessed, and no human aethership had ventured farther into the outer reaches of the solar system than the asteroid belt.

That was assuming any of those ancient legends were true at all. Edward was a bit skeptical himself, but tried to keep an open mind on the subject. Seeing this immense complex of tunnels and chambers was making it much easier to do so. The labor involved made the construction of the Egyptian pyramids seem like the work of children on a beach building sand castles. It was a labyrinth that dwarfed anything of the sort ever constructed on Earth. At any moment, Edward almost expected to hear the distant bellow of a minotaur.

Only the first few miles of the corridors were used to house texts and other relics and artifacts. Thereafter, the tunnels fell into darkness and went...wherever they went, and however far that might be.

Smiling, he turned to his companion. "And what do you think of all this, Vera?"

What she thought didn't bear speaking aloud, at least not to Edward—and certainly not in front of his children.

What I think is that Grigory Gershuni was right. We can forge a revolutionary movement in this vast labyrinth that no human regime will ever be able to eradicate. With the right alliances with other human movements and good relations where needed with Martian authorities, we will be indestructible.

That had been Gershuni's hope, and one of the reasons the SRP leader had sent Duchesne on this mission. A Quixotic mission, she'd thought, and had only agreed because of the imperative logic of the other mission he'd given her on this voyage. But now that she had seen the reality for herself, she was fully persuaded.

And deeply relieved. Reconciling her missions with her growing sentiments for Edward and his children had seemed a well-nigh insurmountable challenge. Now...

It would be quite possible, she thought. Not easy, perhaps, but definitely possible.

As if seeking comfort from the vast solitude of the tunnels, her hand found its way into Edward's. And stayed there.

"This is so marvelous," enthused Adrian Luff. "I bet there are monsters somewhere down here. Just think, Charlotte! Minotaurs. Well, Martian versions, anyway."

Leave it to her brother to take glee in the prospect of

seeing someone devoured by a carnivorous quasi-bovine.

With any luck, if such a creature existed down here, it would choose Adrian for its first meal. Charlotte could make her escape while the monster shredded her brother's flesh and plucked bone from annoying bone.

CHAPTER 13

The food was . . .

Interesting. That was the term Charlotte settled upon, after trying out a number of others. It seemed a more productive way of becoming accustomed to Martian cuisine than such terms as revolting and nauseating.

It helped not to consider the exact source of the provender. Vegetable, animal, fruit—who could say? The course they were dining upon at the moment, if Charlotte were foolish enough to analyze it, seemed to be a cross between an African horned melon she'd once eaten on a dare and some sort of arthropod. Most likely a lobster equivalent, she told herself, thereby avoiding such terms as giant cockroach.

She could stand to lose some weight. She was a bit distressed at the way her body was developing of late. Given its location, the adipose tissue she'd been acquiring was aesthetically acceptable—even pleasing, apparently, to men—but she felt increasingly awkward. Madame Duchesne was a hefty woman in all proportions, so her bust was counter-balanced by her abdomen. Charlotte, on the other hand, retained her slender girlish figure everywhere . . . except.

She felt top-heavy. As if she might topple over due to a minor stumble.

Her brother was starting to make stupid remarks on the subject, too.

She decided not to finish the meal. She'd eaten enough for propriety's sake, she figured. Besides, the two Martian dignitaries seated at one end of the table didn't seem to care much whether humans enjoyed their food or not. They were every bit as engrossed in the scholarly discussion/debate/dispute taking place at the table as her father, Joedheg, and the Shankar couple. They probably wouldn't even notice when the servants took the plates away.

"—can't refer to the indigenes of the tablelands," Mr. Shankar was insisting. "None of them is in the least bit blueish, and even their reddish coloration is more in the way of a brown ochre than anything which can properly be labeled 'red,' or even 'brick-colored.'"

The larger of the two Martian dignitaries leaned forward, gesticulating vigorously. That seemed to be a common characteristic of the red planet's natives. It was as if they viewed gestures as necessary auxiliary verbs.

"But you are overlooking the obvious, Vijay," said Th'taba. "The tableland natives are most likely devolved from their earlier forms. As you'd expect of a declining species, their coloration has changed to enable them to blend more easily into the landscape."

Charlotte's father cleared his throat. "Assuming these 'native indigenes' exist at all. You said yourself, Th'taba, that reports of their sighting are few and sketchy."

Th'taba made the Martian wrist-rolling gesture. "Yes,

yes—but that just further buttresses my argument. If the indigenes are a figment of the imagination, then obviously they are not the beings referred to in various passages of the Vedas."

He gave Mr. Shankar a look that Charlotte would have called "beady-eyed" if a human had bestowed it upon him. But she had no idea what that expression signified on a Martian's face.

"Not to mention that Vijay is but playing at the devil's avocation." The Martian paused for a moment. "Is that how you say it?"

"Playing the devil's advocate," Vera supplied.

"Yes, that. I don't think he believes any more than I do that the references in the Vedas are to anything but the Old Ones."

Mr. Shankar smiled. "Well, no, I don't. But someone has to put the squeeze on notions to make sure they aren't—"

He was interrupted by a great crashing noise. A moment later, the door to the dining hall was flung open and two men barged in.

The one in front had a fierce look on his face and was brandishing a revolver. Charlotte recognized him as one of the passengers she'd seen on the *Agincourt*, although she hadn't taken much notice of him at the time. The man just behind him was wearing some sort of uniform and was carrying a rifle, but seemed uncertain of himself.

The smaller Martian rose abruptly to his feet. That was Jhu Klagna, the owner of the building they were dining in. "Jhu" was a title, not a name. He was one of Ghlaktora's officials; something between a magistrate and a tax assessor, as near as Charlotte could figure out.

"This is irregular!" Klagna exclaimed. "Grievances must be—"

He got no further. The man in front struck him in the forehead with the revolver butt, knocking him to the floor. There, the official moaned softly and rolled over on his side. He seemed semi-conscious at best.

"Everyone sit still—and be silent!" commanded the man wielding the revolver. "Or I'll shoot!"

He waved the revolver about in a menacing manner, then lowered it to point at Charlotte's father.

"Get up, Savinkov—or whatever name you go by." He made a jerking motion with the weapon, as if to pull Edward Luff to his feet by sheer force of will. "Get up, I say!"

Slowly, Charlotte's father came to his feet, his fingertips spread out on the tabletop. "What is this all about, if I might ask?" His tone was mild. "I believe you've mistaken me for someone else."

The man with the revolver began to reply but was distracted by Th'taba, who was now rising to his own feet.

"Sit still, I said!"

"I am not bound by irregular conduct," the Martian replied, with great dignity.

Snarling, the man glanced at the soldier and jerked his free hand toward Th'taba. "Keep your weapon on him, Kapral Baranovsky. If he makes a threatening move of any kind, shoot him."

"Yes, Captain Drezhner." The soldier did as he was told, holding his rifle against his hip and pointed in the direction of Th'taba.

At least the madman now had a name. Charlotte clutched at that fact as a way to keep from panicking.

Seated next to her, out of the corner of her eye, she saw that Vera had lowered her gaze and placed her hands in her lap. She looked to be praying. That surprised Charlotte a bit, since the woman had never indicated any religious sentiment previously.

Drezhner turned his attention back to Edward Luff. "Here's how it will be," he said coldly. "You will accompany me and Kapral Baranovsky to the plaza—whatever it's called—where we have an airship waiting. We will take you to the embassy at Crenex, since that's the nearest. There—"

"Whose embassy?" her father asked, still in that mild tone of voice.

Drezhner's face tightened with anger. "Don't play the fool, Savinkov! Whoever you are. The Russian embassy, of course."

Suddenly, Charlotte's brother erupted from his chair. "You leave Father alone!" he cried, picking up a Martian utensil that was a cross between a spoon and a butter knife and hurling it at Drezhner.

Adrian's aim was good. The utensil would have struck Drezhner in the face except he brought up his arm in time to deflect it away.

Not the arm holding the revolver, though. Whoever he was, Drezhner was no stranger to violence.

Adrian was now coming around the table, snatching up another utensil and brandishing it as if it were a sword.

"Adrian!" their father cried.

It was an insane thing to do, but Charlotte felt a surge of admiration for her little brother. Followed instantly by a still greater surge of fear.

Drezhner's face was still, cold. He aimed the revolver and fired.

Blessedly, he was not shooting to kill. The bullet struck Adrian in the meaty part of the upper thigh, just to the side of the bone. Her brother was sent flying, his leg a bloody mess.

Now Charlotte's father, his own face filled with fury, began coming around the table on the other side.

"Stand, Savinkov!" Drezhner shouted. "Stand or I'll shoot!"

His attention was entirely fixed on Edward Luff. Charlotte was paralyzed, not knowing what to do.

The matter was taken out of her hands. Vera's hand seized her by the shoulder and dragged her down, the chair coming with her. Dear God, the woman was strong!

BOOM! BOOM!

Half on her back, Charlotte stared up. Duchesne was now standing, a revolver in her own hand which she had pointing forward. Her face was like a carven idol; not quite human. Her eyes were fixed on something or someone Charlotte couldn't see.

Drezhner, of course. Again, Vera fired the revolver. BOOM! BOOM! Two shots, quick but not hurried. Dimly, Charlotte realized she was observing someone quite familiar with the use of sidearms.

She heard a muffled thud, a sigh, as if a body had fallen in a heap to the floor. Then saw Vera swivel slightly to bring the revolver to bear elsewhere.

"Do. Not. Move. Kapral Baranovsky. Be assured I will shoot to kill. And as you can see, I am an excellent shot."

There was a moment of silence. Vera seemed to relax

a bit. "Edward, if you would be so kind, please disarm the corporal. I believe he has seen reason."

Charlotte couldn't stop herself from giggling. If Drezhner was in the condition she suspected he was—with four bullet holes in him and dead, dead, dead—she didn't doubt herself that the corporal was now the very font of logic. He seemed quite young, no more than twenty or so. And probably repeating to himself over and over: I'm too young to die.

A few seconds passed. Then Vera stretched down her left hand to Charlotte. That was the one not holding the revolver, of course. The revolver itself stayed level and steady, as if it were held by a machine.

Charlotte took the hand and Vera lifted her to her feet. Displaying, again, that rather incredible strength of body.

Now able to see the whole room again, Charlotte immediately spotted Drezhner's body, lying sprawled against the far wall.

Drezhner's corpse, rather. There was no question that he was dead. His whole shirt was soaked in blood from the collar down. Every bullet fired by Madame Duchesne seemed to have struck him squarely in the chest. At least one of them, quite possibly more, must have penetrated his heart.

Charlotte felt no grief for the man. He'd been a ghastly brute. Still, she was shaken. She was trembling, in fact.

Where had Vera Duchesne learned to shoot like that? Charlotte hadn't even known the woman possessed a gun. Yet, she must have had it hidden somewhere on her person. True, it was a very ample person and the revolver did not seem like an especially large one. Still . . .

She shook her head, trying to clear it. A yelp of pain from a different part of the room drew her attention from Drezhner's bloody corpse. She saw that her father was now attending to Adrian.

Trying to, rather. From the helpless look on his face, it was apparent that the skills of a scholar did not extend to emergency medicine.

Madame Duchesne headed toward him, glancing toward Kapral Baranovsky on the way. It was a brief glance. The young soldier had been disarmed and was looking even more helpless than Edward Luff.

Vijay Shankar had taken the man's rifle and was holding it in the very gingerly manner that someone who has no familiarity with guns does such a thing. But Shankar wasn't the one holding the corporal at bay—if the term "holding at bay" applied at all. That was being done by Th'taba, who had drawn a very wicked-looking dagger (dirk? Charlotte had no idea) from somewhere on his person. He seemed to be looming over Baranovsky in a most threatening manner, despite being several inches shorter than the rather tall young soldier. Joedheg was there also, although he did not seem to be armed.

Seeing that Baranovsky no longer posed any danger, Vera turned all her attention to Charlotte's brother and father.

She began with the father.

"Edward, you obviously have no idea what you're doing," she said, sinking to her knees next to Adrian. "Please move back a bit and give me some room."

Still looking helpless, Charlotte's father did as she bade him. Vera then went to work immediately on Adrian.

Charlotte had no idea what she did, exactly. For one thing, she wasn't standing at close hand. All the blood in the room was now making her feel ill and she wanted to keep her distance.

There was some tearing of cloth involved, probably from Madame Duchesne's own dress. Adrian yelped several more times, but then grew quiet. Duchesne murmured what sounded like encouraging words to him.

Charlotte's sentiments veered wildly back and forth. She alternated between wanting to hug her little brother and scream furiously at him. What had the little maniac been thinking?

After a short while, accepting his own inefficacy in the matter, her father came over to her and placed his arm around her shoulder.

"You are unharmed, yes?"

She shook her head. Then burst into tears. It was rather mortifying.

She wondered if Vera Duchesne had ever burst into tears, even once in her life. At first, she didn't think so. But after a time, with further thought, she realized that she must have. Somewhere, completely hidden beneath the iron-mask face and the deadly precision of the shots, must lie a monstrous amount of pain.

Either that, or the woman was a crazed, cold-blooded killer.

Could one be crazed and cold-blooded at the same time? Charlotte wasn't sure.

She'd have to find out. But how would you find out such a thing?

She burst into a half-choked laugh, then. Which was even more mortifying than the tears.

Of course. She'd ask Madame Duchesne. She would know.

CHAPTER 14

By the time Alexander reached Ghlaktora, the international incident he feared had already happened. Drezhner—the monumental ass!—had managed to get himself killed in the process of infuriating the local authorities.

And had accomplished nothing. No, worse. If Luff or anyone in his party had been Savinkov, as unlikely as that was, the assassin was now beyond reach.

Beyond Alexander's reach, certainly, or that of any Russian official on Mars. It was conceivable that Cecil Rhodes could bring enough pressure to bear on whichever petty native potentate ruled Ghlaktora to get them to relinquish a might-be-Savinkov, but would he? Probably not. His own reaction, once he heard of Drezhner's conduct, was far more likely to be hostile to Russians than to Martians. All the more so since the likelihood that Savinkov—no, a Savinkov substitute; Savinkov himself was apparently dead—was actually on Mars was vanishingly small. Alexander was now almost certain that the whole affair had been a ruse on the part of the Esers. Probably to distract everyone while they plotted a strike at some target in Russia.

And besides, even if Rhodes agreed to coerce the local

nawab into removing his protection of maybe-Savinkov-substitute, it probably still wouldn't do any good. From what Alexander had been able to learn about Ghlaktora and the Protei Locus region, it was riddled with underground catacombs and passageways. In the unlikely event there was a maybe-Savinkov-substitute in the city, he'd certainly have the skills to find shelter there.

Judging from what Alexander had heard, it would take an army to search that labyrinth. He had no army at his disposal. Neither did Prince Vorontsov.

For that matter, neither did Cecil Rhodes. The English imperialist maintained his power on the red planet in the same manner he'd established it in the first place. He'd used what you might call the Mongol Method—a ruthless, even savage, application of force and violence precisely because he didn't have a huge army of soldiers and bureaucrats to rule by direct administration.

The Martian authorities were afraid of him, certainly. But that sort of fear did not lend itself to launching a systematic search of gigantic labyrinths. How was Rhodes to know if they carried out such a search effectively, since he'd have no way of overseeing them? If they did it at all, they'd do in a slack and lackadaisical manner.

No, best to just let the whole unsavory affair die a natural death. Had Ghlaktora's authorities tried to keep Kapral Baranovsky under arrest, things would have taken a nasty turn. But they were perfectly willing to turn him over to Alexander's keeping, once he arrived. They even gave the soldier his rifle back, although they kept the ammunition.

No matter. Kapral Baranovsky was even less inclined

than Alexander to stay in Ghlaktora and cause any further trouble.

"I was just assigned to guard the embassy at Crenex," the young corporal said plaintively. "Drezhner made me come with him. He wanted to bring a whole squad of the embassy's guards, but Count Shuvalov wouldn't let him have anyone but me."

He looked aggrieved. "Because I was the youngest, I think."

The youngest—and clearly the least useful, once that imbecile Drezhner forced matters to gunplay.

The one surprising thing Alexander learned was that Drezhner had been killed by the Duchesne woman.

"She terrified me," Baranovsky confessed. "When she turned her gun on me after—after Drezhner died—I was sure she was going to kill me as well. Her eyes . . . They were empty. Just like a snake's."

Alexander wondered . . .

But it made no sense. If Duchesne were an SRP terrorist, she'd surely have killed Baranovsky along with Drezhner in order to silence any witness who could bring the tale back to the Okhrana. Why let him live? Given the circumstances, no one would have blamed her if she'd gunned down the corporal as well. He'd come with Drezhner, armed; he was another threat; he was dealt with.

Case closed.

The fluybakh took them back to Mooktar. From there, within a day or two, they'd be able to find an airship which would fly them to Coprates or Tryddoc Aru. Mooktar was not large enough to have regular service to any other Martian city, but there were a number of small dirigibles that crisscrossed the planet, providing whoever needed it with passage wherever they wanted to go. For a price, of course—usually a steep one, if the customers were human.

Alexander didn't care. He still had sufficient funds and, by now, all he wanted was to leave the miserable planet altogether and return to Paris.

He adored Paris. He couldn't wait to get back.

Everyone else had settled in for the night. Adrian had fallen asleep hours before. Only Charlotte and her father remained awake, along with Mr. and Mrs. Shankar, sharing the domicile's equivalent of a living room with Madame Duchesne.

"Vera…" Edward Luff seemed uncertain of what to say. "This…ah…Savinkov whom Drezhner was raving about…"

"Gavril Savinkov does not exist," said Madame Duchesne. "He never did. He's a figment of the Russian secret police's imagination."

She smiled, thinly. "Admittedly, we did everything in our power to give the Okhrana that illusion—and then to maintain it."

Charlotte's father cleared his throat. "'We' being…"

"The Socialist-Revolutionary Party's Combat Organization. Of which I am, and have been for many years, a member." She wiggled her fingers in a familiar gesture. "Well, not that. The SRP was only formed recently. It came mostly out of the Northern Union of

Socialist Revolutionaries and the Workers' Party of Political Liberation of Russia, which were formed in the 1890s. I was one of the Workers' Party's cadres. Our leaders were—still are, along with Victor Chernov—Catherine Breshkovsky and Grigory Gershuni. But the armed struggle goes back much farther than that, to the days of the Narodnaya Volya."

"Ah. Yes. The 'People's Will' organization. I'd heard of them. Of Catherine Breshkovsky also." Edward Luff was still fumbling. "Vera . . . Ah. When did you . . ."

"After my brother came back from Siberian exile. He'd been ruined by the experience. One of my brothers, rather. The younger one had already died in the Tsar's prisons. He'd been beaten to death."

Her expression was calm; her tone of voice, cold.

"Duchesne is an invented name," she continued. "I was indeed married, but my husband's name was Vladimir Natanson. He was Jewish, one of the founders of the Circle of Tchaikovsky, Land and Liberty. He also died in prison. From disease, in his case."

Her face was masklike again. Moved by a sudden, powerful impulse, Charlotte rose from her seat and went over to sit next to Madame Duchesne—no, Madame Natanson, it now seemed.

She decided she would call her Madame Vera from now on. It seemed less confusing.

She took the older woman's hand in her own. Or maybe she would just call her Vera.

Edward Luff stared at his daughter for a moment, then sighed and ran fingers through his hair.

"I'm sorry, I'm just trying to catch up. So, why did you

come to Mars then, Vera? I assume it was not a simple desire to sightsee."

She chuckled. "Hardly. I'm afraid I'm not actually a rich widow. Widow, yes; well-to-do, no. I've been traveling on the Party's funds. On Party business."

His face looked a bit drawn. "And that business is . . ."

Again, she chuckled. The sound had a harsh ring to it, this time. "Poor Edward! No, I am not here to shoot down some Tsarist official. Not that the stinking bastard wouldn't deserve it. My mission is of a very different nature."

"And—if I might ask—that mission is . . . ?"

Mr. Shankar cleared his throat. "Actually, she's here to see me, Edward. Me and Sumati."

Luff stared at him. "You?"

Shankar made a face. "Please, Edward—don't look quite so shocked. I assure you that Russia is not the only land where the professions of scholar and political activist get combined."

Charlotte's father was still staring at him. The Hindu's expression seemed to harden somewhat.

"Give it a few years under the new dispensation brought by Cecil Rhodes and his thugs, Edward. You may come to understand what it means to be an Indian under English rule."

His wife spoke. "A rule which is now certain to be much harsher, given Rhodes' ascendancy. And it is already not pleasant, for us."

Charlotte grasped the heart of the issue before her father did. She would have clapped her hands except one of them was still being gripped in Vera's.

"Oh, I see! You're here to forge a conspiratorial alliance

between Russian and Indian revolutionaries." Her brother would have been thrilled, if he hadn't been asleep. He adored the thought of conspiracies.

But her mind was racing ahead, as more things fell into place. "And do it on Mars, where you'll be beyond the reach of either the Russian or English police agencies." She pursed her lips. "At least, so long as the Martian authorities look the other way."

Vera's chuckle, this time, was quite rich and full of humor. "'Look the other way!' My dear Charlotte, some of those Martian authorities—including those who oversee all the cities of Protei Locus—have joined the conspiracy themselves. They have no love for Rhodes either."

"Really?"

"Really?" echoed her father.

"Yes," said Sumati Shankar. "It was one of them—our supposed 'guide' Joedheg, as a matter of fact—who first approached us. You may remember that our employer, the Nizam of Hyderabad, visited Mars himself last year. That began the process. The Nizam spoke to us, we communicated with Vera—whom we've known for years, at first through her husband Vladimir—and she discussed the matter with Grigory Gershuni, the head of the SRP's Combat Organization."

"You need to understand the stakes involved for us," said Vera. "With Rhodes' ascendancy in Britain, all the major powers of Europe except France are now controlled by reactionaries, and France is irrelevant because of the chaos of its political affairs. Only the United States remains as a bastion of democracy, and they are across the Atlantic and preoccupied with their own affairs. The pressure on us—on all democratic and revolutionary movements and parties—in Asia and Africa as much as in Europe—is becoming fiercer all the time. The possibility of creating here on Mars a political fortress—a refuge, if you will; a safe haven—which can shield us while we rebuild our strength . . ."

"That is the heart of it," said Mr. Shankar. "That is why we came here."

Vera spread her hands. "And here we are. And now we invite you to join us."

Her father's eyes widened. "Me?"

"Why not, Edward?" said Mr. Shankar. "You plan to be here for years, do you not? By the time you'd have been ready to return to Earth—trust me on this matter—you'll have found England a very different place than the one you know. And by then, there will be Englishmen in our ranks as well."

"What Englishmen?"

"From the military, to start. Have you heard of 'redcoats'?"

Her father rubbed his jaw. "Yes. I have."

So had Charlotte. There were reputed to be elements in the British military, especially the Navy—officers and enlisted men both—who were disaffected with the new regime put in place by Cecil Rhodes and his people. The so-called "blackcoats," named after the color of the new uniforms.

There was silence for a while. Then her father said: "I'll need to think about it."

"Yes, of course."

"In the meantime . . ." He glanced at the handclasp

between Charlotte and Vera. "I must thank you for saving my son, Madame Natanson. And me. And perhaps my daughter as well."

"Oh, please, Edward. I'm still Vera. Not really so different from the one you thought you knew, either."

He smiled at her. "Vera, then."

She smiled back.

Charlotte squeezed her hand. Vera squeezed back.

Adrian awoke then, in the adjoining room. "Where is everyone?" he cried out, plaintively. "I need some help!"

Thereby ruining the moment. It was so exasperating.

CHAPTER 15

As he waited in the aerodrome's guest facilities for the *Blenheim* to land, Alexander spotted someone familiar. It was the portly face and figure of the Luff governess. What was her name? Mrs. Smith, wasn't it? The one who'd come down ill just at the end of the voyage to Mars.

She seemed rather lost. Partly out of natural sympathy and partly out of curiosity, Alexander approached her.

"May I be of help, Mrs. Smith?"

She stared at up at him with blank eyes. Alexander's impression on the voyage had been that the woman was not especially intelligent. That assessment was strengthened by the woman's dull, confused expression.

"I'm Alexander Evalenko. You may remember me from the voyage. I was also on the *Agincourt*."

That seemed to register. "Oh, yes," she said. "I remember you now."

She looked around, clutching her large valise as if it were a life vest. "Do you . . . Mr. Valenkin, is it? Do you know where I could catch the airship to Ghlaktora? I need to rejoin my employer. I was told I should look for something called a 'float back.' Something like that."

"A fluybakh." He turned and pointed toward a distant door in the facilities. "You need to go through there, Mrs. Smith. You'll find a fluybakh available on the grounds beyond. Several of them, most likely."

He decided not to mention that she'd find riding on one of the rather flimsy airships quite a bit more . . . ah, exciting, that she was perhaps expecting.

As she started to move in that direction, Alexander asked her, "Are you feeling better now?"

She turned back, grimacing. "Oh, yes. It was a miserable week or so, but after that everything was fine."

"What was it, do you know? I was told several other people on the ship came down with the sane ailment."

Now, she looked indignant. "They never found out! Would you believe, the silly doctor they had told me he thought I might have been poisoned. Poisoned! Who would do a thing like that to someone like me? It's ridiculous! And he was an English doctor, too. Said he was, anyway. But you have to wonder, coming up with preposterous notions like that."

And off she went, stumping forward vigorously if not gracefully. As a mode of locomotion on Mars, with its low gravity, "stumping" had its drawbacks.

Alexander stared after her.

Poisoned . . .

His mind began to race. What if the Duchesne woman

was an SRP agent with a long-term mission here on Mars? He'd been thinking simply in terms of the usual assassination attempt. Poisoning Mrs. Smith—some sort of mild, non-fatal substance; Alexander could think of two offhand that might have served the purpose—would provide Duchesne with the perfect excuse to join the Luff party after the end of the voyage. That was why Alexander himself had dismissed Drezhner's suspicions.

Then . . .

That would also explain why Duchesne hadn't killed Kapral Baranovsky along with Drezhner. If her mission required remaining on Mars for months, even years, she needed to remain close to the Luff family.

Alexander closed his eyes, picturing the scene as it had been described to him by the young corporal.

Here, Drezhner. There, Duchesne. Firing—one, two; then again, one, two; four shots in all. Three of those shots had been fatal. Even the fourth might have been.

Not one shot had missed its mark. The signs of a skilled and experienced killer.

Over there, watching, was the Charlotte girl. How old was she? Fourteen? Fifteen?

She'd have been shocked by Duchesne's actions. Yet, so far . . .

The woman had just been defending the girl's father and brother. Almost anything could be forgiven—even forgotten, in time—under those circumstances.

But if Duchesne had gone further, had gone on to slaughter a young soldier too confused and frightened to pose a threat . . .

Just to silence an inconvenient witness . . .

No. The girl would never have forgotten that. She'd never have been able to regain her trust in Duchesne. As time went by, the situation would become unmanageable.

Alexander tried to imagine what sort of person could be so calculating, so cold-blooded, as to gauge all that and come to the right decision in the middle of deadly gunfire. Decide instantly, even as he—she—fired shot after unerring shot.

Savinkov. Only an assassin of that caliber could do such a thing.

He began to rise. And then . . .

Sat back down.

This was all speculation. Perhaps wild speculation. Even if he brought the matter to Rachkovsky's attention, and Rachkovsky brought it to Semiakin's, they'd probably decide the notion was preposterous. Alexander's reputation, already bruised by this mess, would be damaged still further.

Worse still, what if they decided the notion was correct?

There'd be no way to apprehend Savinkov, no way to track him—her—down. Not here, not on Mars. All that could be done would be to maintain a more vigilant guard on Prince Vorontsov. Which duty . . .

Would surely fall to Alexander Evalenko himself.

Stuck here on Mars. For months. Years. With no company but that of Cossacks.

Which is to say, the world's premier cavalrymen.

No.

Clearly, it was nothing but a wild surmise on his part.

A silly notion, really. Why would the SRP waste the talents of someone like Savinkov—for months; even years—simply to kill a prince? Russia had lots of princes.

Alexander sighed in soft relief.

"Attention, please. The *Blenheim* has landed. Passengers should prepare to board."

He rose, holding his bag. Paris awaited.

CHAPTER 16

Deception within deception. Such was the nature of the struggle against the Okhrana, driven by harsh necessity. The Tsar's secret police surpassed any other in the world, in their subtlety as well as their brutality. It was they who had forged the *Protocols of the Elders of Zion*; they, also, who had perfected the use of double agents and provocateurs.

So, the SRP's Combat Organization had responded in kind. A traitor had been found, Maxim Pechkin, uncovered by Vladimir Burtsev and his small band of counter-infiltrators. The man would normally have been executed by Eser agents, but this time he was allowed to run free for several years.

Years in which the Combat Organization slowly and carefully built up the legend of the master assassin, Gavril Savinkov. Then, two years ago, Pechkin was finally executed. The deed was done in secret, shortly after the assassination of a provincial governor. The body was left in a place where it could eventually be discovered, with evidence planted that suggested it was the corpse of none other than Savinkov himself. Dead of wounds incurred in the course of the governor's assassination, it seemed.

When the time came, an anonymous source notified the Okhrana of the body's location. The master assassin, gone at last.

Deception within deception. Gavril Savinkov had never existed, and the Okhrana now believed the phantom to be dead. But Savinkov...

That master assassin did exist, and was still quite alive. And now, in position to strike the needed blow when the time finally came.

A time which would certainly take years, before the conditions had matured. Years in which a new and powerful revolutionary alliance could be forged; with Mars as its bastion; an alliance that could finally confront the world's oppressors. Years in which the master assassin could slowly blend into the target's surroundings; learning all that needed to be learned; preparing all that needed to be prepared.

Throughout, the Okhrana would remain blind to the danger, for no Russian was Savinkov's new target. Not even the Tsar himself.

Cecil Rhodes. When the time came and the alliance was finally forged, he would be the one brought down. He was the master of the space-going warcraft that had destroyed the Boers and broken the English Navy's resistance. With him gone, and the great alliance ready to rise up, there would be no power left that could rescue the world's tyrants and autocrats.

• • •

"It's time to go, Vera! It's time!" Adrian Luff was practically dancing with eagerness. "Just think! We've never gone so deep into the labyrinth before! Maybe we'll run across a minotaur!"

Charlotte rolled her eyes. Edward Luff just smiled and extended his hand.

Savinkov took the hand. There was no reason not to enjoy life in the meantime, after all. Wounds were healing, Savinkov's as well as the physical ones Drezhner had inflicted on the boy. The master assassin would make sure the family that provided the ultimate shelter for the mission would emerge unscathed, when the time came.

If it came at all. There was no way to know.

Rhodes might die of natural causes. Or a Martian might kill him. He was hated by a great many.

The possibilities were endless. A horse might even learn to sing.

Appendix:
Eric Flint Bibliography

Author's note:

I've sorted out the various novels and stories I've written according to whichever series they belong to. With the exception of four novels, a short novel with Ryk Spoor, and some short stories I've written over the years for various anthologies, all my work fits into one broader setting or another. I'm an author who much prefers to work in big series. It's just the way my scribbler's mind works.

Standalone stories:

Mother of Demons (1997)
Slow Train to Arcturus, with Dave Freer (2008)
The Gods of Sagittarius, with Mike Resnick (2017)
Iron Angels, with Alistair Kimble (2017)

"The Thief and the Roller Derby Queen," published in *The Chick Is in the Mail*, (2000), ed. Esther Friesner

"The Truth About the Gotterdammerung," published in *Turn the Other Chick* (2004), ed. Esther Friesner

"The Flood Was Fixed," published in *Something Magic This Way Comes* (2008), edited by Marty Greenberg and Sarah Hoyt

"Red Fiddler," with Dave Freer, published in *Bedlam's Edge* (2005), edited by Mercedes Lackey and Rosemary Edghill

"Diamonds Are Forever," with Ryk Spoor, in *Mountain Magic* (2004)

"Conspiracies: A Very Condensed 937-Page Novel," with Mike Resnick, published in *Sideways in Crime*, edited by Lou Anders (2008)

"Pirates of the Suara Sea," with Dave Freer, published in *Fast Ships, Black Sails*, edited by Jeff Vandermeer (2008)

"Operation Xibalba," in Poul Anderson tribute anthology *Multiverse: Exploring Poul Anderson's Worlds*, edited by Gardner Dozois (2014)

"In the Matter of Savinkov," in *The Aethers of Mars*, edited by Mike Resnick (2014)

"Sanctuary," in *By Tooth and Claw*, edited by Bill Fawcett (2015)

"Up On the Roof," in *Black Tide Rising*, edited by John Ringo and Gary Poole (2016)

The Belisarius series (with David Drake)

An Oblique Approach (1998)
In the Heart of Darkness (1998)
Destiny's Shield (1999)

Fortune's Stroke (2000)

The Tide of Victory (2001)

"Islands," originally published in *Warmasters* (2002), edited by Bill Fawcett

The Dance of Time (2006)

The Tyrant (2002) [Note: this is not directly part of the Belisarius series, but is part of the related General series]

The 1632 series

1632 (2000)

1633, with David Weber (2002)

"The Wallenstein Gambit," first published in *Ring of Fire* (2004), edited by Eric Flint

"Portraits," first published in *Grantville Gazette I* (2004), edited by Eric Flint

"Steps in the Dance," first published in *Grantville Gazette II* (2006), edited by Eric Flint

"Postage Due," first published in *Grantville Gazette III* (2007), edited by Eric Flint

1634: The Galileo Affair, with Andrew Dennis (2004)

1634: The Baltic War, with David Weber (2007)

1634: The Ram Rebellion, with Virginia DeMarce (2006)

1634: The Bavarian Crisis, with Virginia DeMarce (2007)

1635: The Cannon Law, with Andrew Dennis (2006)

1635: The Dreeson Incident, with Virginia DeMarce (2008)

1635: A Parcel of Rogues, with Andrew Dennis (2016)

"The Austro-Hungarian Connection," first published in *Ring of Fire II* (2008), edited by Eric Flint

"The Anatomy Lesson," first published in *Grantville Gazette IV* (2008), edited by Eric Flint

"Steady Girl," first published in *Grantville Gazette V* (2009), edited by Eric Flint

1635: The Eastern Front (2010)

1636: The Saxon Uprising (2011)

"Four Days on the Danube," first published in *Ring of Fire III* (2011), edited by Eric Flint

"The Masque," first published in *Grantville Gazette VI* (2012), edited by Eric Flint and Paula Goodlett

1636: The Kremlin Games, with Gorg Huff and Paula Goodlett (2012)

1636: The Devil's Opera, with David Carrico (2013)

1636: Commander Cantrell in the West Indies, with Charles E. Gannon (2014)

1636: The Viennese Waltz, with Paula Goodlett and Gorg Huff (2014)

1636: The Cardinal Virtues, with Walter H. Hunt (2015)

"An Aukward Situation," first published in *Grantville Gazette VII* (2015), edited by Eric Flint and Paula Goodlett

"A Cardinal Relief," first published in *Grantville Gazette VII* (2015), edited by Eric Flint and Paula Goodlett

1635: A Parcel of Rogues, with Andrew Dennis (2016)

"Scarface," first published in *Ring of Fire IV* (2016), edited by Eric Flint

1636: The Ottoman Onslaught (2017)

1636: Mission to the Mughals, with Griffin Barber (2017)

1636: The Vatican Sanction, with Charles E. Gannon (2017)

1637: The Volga Rules, with Paula Goodlett and Gorg Huff (2018)

"Descartes Before the Whores," first published in *Grantville Gazette VIII* (2018), edited by Eric Flint and Walt Boyes

1637: The Polish Maelstrom (2019)

In addition to the above, there have been almost eighty issues published of the *Grantville Gazette* bi-monthly electronic magazine.

Connected to the 1632 series is another series which I'm calling the Assiti Shards series. The first book in that series is *Timespike*, which I coauthored with Marilyn Kosmatka (2008). The second volume is *The Alexander Inheritance*, with Gorg Huff and Paula Goodlett (2017).

The Honor Harrington series (by David Weber)

"From the Highlands," first published in *Changer of Worlds: Worlds of Honor #3* (2001), edited by David Weber

"Fanatic," first published in *The Service of the Sword: Worlds of Honor #4* (2003), edited by David Weber

Crown of Slaves, with David Weber (2003)

Torch of Freedom, with David Weber (2009)

Cauldron of Ghosts, with David Weber (2014)

The Trail of Glory series

  1812: The Rivers of War (2005)
  1824: The Arkansas War (2006)

The Joe's World series

  "Entropy, and the Strangler," first published in
    Writers of the Future, Volume IX (1993), edited by
    Dave Wolverton
  The Philosophical Strangler (2001)
  Forward the Mage, with Richard Roach (2002)
  A Desperate and Despicable Dwarf (forthcoming)

The Rats, Bats & Vats series (with Dave Freer)

  "Genie Out of the Bottle," first published in *Cosmic
    Tales II: Adventures in Far Futures* (2205), edited
    by Toni Weisskopf
  Rats, Bats & Vats (2000)
  The Rats, the Bats & the Ugly (2004)
  "Crawlspace," first published in *Jim Baen's Universe*,
    April 2007.

The Pyramid series (with Dave Freer)

  Pyramid Scheme (2001)
  Pyramid Power (2007)

The Heirs of Alexandria series

The Shadow of the Lion, with Mercedes Lackey and Dave Freer (2002)

A Mankind Witch (2005) [Note: this is a solo novel in the series by Dave Freer]

This Rough Magic, with Mercedes Lackey and Dave Freer (2003)

Much Fall of Blood, with Mercedes Lackey and Dave Freer (2010)

"The Witch's Murder," with Dave Freer, first published in *The Dragon Done It*, edited by Eric Flint and Mike Resnick (2008)

Burdens of the Dead, with Mercedes Lackey and Dave Freer (2013)

All the Plagues of Hell, with Dave Freer (2018)

The Witches of Karres series (created by James H. Schmitz)

The Wizard of Karres, with Mercedes Lacky and Dave Freer (2004)

The Sorceress of Karres, with Dave Freer (2010)

The Boundary series (with Ryk Spoor)

Boundary (2006)
Threshold (2010)
Portal (2013)
Castaway Planet (2015)
Castaway Odyssey (2016)

The Jao series
(with K.D. Wentworth and David Carrico)

The Course of Empire (2003)
The Crucible of Empire (2010)
The Span of Empire (2016)

• • •

In addition to my own work as an author, I've edited a lot of anthologies. Most of these involve multi-volume reissues of authors from times past. I'm listing them below

Complete Works of James H. Schmitz
(with Guy Gordon, coeditor)

Telzey Amberdon (2000)
TnT: Telzey and Trigger Together (2000)
Trigger and Friends (2001)
Dangerous Territory: The Federation of the Hub (2001)
Agent of Vega & Other Stories (2001)
Eternal Frontier (2002)
The Witches of Karres (2005)

Complete Works of Christopher Anvil

Pandora's Legions (2002)
The Interstellar Patrol (2003)
The Interstellar Patrol II: The Federation of Humanity
   (2005)
The Trouble with Aliens (2006)
The Trouble with Humans (2007)

War Games (2008)
Prescription for Chaos (2009)
The Power of Illusion (2010)

Works of Keith Laumer

Retief! (2002)
Odyssey (2002)
Keith Laumer: The Lighter Side (2002)
A Plague of Demons (2003)
Future Imperfect (2003)
Legions of Space (2004)
Imperium (2005)
The Long Twilight & Other Stories (2007)
Earthblood & Other Stories (2008)
The Universe Twister (2008)

Works of Murray Leinster

Med Ship (2002)
Planets of Adventure (2003)
A Logic Named Joe (2005)

Complete Works of Howard L. Myers
(with Guy Gordon, coeditor)

The Creatures of Man (2003)
A Sense of Infinity (2009)

Other anthologies

Tom Godwin, *The Cold Equations & Other Stories* (2003)

Randall Garrett, *Lord Darcy,* with Guy Gordon, coeditor (2002)

The World Turned Upside Down, coedited with David Drake and Jim Baen (2005)

The Best of Jim Baen's Universe (2007)

The Dragon Done It, coedited with Mike Resnick (2008)

The Best of Jim Baen's Universe II, coedited with Mike Resnick (2008)